FIRST STRIKE

Everything happened at once.

Kenhodan's brain seized a brief image of the door as it flew inward in an explosion of splinters and broken bolts. An iron shard gashed his cheek, hissing past to bury its length in the wall. Windows and shutters cascaded inward in the same moment, showering the sawdust with diamond-bright glass. Broken bits of pane winked in the fire like rubies, ringing as they bounced over tabletops and benches. A shadow filled the doorway, and cold rolled from it like acid. A flash of brilliance washed his shoulder as Wencit muttered a semi-audible incantation and his blade pulsed with savage light in time with the words. The chill withdrew slightly, and Bahzell's breath snorted, pluming like frost, as his huge sword swung up in a silvery arc, as if saluting his foes.

Then the shadows were upon them.

Despite his scars, this was in a very real sense Kenhodan's first combat, yet there was time for him to realize he felt no fear. Time for him to wonder what that said about the man he'd forgotten. And then a strange, consuming rage roused within him. It filled him with a fury which demanded blood, and it had an endless depth that staggered the mind. He had no idea where it had come from, and if there'd been time to think about it, its fiery strength would have terrified him. But now, at this moment, he was conscious only of his own burning hunger, and his lips drew back in a feral snarl as the shadows attacked.

BAEN BOOKS by DAVID WEBER

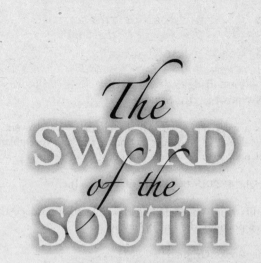

The SWORD of the SOUTH

DAVID WEBER

A Baen Books Original

Baen Publishing Enterprises
P.O. Box 1403
Riverdale, NY 10471
www.baen.com

ISBN: 978-1-4814-8236-3

Cover art by Kurt Miller
Maps by Randy Asplund

First Baen Mass Market Paperback printing, February 2017

Library of Congress Catalog Number: 2015009698

Distributed by Simon & Schuster
1230 Avenue of the Americas
New York, NY 10020

Pages by Joy Freeman (www.pagesbyjoy.com)
Printed in the United States of America

"To all the old—and new—friends who
have fussed at me over the pacemaker.
Many thanks for giving me a hard time...
and the doctor promises Sharon the pulse rate
will never fall below sixty again!"

Contents

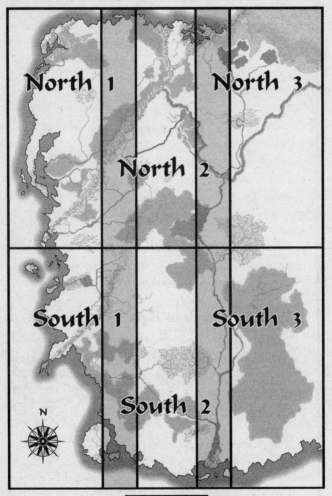

North 1

North 3

North 2

South 1

South 3

South 2

N

0 1000 2000 3000
Miles

Norfressa
Key

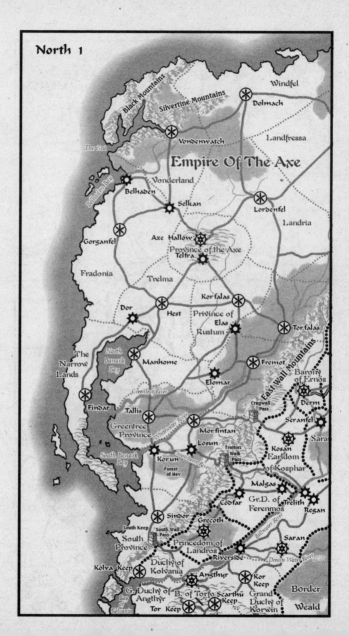

North 1

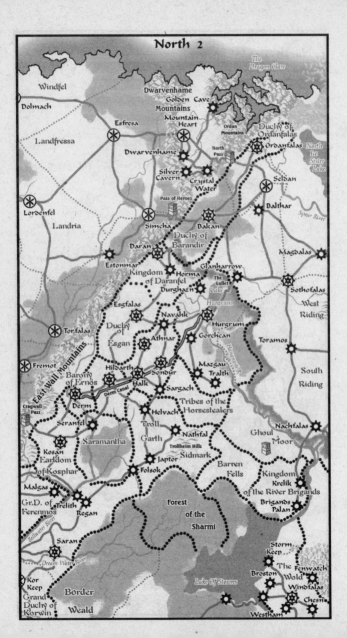

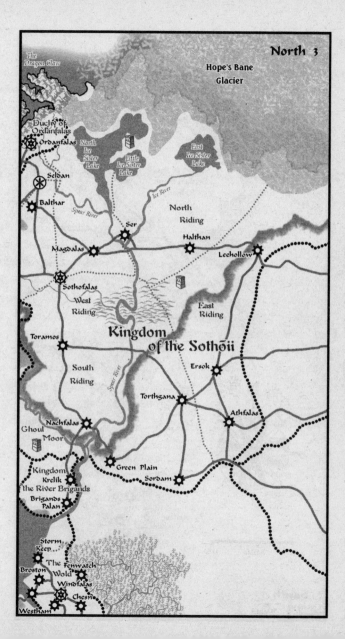

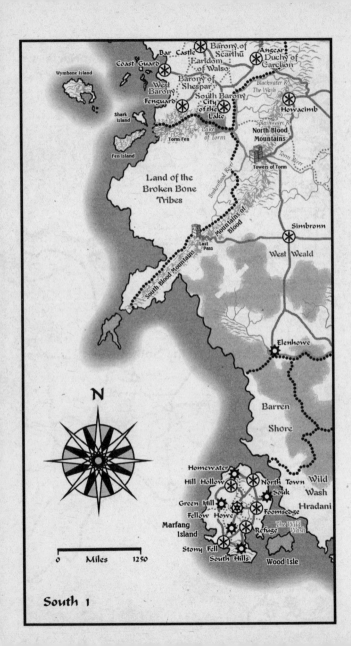

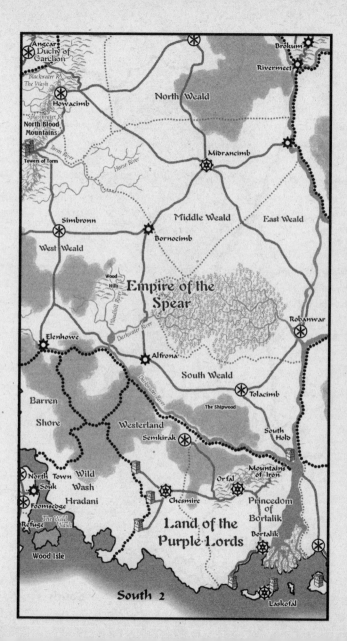

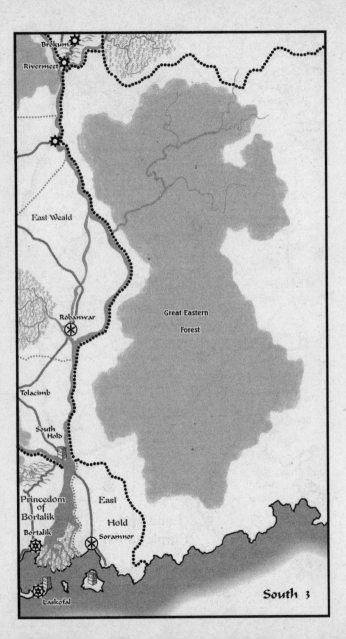

The
SWORD
of the
SOUTH

Lost Hope

Wencit of Rūm's face flickered in the eerie glow of the crystal's heart, and his eyes flamed with their own light as he watched the ghastly carnage. It had raged for hours, but the end was near...and drawing nearer. The Gryphon Guard stood at bay atop a hill, cut off from its final frail hope of retreat. Its men had fought and died for year after year to protect the ports from which so many thousands upon thousands of refugees had fled to distant Norfressa, and one by one, those ports had fallen. Only the great harbor city of Gayrtherym remained now, manned by a skeleton garrison and the last, threadbare fleet awaiting the Light's defenders. But there was no one in all of Kontovar to aid them in their fight to reach it, and Wencit's fists clenched as his viewpoint hovered above their desperate ring of steel. The Guard fought with the valor of brave men who knew they could not win, yet had they faced only mortal foes, they might still have hoped to cut a path to the sea.

1

But sorcery streaked the sky, its unearthly glow glittering on the red and gold badges of the House of Ottovar. The protective wards wrought by the Council grew steadily weaker as the dark art gnawed their foundations. They would break soon.

A flank company of the Guard collapsed, the flood of attackers pausing only to hew the fallen before they climbed the slope over the bodies of imperial veterans. Red blades waved at the violet sky, the reflected streamers of arcane wrath gory in their wetness, and the Emperor summoned his last reserve. He charged at the head of a scant, threadbare company—little more than three cobbled-together platoons—to meet the threat, his personal banner leading the men whose fidelity had never wavered, who'd never once failed to follow wherever that banner led. Nor did they fail it now, and Wencit's eyes burned with unshed tears as they fastened on Toren's gryphon-crowned helm and bloody skill, watching the last Emperor of Kontovar win the last victory of his empire's long life...a life measured now in minutes. The reserve slashed the breakthrough apart in crimson steel, and its remnants sealed the hole in the steadily shrinking line.

Air hissed in Wencit's nostrils as the misshapen blackness he'd awaited suddenly appeared. It radiated black lightnings, cored with the corrosive green taint of corruption, as it scaled the hill, and the barriers of the white wizards trembled at the defiled sorcery which shrouded it. Even the Gryphon Guard quailed before its menace.

Nails drew blood from Wencit's palms as he fought the hunger to match his own might against the Empire's foe. The Lord of Carnadosa was a wild wizard, of a house which had produced dozens of wild wizards, and his strength was unfathomable. Yet Wencit had been schooled far longer in the hard lore of wizardry; in his heart, he believed he could outmatch his foe...but he dared not test that belief. He dared not! Too much was at stake for him to tamper here, even though his restraint spelled ruin and death for untold multitudes.

He groaned and thrust himself back from the crystal. He knew what the end must be, and it was more than he could bear.

He turned away as the stone's tiny Emperor pivoted to face the blackness. A full battalion of the Guard fell, life riven away by the deadly kiss of twisted magic, as their nightmare foe reached their shieldwall. The blackness passed over them and stooped upon the Emperor as Wencit opened the door, and Toren's glowing sword vanished in the darkness. The stubborn line about his banner bent at last, yielding the ground soaked by its blood inch by savagely fought inch as its ring contracted toward the spot where arch-wizard and Emperor fought to the death.

Wencit opened the council chamber door and met the eyes of his fellows. In his unwatched crystal, the last Guardsman took his stand, his back to the tormented cloud which had engulfed his liege. His left hand held the staff of the Emperor's banner, and the gryphon stirred sullenly on an angry wind, red silk sodden with a darker red, as the massive, wounded hradani—last captain of the Gryphon Guard of Ottovar—lashed out at his enemies. He reaped a gory harvest, but he was one and they were many. He fell before their hewing blades and the bodies of the Guard formed a ragged circle about the power-spewing blackness atop the hill. Violet lightning flashed from the duel raging at its heart, and the arch-wizard's own troops died in scores, screaming at their touch.

Wencit of Rūm, Last Lord of the Council of Ottovar, locked his glowing gaze with the somber eyes of the Council's members and slowly, slowly raised his hands. Candlelight glimmered on the old scars which seamed his strong fingers, and his fellows rose to join his gesture and his power. Arcane tension crackled as the Council was joined in turn by every wizard on the Isle of Rūm, the tattered survivors of the white wizardry of a continent. Their massed might rose high, focused in a storm of strength fit to drain life itself from those who spawned it. Yet they were the white wizards of Kontovar, the heirs of Ottovar and Gwynytha the Great, loyal beyond death. They knew what price this night's work would demand of them, but they'd lived as wizards; as wizards they would die, spending themselves against the evil they'd allowed to live. Their joint strength was far too little for victory, but it was enough for the single purpose which remained to them.

Wencit gathered the deadly power in his hands, his fingers quivering with the essence of destruction. He had but one more task before he loosed devastation upon his enemies, and his lips parted to begin the final spell.

• CHAPTER ONE •

Belhadan

"Out of the way, you idiot!"

The drayman snarled, the heavy goods wagon swerved, and a redhaired man slid from under the horses' very hooves into the gutter. The wagoneer's round Belhadan accent drifted back in a picturesque curse, but the grating roar of iron-shod wheels drowned his profanity. And despite his anger, the wagon neither slowed nor stopped, for this was Belhadan, commercial hub of the north. Those who served the port's voracity had little time for idle pleasantries with strangers.

Muddy water flowed over the pedestrian's legs as the stamp of horses and rattle of wheels faded. The mingled smells of salt, tar, and garbage overlaid the scents of hemp and fresh timber, and thunder muttered. Night cooking smells rode a sullen breeze from the west, but their comfortable aroma couldn't cloak the sharp, damp smell of the looming tempest. There was thunder in those clouds, and lightning, and the promise of cold, drenching rain.

The redhaired man shook his head and rose. He dabbed at his worn clothing, but it would never again attain sartorial splendor and he gave up with a shrug and peered into the wind. Gusts fingered his hair, and he leaned into them, feeling the approaching storm on his cheekbones. Belhadan loomed before him, laced with strands of glowing streetlamps, windows gleaming against the darkness. Much of the dwarven-designed city was buried in the bedrock of the steep mountainside and foothills its walls and fortifications crowned, but its broad streets were thickly lined with the above-ground houses, shops, and taverns preferred by the other Races of Man. Now the redhaired man scratched his jaw thoughtfully, then moved off towards the streetlamps leading towards the city's heart.

He wasn't alone. An old man in an alley straightened from his slouch against a handy wall and squinted warily at the low-bellied clouds. Then he raised the hood of his Sothōii-style poncho with resigned hands and waited until the redhaired man had half-vanished into the dark before he hitched up the sword belt under that poncho and followed softly over the paving.

◆   ◆   ◆

The thunder's mumbled promise was redeemed in a downpour. The wind died in a moment, leaving the air still and hushed, prickly and humming. The next instant was born in the stutter of lightning and the hiss of rain. The wind returned, refreshed by its pause, billowing the skirts of the old man's poncho and forcing the redhaired man to hunch into the raindrops which rode it.

The old man muttered balefully into his neatly trimmed beard as the younger man continued at the same pace. Tolerance for thunderstorms was a youth-ful vice sensible old bones no longer boasted. Rain pelted the old man's shoulders like pebbles and wind threatened to snatch the hood from his head, but he grunted with something like satisfaction as he peered at a passing corner marker.

Ahead of him, the redhaired man scanned the darkened shops and warehouses as he trudged into the downpour, shielding his eyes against the rain with a cupped palm as he sought a haven. No one walked the streets in such weather—indeed, the approaching storm helped explain the drayman's surly haste—but he glanced constantly over his shoulder, as if somehow aware he wasn't alone on the deserted street. Yet no matter how quickly he looked, the old man always contrived to place a corner, a shutter, or an out-thrust stone buttress between them just before he turned.

His present neighborhood seemed singularly lack-ing in the shelter for which he searched, and the water gushing from rooftops and downspouts filled the street's gutters. They were well designed, those gutters, yet the last month had been rainy. They were already half-filled by older runoff, and the sudden, massive deluge flooded them and sent a sheet of water swirling out across the hard-paved street. It washed about the redhaired man's ankles, and he grimaced as its icy outriders found the leaks in his worn-out boots. His feet squelched with every step, adding a fresh stratum of wretchedness to the night's misery.

He turned a corner and paused suddenly as diamond-paned windows poured light out into the night, turning raindrops into plunging topazes in the instant before they slammed into the flooded street in dimpled explosions of spray. Then a door opened between two of those windows, spilling light and laughter, and a pair of sailors staggered out of it, arms draped about one another, loudly proclaiming their disdain for such a paltry zephyr.

They wandered down the street, drunkenly bellowing an utterly reprehensible ditty to the thunder, and the redhaired man's smile was etched in the welcoming light before the door slammed once more. Taverns offered warmth, even to those with empty purses, he thought, provided one didn't attract too much attention to one's poverty.

He crossed the street and relief sighed from the old man's lips, but he didn't follow into that oasis of light and warmth. He watched the redhaired man enter the tavern without him, instead, for he knew something more than tempest prowled the night. He'd searched his mind at length and found no hint of what was to come, which was even more worrisome than it was unusual, but he cocked one eye speculatively upward and probed the storm for clues once more.

Finally, he shook his head, muttered something under his breath, and clapped his hands once, sharply. The sound of his clap vanished in a roll of thunder—a roll unaccompanied by any flash of lightning—and a blue hemisphere whuffed into existence about him. It was faint, its glow more sensed than seen even in the darkness, yet rain hissed into steam upon its surface, and he peered about alertly, eyes slitted against the faint blue haze. A longsword materialized in his gnarled, scarred hand, swinging easily, edged with a glitter of silver-blue radiance.

Something, yes... but what? His enemies wouldn't wish to draw attention to their art: not in Belhadan.

Wizards might be tolerated—barely—in some realms; with one notable exception, however, they received short shrift and a long rope in Belhadan. So what form would the attack take?

His eyes flicked to the clouds, and he grinned. Of course. He lifted his sword's tip to touch the underside of the hemisphere, then closed his eyes and murmured more words under his breath. Power welled, filling the blue shield with vibrating urgency, and the old man smiled at the familiar tingle and cracked his left eye to scan the clouds.

Nothing.

Well, such things took time. He closed both eyes and settled into a hunched-shoulder wait. He was reasonably certain what was about to happen, and he had no wish to carry it into the tavern. Indeed, he had every reason to keep any danger away from that inn. And at least his wards kept off the rain.

His wait was shorter than he'd feared. Thunder rumbled again, and a lance of lightning, blue-white and screaming, forked from the clouds. It smashed into his shield, rupturing the rain-shrouded darkness with prominences of destruction that splintered back towards the heavens which had birthed them. The old man swayed, and his grip on the sword hilt went white-knuckled as the lightning sheeted back in clinging waves of flame. The shaft of brilliance lingered unnaturally, ramming sullenly against the old man. It seemed to endure for hours, shifting and probing at his defenses with self-aware malevolence while his mind flashed through the calculations of a wizard lord, beating back the attack with his own shifting strength. The battle swayed back and forth as minds and wills clashed and struck like edged steel in skilled hands.

And then, finally, unwillingly, the bolt of light withdrew into the clouds and the savagery at its heart bled away into the all-absorbent earth. The old man straightened and opened his eyes, grinning up at the storm lashed clouds.

"Nicely played," he told the storm calmly, sheathing his blade with a snap. "A lightning bolt. What could be more natural? A nice touch, but not, I think, quite good enough, Milady!"

He bowed ironically to the raging sky and crossed to the tavern. The blue light retreated into his body as he touched the latch. It clung for a moment, like glittering blue frost, then vanished as he opened the door.

✦   ✦   ✦

The redhaired man paused inside the door and peered about. The place was crowded, the air thick with the smell of food and drink. Pipe smoke hazed the rafters, drifting overhead in a lazy canopy, and freshly spread sawdust covered the floor. Voices rumbled, glass clinked, and eating utensils clattered about him.

Most of the Races of Man seemed represented. Stocky dwarves brushed shoulders with ivory-horned halflings and the tall, broad-shouldered men of the northern provinces. There were even half a dozen patrons with the slashed eyebrows of the half-elven, and the dark-faced harper perched on the end of the bar boasted Wakūo blood, to judge by his hooked nose and bold, black eyes. Slashed doublets and silk breeches matched their finery against the plain shirts and canvas trousers of seamen while life and vitality bubbled like simmering porridge, rising even stronger and more welcomingly against the pound of rain on roof slates and the echoing rolls of thunder beyond the tavern's stout eaves. It all made the redhaired man even more aware of his own bedraggled appearance, and he hesitated before plunging into the press in search of some corner in which a man with an empty purse might find a haven from the storm.

"Ho! Look what the wind's blown in!"

The redhaired man turned towards the deep, jovial bellow...and froze in mid stride, as he found himself face-to-face with two fathoms of midnight-black death. He stood there, not daring even to breathe, as the immense direcat gazed up at him out of amber eyes. It was one of the great direcats of the plains, almost seven feet in length, not counting its tail, and well over three feet at the shoulder, with five-inch bone-white fangs. It was also the most feared predator of Norfressa, with absolutely no business in a Belhadan tavern.

He waited, frozen, anticipating its spring. But it merely seated itself and wrapped its yard-long tail neatly about its toes, like some enormous house cat. It cocked its massive head to gaze straight across at him out of those frighteningly intelligent yellow eyes. And as it did, he realized no one else in the entire tavern seemed to consider its deadly presence the least bit out of the ordinary.

He inhaled cautiously, pulling his gaze away from the direcat by sheer force of will to look at whoever had spoken, and his nostrils widened in fresh astonishment. No stripling himself, he was overtopped by the man he faced, and his green eyes widened as he recognized a hradani. Not just any hradani, either.

This was a giant among them; at six and a half feet, the redhaired man's head barely topped the other's shoulder. The white apron over the leathers of a fighting man—and the sheathed Wakūo hook knife at his hip—only added to the aura of unreality, for the hradani were the only foes more savage in combat than the huge direcat which sat with such bizarre daintiness at the giant's side.

"It's a powerful thirst as brings a man out on a night like this!" The hradani laughed, and the redhaired man studied the massive figure carefully, reassured by the other's cheerful manner . . . and the fact that the direcat hadn't yet pounced. He glanced back at the beast, and it yawned through its fangs as it returned his regard.

"Not thirst so much as an excess of drinking water," he said, kicking his wits back to life, and smiled. The hradani's tufted ears, foxlike and mobile, twitched in amusement, and his huge laugh bounced back from the rafters like enclosed thunder.

"Aye, I'm thinking Chemalka and Khalifrio are after having their heads together this night," he agreed. "Myself, I'm one as prefers my drink in a mug and not so cold! If it's something stronger than water you're seeking, you've come to the right place in the Iron Axe."

"I may have, but I fear the contents of my purse haven't," the redhaired man confessed candidly.

"No money?" The hradani eyed him thoughtfully, then shrugged. "No matter. I'll not turn any man out on a night such as this. We'll fire your belly with rockfish stew while the fire's after drying your hide."

He chuckled rumblingly at his own humor and turned to plow through the crowded taproom like a barque under full sail. The press parted before him like foam, and the redhaired man trailed gratefully in his wake. He stayed carefully clear of the direcat, but the beast only glanced at him as he passed and began grooming a scimitared paw. The redhaired man met its incurious gaze respectfully, for the cat must have weighed at least eight hundred pounds, which made it worthy of all the respect he could muster.

"Leeana! Leeana!"

The hradani's bass bellow was as loud as before, and the redhaired man wondered if he ever spoke at less than full volume. Even as he wondered, however, his strange host was answered by a sweet contralto. The contrast was astonishing, but the volume of the response almost matched that of the summons.

"'Leeana,' yourself! What now? Another drinking bout to oversee?"

Customers moved aside to let the speaker pass. She was tall for a woman, within three inches or so of the redhaired man's own height, though she seemed tiny beside the giant, and her red-gold braids fell below her waist. A flowing skirt of deep green wool swirled about her ankles, covered by a spotless apron; opals gleamed in the silver bracelet clasped around her left wrist; and a massive golden necklet set with a single ruby flashed about her slender throat. The redhaired man's eyes flickered past her leather headband, then returned with a jerk. What had seemed a simple band was in fact many windings of a thick rawhide thong, and what he'd taken for large wooden earrings were carved wooden *grips*, instead. He eyed her with the same respect he'd shown the direcat as he recognized the Sothōii garrote for what it was.

"And what are you and your cronies up to now?" she demanded, hands on hips as she gazed up at the towering hradani through green eyes a shade darker than the redhaired man's own.

"No cronies this time, love...though Wencit did say it might be he'd drop by for a visit."

The hradani swept her off the floor, huge hands more than spanning her slender waist, and kissed her enthusiastically before he set her down and tucked her comfortably under his left arm. Then he turned with her to face the redhaired man...who noticed the matching silver bracelet around the hradani's left wrist.

"No, lass," he said. "We've a guest without the price of a pot of ale in his pocket. Surely there's after being a place by the fire and a bit of something in the stew pot still?"

"I'm certain I can find both, if you'll take the time from your lowborn friends to watch the bar for me."

"To be sure," the big hradani murmured, tugging his forelock respectfully. His dark face was alight with humor as he kissed the top of her head and swatted her behind gently—two liberties the redhaired man would never have dared with someone who carried a Sothōii garrote. She fisted him in the ribs and spun away like a dancer, and even the roughest-looking patron moved respectfully from her path.

She smiled and gestured to the redhaired man, and he followed her through an arched doorway and down a short, stone-flagged passage into an enormous kitchen. He was puzzled by how silently she moved until the hem of her skirt swirled to show him that she wore no shoes.

The kitchen was almost uncomfortably warm, for

a fire crackled and seethed in a hearth large enough for a ship's mast. Wind roared across the chimney tops like a hunting beast, and rain hissed and spat in the flames as drops found their way down the flue. The rumbling storm was barely audible, yet he felt a warm puff of damp breeze on his neck and turned cautiously, then held very still as the direcat padded past, prick-eared head almost level with his own chest. The beast ignored him to curl neatly beneath a high trestle table, and the redhaired man drew a deep breath of quiet relief.

Leeana waved him towards another table while a half-dozen or so aproned women and a trio of men looked up briefly from their tasks, then nodded respectfully to Leeana and returned to chopping vegetables, peeling potatoes, turning the spit before the main fireplace, or tending pots and kettles on the immense stove which formed an island in the center of the room. Half of the kitchen staff were hradani, as well, he realized with a brain becoming inured to (or at least numbed by) repeated shocks. That mix was certainly odd, though not inherently impossible, he supposed. It was merely unheard of for humans and hradani to keep their swords out of one another long enough to discuss coexistence. But the girl who ran to meet Leeana, pausing in passing to lavish a rough caress on the deadly direcat, resolved any doubt as to how well *this* human got along with at least one hradani. Her flaming hair and foxlike ears marked her as Leeana's daughter by the unlikely tavern keeper.

"Sit. Sit!" Leeana told him briskly. "Fetch a bowl of stew, Gwynna. And you, sir—haul off that wet jerkin and set it aside to dry."

"You're too kind," the redhaired man protested. "I can't repay the courtesy you show me."

"Nonsense!" Leeana snorted. "It does my layabout of a husband good to have a guest about the house. And I'd rather feed one man in the kitchen than wait bar for half a hundred," she added with a sly smile. "You did me a favor there. It's my night to tend bar and his to circulate, so you can see I actually stand in *your* debt."

"I'm relieved to have paid my score, then." He chuckled, shrugging out of his jerkin gratefully. Steam rose gently as he spread it across the back of an unoccupied chair before the flames, and he unlaced his tunic as well, hanging both by the hearth. He rubbed his hands, offering them to the heat and feeling the welcome warmth against his rain-chilled skin and—

Shattering crockery snatched his head towards the girl, Gwynna. She was a striking child, for all her mixed blood, with the mobile, tufted ears of her father's people pricking piquantly through the rich red and golden hair of her mother. Her proud cheekbones were lightly dusted with freckles, and huge, dark eyes of midnight blue shone under delicate lashes. Though she was only a child, her face already showed the elegant beauty to come, yet at the moment, that beauty was clouded by shock.

He had only a second to realize that before a sound of tearing canvas ripped from his left as the direcat surged to its feet. The table under which it had lain crashed aside as the beast rose, lips drawn back, mouth gaping in fanged, bristling challenge. It bounded to the girl's side—seven feet of midnight menace rumbling a deadly snarl that chilled the redhaired man's blood.

"Stand, Blanchrach!"

Leeana's voice whiplashed through the sudden tension, and the cat paused, tensed as if against an invisible leash. The redhaired man stared into its amber eyes and felt sweat on his brow, but the cat only edged forward, placing itself protectively between himself and the girl.

"Your pardon, sir," Leeana said more calmly. "I beg your pardon—for myself, as well as for my daughter and her friend. But I've never seen such scars. Not even on Bahzell."

"Scars?" he asked blankly.

Her eyes led his own down over his chest and belly, and he sucked in wind and thudded onto the bench like a string-cut puppet. His torso was seamed and ridged, scars running in all directions across hard-muscled flash. Craggy peaks and valleys turned his body into a livid mountain range, and the firelight traced lines of shadow along their curves. He touched them fearfully, and his face blanched.

A tiny sound pierced his shock. He glanced up, green eyes stunned and confused, and adrenaline spurted afresh as he saw the garrote in Leeana's hands, the balls of her thumbs poised on the wooden grips.

"You didn't know about your own scars."

It wasn't a question, and he shook his head numbly. Her face hardened, her eyes flicked to her daughter, and she spat a brief sentence in a strange tongue. Gwynna's hands lowered from her mouth instantly, and she stepped behind her mother, her own eyes wide as the direcat crouched, tail lashing, and its deep rumble pulsed. The others in the kitchen—including two powerful, dagger-armed hradani—stepped back to give Leeana and the cat room.

"What manner of man are you?" Leeana's words were courteous, but her voice was cold and her eyes bored into his. "What do you call yourself? Where do you come from, and why are you here?"

"I—"

He stared at her, his eyes half-glazed, and tried again.

"I—"

His tongue clove to the roof of his mouth and an expression of utter helplessness flashed over his face. He sought desperately for answers, knowing his life rode upon them, yet his mind spun from the surface of his thoughts into an endless well of silence. He licked his lips and sagged down on the bench, the roaring fire fingering his back with heat, and shook his head slowly, fear for his life overridden by a terror infinitely worse.

"In the names of all the gods," he said hoarsely. "I don't know."

Wind howled in the chimney tops, and the flames danced behind him, laughing with the ageless malice of burning wood. His gaze locked with Leeana's, and his voice was a cry of anguish.

"I don't know!"

◆   ◆   ◆

A trio of dwarves filled the door, gripping a protesting halfling with ungentle hands, and the old man stepped smartly aside. One dwarf's sliced pursestrings told their own tale, though the halfling continued to protest his innocence. His protests grew more forceful as he smelled the pounding rain, and the old man swallowed a smile as the dismally wailing thief arced gracefully outward. He landed in the far gutter with a terrific splash, his cries quenched in flying spray, and the old man nodded to the dwarves as they stood just inside the door, exchanging comments on the thief's probable ancestry. Their imaginative speculations held his amused attention for several seconds before he turned away.

He picked a path through the crowd, sniffing the pipe smoke while his eyes flitted about like a hunting cat's, and a pocket of silence moved with him as people recognized him. He hid another smile and eyed the crowd speculatively, estimating the sums which would change hands as they paid their shots. It would be a tidy amount, but no more than it was worth.

The Iron Axe Tavern was always busy, but tonight it was packed. The tavern was known for song, good food, and better drink...and the fact that no one's throat was ever slit within it. When bad weather stalked Belhadan, the Iron Axe filled as though by magic.

His eyes searched busily. Bahzell had to be somewhere, but where? Normally, he stood out like a tower, yet now he was nowhere to be seen.

Ah! The old man grinned as a bellow arose in the rear taproom. He should've known he could find his host by following his ears to the loudest noise in the vicinity! He made his way quickly into the rear room and headed for the long, polished bar.

"Wencit!" the big hradani called, thumping the oaken surface. "Come in! It's a right soaking you've had this evening, but I've some Granservan Grand Reserve put by for nights such as this. Let me be pouring some of it down your throat."

"Good evening, Bahzell," the old man replied more sedately, pushing back his dripping poncho's hood, and wedged up to the bar.

Other customers pushed back to give him elbow room. Most Belhadans knew him, either by sight or description, and respected his reputation, but wizards were chancy companions at best. No one wished to crowd one unduly; not even one who was their host's longtime friend. Besides, one glance at his peculiar eyes deterred even the hardiest of strangers.

Bahzell reached under the bar for a bottle encased in old leather, tooled and warm with the polish of years, and his brown eyes laughed as he carefully filled a glass and set it before the old man.

"Drink up and be telling me why you're here," he ordered. "It was urgent enough your message sounded, yet here you come like a drowned cat. Not the best image for a master wizard, I'm thinking!"

"Even master wizards melt in the rain," Wencit said sourly, toasting the hradani gratefully before sipping the amber, honeyed fire. "And nights like this," he sighed, lowering the glass after one long swallow, "would wet Tolomos himself."

"Aye, true enough," Bahzell nodded. "And you're not the first drowned cat as scratched at my door this night. There's a redhead back in the kitchen who looked as if he'd been after swimming the Spear— north to south."

"A redhead, you say?" Wencit cocked a bushy eyebrow over his wildfire eyes. "A tall young fellow? Perhaps thirty years old?"

"The very man." Bahzell sounded unsurprised. "A friend of yours, is it?"

"You might say so," Wencit smiled, "although he doesn't know it yet. The kitchen, you say?"

"Aye, he'd no coin for drink, so I gave him meat.

Leeana's stew will be taking the chill from him. He reminded me of someone..." The hradani drummed on the bar for a moment, head cocked, eyes intent upon the wizard. "Would it happen I'd be after knowing him, Wencit?"

"I doubt it. You know a great many very odd people, Bahzell, but this fellow's outside the circle even of your acquaintance." Wencit met Bahzell's measuring gaze levelly. "I've no doubt he does remind you of someone, but I give you my word you've never met him before."

Bahzell regarded him steadily for another brace of heartbeats. Then he flicked his mobile ears and nodded. It was a strange sort of nod, one which seemed to acknowledge more than Wencit had actually said.

"Well, that being so, I'm thinking there's naught more to say," he said out loud, and it was Wencit's turn to nod.

The wizard finished his whiskey and straightened.

"With your permission, I'll take myself off to the kitchen."

"Aye, you be doing that." The hradani's expressive ears twitched in combined amusement and resignation. "You've something deep in mind. But then, you always do, don't you just?"

"As you say, I'm a master wizard. Master wizards always have something deep in mind."

Bahzell's lips quirked and he snorted.

"Well, be off with you! I've a full bar, and you'll say naught till it suits you, as well I know."

"Alas for my reputation," Wencit mourned, then grinned and pushed off through the crowd.

He found his way to the Iron Axe's kitchens with the

ease of long familiarity, and his boots clumped down the passage, but none of the kitchen staff noticed. They were too intent on the confrontation between Leeana and the redhaired man. Wencit felt the tension as he entered the kitchen, but no sign of it colored his voice or expression.

"Good evening to you, Leeana Flame Hair," he called pleasantly. "The mountain behind the bar told me I'd find you here."

"Wencit!" Leeana twitched in surprise, but there was relief in her voice. Only two pairs of eyes did not turn to the wizard: the redhaired man's, which stared sickly at the tabletop, and the rumbling direcat's, which watched the redhaired man unblinkingly.

Wencit glanced quizzically from the taut garrote to the redhaired man's ashen face. His expression softened as the man's trembling fingers traced his cruel scars, then the old man extended a hand to Gwynna.

"And good evening to you, young Gwynna," he said gently. The girl scampered over to hug him tightly, her face alight with welcome, but the light faded as she looked back at the man whose scars had startled her.

"I'm more pleased than usual to see you," Leeana said frankly. She allowed the garrote to slacken, raised her eyebrows at the wizard, and twitched her head sideways at the man seated before her fire.

"Indeed?"

"Indeed," she replied firmly. "Bahzell offered this man hospitality, but now he can't—or won't—even tell me his name."

"Strange, but not surprising," Wencit said cryptically.

"Oh, thank you *ever* so much!" Leeana said, then snorted. "Have you ever in your entire life given someone a straight answer?" she demanded, yet her voice was more cheerful, as if she drew reassurance from his presence.

"Wizards always give straight answers—those of us who claim to be honest, that is. But our affairs are usually so tangled the straightest answers appear most crooked." He lifted Gwynna's chin with a gentle forefinger and smiled into her eyes. "Tell me, young Gwynna. Could you fetch another bowl of stew for my friend? And perhaps one for me, as well? And—" his smile widened gently "—*not* drop them?"

"I never drop bowls!" Gwynna said indignantly.

"Ah?" Wencit's eyebrows crinkled as his gaze rested on the broken crockery on the flagstone floor. "Did it fly, then, young Gwynna?"

"Well," she twinkled up at him, "*hardly* ever."

"Very good. My supper will doubtless arrive intact, which is a great relief to my mind."

He pushed her gently towards the stewpot and shifted his gaze once more to the redhaired man.

"Wencit, *do* you know him?" Leeana asked quietly.

"Yes and no." His raised hand forestalled her indignant retort. "I know a great deal about him, Leeana, but he doesn't know me."

"Is he all right?" Her anxious eyes edged meaningfully to Gwynna.

"You, of all people, should know it's seldom 'all right' to be of interest to a wizard, Leeana Hanathafressa," Wencit said gently. "But I think no harm will come to Gwynna from him."

Leeana peered into the multicolored depths of his strange eyes. Something deep and hidden looked back from their whirling depths, and she nodded. He'd answered her as fully as he would. He wasn't telling everything—he never did—but she trusted him. Especially where Gwynna was concerned. There was some link between the wizard and her daughter, one Leeana had never understood but whose strength she could not doubt. Her hands moved precisely, rewrapping the garrote around her head, and Wencit sighed inwardly at her affirmation of confidence.

"Let me sit and eat with him," he said softly. "I have to speak with him, and this is the best time. Besides—" he smiled teasingly "—it will convince you of his harmlessness."

"Japester!" She stabbed his ribs with a stiff index finger and he whuffed. Then she tossed a word at the direcat, and the great beast retreated slowly into his original place. He lay down neatly, chin on massive forepaws, but his eyes remained on the redhaired man.

"I'll see you're not disturbed," she said softly, "but you won't leave this house until you tell me more than you have!"

"All that I can," he promised, touching her forehead gently. She gripped his forearm tight.

"Ha! You mean all you want me to know!"

"It's the same thing, my dear," he said, smiling faintly.

"Here!" Gwynna dashed up, a full bowl in either hand.

"Am I supposed to stand in the corner and eat with one hand?" Wencit demanded. "The table, you little wretch!"

Gwynna laughed and ran to set the bowls in place. The red-haired man scarcely noticed her, though she stared at him with frank curiosity, certain it was safe to do so now that Wencit had come.

Leeana gathered up her daughter and moved into

the scullery, setting the girl to washing trenchers and glasses. She bustled the kitchen staff back to its tasks and took her own turn at the great sinks, but her eyes returned ever and again to the redhaired man and the old wizard by the fire, and a puzzled frown creased her brow.

✦   ✦   ✦

"Give you good evening, young sir."

The redhaired man looked up at the soft voice and saw an old man with a face creased by laughter, tears, and weather. Hair white as snow but thick and healthy was held back by a tooled leather headband, and bushy eyebrows moved expressively above strange eyes—*glowing* eyes that seemed all colors yet called no color their own. The old man's body looked younger than his face, and he had the scarred, powerful hands and wrists of a swordsman. He stood as tall as the redhaired man himself, and under his wet poncho he wore the sheathed weapons of a warrior. His appearance was shabby, yet an indefinable sense of power clung to his deep voice and ancient frame.

"I beg your pardon," the redhaired man made himself mutter. "I'm afraid I feel...unwell."

"Hardly surprising." The old man sat opposite him and spooned up stew, regarding him through the aromatic steam. "It's...unpleasant to realize one has no past."

"Yes," the younger man said softly. "I don't—" Then he broke off.

"How did you know?" he whispered, his right hand searching his belt for something that wasn't there.

"It's my job to know things," the old man said lightly. "I'm a wizard."

"*Wizard?*" The word was a hiss, and those searching fingers closed convulsively on a missing hilt. The old man only laughed and pushed the second bowl towards him.

"Indeed. Come now, man! Not all wizards have been evil, though I grant the breed has an evil name these days. But Bahzell Bloody Hand would have no dark wizard in *his* house!"

"Possibly not." The redhaired man's voice was harsh as he reached blindly for a spoon, eyes on the wizard's face. "Only I've never even heard of any 'Bloody Hand,' and even if I had, it wouldn't follow that any wizard was worthy of my trust."

"But you've met Bahzell," the old man said. "Come. Eat! His lady's made you free of her kitchen, and that's not a privilege that's easily come by."

"No, I imagine it isn't." The redhaired man smiled unwillingly. It was a thin smile, edged with bitter uncertainty, yet a smile for all of that, and he dipped his spoon into his own bowl. "A daunting lady indeed."

"The Sothōii war maids have their little ways," the old man said dryly.

"Sothōii war maids?" The redhaired man looked back up sharply. "They're pledged never to wed!"

"So they are. Or were, at any rate." The old man shrugged. "Their charter was . . . revised slightly in that respect some years ago. In fact, Leeana had a bit to do with that. Or her example did, anyway." He smiled. "She does rather tend to set the entire world on its ear just when the people around her think it's safe to take their eye off her. Of course, she comes by it naturally, I suppose." He shook his head. "Surely you've realized our Leeana is special in every way?

This whole household's special, my friend, and Leeana carries the rank of a commander of one thousand."

The redhaired man's eyes went back to the tall, slender woman with something like awe. War maids were seldom seen beyond the borders of the Wind Plain, but their reputation as fighters was second to none. The Sothōii's splendid cavalry was the terror of their enemies, yet the war maids—for all that they'd never been considered truly "respectable" by most Sothōii—were equally skilled in their chosen role as light infantry, scouts, and mistresses of irregular warfare. If Leeana had led a thousand of them in battle, she was a force to be reckoned with. No wonder men stepped aside when she crossed a room! But what was she doing wed to a hradani, one of the Sothōii's hereditary enemies? And why did the two of them manage a tavern in the Empire of the Axe, of all places?

He turned eyes filled with questions to the wizard across the table, but the other man shook his head ever so slightly.

"Your curiosity's apparent," he said softly, "but it isn't my right to enlighten you. Not that it isn't a tale well worth the telling—or that half the bards in Norfressa haven't already tried their hands at telling it, for that matter—but none of the ballads get it quite right. Except for Brandark's, perhaps." The old man's lips twitched on the edge of what looked like a smile. "Just understand that all the questions you've already imagined about them fall well short of the reality. If there's time later, I'm sure they'll be willing to tell you more, although it's unlikely there *will* be time for it tonight. The evening's schedule is likely to be a bit too much on the . . . full side for long stories, however good they may be. One word of caution I will give, however: offer no harm to anyone under this roof. Especially not to Gwynna Bahzelldaughter! If you do, no power on earth will save you."

The redhaired man shivered as the wizard's expression offered the second part of his warning—that Bahzell and his redoubtable wife might be the least of his dangers if he posed a threat to the child. He couldn't understand why that might be, but the cold certainty of it burned his nerves. Then the wizard's expression relented and he smiled crookedly.

"But we should speak of you, shouldn't we?" he said more lightly.

"What about me?" the redhaired man asked warily.

"Don't be foolish. A blind man could see you're troubled, and I'm far from blind. Besides, I'm a wizard. I may know more about you than *you* do."

"You know who I am?"

The younger man's spoon dropped and his hand locked on the wizard's wrist with bruising strength. The rumble of Blanchrach's displeasure rose, and the direcat's head lifted from his paws.

"Softly, my friend. Softly!"

Wencit's eyes compelled the redhaired man back onto his bench.

"You know who I am!" he insisted desperately.

"Who you are?" The old man toyed with the words, not tauntingly, but is if tasting their meaning. "Who can say *who* a man is? Not I! I can't even tell you who I am myself—not accurately. Tomorrow I'll no longer be the man I am today, and the me of yesterday has already died. No, I can't tell you who you

are, but perhaps I can tell you *what* you are, and
that's almost as good." He paused and eyed the other
levelly. "Almost."

"I see." The redhaired man smiled, and it was not
a pleasant expression. "Isn't there a proverb about
asking wizards questions?"

"A great many of them, actually. But I think the
one you want says 'Ask a wizard a question only if
you know the answer—and even then, *his* answer will
confuse you.'"

"You're right. That's the one I was trying to recall."

"I thought it might be. Do you want an answer?"

"Will it confuse me?"

"Undoubtedly," the wizard said calmly, spooning
up more stew.

The redhaired man regarded him across the table,
filled with a queer calm, like ice over a fire. He hadn't
known he was a stranger to himself before Gwynna
reacted to his scars, and the aftershock of finding
that he had no past still echoed in his soul. He had
no idea of who or what he was, no idea of what he
might have done. Was he a criminal? An outlawed
man with a price on his head? He remembered no
crimes—and wouldn't *that* be a poor defense? Did
he have a wife of his own? A family who'd become
less than ghosts as they vanished from his memory?
Was someone desperately searching for him, or did
no one in all the world care what might have become
of him? All those questions, and a thousand more
besides, poured through him, yet the old man seemed
unconcerned by his anguished confusion. He sat playing word games and swallowing stew as if things like
this happened every day! Perhaps they did happen to

wizards, but the redhaired man was ill prepared to cope with disaster on such a scale. If the wizard had the smallest clue to this...this *absence*, this negation of his past, of course he wanted to hear it. However confusing or frightening it might be.

"Tell me, then, Wizard." He made his voice mocking, though it took more courage than he'd thought he had. "What am I?"

"An important piece of a very large puzzle," the old man replied.

"You're right." The redhaired man snorted, green eyes dark with disappointment. "I'm confused."

"It's generally confusing to be a puzzle piece," the other man agreed. "Especially when the puzzle is vaster than you can possibly imagine."

"Really? Just how does this piece fit in? What makes me so important that a wizard chooses to play riddle games with me? Or is that question permitted?" the redhaired man asked bitterly.

"The question's permitted," the old man said, suddenly serious, "but I can't answer it now. Not in full, though I can tell you some things."

"Such as?" The redhaired man bent across the table, unable to hide the eagerness in his eyes.

"I will tell you this much. You're a fighting man, as your scars proclaim, but you're also much more than that, my friend. You're a man people will find it easy to like—perhaps even to follow—and such men are always dangerous, not least to themselves. You have strengths of which you're not aware, strengths which are hidden deep within you, and they make you a sharp-edged tool for a knowing hand."

"Wonderful," the redhaired man said bitterly. "Are

you *trying* to confuse me? Isn't simple ignorance enough for you? Why can't you give me something *useful?*"

"I have." The old man swallowed and waved his spoon. "Put it together. I'm a wizard, and wizards' answers are limited because we know too much. An injudicious word, a hint too much, and the damage is done. An entire series of plans, of strategies—years of effort—can slide down into ruin because we said one word too many."

His spoon cut the air to strike the table with a crack, and the redhaired man snorted angrily.

"I don't recall asking to be included in any strategies!"

"But then, you don't remember everything, do you?" The question was asked gently, and the younger man stiffened. "Perhaps you *did* ask...once. And consider this—your memory loss is selective, my friend. You know what hradani are, and direcats. You've heard of war maids. *Selective* amnesia's probably no accident."

"You mean...You're saying someone *took* my memory?"

"Precisely. And that means you're already part of *someone's* plans."

"But...why?" The younger man shook his head, eyes dark.

"For any number of reasons. I can't tell you much, but this much I will say: all wizards are puzzle solvers at heart, and most of us cheat. We may not like the way a puzzle fits together, so we change the pieces or rearrange their patterns. For every wizard who seeks one solution another wants a different answer, or simply for it to remain unsolved. It wasn't always so, but the past is the past. We have to deal with what *is*, not what we'd like to be."

The old man paused to stare into the fire. When he spoke again, his voice was softer.

"Some of us try to believe our solutions are in the best interest of all, or at least of the greatest possible number, but we're all quite ruthless. As for you, it would seem someone wants you ignorant of the part you might play if you still had a past."

"But what makes me important? Who *did* this to me? You say you're a wizard—how do I know it wasn't you?"

"It could have been," the old man agreed, his spoon chasing the last stew around his bowl, "but if I wanted you removed, it would've been easy enough to simply kill you."

He looked up and met the younger man's eyes levelly. The redhaired man swallowed, and nodded with a jerk.

"Then what *is* your interest in me?" he asked softly.

"At this moment? To keep you alive," the wizard said simply.

"Really?" The hairs rose on the back of the red-haired man's neck. "And why shouldn't I stay that way on my own?"

"Because ignorance doesn't change what you are. You're a danger to too many who follow the tradition of the Dark Lords of Carnadosa. Perhaps you're safe from the one who stole your memory, but there are others who not only can but certainly will kill you if they even suspect you're alive. And the reason will be simple. You threaten them, whatever you know or don't know...so long as you remain alive."

"So." The younger man studied the wizard as the fire roared to the gusts sucking across the chimney. "You may be telling the truth—or *a* truth, at least. But how do I know your truth is one I'd like?"

"No one wishes to know *all* the truth." The wizard's voice went gray and old. "Believe that, young sir."

"I do," the redhaired man said softly, "but I can't just take the word of the first wizard I meet. I remember another proverb. 'Trust not in wizards. The best are none too good, and most of them are evil.'"

"All proverbs have a core of truth," the old man agreed. "The art's fallen on sad times. There's no Council, and the majority of my brothers and sisters in the art are at best some shade of gray. But if you *don't* trust me, you'll be dead within twenty-four hours.

"Not by my hand," he went on quickly, raising a palm against green eyes that were suddenly burning ice. "If I wanted you dead, not even Bahzell could keep me from killing you now, while you're too ignorant even to understand the reason for your death." Power seemed to smoke above him, and the redhaired man's mouth dried as the shabby old man suddenly became a perilous menace that belied his wet, bedraggled appearance. Danger hovered about him like some invisible fog, but then he shook his head, smiled, and the peril withdrew. Yet it never quite disappeared entirely, and his flaming eyes gleamed between his lashes.

"As it happens, however, the last thing I want would be your death," he said. "If you die, I'll undoubtedly accompany you to Isvaria, and I still have much to do. I'll admit to selfish as well as selfless motives, but you have enemies, both mortal and of the art. Your own skills may protect you against the former, but only I can aid you against the latter."

"But *why*?" The redhaired man half-shouted. "Damn you *and* your cryptic hints!" He mastered himself with a visible effort. "At least answer me this much Wizard—how did you find your 'puzzle piece'?"

"I didn't *find* you; I waited for you."

"Very helpful." The younger man drummed on the table, frowning, and tried another approach. "Give me one good reason to trust you—one reason I can understand now, Wizard!"

"I still honor the Strictures of Ottovar," the flame-eyed old man said softly.

"Words! This is my *life*, Wizard! I don't know one single thing about you, and even less about your damned puzzles. I know nothing at all about altogether too much, so give me a better answer. How will trusting you keep me alive? Tell me, *Wizard!*"

"I never said it would." The old man's voice deepened and his fiery eyes flashed. "But if you trust me, you won't be the first, and no man who's ever trusted me has been betrayed, though many have died of knowing me. They died attempting to aid me, or simply because they came too close to my world of darkness and half-shadows. Don't mistake me! I offer you no promise of life, only a *choice*. I live in the shadows at the edge of what you're pleased to call 'the world,' and I've lived there a very long time. But I'm not part of the darkness."

"How can I know that?" the redhaired man whispered. "I want to trust you—the gods know I'd sell my soul to know who I am! But I don't know *how* to trust you. I don't even know who you are!"

"Remember what I said about asking 'who,'" the old man said gently. "I can't tell you that, but I can tell you what men call me. After that, you must judge for yourself. Perhaps you may even know my name. But beware! Reputation is only hearsay, and even if I mean you no ill, you may yet come to curse the day we met."

He paused, his face cold with warning, and the red-haired man felt a sudden urge to disavow his questions before he could hear their answers. The strange eyes burned brightly, their polychromatic depths dancing, and when the wizard spoke again, his deep, measured voice rang like iron on an anvil.

"I am called Wencit of Rūm, last Lord of the Council of Ottovar, Keeper of the Strictures of Ottovar, Chief Councilor to the Gryphon Throne of Kontovar, and I've waited fourteen centuries for this conversation!"

CHAPTER TWO

Friends at Need

"*Wencit of* Rūm*!*" The redhaired man stared open-mouthed for at least ten seconds, then shook himself as if to fight his shock physically. "*You're* the wizard who destroyed Kontovar?"

"Like all tales, that one's less than completely accurate." Wencit sighed, turning his head to look into the fire. "But, yes. I spoke the Word of Unbinding, yes, and freed the Council from the Strictures to let us strike our enemies."

He sat silent for a long, still moment, as if his wildfire eyes saw memories in the flames, then looked back at the younger man.

"We were three hundred strong, and we were powerful. Oh, yes! We were *powerful*, my friend." His voice was soft, and he sighed again. "And we poured out our strength like water and wasted our lives like fire. The world had never seen a working like it, not since Ottovar ended the great Wizard Wars ten thousand years and more before ... and when we finished, there were four white wizards in all the world. Just four, and two of them were mad...."

His face was wrung by an ancient pain as his flaming eyes bored into the redhaired man like augurs.

"Kontovar was destroyed," he said, still softly, "but only its corpse. Everything which had ever *made* it Kontovar, the Kontovar Ottovar and Gwynytha carved out of the darkness and brought into the light, had died already. Fire had consumed the Gryphon Throne. Trōfrōlantha, the city of Ottovar and Gwynytha, lay in ruins, the Dark Lords had triumphed, and they were poised to pursue the refugees even here, even to Norfressa, to complete the Dark Gods' victory. The only hope of those who'd fled was for us to cripple the victors, because we lacked the power to kill them, though we did our best." He laughed mirthlessly. "Oh, yes, we certainly did do our best! But we couldn't kill them all. Only the gods themselves know how many of their slaves we *did* kill, or how many lesser wizards died, but too many of the arch-wizards lived. Hacromanthi they called Kontovar after that—the Grave of Evil—but not even the grave truly lasts forever, and the evil wasn't dead. It only slept, and that sleep was uneasy."

He fell silent, staring into the fire again, and the redhaired man fought to comprehend the impossibility the old man represented. Somehow he couldn't doubt the word of his strange, shabby-majestic companion, yet it was preposterous. The second most fabled wizard of history wasn't supposed to be found in a tavern kitchen! And yet... and yet...

He watched tiny motes of wildfire hang before the wizard's glowing eyes and knew he heard the truth.

And that terrified him to the marrow of his bones, for what conceivable business had he with a man who'd brought death to an entire continent? And then an even worse thought occurred to him. If Wencit of Rūm himself required his services, could he even hope to refuse?

"And now," Wencit shook himself, rousing from a moody inspection of the flames, "I'm the last white wizard of Kontovar—may my friends recall me with fondness in Isvaria's halls! The gods know I gave them grief enough when they were alive!" He smiled at memories, then frowned. "But if their tasks are ended, mine isn't, and I need your help. I said you were an important puzzle piece, but that isn't entirely accurate. Or, rather, it's not *specific* enough, because the truth is that you're a key piece. I might almost say *the* key piece."

"But—" The redhaired man swallowed sharply. "I still don't understand," he went on, his voice much quieter, almost plaintive, his anger supplanted by confusion. "You're Wencit of Rūm! Every schoolboy knows the legends about you, the things you've accomplished. You can't need *me!*"

"Wencit of Rūm is my name, not what I am," Wencit said. "Not necessarily, at least. I'm many things to many people—and for you, at this moment, I'm far more important than a maker of legends." He snorted in self-derision. "Nor is legend-making all it's said to be, my friend! They're uncomfortable things, legends. They're usually made by people who wish with all their heart they were somewhere else, and any sane person avoids them like the plague. But that's beside the point, because whatever I am to other people, to you I'm the only man who knows how you fit into the struggles of wizards. I know a path through them, though honesty compels me to warn you that there aren't any easy roads, and a journey with me won't be pleasant. Oh, it may have its moments, but you'll curse me as often as you thank me." He grinned suddenly. "Bahzell could tell you I'm not the easiest trail companion even under the best of conditions, but you're committed to *a* journey, no matter what. Unfortunately, it will almost certainly be a very short trip if you leave this tavern without me. For that matter, honesty compels me to admit that the odds are against survival whatever you do, I'm afraid. The only absolute certainty I can give you is that you *won't* survive without me; the rest of the outcome is still... to be determined."

The redhaired man blinked, but his green eyes had lost their glaze of shock. He rubbed his scarred chest absently, considering Wencit's words. Then he surprised himself by smiling suddenly.

"Well, you're plainspoken—in some things—for a wizard," he chuckled. "Basically, I'm damned if I trust you, but doomed if I don't!"

"Not a pleasant choice," Wencit conceded. He fished out a battered pipe and filled it, his fiery eyes watching the younger man unreadably. Then he kindled a splinter at the fire and lit the pipe with care.

"If you can't tell me who I am," the redhaired man said in a strangely dignified voice, "can you at least tell me what I'm supposed to *do*?"

"Not entirely." Wencit blew blue smoke at the waxed cheeses hanging from the kitchen rafters, yet his voice was compassionate. "I can only repeat what

I said before. You're a fighting man, and fighting men are always useful. But you're much more than that, as well—potentially, at least—and there are things within you which I dare not disturb. Things which may make you of incalculable importance."

Gwynna delivered two mugs of hot tea, and the redhaired man thanked her and sniffed the steam, grateful for the interruption while he grappled with the wizard's words and his maimed memory. He couldn't believe anything special was hidden within himself, yet with only an empty void for a past, neither could he refute Wencit's statements.

He watched the grim figure of legend solemnly produce a silver whistle from one of Gwynna's tufted ears, and he smiled as the girl clapped her hands in delight. She hugged the wizard's neck tightly, whispering into his ear before she took her new treasure to show her mother.

Leeana paused to admire the whistle properly and then touched the red-gold hair gently as she released Gwynna from her tasks. The girl curled down with the direcat, and the huge beast lifted his head from his paws to let her perch comfortably upon his forelegs and lean casually back against his chest. Blanchrach's head was almost the size of her entire torso, but he rumbled with a powerful purr and rested his chin on her slight shoulder, amber eyes half-slitted.

Wencit's glowing eyes followed Gwynna, and the redhaired man recognized the fierce tenderness in the wizard's momentarily unguarded expression. It did more than any words to win his heart, that tenderness, but he wasn't prepared to surrender his doubt just yet.

"Suppose," he said quietly, leaning forward, "suppose

I accept you're who you say you are and that, impossible as it seems, I really am important. Let's even say I *have* to trust you. If I do, though, what—if it doesn't sound self-serving—is in it for me?"

"A reasonable question," Wencit said gently. "And a simple one. But I have no simple answer. I can't even promise you your life, only the meaning of it."

"Riddles within riddles." The redhaired man sighed.

"Of course!" Wencit chuckled suddenly. "I'm a wizard, after all." Then he fixed the younger man with a kinder gaze. "But I will promise you this. I swear by my art that someday, if we both live, you'll know your own name and the reason for all my actions. For now, I can't tell you any more than that. Not *won't* tell you, but *can't* tell you."

"I'm afraid I believe that," the redhaired man said unwillingly.

"And, believing it, will you let me guide you?"

"What other choice do I have?"

"Only those I've described to you," Wencit said softly.

"Then what can't be cured must be endured, mustn't it?"

"I'm pleased you take it so well." The wizard's tone was desert dry.

"I wouldn't if I could help it!"

"I expect not."

Wencit fell silent and sipped tea while the redhaired man slowly digested what had been said and tried to envision the implications of his own agreement. Wencit's pipe smoke curled in strange swirls and patterned clouds that seemed to hold secret meanings just beyond comprehension, and it was the wizard who finally broke the silence.

"I suppose you need a name, don't you?"

"It might be useful," the redhaired man said tartly, stretching his arms high in a spine-arching yawn. He held the stretch for a heartbeat or two, then settled back on his bench. "I can't go on being 'my friend' forever. But a man's name should say something about his life. So would you care to suggest one?"

Unveiled irony glittered in his tone, but Wencit declined the bait.

"Names are very personal," he demurred. "I suggest you pick one for yourself."

"All right," the redhaired man agreed, concealing any trace of disappointment as his probe bounced off the armor of the wizard's silence. "How does 'Kenhodan' strike you?" he asked finally, green eyes glinting with bitter humor.

"So you remember the Old Tongue," Wencit said.

"Some of it."

"A good choice, then," the wizard agreed calmly, and silence fell once more, emphasized by the crackle of the fire and the hiss of raindrops dying in its flame. Both men knew the name was both acceptance and challenge, for in the Old Tongue of High Kontovaran, "Kenhodan" meant "born out of silence."

◆　　◆　　◆

A conspiracy of thunder, wind, and lightning-shot rain ruled Belhadan as the night dragged towards a stormy climax. Even the most optimistic finally abandoned hope of a lull, and one by one the Iron Axe's patrons paid their scores and made their unhappy ways out into the blustering dark. In the end, only a handful of diehards remained, and Bahzell gave up the bar to an assistant and joined his guests in the kitchen.

The staff had withdrawn, leaving their mistress with her daughter and guests. Gwynna's bedtime had been extended in honor of the visitors, and she half lay across the direcat's forelegs with the fanged head laid gently but watchfully across her lap. She drowsed sleepily, but her mother sat in deep conversation with Wencit and the man now called Kenhodan.

Leeana's distrust had been conquered by Wencit's acceptance of the stranger, and now she sat across the table from Kenhodan, beside Wencit with her head propped against the wizard's shoulder as she sipped tea and sought to help Kenhodan come to terms with his maimed memory. She couldn't be many years older than he was himself, yet she approached the mystery of his amnesia with a calm far beyond her years. Her lively sense of humor was never far from the surface, but her verbal jabs were reserved for Wencit, not Kenhodan, and there was something almost . . . maternal about her. That wasn't the right word, but it came closer than any of the others he could think of, for there was a wisdom behind her compassion which seemed oddly out of place in someone who couldn't possibly be a day over thirty—thirty-five at the most. Whatever the "right" word might have been, however, he certainly wasn't about to complain. He found her quiet sympathy and acceptance, now that Wencit had vouched for him, soothing to the raw wound in his mind, and the little group floated in the warm comfort of people who hear violent weather rage beyond a snug roof.

And then Bahzell burst upon the quiet like a jovial thunderbolt, his deep voice echoing until Gwynna roused enough to demand her father's lap while Leeana shushed them both. Bahzell lifted his daughter from her perch on the direcat, and Blanchrach's deep purr rumbled as his head butted the hradani's knee affectionately. Gwynna snuggled her arms about her father's thick neck as he swung a mighty leg over Wencit's bench and cuddled her close. Leeana poured tea for him, and their eyes met warmly.

"And would it happen you've been and unraveled our mystery, love?" Bahzell asked, bussing her heartily and pressing another kiss to his daughter's hair.

"Bits and pieces of it," Leeana replied serenely. "At least our guest has a name and he and Wencit have reached an understanding."

"As far as we may in a single night," Wencit threw in, rotating his head slowly to stretch stiff muscles.

"And who could be asking more? By the Sword, though, it's enough to make a man come all over nervous to hear Wencit of Rūm admit a limitation!"

"I've never claimed omnipotence," Wencit said mildly.

"Just acted the part!" The hradani snorted. "I'm not complaining, mind. It's more than one scrape you've gotten me out of with my hide in one piece—more or less—over the years."

"But it's such a large hide," Wencit said wistfully. "Surely you don't begrudge a little piece of it every so often?"

"It's in my mind Tomanāk never promised I'd not bleed a bit now and again," Bahzell replied cheerfully. "It's welcome enough any foe of mine is to my blood, if it should so happen he can get it."

"A hazardous undertaking," Wencit murmured. "But enough pleasantry. Bahzell, this is Kenhodan, another servant of the Sword God. Kenhodan, I realize it may seem unlikely, but this lump of muscle is both a

champion of Tomanāk and swordmaster of the Belhadan
Chapter of the Order of Tomanāk. He had too little
wit to choose a safe god, so don't ask his advice about
anything important. But if you need counsel on the
shedding of blood, you couldn't find a better advisor."

Wencit's warning about the nature of this peculiar
household stood Kenhodan in good stead. So did the
fact that he'd encountered sufficient impossibilities
already for his preconceptions to have acquired a certain
punch-drunk elasticity. None of which was enough to
keep his eyes from widening in an echo of his astonishment. A Sothōii war maid might have no business
in the Empire of the Axe, especially wed to a hradani,
yet that was a mere bagatelle beside the notion of a
hradani champion of Tomanāk! Of any God of Light,
to be fair, but of *Tomanāk?*

Yet as he met the sharp, estimating gaze the hradani
turned upon him, he discovered he wasn't even tempted
to doubt Wencit's cheerful introduction. Those brown
eyes were sharp as daggers, looking out from behind
the façade of boisterous laughter and the tavern-keeper
mask Bahzell had chosen to assume for some reason,
and there was nothing in them of the barbarian brigand
which was the hradani stereotype among the other Races
of Man. There was intelligence, humor, confidence,
and a mind as sharp and as straight as Tomanāk's own
sword. They were the farthest thing imaginable from
a barbarian's, those eyes, and yet deep within them,
beyond the humor and part of the compassion, lurked
something more implacable than steel and merciless
as the war god's mace. Something that told him that,
preposterous though the very notion must be, Bahzell
Bloody Hand truly *was* a champion of Tomanāk.

Kenhodan had no idea how that might have come about. If anyone had asked him, he would have sworn it *couldn't* have come about, yet as his mind adjusted itself to the fresh shock, he realized he could actually see how a hradani—especially one like the giant seated across the table from him—might have been drawn to Tomanāk's service.

Tomanāk was a stern god, the keeper of the soldier's code, yet that was but one of his duties, and far from the most important. The third child of Orr and Kontifrio and second only to Orr himself in power, he was Captain General of the Gods of Light, the god whose hand had cast down Phrobus himself when he rebelled against Orr's authority. Beyond that, he was also the patron of justice, the Judge of Princes and the Sword of Light, entrusted by his father with the task of overseeing the balance of the Scales of Orr. And just as he himself was more than a simple patron of warriors, so were his champions. True, they were famed for their battle craft, but their true function was to be his Swords in the world of mortals, weapons ready to his hand for the protection of the weak and the administration of justice.

As a champion of Tomanāk, Bahzell was certainly a fit mate for a Sothōii war maid, and he also held rank equal to that of a Knight Grand Cross of the Legion of the Axe. More to the point, he was entitled to a lucrative income from the Order's coffers, which only deepened the mystery of why he kept a tavern.

Of course, that last was a minor, virtually insignificant question compared to all the other mysteries chasing themselves about under the tavern in question's roof.

"A warrior, are you?" the hradani mused. "Aye,

you've the thews for hard knocks, but is it the skill you have?"

"Wencit says I do, but I'm afraid I have to take his word for it." Kenhodan shrugged. "I've no memory to judge by."

"Faugh!" Bahzell thumped his tea mug down. "It's naught I know of lost memories, and little more of wizardry—and that too much for comfort—even allowing as I've questionable taste in friends! But this I *do* know. Take no man's word for your own sword skill, Kenhodan. It's advice or opinions you can ask on a ship, a house, or an investment, but know your own worth with a blade or expect a short life! Have you a sword?"

"I've nothing but what you see. Not even a past."

"Well, as to that, it's not so very much I can do about pasts." Bahzell waved a callused, oddly compassionate hand against the bitter self-deprecation of Kenhodan's words. "But if it's a sword that's wanted, we might be doing a mite about such as that." His bright eyes flickered to Wencit, alive with surmise, and then to his wife. "And where was it you were after storing Brandark's old sword, love?"

"In that rusting collection of ironmongery in your strong room, along with every other weapon you've ever collected," Leeana replied with a certain degree of asperity.

"Well, be a good lass and fetch it out! Here's a man of deeds without a blade, and I'm thinking it'd please the little man right down to the ground if we used his sword to set that right."

"All right, but don't let your tea cool while you wait. You keep that place in such a state it may take me hours to find it."

She rose gracefully and swept off, the light of battle in her eyes, and Bahzell threw a glance after her before he leaned closer to his guests. He grinned and spoke in a lowered voice.

"Tomanāk knows what I'd do without her, and whatever it is you might be seeking in this tavern, she can find it in a dark room with her eyes closed. But she does like to prod me now and again. And she's cause enough, truth to tell, for she's the only person can ever find aught in that strong room. Still, she's after enjoying the game as much as I do...I think."

"And the fact that you'd have to get your own swords if the game ever ended never enters your head?" Wencit asked innocently.

"Of course not!" Bahzell took another long pull from his cup and chuckled deep in his chest, ears half-flattened in amusement. It was a resonant, rumbling chuckle—an earthquake sort of a chuckle—but Kenhodan noticed that Gwynna drowsed right through it with the ease of long practice. She merely shifted to one side of her father's neck to avoid jostling, and her lips curved in a sleepy smile as she curled more tightly against him. Yet another deathblow to the hradani stereotype, the redhaired man thought dryly.

"Here." Leeana returned with a long scabbard tucked under her arm. Its black leather was clasped with silver bands overlaid with a patina of vast age, and despite her comments about "rusting ironmongery," the leather was well oiled and the silver gleamed without a trace of tarnish. "Miracles still happen. It was where it was supposed to be!"

"You see?" Bahzell beamed at her. "The serving wenches and I, we're after keeping this place in neat-pin order and all you need do is lord over it like a noblewoman born." His deep voice teased her gently, and his eyes glinted as if they shared some hidden joke.

Leeana made a face and handed Bahzell the sword. He gripped the basket hilt and drew six inches of shining steel, examining it critically before he slammed it back. He looped an index finger through the baldric ring to hold the scabbard in place and then flicked his wrist idly, and the sheathed weapon hissed as it cut the air.

"A nice balance," he observed idly, balancing it easily in the crook of one finger. "An ancient blade, Kontovaran work and made for the Gryphon Guard, or I'm a Purple Lord."

Kenhodan blinked as light reflected from the silver bands. The runes etched into them were far too worn and faint for any eye to read, yet they teased him with an elusive familiarity. The openwork of the basket was a finely fretted steel cage, affixed to the cross guard and knucklebow rather than directly to the hilt, as was the more common Norfressan practice, and the pommel knob was a plain steel ball. It also seemed younger than the rest of the weapon, which made sense if Bahzell was correct about its origins. If the hradani's guess was accurate, that pommel knob had once been a stylized gryphon's head, beak gaping in challenge.

"See how your hand likes its weight, Kenhodan."

Bahzell tossed the sheathed blade across the table with absolutely no other warning, and Kenhodan's right hand shot up like a striking snake. His fingers slipped into the basket to grip the ridged wire of the hilt in sheer, automatic reflex as he plucked the weapon from the air. Only then did he realize he'd gone for the difficult hilt catch rather than reaching for the scabbard, and Bahzell nodded, ears pricked forward in approval.

"A swordsman's speed right enough, by the Mace."

"And a risky way to prove it," Kenhodan said tartly. "I'd be missing teeth if I'd missed that catch!"

"Truer words were never spoken," Bahzell acknowledged. "But I'm thinking Wencit might've been wrong, you see, though that's rare enough to be worth the noting. Any swordsman's after needing speed of hand and quickness of eye, and it's in my mind you'd best be finding out if you've both of them early rather than late."

"And I'm sure one of Tomanāk's champions wouldn't have minded healing you if you *hadn't* caught it," Wencit said a bit repressively.

"Oh, aye, no doubt at all," Bahzell agreed, flipping his ears impudently at the wizard. Then he turned back to Kenhodan, and his expression was more serious.

"Best be drawing it to see what you think, lad," he said. "Brandark and I had it off a Shith Kiri corsair the best part of forty years back, and it's served him well it did, until he found a blade as pleased him even more."

Once again, Kenhodan had the sense of tales yet untold eddying under the surface, but he only cocked an eyebrow and rose, and thirty-eight inches of steel licked from the sheath with a soft, competent whine. It glittered in the lamplight and shadows like blue winter ice, and a strange, distant light kindled in his eyes. His face lost all expression as his nerves and muscles felt out the weight of the blade, and a sudden thrill ran through him as the steel melted into an extension of his hand and arm.

The double-edged blade was worn with use and honing, but the burnished, lovingly cared for metal was bright. The lancet tip shot back the fire glow like the crimson heart of a star, and his grip was light, as natural as instinct, as he moved slowly to the center of the kitchen. He fell into a guard position that raised Bahzell's eyebrows, but before the hradani could speak, Kenhodan lashed out in a lightning lunge and recovery so swift he seemed hardly to have moved.

Bahzell and Leeana eyed one another speculatively.

"Good," the hradani said quietly. "*Very* good."

He glanced at Wencit's impassive face, but the wizard seemed not to notice, and Bahzell returned his critical gaze to Kenhodan.

Steel flickered as the redhaired man flashed through a dazzling series of cuts, thrusts, parries, and feints. The blade hissed, and his movements flowed so quickly and deftly that only a highly trained eye could follow the glittering blade or the supple smoothness, speed, and perfect balance of his footwork.

"Excellent," Bahzell murmured. "Clean and sharp... and controlled. He's one as could lunge against a grape without breaking the skin, by the Sword! And I'm thinking—" he shot another glance at the wizard "—that it's somewhere else I've seen a similar style before this."

Wencit showed him a raised eyebrow, and Bahzell hid a smile as Kenhodan finished with a whirring parry and blinding backhand cut to the side. Then the blade whipped up, sketched a salute, and snicked into the scabbard in a single, flowing motion, and he returned to the table, breathing slightly faster.

"It's no more I know of your past than you do," Bahzell said quietly "but it's in my mind you've handled steel before."

"Yes." Kenhodan's voice was distant, as if he found it difficult to recover a focus on the present. "It came *alive* in my hand...."

"Aye," Bahzell said. "It's a master you were taught by, and I'm thinking such as that could lead to your past. Find the hand as trained you, remember whose it was, and it's not so very far from him you'll find your past, as well."

"I don't remember," Kenhodan said hesitantly. "Maybe no one taught me. It felt so...so much like a part of me...."

"And so it should," Bahzell rumbled, "but I'm thinking someone taught you, and taught you well. The fingers remember, whatever the mind may do, and sword skill runs in the muscles and the bone. A master swordsman's arm—" he eyed Kenhodan with that same measuring gaze "—is one as knows an art no other can imitate."

"High praise from a champion of Tomanāk," Wencit said quietly.

"That's as may be." Bahzell shrugged. "I've yet to see him in action, you understand, but I'd make no wagers against him."

"In so little you see so much?" Wencit teased, and Bahzell snorted.

"Laugh if you've a mind to, but I'm thinking you, of all people, know how much swordplay I've seen, both in practice and in earnest." Bahzell's voice hinted at more than his words said, but this time Kenhodan was too bemused to notice.

"I do." Wencit's nod seemed to respond to Bahzell's tone as much as to his words. "But I told you he was a warrior, didn't I?"

"So you did, and it's not a term you're in the way of using lightly." Bahzell leaned back, cradling his sleeping daughter, and regarded the wizard. "I've a mind to see the man in action, Wencit. So could you be so very kind as to be telling me your plans?"

"Actually, that sounds like an excellent idea to me, as well," Kenhodan said pointedly, laying the sheathed sword gently on the table. "How does this puzzle piece—" he smiled mockingly "—fit into your plans, O Wizard?"

"I need you close to me," Wencit replied. "Most pressingly, at the moment, to fend off attacks directed at you through the art. But the time will come when I need your aid every bit as much as you need mine. In a sense, you and I are part of the same puzzle piece. Neither can succeed without the other, and I'll soon need a strong swordarm. I hope you'll provide it."

"What choice do I have? You seem to know who I am—I'd be a fool to let you out of my sight. But why does a wizard need a swordsman?"

"I have an errand to the south," Wencit said easily. "Another puzzle piece to recover, so to speak. I know where it is, but laying hold of it may be a little . . . difficult."

"'Difficult' is it?" Bahzell's ears pricked at the wizard. "That's a word you use too seldom for me to rest all easy when I hear it, Wencit. It's nothing I know about this puzzle, but the south I do know.

Of course, it's most of the Empire lies south of Belhadan, not to mention the Border Kingdoms and the Empire of the Spear. Aye, and let's not be forgetting the Purple Lords, come to that! So just where would it be, if you don't mind me asking, as you have in mind to be going?"

Wencit eyed him expressionlessly, clearly weighing his answer, and Bahzell's lip curled knowingly. He waved his free hand.

"And don't you be turning that sour face on me, Wizard! I've the cost of a good meal and a better sword in our friend here. I'm thinking as how I might just find myself needing to protect my investment."

"Perhaps," Wencit said tonelessly.

"No perhaps, Wencit. Spit it out—and none of your evasions! You'd not be beating about the bush so unless no one with sense would be so very happy about your destination, now would you?"

"I'm afraid I can't deny that." Wencit's face crinkled in an answering grin and he gave up. "I'm bound for Angthyr. The Scarthū Hills, to be precise."

"Angthyr!" Bahzell sat back on the bench. "And just what sort of 'puzzle' might it be as takes you into that vipers' nest? It's more than enough I've heard—from Chanharsa and Barodahn's factors, and not just the Order—to know Prince Altho'll be at open blows with Ranalf of Carchon and Wulfra of Torfo by high summer. Aye, and past time he was about it, come to that!"

"I don't doubt it. Despite which, I have to go. I'll stay well clear of Carchon, though. I'm afraid the duke remembers our last encounter, and I don't have time to waste avoiding his guards."

"As to that, no doubt you'll know your own business best." Another grin tugged at Bahzell's lips and flattened his ears ever so slightly. "But it's in my mind you and Brandark are too much alike under the skin. I'm sure I've no least idea who it was went around enchanting every harp in the duchy to sing about the duke's bastardy. And I'm not so very sure his guardsmen would find themselves happy at all, at all, if it happened they were so unlucky as to lay you by the heels, come to that. But it's in my mind Wulfra's twice the man Ranalf is, and her barony lies right along the West Scarthū, Wencit! Just how was it you were thinking to avoid *her*?"

"I don't intend to avoid the lady. In point of fact, my business lies with her."

"Wencit, you're mad!" Leeana's arm circled the free side of Bahzell's neck as she leaned against him. Sitting, he was almost as tall as she was standing. "The baroness is no enemy to take lightly!"

"Aye." Bahzell eyed the wizard intently. "I'd not go calling on her without an army at my back—not if it so happened I had the choice. And don't you be telling me you don't know as well as I do what she's been about these past twenty years! If it should happen you don't, then you'd best drop by the Academy for a wee chat with Master Lentos. It's happy the Order of Semkirk would be to fill in those tiny gaps for you."

"I'm perfectly well aware that the baroness is a practitioner of the art, Bahzell," Wencit said calmly. "And that she was . . . rather less than honest when she convinced King Faltho she and that whole little circle of hers honor the Strictures." His expression was bleak. "I warned him allowing her to practice the art openly in Angthyr would be unwise, and so did the magi. Unfortunately, he chose to listen to the Purple Lords, instead."

"It wasn't just the money, Wencit," Leeana put in quietly. "Not entirely. Wulfra can charm an adder out of its hole when she chooses to. Faltho truly believed she was loyal to the throne. And so did Fallona after her father died."

"At least until the magi started looking into exactly how that 'mysterious illness' of his might have come about," Wencit pointed out.

"Aye, and that's one reason—one among many, I'm thinking—Prince Altho's after wanting her head on a pike!" Bahzell flattened his ears in emphasis. "But she's still one of the kingdom's great nobles, the law's still the law, and Ranalf's daft enough to support her still. Whatever it might be as Altho *wants*, it's careful he'll have to be, at least until he's *proof* of treason or blood sorcery, and Carnadosa only knows what deviltry she'll be hatching in that tower of hers until he finds it. Don't you go taking her for a lackweight, Wencit! She's one to walk wary of."

"And I'm not?" Wencit's multihued eyes flamed. "I'll admit she commands a portion of the art, but she's not my equal yet!"

"You've no need to be someone's equal for your henchmen to be putting an arrow in his back if he's daft enough to go riding past your front gate," Bahzell said succinctly.

"Granted." Wencit raised a pacific hand. "But more rides on this than you know, Bahzell, and Wulfra's mocked the Strictures too long. Besides, she has something of mine, and I want it back."

"Ha!" Bahzell's face lit. "I'm thinking you've always been a busy man, Wencit, but truth to tell, it's in my mind you've waited overlong to deal with her. Is it a formal duel you'll challenge her to, then?"

"And get that arrow you were just talking about in my back when I ride up to her gate to call her to account?" Wencit laughed derisively. "No, I've no desire to let the baroness see me coming. And while I don't doubt the time will come to settle that account of hers in full, that's not the reason for this little jaunt." There was no amusement in Wencit's expression now, and he shook his head grimly. "Truth to tell, it's an account badly in need of settling—you're right enough about *that*, Bahzell—and I've had to wait too long to see to that, for a lot of reasons. I won't pretend I'm not looking forward to...repairing that omission, but this is rather more important than showing her the error of her ways. To be honest, I'd prefer to be in and out again before she even knows I've been there."

"But where do I fit in?" Kenhodan demanded. "What use is a sword in a confrontation between wizards?"

"The objective is to *avoid* an arcane confrontation, if possible," Wencit answered. "I doubt we can avoid the art entirely, but the Barony of Torfo is two thousand leagues and more south of here. Even if I can reach it without open sorcery, the sheer length of the journey gives an enemy too many chances to arrange misadventures along the way. I don't doubt we'll meet opposition in the art—after all, several weaker wizards run at Wulfra's heels these days; she'd gladly risk *them*, and despite all her protests, I've caught the scent of Kontovar wafting north from time to time, as well—but most of what we encounter will be mortal enough for cold steel."

"That's your whole reason for taking me?" Kenhodan sounded skeptical.

"Wizards always have many reasons," Wencit said gently. "Don't ask for all of them. You wouldn't like what you might hear. In fact, I don't like knowing them all myself."

"It's a kormak or two I'd give to see the baroness brought down a peg," Bahzell said thoughtfully.

"Bahzell...!" Leeana's tone was sharp.

"Now, lass. It's not as if the Order hasn't heard the same sorts of tales as Wencit and the magi, and well you know it. And as Wencit says, it's time and past time she was seen to." The big hradani's expression had turned grim. "It's in my mind it's no coincidence he and Kenhodan were after washing up on our doorstep tonight."

"And have you heard a single word from Him about it?" she demanded.

"No, that I haven't. But himself's not the sort as leads people about by the hand, now is he, lass? It's a mind of my own I have, and I'm thinking he expects me to be using my head for more than a hat rack, time to time."

Leeana glared at him for a long, still moment, then turned an even more sulfurous glare on the wizard.

"Wencit, if you encourage this great idiot to wander off without me and get himself killed just now—!"

Leeana's eyes seemed to stray to Gwynna for a moment before she caught them and returned her gaze to the wizard.

"Leeana, talking sense to either of you is like trying

to swim the Western Sea. I don't even try anymore. After all these years, you'd think at least one of you would have gotten a *little* less stubborn, but no! And don't even get me started on champions of Tomanāk and how unreasonable *they* can be. Even the ones who *aren't* hradani on top of everything else!"

"Wizards! You dangle the carrot in front of the ox, but it's never *your* fault the poor beast follows after it!"

"Very well." Wencit turned to Bahzell. "Comforting as your sword and your presence have been in their time, I believe I can safely dispense with them. Kenhodan and I can see to our own safety, thank you. You and the Order have done more than enough for me in the past, Bahzell. And Leeana's right that this is no time for you to be away from Belhadan."

"Spoilsport!" Bahzell's tone was wry, but his brown eyes were warm as they met Leeana's worried green gaze.

"Perhaps, but I'd sooner have neither you nor Leeana in this. No, hear me out!" Wencit raised his voice, overriding Bahzell's attempt to interrupt. "You've been good friends, among the best I've ever had, but too many pay for my friendship with their lives. I won't have you do so when there's no need. Kenhodan and I have to go, but you don't. Not this time. The time may come when I have to ask you to risk your lives again—yes, and lose them, too—but not yet, Bahzell. Not yet! Gwynna needs both parents now, more than ever, and I tell you that if you mix in this venture, you'll take a step you can never untake. The time will come when you curse the day you heard my name, Bahzell Bloody Hand."

"Ominous words!" The hradani laughed, but then he shook his head, and his eyes were very serious.

"It's not so very many of himself's champions as die in bed, Wencit. It might be you'll recall a time or two we've had that selfsame discussion. And it's in my mind there's a risk or three you've run for other folk your own self over the last fourteen hundred years or so. You'll not be frightening me—no, nor Leeana come to that—with warnings such as that."

"Perhaps not, but don't expect me not to try, you overgrown lummox!"

"Sure and life would come all over boring if you didn't," Bahzell replied with a slow smile, ears cocked in amusement.

"I'm so happy I've been able to keep you entertained. But that doesn't change anything I just said about Gwynna needing both of you. Nor do I have any intention of exposing *her* to any sort of danger. In fact," Wencit raised his head and sniffed, "we should leave now. I've lingered too long already. Farewell."

He started to rise, but Bahzell's palm slammed the table like a hammer. Kenhodan flinched as bowls and mugs jumped, and the towering hradani's ears lay half flattened, his big, square teeth bared in something no one would ever mistake for a smile.

"Now that you'll not do!" he rumbled. "My house is yours, and has been these sixty years! D'you think Leeana and I are after forgetting all you've done for us and ours? Who was it brought Tellian and me face-to-face and laid out the truth about the hate betwixt hradani and Sothōii for anyone with eyes to be seeing? And who was it saved my arse—aye, and Master Trayn's, come to that—time and again? Who was it warned us of the mage power? No, Wencit of Rūm! I'm thinking it's one thing to leave me out of your journeyings, but you'll not be leaving my roof under threat! Not if I have to knock you senseless myself!"

"We're entering a time of great peril, Bahzell," Wencit said tautly. "Great evil may come to this house and all in it if we linger under your roof. I know you're a champion of Tomanāk. I know what that means—none better. But great evil is coming to us all, more than enough for a dozen champions. Yet this is no demon, no devil—nothing that . . . simple and above board, and I tell you this now. You may meet your sorrow sooner if we stay, Bahzell. Believe me."

"I do," Bahzell said simply but unyieldingly. "What evil?"

"Bahzell, can't you just take my word and let me go?" Wencit was half-pleading now. "Just this once, please. I will *not* involve you in this!"

"And you'll not leave until you tell me," Bahzell said inflexibly. "What evil would be after threatening this house if you stay?"

"An attempt was made on my life earlier tonight," Wencit said unwillingly. "I expect another shortly, and Kenhodan's presence may increase the probability."

"All the more reason to stay," Bahzell insisted. "It's little liking I have for assassins, and it's cold welcome dog brothers will find in my house!"

"Assassins, yes. If that were my only fear, then no place could be safer, and I wouldn't worry about you. But my enemies command the art, as well. They won't rely on mortal killers."

"And whatever it happens they *do* rely on, it's in my mind it won't be so very happy to be meeting with a champion of Tomanāk. Best you be meeting it here, under a roof, with extra eyes to guard and the entire Order ready to hand, come to that. I'm thinking there's little even such as she could be getting past that!"

"I can't involve the Order at this time, Bahzell," Wencit said flatly. Bahzell's mobile ears flattened in obvious surprise and the wizard sighed. "There are too many factors in play," he said. "I can't explain all of them to you, for a lot of reasons, but if the Order's drawn into this—if it's given proof someone is openly using the art against subjects of the King Emperor—you'll have no choice but to move openly against Wulfra. And if you move openly against her, my only chance to retrieve what I need from her will disappear. You're right that I do know even better than the Order of Semkirk just how vile she is, how much damage she's already done. I *know* that, but believe me when I tell you that getting into Torfo and back out again is far more important than punishing her crimes. It's even more important than preventing future crimes."

"I've no need to involve the entire Order," Bahzell said in that same unyielding tone. "But I'm himself's champion, Wencit. And do you think it's so very happy he'd be with me if it should happen I went and left you and Kenhodan to deal with this attack on your own?"

"I don't *want* your protection!" Wencit snapped. "And I've been protecting myself quite handily since before the Fall! I know you're a champion of Tomanāk, and I *know* your skull is thicker than the East Walls, but d'you think I want to expose Gwynna and Leeana to black sorcery? Give me enough credit—"

He stopped suddenly, as if aware he'd made a grave tactical error, and so he had.

"Leeana is the daughter of Tellian and Hanatha

of Balthar," Leeana said proudly, "and Gwynna is the daughter of Bahzell Bahnakson and Leeana Hanathafressa. Will you have it said we turned away guests and friends in time of danger? Would you dishonor us so, Wencit?"

"Some things are more dangerous than others." Wencit picked his words with care. "Believe me. Any attack on this house will be...extreme. Possibly extreme enough to require the rest of Bahzell's chapter when I can't afford—I literally *cannot* afford—to risk involving the Order of Tomanāk *or* the Order of Semkirk. Honor doesn't require you to accept such risks for your daughter, Leeana. Especially not when the guest prefers to leave before his enemies strike."

"Honor requires what we believe it requires." Leeana sounded as if she were reciting a creed. "You were our friend even before we ever met. You were the one person who helped Bahzell and Father put an end to almost a thousand years of slaughter between Sothōii and hradani. You hammered those diehard idiots in the Kraithâlyr when they tried to fight King Markhos' decision to revise the war maids' charter. You warned us about Sharlassa's mage gift, and you held my hand when Gwynna was born and Bahzell couldn't come. You've *always* been our friend, you're our friend now, and we do not desert our friends, Wencit of Rūm! We offer you the protection of our roof, and you will offend and dishonor us if you refuse."

Wind roared around the eaves as Wencit stared at her determined face. When he spoke again, he was through arguing. He was pleading.

"Leeana, listen to me. A time is coming when those dear to me will pay for their love and courage.

I *know* they will, and I thought I could accept it. I was wrong. Some things are more important than all a wizard's schemes. I should never have let you come so close to me, but I was...lonely. Now I want this danger away from you. From Gwynna." He sounded hesitant, almost beaten, as if tormented by something the others couldn't see. "I've risked you both before, and I'd back you against a hundred assassins. You know that. But I don't choose to involve you in this. What's begun tonight is worse than assassins could ever be, Leeana. As bad as anything Bahzell has ever faced in Tomanāk's service and, yes, worse even than that. Believe me, please."

Leeana rested her hand on her husband's shoulder and listened to Wencit's words. Then she looked into Bahzell's face, eyebrows lifted. Brown eyes met green and reached silent agreement.

"Then I'd best get my sword," Bahzell said simply.

CHAPTER THREE

Shadows by Night

The storm prowled the city like a conquering army as night guttered towards a close. The City Guard changed, new men tramping miserably to their sodden posts through sheets of windy rain while others hurried back to the welcome comfort of barracks fires and hot food. Water chuckled and laughed through downspouts, then gurgled and chattered in the deep gutters, its voice lost in the storm as it spouted and fumed headlong for the sea.

Tiny lights gleamed in a smooth crystal. Their wash illuminated the stern face of a blonde-haired woman as she peered past the lights at the water-washed Belhadan streets. Her eyes were intent, her gaze questing for signs of her servants' progress. Long, slow minutes dragged past, and she endured them with a hard-learned patience which was foreign to her nature. Fresh lightning flared, washing the gramerhain crystal's images with blue-white glare that flickered and crackled, and her search ended abruptly. She leaned close—so close her breath misted the stone—and a hard glitter of anticipation burnished her eyes while an unpleasant smile curled her full, red lips.

Shadows gathered in the rainswept night. They moved silently through the maze of streets and alleys, picking an unseen way towards a certain tavern. Deeper dark and blackly solid, they filtered noiselessly through the wind-slashed night while Baroness Wulfra smiled upon them.

✦   ✦   ✦

Bahzell Bahnakson leaned back comfortably in a chair propped against the taproom wall. The tavern keeper's apron had vanished, hanging on its peg and replaced by the chain mail hauberk, breastplate, and deep green surcoat of his order. The crossed mace and sword of Tomanāk on that surcoat's breast gleamed fitfully golden through the dimness of the turned-down lamps as the hearth fire tossed fitful spits of flame among the embers. An enormous sword leaned against the wall beside him, and his eyes were thoughtful as he gazed past the spiral of smoke rising from the bowl of his carven, silver inlaid Dwarvenhame meerschaum. That pipe was a gift from a friend long dead, and its heat-colored stone was hand-polished to a fine gloss from long years of use.

The redhaired man who'd named himself Kenhodan sat across the taproom from him, the bare blade of his new sword gleaming across his thighs. The Iron Axe was quiet despite the tumult rushing and bellowing about the heavens, and the quiet ticking of the clock above the bar was clearly audible.

Bahzell frowned mentally, although his expression never flickered, as he considered the younger man and wondered what might be passing through his mind as they sat waiting for the peril of which Wencit had warned. Bahzell had learned, over the many years of their acquaintance, that one thing Wencit of Rūm seldom did was to overstate a danger or a threat. That was the reason he'd bustled the last few, diehard guests into the rainy dark and sent the staff to find lodging elsewhere. Not without protests, although the guests' complaints had died with remarkable speed when Bahzell twitched his head sideways at Wencit and his wildfire eyes. The staff had been a bit more difficult. None of them had been willing to "desert" Bahzell and Leeana in the face of danger, and against a purely mortal threat, he would have allowed them to stay. Against *this* threat he'd overridden their protests with the ruthless authority of a hradani chieftain... and a champion of Tomanāk. In fact, he rather wished he'd had the intestinal fortitude to send Leeana off to safety with Gwynna, as well.

<*And what, in all the years of your marriage, suggests to you that you could send Leeana Flame Hair* anywhere *she chose not to go?*> a deep, silent voice rumbled in the back of his brain.

<*As to that,*> he replied a bit tartly, <*I'm thinking I'd've had a better chance convincing her she ought to take Gwynna to the chapter house or the Academy if she'd not gone and climbed up on that high Sothōii horse about honor.*>

<*Oh,* please, *Bahzell!*> A laugh rolled like fond thunder. <*She* climbed up on a high horse about honor? *And what, exactly, were* you *saying at the moment, pray tell, my Sword? I wonder whatever happened to that pragmatic, no-time-for-nonsense hradani*

I "pestered" into becoming one of my champions all those years ago? Rather Vaijon-ish you've become in your old age, isn't it?>

Bahzell was a wise and canny tactician. That undoubtedly explained why he chose not to reply to any of those questions, and he felt someone else's fresh amusement at his discretion.

<Well, I'm thinking that's all well and good,> he said then, his mood considerably more sober than it had been a moment earlier. *<And, truth to tell, one thing I've learned is if there's one person in the entire world as can out-stubborn me, it's Leeana, so it's not a task I turn to any oftener than needs must. But it's also in my mind as Wencit might just have chosen his words a mite carefully earlier tonight.>*

There was silence for a moment, and when that deep, rumbling voice, its depths pregnant with a power before which most mortals would have quailed, spoke once again, its humor had faded.

<Wencit is a wizard, as I believe he's mentioned to you a time or two before,> Tomanāk Orfro, God of War and Judge of Princes, said quietly. *<He always chooses his words with care. Indeed, with more care than he's allowed even you and Leeana to realize, Bahzell. But he told you no more than the truth. You and Kenhodan have never met.>*

<But that's not to be saying as how I've never met a man he might have been, is it now?>

<No, it's not,> Tomanāk acknowledged. *<And I did tell you that you and he would meet again someday. I can't tell you everything about Kenhodan—who he is, why he's so important to Wencit—and I know you understand why I can't. But you're right. You*

have *met the man he would have been in another time, another universe. And this much I will tell you, Bahzell Bahnakson: the man he is this night, the man sitting in your taproom, is just as much one of my own as Sergeant Houghton ever was, even if he doesn't know it. He isn't Sergeant Houghton, but in the sense you mean it, you're right. You may not have met, but you do know him. Or, put another way, perhaps, you do know what lives inside him and makes him who he is.>*

<Then that's after being good enough for me,> Bahzell said simply, and felt a vast, immaterial hand rest lightly on his shoulder.

<I knew it would be, my Sword. But Wencit also spoke nothing but truth about the peril you and Leeana—and Gwynna—will face because Kenhodan's come into your lives. I'm not speaking just about tonight, Bahzell. I know the temper of the steel in you and Leeana, and I have no fear either of you will fail the Light. But know this. The moment which I warned you so long ago was coming is almost here. Events are in motion, and the confusion and the possibilities and the echoes of what might be are so sharp, so strong, that not even a god can see them clearly. The final campaign of the war between Kontovar and Norfressa—between those who stand with the Light and those who have given themselves to the Dark—begins this night in your tavern, Bahzell Bahnakson. This is the battle for which you were truly born, the challenge for which you and Leeana were bred and trained and tempered on the anvil of love and honor, and it will cost you dear. I can't see all ends, and of those I can see, I have no way to

*predict which one you and she will experience, but
the price will be high.>*

There was no flinch, no effort to temporize, in that
earthquake voice. There never had been, and Bahzell
had never flinched from the iron fidelity of its truth.
Nor did he flinch now. He only drew on his pipe for
a moment, then blew out a thin, fragrant jet of smoke.

*<Then I'm thinking it's as well as I've my sword
handy,>* he told his deity simply.

◆   ◆   ◆

Kenhodan's fingers caressed the wire-wound hilt of
the sword lying naked across his thighs and he looked
across the taproom at his host.

If not for the smoke curling from Bahzell's pipe, he
would have been tempted to think the huge hradani
was asleep. But thoughtful brown eyes gleamed in
the light-flickers from the hearth, and Bahzell's ears
were half-cocked as if he were considering the pieces
of a puzzle.

Or perhaps *the* piece of a puzzle.

If Kenhodan had been remotely tempted to doubt
Wencit of Rūm's word about Bahzell Bahnakson's status
as a champion of Tomanāk, he would have abandoned
that doubt as Bahzell crisply—and ruthlessly—ordered
the rest of the Iron Axe's staff out of danger. They'd
dispersed to other houses—and it said a great deal
about Bahzell's stature in Belhadan that those other
houses had taken in hradani without even a murmur of
protest—but Kenhodan suspected few of them would
get much sleep this night. He'd needed no memory to
understand the unwillingness with which they'd abandoned their chieftain and lady, and their reluctance had
raised Bahzell and Leeana still higher in his esteem.

Now he sat quietly, waiting, wondering what was about to happen. He'd had no armor to climb into as Bahzell had, and he eyed the great, two-handed sword propped beside the hradani with profound respect. Its five-foot blade and long hilt almost matched Kenhodan's own height, and its hard edges were lovingly honed. The crossed mace and sword of the war god were etched below the quillons, and while Kenhodan would never have attempted to flourish so much steel about, Bahzell handled it like a cavalry saber.

The other defenders were spread about the building. Wencit sat alone in the kitchen, his own sword bare on the table while a tiny globe of witchfire danced slowly up and down it. The globe pulsed gently in time with his breathing, and his hooded eyes never left it.

A lamp glowed in a bedroom high under the eaves. It wasn't Gwynna's normal room, but it had no windows and only one door. Leeana, Kenhodan knew, sat in a chair between her daughter and the door, clad now in the traditional short, kiltlike chari and leather yathu of the war maids, and matching short swords hung at either hip while Blanchrach prowled the upper halls, long fangs gleaming in the lightning flashes the windows admitted. Gwynna was well protected, yet Kenhodan wished she'd been sent with the others. He suspected Wencit agreed with him, but there'd been little they could do. And perhaps Bahzell and Leeana were right. A child with her parents would do well to learn to share the risks and the love early.

The tavern felt like a huge beast around him, shoulders hunched in uneasy sleep while wind and rain pelted its flanks. The tranquility which always seemed to infuse a warm, snug roof while rain drummed upon it hovered in the corners. Yet for all its peacefulness, Kenhodan felt the farthest thing in the world from soothed. He wondered what form the attack would take, but he never doubted it *would* come.

He snorted restlessly and shifted position.

In a sense, his life had begun this evening. He had no past, no knowledge of what he might have been or done or accomplished in those lost years, but now he was locked into a game whose rules were understood only by an enigmatic wizard with flaming eyes that radiated sincerity. It angered him to be so helpless, and the cold chill of ignorance simmered in his blood like sea ice.

He glanced back at Bahzell and smiled wryly. His harrowed and riven memory told him enough about the hradani tribes to know Bahzell's position in the heart of Belhadan was virtually impossible, champion of Tomanāk or not. For that matter, the notion of a hradani champion of Tomanāk was even less likely than that. The hradani were masters of ambush and accomplished raiders who happened to be the Sothōii's most bitter enemies. The hatred between them and the Sothōii—who just happened to be the Empire of the Axe's most important allies—was cold, focused, and deeper than the sea, a thing of centuries filled with mutual slaughter. Yet Bahzell was not only a champion of Tomanāk but wedded to a war maid! The gods only knew how *that* pairing had occurred or how the ill-matched couple had found their way to Belhadan. He gathered Wencit had played no small part in their lives, and perhaps someday he'd learn how it all had happened. He hoped so; it promised to be a rare tale.

His thoughts returned to himself and his smile vanished. Who and what was he? One thing he'd already learned was that it cut across his grain to sit and await attack, especially when it endangered those who'd gone from strangers to friends in mere hours and of their own free will in time of peril. And he'd also learned that it galled him to take orders, even when he knew he must...and even from someone as powerful as Wencit of Rūm.

Not, he thought with another snort, that he had a choice. He was a chip in a millrace, careening into an unknown future from a forgotten past, and it was a journey he would not survive without the wizard. Much as he would have preferred to, he couldn't doubt that truth any more than he doubted that Wencit truly knew who he was. That truth, and Wencit's knowledge, bound Kenhodan to him like a chain.

He straightened in the chair, pressing his spine against its back, inflating his lungs and tightening his arm muscles in a seated, joint-popping release of tension. He suppressed the need to run mental fingers over the raw wound of his forgotten past yet again and, instead, stroked the hilt of his sword and traced its razor edge. He found himself hoping the attackers would arrive soon. They'd be coming sooner or later anyway, and it might ease his frustration to cleave a few hostile skulls.

◆   ◆   ◆

More shadows flitted through the rain, converging on a cloaked figure in the Street of Wharves. The shadows' movements melded into a single, perfectly coordinated whole, yet no word was spoken. A bitter cold hovered about them like arctic mist, streaming through the rain with invisible menace. The dimly lit windows of a tavern were shuttered, squeezed squint-eyed and smiling into the night through the open louvers, and their reflection gleamed on the street's streaming pavement. The shadows halted, clustered about the living human who'd summoned them, and menace flickered in the topaz raindrops as they stood in silent communion with their master just outside the spill of light.

♦   ♦   ♦

Wencit's eyes narrowed as his ball of witchlight blazed purple-red. He lifted his sword in a sparse, economic motion, and the blade whined softly, as though possessed of a life of its own in his sinewy hand. Blue light shimmered briefly down its edge, like a reflection of his fiery eyes, as he paused to throw a warning to the bedroom beneath the eaves before he turned to the taproom.

Leeana looked up at the touch of his magic, her green eyes calm. She stood, and his mind saw her garbed for war. Steel-fanged throwing stars glittered at her belt, and Wencit nodded approval as she loosened the restraining thongs on her sword hilts. Then he opened the taproom door.

Kenhodan rose on catlike feet as the wizard entered. The borrowed sword balanced expertly in his hand, ready to strike, and Wencit stood motionless until the redhaired man relaxed in recognition. Then he glanced across at Bahzell.

The big hradani cocked his head, mobile ears half-flattened, and took his pipe from his mouth.

"I'm thinking you've the look of a man as has a mission," he rumbled calmly.

"I always knew you were smarter than you looked," Wencit replied with an edged smile.

"It's here they are, then?" Bahzell laid the pipe on a table at his elbow and rose, stretching his arms in a mighty yawn while his ears shifted back and forth, alert for any sound through the pound of rain.

"Outside." Wencit jerked his head at the windows. "Something's out there, anyway. Part of it's easy enough to recognize, but there's something strange, too. Difficult to place." He sounded almost meditative.

"What kind of attack do you expect?" Kenhodan asked tautly.

"Shadowmen, I think—and whatever else it is I sense."

"Ahhhh!" Bahzell let out his breath in a sigh that mingled understanding with something very like anticipation. "At least your wizard friends've been good enough to send me something as I can get steel into."

"So they have," Wencit said grimly, "and one of them's come himself—Alwith, I think. But remember: if you can get steel into them, they can do the same for you. And they'll attack without fear, as well, so they've got a good chance of doing it."

"It's been done," Bahzell said simply, "but never twice by the same person."

"Gods send me strength!" Wencit snapped in exasperation. "Tomanāk knows you're almost as good as you think you are, but try to remember these aren't mortal enemies!"

"But if I can be killing them, they aren't after being *im*mortal, either, are they now? And I'm thinking whatever it may be you've sensed out yonder in the rain, it's not so very likely to be a demon or a devil. Not unless Wulfra's run clean mad and decided as how she *wants* to see an Axeman army burning its way across Angthyr to take her head, any road." He wiggled his ears and reached for the helmet lying on the table beside his pipe. "Taking the rough with the smooth, that's not so very bad an outcome, Wencit!"

Wencit eyed him sourly and turned to Kenhodan.

"They'll concentrate on you and me," he warned.

"It'll be a relief to have a problem I can deal with." Kenhodan grinned, meeting Bahzell's eyes in the dimness, and Wencit snorted.

"Solid bone between the ears, the pair of you! It's to be hoped it at least makes your heads harder to split!" His voice was tart, but his hand squeezed Kenhodan's forearm in approval.

"Leeana?" Bahzell had his helmet on, and his enormous sword's edges glittered in the fitful firelight. Now he moved to Kenhodan's left, facing the windows while Wencit turned to the kitchen hall and Kenhodan confronted the front door. They formed a hollow triangle of ready steel.

"She's awake and ready," Wencit murmured, "and Blanchrach's in the hall. But I doubt she'll see much of them compared to us."

"Aye." Bahzell shifted the great sword to his right hand and drew the hook knife with his left. "Well, as to that, they've business with us, tonight. And since they do, I'm thinking it's only courteous to be giving them a belly full of commerce." His smile was unpleasant.

"I approve," Wencit said briefly. Kenhodan only grunted, his eyes sweeping the front of the tavern, swinging from the barred door to the corner of the windows. A flicker of light caught at the corner of his eye, and he glanced over to see red and gold runes dance quickly down Wencit's sword, confusing the gaze that tried to follow them.

"Ready!" the wizard hissed.

✦　　✦　　✦

Shadows conferred silently outside the tavern. Lightning whipped the clouds, shattering blue-white above their silent forms, and the spalling electricity etched two shapes which stood apart from the others. The human's sodden cape lashed from his shoulders in the gusting wind, and the lightning leapt back from the ebon staff he bore. The other was a shadow, taller and somehow more solid than the others. A rod of polished steel or dull silver winked at the lightning from its left hand, its metallic glitter broken by patterns of jagged, deeply carved runes from no alphabet ever used on Orfressa.

The human's staff pointed at the tavern, his lips moved in unheard words, and the shadow's black head bent. Its rod touched the staff, and a speck of eye-searing blackness leapt from the staff to the metal and vanished. Then the shadow turned and gestured to its fellows.

Lesser shadows moved to obey silent commands. Some flitted to the shutters and doors. Some lifted gently into the rainy night, borne by the wind to chimney openings and upper windows. Lightning cracked again, its jagged light vanishing into the dark forms, and the taller shadow waited another moment, then stretched an arm to point at the tavern and its finger glowed dully.

✦　　✦　　✦

Everything happened at once.

Kenhodan's brain seized a brief image of the door as it flew inward in an explosion of splinters and broken bolts. An iron shard gashed his cheek, hissing past to bury its length in the wall. Windows and shutters cascaded inward in the same moment, showering the sawdust with diamond-bright glass. Broken bits of pane winked in the fire like rubies, ringing as they bounced over tabletops and benches. A shadow filled the doorway, and cold rolled from it like acid. A flash of brilliance washed his shoulder as Wencit muttered a semi-audible incantation and his blade pulsed with savage light in time with the words. The chill withdrew slightly, and Bahzell's breath snorted, pluming like frost, as his huge sword swung up in a silvery arc, as if saluting his foes.

Then the shadows were upon them.

Despite his scars, this was in a very real sense Kenhodan's first combat, yet there was time for him to realize he felt no fear. Time for him to wonder what that said about the man he'd forgotten. And then a strange, consuming rage roused within him. It filled him with a fury which demanded blood, and it had an endless depth that staggered the mind. He had no idea where it had come from, and if there'd been time to think about it, its fiery strength would have terrified him. But now, at this moment, he was conscious only of his own burning hunger, and his lips drew back in a feral snarl as the shadows attacked.

"Tomanāk!" Bahzell's bull-throated bellow roared through the taproom, and a shadow loomed close, a scimitar of blackness reaching for Kenhodan like an extrusion of its own substance. Instinct prompted and

reaction obeyed. His own blade darted to engage the scimitar, driving it wide, then recovered in a straight backhand that raked the shadow from crotch to throat. He felt a fleeting resistance, and the shadow fell back with a thin, ear-hurting wail. It dissolved in streamers of noisome fog before it hit the floor.

Another eluded the sweep of Bahzell's knife and charged Kenhodan from the left while the hradani's sword engaged two more. Kenhodan's blade flashed across his own vision as if he were a spectator. Black scimitar crashed on razor-blue steel. Wrist and arm throbbed, and his booted heel slammed into the shadow's midsection as he heaved the scimitar away from his flesh. Acid cold stabbed as high as his thigh and burned in his hip with a pain that wrung an anguished gasp from him, but his sword whistled back against the shadowy neck. A half-seen head flew, and another high death wail pierced his ears.

Sorcerous they undoubtedly were, he thought grimly, but they were as killable as he was.

"Tomanāk! *Tomanāk!*"

Bahzell's thunderous war cry rose over the clash of blades. Kenhodan leaned away from a slash and caught a glimpse of the hradani in the full, murderous action of a champion of the war god. His greatsword avalanched down in an overhand blow, propelled by the muscles of an arm as thick as Kenhodan's thigh. It smashed clean through a scimitar to cleave a shadow in two, then whistled up in a perfect backhand, preposterously swift for a blade of its dimensions, that split another shadowy head. The hook knife darted, gutting a third while the first two fell away. Every move, every shift of weight, was perfect, like some choreographed exercise, with a deadly efficiency which had to be seen to be believed, and a bright yet half-imagined blue glitter wrapped itself around the towering hradani.

Kenhodan spared a thought for the old wizard, but the ring of blades and the odd wails of dying shadows came from his rear as well. It was reassuring evidence of Wencit's condition, yet the moment of inattention was almost his own undoing. The brief break in the flow of his rage snapped his automatic reactions. His waking mind intruded on his trained body, and cold fire burned his shoulder, tracing a line of hot blood edged with ice. He staggered, momentarily convulsed by the awful cold pulsing through his body. But he dragged himself back on balance and his elbow smashed the attacking shadow. Another burst of cold slashed through him, but this time he was prepared. He shook it off and shattered his foe's head, recovered, and slid two feet of steel through another's chest. That shadow, too, fell away, winning him the tiny moment he needed to beat the last cold shudders from his muscles. A shadow sprawled to his right rear, and Wencit's blade burned with dangerous fire, consuming his foe as it struck.

There seemed no end to that first rush. Kenhodan lost track of the number he struck down in a wild flurry of blows, counter blows, and hairbreadth escapes. Yet there was a break in the attack wave at last. He smashed the guard of a final foe and lunged through its throat, then stood back, panting, as the remaining shadows fell away.

They stood just beyond reach, like a circle of icebergs, their silence taunting him, and that fierce rage roared within him. It gripped like bands of hot iron, and he leapt to the attack. But Bahzell dropped his knife. His hand darted out to fasten on his shoulder like a steel vise, and Kenhodan's eyes flared at the immense strength which stopped his lunge as if he were a child.

"No, lad!" The hradani rasped, holding him effortlessly in the defensive triangle. "This one's Wencit's!"

Kenhodan froze, then nodded tightly, panting for breath as a single shadow glided over the sawdust. A metal rod glimmered sullenly in one hand, and a black scimitar burned in the other. A dim flow of light from half-guessed eyes mocked the wildfire of Wencit's gaze, and Kenhodan shuddered to see it.

The defenders pivoted slowly, Kenhodan compelled by the hradani's grasp, until Wencit faced the new threat. Bahzell paused just long enough to recover his hook knife, then faced the shattered door, content to leave the main fight in Wencit's hands. Kenhodan knew he should echo the hradani's detachment, but he found his attention split between the kitchen arch and the arcane confrontation of wizard and shadow.

"You've been lied to," Wencit said levelly, the words drifting in puffs of vapor in the icy chill radiating from the shadows. "Your power here is less than you think. You're overmatched. Be gone or die!"

The shadow continued its silent advance. The metal rod traced an intricate pattern, its tip glowing like a dull ember that left a brief, sullen line of flame in its wake. Wencit's glowing blade moaned a sub-audible shriek that grated in the bones of Kenhodan's skull like the howl of a hunting animal, but the wizard made no move.

Ruby light spat suddenly from the tip of the rod

in a quasi-solid pencil that lashed at the wizard with the speed of thought, but Wencit's sword flashed up. It parried the light with a sweeping gesture and red sparks flew, burning through Kenhodan's jerkin. Wencit's blade wailed hungrily, and the wizard twisted his wrist, wrapping the light about his weapon like a cord. He jerked, and the rod snapped from the shadow's grasp. It bounced into the sawdust with an unnatural ringing sound, as if it had struck stone.

The shadow leapt forward as its rod flew free. Its scimitar scythed at Wencit's torso, but the wizard spun on his toes in a graceful dance that carried him out of the blade's path and behind its wielder. The shadow lurched silently forward, committed to its attack. Its free arm flailed as if for balance, and the shadow head snapped silently towards Wencit.

The wizard continued his swirling motion. He grasped his hilt two-handed, lowering the blade to waist level, and completed his circle. Eldritch steel smashed squarely through the shadow, cleaving it into unequal halves that tumbled grotesquely to the floor. This death wail was louder and more vicious, and the bits of shadow didn't dissipate. Instead, white fire blazed through them, tearing at their darkness, flaring bright and hot. It seemed to last for minutes, but it couldn't have been more than a handful of seconds before those flames dwindled once more, taking the shadow's broken pieces with them in a stink of burning sawdust and something worse.

The remaining shadows snarled as the stench of burning rose, and scimitars lifted in the firelight. Kenhodan gripped the wizard frantically, dragging him back into formation. There was something ominous in that snarl from their hitherto silent enemies, and dread burned through his rage as he fought to reposition Wencit. But the wizard was badly out of position, and he'd barely begun to move before the charge began.

Only Bahzell seemed unconcerned as the shadows gave tongue. He simply leaned sideways, peering intently into the rain beyond the shattered door. And then, as the shadows surged forward, his left hand snapped like the idle flick of a whip. The hook knife hissed from his fingers into the outer darkness, a short, bubbling scream erupted, and the shadows halted, frozen in mid stride. As Kenhodan watched in amazement, they faded slowly and the flames of their fallen chieftain sank back into smoldering sawdust.

"I'm hoping I've not violated etiquette," Bahzell grumbled calmly, "but it's in my mind yonder wizard wasn't one as worried his head over the rules for wizards' duels, Wencit. If he'd no wish to bother with such as that, why, I'd no reason not to be obliging him."

◆　◆　◆

Wulfra of Torfo cursed as the haze of Wencit's masking glamour filled her crystal with a gray and silver mist her strongest spells couldn't pierce. Alwith must be dead or dying, and with the cord of his thought went her ability to breach the wild wizard's defenses.

She sighed and sat back in her exquisitely comfortable chair, massaging her delicate brows. The outcome was hardly surprising, much though she might have wished it otherwise. Still, Alwith had been grossly overconfident. Even a direct order might not have stayed his hand, so she'd made a virtue of his arrogance and given him the spells for which he'd asked. He'd thought Wencit was overrated, had he? That the old man was "past it" and sinking into decline? Well, he knew better now—whatever hell he was in. Yet she had to admit he'd come close...very close. Without the hradani and the unexpected redhaired stranger, he might have succeeded after all.

She frowned thoughtfully, then leaned over the crystal again. She retained two servants in the area, and if Harlich was weaker than Alwith, he was also more cunning. Forewarned about Wencit's allies, he might prove more fortunate, especially since he possessed the madwind incantation.

And if he proved equally *un*fortunate, well, tools were made to be used, and sometimes they broke in the using.

❖   ❖   ❖

Bahzell raked the metal rod through the sawdust with a cautious boot, studying it thoughtfully before he turned to Wencit.

"Well struck, Wencit," he said formally.

"You weren't so bad yourself, Mountain," Wencit retorted with a grin. "But the shadowmage was outclassed." He bent over the rod and lifted it cautiously. "I'll take care of this," he said more sharply. "See to your lady, Bahzell. Kenhodan and I can finish here."

"Aye."

Bahzell turned quickly to the stair, sword still in his hand, and Kenhodan watched Wencit draw the rod slowly through his fingers. The wizard's lips moved silently, his eyes flared briefly, and then answering light burst from the rune-graven metal. As Kenhodan watched, it glowed bright and fierce, and when Wencit opened his hands the enspelled metal curled upward in a thin stream of stinking smoke and vanished.

Kenhodan raised an eyebrow, and the wizard smiled faintly and dusted his hands on his tunic. Then he turned to the door, and Kenhodan followed, standing at the wizard's shoulder and peering out into the night. Rain blew into their faces through the shattered door and windows, but the lightning had ceased and the wind was falling away at last.

"And now there are three...." Wencit murmured.

"What?" Kenhodan turned to look at him, and Wencit shrugged.

"Now there are three," he repeated, gesturing to a sprawled body just visible in the light spilling from the open door. Bahzell's knife stood in the dead throat, surrounded by a thinning pool of rain-diluted blood.

"That was one of Wulfra's allies. Now there are only three: Wulfra, Thardon, and Harlich. I suppose we should consider this a good start, so early in the game, but they shouldn't have found me so quickly."

Wencit sheathed his weapon and straightened. The sword's dangerous light had vanished, and Kenhodan wondered how it could look so normal one moment and burn with arcane fury in the next. There was something frightening about a weapon like that, even when it fought on his side. Then he realized his own madness had vanished just as completely, and the parallel chilled him. He was going to have to come to grips with that blind rage, and the thought of it was far more disturbing than Wencit's blade.

He shook himself and sought a lighter note.

"It seemed less than crushing for a wizard's attack," he ventured.

"You think so?" Wencit turned to him, his voice thoughtful. "No attack's crushing once you defeat it, but what about that score on your shoulder? What about the gash on your cheek? The cold that nearly crippled you?" Kenhodan blinked, startled by the wizard's ability to catalog his hurts, but Wencit gave him no time to consider it. "A second later ducking, an inch to the side, a moment earlier with no counter spell ready—then what? And for each you or I killed, Bahzell took two. Don't underestimate our enemies, Kenhodan. Consider what would've happened if they'd surprised us in the open, alone, with no warning. Not so easy to beat them off then, eh? And remember—the most deadly fighter's still mortal, and the clumsiest foe can kill him with one lucky blow."

"I take your point." Kenhodan knelt to examine the sawdust where the shadow had burned. "What were they, anyway?"

"Shadows of another world. Much the same place demons and devils come from, actually, although shadowmen are far weaker than those are. That's the reason they can flow through the cracks and escape notice so much more easily on their way. It's not difficult to search the worlds that might have been for the fighters you seek. Transferring them, especially in numbers great enough to make them truly dangerous to someone like a wizard lord or a champion of Tomanāk, takes power and a willingness to dabble in sorcery as foul as Krahana herself, but the technique's simple enough."

"For some, no doubt," Kenhodan said dryly.

"True. And even though shadows lose much of their intelligence when they're ripped from their rightful places, they still make deadly foes. That cold is the cold of the void they cross to come here. If you'd felt it without the protection of my wards, your heart would've stopped instantly." Wencit shrugged. "They have other powers, too. They aren't truly of this world, and its presences are, to them, the shadows they are to us. But they also have limitations, because the shock of crossing the void destroys their wills and leaves them as little more than extensions of their summoner. They can't remain if his will is—" he gestured toward the body "—withdrawn."

The wizard paused, scuffing a boot through the scorched sawdust, and his brows knitted thoughtfully.

"But the shadowmage bears thinking on. Shadows aren't normally drawn from among the great and powerful of their worlds—people like that are too deeply rooted in their own time and place to readily answer the summons of anything short of a deity. Yet the shadowmage was a wild wizard in his own world. It takes a very powerful wizard to wrench someone like *that* across the abyss, and the guardians who prevent that sort of thing should have seen the shadowmage coming. Unlike the others, he was powerful enough to stand out clearly and be intercepted. Bringing him through at all would have been difficult enough. Bringing him through undetected *and* with the power to strike with the art once he got here . . . ?"

His voice trailed off and he frowned.

"So it must've taken a wizard more powerful than this Wulfra? Is that what you're saying?" Kenhodan asked slowly.

He didn't care for the implications of that thought, and he cared still less for Wencit's slow nod. Wind gusted through the broken door, touching them with rain and muddying the sawdust. The old wizard sighed resignedly and reached for his poncho.

"Let's go take a look at Alwith."

Kenhodan followed him into the dying storm. Rain soaked his hair and trickled down his face, but it lacked its earlier fury, and Wencit knelt beside the body and rolled it over. The knife hilt described an ominous arc and Alwith's dead eyes looked glassily into Kenhodan's.

"He looks surprised," he observed.

"No doubt he was." Wencit examined a charred staff that crumbled to ashes when he touched it, then scraped its ruin distastefully into the bubbling gutter. "Alwith preferred to avoid physical combat. He probably forgot the lightning might give Bahzell a clear target."

"He won't make that mistake again."

Kenhodan wiped rain from his face and looked back at the tavern. Perhaps Alwith might be pardoned for his misjudgment, he thought, for there were clear targets and then there were clear targets. Bahzell's knife had traveled twenty yards through rain-filled darkness to arrive exactly on its mark... thrown left-handed. He raised a thoughtful eyebrow and wrenched the heavy blade from the grisly ruin of Alwith's throat.

"No, he won't be making *any* mistakes again," Wencit agreed, sitting back on his heels in the rain, but his expression was... not precisely worried, but *perplexed*, perhaps. "There should be *something* more than the ash of his staff, but I don't see what."

"How could you expect to find it if you don't know what it is?"

"Are you a wizard?" Wencit asked patiently, and Kenhodan shook his head in quick disavowal. "Then don't ask me to explain the art on a moment's notice."

He puffed his lips and Kenhodan had the definite sense that the unseen eyes behind his witchfire gaze had just rolled. "You can't *imagine* how many times someone's asked me to do that! But my point at the moment is that I just can't believe the shadows were all Wulfra sent with him. Her henchmen could've managed the earlier attack alone, with her to coach them and provide the information they needed to target it. But she clearly realized it might fail, which is why Alwith was ready to follow it up, and I can't accept that she gave him and the other two no special aid beyond the shadows! I was hoping for a clue to whatever else she might've given them. If I'd found it, I would've recognized it."

"Suit yourself." Kenhodan shrugged.

"It doesn't suit me a bit. Something's missing, and that bothers me as much as whatever's behind her new tactics. There's been an addition or change, and I want to know what it is and how it happened."

"What do you mean?"

"If anyone had asked me, I would've said it was impossible for her to summon something like the shadowmage even with her students' power joined with hers. On top of that, it's not like her to give such a weapon to another. Especially not someone like Alwith, who might turn on his teacher. It worries me to find her doing unanticipated things."

"Don't most wizards know about these shadows? How can you be sure it's beyond her strength?"

"The art isn't a campfire you build higher or lower with a stick of wood!" Wencit turned suddenly snappish. "*Someone*—Alwith or Wulfra or one of the others— must've rummaged through the shadow lines for our opponents. You never know what you'll meet out there, and moving something like the shadowmage increases the odds of attracting some very powerful entities between the worlds. Some of them, like Tomanāk, would simply obliterate someone like Wulfra with a thought. Others would take their time devouring her soul one inch at a time." He shook his head. "Taking chances like that isn't like the baroness."

"But would it be impossible for her?" Kenhodan asked.

"Whatever she may have told the world, she practices blood magic," Wencit said grimly. "That means she could *raise* the power, but controlling it—that's something else entirely. It's her will I question. She'd have precious little margin for error, and if her will wavered even for an instant there'd be a smoking crater where her castle stands. That means it took more courage than she normally displays." He stood and frowned. "No, that's not really fair. She's willing to take risks if she has to, but she's cautious. She wouldn't take such a chance unless she thought she absolutely must. That's what's so strange about it."

They reentered the tavern, wiping rain from their hair, and Wencit leaned over the bar for a squat bottle and two glasses. He poured pungent, cinnamon spiced Belhadan rum and handed one glass to Kenhodan, who sipped the strong spirits thoughtfully.

"So how do you explain it?" he asked finally.

"I can't." Wencit leaned one elbow on the bar and frowned. "At least not in a way that makes sense and doesn't scare me."

He sipped slowly, then shrugged.

"I see two possibilities. Either she thinks our

confrontation justifies extraordinary risks—which isn't like her, when she can't yet know exactly what I'm up to—or else she's found a way to augment her power. To be honest, I like that answer less than the first. Increasing her power would certainly lessen her risk, and I'm afraid I can think of at least one way she might have done it, but I hope to all the gods I'm wrong!" He frowned again. "But unless I can learn more, I can't be sure what she's done. Still, I'd have taken an oath that she didn't have the nerve for *that*, either...."

"Well, *something* must've happened," Kenhodan said carefully as the wizard's voice trailed away in thought.

"Obviously." Wencit shook himself. "Well, of the two, I have to vote for the second possibility, much as I'd prefer not to. Wizards don't change their styles easily, but they can gain power in a number of ways—not all of them pleasant."

"Aye, I'm thinking I've heard that tale before."

Bahzell's voice startled them, and Kenhodan blushed slightly as the hradani eyed the glass in his fist with a twinkle. He and Leeana had entered the taproom silently, a nightgowned Gwynna riding sleepily on her father's hip. The immense direcat padded in behind them and sat gracefully, then convulsed in a violent sneeze.

"You heard?" Wencit sounded unsurprised.

"Aye. It's sharp ears hradani have—and noses, come to that." He sniffed loudly at the rum and chuckled. "Best be pouring out two more glasses, Wencit, seeing as you've made so free with my stock."

"Of course," Wencit said courteously. He filled a

fresh pair of glasses and handed them to his host and hostess.

"So your friend Wulfra's not performing as expected?" Bahzell rumbled. "And you're not liking the smell of things overmuch, I take it?"

"No." Wencit shook his head, then grinned. "On the other hand, wizards seldom perform as expected. Or so I hear."

"*I've* not known one as did, any road," Bahzell agreed pleasantly.

"I thank you." Wencit bowed to him, then turned to Leeana. "I see you suffered no mischief, Leeana."

"Only three of them got as far as the bedroom, and they could only come at me one at a time," she said simply.

"And young Gwynna?"

"Slept through the whole affair," Bahzell chuckled.

"Did not!" the girl protested sleepily.

"Did so," Leeana corrected, touching her nose gently.

"Well . . . maybe," Gwynna admitted with a grin.

"As well for the shadows, I'm thinking."

Her father smiled, easing her onto the bar, and reclaimed his knife. He wiped it before clicking it back into its sheath.

"At least wizards're after having honest blood, though I'm thinking it's the only honest thing as most of them do have. No need to be wiping shadow blood from a blade."

"Yes, they were very considerate," Kenhodan agreed guilelessly.

Bahzell eyed him suspiciously, and then chuckled and clouted Kenhodan's left shoulder so hard he staggered. He opened his mouth, but the direcat went

into a fresh sneezing fit before he could shoot back
a smart remark.

"What's his problem?" he asked instead, nodding
at the cat while his right hand checked his shoulder
for broken bones.

"He says shadows taste funny," Gwynna said sleepily.
"We bit six of them, and he's been sneezing ever since."

Kenhodan glanced up, ready to smile, but the look
on Bahzell's face stopped him. He swallowed his humor
as he realized Bahzell actually believed his daughter
could talk to the cat! The hradani's expression mingled
acceptance and pride with an edge of concern, and
Kenhodan reminded himself—again—that he was in
no position to say *what* this peculiar family could do.

"Don't worry, young Gwynna," Wencit reassured
her. "The sneezing will pass."

"I already told him so," Gwynna nodded. "I did
when we bit them. He just says he wants it to hurry
up. You know how he is, Wencit."

"Yes."

The wizard moved to the broken windows and
peered out, and Kenhodan sighed mentally and refused
to ask questions. Everything else about this household
was preposterous. Why shouldn't Gwynna talk to the
cat? But what about this "*we* bit them" business?
Surely she didn't mean—?

He put a firm lock on his curiosity and joined
Wencit by the windows.

The first faint light of a blustery dawn glinted on
the wizard's silver hair. He sniffed deeply, wrinkling
his nose, and nodded to himself.

"Time Kenhodan and I were gone. This may have
set them back enough for us to make a clean break."

"Aye, and you've come with your usual luck, Wencit," Bahzell said. "It's just this week Brandark raised Belhadan. We'll be finding him at the docks, and he'll find us a way south. I'm thinking we'll make better time by sea than afoot, seeing as how Walsharno's taken it into his head to be visiting the Wind Plain right this very moment. Aye, and Gayrfressa with him."

"No!" Wencit spun to his host accusingly. "I thought I made it clear you weren't included in this little episode!"

"And so you did, or tried to. But that was then, and now's after being now," Bahzell said calmly. "You could refuse to invite me before these enemies of yours were after violating my roof and raising weapons against my guests. Now?"

His expression was as calm as his voice, but his ears were half-flattened and his brown eyes were hard. Wencit looked into that unwavering gaze for a moment, then turned to his wife.

"Leeana?" Wencit appealed to her without much hope in his voice.

"He's right, and you know it." Leeana reached up to rest a hand on her husband's bulging biceps with no sign of her earlier resistance. "You know our customs. Honor demands that one or both of us accompany you against anyone who violates our roof."

"I might point out that you invited the attack by extending your hospitality against my wishes! Honor shouldn't demand you risk your lives in my quarrel, and I won't have you doing it!"

"Honor requires what we believe it requires." Bahzell repeated Leeana's earlier words softly. "We can't be picking and choosing on the basis of safety, Wencit. Not with honor."

"But it's not your quarrel! It's *mine*—mine and Kenhodan's!"

"Wencit, if you try much harder, you'll be after making me angry," Bahzell said. "I remember a wizard as made mine and Leeana's quarrel *his* fight, once upon a time."

"That was different! This is—"

"Oh, admit it, you old horse thief! You're not so senile yet as to not want me along! Who else is it as might be keeping your ancient and venerable hide in one piece?"

"Kenhodan might! And I might be ancient and venerable, but I'm not exactly a dotard yet myself!"

"Aye, and Kenhodan's one as swings a pretty blade. But if two swords are good, why, three are after being better. Besides, if you're not minded to let me come with you, I'll have to be following on my own. And if you're daft enough to be making me do that, how is it you expect me to talk Leeana into staying home with Gwynna? You know she's the better tracker."

Wencit swelled with frustration, but then Bahzell put one hand lightly on his shoulder.

"And laying all that aside," he said softly, "I'd a talk with himself whilst waiting for your friends the shadows."

Wencit glared at him for an instant, then exhaled sharply.

"All right. All right!" He shook his head resignedly. "Tomanāk knows you're handy with that cleaver, but don't blame me if you wake up dead one morning!"

"Oh, I wouldn't be blaming you for that. Why, if such as that was to happen, it would mean someone'd managed to be sneaking up on me in my sleep. And if that's after being the case—" his left hand blurred and the hook knife whined from its sheath to sink four inches deep into the far wall "—it's only myself I'll have to blame, isn't it now?"

Kenhodan thought he heard Wencit mutter something about the thickness of skulls under his breath... but he might have been mistaken.

◆   ◆   ◆

Wulfra of Torfo flinched as the icily incisive thought speared her brain. She herself required a crystal at both ends to communicate with someone else, though she could observe others with her unaided gramerhain. The ability of that ice and iron mind to reach her anytime and under any circumstances mocked her power, and the implications of such strength made her nervous.

The shape of two eyes, slitted and yellow like a cat's, glittered in her thoughts, and the mental voice was a chill purr of malice.

"Your minion failed."

"He was outclassed. Just as I'd be if I faced Wencit personally. You knew that when you agreed to let Alwith attack."

"True. But having tested the mettle of your opponents and counted their number, my dear, I suggest you deal with them from a distance."

The biting thought's malicious amusement angered Wulfra, but she pushed the emotion carefully aside.

"I have to know where he is for that. His glamour's too strong for me to pierce without a link to someone inside it. You know *that*, too."

"To be sure. Wasn't it *I* who found him for your lightning strike? Yet even I dare not take liberties when he's fresh," the cold voice whispered. "If your minions bungle their attacks too often, he may begin to suspect I'm observing him despite his glamour, and neither of us would like that, would we?" The mental purr became a chuckle. "Still, at the moment he's too tired to detect my prying. Alwith was a fool, but he wasn't *completely* wrong. Our Wencit's less young than he was."

"Do you have a suggestion?" Wulfra kept her mental tone respectful, but the cat-eyed wizard sensed her impatience.

"Patience, Wulfra. Patience! Revenge is best taken slowly, distilled in small sips. But, yes, I have both information and a suggestion. You might like to know that our Wencit is highly perturbed by your recent display of power. Isn't that amusing?"

"Do you mean—?"

Wulfra's thoughts were suddenly icy with fear. If Wencit ever guessed who she was dealing with, her fate was sealed, indeed.

"Calmly, dear Wulfra! Of course he doesn't suspect *that*; how could he? But he's anxious—*very* anxious. I believe he fears you've tapped the sword's power, or a part of it. Of course, we know better, don't we?"

Wulfra's racing fear became the coal of anger the cat-eyed wizard could so easily ignite. Of course she hadn't mastered the sword! And neither, she thought in a secret part of her brain, had her patron. If he could have done so, he would have had no need for her.

"But that's neither here nor there," the cat-eyed wizard purred, "and I do have information. Look for a ship, my Wulfra. A ship of Belhadan captained by a hradani named Brandark. There now! Even you should be able to find so singular a vessel."

Communication ceased and the mind link snapped, leaving Wulfra to feel dismissed . . . and angry. She was no child to be so discounted! She'd won her power the hard way, through acts which would have led to instant execution had they been known at the time. And her cat-eyed patron needed her—needed her badly! How dared he to treat her so?

But deep inside, she knew how he dared. It was because for all her knowledge, she *was* a child beside him. Yet perhaps he'd forgotten that children grew up and some surpassed their tutors. . . .

She forced herself to undertake several minutes of carefully calm thought, banishing her rage. It was many minutes before she could unclench her fists in a semblance of normality, but then she brushed back her golden hair brusquely and moved to her crystal. Purposeful concentration carried her rapidly through the energizing incantation. Whatever the cat-eyed wizard thought of her, it was she who must bear the brunt of any failure . . . well, she and her allies.

She bent closer to the stone and formed a mental image of Harlich's face. He should be alert for her regular contact.

He was. The face she'd pictured appeared in the stone, masklike for just a moment. Then the mask's eyes opened. Harlich himself blinked into existence in its place, and his eyebrows rose in question. She shook her head, and he shrugged. He'd never cared much for Alwith anyway.

"There's a ship," Wulfra began carefully. "You have to find it. And then . . ."

CHAPTER FOUR

Designs and Departures

Wencit might have accepted that he had no hope of convincing Bahzell to stay home in Belhadan, but he remained determined to set out as quickly as possible. Personally, Kenhodan would have preferred to let the last of the rain wear itself out, and he wouldn't have objected to a few hours sleep, either.

Bahzell, obviously, agreed with him, and unlike the majority of people faced with Wencit of Rūm, he was completely prepared to argue the point. In fact, he spent fifteen minutes trying to convince Wencit to send a messenger to Brandark while the prospective travelers got some of that badly needed sleep for which Kenhodan longed. Kenhodan lent his own arguments to the effort, but Wencit was adamant. Speed was evasion, and evasion was salvation. They must leave at once! When Bahzell (inevitably) proved stubborn, the wizard turned to Leeana.

". . . so you can see why we have to hurry, can't you, Leeana?"

"No." Leeana's response robbed Wencit of breath—momentarily, at least—and she pressed her advantage ruthlessly. "For once, my rock-headed husband is right. Not even you can speed the tide, Wencit, and you know perfectly well no ships will leave harbor before the ebb." She shrugged. "Since that's true, there's no point sending you out exhausted, especially when Brandark doesn't even know you're coming yet! I'll choose a discreet messenger to find him and warn him about what you have in mind while you three sleep."

"But—"

"Best be giving it up, Wencit," Bahzell rumbled. "There's no budging her when she's after using *that* tone of voice. Tomanāk knows it's often enough I've tried, and I can't recall as I ever succeeded."

"Once," Leeana told him, green eyes glinting with humor. "Twenty-five years ago, I think it was."

Bahzell flattened his ears impudently at her, and she grinned, then folded her arms and returned her gaze to Wencit. There was much less humor in it now, and the toe of her right foot tapped gently on the floor as she waited courteously for his response.

The wizard looked back and forth between his hosts for perhaps fifteen seconds. Then he puffed his lips and threw up his hands.

"Oh, all right!" he said with scant grace . . . and yawned. His eyes widened, and then he smiled sheepishly. "Maybe you're right. The gods know I can use some sleep, too. Where's my room?"

Leeana smiled back serenely and pointed at the stairs.

✦　✦　✦

Kenhodan needed sleep badly, but his rest was uneasy. Dying mutters of thunder thrust him into a

dream world of unfamiliar sights and sounds—sights
and sounds he knew even as he dreamed that he
should have recognized...and would be unable to
recall clearly when he woke. Nor could he. His only
memories were images of war: blows and counter
blows, death and destruction, and a haunting, crippling
sense of guilt, as if he were personally responsible for
all the blood and suffering of the world....

He soaked his blankets in sweat and half-woke endlessly, but always fell back into haunted slumber. None
of it meant anything to him, yet he sensed uneasily
that it should have. It was tempting to ascribe it all
to the taproom battle, but he couldn't. Somehow he
knew the vague, terrifying dreams spoke directly to
his maimed memory...or to his unknown future.

When Leeana finally called him to breakfast, he was
at least somewhat rested, physically, but his inward
exhaustion was even worse. It showed in his weary
eyes and slow responses, and Leeana cocked her head
sympathetically at him.

"You slept poorly?" she asked as she and Gwynna
bustled about the kitchen. Others might cook, but only
she and her daughter served food to their guests. It
was that sort of kitchen.

"I had dreams," he replied evasively.

"Dreams?" Wencit arched an eyebrow. "What sort
of dreams?"

"Unpleasant ones," Kenhodan said shortly.

"Never have bad dreams myself," Bahzell said cheerfully around a thick chunk of rare beef. He swallowed
and downed half a tankard of ale. "Would it happen
they told you aught of your past?"

"I don't know," Kenhodan said slowly. "Maybe. If

they did, I'm not surprised by all the scars anymore. They were . . . violent."

Wencit chewed expressionlessly, and Kenhodan felt a fresh stab of frustration. He had no choice but to accept that some compelling reason kept Wencit from telling him more, but what possible threat *could* force the world's premier white wizard to keep silent on so vital a question?

A flash of humor came to his rescue as he considered what he'd just asked himself and reevaluated his own importance to the world. But it was still vital to *him*, he thought wryly, even if no one else cared.

"You and Poppa are going on a trip, aren't you?" Gwynna's voice broke into his thoughts as she climbed onto the bench beside him.

"Yes, we are." He made room for the long-legged child, struck once again by a prevision of the lovely woman she would one day make.

"Momma told me," Gwynna confided. "She wanted to go, too, but Poppa said no. They had what Momma calls a 'discussion' about it. A *loud* one."

She grinned, and Kenhodan almost choked on a mouthful of exquisitely fried potatoes. He swallowed, then looked at her.

"A discussion?" he repeated carefully.

"Yes. That's when they spend an hour telling each other the same things over and over and then decide to do what they knew they were going to do all along. When *I* have a discussion like that, Momma calls it a quarrel."

"I see." Kenhodan managed to keep his voice level, but his face ached from suppressing his grin when he tried to picture Bahzell as a harassed husband "discussing" things with the cool and independent Leeana. It was surprisingly easy. What was hard was imagining him winning the argument, but Gwynna's next words explained it.

"Momma doesn't travel with Poppa as much as she used to. I think she's worried about leaving me with Farmah and Lentos. She says I'll drive anyone mad if they have to take care of me long without being rescued."

"I can understand that," he said feelingly.

"Me, too."

She wiggled her ears at him, disturbingly like her father, and grinned impishly.

"Let me see," Kenhodan said. "I've met Farmah—that's her over there, isn't it?" He gestured at a middle aged hradani woman with dark hair and a checked apron, and Gwynna nodded. "But I don't think I've met Lentos."

"Oh, he's away this week. He's my teacher, from the Academy. He's nice, but he must be almost as old as Wencit, and he gives such good advice I can hardly stand it."

"I see," Kenhodan said politely. It hadn't occurred to him that Gwynna might be old enough for a tutor. He smiled at her, touched by her mixture of precocity and whimsy—and privately sympathizing with the tutor responsible for her. "I'm sure he only does it because it's something you should know."

"Oh, I understand that." Gwynna waved airily. "But I really wanted to talk about last night. I wanted to apologize for dropping your stew."

"That's all right. You did bring me another bowl."

"I know. I just wanted you to understand it was

only because your scars surprised me. I mean, Poppa has a lot, too, but not like those." Her brows knitted in a troubled frown, but his smiling nod erased it magically. "Good! I wouldn't want you to think your scars scared me or anything. Well, not much, anyway."

"They surprised me, too," he told her with a certain edge of sincerity.

"Then you're not mad at me? Really?"

"Really," he assured her, and she heaved a sigh of relief and smiled.

"Good! Because I'd like you to do something for me when you go with Poppa."

"Do what?"

He was amused by her assumption that he was going with Bahzell rather than the reverse, but he concealed it carefully.

"Well..." Gwynna doodled a fingertip on the table, studying her invisible design intensely. "Farmah knows lots of stories, and she tells them in the kitchen sometimes. Lentos knows more, but his aren't as interesting, because he only ever tells what really happened. But Farmah says warriors used to carry things with them to remember ladies back home. She says they called them 'favors' and they were things like handkerchiefs or veils." Her lip curled disdainfully. "I think those are dumb things to take on an adventure!"

"So do I," he said gravely, and she regarded him suspiciously.

"Well, it *is* dumb to take useless things. What good's a handkerchief, unless you need to blow your nose? But I thought it would be nice to have someone carry *my* favor. I know I'm not a lady yet—" She broke off with a silvery giggle. "Momma says I'll *never* be a lady, but I think she's wrong, and so does Wencit. Anyway, I wondered if *you'd* carry my favor?"

Her blue eyes looked up very seriously, and he was deeply touched, as if a warm finger had brushed his cold amnesiac world. He felt a surge of grateful tenderness...and protectiveness.

"I'd be honored to carry your favor, Lady Gwynna."

"You don't mind I'm only ten?" she asked anxiously. "I'll be eleven in a few weeks."

"I don't mind at all," he told her solemnly.

"Well, good! I mean, you're the only one I can ask. I can't ask Poppa, because he's already Poppa. And Wencit is...well, he's just *Wencit*. I can't imagine him being anyone else. Not even for me."

"I understand," Kenhodan said, but he didn't, really. He could feel the girl's presence himself, an acute awareness of the happy deviltry which followed her around. He wasn't even surprised by his own sense of protectiveness, yet it seemed strange to see such tenderness from the ancient wizard, and Gwynna's choice of words suggested something even deeper.

Don't go reading too much into things, he chided himself. *It's obvious he and Bahzell and Leeana are close. It's probably just friendship.*

"I thought you would," Gwynna said cheerfully, "and I won't give you anything dumb, either. I brought something special. Here!"

She handed him a straight, heavy object fifteen or sixteen inches long. It was wrapped in oiled silk and weighted his hand with the solidity of tempered steel. He recognized the dagger instantly, and his eyebrows rose.

"Momma and Poppa gave it to me two years ago. If we were still on the Windy Plain I'd already be training as a war maid, so Momma said I might as well start here, and Lentos agreed. It's hard, but it's fun, too. But this is special—a corsair dagger Captain Brandark brought back from his last big sea fight when he was still captain of Poppa's ship. He gave it to Momma as a souvenir when he bought *his* first ship. I thought you'd like to have it, since you already have his old sword. And it'll be lots more useful than a stupid old *handkerchief!*"

Her scorn was withering.

"I agree," he said, touched by her hardheaded practicality.

He unwrapped the sheathed dagger, drew the blade, and examined it carefully. It might have come from a corsair, he realized, but it was dwarven work, and an outstanding example of it. It carried the rippled pattern of water steel, and the double-edged blade was sharp enough to slice the wind.

He looked up to find her gazing at him just a bit anxiously and slid the weapon back into its scabbard. Then he stood, unbuckled his belt, and threaded the free end through the sheath's belt loop. He re-fastened it and sat back down on the bench.

"I shall carry your favor everywhere, Lady Gwynna," he told her gravely.

"Good!"

She patted his elbow and climbed down to help clear the table, and Kenhodan looked up to meet Bahzell's eyes. The hradani's gaze measured him thoughtfully, then moved to his daughter. Kenhodan felt a little abashed by the fierce love on Bahzell's face, but there was something else there, too. An inexplicable sadness, perhaps.

"It's a good lass she is," Bahzell said softly.

"Yes, she is," Kenhodan agreed.

Bahzell nodded sharply. Then he drained his tankard noisily, thumped it to the table empty, caught Wencit's eye, and jerked his head at the door.

"Young Frolach was after finding Brandark. He says Brandark told him it's pleased he'll be to give us ship room as far as Manhome, as he's a cargo bound there. If we're wishful, he'll bear us farther—to Coast Guard, say. But it's in my mind you'd be minded to go the last bit by land?"

"Good thinking," Wencit agreed. "Angthyr's so unsettled merchants will shun the ports, so any arrivals by ship will certainly attract attention. We can go overland through South Pass, instead."

"So I thought my own self," Bahzell nodded. "What do you say, Kenhodan?"

"One route's the same as another." Kenhodan shrugged "I seem to recall a little about Angthyr, but not enough to make suggestions."

"Aye." Bahzell tugged a watch from his pocket and glanced at it, then rose. "Well, let's be taking our leave, then, and I'll be telling you what I can about Angthyr as we're walking."

Kenhodan and Wencit rose with him and began gathering the gear Leeana had chosen while they slept. Each had his personal weapons, but Leeana had also provided Kenhodan with a longbow of Vonderland yew. Bahzell carried a huge composite horse bow (one far beyond his own strength, Kenhodan suspected), but Wencit had neither requested nor been offered a missile weapon.

The new bow suited Kenhodan. It was a magnificent

weapon, and though he'd had no opportunity yet to try it, he'd felt a sort of natural affinity for it—almost, but not quite, like the one he'd felt the night before for Brandark's old sword—the moment he touched it. It wasn't quite the heaviest he could pull, but it felt good in his hands, and he liked the supple way the wood yielded to his muscles. Vonderland provided the best of the Empire's archers, and they were one reason even the heaviest cavalry extended profound respect to an Axeman army.

In addition to weapons, each had a heavy pack of concentrated food, two or three changes of clothing, and two blankets, plus other incidentals required for a comfortable camp. Kenhodan belted on his water bottle and checked his coal oil-filled fire striker and the small pouch of medicines Leeana insisted each of them carry. Clearly she knew what was needed for moving quickly but comfortably through rough terrain. Which, he reflected, shouldn't have surprised him in the least in a war maid commander of a thousand.

He glanced doubtfully at his heavy riding boots. They were scarcely new, but they were still serviceable—with a little mending, at any rate—yet they seemed out of place on a ship. Nor did he wish to trudge too many leagues wearing them.

"Don't be worrying," Bahzell said, following his gaze and thoughts. "It might be they're not much for walking, but once we reach Manhome it's horses we'll need."

"Ah, yes. Horses." Kenhodan's tone was noncommittal, and Bahzell grinned at him.

"Don't you be fretting about a thing, Kenhodan. It's years ago Leeana's folk taught me as how they're a sight better under a man's seat than in his belly."

"I wondered about that," Kenhodan admitted.

"Aye, I thought as how you might." Bahzell slapped him on the shoulder. "Mind you, I'm thinking Walsharno and Gayrfressa'd've had a sharp word or three for me if I'd not gotten that straight! But now, if you'll excuse me?"

The hradani swept his wife and daughter into a universal hug. Gwynna brushed away a few tears and hugged him strangulation tight, yet she seemed confident her father could deal with anything he encountered. Leeana was less tearful, but her strained eyes showed a clearer appreciation of the risks.

"Only small pieces of hide this time, now!" she admonished him.

"Not enough to patch a shoe," he promised. "I'm after needing what I have—I've big bones to wrap it around."

"See you remember!" She tugged his ears fiercely, her eyes bright.

"And how should I forget, with you so ready to tan it for me if I should?" He gave her a final kiss and set her on her feet, then turned to his daughter. "Gwynna, you be minding your mother."

"Like always, Poppa," she promised demurely.

"Don't you 'Like always' me, wretch! I said to be *minding* her!"

"Yes, Poppa."

She giggled, and Bahzell frowned at her. She only grinned back, cheeks dimpled and ears twitching gently in amusement. He sighed and closed his eyes in mock exasperation, then smiled back and touched her cheek.

"All right, then," he said more gently, and turned back to his companions. "Let's be off—if we're after missing the tide, Brandark'll tan my hide before Leeana does!"

The trio set out briskly. The rain-fresh air was cool about their ears and the sun was bright. Workmen labored to replace the shattered windows and broken door, their sober expressions eloquent of their opinion of the night's events. It was a common Belhadan belief that offering any sort of violence to *anyone* on Bahzell's premises went far beyond foolishness. An attack on his own family was as near to suicidal as anyone was likely to come. Yet their sobriety stemmed less from the fact that someone had been mad enough to attempt it than from the fact that, for all the damage, only a single body had been delivered to the Guard. But when they set eyes on Wencit, a fresh mutter went up. They all respected Bahzell, and Wencit's reputation was known throughout Norfressa, but they were understandably eager to have such a chancy citizen as far from their city as possible.

Bahzell exchanged words with their foreman before leading off down the street, and Kenhodan was amused by the way the man's eyes followed Wencit in passing. He could almost feel the foreman's fingers itch to sketch a sign against evil, but the man's awe of the wizard clearly held him in check.

Kenhodan was unhappy to leave the Iron Axe. In a sense, it was the only home he'd ever known, and Bahzell and Leeana—and Gwynna—had made him truly welcome. He laid a hand on the dagger hilt at his belt, and a warm awareness of acceptance wrapped itself about the ice of his missing memory. But he noticed that Bahzell never looked back. The hradani's spine was pikestaff straight as he stepped out down the street, yet his ears—expressive as always—were half-turned, as if to catch any sound from behind as he strode away.

Kenhodan wished he remembered having loved someone that much.

◆   ◆   ◆

The busy streets were a waking dream for Kenhodan. Every sight was new, as fresh as the air he breathed, yet none of them were completely out of context. It was as though he'd read bits and pieces about a hundred subjects, not as if he'd actually seen or experienced them. He knew Belhadan was one of the great cities of Norfressa, but the wide, clean street was totally new to him, and the neat buildings with their bright roofs, mingled with the shops and houses burrowed into the mountains' bones, delighted him. The cool air of the northern spring was like wine, and the vitality humming about him gave him a pleasure he couldn't describe. It was almost . . . possessive, as if Belhadan were his and his alone, the product of his own labors.

The absurdity of that thought appealed to him somehow, and he chuckled as he contemplated it.

They turned into the Street of Merchants, a wide avenue of shops and counting houses. The crowds were thicker, and the mingled scents of cargoes from half a hundred ports blended with the morning. Kenhodan shook his head, about to laugh in pure delight, and then they turned another corner.

Blue and silver flashed before him in a wrinkled blanket. They stood high on a steep hillside, the paved street falling away to Hirahim's Wharf and the vast Bay of Belhadan, where the sea thrust deep into the land. The sight hit Kenhodan like a hammer, and his pulse leapt, his eyes glistened, and his throat filled with an indefinable ache of longing that struck him motionless.

He stopped so suddenly that Bahzell walked straight into him. Kenhodan stumbled at the impact—a hradani well over seven feet tall took some stopping—and would have fallen if Bahzell hadn't caught him. The hradani held him upright as he gasped for breath, the wind knocked out of him, then chuckled gently and set him on his feet.

"Well, now," Bahzell said softly. "I'm thinking you're a man might love the sea—and she's enough to strike anyone dumb on a morning like this."

"I never dreamed—" Kenhodan said softly, then chopped off. How could he say what he'd known in dreams? He was a man-shaped emptiness...yet not even the bitterness of that thought could quench his wonder and an awe that was almost reverence.

"Aye," Bahzell said, drawing him into motion once more. "I know. She takes some learning, the sea, and there's some as curse her when they know her, but even they can't leave her. Not and live happy."

Kenhodan glanced up and surprised a look in the brown eyes which humbled him. The hradani looked back down at him and grinned suddenly, driving the longing from his own face, and shook Kenhodan gently.

"Well, now! If it's your feet you've found again, I'm thinking I offered to tell you a mite about Angthyr. Would it happen you're still minded to hear it?"

Kenhodan nodded, grateful for the change of subject. He'd felt as if too much of Bahzell's soul had shown itself when he looked at the sea.

"Now Angthyr, that's after being a tangled subject,"

Bahzell mused, tapping gently on his sword belt and humming for a moment as he ordered his thoughts.

"Aye, then," he said finally. "Angthyr's after being one of the Border Kingdoms, as folk call them—one of the smaller states on the King Emperor's borders. Angthyr's the largest of the lot, and one of the most important, I'm thinking, for it's a buffer 'twixt South Province and the Empire of the Spear. And Emperor Soldan, as took the throne some fifteen years back, is after being as expansionist as old Phrobus himself. Not that he's the first Spearman as thought such as that, you understand. Truth to tell, most of the King Emperor's treaties with the Border Kingdoms are aimed at keeping Soldan at home, if you take my meaning."

"And since Angthyr's the biggest Border Kingdom, it's also the one Soldan wants worst, right?"

"Aye." Bahzell pulled out his pipe and packed it with coarsely cut black tobacco as he went on. "There's naught but two ways to Angthyr from here: the sea and the South Road. The sea route's after taking you to Coast Guard, the capital of Angthyr's West Barony. It's a tall city, that is, strong enough to make armies weep, but we daren't go so far by sea, so I'm thinking we'll take the South Road from Manhome. It's after crossing the East Walls at South Wall Pass, the King Emperor's southernmost fortress."

Bahzell thrust the pipe stem into his mouth, and Kenhodan kindled a light with his fire striker, then sneezed as the strong smoke burned his nose.

"I can see how a journey that long offers plenty of room for attacks," he said, maneuvering to stay upwind. "But just what's going on *inside* Angthyr?"

"Ah, you've set your hand on the meat of the

problem," Bahzell agreed, his eyes gleaming as Kenhodan dodged his smoke. "Angthyr's after having an internal crisis of its own just this minute, you see. King Faltho took and died unexpectedly four years back, and there's some as question the illness that took him off so sudden, as you might be saying. But what's after worrying folk most is that his only heir was a daughter, Fallona."

"Really? Was she crowned?"

Kenhodan found a position which let the wind carry the smoke away and hid a sigh of relief. It wasn't that it smelled all that foul, but simply that it was so *strong*. He wondered what Bahzell was smoking. Condemned cordage came to mind.

"Aye, that she was. But, you see, while there's no law in Angthyr as says a woman can't hold the crown, there's no law as says she *can*, either, and Fallona's succession has the nobles all a-twitter. There's some of them only accepted her to avoid civil war, and even the most of those were none too happy when she wed Prince Altho—or Duke Altho, as he was then. He's after being young, and they'd no mind to see one of their own raised above them. Besides, he's no man to stand for foolishness, and he's a name as a soldier troublemakers aren't so very likely to find comforting."

"Is someone actually disputing the succession, then?"

"In a manner of speaking, but there's the rub. King Faltho's brother up and died as a mere lad and his sister's no child of her own, so there's not a man at all as has any blood claim to the throne. If it's not after being Fallona and Altho, why, then it's every man for himself, and Phrobus take the hindermost."

"Messy."

"It's a gift for understatement you have," Bahzell observed. "I'm thinking it's only the fact no one's sure he'd be the one as ends up on top as has kept swords sheathed this long, and even that's not so likely to keep them there much longer. And to be making bad worse, Soldan's taken an interest. He knows the King Emperor can't be intervening unless the royal house asks it, but Fallona's people daren't ask. One sniff of Axemen in the kingdom and hell wouldn't hold the trouble as would break loose."

"I see. And we're going into *that?*"

"Oh, aye. Wencit's not one to let a little thing like that natter him, lad. And there's more to tell. Don't be blabbing it about in Angthyr unless you've a liking for dungeons, but Soldan's after having his hooks into some of the great nobles. Duke Doral of Korwin's as deep into it with Soldan as Wulfra or Ranalf of Carchon, and Tomanāk only knows about Earl Wullem. I've my doubts as Wullem knows himself! And as for Baron Shaisan—!"

Bahzell removed his pipe from his mouth and spat into the gutter.

"I've the Order's reports about Angthyr, lad, and the way it's looking, the only help Fallona and Altho can be counting on are her mother's kinsmen, Darsil of Scarthū and Baron Rochfro of Coast Guard, and probably Baron Ledo. But Ledo's problems enough of his own for any man along the marshes, and Darsil's as good as at war with Doral already. The blood's always been hot betwixt them, and now it's after starting to flow. And behind it all, Soldan's after sending in money and advice and generally giving the fire a kick whenever it looks like dying down a bit."

"I see," Kenhodan said again. "And Baroness Wulfra?"

"There's one foul enough for Sharnā," Bahzell said bluntly. "A sad thing it is, too, for her father was a good enough man. I knew him well, and her family's one as has served Angthyr well in its time. But she's a bad one. She's one of the few rulers as allows sorcery to be practiced in her lands, and that's after telling you something. Come to that, it's not so very long ago—no more than a year or two before Faltho's death—as Wulfra admitted she practiced it herself, although to be hearing her tell it, *her* magic's white as new fallen snow."

His tone made his opinion of that particular claim abundantly clear.

"She's all sugar to Fallona since Faltho died, but I'm thinking she's only biding her time. They say Fallona trusts her, but Altho's not one to be fooled by her promises to be 'helping' Fallona with sorcery. But what's he to do? Here's Fallona, desperate for friends amongst the nobles, and here's Wulfra, always prating about her loyalty to the throne. Aye, and Phrobus was after being loyal to Orr, too, wasn't he just? She's after being loyal to the throne, right enough, as long as it's in her mind she can ease her own backside onto it! And Altho knows it, too. He and the Queen had a rare set-to in public when he was after wondering—in a formal audience, mind you!—about Faltho's illness. It seems he mentioned the fact that the same strange illness carried off Wulfra's father . . . that and the matter of her older sister's mysterious disappearance long before that. I'm thinking it must've been a rare set out when Fallona took Wulfra's side! Phrobus to pay and no pitch hot, and no mistake about it! Altho only said what needed saying, mind you, but there's no denying as how his timing might've been a mite impolitic. And it's after adding another problem, you see, for Fallona and her consort—who's also her most powerful vassal—don't agree on what to do about their worst enemy. Tomanāk! They're not even after agreeing she *is* an enemy!"

"I begin to question the wisdom of this trip," Kenhodan sighed.

"Wisdom?" Wencit turned his head and spoke suddenly, though he'd seemed unaware of their conversation. "It was never wise. Only necessary."

Bahzell grinned and wiggled his ears at Kenhodan as the old man turned back to the street. Kenhodan chuckled at the hradani's expression, but he couldn't shake a sense of unease as he considered what he'd just heard. There'd been moments during Bahzell's explanation when he'd felt as if he were watching a play he'd seen entirely too many times, which was absurd—wasn't it?—in a man who couldn't remember even his own name!

He shrugged his sword belt more comfortably into place and made himself step back from the problem of the future before it could spoil his walk. After a moment, he even managed to begin whistling through his teeth as they turned a bend at the foot of the hill and fresh-washed cobbles glistened in the light, mocking his qualms while the vast Bay of Belhadan opened wide before him.

It seemed even vaster seen at its own level, dancing in the spring morning. White wave crests chased themselves across the broad bay on a northwesterly breeze that fingered his hair and tightened his throat with an inarticulate longing. Did his hunger mean he'd known deep waters before his memory was stolen? Or was this indeed his first glimpse of tidewater? He stared out over the crinkled blue mirror and smelled the salt—rich as wine and wood smoke—as he searched for his past.

"This way."

Bahzell's voice broke his thoughts as the hradani pointed out a large square rigged ship. She towered above the coasting schooners, her yards proud with the furled yellow sails of Belhadan. A banner snapped briskly at her foremast, displaying a crossed black axe and fouled anchor on a blue field, and the crossed axes and crown of the Empire floated from her mizzen, the banner's red field blood-bright in the morning light.

"*Wave Mistress*," Bahzell said. "Brandark's pride and joy. The axe and anchor's after being his house banner."

"He's a good friend of yours?" Kenhodan asked.

"Well now," Bahzell smiled slowly, "I'm thinking that depends a mite on just exactly what it is you might be meaning by 'friend.' I've a bone or two to pick with the little man, and he's the sort of sense of humor as needs a ready sword to keep its owner alive. But it's a long time the two of us've known each other, and there's not a man alive I'd sooner have at my back in a fight. Aye, and I'm thinking he's the finest ship handler you'll ever meet. He was after captaining *Sword of Tomanāk* for me before he ordered *Wave Mistress* built right here in Belhadan."

"He was your captain?" Kenhodan couldn't keep the surprise out of his voice. Gwynna had said something about "Poppa's ship," but he hadn't actually paid it that much attention. After all, what sort of hradani owned his own ship? He flushed ever so slightly as he considered the implications of his own assumptions, and Bahzell's eyes glinted with laughter.

"Aye, so he was. That's after surprising you, is it?"

"Well..."

"Last count, I had ten captains," Bahzell told him affably, "not counting the Belhadan ships of the Order, but it might be I've fewer. The corsairs've been wicked this past year, curse them, and I'm thinking they've forgotten to leave my ships alone. It won't be so very long before the King Emperor's after having to deal with them, and if he doesn't, I'm thinking as the Order will. Tomanāk knows they're a plague on the sea, and they'll be starting shore raids again if they're not re-taught manners soon. Maybe when we return you and I might take the *Sword* and one or two of the Order's other ships to reeducate them, eh?"

Kenhodan glanced at him, decided he was serious, and filed that thought away with all the other indications that Bahzell was nothing if not direct...and far more powerful than his tavern keeping role suggested. In fact, it suddenly occurred to the redhaired man that as a champion and the local chapter's swordmaster, Bahzell commanded all of the Order of Tomanāk's armed forces in Belhadan, and he reminded himself once more to take nothing for granted where this particular hradani was concerned.

He chewed on that thought while he turned his attention to *Wave Mistress*, and as he studied her, he understood her master's pride. Though she loomed above her smaller neighbors, she had the sleek lines of a greyhound—broad enough in the beam to carry profitable cargoes, but also with the elegant sheer, raked stem, and graceful run of a thoroughbred. Her masts raked sharply, her tall yards and great spread of sail spoke eloquently of her speed and, unlike many smaller ships, her black hull boasted no oar ports, for sweeps would have been little use to a ship her size. Her arrogant masts disdained the strength of anything less mighty than the wind itself, and two large, tarpaulin-shrouded shapes bulked on her decks, one well forward and one just aft of the mainmast. Kenhodan suspected the canvas hid powerful ballistae—heavy armament for a merchantman, but certainly in keeping with the bulwark mountings for dart throwers. *Wave Mistress* was a direcat of the deep, and only the heartiest—or most foolish—of pirates would cross the path of a vessel as heavily armed as most imperial cruisers.

His mouth curved wryly as he pondered the ship and his fragments of assessing memory proved this wasn't the first time he'd seen the sea after all.

"There's Brandark," Bahzell said, and Kenhodan blinked, recalling his earlier thoughts about hradani shipowners.

You really do have to work on that, he told himself. *Of course, no one ever said he wasn't a hradani, but still . . .*

"Never a hradani went willingly to sea before Brandark and I did," Bahzell continued. "Not that we were after going willing just at first! All the swords of the Purple Lords were nipping at our backsides, they were, and it was only a ready tide and a schooner crew we could . . . convince to be giving us room aboard as took us out of their reach. But here we are now, and while

I've not so much seawater in my veins as Brandark, I'll not deny there's little in the world to equal the feel of a deck under my feet. I'm thinking it may be the tales are true and we hradani were after swimming all the way from Kontovar because no one would give us room aboard ship!

"Brandark, now, he went for a sailor years before ever I did. Old Kilthan—Kilthandahknarthas of Silver Cavern, that would be—was after taking him on as one of his ship captains, and truth to tell, he'd reason to be seeking a home elsewhere at the time. It wasn't so very long before that that my Da'd gone and—"

"*Bahzell!*" Brandark's lungs were clearly equal to Bahzell's, Kenhodan thought. "About time you showed your face down here! Come aboard! Or has the salt gone out of your blood?"

Bahzell bounded up the gangway, his weight sending the stout plank into wild gyrations. Wencit and Kenhodan waited for the vibrations to die down before following him more sedately, and Brandark met him at the entry port in an exchange of insults, arm clasps, and back-slapping blows fit to shatter lesser spines. They took the time to do it properly. In fact, they were only getting well started when Kenhodan stepped around them onto the spotless deck.

Brandark was considerably shorter than Bahzell. In fact, he was shorter than Kenhodan, no more than an inch or two over six feet. But his shoulders were far broader and more powerful than the human's, and Kenhodan sighed. He knew he was tall, for a human, but next to Bahzell and Brandark he felt half-grown.

Yet that wasn't the thought foremost in his mind as he studied the shipmaster with a certain degree of resignation, for Brandark was every bit as atypical for a hradani as Bahzell himself.

He bore the marks of his trade—his left cheek was seamed with an age-smoothed scar that drew that corner of his mouth into a slight, perpetual grin, his right ear was shorter than his left, where some long-ago sword had claimed its tip, and he lacked the last two fingers on his left hand—but that wasn't what struck the eye most forcefully. No, that was left to his exquisite tailoring.

Kenhodan shook his head. The thought of a hradani dandy, he'd just discovered, was even more outré, somehow, than the thought of a hradani champion of Tomanāk. Yet outré or not, "dandy" was the only word fit to describe Brandark of Belhadan. He was perfectly groomed, from the soles of his brilliantly polished, hand-tooled boots, with their silver tassels and repeating motif of lotus flowers, to the top of his jauntily plumed velvet cap, and the heavy golden chain of a pocket watch, draped across his magnificently embroidered waistcoat, boasted a handsome, sapphire-set fob. He should have looked like some sort of parody, standing on a ship's deck beside Bahzell's plain hauberk and unornamented steel breastplate, but instead he only managed to look inevitable.

And not all the fine fabric, embroidery, and stylish tailoring in the world could have hidden the toughness they were wrapped about. The scars, the missing fingers, did more than proclaim his violent past; they made him look indestructible, like an ancient tree which had lost limbs without losing an ounce of strength, and Kenhodan saw why one might not trifle with a ship he commanded.

Bahzell interrupted his greetings to introduce his friends.

"My fellow passengers, Brandark. You're after knowing Wencit, of course."

"Of course." Brandark clasped forearms with the wizard. "It's good to see you again, Wencit."

"And you," Wencit agreed, clasping Brandark's forearm in return and simultaneously drawing Kenhodan forward with his free hand. "And this is Kenhodan."

Brandark gripped Kenhodan's arm in turn, and smiled as he saw the sword he wore.

"Kenhodan," Bahzell said, "Brandark was after carrying that blade once, and a mercy he didn't lose fingers to it. Bloody Sword or no, it's in my mind as a proper blade...overtaxed him, just a mite. An axe is more his speed, I'm thinking. No sharp edges near the hilt."

"Bilge water!" Brandark's laughed. "Welcome aboard, then, Kenhodan! Does me good to see that old sword again."

"And it'll do you even better when you've once seen it used properly for a change," Bahzell assured him solemnly.

"Maybe I will, since someone besides you will be using it!"

"Hah!" Bahzell reached up to slap the hilt of the huge sword across his back and smiled benignly down on the lesser beings clustered about his ankles.

"Well, come below. We've an hour before slack water, so let's find some whiskey while you tell me what in Korthrala's name you're up to this time."

"I don't think old Wave Beard wants to know," Wencit said with a grin.

"Oh ho! It ought to be good, then." Brandark paused in the open hatch to yell at one of his men. "Tobian! Tell Hornos to break out that Old Halahrn—the Grand Reserve, mind you—from Silver Cavern!"

"Aye, Captain!" the crewman acknowledged.

"I think we'll need something special for *this* explanation," Brandark said more quietly to his guests, and waved them below with a toothy grin.

◆　　◆　　◆

"Angthyr?" Brandark sipped from a carved crystal tumbler of whiskey as he considered. "Not the spot I'd fancy for a visit just now, Wencit."

"Agreed."

Wencit's eyes glowed in the dim light, sparkles dancing before them as he nodded, and Kenhodan leaned back comfortably and gazed about the cabin while he listened. Racked books lined the bulkheads and thick carpet covered the deck. Intricately-paned stern and quarter windows flashed with sun on the seaward side, flooding half the cabin with brilliance, but dark shadows covered the larboard side where the wharf blocked the light. Wrought silver lamps hung from the deckhead on chains, and there were at least three cased musical instruments tucked away in various corners.

"Bahzell's right," Brandark said. "You'll do better overland from Manhome, but I can cut your trip forty leagues shorter if I detour up the Whitewater as far as Korun."

"You could," Wencit agreed, "but that takes you far out of your way, and the Whitewater isn't safe so early in the spring."

"Wizards have their art, and seamen have theirs,"

Brandark replied. "If I say I can take you up White-water, then I can take you up Whitewater."

"I don't doubt it, but it still takes you out of your way."

"Don't compound the insult," Brandark said cheerfully. "You're daft to go into Angthyr at all. You know it. Kenhodan knows it. Korthrala, Wencit, even *Bahzell* knows it! But if you have to go to Angthyr, you're more likely to get there intact if you stay away from tidewater ports. If you've got enemies in Belhadan, let them know you've sailed for Manhome in *Wave Mistress*. Let them search there while you go elsewhere. And, Wencit—" he overrode the wizard's attempted interruption "—do me the courtesy of letting me get you there in one piece as quickly as possible. I suspect there's more to this than you're ready to say, and that's your business. But if you think it's important—and if Tomanāk and this overgrown lump think it's important—it's my business, too."

"Very well, but you leave me deep in your debt."

"Oh, please!" Brandark rolled his eyes and flattened his ears. "Do you really think Bahzell and I are keeping *score*?" He snorted. "I could do you favors for the rest of my life without coming close to matching the ones you've done for other people. For that matter, I can think of the few 'favors' you've done for *me* upon occasion. And, come to that, I suppose I might owe the Mountain a favor or two, as well."

"Aye, so you might," Bahzell acknowledged, holding out his empty glass suggestively, and Brandark laughed and poured again.

"To Korun, then." He raised his own glass.

"To Korun, and our thanks," Wencit responded, and all four of them drained their glasses.

"Then if you'll excuse me," Brandark said, setting his glass back down on his deck, "I've got the last of the cargo to stow. You're in luck there, too. Duke Lainton's chartered me to deliver a shipment of bullion, so we'll have the better part of a company of Axe Brothers on board to keep an eye on it."

"Bullion?" Wencit frowned. "Why send it just now, I wonder?"

"Ask Axe Hallow." Brandark shrugged. "When the King Emperor says send bullion, Vonderland sends it. And when the Gut's frozen, they send it overland to Belhadan, then someone has to take it to Manhome so they can send it to Axe Hallow so someone can make coins out of it and send it back to Belhadan. A wonderful thing, high finance."

"The Axe Brothers won't mind your detour?"

"All they worry about is their chests." Brandark chuckled. "How they reach their destination's up to me—and so it should be! Until later, then."

He waved a cheerful hand and left.

"I don't like this bullion," Wencit said thoughtfully.

"Why not?" Bahzell asked. "As Brandark says, when the King Emperor commands, folk tend to be doing as he asks. And if I were after being the Duke, there's no captain I'd sooner trust with *my* bullion shipment."

"True, Brandark does have a habit of getting where he sets out to go. But it offers an unfortunate pretext, Bahzell."

"Pretext?" Kenhodan was puzzled.

"For a traceless disappearance he means, I'm thinking," Bahzell murmured.

"Exactly. If someone—with command of the art, let's say—discovers where we are, we may bring Brandark more trouble than he's reckoned for. It would surprise everyone if Brandark failed to complete a normal voyage . . . but if we don't arrive now, people will simply assume we met more corsairs than even he could handle. And the bullion offers a perfect bait for an ill-intentioned wizard to inspire the corsairs to make the attempt."

"And be helping us to the bottom by *un*natural means with no one the wiser," Bahzell grunted.

"But why?" Kenhodan asked. "I mean, why should anyone need a 'pretext'? You're a wizard—a *white* wizard—and you've spent the gods only know how long dealing with one rogue wizard after another. Surely no one would be surprised if one of those rogue wizards used sorcery against you."

"Surprised, no," Wencit agreed. "But angry? Yes."

"If they're worried about making someone angry, then why did they use sorcery last night?"

"As far as last night goes, that was very carefully *chosen* sorcery," Wencit replied. "Shadow chill is lethal, but they also carried swords. The shadowmage was a last-ditch weapon they didn't want to use, because what he would've done would have been unmistakable sorcery. But if we'd been cut down by blades, who could prove they hadn't been honest steel?"

"But why would it matter? Let's face it, Wencit. If they'd *succeeded* in killing you, who'd be in a position to do anything about it?"

"The Council of Semkirk, lad," Bahzell said. "They'd not be so very happy about that at all, at all. I'm thinking they'd have no choice but to stand by and watch if someone was after being so cork-brained as to be challenging our Wencit to a formal duel. They'd not like it, you understand, but it's little choice they'd have. But a sorcerous attack without challenge? In the middle of a city with never a wizard of its own? No, they'd not be standing for that, and I'd not like to be the black wizard as got the lot of them set on my trail."

"What's the Council of Semkirk?" Kenhodan was puzzled. Semkirk was the god of wisdom and mental and physical discipline. It was true that, before the Fall of Kontovar, he'd been the patron of white wizardry, as well, but the art of wizardry had fallen on hard times since. He rather doubted any of the Gods of Light would have desired the worship of most of sorcery's present practitioners.

"The council of mishuki and magi sworn to destroy black sorcery and any who practice it," Bahzell replied grimly.

"Magi? Isn't that just another name for wizards?"

"I'm thinking your memory *is* after having some holes," Bahzell said gently, yet with an edge in his voice. Not one aimed at him, Kenhodan was sure, but it sounded like hurt...or fear. "No one's been after using 'mage' that way in centuries."

"No? Then what does it mean now? And why should wizards be afraid of mishuki? They're only weaponless combat experts, aren't they?"

"As to fearing mishuki, why, *I'm* more than a little fearful of such as they!" Bahzell's levity felt strangely flat, and he went on more slowly. "As for magi, now, that's another matter. A mage is after being a mental adept, one as can do some of the things a wizard can, although it's not the same thing at all, at all."

"Indeed," Wencit said dryly.

"Magi can duplicate some wizard's powers," Bahzell

said slowly, "but sorcery's after being the furthest
thing from their way. And most folk think of them as
natural allies against wizards. There're after being...
exceptions, though." His voice was suddenly very low.
"And a mage pays for his power."

His soft voice faded, lost in the faint background
noise of shouting longshoreman as they swayed the
last of *Wave Mistress'* cargo aboard. Kenhodan felt
the hradani's withdrawal without understanding it, but
something in Bahzell's face kept him from probing.
Instead, he simply waited, and finally Bahzell shook
himself and resumed more briskly.

"But to be answering your question, lad, both
mage and mishuk follow Semkirk, and his Council's a
powerful thing. Black wizards fear it like death, with
good reason, and I'm thinking the Council would be
after taking violent exception to our unnatural ends.
Especially if someone else was after going with us."

"Then why hasn't it already gone after Wulfra?"
Kenhodan demanded.

"Because the Council bears the King Emperor's
commission," Wencit said sternly, "and such responsibilities have limits which may not be overstepped.
Magi may be born anywhere in Norfressa, Kenhodan,
but all of the major academies are either located in
the Empire of the Axe or—like the Jashân Academy
in the Empire of the Spear—were founded by and
associated with one of the Axeman academies. Whether
the Council likes it or not, it's firmly associated with
the Axe in the mind of every Norfressan, and the King
Emperor recognized that two hundred years ago when
he formally vested it with the authority to investigate
charges of black wizardry anywhere in his territory.

"But because he gave them that authority within the Empire, and because that means they act in *his* name when they exercise it, they can never act beyond his borders without the permission of the ruler whose land they'd enter . . . or on the King Emperor's direct orders. Obviously Fallona won't ask them to attack someone she thinks is her friend! And the King Emperor can't send them in against her will unless he has an iron-bound case. Mind you, if he *had* that ironbound case, he probably would; black wizardry's something the Axe has never tolerated anywhere on—or near—its soil. Of course, that would be an act of war, however justified it might be, and he could be confident Soldan would invade Angthyr to 'protect' it."

"And so far, Wulfra's avoided any open violations of the Strictures where there's eyes as might see and tongues as might wag," Bahzell observed gloomily.

"Indeed she has," Wencit agreed. "Officially, her magic's white as the snow, though it stinks of the Dark to another wizard, and I doubt she could hide the evidence of her use of the Dark if anyone with mage or wizard's training got close enough to Castle Torfo to see it. But as baroness, she has the authority to bar magi from Torfo unless the Queen herself overrules her, which means none of the Council's wizard sniffers are likely to get close enough to provide the proof of that. That means it would be my word against hers, and more than a wizard's word—even if one of the wizards is me—is needed to launch the Council at someone's throat. Wulfra won't give me that. She was leagues away when Alwith attacked us. *She* had nothing to do with such a heinous act! Why, if *she* wanted me dead, she'd use the Duel Arcane, exactly as the Strictures allow!"

Wencit's sarcasm was withering.

"I'm assuming from your tone that she's . . . unlikely to do anything that open," Kenhodan said. "If she were, though, how would it work?"

His curiosity was obvious, and Wencit's nostrils flared.

"Not well for her," he said flatly. "The Duel Arcane is a formal challenge to combat to the death between two wizards. The Strictures permit it, although mass combat's forbidden, along with anything which might endanger non-wizards. I've . . . had a few of those of my own, over the centuries, but if another wizard wanted to challenge *me* formally, the Council would have to be consulted.

"You see, after the flight to Norfressa, they were too few white wizards to police the new lands against black wizardry, and even if there'd been more of us, it really wouldn't have mattered. I told you what it cost us to strafe Kontovar. After that, there was no one to form a new White Council with me, and there were few new wizards in the years that followed. The refugees saw to that; enraged and terrified people take few chances. It was almost three hundred years before any of the new rulers in Norfressa were willing to trust even *me*, Kenhodan, outside of the House of Kormak, at least, and even Kormak and his son were unwilling to trust me openly, for fear of how their people might have reacted. It took that long for the survivors' children to forgive me for the Council of Ottovar's failure—*my* failure—to prevent the Fall. By that time, virtually all knowledge of the art had been lost in Norfressa, and to be honest, none of the new realms *wanted* that knowledge rediscovered. Yet they knew at least some scraps of various wizards' libraries had made it out of

Kontovar—some people will seek any means to power, however dark, after all. So when the magi emerged, we turned to the Council of Semkirk to assume the duties the White Council could no longer discharge. In fact, the two councils merged, after a manner of speaking. I'm the last member of the White Council, whose authority's never been revoked, and I'm also the only non-mage member of the Council of Semkirk. I can do—and I've done—things in my persona as the Last Lord of the Council of Ottovar that the magi can't do, though, because for the reasons I've already explained, the Council of Semkirk's authority—its 'reach,' if you will—is far less extensive and far more hemmed in by restrictions than the White Council's authority was under the House of Ottovar."

"But there's still provision for the Duel Arcane?" Kenhodan asked. Wencit nodded, and the redhaired man shrugged. "So why doesn't someone challenge you and have done with it?"

"I'm thinking there'd be few dark wizards left if it so happened they were stupid enough to be doing that!" Bahzell snorted.

"I see." Kenhodan considered that statement. "Look," he said finally, "I understand that sorcery isn't something you can explain in an afternoon, Wencit. But if I'm going to be mixed up with wizards, can't you give me at least *some* idea about how it works?"

"I imagine I could give you a fair idea in a decade or two," Wencit said.

"Once over lightly's all I need, thank you!"

"All right, let's see how simpleminded I can make it."

Wencit steepled his fingers under his beard and smiled, then cleared his throat.

"Wizardry is a human talent," he began, "All wizards have been either entirely human or at least partially so, just as all sarthnaisks—'stone herds'—have been dwarvish or half-dwarvish, and there are three kinds of them. Once there were four, but the ancestors of the elves traded their special art for long life when Ottovar and Gwynytha declared the Strictures. So, these days, there are first, warlocks and witches, then come wand wizards—often called 'sorcerers' or 'sorceresses'—and, finally, wild wizards. Of the three, the first two are most feared by normal folk, but the wild wizard is most feared by those of the art.

"Warlocks have an inborn sensitivity to the art. Not so great as the elves once had, but enough for them to use it as naturally as their hands or feet, without formal training. To be honest, the vast majority of them don't even realize they're using the art at all. They simply think they have an odd 'talent' or two that works for them. Only a relative handful of them ever actually progress to a deliberate, conscious manipulation of the art.

"Because of that, because they're untrained, they're actually less powerful than wand wizards. True wizardry requires discipline and acquired skills, which warlocks simply don't have. But that lack of training also means they seldom know the Strictures, and they often gravitate towards the dark side of the art. Few of them would knowingly lend themselves to the sort of foulness Wulfra embraces, but the best of them are varying shades of gray.

"Wand wizards, on the other hand, have little native sensitivity. More than non-wizards, but less than warlocks. Sorcerers gain their mastery through long, hard, sometimes fatal study. They used to be well taught in their responsibilities along the way, but even then the difficulty of their studies often led them to use a little of the dark side to survive perilous moments... physically at least. But there's no such thing as 'a little' of the Dark. If you use it even once, you open a chink in your armor; it's always easier to slip a second time. The step from white wizardry to blood magic and death magic is seldom a one-time choice, Kenhodan. It comes from slow, steady corruption, and that's what makes it entirely too easy for all too many wand wizards to slide into the black ranks one step at a time. Few escape that fate today. Indeed, I've known men and women who could have been powerful wand wizards but renounced their birthright, agonizing as that was, rather than risk falling into evil.

"The last sort, the wild wizards, are another case entirely. They have no native sensitivity at all, nor do they suspect even for an instant that they might ever become wizards, so they're totally untrained for it when it happens. Instead, their power wakes suddenly, usually under terrible stress."

He sighed sadly and reached for Brandark's whiskey bottle. He poured the amber liquid into his tumbler and held it up against the light from the starboard quarter windows. He gazed at it for a moment, then threw it back in a single swallow and returned his gaze to Kenhodan.

"Wild wizards are very...elemental," he said. "Their power comes on them only if they have no alternative. When all hope is gone, when grief and despair bite deepest, then a wild wizard feels the birth of a power he never knew he had. It can never be anticipated...

and it always comes with a price of pain, or grief—or hate—which few sane people would willingly pay.

"Only a strong personality can assimilate such power," Wencit said softly. "Not even another wild wizard can help in that moment. The new wizard's alone, and the wild magic will destroy him unless he has a powerful will and realizes what's happening. Yet if he survives, he comes into such power as neither warlock nor sorcerer can ever wield."

"And what is the 'wild magic'?" Kenhodan asked, green eyes intent.

"It can't be described," Wencit said bluntly. "Other wizards command a tiny part of the force that binds the entire world together, and they learn to do that by carefully and cautiously learning specific incantations, spells, workings...ways to bridle and constrain that force. But wild wizards need no bridles, no spells to chain the wild magic to their will. They *ride* it. They can tap it all, if you will, and that means they can manipulate the very essences of objects, creatures... persons. They can bind and unbind them, or reduce them to dust and rip the life from them.

"But it's a raw, brutal application of power. There's little finesse to the wild magic, and the wild wizard's strength is limited only by the stress he can endure. Most dangerous of all is the *young* wild wizard, because his body's strong enough to absorb and channel so much power. Wild wizards live a very long time, but as they age their failing bodies finally limit their power, though even in old age they remain frighteningly strong. In combat, they generally disdain technique, at least until failing strength requires subtlety to compensate. Until then, they simply throw raw power at opponents.

Their control's instinctive, not a product of training, and their power's virtually limitless."

"But it can be trained?"

"Of course it can, once you know you've got it!" Wencit snorted. "It simply never awakens that way. Nor does it need to."

"I can see that." Kenhodan pursed his lips. "Can non-wizards recognize wild wizards?"

"Oh, yes," Wencit said softly.

"How?"

"By their eyes," Wencit said, almost whispering. "By their eyes."

◆　　◆　　◆

Harlich of Torfo and Thardon of the Purple Lords stood in the shadow of a warehouse wall and studied *Wave Mistress*.

Short, chunky Thardon looked reassuringly harmless with his plump face and curly hair. Not even the dark violet eyes and angled eyebrows of the half-elven could change that, and he'd used that appearance to good purpose upon occasion. His companion was different, for no shadow could hide the lean, angular menace of Harlich's sparse frame. Of course, once one knew them, it was another matter. Harlich's brown eyes were merely hard and thoughtful; Thardon's purple gaze flickered with a hungry light.

"So that's the redoubtable Brandark's ship," Harlich mused.

"Yes." Thardon's nod was choppy, abrupt with compulsive energy. "My informant says the bullion's already on board. They sail within the hour."

"I see. And a full company of Axe Brothers?"

"Almost. They're one platoon understrength, but

they're drawn from Captain Forstan's company. Picked men, I hear, though I haven't probed them to check. Too much chance of Wencit noticing."

"To be sure." Harlich seldom hid his contempt for Thardon's penchant for stating the obvious. Now he tapped his teeth, brow furrowed.

"We've found them," Thardon sulked. "There has to be a way! Once they put to sea, there won't be any place for them to find help."

"True, but opportunity doesn't guarantee *success*, or someone would have killed Wencit centuries ago. Admittedly, they'd be isolated—but so would we, Thardon. And three-score Axe Brothers seem adequate protection, I think."

"Not against the art!"

"No, but what about Wencit? Or do you fancy stepping out on the wharf to challenge him?" Harlich waved gently at the bright sunlight beyond their band of shadow. "Feel free, Thardon. I'll be happy to notify your next of kin."

Thardon flushed. The taller wizard's disparagement was a burden he'd grown accustomed to without ever accepting. Someday he'd show Harlich how far he could be pushed . . . but not today. Not unless he wanted to challenge Wulfra by violating her orders. Or—even worse!—to anger her mysterious patron. And so he gritted his teeth and held his tongue with difficulty.

"Still, your idea has some merit," Harlich finally conceded. "It's a matter of using our advantages at the proper time. That bullion, now. That might be turned to use. It could provide an excellent cover, if we can capitalize on it. And I rather think we can, Thardon."

"How?" Thardon asked sullenly.

"Come, now! We have the madwind, and not even Wencit can use the art and keep someone's sword out of his throat at the same time. What we *need*, Thardon, is someone to supply the sword."

"Who?"

"I think Tolgrim might be our man. You *can* find him, can't you?"

Thardon's face lit with understanding.

"It may take a few days," he said.

"No matter. If Tolgrim's ships are available, we can speed them on their way. After all—" Harlich smiled gently "—the Strictures prevent *Wencit* from meddling unduly with nature. Not us."

Thardon nodded and turned away, but Harlich gripped his shoulder. The tall wizard's eyes were bleak, but his lips shaped another gentle smile.

"Yes?" Thardon asked impatiently.

"I'm sure Tolgrim will be eager to seize the bullion, Thardon, and I see no reason to cool his ardor. Don't overburden him with information."

"You mean—?"

"Precisely. There's no need to mention the Axe Brothers or Bahzell. After all, we wouldn't want to cause our good pirate to fret, would we?"

Thardon nodded slowly, and for once the smile with which he favored his companion was bright with understanding and approval.

✦ ✦ ✦

Wind whipped Kenhodan's hair as *Wave Mistress* nosed out of the bay and crewmen darted about, adjusting downhauls and braces. A steep hill loomed out of the sea to the west, craggy flanks yielding unwillingly to wind-blighted trees. The Isle of Cardos' forbidding slopes shielded the harbor from the worst of the sometimes savage northwesterlies, and its weather-gnawed sides showed what the northern winter could do.

Beyond Cardos, a stiff breeze whipped out of the eye of the north, overpowering the easterly which had wafted them from the wharf. The wind bit with the last feeble fangs of Vonderland's ice, and Kenhodan burrowed deep into his borrowed coat as he sniffed the salt air.

"See that orange buoy?" Kenhodan nodded as Bahzell pointed to the bell-crowned buoy. "Once we've cleared that, it's into the Fradonian Channel we'll be. We'll follow that south to Cape Storm, then bear well away to the west for a day or two before we make our southing."

"Why?"

"Because this whole coast's after being fanged with reefs. North to south, the Fradonian Banks stretch nearly a hundred leagues, and every mortal mile of them dotted with ships' bones. Korthrala's Teeth, folk call them."

"So." Kenhodan felt the grain of the rail with an index finger. "And when do we reach Cape Storm?"

"It's over a hundred leagues, but—" Bahzell squinted at the yards "—*Wave Mistress*'s after being almost as fast as Brandark boasts, and the wind's after being fair . . . Late this time tomorrow, if Korthrala heeds our prayers. Which, like as not, he won't."

"And from there to Korun?"

"Now that's after being harder to say. The winds are fluky in the spring, and the trade season's just starting, so it's likely enough the corsairs will be out after a hungry winter. It might be as they're even hungry enough to be tackling *Wave Mistress*."

Bahzell sniffed the salt appreciatively and tapped his sword belt with a cheerful smile.

"Call it fifteen days to the Whitewater and you'll not be too far out," he said finally. "And maybe two more days upriver to Korun, with the spring flood in our teeth. Then best add in a day or two for calms and the like. Say twenty days."

"I'll be sorry to see it end," Kenhodan said wistfully.

"Hah! It's kind the sea's been to you so far, my lad! Best be taking my word for it—a seaman's lot is hard when Korthrala's after growing absentminded and lets the storms loose! I've seen ships this size stand on their heads and curtsy while they waved their backsides at the clouds. You won't be finding *that* so pleasant!"

"I suppose not. But for now..."

They watched a white hurricane of gulls dive at the wake, their voices a shrill threnody across the wind, their wings a ruffle of thunder. The sky gleamed, swept and polished by the night's storm, and the crisp wind flowed chill from the north, stinging their cheeks as the Western Sea breathed and *Wave Mistress* pitched beneath them. The figurehead of Myrea, Korthrala's mortal mistress, moved with the ship, light flickering from the gilded trident she'd "borrowed" from her lover, and Kenhodan's heart rose despite the nagging loss of his past as his lungs ached with the savor of salt.

"Aye." Bahzell sounded thoughtful. "My folk live inland, and other folk aren't so wrong as I'd like to think when they're after calling us barbarians. Mind, times change, and it's not so barbarian we are these days, thanks to my Da and Leeana's. Yet there it is.

It's not so easy to forget twelve hundred years and more of history, and I'm thinking—sometimes, any road—that we were after losing all those years because we lived away from the sea." He smiled sadly. "The salt's in our blood, Kenhodan, and we've the hearts and thews to fight old Wave Beard himself tooth and nail, and we never even guessed it. Instead, we were after wasting our blood and bone against folk we might've lived in peace with when we should have been measuring ourselves against this."

He waved at the sea and fell silent, his mobile ears half-flattened. Kenhodan could just catch the thread of sailor's chantey he hummed under his breath, and he felt oddly like an intruder. He turned silently to leave, but Bahzell roused and clouted him staggeringly on the shoulder before he'd taken a second step.

"Here, now! That's no way for a champion of Tomanāk to be talking! Come on. Let's you and I gather up some of these lubbers and be about teaching them which end of the sword's after having the pointy bit. Who knows? It might be as they'll need it soon, eh?"

CHAPTER FIVE

A Bit of Insight

"You and Bahzell really have been friends for a long time, haven't you, Brandark?"

The hradani laid his book in his lap and looked up, cocking his ears at Kenhodan. The human sat across the table from him in his shirt sleeves, slowly and carefully polishing the fine-grained wood of a small harp in the golden pool of light pouring in through the cabin skylight, and Brandark smiled.

"You might say that," he acknowledged. "Mind you, I didn't expect our friendship to last this long when we first met. Mostly because I didn't expect *Bahzell* to last very long! I know you haven't known him as long as I have, but I'm pretty sure you can already see why he didn't make exactly the most . . . circumspectly behaved diplomatic hostage in history."

"Diplomatic hostage?" Kenhodan's moving hands paused. "Bahzell was a *diplomatic hostage?*"

"Of course he was."

Brandark seemed a bit taken aback by Kenhodan's

surprise, and Kenhodan set down his polishing cloth, sat back in his chair, and placed both hands on the table, rather like a man bracing himself.

In some ways, he and Brandark had become even closer than he'd come to Bahzell or Wencit. Even though he couldn't imagine what the reason was, he'd been forced to accept that there truly *was* a reason Wencit couldn't fill the yawning void where his memory should have been. He didn't like it, he couldn't truly accept it, yet he'd come to the conclusion that he had no choice but to *endure* it . . . and to console himself with the belief that sooner or later, if they both survived, Wencit truly would tell him what he needed to know. In the meantime, however, the wizard's silence was there between them, a hidden core of tension at the heart of their relationship.

Bahzell didn't know any more about Kenhodan's past than Kenhodan himself, and he regarded Kenhodan's amnesia the same way he regarded the redhaired man's physical scars. It was simply part of who Kenhodan was, a wound to be accepted with sympathy and compassion, but not some dread secret he had to juggle against other, awesome responsibilities. He'd become a trusted companion, a friend, and a source of strength, yet there was something, some constraint, in *his* relationship with Kenhodan, as well. It had nothing at all to do with the human's amnesia; Kenhodan was certain of that. But at the same time, without knowing why, he was positive Bahzell had his own reasons—quite possibly reasons related to his champion's duty to Tomanāk—that made him occasionally watch his words very, very carefully. There was no way in the universe Bahzell Bahnakson would ever *lie* to him; Kenhodan was certain of that, as well. But not lying wasn't remotely the same thing as telling the *whole* truth. Kenhodan often wondered if his hypersensitivity to his amnesia was causing him to imagine that faint edge of constraint in Bahzell, yet each time he considered it, he came back to the conclusion that it wasn't.

But Brandark was no champion of Tomanāk, and he certainly wasn't a wizard. Like Bahzell, he knew no more about Kenhodan's past than Kenhodan himself did, yet he had no secrets to protect and no divine instruction to treat Kenhodan as anything other than one of his closest friends' comrade and sword companion. And, also like Bahzell, he accepted Kenhodan's amnesia the way he would have accepted any other wound, and he'd extended his welcome to Kenhodan the same way he would have welcomed any of Bahzell's other friends.

That was important. Kenhodan very much doubted Brandark even began to fully realize *how* important it was. To have *anyone* treat him the same way they would have treated anyone else would have been more than enough to make him prayerfully grateful for Brandark, but Brandark wasn't just "anyone."

Kenhodan had quickly discovered that *Wave Mistress'* captain was even more of a challenge to the hradani stereotype than he'd first thought. He'd recognized at their first meeting that Brandark had a remarkably acute brain, but after an evening listening to the hradani and Wencit argue philosophy and ancient history, he'd realized Brandark was also a serious scholar, sufficiently informed, polished, literate, and widely read to debate Wencit of Rūm head-to-head . . . and win. *That* was scarcely part of the traditional hradani image!

As if that wasn't enough, Brandark was also an

astonishingly accomplished musician. Kenhodan had noticed three instrument cases that first morning; since then, Brandark had pulled out another half-dozen, and Kenhodan suspected there might be still more tucked away and overlooked in a corner somewhere. And that was another reason for his comfort with Brandark, for he'd discovered that he, too, was a musician.

It was like his sword skill, something he had no memory of acquiring . . . and that he'd never suspected he possessed until he saw the harp. Brandark had brought it out on their second night aboard, and something like an icicle of lightning had gone through Kenhodan when he saw it. He'd reached out without asking permission—without even *thinking*—and taken the harp from Brandark's surprised hands. The hradani had started to ask a question, undoubtedly for an explanation, but then Kenhodan's hands had swept across the harp strings and Brandark had sat back in his chair, his eyes wide and his ears half-flattened in pleasure, as the music poured across him.

Kenhodan didn't really remember much from that night. The notes and the melody had flowed through him, playing him as if *he'd* been the harp, sweeping him out of *Wave Mistress'* great cabin and into a place where, for at least those few moments, his maimed past meant nothing. A place where he was simultaneously only a single ripple of notes lost in the greater melody flooding from the harp and yet simultaneously whole—complete and at peace as he'd never been since the moment Leeana first asked him about the scars he hadn't known he had.

That love for music was a link, a bond, between him and Brandark that went straight to the soul, and its discovery was a gift beyond price. When Kenhodan had finally floated once more to the surface of the music, opened his eyes upon the cabin once again, he'd seen the others—even Wencit—gazing at him with the rapt expressions of men who'd been transported beyond themselves on the wings of Chesmirsa herself. He'd looked back at them, wondering what had happened, his mind still hazed by a glissando of harp notes, and realized—finally—that he'd somehow ended up with Brandark's harp in his hands. He'd flushed in embarrassment and held it out quickly, but Brandark had only sighed and shaken his head.

"No," he'd said softly, his eyes darkly serious yet somehow brilliant. "That harp's exactly where it ought to be. A man who can play like that needs an instrument worthy of him. Do me the honor of allowing me to give him one."

It was only later, from Wencit, that Kenhodan learned the harp Brandark had given him had been crafted in Saramantha over six centuries before by the legendary elven harpist Wenfranos.

The memory of that moment of discovery, and of Brandark's flat refusal to allow him to return an instrument which was literally priceless, flowed through him as he looked back across the table top and the harp at the captain, yet it wasn't enough to damp his surprise at what Brandark had just told him.

"I wasn't aware the Order of Tomanāk ever gave 'diplomatic hostages,'" he said.

"Oh, it wasn't the *Order*." Brandark sat back in his own chair and shook his head. "It was his father."

"His *father?*" Kenhodan blinked. Bahzell had mentioned his "Da" a time or two in passing, and it was obvious he'd respected his father a great deal, but what sort of—?

"His father," Brandark repeated. "Prince Bahnak."

"*Prince* Bahnak? You mean Bahzell is the son of a prince?"

"I mean Bahzell's a prince in his own right, as well as a champion of Tomanāk. You didn't know?"

"No," Kenhodan said with commendable restraint. "Somehow he and Wencit—and Leeana, now that I think about it—failed to share that particular tidbit with me."

"Um. Should I, ah, assume then that they also 'failed to share' the fact that Leeana was born Leeana Bowmaster, the only daughter of *Tellian* Bowmaster, Baron of Balthar and Lord Warden of the West Riding?"

Kenhodan's nostrils flared as he inhaled deeply. The title of "baron" meant different things in different realms; among the Sothōii, it just happened to be the highest and most noble title short of the king himself, the feudal lord and governor of one of their "ridings." The Kingdom of the Sothōii took in the entire Wind Plain, and quite a few thousand square leagues around the base of that mighty plateau, and there were only four Sothōii ridings.

Which meant Leeana's father's demesne had been about the size of the complete Kingdom of Angthyr.

"Yes, I believe you should assume it somehow slipped their mind to mention *that* to me, either," he said after a moment. "How in the names of all the gods did she and Bahzell end up married? For that matter how did the daughter of a Sothōii *baron* end up a war maid? And how did a war maid end up marrying *anyone*?"

"Forgive me, Kenhodan," Brandark said after a moment, his tone oddly gentle, "but there appear to be even larger...gaps in your memory than I'd realized. You truly don't know who Bahzell and Leeana are, do you?"

"Beyond being two people who gave shelter and protection to Wencit and a man who has no idea who he used to be, no. I don't know who they are—*what* they are. But it's just become evident to me that I know even less about them than I'd thought I did."

"You've never heard why Bahzell's called 'Bloody Hand,' then?"

For some reason, Kenhodan's headshake seemed to take Brandark aback for just a moment, but then the hradani shook it off and grinned.

"Actually," he said, "there's an entire lengthy ballad about him. Quite flattering, as a matter of fact, and I personally think it was quite well written. You might almost say *brilliantly* written, now that I think about it. If you'd like, I'll play it for you later tonight. Probably wouldn't be a bad idea to get a couple of the lads in to sing the words, though—Garuth and Yairdain, perhaps. My playing's better than my singing voice, and I'm sure Bahzell would like you to hear it for the first time properly presented."

"I'm sure he would," Kenhodan replied just a bit warily, and Brandark chuckled. Then the hradani's expression sobered and he crossed his legs, resting one mirror-bright boot on the opposite knee, propped his elbows on the arms of his chair, and steepled his fingers under his chin.

"All right," he said after a moment. "I'll tell you about Bahzell, how we met, and who he is. But if

I do, you have to promise not to keep interrupting with admiring exclamations like 'You don't say!' or 'I never would've guessed *that!*' Trust me, if you don't, this could take all afternoon, and we won't have that long before Bahzell gets done swapping stories with Captain Forstan. Besides, if he gets back while we're talking about it, he'll insist on inserting all sorts of minor, pointless clarifications that'll just slow down the narrative and confuse you. I love him like a brother, but he has absolutely no sense of the storyteller's art. Understood?"

"Understood," Kenhodan replied, settling back in his chair.

"All right," Brandark said again. "First, I'm a Bloody Sword and Bahzell's a Horse Stealer. Do you remember what *that* means?"

Kenhodan nodded . . . and sternly reminded himself of his promise not to interrupt. It was hard to keep it in the face of that simple statement. Although he more than suspected there'd be plenty of other surprises along the way, this one was quite enough to be starting with. The towering hatred, competition, and blood feuds between the Bloody Sword hradani clans and their Horse Stealer rivals were fierce enough to be the stuff of legends far beyond the limits of their northern homelands.

"Since you don't know the deep, dark secrets of Bahzell's past, however," Brandark continued, "I'm assuming you don't have any specific memories of recent political events among the northern hradani, either. Am I correct?"

Kenhodan thought for a moment, then nodded again as he realized he genuinely didn't.

"Well, some decades back, Bahzell's father, Prince Bahnak, decided to put an end to all the nonsense our clans had been inflicting on one another for the odd eight or nine hundred years. Unfortunately, hradani being hradani, the only way to do that was for one of us to finally conquer the other one once and for all, and for some strange reason he wasn't especially interested in being the one who got conquered. That meant conquering the Bloody Swords, instead, to which—for some equally strange reason—the Bloody Swords objected. There was a war. In fact, there were two or three of them, and after one of them—one Bahnak won handily, as a matter of fact—Prince Churnazh of Navahk—who was *not* a nice person, even if he was a Bloody Sword—was forced to accept Bahnak's terms. Unfortunately, his defeat hadn't been sufficiently severe, and he had too many allies, for Bahnak to demand his outright capitulation. Everyone knew there'd be another war, but both sides had reason to postpone it while they tried to build up their strength, so there was a treaty and an exchange of hostages, and as Bahnak's youngest son, Bahzell was sent to Navahk. Clear so far?"

"So far."

"Good, because this is where it gets interesting, since this is the point at which *I* enter the picture." Brandark lifted his nose, flicked his ears, and grinned. "You see, much as it pains me to admit it, Churnazh was a member of my own Bloody Sword clan, the Raven Talons, and my father, another Brandark, was a powerful Raven Talon chieftain. Powerful enough Churnazh didn't quite dare try crushing him the way he had his other Bloody Sword rivals despite the fact that I'm afraid I'd made myself just a *tiny* bit unpopular with Churnazh. I was young and impulsive in those days, not the staid and sober fellow you know today, and, as I said, he wasn't a nice person. He was also remarkably lacking in culture, even for an old-style hradani warlord, and he had no appreciation at all for original musical compositions."

Kenhodan winced. He'd been aboard *Wave Mistress* for less than a week, yet he'd come to know Brandark well enough to have a shrewd notion of the sorts of "original musical compositions" he must have produced about the "old-style hradani warlord" he'd just described.

"Because of that, Bahzell and I somehow became friends. My father always said I only did it to piss Churnazh off, but I'm sure he was wrong. And whether or not that was the way it started, it turned into a genuine friendship quickly enough. The oversized lump of bone and gristle has that effect on people. So, when he half-killed one of Churnazh's sons for raping a serving wench and had to flee, of course I went with him. Although," Brandark admitted judiciously, "he was rude enough not to *invite* me to come along. It took me several days to track him down and catch up with him.

"I managed, though, and after many adventures in which I, of course, played a sterling part—but with which I won't bore you at this moment, due to my towering and always understated modesty—Bahzell managed to become a champion of Tomanāk, to rescue the daughter of a Spearman duke from assassins, black wizards, and the Purple Lords; kill a demon single-handed; get both of us outlawed in the Land of the Purple Lords; defeat Churnazh's son Harnak, who happened to be armed with a cursed sword enspelled by Sharnā himself; hijack—well, 'hijack' is probably putting it a bit too strongly—a Marfang Island schooner from Bortalik Bay; sail to Belhadan; outrage a sizable minority of the Belhadan chapter of the Order of Tomanāk; march home cross-country in the middle of winter by way of Dwarvenhame; kill *another* demon and exterminate an entire temple of Sharnā in Navahk; organize the first hradani chapter of the Order of Tomanāk in history; and as an encore—probably just to keep from being bored, you understand—bring an end to the seven or eight centuries of mutual slaughter our people had been enjoying with the Sothōii."

He paused with a benign smile while Kenhodan tried to get his mouth closed.

"While he was involved with all those other minor details," Brandark continued after a moment, "he and I wound up adopted into the family of the Duke of Jashân in the Empire of the Spear and first made the acquaintance of Wencit, which didn't really do a lot to make our lives more tranquil, for some reason. But while he and I were off with the eighty or so members of his brand-new chapter of the Order accepting the surrender of several thousand Sothōii warriors—from Baron Tellian himself, as a matter of fact—Prince Bahnak was tidying up the annoying little details involved in conquering the Bloody Swords and uniting all the northern clans into his Northern Confederation. Bahzell obviously had to go home with Tellian to oversee the conditions of Tellian's parole—don't get me started at this point on just *why* Tellian chose to

surrender to us; let's just say that Wencit's version of
the history between the hradani and the Sothōii gave
us all plenty of food for thought—and since he was
his father's son as well as a champion of Tomanāk,
he became the logical—although I *really* hesitate
to use the word 'logical' too often where Bahzell is
concerned—hradani ambassador to the Sothōii. Which
obviously led to no end of additional alarms, excursions,
and adventures, including a confrontation with not
one, not two, but three of Krashnark's greater devils
on the Ghoul Moor. That," he added kindly, smiling
brightly at Kenhodan's sandbagged expression, "was as
part of the military expedition to clear the line of the
Hangnysti River so the canal from Dwarvenhame to
Hurgrum, Bahzell's hometown, could connect direct
to the Spear River, which completely destroyed the
Purple Lords' monopoly on trade up and down the
river and, particularly, with the Empire of the Spear.
Oh, and all of that predated the formal treaty of alliance between the Northern Confederation and the
Kingdom of the Sothōii."

He paused, still smiling at Kenhodan, and the
redhaired man drew a deep breath and gave himself
a shake.

"I...see," he said after a moment. "And I assume
it was while all of that was going on that he and
Leeana met?"

"Of course. Mind you, she was only—what? thirteen
or fourteen at the time, I think—and any relationship
between the two of them would have been grossly
inappropriate. He knew that, too. And with that excess
of nobility he takes such pains to conceal, he was
determined not to let anything...improper happen.

Unfortunately for his noble intentions, she ran off to become a war maid—political reasons," he raised one hand, waggling his fingers in an airy brushing away motion, "you'd probably be bored by them—and grew up. Then she came back and tripped him into bed."

Kenhodan surprised himself with a chuckle, but it was entirely too easy for him to picture Leeana doing exactly that.

"That was just before the bit with Krashnark and the devils," Brandark continued helpfully. "Oh, and before Baron Cassan, the Lord Warden of the South Riding attempted to assassinate Tellian and King Markhos to stop the canal project—remember, I mentioned that earlier?—which Bahzell's father, Tellian, and Kilthandahknarthas of Silver Cavern had hatched between them. Would've worked, too, if Leeana hadn't become the first female wind rider in Sothōii history, reached her father and the King with a warning in time, and—eventually—personally taken Cassan's head. Well, it still almost worked, but the war maids from Kalatha came along to help Trisu of Lorham thwart the assassination, which had a little something to do with certain revisions to the war maid charter that followed a few years later." He smiled brightly. "Aside from continuing to snuff out the odd demon, help Wencit eradicate the occasional circle of black wizards, trounce an infestation of corsairs from time to time, negotiate with the Spearmen for his father and the Sothōii, and mete out Scale Balancer's justice upon occasion, he really hasn't done much except rest on his laurels ever since."

He paused again, his eyes bright and his ears shifting back and forth in gentle amusement as he watched Kenhodan grapple with his concise, irreverent, but obviously very, very sincere encapsulation of Bahzell's career. It took the human several minutes to do that grappling.

"And the tavern in Belhadan? The Iron Axe? What are a hradani prince, who's also a champion of Tomanāk, and a war maid, who's also the daughter of one of the four most powerful Sothōii nobles in existence, doing running a *tavern* in the Empire of the Axe?"

"Bahzell's never been the sort to sit around and just collect a stipend, even from something like the Order of Tomanāk, no matter how often the Order's pressed him to accept one," Brandark said at least a bit more seriously. "He had his own reasons for relocating to Belhadan in the first place, and he and Leeana have had very good reasons to stay there, but I suspect the real reason for the tavern—he named it for his clan back home, of course—is Gwynna."

"Gwynna?" Kenhodan's eyebrows rose.

"Even today, there's a lot of prejudice against hradani, Kenhodan." Brandark was entirely serious now. "Bahzell—and I, to a lesser extent—are . . . outside that prejudice. We're what some people have taken to calling 'white hradani,' hradani who've demonstrated they don't fit the stereotype of the Rage-crazed hradani berserker. And to be fair, I'd say the prejudice is beginning to fade, although—as ridiculous as it would have seemed once upon a time—it's faded the most among the *Sothōii*, not the Axemen or the Spearmen. But human-hradani marriages, like Bahzell and Leeana's, are still virtually unheard of. I could probably count all of them without taking my boots off, and the one crime we hradani have the least tolerance for is rape. That means there have been precious few human-hradani children ever born in Norfressa."

Brandark leaned back in his chair, his voice soft, and shook his head.

"Wencit says children like that were more common back in Kontovar, before the Rage—before the Fall and the things the Lords of Carnadosa forced enspelled hradani to do burned the hatred of us so deeply into the hearts and minds of the other Races of Man. But today?" He shook his head. "She's a lovely, darling girl, dearer to me than my own nieces and nephews—though I'd never dare to admit that back home!—but just being what she is is more than enough to make all too many bigots—not all of them human, by any means—hate and despise her. So I think one reason Bahzell and Leeana bought the tavern—and one reason they've chosen to be who they are rather than who birth and accomplishment tried to make them—is to provide Gwynna simultaneously with as close to a 'normal' childhood as someone like her could possibly hope to have and with a window into a world where too many people will look at her askance."

"That . . . actually makes sense," Kenhodan said after a moment, his voice equally soft. "I wonder how many other parents would have made a similar decision?"

"Bahzell and Leeana see more deeply—and *care* more deeply—than almost anyone else I know," Brandark said simply. "I expect there are more parents than I think who'd make that sort of decision for the same reasons, but to be honest, I don't see how *they* could've made any other one."

Kenhodan nodded slowly, but then he frowned.

"I know I promised not to interrupt, and I'm sure I could keep you busy answering questions all the way from here to Korun. But I'm a little confused about one point—well, about *several* points, actually, but one that comes especially to mind."

"And that point would be?"

"Having come to know Bahzell, having met Leeana, seeing the two of them arguing with *Wencit of Rūm*—and winning!—I have much less trouble than I might have expected believing the two of them could've accomplished everything you've just rattled off. But how did they manage to fit it all *in*?"

"'Fit it in'?" Brandark repeated, arching his eyebrows.

"How did they have *time* for it all?" Kenhodan amplified. "I'd've thought it would've taken decades to do all that!"

"It did." Brandark leaned back, his expression surprised. "I thought I made that clear."

"But—" Kenhodan shook his head, and Brandark frowned. Then, suddenly, the hradani's face cleared.

"Kenhodan," he said almost gently, "how old is Leeana?"

"What?" Kenhodan blinked. Then he thought about it for a moment. "I don't know. In her thirties—*maybe* her early forties?" he said, pushing the upper end of his estimate hard.

"She's ninety-three, Kenhodan."

"*What?*" Kenhodan stared at him, and Brandark nodded.

"She and Bahzell have been married for over seventy years," he said calmly. "In fact, Bahzell's only a couple of years older than I am, and I'll be a hundred and twenty-five this summer."

Kenhodan went right on staring at him. He could readily believe Brandark and Bahzell were well into their second centuries, since hradani routinely lived to be two hundred years old or better, assuming they managed to avoid death by violence along the way, and they tended to remain hale, hardy, and active right up to the end. But it was starkly preposterous to claim that *Leeana* was over ninety! She might be married to a hradani, but she was obviously a human, after all.

"That's—" he began.

"Impossible?" Brandark interrupted, and snorted. "Kenhodan, you're planning to travel to Angthyr with a wizard who's well over *fourteen hundred* years old!"

"But...but he's *Wencit of Rūm!*"

"Yes, he is, but what you seem not to have grasped is that *she's* Leeana Flame Hair. Tell me, have you noticed her and Bahzell's wedding bracelets?"

"Of course I have."

"Well, you might want to take a closer look at Bahzell's this evening. Most upper-class Sothōii wedding bracelets are made out of gold, not silver, you know. And they're not set with opals, either. For that matter, most of them don't have Tomanāk's mace and sword and Lillinara's moon on them, either."

"Obviously that's significant," Kenhodan said slowly.

"You might say that." Brandark snorted. "You asked how a war maid ended up married to a hradani when their own charter prohibited then from marrying under the law? Well, when Tomanāk and Lillinara appear—*in person*—to pronounce a couple are man and wife, it takes a hardy soul to argue with Them. And just in case anyone was inclined to doubt Their position in this little matter, They gave Bahzell and Leeana their bracelets. And they're very...*interesting* bracelets, too. He and Leeana have convinced them not to glow without their specific permission—which took a while; they're almost as stubborn as hradani, those bracelets—but as nearly as I can understand what the two of them and Wencit have told me over the years, when Tomanāk and Lillinara put those bracelets on their wrists, They united more than just their lives, Kenhodan. They united their *souls*. Something I didn't know until Wencit explained it to us is that hradani—and, for that matter, Sothōii coursers—live as long as we do because we're ... directly connected to what Wencit calls the wild magic. And now, thanks to her union with Bahzell, so is Leeana."

"But why—?"

"Why did They do it for Leeana and no one else?" Brandark shrugged. "I don't have an answer for that one, Kenhodan. My best guess? The gods have something they need her to do. Probably her and Bahzell together, actually. Mind you, I don't know two people on the face of Orfressa who could possibly deserve the extra years Leeana's been given more than the two of them do. But I don't think it's that simple. I think the two of them have been chosen to accomplish something so important that everything they've already done has only been preparation."

The hradani's eyes were deadly serious now, and they held Kenhodan like a wizard's spell.

"That's what *I* think, Kenhodan, and I think you've been chosen to be a part of that same task, whatever it is."

Kenhodan stared back, desperate to deny the possibility. To protest that Brandark *had* to be wrong. He opened his mouth, reached for the words to tell the captain precisely that.

And he couldn't.

· CHAPTER SIX ·

A Sailor's Lot

In addition to all his other manifold talents, Bahzell Bahnakson was an accurate weather prophet.

The fluky winds he'd warned of had shown themselves—or their absence—over the last three days, and Kenhodan was heartily sick of it. Now *Wave Mistress* moved unhappily as another slow wave heaved sullenly under her hull. She was bred to spe ed, and motionlessness made her uneasy...especially this *sort* of motionlessness. For the first two days of dead calm the sea had been a breathless mirror, unusual for this time of year but hardly unheard of. That had changed earlier this morning, however, and the weather-wise among her crew didn't like what they were seeing. Whatever drove the swell was far away, for not a breeze stirred her silent canvas and the brisk chill had become a cold dampness that coated a man's skin like oil, but those swells had grown steadily steeper since dawn. It was as if something was creeping up on them.

Kenhodan sat on the deck, leaning against the foremast, plucking at the harp Brandark had given him, and watched Bahzell and Captain Forstan fence with blunted weapons for the edification—and distraction—of guards and crew. The dull sounds of their blows and parries struck his ear distantly, for his mind was far away as he tuned a discordant string and thought.

His skill at the harp was far more than merely satisfying, even if he had no memory of acquiring it. Nor did he remember learning any of the melodies which bubbled up on their own from the shadow of his lost past if he simply let them. He couldn't *force* them, but they came anyway, as if called by something outside him, and while they lasted, he was whole once more . . . until they released him and he returned to the world about him. It was eerie, he supposed, but it was an eeriness he welcomed and one he'd learned to accept as he accepted Wencit and Bahzell.

He considered his strangely maturing relationship with the wizard. Brandark's tales of Bahzell's doings had put a final seal on Kenhodan's acceptance, for if a champion of Tomanāk—one who'd managed to achieve even a tenth of Bahzell's accomplishments—not only trusted the wizard but accepted him as a close personal friend, how could Kenhodan distrust him? Besides, if Wencit of Rūm couldn't be trusted, no man could. All the tales agreed on that. But that didn't end the tension between them, for Kenhodan had discovered that his willful, imperious streak bitterly resented his inability to control his own life. He didn't know if that willfulness was the product of his amnesia or if it had always been a part of him, but he knew it was there, and so did Wencit.

The wizard was painfully careful to share everything he could, and both he and Bahzell sought Kenhodan's opinions as if he actually had enough memory to make them worth hearing. Kenhodan suspected it was out of kindness, which was yet one more reason he was attracted to Brandark. When the shipmaster asked a question, it was to get an answer, not because he was being kind.

He straightened and moved his feet out of the way as the port and starboard watches thundered past to race one another up the ratlines. They'd been carrying out a lot of competitions like that over the last couple of days. To lie becalmed could try the patience of a saint, and there were precious few saints in Brandark's crew. The captain believed in keeping idle hands too busy for mischief, especially on a day with weather as strange as this one's.

Kenhodan agreed, for *Wave Mistress* carried as mixed a crew as ever there was. Men with . . . problematical pasts had always found the sea a convenient hiding place, and Kenhodan was confident that was true for at least some of Brandark's men. Certainly every Race of Man was represented, including some who were virtually never found at sea, in a blending that defied an orderly imagination. The officers were taut professionals, yet the racial prejudices of so heterogeneous a crew could have been fertile soil for trouble if not for their respect for and fierce (if unadmitted) devotion to their captain. Yet not even that strong cement could fully overcome their internal tensions.

The boatswain, for example, was a Marfang Island halfling. Although he sprang from a sorcery-spawned race many distrusted, he was a pleasant sort, with more experience than any other three crewmen. But he was also less than four feet tall and touchy about his size. He was fast with a dagger hilt, too; even the largest seaman avoided him when he was in an ugly mood. Besides, it was said he felt wind changes in his ivory horns, which earned him the respect due any prophet of Chemalka.

The rest were an inextricable mass. There were humans (including a surly ex-officer from Emperor Soldan's army who captained the main top), two dozen hradani (who regarded themselves as Brandark's elite corps, though he was prone to crack heads if they became too vocal about it), a round dozen dwarves (who'd clearly found it expedient to be elsewhere in a hurry and loudly missed their mountain tunnels), and even one elf—Hornos, who served as first officer and never mentioned his past.

"Ho, Kenhodan!" The lookout's hail broke into his reverie, shaking him back into the present.

"Ho, yourself!" he shouted back up at the man perched at the topmast crosstrees while the mastheads traced slow, uneasy circles against the sky.

"If you must pluck that thing, at least give us a tune!"

"What would you like to hear?"

"D'you know 'Torloss Troubled Heart'?"

Kenhodan let his hands lie limp on the strings, waiting to see if this was one of the tunes which lurked in the reefs of his memory like ships' bones on the Fradonian Banks, ready to bob to the surface on a passing current when tickled by their names or hummed melodies. A handful of seconds passed, and then his fingers moved suddenly and a rollicking ditty sprang from the harp, laughing over the decks. After a moment, his voice began the song of the sailor, the barmaid, and Hirahim Lightfoot, the laughing god. He'd just reached the verse in which Torloss discovered that his rival for the maid's favors was none other than the god of seductions himself, when a hail from above broke his concentration.

"Sail hooooooo!" the same lookout called. "Three sail—no, *four*, by the Trident! Two points off the starboard quarter, and closing like the wrath of Phrobus!"

"What?" Brandark had joined the crowd enjoying Kenhodan's song. Now he wheeled, staring astern towards the sails invisible from deck level, and his mobile ears were half-flattened.

"What's wrong?" Kenhodan stilled the strings with his hand. Brandark's alarm clearly stemmed from more than the mere number of strangers.

"Maybe nothing." Brandark tugged his shortened ear and peered up at the lookout. "But there's no telling who you'll meet out here, and I don't like it that they're closing—not if they're under canvas."

His fingers flicked at *Wave Mistress'* lifeless sails.

"I see your point."

Kenhodan reached for the harp case and began fitting the instrument into it, conscious of the sword that wasn't at his side at the moment.

Bahzell scampered up the ratlines with apelike speed, and Brandark propped his fists on his hips and stared upward as the other hradani carefully peered along the line of the lookout's pointing hand, exchanging observations with the seaman. Then Bahzell gave an emphatic nod, clapped the man on the shoulder, and reached for a stay. He wrapped his legs around it and plunged down to thump heavily on deck, then wiped his stinging palms on his breeches and clumped to Brandark's side.

"You've a good man up there, Brandark," he said quietly. "I'm thinking he spotted them as they broke the horizon, but they'll be up to us soon. They're after coming with the whips of Fiendark behind them, and no mistake. Corsairs. Black sails."

"No quarter, then," Brandark muttered. He stroked his chin with callused fingers. "And they're moving under sail, not oars?"

"They are, Captain." Heads turned as Wencit emerged from the maindeck hatch, eyes flaming. "But not on the winds of *this* world."

"Sorcery!" Brandark spat. "May all the wizards of the world cut each others' throats! Except yours, of course!" he added hastily.

"I applaud your sentiments, but we have more pressing problems."

"Aye." Bahzell was thoughtful. "Boarders or sorcery, are you thinking?"

"Both. There are at least two wizards over there, and there's something more than a wizard wind with them. It won't be shadows this time—too much light— but it's something evil, and strong enough I may be hard-pressed to counter it. And since I can't use the art if I have to fight at the same time, they'll send boarders to break my concentration."

"My thought, as well," Brandark said grimly. "I've good lads, Wencit—not many you'd take home to your mother, maybe, but good lads in a fight. Unfortunately, I don't have as many as I'd like against four ships, even with the Axe Brothers."

"When you're surrounded, you've more targets," Bahzell said philosophically. His hard, calculating eyes belied his light tone. "At least they'll not try to sink or burn us—not if those are after being real corsairs. I'm thinking they've come for your bullion, Brandark, and it won't buy a pot of poor ale on the seabed."

"Well, I don't have any such compunctions where they're concerned!" Brandark grunted, and the scholar was buried deep in the elemental hradani. "Black sails, is it? If that's what they want, I'll stretch myself to give it to them!" He raised his voice. "Hornos! Captain Forstan!"

His lieutenant and the imperial commander arrived together. Hornos' habitual expression of gentle melancholy was unchanged, but his sword was at his side, an extra dagger had materialized on his belt, and he wore a scale mail hauberk. The Axe Brothers' captain looked more anxious than the elf as he tightened his breastplate over the black and gold tunic of the Empire's crack heavy infantry. Kenhodan wasn't surprised; ultimate responsibility for the treasure was his.

"Those gentlemen mean to relieve us of your cargo, Captain," Brandark said levelly, "and they may have the strength to do it. I'd be obliged if your men would muster on the starboard side."

"At once."

Forstan nodded and wheeled away, bellowing orders as boots stamped and armor clanged. Most seamen eschewed armor, for its weight would drag a swimmer swiftly under, but the Axe Brothers were no sailors. They wore plate and carried the double-bitted great axes of the King Emperor's elite, and Kenhodan smiled grimly at the surprise awaiting the corsairs if their allies hadn't warned them what to expect.

"The crew will take the port rail," Brandark went on, laying out his plans for Hornos. "Clear away and load with banefire—but for Korthrala's sake, don't fire the loads before I tell you! The last thing we need is flaming rigging around our ears when we're outnumbered four-to-one!"

"Aye, Sir!"

"Seldwyn," Brandark turned to his archery captain. "Load the dart throwers, but save them till they close. There's no way to dance and run with them when they've got a wind and we don't, so wait till they're right on top of us, then sweep their quarter decks. If there's a wizard on deck, that's where he'll be, and if we put a javelin in *his* belly, so much the better."

"Aye, Sir!" Seldwyn turned away, but Brandark caught his jerkin.

"Wait a minute. Put the archers on the quarterdeck; they won't try coming over the bow—their bulwarks are too low and the foredeck's taper favors us too much—so they'll run alongside to keep us busy, then try to break into the quarter galleys and come over the stern. Don't wait there—start hitting them the moment they're in range."

"Aye, Sir!" Seldwyn repeated, and this time Brandark let him go.

Kenhodan watched the crew come alive with purposeful fury. Outnumbered they might be, and more than a bit unhappy at the odds, yet they appeared to be dominated by anger, not fear. Indeed, they seemed almost to welcome the appearance of enemies they could deal with instead of the bizarre weather they'd been unable to understand . . . until now. Hornos' tenor voice lacked the volume of Brandark's bellow, but it was clear, cutting through the tumult like a trumpet, and the crew's bare feet added a pattering urgency to the din, counterpointing the soldiers' boots and the crash of opening arms chests. He watched a dwarf test an axe edge with grim delight while a brawny topman made a cutlass whistle.

"Bahzell," Brandark ignored the rush as he continued to plan his defense, "Captain Forstan can see to the starboard side. I'd like you with me and the crew on the other bulwark. Hornos will command the ballistae, and he can lead the artillerists wherever they're needed once the bastards close with us. Seldwyn will command the archers and the afterguard."

"Good enough," Bahzell replied. "Best I go find my gear, I'm thinking."

He nodded sharply to the captain and headed below just as one of Brandark's younger seamen ran up to him with a daggered axe on a baldric. It wasn't the traditional great axe of Bahzell's people, for it had only a single blade, but the back of its head ended in a wicked spike, suitable for piercing armor, and the entire weapon had a lean, lethal look. Brandark took it with a nod of thanks, looped the baldric over his head, and settled the axe on his back.

"Where do you want me?" Kenhodan demanded.

"You draw a heavy bow," Brandark replied. "Join the archers, if you please. But make it your special duty to look after Wencit. He'll be on deck to counter whatever deviltry's brewing over there, and you can bet whatever you own they'll try to mark him down early to stop him."

"Fine."

Kenhodan darted down the main hatch to his cabin. He had to dodge the last few crewmen as they boiled up, but he made good time despite the obstacles. He took time to stow the precious harp carefully before he buckled his sword belt, settled the sword and Gwynna's dagger at his side, and slid his quiver over his shoulder. Then he bent the bow stave with a quick motion, seating the resined string in its grooves, and plucked it gently. It hummed as musically as his harp, and he raced for the quarterdeck.

He was one of the last to arrive, and he scanned the deck carefully, fixing the defenders' positions in his mind. The corsairs were well above the horizon now, storming across the water at an unbelievable speed, and twenty other bowmen stood with him, watching them sweep closer. Black sails groaned on their yards, hard-bellied with angry wind, but still no breeze stirred over *Wave Mistress*.

Kenhodan sneezed on noxious fumes as Hornos bent over the after ballista, speaking quietly to his men. The heavy weapon crouched on its turntable like a vast crossbow, loaded with a long, vaned shaft. Its yard-long, hollow iron head was already loaded with deadly banefire—now Hornos stood ready to ignite the evil mixture of pitch, sulfur, naphtha, turpentine, and quicklime. Bahzell stood well forward, abreast the foremast with one foot on the bulwark, and the sun winked on the crossed sword and mace of his surcoat as he studied the enemy. Two halflings crouched over a dart thrower beside him, laying the five-foot javelins into the grooved firing tray. The heavy spring steel firing bar would drive all eight shafts at the jerk of a lanyard, and while the weapon was slow firing, at close range its missiles would pierce ten inches of seasoned oak.

Kenhodan searched for his special charge and saw

Wencit leaning against the mainmast. He'd drawn his sword, but his expression was blank with intensity and his multihued eyes gazed sightlessly at nothing as mind and will sought for the telltale tendrils of sorcery directed against the ship.

Once certain of Wencit's exact position, Kenhodan turned back to starboard and nocked an arrow. They'd enter longbow range soon, and—

His thoughts broke off and he blinked, almost staggering as a hammer struck his brain and sudden fury exploded within him. He shook his head drunkenly, fighting the shock of rage. It was the same anger he'd felt in the taproom, only stronger even than it had been then, and it was neither fear nor the zest Bahzell seemed to feel. It was a *personal* hatred, a loathing, as if the corsairs represented some hideous disease, and it was so much stronger than the hate of Brandark's crew that his bones burned like ice. It lent him a frightening strength—strength all the more frightening because he didn't understand it. Yet he saw its danger, as well, for this fury was blind. It could destroy him as easily as any blade ... unless he could use it rather than be used *by* it. Berserkers made deadly foes, but they also expended themselves like unthinking weapons, and the thought of dying in a mad frenzy of butchery was almost as terrifying as it was seductive.

He knew that, sensed his capacity for destruction and a deep, almost ecstatic need to embrace his *own* destruction, and saw the maelstrom spinning its vortex of bloodshed and thunder at his very core. Its power appalled him, and he made himself breathe deeply, fighting for control.

He won—barely. His pulse slowed and the pounding

in his temples slipped back towards normal. He took his hands from his bow one at a time and dried his palms carefully on his trousers, and the bloodlust bubbling in his brain had been chained to his purpose. It flickered like fire walled in ice, uneasy, unwilling to yield, yet it was *his* now, and he was no longer *its*. He still felt the crawling need to kill or be killed, but he commanded himself once more.

And just in time.

His lips drew back in a snarl as the corsairs swept closer. Little more than half *Wave Mistress'* length, they were low, lean, and wicked, and spray burst over their raked stems in green and cream as they leaned to the breath of their private tempest. Despite their smaller size, each carried almost as many men as *Wave Mistress*, even counting Forstan's Axe Brothers, for their crews greatly outnumbered those of any honest vessel their size, and Kenhodan studied their sleek lines—lines that ruthlessly subordinated cargo space to speed. After all, he thought grimly, pirates sought small bulk, high-value prizes; they could afford the sharp ferocity of those speed-hungry hulls.

"Ready your bows!" Seldwyn ripped out the words and raised his hand, his feet spread wide for balance while his eyes measured the range, the pitch of the hulls, and the priority he should assign each target.

"The lead ship!" he shouted harshly. "Gut me those archers!"

Kenhodan felt the sun's kiss, distant through the cold air, as his bow rose with the others. Salt, pitch, and hemp hung in his nostrils. One corsair had strayed four full lengths before her consorts, a temerity which marked her as the first target for *Wave Mistress'* wrath.

"Loooooose!"

Kenhodan sighted, drew, and released. The string whacked his leather arm guard, and his bow lifted as a cloud of arrows snarled up, fletching howling, and hissed above the sea. They sheeted down on the foremost corsair, barbed heads hungry for blood, and Kenhodan grinned fiercely, rage snarling in his brain as he followed their lethal flight. Then black figures tumbled aside under the beat of the arrow storm, and his nerves quivered ecstatically at the sight.

The return fire was late and short as their bitter points drove into the corsairs' faces. Dozens of out-ranged shafts plunged into the sea in flashes of white, far short of *Wave Mistress'* deck. To rate archer under Brandark Brandarkson, a bowman must be skilled with a longbow, rather than the short bow or crossbow most seamen favored, and his lieutenants were chosen as much for battle skill as sea craft. Seldwyn's keen eye had gauged the range more accurately than his corsair counterpart's, and his bowmen fell into the deadly rhythm of the Vonderland archer: twelve aimed shafts in a minute. Arrows slashed across the corsair like spume, sweeping the packed deck, heaping it with dead and writhing bodies and spattering it with blood.

The corsair archers were no match for that fire. They were cut down before they could reply effectively, but their consorts hastened to their aid. They began to find the range, and arrows whined and licked among the crew. Kenhodan heard them shriek in baffled rage from the Axe Brothers' armor, but too many sank into flesh with dull, meaty thuds, and gasps and screams erupted as men fell about him. He saw and heard it through the fury in his brain, but it was distant, far away and happening somewhere else as he concentrated on the strength of his arm, the keenness of his eye, and the limber strength of his magnificent, killing Vonderland bow.

Two corsairs bore straight for the starboard side. A third circled, storming up to port, while the fourth—hull lined with pike-waving pirates—lunged straight for the stern, exactly as Brandark had predicted.

"Now, Hornos! *Now!*"

Brandark's bellow split his crew's snarl as they sighted the corsairs' bare steel. The halfling boatswain's hands slashed, and the spring engines thudded. Their long, slim missiles howled through shield and pirate alike, and Seldwyn's remaining archers pivoted, hurling their arrows over the rail into the teeth of the boarding pirates.

But it was Hornos who unleashed the most devastating blow. Corsair arrows hissed among his men like feeding sharks, but they waited grimly as Hornos and a grizzled hradani seaman pressed torches to the banefire and leapt aside. Fire geysered and the artillery thudded far more loudly than the dart throwers had. The long missiles soared, trailing stinking smoke and flame in a smudgy line above the sea, and the gunners snatched up swords and boarding pikes and formed behind Hornos as their missiles streaked for their foes.

The seaman's shot slammed into the portside pirate's bulwark. It smashed clean through the thick planking in a shower of splinters and porpoised across the deck, but the head failed to shatter. Liquid fire dribbled from it, but a howling corsair—mad with battle lust or supremely courageous—levered it over the side.

The terrible substance ignited his clothing, clinging like death, and his flaming figure hurtled overboard behind the banefire even as his ship lunged across the final few dozen yards to *Wave Mistress*. His screaming body was crushed between the grinding hulls, yet his sacrifice saved his ship, and his mates surged up the side, pikeheads shining in the smoke.

And smoke there was, for Hornos' shot had crashed into the oardeck of the lead ship to starboard, and crewmen scattered wildly as the projectile shattered into fiery fragments. Water was less than useless against the quicklime-charged banefire, and it spread too quickly for sand buckets to quench. Smoke billowed and fire licked up the masts. Sails and tarred rigging burst into towers of flame, and screams told their own tale as the pirate ship bucked out of control, showering the sea with charred flecks of canvas and burning paint.

The corsair sheared away, wrapped in destruction, and the wizard wind became a two-edged weapon, blowing her to her doom. Wind bellied the untouched sails and fanned the flames to furnace fury. Bitter heat drove the helmsmen from their stations, unable to control their hurtling vessel, and desperate figures flung themselves overboard, only to be smashed back against the hull and battered beneath the waves by their ship's speed.

An ugly cheer rumbled from Brandark's crew as the three survivors struck home. Grapnels whipped up to sink iron teeth in *Wave Mistress'* timbers. Hulls groaned in protest, surging together in a thunder of oaken planking, and corsairs sprang up onto their lower bulwarks, thrusting at the defenders. Pikes crashed on armor as the pirates to starboard met the unexpected, plated axemen, but the other two ships disgorged hordes of howling warriors that frothed up too thick and fast to be stopped.

A wave of boarders broke into the cabins through the stern windows and boiled over the after rail. They were too close for bow work, and Kenhodan fired his last shaft into an officer's mouth before he whipped out his blade. He backed quickly towards Wencit, desperate to protect the wizard from the steel fanging the press of fighting men, and the wizard's voice rose behind him. His words were unintelligible, but the power crackling at their core prickled the nape of Kenhodan's neck.

Wencit's chant rose, yet for all its potency, the power in its words was hidden, pale beside the visible menace pluming up from two of the corsair ships. Twin darknesses loomed—fistlike, merging into one vast, tentacled mass of midnight-dark murder, pregnant with destruction and groping for prey like a living enemy, and the corsairs howled triumphantly at the evidence of their arcane allies.

They were protected from its touch; *Wave Mistress'* crew was not.

A black tendril reached the ship, stretching out before its fellows, and brushed one of Brandark's seamen as he buried his cutlass in a pirate's chest. The black caress transfixed him. For a moment he stood, a rock of stillness in the whirling melee, and then he dropped his weapon and his hands fastened on his own throat.

He screamed in agonized terror as his own fingers throttled away his life.

Kenhodan looked away sickly, and the defenders

wavered. Clean death was one thing; this abomination was more than mere courage could withstand. Yet they didn't break, for a voice rose like sea thunder from somewhere forward.

"Tomanāk! *Tomanāk!*"

Bahzell Bahnakson's bull-throated challenge roared, and a brilliant azure glow reached out from *Wave Mistress'* planking. The tendrils of sorcery hissed, recoiling, disintegrating into smoke at its touch, and the crew's resistance stiffened. Yet the spell was only baffled; it wasn't dismissed, and it gathered its strength anew. The many serpents of darkness withdrew, merged, combined into a single mighty column...and then smashed into the protective blue radiance like a battering ram of steel.

The shield cracked. It didn't fail, but the battering ram slammed silently into it, and Kenhodan felt the hatred, fell purpose, and power radiating from it like the breath of a Dwarvenhame blast furnace. It opened a crack—a tiny thing, no bigger than a man's hand—and the corsairs bellowed in fresh triumph as the blackness poured through the tiny breach, spilling onto the deck like oil, spreading like poison.

A lance of white light thrust suddenly into the darkness from the steel of Wencit's sword—steel writhing with a crawling arabesque of red and gold runes. It ignored the blackness spilling across the deck; instead, the beam pierced the column which drove that blackness onward. It struck like a flaming arrow and tore through it, seeking its heart, and Kenhodan's head throbbed to the sound of an animal scream of rage. It came, he knew, from Wencit's sorcery, and it terrified him.

Madness raged as light and blackness met, and the cloud recoiled, hissing. The white light ripped deeper, flaming against the darkness, and Kenhodan stared in fascination as sorcery fought sorcery. The ebon poison on the deck dissipated, drawing back into the battering ram behind it, and that battering ram drifted away from the ship as Wencit's voice rose higher. It was as if the light were a pole with which the wizard thrust danger away from the ship, but the blackness was only baffled. It was not yet defeated, and the balance wavered precariously back and forth.

The defenders gripped their weapons with renewed hope. As long as Bahzell and Wencit stood, they shielded *Wave Mistress* from the darkness, and as long as it was a matter of blood and blades, Brandark's crew knew itself equal to any threat. But the corsairs knew who'd thwarted their allies, and they hurled themselves forward to reach and kill them both.

"Tomanāk!"

Bahzell's voice roared out above the tumult as he met the rush sweeping up *Wave Mistress'* port side forward of the mainmast. His enormous sword flashed, wielded one-handed despite its size and weight, and heads flew. His hook knife was in his other hand and it struck like a steel serpent as one of Brandark's human crewmen went down beside him and a corsair leapt into the gap. His concentration never wavered, the blue glow around *Wave Mistress* grew stronger, and it made no difference at all to the lethality of his swordplay. His ears were flat, his brown eyes glittered, and blood flew in crimson spray as he reaped the gory harvest of a champion of Tomanāk at war.

Many of the corsairs gave ground as they realized

what—and who—they faced, but others swarmed forward. Say what one might about the Shith Kiri Corsairs, there were few cowards among them, and desperation made them bold. They flung themselves at Bahzell, swarming over the crewmen about him, and those crewmen gave ground, driven back by sheer force of numbers.

"Tomanāk!"

There was no hesitation, no compromise, in that thunderous war cry, and bodies and bits of bodies flew from the vortex of destruction called Bahzell Bahnakson. Blood coated *Wave Mistress'* planking as he built a breastwork of dead men, yet still the corsairs pressed forward.

A whine warned Kenhodan, and he ducked under a blade as the quarterdeck defenders went down in a tide of red steel. He thrust through a throat, recovered with a clean, deft flourish, and stood alone in the center of the deck, facing the stern rail, between it and Wencit. His opponents crowded one another, hampering themselves, giving him a precious edge, yet he was only one man. The corsairs knew who they had to kill...and that no one man could hold so many for long.

They poured forward like the tide.

Captain Forstan saw Kenhodan's peril and curled the after end of his Axe Brothers inward, covering half the deck with a wall of armor. The Axe Brothers smashed their enemies aside, but the unarmored seamen to port were unequal to the task. They strove to reach Kenhodan, but they were cut down or driven back by the howling corsairs.

Hornos hurtled aft at the head of his artillerists,

his sword carving a path for the men behind him, but the surge of pirates was too thick. Each corsair he cut down only gave sword room to two more, and the seamen were unarmored. Hornos' men were cut off behind him as he slashed a way through his foes, and Brandark's bleeding men gave ground—slowly, sullenly, cutting down their enemies as they went—but with chilling inevitability.

The corsair captains knew Wencit's death would give them *Wave Mistress* even more surely than Bahzell's would. They funneled their men to the attack with ruthless disregard for losses, willing to spend as many lives as necessary to thrust a foot of steel through the wizard, and only Kenhodan barred their way.

The redhaired man stood no chance. He knew it as well as the corsairs did...and he didn't care. He reached down inside himself and deliberately freed his inner rage, yet even now it was no berserker's fury. He couldn't understand what he was doing—or how—even as he did it, and it didn't matter. It was as if something within him watched an inner gauge, measuring that terrible anger as it pulsed through him, allowing just enough of it to fill his brain, pour into his muscles and blaze in the secret places of his soul.

He changed. His enemies saw his green eyes freeze into emerald ice, his lips drew back in a direcat's fierce, hungry snarl, and his sword was a blood-spattering scythe. He watched the seamen to his right go down, and then the corsairs poured through the breach at the port bulwark like a breaker, its crest edged with steel, not foam. He saw them come...and launched himself into them, laughing, for how could he kill them unless they came within his reach?

A bright pikehead gleamed, ignoring him to dart at Wencit, and Kenhodan thrust the pike wide with his left arm while his sword sliced across a throat like fire. The pikehead fell, and Kenhodan slid into the path of the dead man's companions like a machine of wire and steel . . . and vengeance.

"Tomanāk! Tomanāk!"

Kenhodan heard the thunder of Bahzell's deep-throated war cry, but it scarcely registered as a pirate came at him from the right. The corsair lunged with desperate speed, and yet he moved so *slowly*, like a man in a dream. Kenhodan dodged the thrust with a simple twist of his torso, tripped his man, and smashed his spine as he fell. The wounded man crawled on his arms, screaming, sliming the deck with his blood, and his agony scarcely touched the surface of Kenhodan's exalted fury.

The defending line to port crumbled into knots of cursing, striking fighters, and chaos reigned on *Wave Mistress'* deck. The battle degenerated into a savage dogfight, a frothing madness of bloodshed and death, and the skilled were as much at risk as the clumsy, for no man could guard in all directions at once.

Hornos cut his way to Kenhodan's side, trying to guard the wizard's flank. The lieutenant lopped off a corsair's sword hand and dropped another with a straight head cut. His recovery ripped the throat from a third, and a straight thrust killed a fourth. Red spray fanned from his blade, but the detached melancholy in his eyes never changed—not even as the fifth corsair rammed a pike through his hauberk to still his ancient heart forever. He fell without a sound, and Kenhodan roared with fury as he split the killer's head.

Hornos' death removed his last support, and he

staggered, off-balance, as yet another corsair came at him with a grin. Red steel surged towards him, and he writhed aside, barely in time. The corsair cursed and shortened his weapon for another thrust, but Brandark appeared from nowhere and smashed the pikeman to the deck. His axe hummed, flaring with blue light that mirrored the shield around his ship. Its glaring nimbus lit his face, and the savage glitter in his eyes reflected that hungry flame. A corsair officer leapt at *Wave Mistress'* master and fell back, cloven cleanly in two, dead mouth open in surprise.

Kenhodan dodged a swordsman, kicked him in the belly, and crushed his skull with his hilt. Sweat stung his eyes, he bled from a dozen shallow cuts, and he was bloody to the elbow, and he didn't care. More blades reached for him from every side, yet his unchained fury bore him up, and behind him the remote voice of the wizard still rose.

Kenhodan dared not look to see what might threaten Wencit's other flank. His full attention was focused on the enemies before him, and to look away was to die, yet the fierce shriek of Wencit's magic clawed at his blood. It boiled in his marrow with his rage, and his enemies died screaming.

A shout announced that the starboard attacker had cut her lines and veered off. The Axe Brothers had been too much for her unarmored men, and the water alongside was scarlet with the flotsam of their bodies. Some of the Axemen were down, but not many, and harsh commands rang out as Forstan mustered his sections and brought them avalanching aft by squads.

Kenhodan's blade jammed in a corsair's ribs, and the dead man's companion came at him desperately.

He flinched out of the path of the first stroke, but the pirate recovered with an animal snarl. His sword hissed back around, slicing towards Kenhodan's neck, and Kenhodan's hand flashed to his belt. His fingers found the hilt of Gwynna's dagger, and he buried it in his enemy's belly as he dodged the blow. The pirate shrieked and fell, intestines spilling, and a fresh pike licked over his falling body.

A thunderbolt of gory steel flashed, and the pikeman's head exploded. Bahzell kicked the body aside and moved in on Kenhodan's left.

They stood together: Bahzell, Kenhodan, and Brandark. Forstan's men closed in from the sides, cutting off the corsairs' retreat, but no one could come to their aid. Wencit stood against the mast behind them, distant as the stars, his voice their only weapon against far worse than sword or axe, and their own weapons flashed before them.

It was a simple choice for the pirates within the net of the Axe Brothers. If Bahzell and the wizard lived, they died, whatever the fate of the ship; if the wizard or the champion died, sorcery would save them from their foes.

They attacked in a wave of steel.

Kenhodan swept the legs from one man and brought his blade shrieking back to claim another's head. He daggered a third while Bahzell dropped two men with one blow, smashing them into ruin to gain elbow room to throw his hook knife into a pirate charging Brandark's back. Brandark's axe crunched through the ribs of a pike-armed pirate chieftain as the man tried to use his weapon to vault over the heads of Wencit's defenders, and the corsair fell shrieking.

Kenhodan sucked in air. Hot blood sprayed his face. Not even he and his companions could stand against so many, and they gave back a step in unison, as if it were a drill field maneuver. And then, impossibly, they stopped once more, throwing the corsairs aside in steaming blood and shattered limbs.

Forstan's men crunched into the melee, axes flashing. Their voices rose in the terrible song of the Brothers of the Axe at war, and pirates tumbled back in bloody wreckage from the precise axe work of their advancing wedge.

The pressure eased. The three companions gained back the space they'd yielded, and Brandark dropped behind to deal with whatever might slip past Bahzell and Kenhodan. Seldwyn, blood streaming from a cut forehead, rallied his surviving archers and charged across the bloody deck, and the corsairs were suddenly hemmed into a tiny pocket, growing smaller as death harvested their numbers.

And then Kenhodan leaned on his sword, gasping as soldiers and seamen met in the center of the deck. The boarders had offered no quarter; they were given none.

Wencit's chant peaked suddenly and died, and Kenhodan wiped bloody sweat from his eyes and stared in hypnotized horror as the blackness split once more and one cloud was driven back on the ship which had spawned it. Screams rose from her deck as fire and darkness consumed her. Her back broke with a crunch of timbers, and the outraged sea rose, a vortex raging about the broken ship like Korthrala's own wrath to suck her screaming crew and shattered planking deep.

Whoever controlled the other ship's sorcery took heed of his consort's fate, and the blackness vanished

suddenly as he dispelled his own attack before it could
be turned against him. White light streaked unopposed
over his vessel, and the clash of wizardry ended in
a twanging chorus of riven lines as the remaining
corsairs slashed their own grapnels free.

The two survivors wheeled away, carrying the tattered rags of the wizard wind with them. Near silence
fell on Brandark's ship, broken only by the moans of
the wounded, and Kenhodan stared about, abruptly
appalled by the carnage. His muscles slackened as the
rage flowed away as swiftly and suddenly as it had
invaded him, taking with it the exultation and leaving
only sorrow—and horrified revulsion as he realized his
sorrow arose not from the loss of life, but from the
fact that any of the corsairs had eluded him.

He stared at the bloody deck in anguish and gripped
his sword white-knuckled. What was he? In the names
of all the gods, what kind of blood-mad killer *was* he?

◆   ◆   ◆

Splashes roused him as the crew tumbled their
enemies to Korthrala's mercy. He watched the bodies slide over the side, and his hands trembled as he
mechanically cleaned his weapons on a fallen pirate's
tunic and sheathed them. He frowned down at his
fingers, filled with an ageless weariness that gnawed
the vitals of his soul. Then he clenched them into fists
to still their quiver and leaned against the bulwark.
He watched flames eat to the waterline of the ship
Hornos had set alight, and the horror of what he was
burned like a mortal wound.

Bahzell's heavy hand gripped his shoulder, dragging
him up out of the icy wastes of his soul. He drew
strength and warmth from the touch, and the hradani's

elemental vitality seemed to flash through him like a
cleansing fire. It wasn't enough to erase his fear of
himself, but it gave him control once more. He sighed,
surveying the slaughterhouse deck from Bahzell's side,
and felt life return unwillingly to his battered mind.
He would have to face his demon again, come to grips
with it somehow, but this wasn't the time. Instead, he
looked up at Bahzell and actually managed a smile.

"You were right, you know," he said, and his voice
was almost normal.

"Was I, now? And what would it happen as I was
being right about?" The hradani raised an eyebrow
above an eye that still smoldered with the cinders
of battle.

"What you said that first day."

Kenhodan watched Brandark's surgeon and his
assistants bending over the wounded, and his throat
ached. They were sorting out the most badly injured,
carrying them towards Bahzell, and Kenhodan recalled
the healing gift granted by Tomanāk to his champions.
He could feel Bahzell putting aside the fury of battle,
reaching for that far more joyous gift, but the hradani's
gaze was still on him, the eyebrow still raised, the
ears still cocked, and he smiled sadly.

"What you said that first day," he repeated. "A
sailor's lot *is* hard."

✦   ✦   ✦

Tolgrim of the Shith Kiri wore a grim expression,
directed in sidelong glances at the wizard by the rail.
Sea Scimitar quivered to the wizard wind, and only
that kept his dagger from Harlich of Torfo's back.

"I don't recall your mentioning those imperial troops,
Wizard! Or that bastard Bahzell, for that matter!"

"No," Harlich said smoothly. "I didn't know about them, Captain. I suppose the bullion should have led us all to anticipate the Axe Brothers, at least. But trust me, if I'd known Bahzell Bloody Hand was anywhere about, I'd never have gone anywhere near this entire business!"

"Pretty words!" Tolgrim snarled. "Pretty words indeed that cost me half my ships and three quarters of my men!"

"I can only apologize, Captain. It was my companion's task to obtain information. Apparently his spies were less thorough than he thought."

"Aye?" Tolgrim spat over the side, scowling back at the vanishing *Wave Mistress*. "Your scummy friend's cost the Islands dear this day! And I daresay you won't be any too popular back home yourself." He grinned sourly, obviously pleased by the thought.

"No, I don't suppose so. But when you condemn poor Thardon, recall that he shared the fate of your men. His mistake cost him as dearly as it did them."

"May the fish lick his bones!"

Tolgrim hissed the traditional curse savagely and took a jerky turn about his quarterdeck to regain control. Harlich stood motionless, his attention seemingly on the swelling sails. His life hung on a thread, for his art couldn't protect him from the baffled rage of Tolgrim's survivors if they turned on him, yet nothing in his face or manner betrayed any awareness of his danger.

"Well, Wizard," Tolgrim said at last, "it seems we've both failed. At least I can tell the Council of Captains my precious allies let me down—but what will you tell *your* bitch mistress, hey?"

"An excellent question." Harlich took care to conceal his relief at Tolgrim's implication that he still had a future in which to report.

"Aye, she won't be any too pleased, I'll wager." Tolgrim seemed to find grim satisfaction in the thought. "Well, we'll set you ashore near Belhadan as we promised, and it's glad I'll be to see the back of you!"

"Thank you, Captain," Harlich said carefully, "but I feel we've let you down badly. I'd rather see you all safely home with the wizard wind, lest more difficulties befall you. After all, your captains and the baroness have been good friends for many years. I'd like to do what I can to preserve that friendship."

"You would, would you?" Tolgrim's eyes gleamed. "I'm not so sure that would be wise. The Council might not be so understanding as I am. They might be almost as dangerous as yonder wizard."

His thumb jerked at their wake.

"Of course the Council will need an explanation. That's why it might be to your advantage to take me along. My word that you were misled—by mistake, of course!—and that you did all any man could do to save the day, might bolster your own position, I should think."

"Might it now? And in return?"

"You might extend hospitality to a poor weary wizard for the next...shall we say four months?"

"Four months, is it?" Tolgrim tugged his beard. "So you reckon it'll all be over by then, do you?"

"Over?" Harlich looked blank. "I'm afraid I don't understand."

"Of course not. Of course not."

Tolgrim tucked his thumbs into his sword belt and

rocked on his heels, studying the wizard. He still didn't care for this Harlich above half, but it was true another's words might stand him in good stead before the Council.

"All right, Wizard," he said abruptly. "I'll take you, and if I keep my head and you keep yours, I'll put you up for four months. But not a day longer! And may Phrobus take me if ever I have dealings with you again!"

"Thank you, Captain."

Tolgrim stumped off to pass among his remaining men, and Harlich watched him exchange hand clasps with them, speak to the wounded, and generally set about shoring up his damaged prestige. He'd be busy at that throughout the voyage, for corsair captains depended upon their men's acceptance for survival. If they lost the power of their reputations, they never commanded at sea again . . . if they were fortunate enough to reach home alive at all.

And Harlich's survival?

He looked out over the sea. *Wave Mistress* had vanished, for which he was profoundly grateful. He still felt the terrible power of Wencit's will, and it was nothing he ever wanted to feel again. Counterspells were one thing, but Wencit had shown him a new dimension of the art. It was impossible to invade another's spell and seize control of it—every wizard knew that—yet Wencit had done it anyway. Harlich shivered in memory, for the wild wizard had done even more. Whatever had destroyed the *Shark* had been more than the madwind alone, and Harlich had no desire to face Wencit again, whatever Wulfra wanted.

The Corsair Isles were far from Torfo—far enough

to be safe from Wulfra's vengeance. There was always the bothersome matter of her sponsor, of course, but Harlich suspected that he—whoever "he" was—wouldn't bother to destroy one of Wulfra's straying minions. After all, Harlich might prove useful to him one day . . . perhaps one day soon, if Wulfra was unfortunate enough to meet Wencit in arcane combat.

Of course, Wulfra would feel he'd deserted her, but he could live with that. She wasn't that much more powerful than he. Even if she managed to come within striking range, he had a better than even chance of surviving whatever she cared to attempt.

And that, after all, was the point: survival. Harlich recalled Thardon's eagerness and shook his head. Let Thardon and those like him believe the objective was power; Harlich knew better now. Power was secondary, useless unless a man survived to wield it.

Three times Wulfra's servants had clashed with Wencit, and Alwith and Thardon were dead. Harlich had no wish to offer Wencit a clean sweep. Oh, no! If Wulfra wanted the wild wizard dead, let *her* kill him. Harlich had had enough, and if Wulfra wanted to punish him for that, she could always look them up in the future.

After four months, say . . . if she was still alive to do it.

CHAPTER SEVEN

The Cost of Love

Brandark cradled his sextant in a bandaged hand and touched an index finger to the chart under the cabin skylight.

"Right here," he said confidently. "We'll raise Cape Banark tomorrow and enter South Banark Bay on the flood."

"I'll be relieved to rest my weary bones on something that doesn't move constantly," Wencit said.

"Hah!" Bahzell's derision was majestic. "You'll change your tune soon enough, I'm betting. If it's choose between a moving deck underfoot and a moving horse under your backside, there's no doubt in my mind at all, at all, which you'll be after preferring in a few days!"

"No one made you come," Wencit said pointedly, "but now that you have, you might at least show some respect for my old gray hairs."

"Come now, Wencit!" Brandark grinned and nudged Kenhodan in the ribs. "You really did invite him, you know."

"I did no such thing," Wencit said tartly. "In fact, I told him he might get himself killed if he insisted on coming!"

"That's what I meant. You know champions of Tomanāk are disgraced if they die in bed—especially the feeble-witted hradani ones. Warning Bahzell he could get killed was like sending him an engraved invitation! Don't begrudge him another chance to earn Scale Balancer's favor."

"Aye," Bahzell rumbled, eyes glinting at the wizard's discomfiture. "Especially not when I'll have to be accounting to him for having friends like this namby-pamby ship's captain. Sure, and it's a hard thing when a hradani's after playing dress-up and wasting time on silly, addlepated things like books."

"You two are remarkable," Wencit retorted. "You're the only people I know with such thick skulls you don't need helmets!"

"Aye? Well then, I've no doubt that's why we're after being *your* friends!"

Bahzell chuckled and slapped Brandark's shoulder in appreciation of his own wit.

"Out! Both of you—out!" Wencit clenched his fist and a blue glow danced on his knuckles. "*Out!* Or by Isvaria's Axe, I'll fry your hairy backsides over a slow fire! We'll see who doesn't like saddles then!"

The two hradani beat a hasty retreat, still laughing, and Kenhodan grinned after them. But when he looked back at Wencit his smile died, for the wizard's wildfire eyes were half-shut, his face wrung with pain, as he unclenched his fist and let the glow float above his seamed palm.

"Wencit? What's wrong?"

"*Nothing!*"

The glow leapt and died as Wencit's hand chopped the air sharply. His palm slapped down on the chart table with a sharp, explosive sound, and Kenhodan frowned in bafflement. Tension had hovered about the old man for days, screwing tighter and tighter with passing time. Kenhodan had no idea what its source might be, but his own fear of the rage hiding within him made him sensitive to the wizard's mood, and it felt as if Wencit's defenses had been eroded in some unfathomable manner. The wizard's . . . vulnerability worried him, and not knowing its cause only made it worse.

Silence hovered between them, framed in the sounds of a sailing ship underway—the steady creak of timbers, the rush of water, the distant voices of *Wave Mistress*' crew, and the even more distant voices of the seagulls who'd swept out from the approaching land to greet them. Then, finally, Wencit sighed, propped his elbows on the chart, and leaned his face into his palms.

"I'm sorry I snapped at you, Kenhodan," he said into them, his voice weary. "I'll ask your pardon for that."

"What's bothering you, Wencit?" Kenhodan asked gently, his tone an acceptance of the wizard's apology.

"Many things." Wencit lowered his hands, leaned back, and stared at the deckhead, his expression bleak, and his voice seemed to come from far away. "When you live a long time, you find too many things to regret, Kenhodan."

His suddenly desolate tone frightened Kenhodan, as if the sea had admitted an end to its strength. He'd come to share Bahzell's faith in Wencit's complete capability, but this strange depression had stripped away the veils of legend and reminded Kenhodan that for all his power, the last white wizard of Kontovar was but a man...a very old man.

"What's brought that on just now?" he asked finally, and Wencit hesitated, then shrugged.

"Bahzell. Brandark. They're so full of life—and they're my friends." The wildfire eyes lowered suddenly, stabbing Kenhodan. "It's bad enough to lose friends," he said softly, "but it's worse to know you won't be joining them. And worse yet to know *your* actions, *your* decisions, will cut their lives still shorter."

Kenhodan nodded slowly, suddenly aware that he and the wizard were two sides of a single coin. He couldn't remember...but Wencit couldn't *forget*, and he wondered, now, which was the heavier burden.

"It's terrible to be afraid to make friends, to love, because anyone you love will die...probably because they got too close to *you*, and it killed them," Wencit went on. "You can accept the pattern of the world, of time...but not for those you love."

His voice was old, his face drawn, as he crossed his arms and rocked gently, cradling the memory of all his dead. Kenhodan shivered and strained to catch the last words he whispered to himself.

"Love tears holes in you, and it happens over and over, until—after a time—you can't even weep...."

◆   ◆   ◆

Night ruled Belhadan like a gentle tyrant. Stars burned bright, moon-silvered clouds drifted gently across a cobalt dome, and a cool breeze blew through empty streets. Silence gripped the Iron Axe Tavern, broken only by the even breathing of its inhabitants, and Leeana Hanathafressa slept deeply, her dreams far away with her husband in the south.

Slowly, ever so slowly, a tiny sound crept into those dreams. The sleeping mind tried to ignore it, but the sound persisted, hanging on the very edge of existence. Normal ears wouldn't have heard it, but Leeana's hearing was far from normal.

The small sound continued, and her eyes opened. Like Bahzell, she woke fully, completely, with no lingering on the edge of sleep. She sat up and her brow furrowed as she listened intently.

For one moment she sat; then confusion became knowledge ... and fear. She vaulted up and fled the room, the hem of her gown flying as she sped down the darkened hall like the wind.

She halted outside Gwynna's room, and her face twisted with a fear no enemy had ever seen as her trembling hand opened the door slowly.

Moonlight washed the bedroom through windows on three sides. It was a pleasant, blue-walled place with a thick rug, and the huge direcat slept on that rug, his black coat a slab of midnight in the moonlight. He lay almost motionless, but his forefeet moved slowly, scrabbling silently at an unseen barrier, and his breathing was quick and shallow. He didn't even stir at her arrival, and Leeana's heart quailed. No natural sleep would prevent Blanchrach from rousing at the quiet sound of that opening door.

She glided to the edge of the bed. Gwynna lay very still, huge blue eyes staring blindly into the darkness. Her small fists were clenched at her sides, as if to nail down the coverlet, and her lips moved slowly.

Leeana bent fearfully to the tiny, thready whisper which had drawn her here.

"No, Poppa. No. It's not safe, Poppa. No, Poppa, please...."

"Gwynna?"

Leeana's cool fingers brushed Gwynna's forehead, but her daughter's eyes were fixed and open. She never even blinked, and her lips only whispered their warning again. Leeana's blood ran cold, and she shook the girl gently.

"Gwynna! It's Momma, Gwynna! Wake up!" she commanded, and the child rolled under her hand. But when Leeana released her, she lay still, her whispered litany unbroken, and Leeana Flame Hair, wind rider, war maid of the Sothōii, daughter of the House of Bowmaster, victor in a score of battles, wife to a champion of Tomanāk, pressed her knuckles to her mouth and bit them bloody.

"Lillinara, Friend of Women," she whispered, and her voice was a bitter prayer, "must I lose my child so soon?"

She bent over the bed a moment longer, tears glistening under the moon to splash Gwynna's face, but the girl slept heedlessly on. Leeana's finger traced one ivory-knuckled fist. Then she patted the small hand with infinite tenderness, turned, and left the room with a firm tread. Her face was composed, her shoulders squared, but she went down the hall with a deliberate stride unlike her normal gliding grace. She descended a flight of stairs to another door and struck the wood imperatively.

"Farmah!" She pitched her voice low and knocked again. "Farmah!"

After a long moment, someone stirred behind the door. The latch clicked, and the door swung quickly wide. A hradani woman looked out, her eyes bleary, her hair hanging unbraided, and her ears cocked in confusion.

"Lady Leeana! W-What is it?"

"Wake Frolach." Leeana's chin rose as if she faced an enemy. "Send him to the Academy. Tell him not to come back without Lentos himself."

"Lentos?" Farmah blinked away sleep. "It's the middle of the night, Milady! Why? What's hap—" She broke off, eyes flying wide as the last trace of sleep departed, and her hand rose to her mouth. "No, Milady!"

"I can't wake her," Leeana said bleakly. "We need Lentos."

Farmah's brown eyes were suddenly strained. Her ears flattened and her own lips trembled.

"But perhaps it's only a dream, Milady! Perhaps—"

"I tried to wake her!" An edge of desperation sharpened Leeana's voice. "And Blanchrach won't wake, either. It's no dream. Send for Lentos now!"

"At once, Milady!" Farmah gasped, bobbing a quick curtsy.

"Good." Leeana turned and walked away with the same slow, deliberate stride, and Farmah gazed after her in confusion and dread.

"But, Milady, w-what should *we* do?" she whispered.

"I'm going to my daughter," Leeana said softly, without turning. "No childhood should die unwatched. Hurry, Farmah."

And Leeana Hanathafressa passed through the stillness of her home as silently as any ghost.

✦   ✦   ✦

"That's the mouth of the Whitewater."

Brandark pointed across the starboard bow in the morning light, and Kenhodan strained his eyes. The shore was still distant, but he saw a broad, tan stain on the blue bay where silt fanned outward.

"I see it."

"It's a wicked channel," Brandark said idly, eyes on the dwarf perched on the bowsprit with a swinging leadline. "There's a nasty shifting mud bank that reaches out like an underwater delta. I once saw a ship almost our size go to pieces on it right about here. We're lucky it's still early spring—from the middle of Yienkonto to the beginning of Haniyean water boils out of there like the wrath of Korthrala. It's the snowpack in the East Walls that does it. It takes a while to reach this far, but when it comes it brings trees the size of houses with it."

"I can imagine."

"Not if you haven't seen it," Brandark said grimly.

"Perhaps not," Kenhodan admitted.

"No offense," Brandark said quickly. "I'm always nervous too near the Whitewater this time of year—especially with a crew understrength with dead and wounded. I'd rather face corsairs!" Then he shook himself and laughed. "Listen to me, will you? Carrying on like an old woman over a trip I've made dozens of times!" He clouted Kenhodan's shoulder. "Come on, then. If it's ships and the sea you want to learn, there's no better school than this. Come watch a captain reap the true reward of command while he feels his way blindfolded up yonder creek!"

And the two of them moved aft to the helmsman, laughing in the sunlight.

◆   ◆   ◆

Leeana looked up as Lentos entered the room. The golden scepter of Semkirk gleamed on his blue tunic, and his face—normally smooth and unreasonably young looking for a man of his years—was taut. He was younger than Leeana, but no gods-granted bracelet encircled his wrist, and he'd seen eight decades. Now the weight of all of them seemed to crush his shoulders as he regarded her with compassionate gray eyes.

"Well, Master Lentos?" Her voice was brittle in the sunlight.

"The crisis is approaching, Leeana."

His voice sounded as if it had been planed down into something which could offer only truth, and he drew out a chair and sat with an almost painful economy of movement.

"'The crisis is approaching,'" Leeana repeated bitterly, and her hands tightened into fists in her lap. "How much longer?"

"I can't say. She's young—very young for this."

"How well I know it." Leeana averted her eyes, speaking with quiet difficulty. "All her life we've known she'd be 'young' for this, and we thought we understood. But I *didn't*, Lentos. Not really. Now it's here, and her father's far from home. I-I'm not strong enough for this."

"You are," Lentos denied gently.

"I'm not!" Leeana thrust herself up, her fingers curved into weapons. "If it were an enemy—that I could fight for her! *That* I could stand! But *this*—! I don't have the courage to face this, Lentos!"

"No one's ever ready for this moment, Milady," Lentos said levelly, addressing her with grave, unusual formality. "Waiting. Helplessness. Those are hard to bear, and hardest for those who love her. But at least you woke and summoned us in time, and Trayn is the finest empath we have. We're as well prepared as we could possibly hope to be."

"I know." Her mouth quivered. "But I feel so *useless!*"

"As we all do," Lentos said gently. "But remember this, Lady Leeana, Flame Hair of the Sothōii, we of the Academy have let ourselves love her. We wouldn't have if we'd believed she'd fail and diminish our lives."

"True." Leeana's mouth eased, and she touched his shoulder gently, then spoke more briskly. "But did you leave her just to comfort me?"

"No. I need your permission to give Blanchrach ephinos."

"Ephinos? But why?" Leeana looked at him blankly.

"He's linked to her," Lentos said softly. "If they remain linked when her barriers break, he'll share her convulsions. We can't restrain them both."

"Of course." Leeana blanched and her voice sank. "You have my permission, Lentos . . . and may Lillinara be with her now."

She turned away and buried her face in her hands.

◆　　　◆　　　◆

Wave Mistress shouldered up the river on a favoring wind and an incoming tide. Kenhodan stood out of the way on the quarterdeck, listening to Brandark volley orders to his helmsman, and decided that if this was only a preliminary to the true spring floods he had no desire to see the river in full spate. Away from the bay, the Whitewater belied its name, for it was dark with mud and flotsam of every sort rode its current.

The hull shuddered with glancing blows as Brandark fought the river, and Kenhodan didn't envy his task.

Trees, logs, rafted jams of branches and timbers—all rolled slowly down the hungry river, mingled with occasional floating barns and other waterlogged structures. And Brandark had assured him the Whitewater wasn't a large river by Norfressan standards. It was far smaller than the Geen Leaf, to the north, or the mighty River of the Spear, to the east, but the hradani admitted that the Whitewater had to accept more snowmelt than the Geen Leaf, and its narrower bed produced a swifter, fiercer current.

Bahzell joined him as they crawled upstream, pointing out spots of interest along the side and banks. It seemed to Kenhodan that there wasn't a square foot of Norfressa which Bahzell hadn't trodden, ridden over, or had described to him, and far too many of those anecdotes were punctuated by battle.

"I wish I shared your delight in warfare," he said finally, shaking his head over the cold fear of his remembered rage. "It would help."

"Delight?" Bahzell rumbled thoughtfully. "Now there's a word I'd not use myself, lad."

"What other word *can* you use?" Kenhodan asked curiously.

"Whatever it may be you're thinking," Bahzell said soberly, turning to face him squarely, "there's not a sane man as ever lived who's seen battle, lost folk dear to him, taken too many lives himself, and still thinks it's anything but ugly, vile, and vicious, lad. It may be you'll find this hard to believe, but it's happier I'd be if it happened I'd never see another. Yet whatever it might be would make me happy, it's not something

as is going to happen, for the truth is, there's things
worse—*far* worse—than they are."

He turned away to look out over the river.

"It's a champion of Tomanāk I've been these eighty
years and more, Kenhodan, and not something as
ever crossed my mind might happen when I was
a lad. And well it shouldn't have, for there'd not
been a hradani champion—of *any* god, much less
himself—in twelve mortal centuries since the Fall.
It wasn't so very happy I was to discover himself
was after wanting *me* to be one, either, and yet to
speak truth, himself had the right of it from the start.
Folk call us his Swords, and so we are, for it's us
he sends against those things as are worse. It's not
so many of his champions die in bed, Kenhodan,
but this we do have. If die we must, it's with a
sword in our hand, our back to those we love, and
our face to anything—*anything*—as threatens them.
And when all's said and done, that's not so very bad
a way for any man's life to end."

"No," Kenhodan said softly. "No, I can see that."

"And, to speak another truth," Bahzell said, turning
back to him, "it's not so bad a thing to be a hradani
when swords are out. It's too many centuries the Rage's
been the curse of my folk, but it's a weapon ready
to hand, as well, one as fits us to battle the way a
dwarf fits hammer and anvil. Especially since himself
was after telling us the truth about it."

Kenhodan nodded, but he also hesitated. The Rage
was the curse of the hradani, the sudden, often unpre-
dictable eruption of bloodlust and massacre which did
so much to explain the wariness with which the other
Races of Man regarded them. And since the battle

against the corsairs, he'd wondered if what he'd felt then was what so many generations of hradani had felt.

"What 'truth'?" he asked finally.

"About the Rage?" Bahzell cocked his ears, and Kenhodan nodded again. "Well, as to that, how much is it you remember about it?"

"Not much," Kenhodan admitted. Practice had made it easier for him to face and admit the yawning gaps in his memory, but it hadn't become any more pleasant. "I know it's afflicted your people for a long time, and I know it came out of Kontovar. I don't really know how it came to be, or why."

"Ah."

Bahzell looked over the side at the flooded river for several minutes, clearly considering what Kenhodan had said. Then he turned back to the redhaired man.

"You've the right that the Rage's been the bane of my folk from the Fall itself," he said quietly. "As to why that might be, why, the answer's not so very hard to find. In the final Wizards War, after the Dark Lords were after setting up the Council of Carnadosa and turned openly to black sorcery, there weren't so very many things they'd stop short of doing.

"It's said the last two emperors of the Empire of Ottovar stood strong for the Light, but by then the rot had set too deep for them to stop it. Toren—him as they call 'Toren Swordarm'—was the last emperor, but he'd no hope of holding the Empire together, and he knew it. So he and Wencit were after putting their heads together with Duke Kormak of the Crystal Cave dwarves and hatched a plan to save what little they could, but they couldn't save *my* folk.

"It's often I've wished I'd known Toren," the hradani

said softly. "Forty years he was in the field, year after year, with no pause, no summer when there were no armies after marching, no towns and cities after burning. Forty years, Kenhodan, and it was only four battles—*four*, in all those years—as he lost. Yet for all that, it was too little and it was too late, and he fought all those years *knowing* as it was. He'd win a battle, lose men, fight another battle, and lose more men, then turn to the next campaign and lose still more men. In the end, he ran out of men—and time—yet he'd held long enough to cover the Long Retreat."

Bahzell paused again and reached for his pipe. He filled it slowly, and as his words cast a pall over Kenhodan, the redhaired man fancied he smelled the smoke of a burning land when Bahzell lit the tobacco.

"All Wencit and Toren ever hoped for was a rearguard action," Bahzell said quietly. "Just to hang on long enough to be getting out as many as they might. There'd been coastal colonies in Norfressa for two hundred years before ever Toren named Kormak their governor and put him in charge of sorting out the refugees. And whatever else, he'd the right man in the right place, for Kormak was one as did his job well. It's no accident the Empire of the Axe is the strongest Norfressan realm even today, Kenhodan. Kormak's house was one as *earned* its crown, by the Sword!

"And to my mind—" Bahzell jabbed his pipe stem at Kenhodan "—the fact that Toren was after naming Kormak 'King of Manhome'—it was Kormak's grandson as added 'Emperor' to his title—proves as how Toren never planned to leave Kontovar his own self. And I'm thinking I understand that, too. Without his army, the evacuation ports would fall, and the army wouldn't last a year without him to lead it. But that was an army as would die where it stood if *he* stood with it, lad. So he and his troops, they were after *holding* those ports for forty years, and when his army died, he died with it, fighting at its head. He nodded slowly. "That was no easy thing to do, lad, not when every man of them knew how it had to end. Tomanāk's way can be hard, but Toren was a man as understood why that is, and he served himself well.

"Yet true as that may be, true as death, it was also Toren's fight as brought the Rage upon my folk. You wonder about it?" Bahzell's voice hardened. "Well, it's not so very hard an answer, for the Dark Lords never counted on Toren and his army. And when that army was after refusing to break, refusing to lie down and die, why, they needed something to smash it, and so they found it.

"It was our size, d'you see? Our strength. We make good troops, we hradani, for it's a mortal lot of killing we take. Many of us were after fighting for Toren, for we were loyal as any. The last three commanders of the Gryphon Guard were hradani, every one of them—but is there anyone today as remembers Forhaiden died holding the imperial standard?" Bahzell spat over the rail and shook his head, ears flat. "All it is they remember is that we were after fighting for the Dark Lords, and that we did. Aye, Kenhodan, that we did."

He brooded darkly at the river, his nostrils flared.

"The Dark Lords needed an army as could break the Gryphon Guard, and if it happened we wanted no part of treason, why there was always some damned wizard as could encourage us with a little sorcery. Just a little thing. Only a spell as turned us into blood-crazed beasts—that was all.

"We remember, Kenhodan. In our old tales, we remember we were peaceful as any, once. No better, mind you, but no worse. Until that wizardry got into our blood and bone. Until it was after *twisting* something inside us, and it's the Rage we've carried with us ever since."

He stood silent for several long seconds, and then he shook himself.

"That's what the Rage is," he said softly. "Why we were after betraying our emperor, why it was as armies of hradani looted Trōfrōlantha and butchered any as stood in their way. And it's why my folk have been who we've been for fourteen hundred years while no one cared. No one but Wencit.

"And then himself chose me as his champion, for it was time."

"Time?" Kenhodan's voice was quiet, shadowed by the way Bahzell's explanation echoed his own strange, bottomless fury.

"Aye." Bahzell nodded. "The Rage isn't something as leaves a folk untouched, and it's there in our souls, the knowing other folk aren't far wrong to fear us as little more than beasts when the Rage's upon us. But the truth is time's a way of changing almost anything, Kenhodan, even the Rage, for the Rage we have today's not the one those blackhearted bastards were after giving us. It's a terrible thing, the Rage, and not least because when it comes on a man, it's after making him more than he'd ever be in his life entire without it. Even when the blood hunger burns hottest, there's a . . . splendor to the Rage. Everything he's after having inside him, every ounce of strength, every breath of passion—*all* of it—why, it comes together, burning inside him like a Dwarvenhame furnace. There's some among us as crave that the way a drunkard craves drink, for there's a power to it no one as never tasted it can truly understand. I'm thinking it must be a bit like Wencit's descriptions of wizards and wizardry—a thing as some men give themselves to even knowing as how it's like to destroy them in the end.

"And such the Rage is, for when it comes on a man all unexpected, when it's after taking him by the throat, all of that focus bends itself to blood and killing, and there's naught will stop him but his own death. That's the reason so many of my folk spent so many centuries fighting the Rage, for we'd seen what it did to those as opened the door, let it in and let it take them. But when himself first spoke to me, he told me as how the Rage has changed. The old Rage is with us still, and will be. Still waiting to take us down into the madness and drown us in blood. But when a man as knows what he's about, as makes the choice himself, *summons* the Rage, *gives* himself to it instead of letting it simply *take* him, why then *he* commands *it*. It's after being his, and not him being its, and all that focus and all that power and passion are after lifting him up, not dragging him down amongst the beasts and worse than beasts. It's become a tool, another weapon against the Dark." Bahzell smiled grimly. "And there's Hirahim's own joke on the Dark Lords in that!"

Kenhodan looked up into that strong, grim face and tasted the centuries of bloodshed, grief, and horror the Rage had inflicted upon the hradani since the Fall. The parallel between the Rage—the "*old*" Rage—and the fury which had filled him as the corsairs attacked was terrifying, and he wondered if Bahzell even suspected that there might be at least one human who understood exactly what a hradani felt in that moment of passionate power and carnage. Yet strands of hope wove themselves through the terror, for in the end, hadn't he done precisely what Bahzell had just described? He'd embraced the fury, used it rather than allowing it to use him.

"Thank you for explaining that to me," he said finally. "I didn't know—or else it's another thing I've forgotten—how the Rage came upon your people, Bahzell. But you're right," he smiled thinly, thinking about how slowly the corsairs had seemed to move, the way he'd gone through them like a direcat, "it *is* Hirahim's own joke against the Dark."

◆   ◆   ◆

Thousands of leagues from the Whitewater, a cat-eyed wizard shook with silent mirth. He would never have believed a hradani could be so eloquent!

His cheeks sparkled with tears of laughter as he blanked his crystal. Let the hradani maunder about the woes of his people—he had greater woes in Belhadan, if only he knew. The cat-eyed wizard toyed with the idea of sending Bahzell images of what passed there, yet he put it aside. Bahzell might be a hradani, and so, by definition, little more than the beasts of the field, but the cat-eyed wizard was unprepared to estimate him too lightly. The Council of Carnadosa had spent the better part of seven decades in periodic attempts to eliminate him with a deplorable lack of success. Whatever else might be true, Bahzell clearly was a champion of Tomanāk, and Tomanāk had taken excellent care of his tool. Fortunately, there were other gods who were prepared to take excellent care of *Their* tools, and the tide was setting heavily in Their favor.

Of course, Tomanāk wasn't the only one who'd taken care for Bahzell and his family, and the cat-eyed wizard frowned slightly as he reflected upon that unpalatable fact. Even after all these years, he was no closer to discovering what Wencit had expected of the hradani, his wife, and their halfbreed daughter. It was clear they were important, for Wencit had been quick to smash every probe directed at Bahzell's family over the years. Indeed, he'd threatened to reopen the spells which had strafed Kontovar—to unleash that devastation a second time, even at the cost of his own life—if the Council ever again so much as attempted to use the art against Leeana Hanathafressa. No one on the Council had been able to understand why the ancient wild wizard would make that threat on Leeana's behalf—and only on her behalf—after over twelve hundred years. Until her daughter was born, that was. Precisely what part Wencit had expected Gwynna Bahzelldaughter to play remained unclear—not even the cat-eyed wizard's divine patrons seemed to have the answer to that—but clearly his threat had been intended to protect the vessel of the girl's birth.

The Council's repeated efforts to determine what he'd thought was so important about a single halfbreed brat had met with universal failure, for one dared not thrust too hard where Wencit was concerned. But the manner in which he'd protected them proved they were important.

Not that it mattered. The little bitch was dying, and champion of Tomanāk or not, Bahzell's only true value could be as a fighting tool. True, he was a *dangerous* fighting tool, one which had proved its worth in the destruction of demons and even greater devils, and the cat-eyed wizard acknowledged his importance to the Council's foes as a rallying point and a potential leader of resistance to its plans. Yet in the end, it didn't matter how good a fighting machine the beast might be; enough warriors, backed by enough of the art, could overwhelm anyone.

No. In the end, Bahzell could be no more than an inconvenience, and it would not be useful to worry him. No one could save his precious daughter now, and the poor beast had little enough time left to worry about anything. It might be pleasant to let him know her plight, but it was a mark of discipline to hold one's revenge to a manageable level.

◆　　◆　　◆

Leeana stared dry-eyed at the small, twisting body. Her face was drawn with anguish, and her trembling hands rested on Blanchrach's ruff, feeling his muscles fight the ephinos. Had those muscles been free to answer the tumult in Gwynna's brain, he would have killed them all. She knew that, and her heart was a frozen, aching lump in her chest, but she'd spent her tears.

Master Trayn bent over the bed. His eyes were distant, but his cheeks quivered under the hurricane of emotions blasting out of the girl. He fought to reach her, to lead her out of the horror, but her barriers were too strong.

Farmah and Lentos knelt on opposite sides of the bed, their jaws tight as they fought the convulsions lashing through Gwynna. The straps about her arms and torso wrung Leeana's frozen heart, but Gwynna had turned her own nails against herself in a frenzied effort to destroy the madness in her head. Her eyes were wild and staring as her struggles wrenched the heavier adults this way and that, her lips were bitten bloody, and her sweat soaked the bedding and glued her hair to her face in streaks.

"Momma! *Mommaaaaaaaa!*"

Gwynna's screams rose as another peak approached, and Leeana ached to touch her. But Lentos forbade it. Gwynna was desperate for her mother, but the touch of Leeana's hand might open a direct link, pouring her personality into the child. It was the inflooding of foreign thoughts and minds which had driven Gwynna to this extremity; the closer embrace of any mind, even Leeana's, would break her sanity forever. Even Master Trayn dared not open his mind to hers fully lest it destroy them both.

"Momma! Poppa! No, Poppa! Don't *go* there!!"

Gwynna fought the maelstrom, writhing in exquisite agony as the wash of alien minds ripped through her and she flinched away from the hurtful edges of concepts and images which were not hers. Her selfhood twisted on the edge of dissolution, exposed to too many other selves, too many other perceptions, too much beauty and ugliness, and her heart hammered destructively, perilously near death. Her agony was mirrored on the magi's faces, yet their training blocked all but a shadow of the torment she faced alone and terrified.

Trayn Aldarfro relaxed for a moment. He had to, lest he burn out his talent, yet only his trained sensitivity had any chance of breaking through to her. He forced his own heart to slow, and his eyes met Lentos', filled with fear. Not for himself, but for Gwynna.

Lentos' own face was calm, but his heart ached, for the Academy had been wrong.

Gwynna was dying.

Sorrow twisted him, but he faced it squarely. The girl's powers were simply too great. They surpassed the mightiest savants of the Academy . . . and no one had quite believed they could. She'd writhed in isolated madness for over ten hours, and *still* her barriers stood! She couldn't screen out the visions driving her to destruction, but she could lock out the guidance which might have led her back to life.

He bent his head. The greatest gift he could give her now would be to stop her heart, yet that was forbidden so long as an ember lingered with the glimmer of a hope that she might survive to inherit the bounty of her talents. But he knew it would be the kindest course, and not just to the child he loved. How much more of Gwynna's suffering must Leeana endure before it ended in death?

He drew a deep breath and nodded to Trayn, and the empath closed his eyes, marshaling his strength once more for the hopeless task. He was forty years Lentos' junior, yet he could no more abandon the battle than Lentos could have, even though continuing might well cost his own sanity when Gwynna finally, mercifully, died.

The girl screamed as fresh visions assailed her— more and worse than the minute-to-minute flow of thoughts about her. Images of past and present flared behind her eyes, brilliant, incomprehensible . . .

terrifying. She whimpered and tried to thrust them away, her brain flailing blindly, self-destructively, in her extremity, but there was nowhere she might hide from the madness.

She saw her father surrounded by blades, standing astride her fallen mother. She saw a terrible, glittering storm of wizardry blasting through forgotten caverns. She saw leering yellow eyes, slitted like a cat's, promising death and worse than death. She saw heaps of dead and carrion crows, saw a tattered standard of gryphon and crown, its staff clutched in the stiff hand of a fallen hradani. She saw—

She didn't know what she saw. She had no way to comprehend it, and the images stuttered in her thoughts like lightning. They were too close-paced, too violent. They merged and overlapped into a maddening whole she could neither grasp nor endure. Her head went back and her eyes bulged, and behind everything was the glare of the wild magic, scattering its violence as it gouged and fought over twice a thousand years and more of time.

The glittering sorcery terrified her, but it also touched a last strand of her fraying selfness. The wildfire! She knew the wildfire—had *always* known it!

Her mouth opened and blood flew from her bitten lips as she screamed to the wildfire presence which had always loved and protected her.

"Wennncittttttttt!"

◆   ◆   ◆

Water chuckled against a wooden hull, and Wencit of Rūm sat in the darkened cabin, its scuttles and quarter windows shuttered against the afternoon light. His haunted face was streaked with sweat in the glow of his wards, and he clutched his sword hilt in trembling hands as his power reached out with all the strength and desperation of his ancient heart.

Belhadan lay seven hundred leagues to the north, and he knew what struggle raged in a cheerful bedroom there. His might hammered at the distance, frantic to smash the resistance which blocked him from that room, and his nerves groaned with the long strain of his effort. Wild magic danced in his blood like fire and his art racked him with agony, yet he dared not blink, could not relent for an instant.

If the moment came, it would be fleeting.

And then, far to the north, Gwynna's shattering mind turned to the wild wizard. Even as she screamed his name, her terrified thought winged across the miles in an agonized search for safety.

Wencit stiffened. His eyes flared, their glare spangling the bulkheads, and the cabin seemed to rock to the blinding fluorescence and silent explosion of his effort. Sorcery shaped and honed to fight for a world slammed across the leagues in a reckless race to save one small and precious life. His might smashed into her barriers with the power of a hurricane and the delicacy of a hummingbird, and across the width and breadth of two continents, every soul sensitive to the art winced and hissed for breath before the uncounting prodigality with which he poured out his power like fire and shaped it with his very life.

◆   ◆   ◆

Gwynna shrieked, and Leeana lurched up at the sound of her daughter's unadulterated agony. Her hands flew out, but Lentos' warning shout stopped her fingers inches from the twisting body. She went to her knees beside the bed, her lips trembled, and her eyes burned, but she dared not touch her.

Master Trayn's head snapped back as if he'd been clubbed. He slid to his knees, shrugged aside by the cable of power driving at Gwynna's crumbling defenses. Lentos gasped in anguish as he caught the backlash of the blow, yet he shook his head, clinging desperately to the jerking body while his brain blazed with wonder and confusion.

Gwynna hung timelessly above an abyss, and the darkness beckoned to her. It promised rest, an end to torment and terror and confusion, and she yearned towards the peace of nonbeing. Its welcoming embrace reached out to her, and her hold on life shattered cleanly.

She began the slide down the slope of death, but streamers of wild magic and something more—something stronger than sorcery, deeper than mage power—clawed at her barriers with desperate delicacy. World-crushing strength compressed them, and a strand suddenly snapped. Her web of thought whipped, unraveling like an overstressed stay, and an alien presence, strong and ancient, thundered into her. It seized her with ruthless love—caught her, like fingers in her hair, dragging her back from the brink of peace inch by agonized inch. She fought it, hurling herself away from it, seeking the dreamless sleep, but it refused to release her.

She hesitated. She had the power to embrace the darkness. Not even that titanic strength could stop her from ending her torment. But if she did, that ancient might would go with her. She would take that other—that warm, fiercely loving other—with her, for it would never surrender her to death . . . and would never let her go alone.

She teetered on the cusp of decision, and it was a choice no child could make. Dim perceptions of endless struggles and subtle plans beat her with mallets of fire, twisted her upon a rack of horrified understanding and the deathless hope of that other. She fought to reject its strength. She fought to retain her childhood, even at the price of death, for if she lived she would never be free of her own power and the ageless torment of her visions. But innocence was a treasure she could keep only if she chose death for that other, as well. And somehow, even in that moment of chaos and anguish, she knew she could no more refuse the love which would not let her go than it could abandon her.

She relinquished childhood, abandoned the quest for peace. She turned once more to the agonizing struggle for life, and steel-strong bands of love locked her close. They raised her out of her torment like powerful arms, and she surrendered her inner self to them, her last barriers crashing into ruin while warm wildfire eyes bore her up through blackness and worse than blackness into sleep.

✦　　✦　　✦

Wencit collapsed.

His sword rang on the deck, and his head rolled slackly as he searched for the glow of his wards. If they failed, he died, for he was drained, his power muted by an application far beyond even its limits. The plans and hopes of five millennia hung upon defenses he could strengthen no further, yet he felt no regret. Even a wild wizard was entitled to risk his life for one dearer to him than continents.

His half-blind eyes found the wards. They glowed

still, protecting him, and he sighed gratefully as he
slid down into the darkness.

◆   ◆   ◆

Lentos rose shakily and bent over Gwynna, feeling
the strong, slow pulse in her throat. His face lost its
habitual detachment, and he turned radiant eyes to
Leeana, lifting her to embrace her gently.

"Is—?"

For all her courage, it was a question Leeana
Hanathafressa couldn't frame, and he shook his head
ever so slightly.

"The crisis has passed," he said simply. "*How* is
more than I can say, yet it's passed. Gwynna will
live, Leeana."

"Thank you, Lillinara!" Leeana whispered. "Oh,
thank you, Friend of Women!"

She clung to Lentos, and the hardihood of the war
maid vanished in the tears of a mother.

"Indeed," Lentos said gently, "we all have much
to be thankful for. But now she must come to the
Academy. We must start her on the path of self-
knowledge. She'll someday go where none of us can
follow, but for now we must teach her to protect
herself from the world."

"I understand," Leeana said, sobbing in relief. She
knelt beside the bed once more to stroke a slack
cheek and felt the warmth of life. She laid her head
on Gwynna's chest and gathered her close, cradling
her for long minutes before she laid her back with a
kiss. "Take her, Master Lentos. Teach her. And, when
you can, send her home to me."

"We will, Milady," Lentos said formally. Then he

nodded to an even shakier Master Trayn, and the two magi lifted the limp body in gentle hands.

Leeana followed them from the bedchamber, followed down the stairs, across the deserted taproom, and watched them place the small form carefully into the scepter-badged carriage. She stood erect, her spine straight, her shoulders squared, green eyes bright as the carriage door closed, and then she watched it out of sight, ignoring the hesitant hand Farmah placed upon her shoulder.

Only when the carriage had vanished did she collapse in tears into the other woman's arms.

CHAPTER EIGHT

Korun in the Spring

Korun was a welter of sights, sounds, and smells—a confusion of the senses made even worse because Kenhodan had grown accustomed to the empty Western Sea. The raucous voices and seething life of the city, especially so late in the evening, daunted him.

He stood on the dock, pack on his back, while Bahzell and a curiously serene Wencit bid Brandark farewell. The wizard's strange mood shifts worried Kenhodan. Yesterday, he'd been nervous, irritable and brooding—almost frightened. Now he looked simultaneously exhausted and glad, as if the weight of years had fallen on him in an afternoon, chipping holes in his armor, only to let flickers of some strange, deeply quiet joy shine through the chinks. It was good to see the old man smiling, exchanging cheerful insults and jests with the hradani, yet his changing spirits made the redhaired man vaguely uneasy. Wencit was *Wencit of Rūm*, the bedrock of endless legends and deadly serious history. He wasn't supposed to be as changeable as Vonderland weather or the unstable slopes of some Wakūo volcano, and Kenhodan tried to divert himself from his puzzlement—and, however little he liked admitting it, worry—by studying the scene about him.

The day's embers burned over distant Banark Bay, bathing the sky in blood. *Wave Mistress'* masts bulked black and hard against the light, and lanterns and torches already lit the docks. A crisp breeze cut through the crowd sounds, flapping awnings briskly, snapping and popping *Wave Mistress'* banners. The sunset was an ominous boil of smoke and burning cloud, and he was unpleasantly aware of approaching rain. Was he destined to be rained on in every city he visited?

"Well, lad," Bahzell slapped his shoulder as he joined him, "be welcome to Korun. Not one of the Empire's most respectable cities, I'm thinking, but as good a place as a man might ask to be getting his throat slit for a copper kormak."

"I was just thinking that," Kenhodan agreed, eyeing the motley crowd.

"Oh, it's not so bad as all that." Bahzell inflated his huge chest and grinned. "A bit wild, like all South March towns, but that's the East Walls, I'm thinking. A man never knows what might be after brewing up there, so folk with their wits about them count on it's being something nasty, just to be on the safe side. The worst bandits in the Empire are after making their homes up around the Traitors' Walk, because it'd take half the Army to be rooting them out." He shook his head and grinned, ears half-flattened. "That's a job not even the Order would be so very happy about taking on unless it was to happen we'd no choice about it.

So the Whitewater rivermen are after looking after themselves, and it's a tough, stubborn lot they are. They've a hard trade, and they've a right to their reputation as the south's finest watermen, but there's no one can deny they're folk as make Korun lively."

"I see." Kenhodan watched a cluster of rivermen set upon one another with eye-gouging gusto. "I don't much care how they manage their civic affairs, if they'll just keep their knives out of me."

"Wise of you." Wencit joined them, and the bubble of laughter in his voice drew sidelong glances from both of them, although he seemed unaware of it. "They *are* a bit wild, especially during the Spring Festival, but they're some of the Empire's best fighters, too. And Korun boasts its share of cutpurses and backstabbers. The Thieves Guild thrives here, so bear that in mind."

"You sound as if we're less than welcome," Kenhodan observed.

"I sound as if I've been here before," Wencit corrected cheerfully. "But don't expect gracious welcomes traveling with me. I'll admit I have the odd friend scattered about, but don't count on finding a comfortable fire to prop your feet in front of. Too many would like me dead—and you with me—and there're more than a few in Korun, among other places, who'd cheerfully kill us both at bargain rates, no questions asked."

"I note your deep concern," Kenhodan said dryly. He watched the brawl for a moment, then turned to Bahzell. "You watch the shadows on the left. I'll watch the ones on the right, and Wencit can watch our backs. But who'll watch *his* back?"

"Don't get too cheerful," Wencit growled. "You two

might match any assassin in a fair fight, but neither of you has eyes in the back of his head or a poison-proof belly."

"Aye." Bahzell sounded unusually thoughtful. "I'd not thought of dog brothers, and Korun's after being a likely spot for such as them. Oh, not on the docks, but there's places in Korun as the city guard goes only in platoons."

"In that case, I suggest we finish our business here as quickly as we can," Kenhodan said pointedly.

"Agreed." The hradani checked his bearings. "I'm thinking we'd best head for Lendri Street. There's a man there as owes me a favor who can guarantee a good price on fast horses."

"How can you be sure they'll be fast? Or cheap?"

"Because Fradenhelm's after stealing only the best and he knows as how I know he does," Bahzell said simply.

"I thought you were a champion of Tomanāk," Kenhodan said, quirking an eyebrow at him. "The God of Justice?"

"And so I am," Bahzell agreed genially. "But I've not stopped being a hradani, and my folk are after having what you might be calling 'contacts' in places where little details like bills of sale aren't so very common. And it's never so very bad a thing for a champion to be having an eye inside such goings-on."

"You mean he's an informant?"

"Now 'informant's' a hard, hard word," Bahzell rumbled thoughtfully. "The kind of word as could get a man's throat cut, now I'm thinking on it. So it's in my mind we'd best call Fradenhelm . . . a fount of wisdom, let's be saying."

"I should've guessed," Kenhodan sighed, shaking his head, and Wencit chuckled.

They fell into a loose formation and pushed off along a street so crowded that Kenhodan wondered who ran the city by day. Rough-trousered rivermen rubbed against prosperous merchants in silks, hucksters, food vendors, and itinerant entertainers. They were all there—from veiled lady to corner prostitute, from mime to beggar to magistrate's clerk. They thronged the streets in a wall-to-wall ferment as they celebrated the season of the floods. Here and there a clumsy pickpocket's fumbling gave him away or an intoxicated rowdy gave or took offense, but a path opened miraculously for Bahzell. Kenhodan wondered if the crowd was moved by recognition of who he was and the green surcoat of Tomanāk or if it was simple prudence, given his towering inches and the hradani's reputation. But whatever its reason, the press of people parted and let them move with speed.

They crossed a quarter of the waterfront, then turned down a quieter street, and Kenhodan sighed with relief as the congestion thinned. He heard Wencit chuckle at his soft sound and wondered again what could have produced such cheerfulness.

Lendri Street was a good forty minutes' walk from the docks, where the imperial high road cut through the city's eastern arc of avenues and alleys. The smells of horse dung and hay hung in the air like a signpost as they followed Bahzell to a long, low building bearing the sign of a rearing horse. Bahzell beat on the closed door with a hard-knuckled fist, and the hollow booming woke a nickering equine chorus.

There was no other response, and after a moment, he pounded again—harder.

"Go away!" a nasal voice shouted at last. "We're closed!"

"Not to me, you're not!" Bahzell bellowed back.

"And why not?" the nasal voice snapped pettishly.

"Because I'll be after kicking this door down, wringing your scrawny neck, and booting your thieving backside to Belhadan!"

"Bahzell?" the nasal voice asked incredulously. "Is that you, Bahzell?"

"And who *else* is after having the patience to stand blathering through a closed door? Not, mind you, as I'll be patient much longer!"

"Er...just a moment!"

Voices muttered, then the bolt thumped and the door creaked open. A small, bald man blinked like a mole, rubbing a wisp of straw from his apron, and a nervous stable boy stood a pace or so behind him, fidgeting as he peered around him at the newcomers.

"It *is* Bahzell!"

"Is it, then?" Bahzell retorted sarcastically, and glared at him. "It's horses I need—and I'm after needing them quick. A mount each for Wencit and my friend here, and two pack horses. Would it happen you've got them?"

"Uhhh...Of course! I mean—Well, that's to say I can mount one of your friends at once, Bahzell, but—"

The little man stopped to wring his hands.

"But what?" Bahzell asked ominously.

"I don't have one big enough for *you!*" the small man blurted.

"And were you thinking I'd not've thought on that

myself?" Bahzell snorted. "Rest easy, Fradenhelm. I've a friend on his way to meet me."

"Walsharno?"

It seemed to Kenhodan that Fradenhelm was less than delighted to suggest that name, and he wondered why. In Old Kontovaran, it meant "Battle Dawn" or "Dawn of Battle," which, he admitted, sounded more than faintly ominous, but the stable master's attitude still struck him as a bit odd.

"Aye," Bahzell replied, ears cocked and one eyebrow raised as he considered Fradenhelm. "And where else were you thinking I'd find something with four hooves as was up to my weight?"

"Nowhere," Fradenhelm said hastily. "It's just..."

"Just what?" Wencit asked, and Fradenhelm turned quickly to face the wizard as he entered the conversation.

"I've one mount here that could probably stand the sort of pace Walsharno would set, Milord," he said quickly, "but not two, and I wouldn't want to slow him and Bahzell down."

"And?" Bahzell prompted as the stable master paused, and Fradenhelm's eyes darted back to him.

"Well, I was only thinking it might be wiser for you to wait until I could find another as good as the one I already have. I mean, if you were to take a room at the Lively Vixen while I looked about, I might be able to—"

"You're one as always knows where the best horse-flesh in Korun's after being found," Bahzell interrupted. "So you'd best be saying it straight. Would it happen you've the horses we need? And if you don't, where might such as you lay hands on them?"

"I don't know. I mean, it *is* late, so if you could just find someplace to spend the night, give me until morning, I mean, and then—"

"Fradenhelm," Bahzell said ominously, "you're after being a thief and a cheat, and well we both know it. Korun's not my city, and it's a time or two you've been useful to the Order, so I've not made it my business to be discussing the mayor's matched bays with him...yet. But if it was to so happen you couldn't be finding the mounts we've need of, and quickly, it might just be I'd have time to do it while we lie about waiting."

"What I meant to say," Fradenhelm said hurriedly, "is that I can mount one of your friends suitably right this moment, and if you'd care to wait, I'm sure I can find another mount almost as good despite the hour. I can send Refram here—" he gestured at the silent stable boy "—to check with Cherthan at the city livery and Terahn at the Gray Pony. Terahn had a Sothōii warhorse he wanted me to look at day before yesterday, and if he's found a buyer already—and the gods know he may well have—Cherthan always knows where the best horseflesh's to be found. It may take a while, you understand, but I can guarantee—well, *almost* guarantee—I can find you what you need. *Truly* I can, Bahzell! There's, uh, no need to be bothering the mayor at this time of night. Really there isn't!"

"As to that, it's a few minutes we can spare," Bahzell replied. "And while Refram's after running about town, we'll be looking at this other mount of yours, Fradenhelm. And the pack horses, too. I've a mind to be gone by mid-watch, and I'll not appreciate it if we're not."

"Of course!"

Fradenhelm bowed them in and jerked his head in silent command at the boy, who dashed down the street. Kenhodan watched him go, then followed Bahzell and Wencit into the stable. Somehow, he reflected, Bahzell's . . . bargaining style wasn't quite what he would have anticipated out of a champion of Tomanāk. It did seem to cut right to the heart of things, though.

Fradenhelm scurried about, lighting lanterns in the front half of the stable. The rear half remained shrouded in shadow, but there was light enough to see the open stalls in the front and Kenhodan felt his eyebrows rise. However and wherever Fradenhelm acquired his stock, Bahzell was right about its quality. The stable was full of horses, all above average and some excellent, and Kenhodan gravitated almost unconsciously toward a tall, gray stallion the color of fog under the lantern light. He had a shaggy, mountain mustang's winter coat, but the long, powerful quarters and graceful head of Sothōii breeding, although he stood at least two full hands taller than a normal Sothōii warhorse.

"Ah! I see you've noticed him, young master," Fradenhelm purred as he opened the stall's half door and led the stallion out. "Caught your eye, hasn't he? And well he should! I'll stand behind any horse in this stable, but if you're going to travel with Walsharno, this lad's the only one for you."

"No doubt," Kenhodan said, reaching up to lay one hand on the horse's shoulder, the rough coat marvelously soft against his palm, while he wondered again who the mysterious "Walsharno" might be, "but I'm afraid he's beyond my means."

"By no means! To be sure, such don't come cheap, but I'm sure we can reach agreement if you're Bahzell's friend and travel with Wencit of Rūm."

"You'd be striking a better bargain because he's after being my friend?" Bahzell's eyebrows rose and his ears twitched derisively.

"Not precisely." Fradenhelm coughed into his fist. "I really meant that Wencit of Rūm carries a heavy purse, and you're clearly in a hurry. That should produce a mutually acceptable price, don't you think?"

"Aye, and you've relieved my mind, too," Bahzell told him. "For a moment, I was afraid as how I'd underestimated your greed."

"You don't have to meet my price." Fradenhelm sounded hurt, although the expression of mournful reproach seemed an unnatural fit on his sharp, foxy features.

"Never fear," Wencit said, reaching for his purse. "He's a noble beast, and you're right—we *are* in haste. Name your price."

"Forty gold kormaks," Fradenhelm said promptly.

"Gods!" Bahzell exclaimed. "A noble beast, fair enough, but he's not after being made of gold! Give him twenty, Wencit."

"Thirty-five?" Fradenhelm suggested. "You won't find a finer horse this side of the Wind Plain, Bahzell, and well you know it! He'll carry the young sir all day on a handful of grain, and not hold Walsharno back while he does it. No need for a spare mount with *this* fellow!"

"Hirahim was after leaving a son in *your* father's bed!" Bahzell snorted. "I'd not give thirty-five for a purebred Sothōii warhorse! Still, you're not so very wrong about his quality." The last sentence came out grudgingly, and the hradani reached up to run a huge hand down the stallion's proudly arched neck. "Throw in his saddle, and it might be we'd give you twenty-five."

"Saddle, bridle, saddlebags, and blanket—and not one copper less than thirty kormaks!" Fradenhelm replied indignantly.

"Well . . ."

Bahzell examined the horse thoroughly, skilled hands searching the shaggy coat for hidden infirmities. He peered into the stallion's mouth and examined each hoof and shoe minutely.

"It's robbery without a weapon," he muttered, "but not so much more than he'd be after fetching if it should happen his papers would stand in court! Take it, Wencit."

"Very well: thirty gold kormaks."

Wencit counted the money into Fradenhelm's hand while Bahzell selected suitable equipment from the tack room just inside the stable's entrance and handed the gear to Kenhodan with a grin. Thirty gold kormaks was a princely sum . . . and ludicrously low for such a beast, if he'd been honestly come by.

Kenhodan had become accustomed to finding hidden talents within himself, but it was especially pleasing to learn horsemanship was among them. His hands were gentle as he worked, whispering softly, and a velvet nose pressed his shoulder. The stallion blew softly, and his ears were as expressive as Bahzell's as he and Kenhodan felt one another out.

Wencit and Fradenhelm soon reached agreement on two more horses to serve as pack animals. Both were well above average, but Kenhodan noted smugly that the stable master had spoken no more than the truth when he said neither of them was the equal of his own new beauty. Under normal circumstances, he would have been more than satisfied to accept either of them, however, and he found himself wondering once again what sort of mount the mysterious Walsharno intended to provide Bahzell if they needed an even better horse to go under Wencit's saddle.

Fradenhelm provided two pack frames for a modest fee, and Bahzell and Kenhodan quickly packed their gear onto the horses. In the event, they needn't have hurried, however, for there was no immediate sign of Refram's return, and Bahzell paced slowly, smoking his pipe and stopping occasionally to examine the shaggy-coated stallion. The horse stood behind Kenhodan, resting his jaw on the redhaired man's shoulder with his eyes half-closed as he luxuriated in the fingers reaching up to caress the half-lowered ears.

"I'm thinking you've made a friend," the hradani said.

"And who wouldn't want a friend like this one?" Kenhodan asked cheerfully.

"No one as I'd care to know. Would it be you've a thought about what to call him?"

"I've been thinking about that, but I haven't come up with anything suitable. Why? Do you have a suggestion?"

"As to that, it might be I do. It's after being a Sothōii-ish sort of a name, but I'm thinking it's one as fits. Look at that coat; see how it's after shifting under the light and melting into the shadows like mist? I'm thinking he'll show gray under the sun, but I'll swear to silver under the moon. And if he's not one as outruns the wind, my name's not Bahzell Bahnakson... which would be something of a shock to Leeana, I'm thinking!" He chuckled, then turned serious. "Aye, I think I've a name. How would 'Glamhandro' strike your fancy?"

"Glamhandro." Kenhodan tried it slowly, savoring the sound on his tongue. Like "Walsharno" it was Old Kontovaran, and it meant "gray wind of autumn."

"I like it," he said. He whispered the name in the stallion's ear, and the horse flicked his head as if in agreement. "I swear he understands every word I say!" Kenhodan chuckled delightedly.

"Why, as to that, I'm thinking it's not so unlikely as he does."

Kenhodan eyed Bahzell suspiciously, then glanced at the wizard. Wencit grinned and settled on a bale of hay, settling his poncho about him, and Kenhodan looked back at Bahzell.

"What do you mean?"

"Any fool could be seeing as he's Sothōii blood, and there's no faster, smarter horse ever bred than a Sothōii warhorse. Mind you, I'm thinking this lad is after being something special, however it might be Fradenhelm laid hands on him. He's warhorse blood, sure as death, but I'm thinking there's more than that to him. It's not so very often a courser and one of what they're after calling 'the lesser cousins' mate, but it's not something as *never* happens, either, and it's in my mind as how there might just be a wee drop of courser blood in this lad's family tree. And any wind rider knows any courser's after understanding us 'two-foots' when it happens we speak to one of them."

"Like Blanchrach?" Kenhodan asked, seeing a sudden light.

"Eh?" Bahzell's ears flicked. "No! Coursers are after understanding *anyone*, Kenhodan, though it's true enough that it's only their own wind brothers as can hear them reply."

Kenhodan bit off a sigh. It was frustrating to think he saw a door crack of light only to have it vanish, and that seemed to happen a lot in his case. Gwynna and the direcat confused him, and he longed to understand the child's relationship with the enormous predator. But he refused to pry if Bahzell didn't volunteer information. Still, the hradani's explanation of the coursers left much to be desired, as well.

"So do you mean the coursers read minds?"

"No, I mean they're after understanding two-foots' language. Now, it might be fair to be saying they read their *riders'* minds—and t'other way about, come to that—but that's not the same thing."

"You know the Sothōii well, don't you?" Kenhodan asked curiously, remembering Brandark's explanation of Bahzell's past.

"Aye, you might be saying that," Bahzell acknowledged, and Wencit laughed.

"And you might be saying the Western Sea's a little damp," the wizard said. "Mind you, there was a time—before that unfortunate business in Navahk and his introduction to Tomanāk—when young Bahzell Bahnakson was one of the most accomplished horse thieves in all of Norfressa. Of course, that was before his father put an end to Iron Axe raids on the Sothōii herds. Although I *do* seem to remember that there was that one raid after that, wasn't there, Bahzell? That little business with Lord Warden Resak's prize stud, wasn't it?"

Bahzell ignored him and busied himself tamping the tobacco in his pipe and relighting it from one of the stable lanterns, and Wencit chuckled.

"I've often thought Prince Bahnak had more than one reason for picking young Bahzell as his hostage to Navahk," he said. "Just getting him away from temptation on the Wind Plain probably would've been enough to convince him all by itself. Of course, then Bahzell wandered off and got himself enlisted by Tomanāk, which was a horrid shock to any hradani's system, as I'm sure you can imagine. When he came home again, butter wouldn't have melted in his mouth."

Kenhodan snorted in amusement, trying—and failing spectacularly—to imagine Bahzell as a prim and proper reformed horse thief.

"I'm thinking," Bahzell said to no one in particular, gazing up at the rafters, "as those who're after opening their mouths too wide are like to be finding a boot stuck in them. Aye, and sometimes it's even their own and not someone else's."

"I believe Brandark did mention something about surrenders and paroles," Kenhodan said. "I didn't get much detail, though."

"That's a pity," Wencit replied. "It's worth telling in full, and if we had time, I would. The heart of the matter, though, was that some of Tellian of Balthar's vassals had taken it upon themselves to launch an unauthorized invasion of Hurgrum while Prince Bahnak was occupied fighting the Bloody Swords. Since no one else was available, Bahzell and a few score Horse Stealers who'd taken Tomanāk's service took it upon themselves to block the only good route from the

West Riding to Hurgrum and . . . argue the point with them. Rather emphatically, in fact."

The wizard's humor settled into something rather more serious, and he shook his head.

"The fellow leading the Sothōii was an insufferable young hothead, the sort who thinks with his spurs and his sword instead of his brain—and doesn't have much brain even if he should miraculously try to use if, for that matter—and he got a lot of his supporters killed when he tried to rush the hradani's position. He was getting ready for another try when Tellian arrived. He'd hoped to overtake the idiots before they actually crossed swords with the hradani, and when he realized he was too late for that—that the war he'd been trying to stop had already well and truly started without him—he was sorely tempted to follow through with the attack himself. He had a lot more men with him, as well, and getting the first blow in quick and hard might have made that war a lot shorter, after all. And there's no doubt he could have done just that, although the price tag would've been steep. I happened to have ridden along with him, however—just to do my own bit to prevent the normal sort of Sothōii-hradani 'negotiations'—and I decided the foolishness had gone far enough, so I gave them a little history lesson."

"History lesson?" Kenhodan repeated in a careful tone, and Bahzell snorted thunderously.

"Aye, you might be calling it that. He was after standing the Sothōii's understanding of how the war betwixt us first started on its head."

"He did?"

"In a manner of speaking," Wencit acknowledged.

"And once Tellian understood that it truly had been the *Sothōii* who'd started all those centuries of mutual bloodletting, he found himself in a bit of a quandary."

"Don't you be making light of Tellian, Wencit." Bahzell's tone was dry, but something very like a warning gleamed in his eyes. "It's a good man he was, one of the finest ever I've known."

"Yes. Yes, he was," Wencit agreed. "Unfortunately, the only way anyone could see to bring the confrontation to a close without major bloodshed was for one side to surrender to the other. Logically—although I realize we're talking about Sothōii and hradani here—Bahzell ought to have surrendered to Tellian, given the enormous imbalance in their numbers. I doubt he and his lads were outnumbered by any more than—eighty or ninety to one, would you say, Bahzell?"

The hradani only grunted, and Wencit chuckled softly.

"The problem was that our Bahzell, as you may have noticed, is sometimes a bit on the impulsive side, and it was much worse then. You may not believe it, Kenhodan, but he's actually mellowed quite a bit over the years I've known him. At the time, however, that mellowing process hadn't really taken hold yet, I'm afraid. So he basically informed Tellian that no one had ever taught him how to surrender. Hradani can be a bit stubborn, you know."

Kenhodan felt his lips quiver but managed to restrain the smile as Bahzell snorted in disgust and busied himself unnecessarily adjusting the load of one of the pack horses.

"So what . . . what happened?" Kenhodan asked just a bit unsteadily.

"Well, Tellian was a wind rider, you know, and so

was his sword brother, Hathan Shieldarm. Now, *there* was a stubborn man!"

"And as fine a man as Tellian," Bahzell said over his shoulder. He never looked away from the pack horse, but his voice was dead serious, and Wencit nodded.

"Indeed he was," he said. "Up to that moment, though, Hathan had probably been as staunch a dyed-in-the-wool anti-hradani bigot as you could hope to find. He was as honest as he was stubborn, though, so he climbed down from his courser and told Bahzell that if he didn't know how to surrender, he'd teach him. Which he did... by surrendering to *Bahzell*. At which point Tellian surrendered his entire force to Bahzell, as well."

"He did what?" Kenhodan blinked. Brandark's description hadn't included all of those details, and he looked at Bahzell in disbelief. "At eighty-to-one odds?" Wencit nodded solemnly, and Kenhodan shook his head. "And how did the rest of his men take it?"

"Some of them were a bit... irked," Wencit said with the air of a man seeking exactly the right verb. "Mind you, they got over it eventually. In fact, most of them decided—in the end, not immediately—that it was hilarious. They're all mad, you know."

"Mad they may be," Bahzell growled, "but they're also after being the finest horsemen as ever the gods put on earth!"

"And that they truly are," Wencit agreed. "As Bahzell has better reason than most to know. Their regular warhorses are the finest light and medium cavalry mounts in the world, and no mere horse can compare to a courser."

"I was under the impression that coursers *are* horses," Kenhodan said.

"Aye?" Bahzell turned and cocked his ears at the redhaired man. "And would you be saying Blanchrach and yonder tabby—" he flicked his head at the ragamuffin calico in charge of ridding Fradenhelm's stable of rats "—are both cats?"

"Well..."

"He's right about that, Kenhodan," Wencit said. "Coursers are every bit as intelligent as any of the Races of Man. That's something most non-Sothōii seem to find a bit difficult to grasp, but every Sothōii ever born knows the truth down deep in his bones, and the wind riders are the elite of the Sothōii cavalry."

"How does someone become a wind rider?" Kenhodan asked curiously, and Bahzell snorted again, very softly this time.

"If a courser's after choosing to bear you, then it's a wind rider you are, lad. And if the coursers *don't* choose to bear you, there's no power on earth could make you one."

There was something about the hradani's tone, something that spoke to the heart, even if Kenhodan didn't understand the message.

"There's no bond closer in all the world than that 'twixt courser and rider," Bahzell went on. "Heart and soul, mind and life—all either of them are after being, all poured out together. *That's* what makes a wind rider, and there's naught but death can break that bond."

"So they truly can speak to each other?" Kenhodan asked, and Bahzell nodded.

"Aye, but only to each other. Still, there's signals— calls, you might be calling them—as every wind rider and courser recognize."

"What sort of 'calls'?" Kenhodan asked curiously.

Bahzell glanced at him, then grinned and closed his eyes. His mouth opened, and the sound which came from him startled Kenhodan to his feet, knowing he would remember it even if he forgot everything else he'd ever heard. It was wild and fierce, a wordless cry that mingled wind and the dusty beat of hooves with the whistle of a stallion defending his mares. Glamhandro's head rose high and proud as he nickered a fierce reply, but Kenhodan stared at Bahzell, amazed the hradani could make such a sound.

It was an amazement that became confusion as a whistling scream answered from a closed box stall in the gloomy darkness at the rear of the stable, beyond the lanterns' illumination. Bahzell spun toward the sound in shock, and it came again, louder and fiercer. The hradani launched himself at the stall like a thrown spear as pride and fury whistled from it yet again, followed by the savage beat of steel-shod hooves on wood. The stall's closed door shuddered under the pounding, but its heavy timbers held, and Bahzell reached for the latch. It was padlocked tight, and he caught the lock in one hand. His wrist twisted, metal spanged and cracked explosively, and he tossed the shattered lock aside and flung open the door.

"*Phrobus!*"

That shrill, whistling cry of fury sounded a fourth time, and Bahzell snatched the hook knife from his belt and vanished into the stall. Kenhodan heard the heavy blade thunk against the timbers once, twice—a third time—and then a horse prouder than morning burst from the enclosure, trailing half a dozen heavy, severed leads from a halter which had galled angry welts across a coat of gleaming black. He must have stood at least twenty hands—seven feet at the shoulder, his head towering even over Bahzell—and his eyes were fierce and dark, touched with gold under the lanterns.

Bahzell followed him from the stall, hook knife still in his hand, and the stallion wheeled to face him. He glided closer to the hradani, hooves moving delicately, each stride like newborn grace, and Bahzell sheathed the knife and raised his right hand. He extended it in front of him in an oddly formal salute, and the stallion reached out and touched it with his nose.

"Is that what I think it is?" Kenhodan breathed in Wencit's ear.

"If you think it's a courser," the wizard replied softly.

"Aye." Bahzell heard them and turned, and his ears were flat to his skull, his eyes hard. "Born on the Wind Plain, and nigh on two thousand leagues from home and herd, and he'd not've come this far without his wind brother. And that—" his deep, rumbling voice went harder than his eyes "—makes me wonder."

Kenhodan suddenly realized Fradenhelm was creeping for a side door, and he moved to intercept him. The stable master squealed and broke for the main entrance, but Bahzell caught him in three strides. His massive hand closed on the nape of the scrawny neck like a steel viper, and the little man squealed again, even louder than before, as the hradani snatched him high at arm's length and held his toes a foot from the straw strewn floor.

"And why might it be," Bahzell asked gently, "as you weren't after mentioning this courser to me?"

"I-I-I—" the horsetrader gobbled in terror. Bahzell

shook him gently, and he squealed again. "H-he's sold! I-I'm just h-holding him for the buyer!"

"I'd not be wishful for you to lie to me," Bahzell said softly. "It's angry I've been known to grow when someone's after lying to me, and when I'm angry, I've been known to act hasty, friend."

His fingers tightened, and Fradenhelm's face twisted in pain.

"No, I'd not like to think you'd be so foolish as to try lying to a champion of Tomanāk, Fradenhelm. There's never a Sothōii born as would try to sell a courser. They'd die first—aye, and so would the courser! I've no notion—yet—how it was he found himself in that stall, but that's a thing I *will* know before all's done, and this I know already. However he came to be here, there's not a fool in all the world as would trust you with such as he! What's stolen once can be stolen twice, not but what you know that already. Now—once more—why was it you weren't after telling me?"

"I-I told you! It's the truth!"

"No, you lied." Bahzell's free hand gripped Fradenhelm's left forearm. "They say as how hradani are barbarians, little man, and some tales tell true. I'm wondering how it is you'd like going through life with one arm."

"I told you the *truth*!" the horsetrader whimpered.

"It's many a year I've known you for a thief," Bahzell said softly, almost caressingly, "but I was never after taking you for a fool...until now."

The hradani's fingers tightened, and Fradenhelm shrieked. Kenhodan stepped towards them, appalled by the expression on his friend's merciless face, but Wencit's tiny headshake stopped him.

Kenhodan watched in something like horror as Bahzell tightened his grip and Fradenhelm writhed. He screamed again, setting horses neighing and stamping, but Bahzell's eyes never flickered. Tighter his hand clamped, like a vise of steel. Kenhodan knew what had to happen, but the snap of breaking bone and Fradenhelm's howl of agony made his stomach muscles jump.

Bahzell released the broken arm, visibly bent in the middle. He gripped Fradenhelm's other arm... and smiled.

"*All right!*" the horsetrader shrieked as Bahzell touched him. He sobbed in terror and pain as the hradani released him contemptuously to huddle in a beaten ball. Kenhodan smelled his terror, and he couldn't blame him. For the first time, Kenhodan realized that Bahzell was truly hradani, whatever else he might be.

"Quickly, Fradenhelm," Bahzell said quietly.

"It was...was the wizard. They told me...told me he'd pass through. They said—they said they'd pay... pay five hundred kormaks if I told them w-when he got here...."

"And the courser?" Kenhodan barely recognized Bahzell's icy voice.

"The...the courser?" Fradenhelm cradled his broken arm, whimpering as he looked into Bahzell's stony face.

"This is a courser." Bahzell spoke tonelessly, as if reciting an indictment, and his rustic accent had completely vanished. "No wind rider will abandon his courser, and no more will a courser abandon his rider. They'll die first. So tell me, Fradenhelm—*how did you get this courser?*"

"I-I—" Fradenhelm stuttered helplessly at the whiplash question. "I don't know! Please, Bahzell! They brought him here! They said he'd be good bait to...trap you—"

His gobbling voice broke off in a fresh howl of pain as Bahzell backhanded him. The hradani grabbed the front of his apron and yanked him to his feet, and the hook knife whispered evilly from its sheath.

"Hear me, Fradenhelm. You can play Hirahim's game with the local magistrates whenever you choose, but your life is mine now, little man. This courser came here with a wind rider. I've no idea how you got him fastened in that stall in the first place, but this I do know—you'd never have done it unless his rider was dead first. And that means someone—and it may have been you—killed a wind rider in this stable. But that wasn't wise, d'you see, because *I'm* a wind rider. I don't like people who kill my brothers, and himself doesn't like those who do murder in the dark. So there's no least reason in the world for me to leave your throat uncut. You'd best be thinking of one, and you'd best come up with it fast."

The keen edge of the hook knife touched the side of Fradenhelm's neck delicately.

"It wasn't me!" Fradenhelm shrieked. "It was *them!* They asked after you, and he wanted to know why! *They* killed him, and one of them darted the courser with a blowgun. I don't know what they used on him—I *swear* I don't!—but it left him meek as a kitten. They...they made me put him in the stall. It wasn't my idea! I told them it was madness! I warned them the wind riders would find out! But it was done. It was already *done*, I tell you! I was supposed to get rid of him, but I couldn't. He's worth too much—the Purple Lords would pay a *fortune* for a courser! I didn't even know who they were, or why they were hunting you—not at first! I swear! On my father's life I swear it!"

"You never met your father," Bahzell said coldly, "but that's neither here nor there. Tell it quick and tell it true, Fradenhelm, and it might be you'll live another hour. Who's this 'they' you keep yammering about?"

"Chernion," Fradenhelm whispered ashenly. "It... was Chernion."

Bahzell's lips tightened and he dropped the horse-trader with a thud, then snatched up a blanket and saddle. He turned to the coal black courser, holding up the blanket, and the courser dipped its head, touching its nose to it and then turning broadside to help the hradani throw it across his back.

"Who's Chernion?" Kenhodan demanded, dazed by events, as a saddle followed the blanket.

"Better to ask *what* he is," Wencit said grimly.

"Don't you start any damned word games with me *now!*" Kenhodan snapped.

"Start—Oh, I see." Wencit chuckled humorlessly. "I meant that the important thing is his trade. He's the master of the Assassins Guild."

"*Assassins Guild?* They're outlawed!"

"And would you be telling me what that matters?" Bahzell tossed over his shoulder as he tightened the saddle's girth. "I'm thinking corsairs are after being outlawed, as well, but it's in my mind as how you'll meet them now and again. What's after mattering is that someone's set the best assassin of them all on us—and I'm thinking as how he'll be here soon."

"True. So we'd best leave even sooner," Wencit agreed.

Bahzell nodded curtly and reached up to unbuckle the heavy halter. He hurled it away from him with an ugly expression, then bowed to the courser.

"Will you bear him, Wind Brother?" he asked quietly, and the stallion looked back at him for a heartbeat, then bent his head in an unmistakable nod of agreement.

"My thanks, and Walsharno's as well," Bahzell said, and turned to Wencit. "I'm thinking you've found the mount you were after needing, Wencit."

"I thank you for the trust and the honor." Wencit's voice was deep and measured, and he held out his hand in the same gesture Bahzell had used. The stallion touched it with his nose, and Wencit bowed.

The courser started walking toward the open door. Bahzell gathered up the pack horses' lead reins and followed, and Kenhodan shook himself and began leading Glamhandro in the hradani's wake.

"What about—?" He jutted his chin at Fradenhelm.

"What about him?" Wencit asked. "What more harm can he do? Does he know where we are bound, or why? All he can tell them is that Bahzell's with us, and they know that already, or they wouldn't have murdered the wind rider. Leave him be."

"Aye." Bahzell paused in the open doorway and looked down coldly. "We've had our dealings, Fradenhelm, and it's once or twice you've done me a good turn. I'm remembering that now, and you'd best be grateful. Aye, and be thankful you're a crawling dog, for well I know *you* couldn't kill a wind rider even from behind. But mark me, little man. If ever I see you again, I'll not break your arms; I'll rip them off and feed you the stumps!"

The hradani glared at the horsetrader, and Kenhodan knew he meant it. Bahzell waited for an answer, but Fradenhelm only curled more tightly and moaned. The hradani snarled in disgust and pushed through the door.

Clouds had settled lower, and the air was moist with river mist. Kenhodan sniffed. The promised rain was close, the air was raw and chill, and breeze swirled about him, stirring his hair as he leaned against Glamhandro. Wencit swung into the courser's saddle with a curious formality, and the huge black stallion accepted him, stamping briskly, eager to be off.

"Which way, Wencit?" Bahzell asked.

"East. Make for the Morfintan High Road. Perhaps that will throw them off."

"East it is, then. Mount up, Kenhodan!" Bahzell's deep bellow was rich with laughter. "We've some running to do."

Kenhodan swung up on Glamhandro, and the big gray sidled sideways beneath him. He felt muscles tighten as his thighs gripped the strong barrel, and in that moment, he was a centaur. Elation pounded in his throat, and his head whirled with the staccato pace of the last few minutes.

"What about you?" he asked, looking across at Bahzell, whose head was only a little lower than his own even with Glamhandro under him.

"There's never a horse born as can run a Horse Stealer into the ground, lad!" Bahzell laughed. "A courser, now—*he* might be after doing it, but it won't be happening soon, and I've a suspicion I'll not be stuck afoot long. You just be worrying about your own saddle sores and leave the boot leather to me!"

"Whatever you say." Kenhodan shook his head, and Bahzell laughed again.

"Lead us, Bahzell," Wencit said, and the hradani nodded sharply. Then he turned, impossibly quick— impossibly graceful—for someone of his towering inches and Kenhodan blinked as he disappeared out of the stable yard's front gate at a dead run with the startled packhorses lunging into motion to keep up with him.

The redhaired man looked across at Wencit for a moment, and then—as one—Glamhandro and the courser shot forward, steel shoes sparking on the cobbles in a battering of hooves.

The night swallowed them, and they were gone. The sound of their horses died on the moaning breeze.

· CHAPTER NINE ·

The Road to Morfintan

The sound of hooves had long faded and the moon blinked and vanished in a bank of black and silver cloud as the smell of rain grew stronger. The flooded river's voice was a low, grumbling rush, underpinning the night, and the breeze swirled mist under the stable lantern while the sign creaked.

A dozen figures in black leather slipped through the mist. No blazon marred their black garb, and the feeble light seemed to sink into them and vanish. A concealing hood covered each face and soft buskins slithered noiselessly over the paving. The wind made more noise than they.

Their slim leader paused, head swaying as if to scent the night. An imperiously raised hand halted the others as the leader sidled up to the stable door and paused again. The unbolted panel stirred to the wind's touch, and steel whispered. A longsword gleamed, dull in the moonlight and lantern light, as a buskin toed the door soundlessly open, and six figures filtered through like fog.

Fradenhelm huddled in a corner, propped against the wall, and clutched his arm while whimpers leaked through his teeth. An hour had passed since Bahzell dropped him, but shock and terror gripped him still, sapping his strength.

Five hundred gold kormaks had seemed a fortune, especially with half of it paid in advance, when all he'd had to do was inform the assassins when their victims appeared. Even the murder of the wind rider had been easy, for all he'd done was look the other way. Yet the rider's death rattle had been the first whisper of his own fate, and now he knew what greed might have cost him.

He was marked. As a wind rider, Bahzell shared an obligation with every wind rider of the vast Kingdom of the Sothōii to kill him. The Sothōii had seemed safely far away at the time, but that distance had become cold comfort in the wake of Bahzell's visit. Fradenhelm was only grateful their past dealings had created an offsetting obligation in the hradani's mind. It gave him a chance to flee, and he must run if he wanted to live—run so far and hide so deep that no one, not even Bahzell Bloody Hand, could ever find him again.

Unless the assassins actually managed to kill Bahzell, of course. The chances of which, based on their uniform lack of success in that respect, were no more than even, even with Chernion himself taking the assignment.

None of which considered the fact that he'd violated *Chernion's* instructions, as well, which could mean—

A buskin whispered in straw, and his head jerked up as six assassins materialized about him. His spastic effort to rise ended stillborn as a sword tip waved gently at his terror-dilated eyes.

"Greetings, Horsetrader." The leader's voice was low, carved from melodious, almost effeminate ice, and Fradenhelm trembled as he stared pleadingly into the dark eye-glitter in the hood's slits.

"I received your message ... tardily. You chose a poor messenger, yet he found us at last and bade us come. Behold me. Where are the targets?"

"G-gone," Fradenhelm whispered.

"So I perceive." The voice was gentle. "Weren't you told to hold them here until I could attend to them?"

"I ... They—"

"A simple answer is sufficient, Horsetrader," the assassin purred.

"I tried! Bahzell was in too big a hurry for me to hold them long. I ... I tried to convince them to spend the night here in Korun, but they refused! And ... and I sent you word as soon as they got here!"

"You did—by a halfwitted oaf who took an hour and more to find me. But, yes, you sent word. And your messenger tells me you also kept the courser you were supposed to dispose of." The soft voice sounded almost amused. "You know Bahzell's a wind rider. Were you truly so foolish you thought you could hide a courser from *him*?"

"They—that is, Bahzell—"

"You told them we were coming, didn't you?"

"Bahzell made me! He *tortured* me!" Fradenhelm shrieked.

"So I see," the assassin soothed, "and a man has a right to tell what he knows to end the pain. Even so, Horsetrader, it may have been unwise. You've failed

me, and no one does that twice. Redeem yourself!"
The voice became a lash. "Where did they go?"

"Morfintan! They said Morfintan!" Fradenhelm
offered feverishly, raising his good hand ingratiatingly.
"I-I crawled to the door to listen."

"Morfintan." The assassin considered a moment,
then chuckled. "Foolish of you, Horsetrader. Do you
really believe Bahzell Bloody Hand wouldn't guess
you were there?"

A gloved hand gestured, a knife whispered on
leather as it was drawn, and Fradenhelm shrank back,
moaning as the blade gleamed.

"You're a fool," the leader remarked calmly, nodding to the man with the knife, "and I have no use
for fools. Your greed betrayed us, and your stupidity's
allowed our targets to begin some plan to evade us.
Farewell, Horsetrader."

"*Noooooooooooooooooo!*"

Fradenhelm's scream died in a gurgle, and a small
body slumped to the straw in a spreading fan of red.
The leader had already turned to one of the others.

"Check the gates, Rosper. Check them all. Their
destination's Sindor for the present—I'm sure of it.
But I think this fool told the truth about what he
heard, so perhaps they've chosen an indirect route.
Check the East Gate well; if they *have* gone that way,
we may be able to overtake them on the high road."

"At once, Chernion."

"The rest of you, gather our mounts and meet me
in the Potters' Square. We can ride in any direction
from there."

"Yes, Chernion!" they chorused.

"See to it. And hide your leathers until we ride."

"Yes, Chernion!"

They slapped fists to chests in salute and faded into the mist, and Chernion's emotionless toe pushed the body onto its back. The assassin reached into an inner pocket for a heavy purse, and gold gleamed as the guildmaster emptied two hundred and fifty gold kormaks over the corpse.

Chernion dropped the purse and drew a tiny dagger of hammered silver, its pommel a grinning death's head, from a wrist sheath. The killer drove it through the purse into the dirt, then turned on a heel without glancing back.

Chernion had no use for fools, but examples were another matter. Dog brothers were businessmen, and if mere murder paid no bills, executions for failure built a reputation for ruthless infallibility.

That was worth the kormaks Fradenhelm had been promised.

◆　◆　◆

Two horsemen and a hradani pressed down the high road.

The hradani's ears pricked, as if to pluck any sound of pursuit from the breeze, as he ran with the steady, swinging, tireless endurance of the Horse Stealers. Mist wreathed the horses' knees, so that the riders seemed to float on a sea of vapor that ended at their stirrup irons. Moonlight broke the clouds occasionally, but they'd grown thick; breaks big enough for the moon had become few and far between, and a soft drizzle sifted down.

One of the pack horses stumbled, but Bahzell's iron arm held him. The gelding recovered, yet he breathed heavily as the hradani brought him back up. He was obviously still willing, but he was nearly spent, and the second pack horse was little better, although the courser and Glamhandro appeared fresh enough.

"We'll have to rest them again," Bahzell said so abruptly Kenhodan started in surprise after the speechless hours. He glanced at the drooping gelding and nodded agreement.

"I fear you're right." Wencit rose in the saddle to peer through the depressing mist. The high road was wide and firm, hard paved as it sped across the moor, and a swatch of firm turf ran along either verge for horsemen. The night lay in ashes about them, but dawn was still distant, and fine drops of rain made it hard to see much.

"Over there," he said finally, pointing into the dark. "I see the loom of some trees. We can shelter there for an hour or so."

Bahzell looked carefully in the indicated direction and grunted, then led them through the rainy mist at a more sedate pace, followed by Wencit, the pack horses, and Kenhodan. The redhaired man was uneasy, sensing the pursuit he couldn't see, and his hand brushed his sword hilt. He turned every few minutes to glance cautiously behind, but at least the following breeze favored them. It would carry any sound of pursuit to them and push their own noise ahead... he hoped.

Melting snow and spring's long rains had struck deep into the soil of South March Moor, and sodden ground sucked at the horses' hooves between tussocks of stiff grass. A dense belt of firs bulked wetly, farther from the road than Kenhodan would have guessed. They stood on higher, firmer ground, and he suspected they'd been planted as a windbreak for the high road.

He sighed in relief as he dismounted, and Wencit swung down beside him with an echoing sigh of gratitude.

"Old bones don't take kindly to desperate all-night rides," the wizard observed, stretching until his shoulders popped loudly.

"Old bones, is it?" Bahzell's ears twitched at Wencit in amusement. "I'm thinking as how someone wants an excuse to be lying about while others are after doing the work!"

"You expect a poor old man to work after such a night?" Wencit's voice quavered pitifully. "An old man, worn with his labors and hard riding?"

"Aye," Bahzell answered with a grin.

"The gods will deal with you as you with me," Wencit warned him.

"That's as may be, but it's pleased as punch you've been with yourself all afternoon and night, Wizard. Well, wizard's news is for wizard's ears, they say, so I'll not blame you for not sharing it—though Tomanāk knows it must be after being good indeed to have you grinning like a loon with dog brothers on our heels! But if you'll not share that, you'll at least share the work."

"Learn from this, Kenhodan," Wencit said mournfully. "Never ride with a hradani. He'll either eat your horse or make you tend it like a slave."

The coal black courser snorted. Then his nose pushed the wizard between the shoulders hard enough to make Wencit stumble forward a full stride, and Kenhodan— already busy with Glamhandro—grinned. The wizard turned to the courser, and the huge stallion cocked

his head to one side, turning it to regard Wencit with
a steady eye until he reached up and laid one palm on
the courser's forehead. The stallion pushed against it,
far more gently, and Wencit smiled.

"Old and feeble I may be, Milord, but I'm sure I
can dredge up at least a little energy."

The courser snorted again, and Wencit began loosening the saddle girth.

Kenhodan already had Glamhandro's saddle off, and
the big gray was sweaty enough to need attention in
the chill air. Yet he still spoiled for a run—his ears
were forward, and his left forefoot dug at the damp
turf as Kenhodan stroked his velvet nose, then rubbed
him down briskly. He turned the blanket and replaced
the saddle, then draped his poncho over the horse.
The firs protected him from the rain, and Glamhandro's overheated strength needed warmth more than
he. He eased the bit from the stallion's mouth, and
Glamhandro nuzzled his ear, blowing gently before he
dropped his head to crop the sparse grass.

Kenhodan listened to the sound of grazing for a
moment, then turned to help the others. Bahzell was
just finishing with the first of the pack horses, and he
glanced at Kenhodan with a tight grin as he bent his
great bow and nodded back towards the high road.
Kenhodan nodded in understanding, and the hradani
vanished into the mist. Kenhodan heard his boots
suck in and out of the mud once or twice; then there
was only silence.

The redhaired man removed the second pack horse's
pack frame and set it aside, and the weary gelding—a
gray, darker than Glamhandro with black legs—blew
gratefully. The redhaired man began working the

rubbing cloth over the horse's coat and glanced over his shoulder at Wencit.

The courser was big enough to make it difficult for the wizard to reach his poll without some sort of stool, but the stallion had bent his head to ease the task, and Wencit's hands were gentle on the galled welts his imprisoning halter had left. He wore no bridle, of course. Most coursers wore ornamental hackamores, usually without reins and decorated with ornamental silver work or even gems, but no wind rider would even consider putting a bit into his companion's mouth, and no courser would ever choose a rider who might have contemplated anything of the sort. Kenhodan knew that, yet he'd still found it strange to watch Wencit cantering through the night with his hands resting on his thighs.

Now the wizard finished rubbing down the courser, and the stallion touched him with his nose again in thanks, then moved over beside Glamhandro to tear at the scanty grass.

Kenhodan and Wencit worked together, as silently and smoothly as if they'd practiced it for years, to set the picket pins for the pack animals. Wencit seemed content to trust their security to Bahzell, and after a moment or two of thought, Kenhodan discovered that he shared his confidence. The redhaired man considered what would happen to any pursuers out there in the dark and felt less anxious as he checked the picket rope and turned wearily to Wencit.

"Do we dare risk a fire? Or are they likely to be so close we really need Bahzell out there?"

"Probably not—to both questions." Wencit's silver hair gleamed with the fine raindrops. "For all his banter, Bahzell's cautious. He doesn't really expect to see anyone, but he hasn't lived this long by ignoring remote possibilities. But why were you wanting a fire?"

"Leeana packed plenty of tea. I thought a cup or two . . . ?"

"An excellent idea! And we don't need a fire for that; I'll provide the heat."

There was a stream somewhere near, chuckling softly in the night. Indeed, it was a rare spot on South March Moor where one *didn't* hear running water, but direction was easily lost in the mist. Kenhodan didn't care to stray far on the fog-girt moor, so he unstoppered a canteen to fill Bahzell's blackened camp kettle and dropped in a handful of fragrant tea.

While he did that, Wencit had drawn his sword and turned up the flat of the blade. Now he set the kettle on the inlaid steel, balancing it with his free hand. His brilliant eyes burned even brighter for a moment and a diamond-hard glitter edged the blade, bathing his features in blue luminescence. Kenhodan swallowed a muffled exclamation and moved quickly between the sword and the road to hide its light, but his instinctive protest died as the kettle began to steam. His eyes fastened on the razor edge of light, and his mind echoed with a strange humming noise.

The kettle bubbled at a low boil within seconds, and Kenhodan snatched it from the sword. He hissed as he burned his fingers and set it aside quickly, fumbling a riding glove from his belt to shield his hand from the heat.

Wencit blinked at Kenhodan's muffled curse, and the glow of the sword died instantly, plunging them back into a night all the darker for the brief light. All

Kenhodan could see were the wizard's eyes, floating like disembodied balefires in the gloom.

"Here." Wencit wrapped a corner of his poncho around the kettle handle, and Kenhodan watched bemusedly—wondering why the small, casual sorcery impressed him as deeply as the desperate spells Wencit had used against the corsairs. Watching Wencit of Rūm calmly brew tea on a magical sword seemed somehow . . . inappropriate.

"What was that sound?" he asked curiously.

"Sound?" The glowing eyes shifted to consider him thoughtfully.

"Like a humming. I've heard something every time you've worked sorcery near me, only usually it sounds like some sort of animal."

"Have you now?" Wencit chuckled. "Mightn't it be wiser to say you heard it every time you *knew* I was using the art?"

"Are you trying to evade me?" Kenhodan asked curiously. "If so, I'm perfectly willing to drop it. I was only curious."

"No, that's all right," Wencit said. "Some people can detect the wild magic, although there's no fixed way of perceiving it. Some hear it, some see it—some actually *taste* it. It's possible you truly can hear it."

"Is that significant?" Kenhodan asked nervously.

"I wouldn't count on it," Wencit said dryly. "I once knew a warrior with no more skill in the art than a block of wood. You couldn't even begin to *imagine* how profoundly *un*magical he was! Yet he could hear wild magic from one end of Kontovar to the other. Little good it did him in the end, I'm afraid. There's a vast difference between *detecting* the wild magic and being able to command it, and he went off to the Battle of Lost Hope without ever showing even a hint of the Gift."

"I see." Kenhodan felt a surge of relief. "Good! I don't want—"

"*Idiots!* Idiots the pair of you!" Bahzell filtered out of the mist and glowered at them. "Clear down by the road, I was, and saw that glow like a beacon! I might've been picking you both off, clean and easy as butts at a target match—and tempted I was to do it! Why not be hiring a band the next time you're wishful to draw the dog brothers' eye?"

"There are no eyes out there to see it," Wencit said calmly, "and even if there were, there's far less chance of anyone noticing so brief a light than any fire we might have lit."

"With mortal eyes, maybe." Bahzell gave not an inch. "But what if Wulfra's seen fit to be giving her killers a pet wizard for a guide?"

"Unlikely." Wencit shrugged. "Rumor says Chernion hates all wizards. His Guild has too many secrets, and he wants no wizard meddling with them. Besides, the dog brothers have been hurt too often working with wizardry against you and me alike, Bahzell. Chernion won't want to risk repeating that against *both* of us. But even if he *wanted* a wizard, it's unlikely any of Wulfra's circle would go with him. Whatever else, Chernion's never been afraid to see his victims before he strikes—or even to attack them face-to-face. Do you really think any of the scum running with Wulfra would willingly come close to *me?* I know you're not that stupid, Bahzell."

"All right! Put your pride back in your pack and forget I was after speaking! Wizards! Not a one of 'em but would take time out on the brink of disaster to discuss his peers' failings!" Bahzell turned to Kenhodan before Wencit could take fresh umbrage at the suggestion that another wizard might be his "peer." "If that's tea I'm smelling, pour it out. My belly's colder than a Purple Lord's heart on settling day."

Kenhodan chuckled as he poured into the metal cups, and they squatted, sipping gratefully at the hot, bitter tea of the East Wall mountaineers.

"What time is it?" Kenhodan asked finally, the better part of an hour later.

"About the turn of the morning watch," Bahzell answered. "We're after making good time—we've come over ten leagues, I'm guessing. Say what you will of Fradenhelm, he's an eye for horseflesh and it's not far wrong he was about Glamhandro."

"Then we could camp here?"

"No." Bahzell sipped noisily and shook his head. "I'm thinking we'd best rest a little more, then move on. They'll be after us, and while they'll not be making up much distance, they'll not be many hours back, either."

"Why not?"

"Because friend Fradenhelm was after sending them after us like a shot, lad, to save his own skin. Not but what he wouldn't have done it for pay, anyway. He was after hearing us, and his only chance—and that not a good one—is to be telling them all he can."

"I thought you said he couldn't do any more harm!"

"And so I did, for I wanted him to be thinking I thought that. I'm hopeful of leading the dog brothers astray, and it's mortal hard to lead someone wrong if they don't think as they know where you've gone."

"Why not go south if he sent them east, then? We might've lost them!"

"That we wouldn't have. If we'd taken the South Gate, how long d'you think they'd've taken to be learning just that? We're not after being the very hardest group for folks to notice, and Chernion's the reputation of the best hired killer in Norfressa—not one to be running off on the say-so of such as Fradenhelm! No, Chernion's one as knows his trade as well as I'm after knowing mine. He'll have checked all the gates to be certain, for he's not one to leave anything to chance, either. I'm doubting as it took him all that long to check, but it's surprised I'd be if he could send runners to all of them in much less than an hour. So we're that far ahead, and it may be—though I'd not count on it!—that he's after believing we're truly off to Morfintan."

"Well, we are." Kenhodan paused accusingly. "Aren't we?"

"Lad, the war god loves truth, but himself's also one as loves a cunning mind. In fact, to be cutting a long tale short—" Bahzell's teeth gleamed "—no."

"Then where in Phrobus' name *are* we going?" Kenhodan was on his feet, amazed by the anger exploding within him. "You and this wizard seem to have a means of communication denied to lesser mortals! Am I supposed to consult the birds to divine our future—when I can *find* any birds in this Chemalka-cursed climate? We been riding hard all night, and you haven't even seen fit to tell me where we're really *going?*"

He couldn't see himself, but his companions could, and he no longer looked like a worried young man without a past of his own, for that inner imperiousness he'd already detected within himself had risen to the surface. His green eyes were hard, his jaw taut, and his expression was that of a man accustomed to command, not to obey. The wizard and hradani glanced at one another, and then Bahzell shrugged.

"It's sorry I am, lad," he said calmly. "It was no part of my thinking to be misleading *you*, but you've the right of it—Wencit and I *are* after knowing each other too well. It's not so very often we discuss our plans, because we're in the habit of each knowing the other's thought before he's thought it. It may be as we feel too comfortable with you to be remembering you're a newcomer."

"Well I *am* a newcomer," Kenhodan half-snapped, and felt embarrassment at his own reaction heat his face. He dug a toe angrily into the sodden turf and glowered at them. "I can accept that you can't discuss my past, but you can bloody well discuss the future! And you can start with why we're freezing our arses off in the rain in the middle of nowhere like village halfwits waiting for hired assassins to stick knives in our backs!"

"Now, that's after being a reasonable question."

Bahzell's chuckle snapped the tension—and Kenhodan's anger. He felt suddenly abashed by his words and sank back down, reaching for his cup.

"Sorry," he muttered. "I guess I'm too sensitive, but I feel so damned helpless. So . . . so *uninformed*. And there's so much I need to know!"

"Wencit," Bahzell said more seriously, "the lad's the right of it. And I'm thinking, now I think about it at all, that it's surprised I am he's been patient with us this long."

"You're right," Wencit agreed, then turned to Kenhodan. "You've reason to feel ill used—not least because you know I know more about you than I can tell you—and you certainly have a right to know anything we *can* tell you. Please believe we left you in ignorance out of thoughtlessness and haste, not by design."

Kenhodan nodded, gratified by their reaction but confused by his own. He knew part of it was frustration mixed with fatigue and not a little fear, but he also knew there was more to it. There'd been more than a trace of the rage he'd felt on *Wave Mistress* in that anger, and that worried him. It wasn't the same sort of killing rage...but it wasn't completely different from it, either, and that thought evaporated the last embers of his temper, leaving him shaken and cold, instead. *Did* he have his own share of the hradani's Rage? And if he did, what did that say about him?

He drew a deep breath and clenched his teeth. What he'd been mattered less than what he was *now*. It had to. He couldn't undo his past, even if he'd known what it was, but whatever sparked his fury lay within him. If he couldn't alter what he'd been, at least he could control what he might become, and he *would* control it. He must.

"I'm sorry," he repeated more naturally, "but I really do want to know what we're doing, so tell me, please. At least—" his lips twitched a wry smile "—until my mindreading catches up with yours."

"That's better!" Bahzell clasped his forearms firmly. "Aye, and this old spell-spinner's after speaking for me, as well. It's not that we undervalue you, but sometimes we're after forgetting, d'you see? Forgive us."

"Don't make me feel guilty, you oaf! You'll start it all over again!"

"Tell him, Bahzell!" Wencit laughed. "As you value both our lives, tell him!"

Kenhodan surprised himself with an answering spurt of laughter, and his companions' chuckles erased the last tension as if Wencit had used a spell.

"Aye, I will, then," Bahzell agreed, and knelt as the moon blinked through a fortuitous hole in the cloud drift. He smoothed a patch of soil and put a pebble on it.

"This pebble's after being Korun, Kenhodan. This line's the South Road—" he scribed with a fingertip "—and *this* is the East Road." He jerked a thumb at the mist-hidden high road. "This line's the Morfintan High Road," he went on, scribing in another north-south line to cap the eastern end of the East Road. "If we were to be going clear to the Morfintan High Road, we'd be hitting it here—" his forefinger jabbed "—at Losun, and it's straight south we could turn for Sindor. But that's after being the longer way. It's leagues out of our way it would take us—not but what I'd not be so very unhappy about that, if it should so happen it would be throwing off the dog brothers. Only that's not so likely to happen, I'm thinking.

"But that's not so bad a thing, for we're after *knowing* it won't, so . . ."

He made more lines.

"This is after being the Whitewater, and this other line the Snowborn—a river from the East Walls as meets Whitewater about five leagues from this very spot . . . here. The East Road's after crossing the Snowborn on the Bridge of Eloham, then runs seventy more leagues to the Morfintan High Road."

"All right," Kenhodan said as Bahzell paused and glanced up. "I see where we are, but not why we're here."

"As to that," Bahzell said, sitting back on his haunches, "the answer's at the Bridge of King Emperor Eloham. Right at its west end, there's a trail branches off to follow the Snowborn a league or two before it's after turning back southwest through the Forest of Hev to join the South Road a hundred leagues south of Korun."

"And we take that trail, do we?"

"Aye, and one of two things will be happening. If the dog brothers know the trail, or if they're after figuring it out, like as not they'll follow us. If they're not after knowing or guessing, I'm thinking they'll keep on to the east after ghosts and the wind. Either way, we'll come out to the better."

"I can see where we'd come out ahead if they lose us, but won't we still be in the same fix if they do follow us down the trail?"

"No. First, I've no doubt at all, at all, that our horses—even the pack beasts—are after being better than theirs. Thief and traitor Fradenhelm may be, but he's a master's eye for horseflesh, and it's his best we took. It's not so very likely the dog brothers can match them, and cross-country, they'll not find remounts when their own steeds fail. Holding to the roads, though, they'll be after hiring or buying fresh at every posting station. That's something we can't do, unless we're wishful to abandon the horses we have—aside from the courser, of course—and that I'd not do with all the scorpions of Sharnā nipping at my backside. But cross-country, it's our heels we'll show them, unless it should happen they've plenty of spares."

"And if they do?"

"I'll still not worry overmuch." Bahzell smiled, and his tone was almost hungry as he touched a spot on his crude map. "Right about here," he said almost wistfully, "there's after being a stream. It's not so much a stream it is in summer, but right now it's running deep and fast. Best of all, the west bank's sheer as a temple wall, and the trail's after being steep as heartbreak and narrow as honor. It's a place where horses can be going only in single file, and at the top, why there's a nice cluster of trees. I'm thinking as we might make camp in those trees a day or two, lad."

He met Kenhodan's eyes in the moonlight, and the redhaired man nodded slowly. If he had a killer's soul, who better to unleash it against than assassins? His smile was colder than Bahzell's bright, fierce grin and his eyes were hard.

"That might be nice," he murmured softly.

"Aye. At best, they'll be 'following' us to Morfintan while we cut across the inside of the loop—a little slower, but a lot shorter. We can be waiting two days at the stream and still gain a week over them, and set them a pretty puzzle, too. At worst, they'll follow along the trail and come up with us at a time and place of our choosing, not theirs."

"I like it," Kenhodan said. He supposed he should feel squeamish about cold-bloodedly planning to ambush others, but he couldn't. Hired killers were vermin, and there was only one way to deal with them. Or, at least, there was only one way for *him* to deal with them.

He wondered if he'd always been like that?

"Then—" Bahzell rose and carefully blotted his

diagram with his heel "—I'm thinking we'd best be on our way again."

Wencit and Kenhodan nodded, and the hradani pulled the picket pins and gathered up the pack horses' leads as his companions reclaimed their ponchos, tightened their girths, and climbed back into the saddle. The courser pawed impatiently, tossing his head and ready to be off, and Glamhandro snorted in reply. The pack horses seemed less eager, but their heads came up as the courser gave a shrill whinny. His right forehoof thudded the muddy ground again, and when Bahzell tugged on the lead ropes, they followed him gamely, forging back to the road. Hooves sucked in mud, then thudded on wet, firm turf. Horses and courser gathered themselves, then swung to the east once more, fleeing into the teeth of a misty dawn at the hradani's heels, and rain swallowed them.

✦   ✦   ✦

Fine rain beaded the cloaks and ponchos of a grim group of horsemen. Two of them rode ahead while their ten companions followed respectfully behind. One of the leaders was Chernion; the other was Rosper.

"I wonder why?" Chernion murmured as they rode on through the shredding fog.

"Why what?"

Chernion eyed Rosper thoughtfully. Rosper was craftmaster of the south, second only to Chernion in this part of the Empire, and he'd earned that position. Chernion considered him a little hasty, but he was an able man, and one of only two who knew Chernion's deepest secret.

"Why Morfintan?" the guildmaster said after a moment. "It's not the straight path to Angthyr, Rosper."

"What of it? They're warned now, and they're detouring to avoid pursuit." Rosper shrugged, and water trickled down his cloak.

"Are they?" Chernion's head cocked thoughtfully. "Neither the Bloody Hand nor the wizard is a fool. They knew the horsetrader would be listening, just as they knew he'd betray them the instant he could. No, they left us a message, Rosper. They *want* us to come this way."

"With all respect, I think you're seeing plots that don't exist," Rosper replied. "They're afraid of the Guild. It's that simple."

"No, it's not," Chernion said firmly. "These are no fat merchants or fawning, fat-bellied nobles. Now that they know we're hunting them, neither Wencit nor the Bloody Hand will *fear* us. They have some purpose in mind, whatever it may be."

"I'm not so certain. Not even Bahzell would care to face all of us."

Chernion suppressed a sigh. So Rosper meant to be stubborn, did he? Well, it was Chernion's duty to teach him wisdom, even if it was likely to prove a futile exercise in this instance.

"Bahzell," the guildmaster said bluntly, "could kill half our brothers by himself, and if a quarter of the tales are true, Wencit could kill the rest without a spell. Which says nothing of the third man—and trust me, Rosper; the Bloody Hand and Wencit didn't bring along a man who can't fight."

"And if we take them unaware?" Rosper asked pointedly.

"There are times, Rosper, when you show a glimmer of genius." Chernion's tone was as close to jesting as it ever came. "That's what I hope for, but our best chance was in Korun, before they knew we were hunting them. The Bloody Hand hasn't survived so long without growing eyes in the back of his head, and their guard will be up."

"Let it be! We have two fresh horses each. We'll run them to earth and take them in the dark! Or do you question my dog brothers' stealth?"

"Rosper, you listen like a soldier! I never question the dog brothers' stealthiness; but I fear the Bloody Hand's. You've never hunted a target like him. I wouldn't count on surprising him even if he didn't know anyone was hunting him. But that's the least of it, because he has a plan. I'm as certain of that as if he'd told me so himself."

"What good's a plan against a dozen of us in the dark? Not even Bahzell can see in all directions." Rosper grimaced. "Your pardon, but this sounds like the fluttering of a frightened maid, not the words of an assassin."

"Perhaps," Chernion returned calmly. "But the wizard's eyes aren't like those of other men. Who knows what they see? *I* don't . . . but I'm wise enough to fear them. No. We'll follow, but carefully. Carefully, Rosper!"

"Of course, Chernion."

Rosper slapped his chest in salute and fell back, explaining Chernion's plans quietly to the others, and no listener could have guessed his mind wasn't in complete accord with his words.

Chernion smiled and peered forward, carefully wiping bushy eyebrows and an oddly delicate face as water trickled down them. Rosper! He should have been a warrior, not an assassin. His skill with poison was outstanding, and it was his dart which had paralyzed the courser's will before it could avenge its fallen rider. The drugs he'd supplied after that ought to have *kept* that will paralyzed, as well. Obviously, something had gone wrong with that, but the truth was that Chernion couldn't really blame Fradenhelm for assuming Rosper's concoctions would keep the stallion quiescent and pliant until he could dispose of it. Chernion would have assumed the same. Unfortunately, it would appear there was more truth to the tales about the coursers' vitality and resistance to poison than the guildmaster had believed, and while one could scarcely blame Rosper for not knowing that, the evidence that his potions had failed of their purpose in the end had touched his pride on the quick. That would have been enough to hone the edge of his determination to lay their quarry by the heels, yet the truth was that injured self-esteem was only a part of what pushed him to drive the pursuit.

Despite his well-earned pride in the efficacy of his poisons, there were times the dog brothers' stealthy killing galled Rosper. Times when he wanted to face his prey openly, *see* the knowledge that death had come for them in their eyes. Which was foolish. Assassins were better fighters than most, or they didn't live long, but pride paid no bills and frontal assaults were bad business. Men hired the dog brothers when they needed an enemy to vanish without fuss or bother; any hired bravo with a sword could kill openly.

No, assassins traded in skill and stealth, and the Guild's reputation attracted patrons who didn't relish failure. It was always wise to pick the moment carefully, and Chernion disliked the notion of meeting Bahzell on ground of his own choosing. Assassins were merchants of death, not heroes, and the Guild had long ago learned how expensive it could prove to hunt Bahzell Bahnakson on anything remotely like his own terms.

Norfressa's deadliest killer rode silently onward, lost in thought.

◆   ◆   ◆

Wulfra of Torfo studied her crystal, peering down on Chernion from a great height. She knew Wencit was somewhere ahead of the assassin, but that was all she knew, for the old wizard's glamour was beyond her piercing. Her patron could penetrate it, but he would no longer share his full information with her.

She sighed and gems flashed as she combed slender, ringed fingers through her golden hair, then steepled them under her chin. She might not like the cat-eyed wizard's reasoning, but she understood it.

Wencit knew it was beyond her power to breach his defenses. So far, her minions had attacked only when there was some other reasonable explanation for how they might have tracked him, but if Chernion went unfailingly to him, he'd know he was under close observation. At best he'd strengthen his glamours ... at worst he'd know someone more powerful than Wulfra opposed him, and the cat-eyed wizard refused to alert his ancient enemy.

Anyway, her patron probably disapproved of the dog brothers. Not that Chernion had much chance of succeeding. Wulfra knew that better than most, and she didn't like the exorbitant price the Assassins Guild had charged her, but it was *she* towards whom Wencit rode. Under the circumstances, she was prepared to try anything with a chance, however remote, of success. Besides, Chernion might just be lucky, for the assassin had a formidable record. And if the Guild failed, Wulfra lost nothing but the down payment they'd already received, for the dog brothers guaranteed success. In the rare instances when they failed—and they did fail, from time to time, despite anything their reputation might say—their clients owed nothing.

It was a pity, in a way. Wulfra smiled as she gazed at the assassin. Chernion truly was as capable as they said, and the assassin had already struck down two of Fallona's better generals for Wulfra, though the dog brothers didn't know she was the one who'd hired them. The contract had been negotiated in the name of Ranalf of Carchon, since Wulfra was of no mind to risk her saintly public image just yet. It would be a shame if the assassin's steel was unequal to this task, but even that could be useful, for Bahzell and Wencit were bound to kill at least a few dog brothers along the way. If that happened, the Guild would be more determined than ever to kill them in return, for assassins had no friends. They took care of their own, because it was bad business for dead dog brothers to go unavenged. It was largely fear of inevitable retribution which made brave men hesitate to face them.

Yes, Chernion might yet be a winning card. If not . . . at least the assassin amused her. She enjoyed her link to Chernion's mind, even knowing Chernion would risk anything to destroy her if the assassin ever became aware that link existed. Chernion had secrets, and the guildmaster had killed repeatedly to hide them. It might be dangerous to know them, but Wulfra was willing to risk that.

She did *so* enjoy being on the inside.

◆   ◆   ◆

"I thought you said there was a trail."

Kenhodan's tone was both pointed and sour as he eyed the river. Like the Whitewater, the Snowborn was high with snowmelt, and the road arrowed out into its waters on a broad causeway that melded with a many-arched bridge. Foam boiled through those arches, fretting at the constriction in brawling rage, but the stonework rose like a fortress, throwing back the current in angry ruffles of yellow and brown lace while the river growled its anger.

Day had come, such as it was. There was no sun; clouds shouldered one another in solid, lumpy charcoal billows and misty rain dusted down. The desolate sight of the flooded river glowered at them in the barren gray light.

"Aye, and a trail there is!" Bahzell raised his voice over the bone-numbing roar. "I was never saying as it was easy to reach!"

"Easy isn't all that important, as long as it's possible! Is it?"

"And would I've been after bringing you this way if it wasn't?"

Kenhodan shivered doubtfully. Trees drifted on the current, swirling slowly end for end while water heaved and foamed through broken limbs and roots. The swollen river rose ten feet up oaks and ash trees growing well back from its nominal bank; farther out, the willows along the "shore" were barely visible humps of foam. Two of the bridge's arches were packed with jams of wreckage, but it stood like a cliff, its piers founded firmly in the riverbed. The stonework bore the scars of combat, yet it faced the battle undaunted.

"Show me!" he shouted dubiously.

"Would it happen you see that oak?" Bahzell pointed downstream, and Kenhodan nodded. "It's thirty or forty feet beyond it our trail lies. All we're after needing is to swim the horses from here to there, d'you see?"

"You're joking!" Kenhodan was stunned. "It must be a hundred yards! Look at that current! How are *we* supposed to swim that far—much less the pack horses?"

Bahzell glanced at the weary horses and smiled as the gray gelding raised his head. The pack horse was tired and unsure of what was about to be demanded, but he was willing—though that might change when he confronted the river.

"I'm thinking Wencit will be just fine!" Bahzell shouted over the river. "And so will I. His beauty's strong enough to be towing him—and me, too, come to that—and we'll tie one of the pack horse's leads to his saddle, as well. You and Glamhandro can be coming behind with the other!"

"Brilliant! And what about the current?"

"And what current might that be?" Bahzell pointed smugly into the blowing spray. "The causeway's solid as a Dwarvenhame dam, Kenhodan! The only current's after being out in the middle; along the downstream sides it's smooth as a Saramanthan duck pond!"

"A duck pond!" Kenhodan snorted.

He glowered at the river a moment longer, then shook his head and climbed down to rearrange his equipment. It still sounded insane, but Bahzell was probably right about the current. He hoped so, anyway.

He rechecked the pack saddles, lashing each item individually to the frames, then fastened the gray gelding's lead rope to Glamhandro's saddle. He checked his bow carefully, sealed his extra string in the oiled leather case to protect it, and fastened the quiver to his saddle, trying to keep his arrows' fletching high enough to stay dry. Then he stripped off his sword and tied it behind the cantle. Finally, he dragged off his boots, and the causeway was chill and wet under his stocking feet as he tied them to the pack frame, as well. Last but far from least, he checked the fastenings of his harp's case and hoped Brandark would never hear how he was about to abuse the magnificent instrument.

Bahzell and Wencit had made their own preparations by the time he was finished. Wencit and Kenhodan retained only their daggers, and Bahzell had stripped to his arming doublet and bundled his hauberk and breastplate into an untidy package behind the courser's saddle. Kenhodan grinned as they all stood bootless in the ankle-deep mud, and he wondered how many had ever seen Wencit of Rūm look so ridiculous.

"Ready?" Bahzell's shout cut across the river's roar.

"As close to it as I'll ever be, anyway," Kenhodan replied glumly. Wencit merely nodded.

Bahzell roped the wizard's left wrist to the courser's saddle, fastened the second pack horse's lead to it, as well, then reached up and gripped the saddle horn in his right hand. Water licked against the causeway six feet below its crest, and Kenhodan hoped there was no undertow . . . or underbrush.

"The slope's steep as the price of grain in Vonderland, but the footing's firm!" Bahzell said loudly. "It's after being faced with stone, but grown with grass. Just take it slow and steady! Glamhandro will tell you when he's ready to swim, and the gray will be after following him!"

Kenhodan nodded and watched Wencit and Bahzell slip over the edge. The courser showed no hesitation as he stepped almost gaily over the side and picked his mincing way down the slope more gracefully than the sliding, slipping hradani and wizard, but the pack horse was unhappy. He planted his feet and refused to budge until the courser turned his head with an admonishing whinny, as if chiding a fainthearted companion. The pack horse's ears shifted. Then he tossed his head in unmistakable assent and followed.

The courser trumpeted approval and sprang into the water, the pack horse following with a rush. Bahzell released his grip on the courser's saddle horn and launched out with a powerful breaststroke, and the courser and pack horse followed in his wake. Kenhodan watched anxiously for a moment, then sighed with relief as all of them rode the rippled flood easily.

Then it was his turn. He hesitated a moment, feeling absurdly like the pack horse. He was willing, but he couldn't avoid a qualm. Then Glamhandro nosed him so impatiently he almost stumbled, and Kenhodan looked back in astonishment and burst into laughter as the stallion snorted and tossed his head impatiently. Urged on by his horse! Thank Tomanāk Bahzell was too busy swimming to have witnessed Glamhandro's prodding.

"All right, then! Let's go!" he said, and stepped off the road.

The footing was better than he'd feared. Over the years, a thick skin of sod had covered the ancient stonework, and the dense network of roots offered purchase in the slippery mud if he took it slowly. The gray pack horse was hesitant—it refused to budge until

Glamhandro nipped it sharply—but it kept its feet as both horses finally eased into the river behind him.

The water was bitterly cold, and Kenhodan's teeth chattered the moment his toes touched it. Snowborn! He shuddered. The river deserved its name! He struck out, side-stroking along the stream side of the horses, pacing them to prevent them from straying out into the current.

Glamhandro needed no encouragement. His neck cut the water like a ship's prow, and the pack horse kept up with him, though it clearly had less liking for the challenge than he. The gelding rolled its eyes and swam with a painful, lunging motion, but the stallion's eyes were bright as he fought the river. Personally, even though he had to admit Bahzell had been right about the current, Kenhodan could hardly fault the pack horse for its unhappiness.

By the time they reached the oak, only Glamhandro and the courser seemed in the least cheerful. Kenhodan himself was much the worse for wear, shivering uncontrollably, but Glamhandro appeared to have thrived on the trip. He and the courser touched noses cheerfully, apparently amused by everyone else's misery, but even Bahzell was less ebullient than usual, breathing hard as he leaned against the courser's side.

"Next time let's face the assassins," Kenhodan panted. "At least we'll die dry!"

He wiped his face and coughed. Half the Snowborn seemed to have found its way down his throat, but Bahzell found the breath for a fair imitation of his normal laugh as he wrung river water from his warrior's braid.

"At least we've thrown them off," Kenhodan went on, looking back over the flood with a sort of miserable complacency.

"Not if they know we came this way."

Kenhodan turned at the sound of Wencit's voice, only to find the wizard once more booted. As Kenhodan looked at him, the wizard settled back into his poncho, as well, and began making sharp prodding gestures.

"Come, come! Let's not stand around admiring our own cleverness! They can't be many hours behind."

"So? How'll they follow us past *that*?" Kenhodan waved at the river.

"The same way we did," Wencit said. "Or dry shod, if they want to leave the high road two miles back."

"*What*?" Kenhodan straightened in outrage. "You mean we could've avoided swimming that—that—!"

Words failed him.

"Aye." Bahzell had already squirmed back into his hauberk and buckled his breastplate. Now he nodded as he pulled his boots on. "That we could have, but the trail's after twisting like a broken-backed snake betwixt here and there. It's nigh on three times farther, and we'd've moved slower, too. We're after leaving them further behind by this, and it's possible they may miss us entirely, though I'd not bet on it."

"Well you might've told me!" Kenhodan retorted.

"No, lad, this time I couldn't be doing that," Bahzell disagreed solemnly as he watched Kenhodan stamp into his own boots and buckle his sword belt.

"And why not?" the redhaired man demanded.

"Because you're after being too smart and stubborn." Bahzell grinned. "You'd never have agreed to swim if you'd known as how you'd a choice!"

He and Wencit were still roaring with laughter as they squelched off down the sodden trail.

◆   ◆   ◆

Chernion reached the Bridge of Eloham at midday and drew up to regard the flood sourly. The water's fruitless assault on the bridge seemed to mirror the assassins' efforts to catch their prey, mocking them.

"Let's move on," their leader sighed finally, shifting in the saddle. The strain of so many mounted hours was beginning to tell even on Chernion.

They clattered onto the bridge, the horses rolling nervous eyes at the vibration in the stone. Storm wrack and flotsam left by the Snowborn's wrath covered the road in places, proving the torrent was less than it had been. The pavement was clouded with drifts of fine sand and pools of water, and the misting rain was so fine it scarcely dimpled the puddles.

Chernion neared the center of the bridge and suddenly stopped. One hand rose sharply in command, and the others halted instantly. Some seemed puzzled, but all had worked with Chernion before and waited patiently for the reason to unfold.

"What is it?" Rosper finally asked softly.

"We've lost them," Chernion replied calmly.

"Lost them? How? We found their last rest stop not a quarter-mile back! How can we lose them in the middle of a Sharnā-damned *bridge*?"

"Because they never crossed it, Rosper."

"How do you know?"

"Look for yourself, Brother. This entire span's covered with sand. Where are their hoof marks?"

"Wh—" Rosper leaned from the saddle and looked carefully. Smooth sand smiled blandly back at him. "Could rain have washed them away?"

"It's not heavy enough," Chernion replied.

"Agreed." Rosper nodded curtly. "But where have

they gone, then? There's no other road for them, Chernion."

"No?" Chernion eyed him thoughtfully. "I've said from the start that the Bloody Hand has some plan, and it seems I was correct. Consider: we've become so certain they're on the road before us that we almost failed to notice they'd left it. No, Rosper. There *is* another way."

"Very well, I agree. But where is it?"

"Let's see."

Chernion wheeled and rode back along the bridge, and dark-cloaked assassins crowded aside and then fell in behind. Chernion rejected the north side of the road—leaving in that direction would only have mired their targets in the mud of the Whitewater and pinned them between the two rivers. Bahzell would never be that generous, so he must have gone south along some unknown path the guildmaster didn't really care to follow.

They were well off the bridge when Chernion's dark eyes spied the marks of stockinged feet and hooves on the downslope of the causeway. They were faint in the thick, strong sod, but they were there, and they went straight into the river.

The assassin sighted thoughtfully along their course, and dark eyes lit on a huge oak that loomed like a giant among halflings. The bushy brows quirked. Sloppy of the Bloody Hand, the guildmaster mused.

"There. They swam to that tree for some reason. Send one of your men to confirm it."

"And if the Bloody Hand's waiting with a bow?" Rosper asked.

"No fear of that," Chernion said dryly. "The range is barely a hundred yards. If the Bloody Hand were there with a bow, we'd have bodies to prove it by now."

"He might wait until we're strung out crossing over."

"No. He knows I'll send a scout, and that without a satisfactory report, I won't follow. He's gone on."

"But why? Why leave the road here, this way, instead of a dozen miles back?"

"Because he knows a trail," Chernion said patiently, "and he doesn't care if we follow him, or he would've hidden these marks. I don't know where it leads, but there's no other crossing to the east bank of the Snowborn short of South Bridge. He's gone west into the Forest of Hev."

"So they're still bound for Sindor after all!"

"Of course. It was only a question of their route all along." Rosper flushed as Chernion forbore to recall their earlier discussion. "As I feared, he knows the land better than we do. I only regret letting him lead me so far from the straight way to Sindor, or I might have met him outside its gates."

"But we're here now," Rosper said diffidently. "What should we do?"

Chernion glanced at the craftmaster from the corner of one dark eye. Rosper was chastened, but was he chastened enough? On the other hand, Chernion had no wish to lead dog brothers personally after Bahzell—not in the woods, and not when he obviously knew precisely where he was going.

"Send to that tree to see if there is indeed a trail," Chernion said finally, and a volunteer plunged into the water, carrying one end of a coiled rope. If there was a trail, the rope would aid those who followed—and Chernion knew someone had to follow. There was no alternative.

The swimmer crawled ashore by the tree and clung

to the bank, gasping. After a moment he vanished into the dense undergrowth, only to emerge ten minutes later and wave his arms vigorously in the semaphore of the dog brothers.

"So." Chernion plucked a thoughtful lower lip. "They've taken a path we don't know, headed we don't know where, to take we don't know how long to reach Sindor. I'm afraid we have to split our forces, Rosper.

"You'll take seven brothers and follow them, marking if they turn aside. The four others and I will go to Losun, then south to Sindor. We can buy horses at each step, so we can leave you all of our extra mounts and still make good time. Meanwhile, you'll strike if the opportunity offers. But remember, Rosper: your main duty is to *follow*. Attack only if you can find a way to use your skills and deny them theirs.

"If we don't meet on the road, send word to the Windhawk in Sindor, but stay on their heels wherever they go. Don't let them vanish again. The Bloody Hand's cunning, and if he breaks clear, we may never find him again."

"Yes, Chernion!" Rosper slapped his chest in salute and grinned. "You won't wait long for us in Sindor. We'll bury them in the Forest of Hev."

"Be wary, Brother," Chernion responded coolly, saluting in reply.

"There are only three of them!"

"And only eight of you," Chernion replied. "Be wary, I said. The Bloody Hand is a champion of Tomanāk, and this isn't the first time, or even the second, the Guild's hunted him. We failed to take him before, and each attempt cost the Guild dearly. Never doubt that all he asks is to meet any three dog brothers sword-to-sword! You've served the Guild well, Rosper. It would grieve me if I had to spend precious time selecting a new southern master, so heed me!"

"Very well." Rosper nodded. "I'll be wary and cautious alike."

"Clean killing, then, Rosper."

"Clean killing, Chernion."

They exchanged salutes once more and went their different ways. Chernion and four others pelted across the bridge, using their mounts mercilessly in anticipation of obtaining new ones, while Rosper and his seven took up the sloppy, slippery, slithering pursuit among the trees of the Forest of Hev.

CHAPTER TEN

Unanswered Questions

"Is she awake?" Lentos asked, looking up from the paperwork on his desk as Trayn entered his austere office.

"No, but I think she will be soon. She's tougher than I expected."

"The young are always tough, Trayn—and don't forget her parentage. I'm less surprised she's recovering quickly than that she survived at all."

"Agreed. Agreed." Trayn flopped into a chair and sighed in exhaustion, rubbing his eyes with both hands. "What in Semkirk's name happened, Lentos?"

"I'd rather hoped you might tell me. You were closer to it than I was."

"Closer!" Trayn lowered his hands and looked across the desk at his superior. "I was bouncing off her shields, and you know it. No, Revered Chancellor. You were better placed to observe things than I was."

"Maybe so, but I don't have any idea what it was, either. One moment we were losing her; the next, something ripped her shields apart—without killing her—and knocked us on our highly trained arses. Got any guesses?"

"You don't suppose it was . . . ?" Trayn trailed off delicately.

"I don't know." Lentos toyed with his quill. "I wondered, of course, but it seems too pat, too neat. I was sure it was Wencit for a moment, but be reasonable. Even he can't do the impossible, and sorcery and the mage power can't be *mixed* that way. The gods know he's strong enough to *break* her barriers . . . but to not only avoid killing her himself but actually bring her out again after?"

Lentos shook his head.

"That's the problem, isn't it?" Trayn said slowly. "*Something* happened—something that *couldn't* happen—and given her relationship with Wencit, I don't think we can rule him out. But if he did it, something scares me even more than the fact that he could."

"I know," Lentos said softly. "If he did it, then he's lied to us, at least by implication, for fourteen hundred years."

◆   ◆   ◆

Kenhodan dismounted with a groan and swayed, massaging his posterior with both hands as abused muscles made their unhappiness known. Even Glamhandro seemed glad to stop, and both pack horses trailed with hanging heads. Only the courser seemed anything remotely like fresh, and Wencit's shoulders sagged as he sat in the saddle. For once, even Bahzell's exuberance was quenched, and the hradani spread his arms in an enormous muscle-popping stretch.

Damp trees surrounded them. The foliage was too

thick for the light rain to penetrate, but a wet mist dripped from the saturated upper branches. The trail snaked endlessly onward between dense trunks, narrow, slick, and muddy, but some winter storm had felled a forest giant to make the clearing where they'd finally halted at last.

"Well." Bahzell lowered his arms, put his hands on his hips, and rotated his upper body while Wencit climbed wearily down from his saddle. The courser lipped the wizard's silver hair affectionately, and Glamhandro sighed and blew in relief as Kenhodan removed his bridle and hung it on a branch.

"Well what?" Kenhodan asked after a moment of silence.

"Well," Bahzell sighed, standing on one foot and raising the other to peer down at the sole of his boot, "it's surprised I am I've not worn a hole clean through to the uppers! I'm ready to be stopping over for a while."

"That makes seven of us." Wencit flipped his poncho beneath him and eased down on the fallen tree's dripping coat of moss with a groan of profound relief of his own.

"Seven?" Bahzell repeated.

"Three two-footed travelers and four with four feet."

"I'd say those with four have worked harder," Kenhodan observed, stripping off Glamhandro's saddle and blanket. The stallion shook himself, then rolled in the clearing's wet moss and fallen leaves, and Kenhodan smiled as his legs waved ecstatically.

"True, but they'd had their vengeance." Wencit winced and eased his legs. "Old bones aren't all I have, and everything's gotten a lot older since Korun, somehow."

"Can we really afford to stop, Bahzell?" Kenhodan asked.

"It's a matter of must, lad. The pack horses are after needing the rest."

"All honor to them, but let's have a little sympathy for this party's senior rider, as well!" Wencit protested.

"It's after needing more than a little ride to be killing the likes of you!" Bahzell stripped the saddle from the nearest pack horse, set it aside, and began rubbing down the exhausted gelding. Wencit watched him for a moment, then dragged himself up, limped over to the courser, and began loosening his saddle girth.

"I know you great warriors would never want to weaken my character by showing me pity or suggesting in any way that I'm not as hardy and capable as either of you. Still, I hope you'll be able to see your way to assisting me in caring for this noble creature."

The courser snorted in obvious amusement and swatted the wizard gently with the side of his head.

"I'm not so sure of all that." Bahzell winked at Kenhodan. "I'm thinking as each rider should be caring for his own mount, even if some of 'em are after being a mite bigger than the others."

"Let me rephrase that," Wencit said pleasantly. "I *know* you'll help me look after him properly—and help with both pack horses—just as I know you won't find your breeches full of Saramanthan fire ants."

"Well, now! Put like that, it's after seeming reasonable enough!" Bahzell said hastily.

"While you two start on that, I'll find some dry firewood," Kenhodan offered with equal haste.

"The light's going fast," Wencit said, "so you'd best hurry."

"I imagine you won't have time to do more than groom the horses and throw up a lean-to before I get back," Kenhodan said, and slid into the concealing forest with a grin as the wizard shook a fist at him.

He carried a strung bow, not that he really hoped to chance across anything for the pot in such dim light. Nor did he, but he did find a dead stump, sodden and punky on the outside but dry and hard at its core, and he chopped away the outer husk and cut a plentiful supply of chips and slivers of dry heartwood to nurse wetter fuel alight. Then he bundled the tinder in the skirt of his poncho and moved noiselessly back towards the camp, pausing beside the fallen giant whose death had made their clearing to watch thoughtfully.

Wencit and Bahzell had finished with the courser and the pack horses and started on the lean-to, and he grinned. It wouldn't take them long to finish it, and there was no point distracting them from their work. He found a spot under the fallen trunk and stretched out on the relatively dry moss on his back, with his poncho load of tinder for a pillow, whetting Gwynna's dagger slowly and glancing out occasionally to see how they were coming along.

Bahzell dumped another load of boughs and helped Wencit spread them over the frame, weaving them together into a crude roof that wasn't completely watertight but was close enough to it to keep off the worst of the wet. The hradani glanced up and started to speak as Wencit's hands paused, then stopped as he recognized Wencit's distant expression. No one had *truly* seen Wencit of Rūm's eyes since long before the fall of Kontovar, but he appeared to be gazing off into depths only he could see. Then he began to smile.

"Wencit?"

"A moment, Bahzell." Wencit chuckled and his fingers curled strangely. They seemed to twirl briefly, and his eyes pulsed once. "There," he said with satisfaction. "Let's finish this up; Kenhodan will be back soon."

"And will he now? I'm thinking he's found a comfortable spot to watch us work from, and it's little I blame him."

"That's because you are a charitable soul, Bahzell, while I ... Well, let's just say I'm a little less generous than you."

Wencit's hands paused again and the wizard glanced over his shoulder at the precise moment Bahzell heard a yelp of outrage.

The hradani straightened with a jerk, turning toward the sound and reaching for his hook knife, only to pause in amazement as Kenhodan levitated over the fallen tree and dashed into the camp. Bahzell had never seen him move so quickly, nor had he ever heard sounds quite like those Kenhodan emitted as he ran. The hradani's eyes narrowed as the redhaired man yanked at his belt while he danced in place like a madman.

Bahzell glanced at Wencit as Kenhodan dropped his breeches to stamp on them with both booted feet. Wencit began to chuckle, and Bahzell grinned. Surely not. Even Wencit wouldn't *really*—!?

Kenhodan stopped yelling and stood in his drawers, glaring accusingly as the wizard mastered his chuckles. Wencit looked back imperturbably as the redhaired man picked up a crushed insect and thrust it under his nose.

"And what, do you suppose, might *this* be?" Kenhodan snarled.

"Why," Wencit said innocently, "it looks like a Saramanthan fire ant to me. Did you bring the firewood, Kenhodan?"

◆   ◆   ◆

Kenhodan mopped the last bite of savory stew from his bowl with a piece of bread. Bahzell was an astonishingly good cook, and Kenhodan felt almost human again as the stew warmed his belly. Of course, "almost human" wasn't quite the same thing as "comfortable," and he shifted and fingered the rudely stung portion of his anatomy. He wanted to be angry over it, but he couldn't. He'd deserved it, and the experience had been a sort of initiation. He could no longer doubt he truly was part of the wizard's inner circle, or Wencit would never have done it to him.

He stretched gratefully. Adventures weren't all they were reputed to be, but his present relaxation was all the sweeter because of the strenuous exertion which had preceded it.

"That was delicious, Bahzell," he said lazily, "but I'm a little uneasy about taking things so slow now."

"Never fear, lad. I'm thinking they couldn't've reached the bridge before midmorning, and they've no knowledge at all, at all, of the trail. They'll not be making up much on us through the trees, even if they're mad enough to press on all night." He shook his head. "We'll not see them before sometime tomorrow."

"Then at least we can have a night's rest," Kenhodan said.

He glanced up past the corner of the lean-to and fell silent. Their clearing ripped a hole in the canopy of leaves, and he could see the sky. The misty rain had paused, and as he watched the clouds parted to free the moon. He stared at it, and an inarticulate longing woke within him. It didn't clash with his languorous content; rather, it seemed a part of it, like a soft, sweet ache, and his hand reached for his harp case almost involuntarily.

"Lad," Bahzell rumbled, "I'm not so very sure that's after being wise. It's certain I am in my own mind we're well ahead of them, but—"

"Let him be, Bahzell," Wencit said softly.

The hradani's eyes narrowed, but Kenhodan never noticed. He opened the harp case, his gaze fixed on the moon, and there was a strange, answering glow in his green eyes. He felt himself drifting on the impossibly bright moonlight, and he sensed a distant thrill as something within him stirred.

He sat up, settling the harp on his knee, and his fingers curved to the strings. He touched them with his fingertips, and they seemed to quiver, begging him to give them voice. His brow furrowed dreamily at the thought, for he had no idea what he wanted to play. He had no ideas at all—he'd been emptied of thought by the silver light. Emptied so suddenly and gently he hadn't even noticed.

Yet if he had no idea what to play, he had no choice but to play it anyway. A compulsion was upon him as the wounding beauty of the cloudy moon possessed him, and his fingers struck the strings with a will of their own.

They wrought merciless magic in the night.

Music poured up from the harp, rich and vibrant, singing through the trees. The Forest of Hev hushed. Animals and birds froze in the darkness, as mesmerized as his companions by the loveliness flowing through the quiet, misty aisles of silver struck green and black.

Kenhodan knew no name for the music he made. It was sweeping. Powerful. Too beautiful to endure. He drifted on it, less important than the wind, but even through the wash of notes he saw the glitter of Wencit's eyes. The wizard's seamed fingers quivered as if they, too, longed to caress the strings, yet Wencit's face and body were rigid as the music surged like the sea.

Kenhodan never knew how long he played. He lived with and in the music, floating on it, reaching out through it, and wondering from whence it had come. It poured through him like the sea itself and spent itself in the heart of mystery, and he was one with it, caught up in something greater than himself, wondering where the music ended and he began—or if there was truly a division at all.

And then the harp notes changed abruptly. The melody's haunting beauty remained, yet it took on a darker, harsher, harder edge that hurled him down dizzy corridors of light and dark, flashing towards destruction even while he knew he sat under a dripping lean-to and stroked a harp. Images stabbed him—dreadful images, and he knew they were the half remembered nightmares which haunted his sleep. Cavalry thundered across waving grass, beating it flat, exploding into an army of horrors and soaking the earth with blood. He saw screaming men, dwarves, hradani and elves, hewing and hewn, dying in agony as steel ripped flesh. He saw the boil of sorcery, a red banner with a crowned, golden gryphon, and cities flaming as they were sacked. He saw temples blaze under lurid skies, altars defiled with butchered priests and ravished priestesses.

He saw the ruin and anguish of conquest, and the images filled him with a burning fury more terrifying than any battle madness. They twisted him on a rack of sorrow, and the music raced—furious and savage now, hurtling towards a conclusion far worse than simple death. He saw an island in the sleeping sea, its rugged coasts sheer, and a city of white walls and towers that gleamed under a weeping, blood-red moon. He floated above it, his brain afire with the surge of music, confused as glowworm lights crawled in the sky. They gathered, weaving together, growing stronger, burning like Vonderland's northern lights. He cringed before their power as they hummed and crackled in the night sky, and then they exploded. They streaked away like lightning bolts, and the harp music crested in a crescendo of anger and sorrow that hurled him from his dreams.

The song—if song it was—ended in a wild flurry of perfect notes, and Kenhodan sagged forward across his harp, drained and spent. He was torn by a terrible desolation, his heart ripped by grief and an inexplicable sense of crushing guilt, and tears streaked his face as he crouched over the harp like a wounded animal, gasping, and stared at the wizard.

"You *know*," he whispered. "You understand."

Wencit looked at him for an endless moment, and the night held its breath. The wizard's face was still, calm as iron, yet Kenhodan sensed the effort which kept it so.

"Yes," he said softly at last. "I know."

"But you can't tell me," Kenhodan said bitterly. He was riven by the music, reeling in that strange whirlwind of loss and confusion, yet even as he thought that he realized he'd gained something, as well. He was shaken and drained, but the fissures within him seemed less yawning, as if for the first time his soul was truly his. As if even in his amnesia he'd begun to find himself at last.

"No," Wencit said, and his voice was shadowed with warning. "I can tell you what that song was, if you wish. I can tell you that . . . but not why you played it."

Kenhodan tried to see the wizard clearly, but his vision had dimmed somehow. All he could make out was the glow of Wencit's eyes, blazing in the night, and he heard ghosts flutter in the old man's voice. Fear touched him—a sudden fear that tried to back away, retreat once more into the safety of not knowing—but the one thing, the *only* thing, he couldn't endure was more ignorance.

"Tell me," he croaked.

Wencit bent his head as if all the years of his weary existence pressed down upon him. But when he raised his face once more, it wore a hard-won serenity.

"What you have just played," he said with careful formality, "is an ancient lay. Men call it 'The Fall of Hacromanthi.'"

Kenhodan stared at him, his thoughts swirling. That name . . . That name meant something . . . He gripped the harp, his head throbbing as if to burst, and then he staggered to his feet as another presence filled him. He towered over the wizard, glaring down at him, and his face was twisted with grief and loss and a terrible, terrible torment.

"You didn't warn me, Wizard!" The words seared out of him, spoken by someone else in a voice of molten fury and endless grief. "You didn't warn me about *this!*"

And then he crashed down into a darkness without even dreams.

✦   ✦   ✦

There was no rain in Torfo and glimmering towers reared into a windy darkness that was unseasonably dry, their banners clapping like unseen hands. Starlight gleamed overhead, moonlight poured down from the heavens, and night ruled the land, but night often came unquiet to the fortress of the sorceress Wulfra.

This was such a night, for a golden-haired woman stirred in her darkened room and sat up, pressing her hands to her eyes. She sat that way for several seconds, then lowered her hands slowly, her fingers flickering in a strange gesture, and the chamber's scores of candles lit as one. Baroness Wulfra didn't even blink against the sudden light as she stared into the distance of her thoughts, and her head swung as if in search, though her eyes were closed.

She rose, her body turning, and her lips tightened as she sought to isolate whatever had disturbed her slumber. Her turning slowed and she came to rest facing north. Her hands clenched slowly at her sides, and a bleak expression crossed her stern, willful features.

She shrugged into a blue robe, blonde hair cascading over its silk, and her snapped fingers summoned a silver-blue radiance that rode her shoulder like some exotic pet as she stepped quickly out the door. Its dim glow lit a dark landing as bare feet carried her to a handle-less slab of ebony, and her eyes blanked as she spoke a word and traced a symbol. Her globe of light flared, the door sighed open, and she passed through it like a barefoot ghost.

The room beyond filled half the top of the keep.

Racked scrolls and books covered three walls, and work tables bore half-unrolled scrolls or sheaves of notes in her strong, graceful hand. One corner held an alchemist's workshop of beakers and bottled fluids, and a large pentagram—traced in silver and umber powder—filled the center of the floor. Each angle held a man-high candle of blue-black wax thicker than her own thigh and somehow subtly deformed. A desk stood under a window slit, covered in something too pale for leather and worked with strange symbols in blood-rust red. A wide-bladed knife lay on a golden salver, its blade mottled with dried stains that whispered of horror, and an ebony tripod in the center of the desk held a single crystal, large as a man's head and clear as quartz, but rough shaped and unpolished.

Wulfra sank into a chair and considered possibilities. Her options ranged from the distasteful to the dangerous, and her brain ticked them off one by one as she sought to avoid the worst of them.

But there was no escape, and finally she drew a deep breath and stood, pressing her hands to the slick crystal. Her brows drew together as she spoke another word, and the chamber became very still. An indefinable chill blew past her, but she ignored it.

Lights swirled within the crystal like doomed fireflies. They hovered, then burst apart, speeding away from one another in streamers of flame. They shattered on the boundaries of the stone, spangling the room with brilliance that burst and died, and she peered past the brightness into the gramerhain as tiny scenes flickered by. They moved almost too quickly to be grasped, but Wulfra was well used to scrying and she sought a single target, clinging stubbornly to her purpose as scene after scene dissolved in flickering sprays of light.

The light froze suddenly, and Wulfra gazed at tiny images of men and horses amid dripping trees. The men spoke soundlessly in the stony depths, and water dripped into their fire in puffs of steam. The horses' heads hung miserably, and the men wore black leather, but there were only eight of them.

Wulfra's lips tightened as she studied their faces intently. She identified Rosper, but there was no sign of Chernion. Had disaster overtaken the hunters? Or had they split into groups for some reason?

She frowned and muttered Chernion's name to key the pattern she'd set upon the assassin weeks before. This time the play of light was briefer as the crystal arrowed down the link, and Wulfra smiled as images formed once more. Would Chernion guess? Not that it mattered; the link could kill, as well as spy.

The image steadied above an inn on an imperial high road. Five weary horses stood in its stable, and Wulfra smiled again as her viewpoint dodged into a darkened room. Chernion slept lightly, bushy brows frowning. So her hired killers had simply split to cover more than one trail. Good. Very good.

Chernion stirred uneasily, and Wulfra snapped the link and sat caressing the pale human skin covering her desk while she thought. She longed to scry for Wencit, but that would be both futile and dangerous. The wild wizard was on guard; hammering against his glamour would avail her little and might tell him entirely too much about her own thoughts. Besides, she'd been badly shaken when Wencit wrested the madwind from Thardon and turned it against him;

she had no desire to experience the same thing with a spell linked to her own mind!

She shook her head. She'd learned all she could on her own, but it was too little to discover what had awakened her, and she'd run out of excuses.

Yet it was dangerous to contact her ally. Each effort left her drained, and the time approached when she couldn't afford that weakness. Worse than the drain, though, was the fear she couldn't master, however hard she sought to hide it. She hated admitting that even to herself, yet there was no point pretending otherwise, and she shook herself, banishing her fear-spawned rationalizations by sheer force of will. She was no Harlich to be ruled by temerity!

She touched the chill, lumpy stone once more and closed her eyes while her lips formed the soundless words of an intricate incantation. Power welled, encasing her in a nimbus that burned ever brighter while the silent words sang in her brain. The nimbus gathered and flashed down her arms to her hands, and her long, gem-encrusted fingers vanished in a burst of bitter brilliance like the heart of the sun. It flashed from her windows, and those who saw it guessed their sorcerous mistress practiced her art once more and trembled.

Savage light engulfed the stone for long seconds before the clear depths drank the energy, sucking twin balls of flame into their glassy heart. A flurry of sparks spiraled to the bottom, and two eyes formed—yellow eyes, pupilled like a cat's. They vanished briefly to the blink of unseen lids, then burned anew.

"Yes, Wulfra?" The cold words echoed in her brain like icicles.

"Something's happened." She held her thought level despite the sweat on her brow, yet his power beat at her from the stone, frightening her.

"What?" His question was like northern sea ice.

"I can't be certain. Something woke me—a surge in the art. I don't know what it was, but my mind was attuned to Wencit when I woke. I fear...I fear he's discovered some new power."

"It's not possible for him to increase his power. He peaked long ago; now he declines. I haven't been powerful enough to challenge him in the past, but that will change soon. I've studied his strengths and weaknesses with care; whatever you detected, it wasn't more power awakening in his mind. He's too old for that."

"It must have been! I tell you, my mind sought him even in sleep!"

"Silence!" The voice burned in her mind, and she recoiled. "Must I teach you which of us is the master and which the student? Can't you even understand the implications of what occurred three days ago? The old fool spent himself like a drunkard to save Bahzell's half-breed bitch—it will be *days* before he dares to channel the wild magic again!"

The cat eyes impaled her lingeringly, and Wulfra's veins clogged with ice.

"You were wise to report. Don't waste that credit by reporting nonsense. It may have been his new companion, the one we haven't identified, but it was *not* Wencit."

"It must be as you say," Wulfra said tightly, "but—"

"Enough." The cold voice became calmer. "Perhaps I seemed hasty to you, but I've given Wencit a great deal of thought. Let's turn to another matter. You didn't tell me you'd employed assassins, Wulfra."

"I didn't think it was necessary."

"It would only matter if this time they might succeed." Now the voice was amused. "They won't; any more than they've ever succeeded against Bahzell or Wencit. Still, I had to learn that for myself, and I doubt you'll prove any more costly to the dog brothers than I. And they may keep him off balance if he believes they're the best you can send against him. Don't let me stand in the path of your initiative, my dear."

Wulfra stared into his yellow eyes, well aware of the amused malice in his agreement. Then she flinched as his thoughts came again.

"Very well. Do you have anything further to report?"

"Not at this time," she replied, hiding a nervous qualm as best she could.

"Good. Guard the sword well, Wulfra! It wouldn't be disastrous if he regained it, but it *would* be . . . unfortunate. No one will ever wield its full power again, but it could inconvenience me even as a weapon. See that he doesn't gain it. Farewell."

The eyes spun into one another, coalescing into a brilliant pinprick that lingered for an instant and then blinked suddenly out of existence.

Wulfra leaned forward, arms braced against the desktop in exhaustion. Her hair was heavy with sweat, and her face glistened, but at least he'd been in a fairly good mood. The opposite was too often true when she disturbed him.

She shook herself back under control, slowing her heart and drawing a deep breath. When one reached for power, one must deal with daunting allies, she told herself. She must remember that she was using the cat-eyed wizard as surely as he used her—and it was she who had a foothold on this continent, not he.

She straightened and walked to the door, pausing to glance back at the reassuring array of equipment and the scrolls of painfully amassed knowledge. Somehow the reassurance was less tonight than usual.

She waved out the lights and the massive door closed silently behind her. She stood on the darkened landing, staring into blackness, wrapped in an inner quandary. Did the cat-eyed wizard truly believe that what she'd felt was unimportant? Or—she shivered— was he so confident only because it wasn't he who must face Wencit's wrath?

The rest of her night, she knew, would not be restful.

CHAPTER ELEVEN

Strategies and Ambushes

Rosper of the assassins cursed imaginatively as night settled once again on the dripping forest. He cursed the rain, the mud, the fog, the darkness, the trees, and—last and most comprehensively of all—Bahzell Bloody Hand. Rosper was a skilled tracker, but it scarcely mattered, for Bahzell was making no effort to hide his passage. He seemed prepared to rely solely on speed, and his pace shamed the assassins' best efforts. It was unbelievable that their prey could be so far ahead! Yet they were, and Rosper didn't plan to admit to Chernion that he'd been unable even to stay on Bahzell's heels.

His seven men sat their steaming horses silently while he vented his spleen. It was clear darkness demanded a halt, yet none of them cared to press the point. Instead, they contrived to find other places to cast their eyes.

"Get down!" he snarled finally, chopping with his arms. "Don't sit there like a pack of Sharnā-damned fools! We'll camp here."

"They can't be far ahead, Rosper," one of them ventured. "They only have four horses, and we have three apiece. We'll run them down soon."

"Idiot!" Rosper's voice was made savage by his own thoughts on that very subject. "The Bloody Hand's a hradani—a *Horse Stealer* hradani—and any hradani can run the sun right out of the sky. Worse, the wizard's riding a Sothōii courser, and Sharnā only knows what that cursed redhead is riding! They're not horses— they're devils, fit to leave any four of ours belly-up! Which is just what they're doing!"

"But—"

"Be silent! We'll rest until dawn, then follow those three from here to Bortalik Bay if we have to!" He surveyed his men grimly. "Pick your best horses tomorrow; from now on, we ride them till they drop."

He turned to glower down the dark and muddy trail, his heart pounding with rage at the chase his targets had led him. A few of his men exchanged mutters, but he chose not to hear. He didn't need them to tell him riding so hard would soon leave them afoot, but couldn't they see that if they failed to catch the targets soon they'd lose them entirely? This trail sped south more rapidly than Rosper had believed possible. If Bahzell stayed so far ahead of them, he might reach Sindor even before Chernion!

One or two exchanges were hard to ignore, but he kept his back turned doggedly. They'd ride better in the morning if he let them grumble now.

Rosper knew his impatience was a failing in an assassin, yet even Chernion admitted that it was what made him incomparable in pursuit. If he had to ride every horse to death, then so be it. And their riders, too, if he had to! He *would* overtake Bahzell, and a slow smile twisted his mouth as he touched his hilt and turned to his men, his anger blunted by anticipation.

"All right. Make camp and set a watch. And sharpen your swords."

He smiled grimly and stalked a short way down the trail, as if moving that small distance towards his prey relieved some of his tension. By dawn he'd be calm and cold, he told himself, ready to begin afresh. And when he caught the Bloody Hand, someone would pay for this wallowing journey.

Master of his trade though he was, Rosper had forgotten his promise to his guildmaster. He no longer tracked; he rode for the kill.

◆　　　◆　　　◆

Chernion's sleep was restless. Neither guilt nor compassion troubled the assassin's mind, for ambition and pragmatism were Chernion's constant companions... that and dread that someone might discover the secret.

The guildmaster woke once, with the uncomfortable feeling of being watched, but the room was empty and the assassin drifted back into sleep. Yet even in sleep, that restless mind turned to Rosper. Chernion was half convinced Rosper should have been sent on to Sindor while the guildmaster undertook his task. In fairness, Rosper was a marginally better tracker, but his hastiness had often made the Guild uneasy, and the thought of where that hastiness might lead on this mission made Chernion far more uneasy than usual.

It wasn't that the dog brothers would miss Rosper (though they would), nor even that Rosper had proven entirely reliable over Chernion's vexatious secret. No, the problem was that between them Chernion and he led half the strength of the Korun chapter, and whatever happened to Rosper would probably happen to those he commanded. If impatience mastered him, he and the hradani between them would leave a yawning hole in the Guild's strength, which was bad. But there was worse, for *no one* escaped the assassins.

Chernion knew that wasn't literally true—indeed, this wasn't the first time the Guild had stalked both Wencit and Bahzell, singly or together, and both of them were rather obviously still alive. But failures were few enough to make it *appear* true, and that was one secret of the Guild's success. Unfortunately, Chernion could hardly hide the loss of half the Korun chapter, if it came to that, and the loss of so many men would demand Guild vengeance ... even against Wencit of Rūm and Bahzell Bloody Hand. No, if Rosper died, the Guild—or the current Guild *Council*, at any rate—would feel forced to avenge him rather than simply quietly returning Wulfra of Torfo's down payment.

That was why Chernion had argued against ever accepting this commission. Unlike Rosper, the guild-master had studied the dog brothers' own history, including the record of its failures—and the cost of its attempts—against the two targets Wulfra had hired them to eliminate. It wasn't that Chernion *feared* the hradani or Wencit, champion of Tomanāk and wizard though they might be. It was simply that the guild-master recognized that there were targets ... and then again, there were *targets*, and a competent, pragmatic merchant of death did well to recognize the difference between them.

There were very few merchants of death more

pragmatic than Chernion of the Assassins Guild. Death was a commodity, one Chernion provided without hatred, heat, or passion to those who sought it. Some dog brothers—more than Chernion would have preferred, upon occasion—were drawn to the Guild by bloodlust, the opportunity to slake their thirst for killing and cruelty. The guildmaster recognized that, had learned to use those sorts of dog brothers for the tasks best suited to them, but that had never been Chernion's own way. Even those outside the Guild, who knew Chernion only as a name of terror, also knew that the guildmaster never threatened, never descended into *petty* cruelty, or employed torture. There was no need for the assassin named Chernion to do any of those things. Merciless death handed out for betrayal, yes; that was precisely the reason for Fradenhelm's fate in Korun. Yet over the years, more than a few, both inside and outside the Guild, had survived failing Chernion, for simple terror was a chancy tool. It might inspire obedience, yet men too consumed by fear were men who would forge ahead blindly—stupidly—rather than pause to *think*, and thought was what kept an assassin alive long enough to become master of the Guild.

Chernion understood that that was what made those who failed—and survived—so useful, as long, at least, as there was no fault, no blame for disobedience or willful, avoidable clumsiness. Rosper was prepared to argue even with the master of his Guild precisely because Chernion permitted it. *Encouraged* it, at least within reason, specifically so that other dog brothers might be willing to exercise their own intelligence and modify their instructions when the mission required it rather than obey the letter of their orders slavishly lest they be punished for failing to do so. But then, Chernion was atypical in many ways. The guildmaster was ruthlessly practical and as implacable as an East Walls winter, but never cruel for cruelty's sake, and even the Guild's most bitter foes recognized that Chernion was just as willing to take a target face-to-face as to strike down victims from the shadows. That was one of the things which made the guildmaster so effective, one of the reasons the Guild's ruling council normally sought—and took—Chernion's advice.

But this time the Council had acted *against* that advice, leaving Chernion no choice but to accept the commission which would have been so much better left alone. The guildmaster's distrust of wizards was well known, but emotion, the Council had ruled, must not be allowed to cloud clear judgment. As for the Guild's previous record against Wencit and the Bloody Hand, past failures didn't preclude future successes, and if the Guild succeeded against two targets such as they—or even against only one of them—the dog brothers' reputation would soar to new heights.

Besides, one or two of the Council's members had murmured to one another, if the whispers coming out of the Church of Sharnā were true, the long-delayed moment of decision between Dark and Light might be upon them sooner than any had expected, and the Guild could not afford a victory for the Light. The majority of the dog brothers might have little taste for the wanton cruelty of the Dark Gods, but they had no friends among the Gods of Light, either. In a world ruled by the Dark, there would always be employment for assassins; in one ruled by the Light, the Guild would be hunted, hounded, and probably doomed. Which meant the dog brothers had an interest of their own in killing Wencit of Rūm and Tomanāk's foremost champion, and it was unlikely the Guild would ever have another opportunity like this—ever have another ally like its present employer—if it let this one slip. And so the Council had ruled against its own guildmaster and accepted the commission.

But Chernion knew success was far from certain, and that thought—and the thought of the potential consequences of *not* succeeding—was disturbing to a prudent broker of mortality.

It was to be hoped Rosper appreciated the investment potential he represented.

◆　◆　◆

Far, far to the south, a lynx-eyed wizard contemplated his own plans and leaned back, sipping chilled wine, to reconsider his analysis. Failure was unacceptable; every judgment must be tested and retested.

The redhaired man, for instance. What was he? Certain points could be eliminated, for he was certainly no wizard! Training in the art left traces behind which literally could not be eradicated, however deeply someone might have tried to hide them. Even a working which hid them from the object of the spell himself couldn't hide those traces from anyone who knew what to look for, and the Council of Carnadosa most certainly did. The stranger's surface thoughts had been probed—fleetingly, to be sure; one was wise to expose one's interest in anything or anyone in Wencit's vicinity no more than absolutely necessary—and no whisper of sorcery had been found.

Yet there was *something* deep within him, something

that whispered of danger, and the amnesia was ominous; it prohibited deep probes, for who could read blank pages? But somewhere under that blankness was iron. The man held a ominous capability which simply couldn't be assessed, and that was ... bothersome.

The cat-eyed wizard drummed on a chair arm, wondering which fool had wiped the stranger's mind. Probably a lesser lord had stumbled upon a link to Wencit, acted in panic, and now dared not own the deed for fear of the Council's response to his bungling. It almost had to be a Carnadosan, assuming it was the result of the art. There was no way to be certain of that, and it was certainly possible the redhaired man had fallen afoul of one of the handful of gray wizards or warlocks of Norfressa rather than a Carnadosan. But that comforting possibility struck the cat-eyed wizard as unlikely, and he was profoundly leery of fortuitous coincidences where Wencit was concerned. One thing the Council did know, however, was that the one wizard in all the world who *couldn't* have done it was Wencit of Rūm.

The wild wizard had been monitored for over half a thousand years, ever since the Council of Carnadosa had rebuilt from the ruins of strafed and devastated Kontovar. For the last hundred years, since the cat-eyed wizard had assumed leadership of the Council, the old wild wizard had been monitored literally hour by hour. Oh, there'd been occasional instances when he'd slipped away, like that unfortunate affair with Tremala in the Empire of the Spear. One simply couldn't drive a scrying spell through Wencit's glamours on those occasions when he had cause to bring them to full strength, but those occasions had been few and far between, and in all the time he'd been watched, Wencit had been near no one who even resembled the young stranger. That really left only one of the Dark Lords, and the smallest threat might have led some of the less hardy among them to destroy a man's mind. Few realized it was wiser to leave such alone to see how Wencit would use them, for Wencit was a past master of every trick, a consummate practitioner of deep laid strategies and careful misdirection. He'd certainly demonstrated *that* clearly enough over the centuries. In fact...

The drumming ceased and the cat eyes narrowed. What if the stranger *had* no hidden significance? Suppose Wencit had simply recognized the obvious potential beneath his amnesia—amnesia which might, however unlikely it might appear on the surface, be entirely natural—and enlisted him as a useful man who could also act as a smokescreen?

The cat-eyed wizard examined the thought carefully, for Wencit was no fool. He couldn't know of the cat-eyed wizard's existence—too many precautions guarded against that!—but he knew the Council of Carnadosa survived, and he must also know it watched him like a hawk. That was the reason he'd so often resorted to the tricks of the stage conjurer, using misdirection to cloak his true intent. It was entirely possible that was what he was doing this time, as well—using this Kenhodan to divert attention from his true objective.

The notion was attractive, but it would be unwise to credit Wencit with *too* much duplicity. Better to conclude that the redhead wasn't a presently active threat except inasmuch as he was in Wencit's company. Mark him as an unknown and watch him. Eliminate him if the chance came, just to be safe, but nothing about him presently justified actions which might tell Wencit the cat-eyed wizard himself existed. Or, for that matter, the extent to which the wild wizard's normal glamours had been penetrated by the Council's most recent workings.

But if that dealt with Kenhodan, what else might Wencit be up to? The hradani could be dismissed; when the time came, Bahzell would die, even if the Dark Lords must feed a thousand warriors into his blade first. Champions of Tomanāk made deadly foes, yet there was a limit to how much of their deity's power they could channel, how close an embrace with the divine any mortal could sustain. In the end, against a foe prepared to spend however many lives it might require, even one of Tomanāk's Swords must fail at last. And just as Bahzell would die when the time came, the same for Leeana. She was a handsome wench, who might please a man for quite some time, but the war maids were...stubborn, and any woman who wed a hradani was beneath contempt. No, when the time came for Bahzell to die, his loving wife would die with him.

Actually, their daughter was far more interesting than they. The Dark Lords had never understood the mage power, for it was unknown in Kontovar and the Council had been able to study it only at second hand. Yet they'd learned it was incompatible with sorcery. Like oil and water, they couldn't be mixed—yet Wencit had done just that, or something like it. How? And why?

The why might be easier. Apparently the old man was actually fond of the little bitch. Well, bad cess to them both! The cat-eyed wizard had no use for bastard breeds. At best they were tools, and if Wencit thought otherwise, he was a fool.

But if affection explained why, "how" was more disturbing. Of course, Wencit was the last surviving wizard trained by the Council of Ottovar, which meant—by definition—he was also the best trained wizard alive. But that wasn't the answer. The cat-eyed wizard had sensed the strength the old man had expended, and the feel of it had been...different. On the other hand, there were no current wild wizards in Kontovar, and this might be simply another inexplicable manifestation of the wild magic. Perhaps the wild magic *could* mix oil and water, however briefly. Not that it seemed very useful. The effort had nearly killed him—*would* have killed him if he'd set his wards a shade less well. Not even he could defend himself from the edge of coma.

But the very depth of the danger he'd courted indicated how much he was prepared to risk for the brat. Indeed, it was of a piece with the threat he'd leveled against the Council seventy years ago when he'd returned Malahk Sahrdohr to it, stripped of his gift, with the promise to strafe Kontovar afresh, even at the cost of his own life, if the Dark Lords ever made another arcane attempt against Leeana Hanathafressa. That had shaken the Council—even the cat-eyed wizard, however little he cared to admit it—to the bone. Perhaps the promises he'd made, the dangers he'd courted, to keep Leeana and her daughter alive were simply the whims of an old, old man who must surely recognize that not even wild wizards lived forever. Perhaps his brain truly was softening, becoming a slave to his need for love in his dotage. But perhaps there were other reasons, as well. The unknown potentials of the mage power meant Gwynna must be approached carefully, but she must also be watched closely, if only for her potential as bait. Indeed, there were many reasons to remember young Gwynna. A young mage might be best for study, especially if she might also prove the long-sought chink in Wencit's armor. The cat-eyed wizard smiled. It might even prove a pleasant game on its own merits, if she grew into the beauty of her mother. . . .

He shook off his daydreams. He'd worn his list of enemies smooth with study, and always it came back to Wencit. He was the true enemy. He always had been, and it must be assumed he knew more than he showed.

Yet what *could* he know? He hadn't visited Kontovar since the Fall, and even the best scrying told little at such distances. He undoubtedly knew a great deal about the Council, but he couldn't have learned of the cat-eyed wizard's birth without tripping the Council's alarm spells. Besides, he'd made no effort to measure the cat-eyed wizard's strength, which proved his ignorance. Not even Wencit could be so confident as to feel no need even to *test* his decisive opponent-to-be!

That, after all, was the Council's current purpose: to test *Wencit*. The wild wizard was old. He might be the best trained wizard alive, but there was a limit to the wild magic he could still channel. It would be foolish to underestimate him, but equally so to *over*estimate him. When his power went, it would go quickly, and the Council must not frighten itself into timidity if the major threat had decayed into impotence.

It had taken years to convince the others to test Wencit, until he'd pointed out that they need not approach the old man directly. Once he'd discovered the sword's continued existence and where it lay hidden, the die had been cast and Wulfra had been recruited and groomed for her role.

If she slew Wencit with his and the Council's subtle backing, good. Of course, it was far more probable that she would die, but that was also acceptable, for when she clashed with Wencit, the cat-eyed wizard would watch. Even if she perished, her struggle would reveal Wencit's current capabilities—and though her death would be a minor inconvenience, there were other Norfressans with her aptitude for the art. Her position as a noble made her useful, but it could be lived without. Even the loss of the sword, while regrettable, would be an acceptable price for the information he stood to gain.

He nodded in satisfaction. His plan was sound, and decades of labor would pay off soon. Whatever the outcome, he would be better informed—and thus stronger—when the true game finally began.

He chuckled and set aside his wine glass to amble off to bed. They were all puppets—even Wencit—dancing to his bidding. It was especially amusing to watch the wild wizard, particularly since the prophecy proved the cat-eyed wizard's line couldn't fail of its final destiny. His house *would* triumph in the end, whatever else might happen. True, there was enough ambiguity that one could never be quite sure *when* they would triumph, so it was possible—however unlikely—that he himself would perish without seeing it happen. But he'd already provided his own heirs, just in case, and the possibility of failure was what made life challenging enough to be worth living.

The cat-eyed wizard slept soundly that night.

❖   ❖   ❖

Kenhodan watched red light filter through the upper branches of the Forest of Hev and pondered.

He knew no source for the music he'd played, nor did he understand his own words to Wencit. The riddle of what he was remained, yet his restless night had brought him an unexpected peace.

He yawned and stretched. Gods! He'd gotten some rest, but he felt as if someone had tried to remove the damp by hammering him out to dry. He poked up the fire and considered letting the others sleep, but Bahzell's instructions had been firm.

He watched the smoke rise, and his eyes strayed to his harp case. He wanted to touch it again, yet he dared not. And so turned his thoughts away from it, delving into the depths of his own mind, instead, reaching for the exalted terror the harping had brought, but it wasn't there. His eyebrows rose in surprise at its absence and he turned his thoughts still further inward...only to stiffen as they stopped with an almost physical shock.

He rose to his full height, eyes wide with astonishment. There was a barrier in his mind! It hadn't been there last night...or had it? He blinked, testing his memory, laying mental hands on every event since Belhadan, and all of them were there, open to his touch. He'd lost nothing of the new, yet that featureless wall seemed to seal off some inner core, and that was all the more unsettling because, as far as he knew, there was nothing inside that barrier.

He squatted again, adjusting the kettle. The music. It had to have been the music. Wherever it had come from, it had done...something deep within him. Was that why Wencit had told Bahzell to let him play? Had the wizard *known* this would happen?

That was a disquieting thought, yet the more Kenhodan pondered it, the more convinced he became that Wencit must have known. So it followed that the wizard had wanted it to happen...whatever "it" was.

He considered himself carefully in the dawn and found, rather to his surprise, that much of his gnawing uncertainty had vanished. That strange internal wall was the first change since he'd realized he had no memory, and it lent him a sort of strength, like tangible proof that there truly was *something* at the very heart of him, for if there was something more than emptiness within him, someday he might truly regain his past. He cherished that thought for a long moment, then snorted in amusement as he realized he felt relieved—almost buoyant—to find part of his mind locked against his own entry. It should have frightened him, but even an enigma, it seemed, was better than mere emptiness.

He shook himself, somehow certain this was something he shouldn't discuss even with Wencit. Partly because he was confident Wencit wouldn't have explained it to him even if he'd asked. Whatever made it necessary to conceal his own past from him was unlikely to have simply disappeared overnight. No, he had no choice but to continue as he'd begun until the wizard gave him a positive sign. It might be frustrating, but he'd acquired a certain familiarity with frustration. A little more wouldn't kill him.

He snorted again, then nodded to himself and shook Bahzell's shoulder gently.

The hradani's snores broke instantly and one eye opened.

"No rain today," Kenhodan told him.

"Aye, I'd expected as much." Bahzell stretched. "I

was after smelling a dry dawn last night, and I'm thinking it owes as much to Tomanāk as to Chemalka, lad."

"And why might that be?" Kenhodan asked suspiciously.

"Why, only that it never rains on the days I fight." Wencit stirred behind them and Bahzell glanced at him. "Except, of course," he added hastily "for those times as I've been harnessed up with armies or wizards."

Wencit was still again, and Bahzell glowered. Was the wizard really awake or not?

"So you expect a fight today? You think they're still with us?"

"Some of them, any rate. I'm thinking they'll have marked our trail well enough, and they'll have guessed where it is we're going, but they've no notion how this trail's after getting there. They'll not want to give me long unseen, for they'll know as how they'll not find us again if ever once they're after losing us. It's been two days, lad, but there's some at least as are back there in the mud trying to keep hard on our heels."

"Then wake Wencit and let's be off!"

"Before *breakfast*? Lad, lad! Let's not be panicking over a few assassins! We're well ahead, unless they've gone and sprouted wings. I'm thinking we'll take it slow and easy to the stream; then they've leave to be catching up with us and welcome. Not that what if they've the sense of the Purple Lords, they'll not do it. Still and all, we can always hope, and in the meantime, it's making and eating a good breakfast I'll be, thank you, while you're after feeding the horses."

❖   ❖   ❖

Rosper greeted the same dawn. In fact, he'd awaited it impatiently, begrudging every second. His irritated pacing had filled the night, and when the sun finally rose, he greeted it with a killing grin.

He used his toe liberally as he roused his men. They rolled out slowly, but whiplash orders soon had them moving briskly, if not precisely with joy. They watched him covertly over their hasty meal, but he hardly noticed. Instead, he ate nothing, pacing in a fervor of eagerness, and one or two men exchanged unhappy looks. Assassins killed coldly; the fire in Rosper's eye struck them as a doubtful augury of success.

Yet no one cared to argue with him in this mood. He drove them to mount, and each dog brother chose his toughest horse—horses refreshed by their night of rest and unaware of the cruel usage awaiting them.

Rosper mounted in turn and rose in the stirrups. He surveyed his men once more, then swung his arm, launching them against their prey, and the eight men pressed down the trail in a spatter of mud.

They would meet today. Rosper felt it—almost tasted it. Whether by stealth or frontal attack, he would mark them down today. Sunlight pricked through the trees, brilliant rays of light turning mist into pooled gold under the branch canopy's darkness, but he paid scant heed to their beauty, except to lean from the saddle to search for signs of his quarry's passage.

◆　◆　◆

Chernion breakfasted in a sunny parlor while the others saddled fresh mounts. Then the guildmaster paid for their lodging and horses and the five of them vanished down the high road.

Chernion had accepted, during the night, that sending Rosper had been a mistake, but tears mended no fences, and whether Rosper succeeded or died was in his own hands. All Chernion could do was reach Sindor quickly. If Rosper rode in on Bahzell's heels, so much the better; if he was dead, Chernion would need as much time as possible to prepare.

The assassin's horse sensed his rider's impatience. Although Chernion used neither spur nor whip, the gelding pricked to ever greater speed along the arrow-straight road. The guildmaster's men glanced at one another, then set spurs to their own mounts as the quintet pounded south.

✦　✦　✦

Baroness Wulfra faced the day with renewed confidence, her night fears soothed by enthusiasm and new plans. Worry still hovered under the surface of her thoughts, but now it urged action, not fear.

Her defenses must be strengthened. Doubling the physical patrols was no problem, but arcane measures required more thought. Still, she knew she could strengthen the trap and alarm spells in her fortress. It would cost the lives of a few more special prisoners, but that was what they were for, after all.

But first, breakfast. An empty stomach was a poor beginning to a day of sorcery. Not that Wulfra ever wanted for energy or appetite—or *appetites*, for that matter. She allowed herself a small smile as she summoned her maid, for there were certain perquisites for one who was both noblewoman and sorceress. Like that new guardsman. She was certain he'd enjoy his new duties as he helped her begin the day properly.

Her small smile grew. She'd lived a sorceress and a baroness; she would die that way, if die she must, but for today life was good.

✦　✦　✦

The sun shone bravely in Belhadan. Despite that, the spring shadows remained cool, but the red-haired little girl seemed unaware of the chill. She sat motionless in the shade of the Belhadan Mage Academy's wall, studying a bed of flowers as if their fragile blooms were the most precious things in the universe, and Trayn Aldarfro leaned against the frame of Lentos' window and watched her. He'd watched her almost as long as *she'd* watched the flowers, for she posed questions he couldn't answer. Questions no one in the Academy could answer, and that was both unacceptable and dangerous.

He sighed.

"Problems, Trayn?"

Lentos had entered the office behind him, and Trayn turned.

"Only one, Lentos. Only one."

"Gwynna?" Lentos sat calmly as he asked the question. His expression was serene, but Trayn had no need of his Talent to sense the other mage's disquiet.

"Of course! Lentos, whatever's happening is even stranger than we'd thought."

Trayn awaited the chancellor's response curiously, for his discoveries had stunned him, and he felt a perverse sort of anticipation as he prepared to shatter Lentos' famed, monumental calm.

"There are no strange talents; only unusual ones," Lentos said.

"You don't need to quote the coda to me, Lentos. Perhaps I should say the *situation* is stranger than we'd thought. Although I also think 'unusual' is far too weak an adjective to describe what's going on inside Gwynna's head."

"I see you're bursting with new observations." Lentos leaned back and raised his feet, propping his heels on his desk. "I suppose you'd better tell me, but if you disturb my dreams again tonight you'll regret it, my friend."

"Ha!" Trayn looked back at Gwynna. "All right, let's take it in order.

"First, she should have died in crisis. Something broke her barriers at the last moment, but she was so far gone that just breaking them wasn't enough. Whoever got in had to give her a reason to live, which is a job for a trained empath. But the only trained empath available—me—couldn't do it.

"So far, the only answer I can see is Wencit. I don't know how, but I do know none of *us* could've done it. I'm not the best mage who ever lived, but I'm not exactly the worst, either. I know my job, and saving Gwynna was impossible using mage talent. Ergo, whoever did it didn't *use* mage talent, which leaves only magic, and we *know* wand wizardry and the talent can't meld. We *thought* we knew the wild magic couldn't, either, but since we have proof wand wizardry can't, this had to be done with wild wizardry. And the only living wild wizard just happens to be her second father. However you slice it, it had to be Wencit."

Trayn leaned back expectantly, but Lentos merely nodded and waved for his junior to continue.

"Well," Trayn was a little nettled by Lentos' composure, "let's take it as a given Wencit saved her, then. Forget that he's lied to us by telling us wild magic can't do such a thing and look at Gwynna herself.

"She should have slept for at least three days after

so severe a crisis; she slept less than eighteen hours. She should've awakened disoriented; she was quiet, but she knew exactly where she was and why. New magi can neither shield nor avoid broadcasting before they're trained; she hasn't broadcast a single peep, and I *still* can't get past her outer shields. She either can't—or won't—let me in. She just sits and stares at those flowers without showing any more curiosity about her talents than a rock!" Trayn's voice had risen, and he almost glared at Lentos as he finished. "And if *that* doesn't qualify as strange, then what the bloody hell *does?*" he demanded.

Lentos was silent for several seconds, and when he spoke again, his words took Trayn by surprise.

"Did you know the elders raised the barriers this morning?"

"What?" Trayn blinked. "No. But what about it? Aren't we about due for a drill?"

"Just about." Lentos nodded. "You know the barriers around the academies and imperial fortresses are maintained against the possibility of Kontovar developing mage talents of its own. Of course, we've carried out our drills for nine centuries without any indication that there *are* any magi in Kontovar, but you know that, too."

"So?" Trayn was baffled by the turn of the conversation.

"What you may not know, since we very carefully never discuss it, is that the barriers are also impervious to all known scrying spells."

"What?" Trayn straightened. "Lentos, I'm as upset by Wencit's . . . *duplicity*, I suppose, as you are, but that's no cause to block him out! If," he added thoughtfully, "you really can, assuming he can tamper with mage talent at all."

"You miss my point. We're not blocking *him*; we're blocking all *other* wizards. Specifically, the Council of Carnadosa."

"Why? I don't like being spied on either, but you can't maintain the barriers forever without draining the Academy."

"True. But sit down, Trayn. There are things I have to tell you, and I want your word that you'll seal them."

Trayn settled into one of the office's straight-backed chairs automatically, staring at the Belhadan Academy's chancellor in shock. "Seal" had only one meaning for a mage: mind-blocked. Lentos wanted him to block the part of his mind dealing with whatever he was about to hear, which would bar him from sharing it with anyone but an elder of the academies. He could never let it slip voluntarily, and if it was forced from him under duress, the first syllable would kill him instantly and painlessly. Only the most potent secrets were sealed, and Trayn wanted no more suicide triggers in his brain than he could help. But Lentos hadn't been made chancellor of the Belhadan Academy on a whim. If he requested it, he had a reason, and after a brief hesitation, the master empath nodded slowly.

"Thank you." Lentos smiled warmly at the proof of his trust, then went on. "First, the elders and I have reviewed the records carefully in the last two days. It seems Wencit never actually said he couldn't do what your admirable logic proves he did for Gwynna."

"But it's in every training text! Every mage knows it's impossible!"

"True, but he never said that. He simply never corrected us when we misunderstood him. That's why I advanced the barrier drill so we could discuss this privately.

"We see only two possibilities. Either he didn't know he could do it, or else he *did* know and wanted to hide the possibility. We don't believe he could've been ignorant, so we conclude that he chose to hide his ability to touch the mage talent directly.

"Obviously, the next question was why. Not knowing hasn't cost us anything, but it's kept him from getting all the help from us he might have. We see no reason he would've needed to hide that from *us*, so we think he was hiding it from someone else—someone with ears so sharp that he could hide it only by telling *no one*, including us."

"Wizards," Trayn said, and nodded. "I follow your logic, but would it really have mattered if the Carnadosans had known?"

"It might have," Lentos said. "Because of Gwynna."

"Gwynna?" Trayn shook his head. "Why Gwynna?"

"Really, Trayn! What did you just call him? Her 'second father'? She has the mage talent; magi experience crises when their powers wake; and Wencit loves her. If hers was a severe crisis—which everyone knew it would be—would *you* expect him simply to let her die? Of course not! And the Carnadosans are no less perceptive than we are. They'd've watched her like a hawk, and when her convulsions started, they'd've been waiting. I imagine he protected himself well, but would it have been enough *if they'd known ahead of time?*"

"So he hid it to keep them from knowing? That's the mystery?"

"That's why he hid it, but it definitely isn't the whole mystery."

"I guess not," Trayn said slowly. "They must know now that he can do it, so there's no point pretending he can't. But you raised the barriers, so you think something about it is still worth hiding. I can get that far; I just don't see what it could be."

"Of course you don't. You're a technician, a teacher. That's all you've really wanted to be from the day Mistress Zarantha first started your training. You don't deal with the Council or politics, so you're not devious. But you have to *become* devious, Trayn, because unless I miss my guess, you're about to find yourself involved with Gwynna and Wencit right up to your neck."

"Eh? I'm afraid you'll have to spell that out," Trayn said in a surprised tone.

"Certainly. If we're right, he showed excellent foresight by hiding his ability so as to avoid the Carnadosans' attack, didn't he?"

"Well, of course he did—"

"Foresight so good," Lentos interrupted, "that he began exercising it nine hundred years ago when he told the first academy no '*sorcerer*' could touch the mage talent."

"But that would mean—" Trayn paused as confusion became consternation. "That's ridiculous! Wizards can't pre-cog, Lentos, and not even a mage could pre-cog that far ahead! Or are you saying he fooled us about *that*, too?"

"What I'm saying is even more disturbing. He never outright lied about his ability to touch the mage talent, but he *did* say—and I quote from the records—'not even a wild wizard has the power of precognition.' Pre-cog and prophecy aren't the same thing, of course, and several wizards have produced the latter, but the ability to see future events is quite different from the ambiguities of prophecy.

"Yet Wencit clearly spent centuries preparing for exactly what happened three days ago, which requires something very like pre-cog. He had specific information, and what does that indicate, Trayn?"

Trayn struggled with new data and confusion, and when he spoke his voice was hesitant.

"He knew about Gwynna, but wizards can't pre-cog. He took steps to protect them both long before she was born, which implies he started taking those steps long before he knew love alone might compel him to run such a risk, so he must've had another motive, as well. But that means..."

"I have hopes for you, Trayn," Lentos said softly as the younger mage's voice trailed off. "It means he's moved even more carefully than we thought. He has a plan based on knowledge to which we aren't—and probably can't be—privy. It means he's spent *at least* a thousand years waiting for something which is happening right now, and that your pupil is somehow critical to the success of whatever he plans."

◆　　◆　　◆

Gwynna glanced up, but Master Trayn was no longer in the window, and she looked away, wondering if he and she could work together as they must. It would be hard for both of them, she knew, just as she knew she dared not reveal what she'd learned from Wencit in that searing moment of fusion.

She looked back at the flowers. She couldn't understand all she'd seen, but she knew she'd seen too much. She was simply too young to understand what it all meant.

Many things about what was happening worried her. She couldn't understand how she'd held Master Trayn out of her mind, but she knew *why* she'd done it. Before he could help her learn, she had to convince him certain knowledge couldn't be shared. But how had she stopped him? All she'd done was push at him with her thoughts, and she shouldn't be able to keep a master mage out that way. The one thing she did know was that Wencit hadn't shown her how to do it. He was no mage, and he hadn't taught her to be one, either.

Yet the ability came from somewhere. And how did the gryphon fit in? For that matter, how did she know the magnificent creature of her vision *was* a gryphon? And where did the harp music come from? It was the most beautiful thing she'd ever heard, but it frightened her to know she'd never really *heard* it at all. And whose were the yellow, catlike eyes? They weren't like Blanchrach's, for they were cold and dead. And what was the huge crown? Whose was the big silver horse? What was the recurring image of the sword with the broken hilt? Why did she feel so frightened whenever she thought of her father?

She didn't think Wencit knew all she'd seen, which only made her problem worse. And whatever he'd shown her, it wasn't enough. There was too much in her mind, now. Too many new abilities, too much knowledge she hadn't found yet, hadn't laid mental hands upon. She needed to master those abilities, to discover the secrets hidden in that knowledge, and understand what it meant, why all of it had poured into her and what she was supposed to *do* with it all. And somehow, for any of that to happen, she had to get Master Trayn to help her without showing him what she knew.

The little girl with bottomless blue eyes and a heart of harp music watched the flowers and longed to tell someone all she knew or suspected. But she couldn't. They probably wouldn't believe her even if she did—she wasn't certain she believed it all herself—yet she knew she couldn't tell anyone.

She'd never before been aware of how young she truly was. There was too much she'd never been told, too much she'd taken for granted. The mage crisis was enough to destroy any childhood, but hers had been further ravished by a brief, magnificently terrible melding with a personality thousands of years old. Now she saw herself through two sets of eyes, two minds. One was young, confused, and terrified; the other was ancient, recognizing her youth with a sort of tender, implacable compassion.

Her inexperience could be deadly, and to far more than just her. She knew she'd seen into Wencit's deepest plans . . . and that he'd never meant for it to happen. If she made a single mistake, she might destroy everything he'd ever tried to do, and she lacked the training to know what *not* to do.

She only knew it scared her. It scared her very, very badly.

◆   ◆   ◆

Bahzell jogged through the late morning, setting an easy pace compared to the last three days. Kenhodan was grateful, and though he was concerned lest they be overtaken short of Bahzell's goal, he felt surprisingly at ease.

Before last night, he'd accepted the plan to ambush the assassins largely as a "safe" outlet for the rage within him, and that had changed somehow. He still felt that rage, but something inside his mind's new walls had transformed his perspective. His fury was no longer a threat; he controlled it, as if it were on a short, heavy chain he could slip at will. He found himself regarding it, almost with detachment, as a part of himself...a useful part which *ought* to have frightened him, but no longer did.

Yet the idea of an ambush bothered him even less now than it had when his rage had craved an acceptable outlet. It was the right decision, for one killed assassins any way one could. That proposition was now self-evident, accepted almost dispassionately—without arrogance or self-righteousness, but with something much more like...self-recognition.

And with it came a weariness, as if some of Wencit's ancientness had crept into his bones. Did old trees feel this way? Full of vigor and sap as they faced a storm, yet simultaneously older than the hills? As if they'd always been here and would be here forever?

Or was he a river rock? A stone polished and worn until it had no hard edges, only roundnesses and a core of permanence? He didn't know the answers to those questions, but a sense of balance, of adjustment, gave him a peace he hadn't known since Belhadan, one all the stranger for the feeling of unending strife beneath it, like a volcano mantled in ice and snow.

The noon halt startled him, for he'd ridden lost in thought. Now he shook himself mentally and dismounted to stretch.

"How much farther, Bahzell?" he asked.

"Another hour. I'm thinking we'll reach the stream in no more than half that; it's climbing the far side will eat up the rest of the time."

"And the assassins?" Wencit asked.

"Now that's after being harder to say." Bahzell shrugged. "It's an easy pace I've set them today, and it's surprised I'll be if they haven't closed on us all the while. It's five hours back they might be, or maybe as little as two. Not less than that though, I'm thinking."

"I'd just as soon get it over." Kenhodan sighed, gnawing at a slab of jerky.

"Aye, I'll not disagree with you there, lad. There's after being too many of Sharnā's scum in the world. Best we be showing some of them the way out of it."

"Scum they may be," Wencit said testily, "but they're also skilled fighters. I'd suggest neither of you forget that!"

"Skilled they may be," Bahzell said sternly, "but don't be naming them 'fighters' to me. Any son of Sharnā's after being a disgrace to my blade—though it's happy I'll be to introduce him to it!"

"Just so they don't get steel into you first, Mountain."

"That they won't."

"I suggest you make certain of that, because it won't be *clean* steel."

"Poison?" Kenhodan's skin crawled at the thought.

"Aye," Bahzell said. "To a dog brother's thinking, dead is dead, and killing's naught but a matter of kormaks. And old graybeard's after being right to be wary. But then, I always am." The hradani stood once more, resettling his pack on his shoulders. "And I still say they're no fighting men!"

Kenhodan mounted and followed Bahzell down a

changing trail. The forest giants moved well back, and lower, scrubbier trees filled the gaps between them. Willow and alder became more frequent, and Kenhodan frowned as they reminded him of rivers. He was finally dry, and he'd prefer to remain that way for a day or so.

Unfortunately, the world didn't much seem to care about what he'd prefer.

He heard the threatening rumble of water long before the trail led them to the deep gash of the stream. It started low, that rumble, but it grew steadily louder as they approached, and he wondered what it sounded like later in the spring, when the stream which spawned it was in full spate.

When he finally saw it, he could only shake his head. It was worse than he'd feared.

The brawling stream ran in a wide, unpleasant ravine. The water didn't look deep, but it flowed with appalling speed over tumbled boulders, and white foam and spray made rainbows over the steep shelves of cascading rapids. A necklace of driftwood near the top of the ravine showed it was sometimes a *little* deeper—by some thirty or forty feet, he thought wryly.

The footing in the ravine was bad. The ground sloped, but not enough for good drainage, and the soft ground sucked at the horses' hooves as they picked their way across. There were firm spots, but no trail, and even with Bahzell probing carefully ahead for a path, one packhorse slithered to its knees at one point and had to be rescued.

Once across the morass, they faced the stream itself. It never washed higher than Kenhodan's stirrups, but the current was bad and the footing worse. Bahzell stayed on the upstream side, guiding the packhorses carefully, but they literally had to feel their way across. The courser took it calmly; the packhorses most definitely did not, and even Glamhandro was clearly relieved when he finally emerged on the far side.

But they emerged only to face the trail out, and it reared up from the very bank of the stream, allowing the horses no place to stop and gather themselves for the climb. It writhed up the western cliff like something a snake might disdain, and the western side was more than a hundred feet higher than that to the east. Kenhodan and Wencit dismounted—even the courser would have found the climb taxing with someone in his saddle—and followed Bahzell up that slope on foot. Much of it was almost vertical, and even with its switchbacks the trail was so steep the packhorses were badly blown before they topped out through a deep, narrow notch into a dense clump of willows.

Kenhodan stopped gratefully to survey the ambush site. Bahzell was right; it was perfect. No one could cross the stream quickly, nor could they retreat rapidly under fire once across. The only way out would be up and through their attackers, and the tortuous trail was hardly conducive to that. It was, he thought, admirably suited to their purposes, and he said so.

"Aye," Bahzell agreed. "But if Chernion's after being as good as folk say he is—and I've no doubt at all, at all that he is—we'd best take no chances."

"And you'd better get ready," Wencit said, head cocked as if to listen.

"Ah? So it's on their way they are, then?"

"Some of them, at least. I can only feel one clearly—he seems to be a good hater. Strange. Dog brothers are usually rather dispassionate."

"It's a guess I'll risk at the cause of his anger." Bahzell smiled. "It's no easy pace we've set them, and I've no doubt they'll be feeling it." He looked out over the ravine thoughtfully. "Would it happen we're after wanting prisoners, Wencit?"

"No." The wizard glanced in the direction of Bahzell's gaze. "Even if they swore Oath to Tomanāk, it's unlikely dog brothers would honor it, and you know you can never be certain you've found all their weapons. For that matter, they wouldn't tell us anything without more 'convincing' than Tomanāk would like, Bahzell."

"Aye, no doubt you've the right of that," Bahzell rumbled in agreement. "But if we'll not be keeping any of them, then here's how I'm thinking to handle it, if you're willing."

The others leaned closer, listening, and their smiles were not pleasant.

◆　◆　◆

Rosper couldn't have faulted Bahzell's explanation of his rage, yet it wasn't simply the narrow, twisting trail and mud that infuriated him. No, the signs left by his quarry were even more galling.

They'd slowed. They were no longer fleeing for their lives, but he hadn't realized that until he'd already exhausted his horses. Three of them had foundered, and five more were close to it. If they didn't catch up soon, their remaining stock would go heels over crupper—and Bahzell's decision to slow would show the entire Guild that Rosper had been wrong to expend his mounts.

Rosper didn't know if Bahzell had slowed because he thought he'd shaken the pursuit or because he was now willing to be overtaken. In his present mood, he favored the former thesis, but it no longer mattered. His decisions were already made.

His men sensed it, and they were unhappy. This pursuit was most unassassinlike. Worse, all of them knew Bahzell's and Wencit's reputations, and none were anxious to meet either of them when they were expecting it. It was common knowledge that the Belhadan chapter had tried to kill Bahzell thirty years ago when he'd first settled in Belhadan; there was no Belhadan chapter today. The possible connection was daunting, and while the thought of killing Wencit might be professionally attractive, there were rumors—denied, for the most part, by the Guild's senior members—that it, too, had been tried before.

But the scorpions of Sharnā rode Rosper, and it was risky to cross him in such a mood. He'd cut his way to his present post, and those who roused his ire tended to draw perilous assignments...or meet still speedier ends.

They reached the ravine and halted. The targets' tracks led into it, but not even Rosper was prepared to race blindly into such terrain. He studied the ravine instead, holding himself still with an effort. Either Bahzell was atop the far cliff, or he wasn't—but how to find out without suffering a mischief or wasting time? The day was wearing on, their horses were pulling up lame, and the thought of letting his prey get still farther ahead of him galled his soul.

Rosper considered for another long moment, then grunted.

"Change horses," he ordered brusquely.

"Your pardon, Rosper," one man said nervously, "but these are our last decent mounts. If we lose them out there—" he nodded at the ravine "—we can't pursue on the other side."

"True, Lairdnos," Rosper grated, "but if there's trouble crossing, we'll need fresh horses to get through it. There's only one way to see if they're waiting up there, and I'm not going to sit here forever just in case!"

Lairdnos dismounted unhappily, and he and his fellows exchanged glances as they changed saddles to their freshest horses. None were eager to discover what was waiting for them, and Rosper sensed their uneasy support for Lairdnos' caution. His anger latched on to their unhappiness like igniting banefire.

"Lairdnos!"

The rangy assassin's mouth went dry. He knew what Rosper was about to say, and he bitterly regretted having opened his mouth. Unfortunately, he'd worked too long and too closely with Chernion, who would never have sought revenge on someone for simply questioning the wisdom of one of his plans. Of course, he wouldn't have *had* to question *Chernion's* wisdom in a case like this.

"They may be waiting up there." Rosper pointed to the willows atop the far cliff. "So to be safe, we'll send up a scout. You."

"Yes, Rosper." Lairdnos saluted and obeyed, for his only alternative was death. The dog brothers didn't take mutiny lightly, however questionable an order might be.

He picked his cautious way into the ravine, and his palms were damp as his eyes flickered over the brink of the cliff with a dreadful fascination. He didn't care for how thick those willows were. . . .

He forded the stream in a rush of water and spring birdsong. His bridle jingled, and his horse snorted as it plunged through the rumbling rapids. It caught his fear, and Lairdnos felt it tremble. He tried to soothe it, but his heart wasn't in it, for Lairdnos—dealer in death—had no wish to die here.

The climbing trail was as bad as he'd feared. Like his quarry, he had to dismount and lead his horse, and even then they made heavy going, although the twisting grade was at least clear of loose rock or other treacherous footing. Lairdnos tried to feel grateful for small favors and kept his eyes on the trail. The last thing he needed was for his horse to stumble so that the two of them plummeted back into the depths of the ravine. He'd worry about the top if he reached it.

And then he did reach it, abruptly, and paused nervously under the lip of the ravine. He wanted his horse as recovered as possible before he poked his nose into that narrow notch. If anything happened, he intended to clap in his heels and dash past whatever awaited him. He'd done his part; let the others figure out why he didn't come back to report!

He waited as long as he dared, then remounted, eased his sword in its sheath and clucked to his horse, starting it forward. The smell of horse sweat was strong in his nostrils, and his own sweat trickled down his spine.

He moved into the willow shadows with one hand on his hilt and his nerves on fire, and his sharp, well-trained eyes peered to either side. The westering sun slanted bloodily under the branches, but the inner shadows were dense, and he eyed the darker areas with special care, for the Bloody Hand would have hidden himself well.

Nothing.

He glanced up, searching the canopy of thin branches above the trail, even though willows made unlikely perches for overhead attackers.

Nothing.

He rode a hundred yards, bending to sweep the shadows carefully. Still nothing! Elated by survival, he turned back to the clifftop to report.

Rosper watched his scout reappear in the willow-crowned cleft, arms semaphoring a message, and muffled a curse. His first judgment had been correct; the targets didn't plan to counterattack, or they would never have passed up this spot. Now his over cautiousness had cost another hour of fading light for no good reason, and fresh frustration churned his belly like acid. He waved a return message, then gestured for the others to mount, grinning sourly at their relieved expressions.

Lairdnos watched Rosper's arms intently, reading the order to move on for another three hundred yards to be doubly certain, and swung his horse obediently, pleased to still be breathing.

◆　　◆　　◆

Unfortunately for Lairdnos, anyone who could hide on the Wind Plain found ample scope for concealment in a wood. As the assassin passed a drift of winter willow fronds, piled untidily over a frost-killed branch, a long arm snaked from behind. Before he hit the ground, a hook knife had opened a second mouth across his throat.

Kenhodan slipped from another drift of brush with no more sound than a cat and moved to the brink of the cliff, careful to conceal himself while he bent his bow. He heard a scuffing sound as Bahzell dragged the body aside, and then steel whispered as the hradani drew his greatsword and spoke softly.

"When I take the leader—then start with the last one."

Kenhodan nodded and nocked an arrow, leaning forward to peer through his screen of willow branches.

The remaining assassins had started up the trail, and he heard their voices clearly, small and distant through willow rustle as they discussed the difficulties of the hunt. He inhaled the damp smell of leaves, earth, and fresh breeze, grateful for whatever change had taken place inside him. The berserker in his soul had been tamed. He was like a sword—hard-edged, empty of all except purpose.

Hooves thudded and rattled as the assassins worked steadily upward and Kenhodan studied the leader. The man's lips were tight, his flushed face angry. The way he gripped his hilt showed his eagerness, just as his drooping men and staggering horses showed how ruthlessly he'd driven them.

Kenhodan raised his bow. He heard the blowing of their horses, the jingling of bridles, the creaking of tack. He saw sweat stains on their salt-streaked black leathers and glanced at Bahzell.

◆   ◆   ◆

Rosper's horse heaved over the edge and paused.

The assassin urged him impatiently on, but the horse hesitated. Too late, professional alertness clawed at Rosper's anger and he peered ahead, half-blind as the setting sun slashed his eyes. Another horse stood there, head hanging, and something lay beside it.

Rosper's trade had taught him to recognize a body. He started to shout a warning—and Bahzell loomed from the shadows like an image of death.

Light stabbed under the willows, gleaming on a huge sword that burned red in the sunset, glittering on the gold embroidery of a green surcoat. The hradani's ears were back, his lips drawn up from strong teeth, and an icy dread burned Rosper's spine even as his own sword flew from its sheath.

"Greetings, Dog Brother," Bahzell grated. "Give my regards to Sharnā!"

Normally, a mounted man has the advantage over a foe on foot. He's higher in the air, with advantages of leverage and position. He can use his horse's strength against his opponent while he rains down blows.

Normally.

But Rosper's theoretical advantages were meaningless. Bahzell's height canceled most of them; his strength canceled the rest. And the notch of the trail was too confining for Rosper to evade him.

The assassin had time to shout one warning, then the singing steel was upon him. He blocked the first whistling blow desperately, and his blade rang like an anvil. A bow sang, and he knew Chernion had been right to warn him against his temper.

He'd wanted to meet the Bloody Hand; he would not profit from the meeting.

◆   ◆   ◆

Kenhodan's arrow snapped through the sunlight like a hornet, struck with a lethal beauty. Fletching whined, flashing through an assassin's throat, and the dog brother gave one gurgle of horrified surprise and plummeted to the ravine's floor.

Kenhodan's eyes never flickered. He nocked another arrow.

◆   ◆   ◆

Rosper was outmatched. Worse, he knew it. One touch of his poisoned steel would be enough to kill any human, but Bahzell was a hradani. That wasn't enough to make him *immune* to the deadly toxin, but he seemed unconcerned by the possibility. He flashed his blade about like a fencing master, and Rosper's frantically interposed sword rang as he managed to keep it from his flesh a dozen times, always by the thickness of an eyelash. Sweat poured down his face, and his jaw clenched as he realized the hradani was toying with him. Bahzell wasn't trying to kill him—not really. He was keeping him in play, instead, to block the trail while that deadly bowman picked off his men one by one.

Then the hradani's blade swept around in a flat figure eight, smashing through Rosper's sword three inches from the hilt. The shattered steel whined away, flipping over the ravine's lip with one last flash of reflected sunset, and Bahzell Bahnakson smiled wolfishly upon his enemy.

"Goodbye, Chernion," he said, and his sword screamed in a backhand arc. The assassin's head leapt from his shoulders, and Bahzell watched the corpse topple from the saddle and frowned. He'd expected more sword skill from Norfressa's foremost assassin.

Beside him, Kenhodan's bow sang once more and a scream answered. Then there was silence, and Bahzell glanced up as the bowman stepped from the shadows.

"Six," he said flatly. "All dead."

"Good." Bahzell strode to the edge and looked down. Six bodies lay on the ravine's floor at the foot of the slope, each marked for death by a single arrow. "Neat work, that," he said professionally.

"What next?" Kenhodan unbent his bow, and his voice was very calm.

"I'm thinking we'd best collect your arrows—and their horses. It's not as if we're after needing them, but it's plain murder to leave them, and no fault of theirs they're after being here."

"True, no horse has such poor taste as to carry an assassin willingly," Kenhodan said, his voice returning to normal.

"Except to the gallows," Bahzell agreed grimly. "Except to the gallows."

◆   ◆   ◆

"Krahana fly away with their souls! Sharnā whip them with scorpions!" Wulfra spat the curses as she blanked her gramerhain spitefully. Damn and blast those incompetent, ham-handed, clumsy—!

She bit off the thought and her nostrils flared as she inhaled deeply. She'd lost only the cost of their hire, she reminded herself—high, but not unreasonably so. She hadn't even warned Wencit, for her earlier attacks had already done that, she thought, and smiled sourly with bitter humor.

One good thing had come of it; the assassins had lost too many men for Chernion to give up, whether the Guild was paid or not. Not that Wulfra was even tempted to contemplate reneging; clients didn't short-change the dog brothers.

No, she'd pay . . . and tell Chernion she considered the contract closed. If Chernion—or the Guild Council—wished to continue, that was their affair.

Wulfra smiled more broadly at that thought. It really was amusing, in a grim sort of way. Even if Wencit succeeded in his mission, with a high probability of her own unpleasant demise, the assassins would be waiting. It would almost be as if they were avenging her, and the baroness permitted herself a mirthless chuckle at the thought.

Now how best to phrase the message? It must convey the necessary information with the proper air of condolence, but expressed in a way guaranteed to rouse Chernion's fury.

Fortunately, Wulfra of Torfo was a past mistress of the poisoned pen.

CHAPTER TWELVE

Meetings Along the Way

"Well, at least Chemalka's decided to stop raining on us," Kenhodan said. "For now."

He leaned against Glamhandro's tall side, chewing on the final bite of sandwich from the lunch for which they'd paused. A last tendril of steam rose from the well-quenched ashes of the fire over which tea had been brewed and his head was back as he gazed up into the branches. The massacre of the assassins lay a full day's journey behind them, and he was profoundly glad to see the sun through those branches. The night after the ambush had given way to a morning of hard, driving rain, even more miserable than the misty precipitation they'd endured earlier, but spring weather was nothing if not changeable in the South March. Now sunlight probed down through openings in the canopy, touching the Forest of Hev with a warm golden glow, gleaming on drifts of fallen leaves still glistening with rainwater and touching tree trunks with a soft-edged patina of light. The air was warmer than it had been, as well, and the breeze tossing those overhead branches smelled crisp and clean.

The trail, unfortunately, was still a slick, muddy slot courtesy of all the water which had tumbled out of the sky before the sun deigned to put in its belated appearance. At least they'd left the ravine behind, however, and the lower, secondary growth around the stream had turned back into the towering trunks of a mature old-growth forest. That left more space around each individual tree and made the going much easier on either side of the trail, but the tree canopy also choked out any possibility of undergrowth or grass. That wouldn't have been a problem under most circumstances, but he and his companions had acquired an additional eighteen horses whose riders no longer required their services. The assassins hadn't anticipated a lengthy journey off the high road, away from posting houses and livery stables, and they'd packed relatively little in the way of grain for their mounts. As a consequence, those mounts' new owners had been forced to put all of their recently inflated string of horses on short rations, and the captured animals, already showing the physical consequences of hard usage, weren't likely to find their condition improved under the circumstances.

"Aye," Bahzell agreed, standing on Glamhandro's far side to look up at the same branch-laced sky. "And it's not so very much farther till we'll be breaking out of the trees. I'll not pretend that's something as strikes me as a bad idea."

"Actually, it strikes *me* as a very *good* idea," Wencit put in. The wizard had climbed back into the courser's saddle. Now he looked down at Kenhodan—and across at Bahzell—and twitched his head down the trail ahead of them. "Once we're free of the trees, we can at least graze them at the roadside. And unless memory fails me, there are these people called 'farmers' here and there along the road to Sindor." He smiled briefly. "As Fradenhelm implied in Korun, a fat purse can carry you a long way under the right circumstances, and I'm willing to invest in feeding these fellows. It's not their fault they fell into bad company."

"No, it isn't," Kenhodan agreed, swinging up into his own saddle.

Glamhandro snorted, as if amused by the two-foots' nattering, and tossed his head. He and the courser seemed to be thriving, despite their shorter rations, and the redhaired man leaned forward in the saddle to pat the big gray stallion's shoulder.

"Of course," he continued, "they've fallen into better company now."

"I'd like to be thinking that's the case," Bahzell said, but he sounded a bit distracted. In fact, now that Kenhodan thought about it, the hradani had seemed a little . . . distant all day. Now, as he moved back towards the head of their much enlarged cavalcade, he was gazing along the trail in front of them with his ears pricked as if listening for something no one else could hear.

"Are you all right, Bahzell?" Kenhodan asked.

"Eh?" Bahzell shook himself and turned to look over his shoulder. "What's that?" His ears shifted back to a more normal angle. "Oh! Well, as to that, I've a mite on my mind. I'm after . . . expecting something, as you might be saying."

"*Expecting* something? Out here?" Kenhodan looked around at the cool, breezy, wind-sighing forest. "Bahzell, in case you haven't noticed, we're still stuck in the middle of the woods. And unless I'm mistaken, the last 'something' we had to deal with—you remember, the assassins who were chasing us?—is busy fertilizing those selfsame woods behind us. That doesn't exactly make me delighted by the prospect of _another_ unanticipated encounter. So don't you think that if you're 'expecting something' it might be a good idea to—oh, I don't know, _share_ that minor fact with us?"

"What?" Bahzell grinned. "And be spoiling the surprise?"

"So far most of the 'surprises' on this little jaunt of Wencit's have been less than pleasant," Kenhodan pointed out. "Personally, I've discovered I'm a great fan of boredom."

"Well, as to that, I'm not one as would deny as how boredom's a certain appeal," Bahzell conceded. "But in this case—"

He stopped in midsentence, turning to gaze back along the trail once more, and Wencit's courser looked up. His ears pricked as sharply as the hradani's as he stared in the same direction. Then he tossed his head with a high, somehow jubilant cry, and Glamhandro raised his own head with an echoing trumpet in almost the same instant. The packhorses and the assassins' captured mounts looked back and forth between him and the courser with suddenly sharpened alertness, and Kenhodan blinked, wondering what could possibly have gotten into all of them.

"What's—" he began, then stopped as something moved ahead of them.

It took him a moment to realize what he was seeing... and another, longer moment to _believe_ he was seeing it.

Wencit's courser companion stood twenty hands at the shoulder, the next best thing to seven feet. The enormous blood-red roan cantering—not walking or trotting, but *cantering*—along that narrow, slick, treacherous trail towards them was at least five hands taller than that. Kenhodan had never imagined any horse-shaped creature that huge, and if he had, his imagination couldn't possibly have matched the grace and balance of the reality forging towards them in a steady, rolling splatter of mud.

He started to say something to Bahzell, but the hradani was already in motion himself. He raced down the trail, arms spread wide, then reached high to wrap them around the roan stallion's mighty neck and buried his face against the winter-rough coat.

"Well, I see what he meant about surprises," Kenhodan said after a moment. "Should I assume this is the mysterious Walsharno?"

◆　　　◆　　　◆

<So, here you are!> the silent voice in Bahzell's brain said with loving tartness. *<Correct me if I'm wrong, but I thought He said you were planning to go* straight *from Korun to Sindor?>*

"Aye? And when, if you'd be so very kind to tell me, was the last time as you and I were after doing *anything* the way we'd planned?" Bahzell demanded, reaching up to scratch Walsharno's cheek gently.

<Well, if you're going to be that *way about it!>* Walsharno snorted and lipped the hradani's ears affectionately. *<And, while I'm admitting things, I should probably point out that He was even less specific than usual this time when I got my marching orders.>*

"Well, I'm thinking that's most likely because we've

what you might be calling a delicate situation here," Bahzell said more soberly, his voice low enough only Walsharno could hear him, and twitched his head slightly in the direction of his human companions. "Tell me, is that lad on the gray after reminding you of anyone?"

Walsharno raised his head, looking over Bahzell's shoulder, and his ears pricked forward.

<Now that you mention it, he does,> he said slowly.

"Aye, and himself's as good as said he's one as Sergeant Houghton might've been after becoming in another world. But he's not the least idea—or memory—of who and what it might happen he is in *this* world. And Wencit's after being his same old pain-in-the-arse self about his precious secrets. Still and all, himself's all but told me we're to follow Wencit's guide in this, and I'm thinking he'd not've been nearly so forthcoming if this wasn't after being something we'd best take deadly serious, Brother."

<Do you mean you think this is what we've been waiting for for so long?> Walsharno's mental voice was deeper than usual, slow and measured, and Bahzell reached up to lay one hand on the proud, arched neck.

"Aye," he said simply, and felt the same cold thrill of mingled anticipation and dread go through them both.

<Well there's a thought to curdle a fellow's thinking,> Walsharno said after a moment. *<Still, there is that bit about champions and dying in bed. And I can't say the extra decades haven't been interesting. Which doesn't say a thing—>* he lowered his nose to push Bahzell's shoulder hard enough to send the hradani half a step sideways *<—about the opportunity to finally face those bastards down south instead of just cleaning up the wreckage they leave behind.>*

"There's that," Bahzell agreed with grim satisfaction. "I'm only wishing Kaeritha was after being here to join us."

<I'm sure she and Vaijon will be keeping an eye on us,> Walsharno told him softly, then tossed his head. *<And now, I suppose we should go and let you make the introductions.>*

◆   ◆   ◆

Kenhodan watched Bahzell and the enormous roan exchange greetings, then glanced across at Wencit.

"You failed to mention anything about another courser. Something that just... slipped your mind, was it?"

"Kenhodan, you *heard* Bahzell tell Fradenhelm he was a wind rider himself. It didn't occur to you that a wind rider has to have a courser before he's a wind rider?"

"I'm under the impression that Bahzell's been just about *everything* at some point in his life," Kenhodan replied tartly. "And I don't recall anyone telling me he was *currently* a wind rider. Of course, I was also under the impression until very recently—or, at least, I *assume* I was under the impression until very recently; I seem to have a few blank spots in my memory, you understand—that coursers hated hradani with a blinding passion. Obviously, I'd already figured out that wasn't the case, at least where Bahzell's concerned. But it still seems... odd."

"You mean odder than the fact that Bahzell's a champion of Tomanāk, married to a war maid, and running a tavern in Belhadan?" Wencit asked brightly, and Kenhodan snorted.

"Point taken," he conceded.

"Actually," Wencit said more seriously, his own wildfire eyes watching Bahzell and Walsharno, "the coursers and the hradani have always had far more in common than either of them realized. The same thing that makes the coursers so powerful, gives them such speed and endurance, is what allows hradani to heal so quickly and gives *Bahzell* the endurance to run any other horse ever born into the ground. They're both directly linked to the energy that binds the universe together, Kenhodan. They draw on it, and it sustains them in ways no one else can match. Bahzell was right that assassins use poisoned steel, but unless there's enough of it to kill a hradani instantly, he'll usually not simply survive but recover fully. The same thing's true for the coursers, which says some interesting things about whatever Chernion apparently used on this fellow—" he patted the courser's neck "—in Korun."

"I see," Kenhodan said slowly, digesting the fresh information, and Wencit chuckled. The redhaired man looked at him sharply, and the wizard smiled.

"You *begin* to see," he said. "For instance, Walsharno's the next best thing to a hundred years old, and so is his sister, Gayrfressa. And, no, coursers don't normally live anywhere near that long. Despite which, Walsharno doesn't look particularly decrepit, wouldn't you say?"

"No, I wouldn't call him that." Kenhodan gazed at the sleekly powerful roan courser with a frown, remembering a conversation with Brandark. "Is this the same sort of thing that applies to Leeana?"

"It certainly seems to be, doesn't it? And right off the top of my head, I can't recall another time anything like that 'same sort of thing' has ever happened. Which, given the fact that Walsharno is also a champion of Tomanāk, gives one furiously to think."

"Wait a minute." Kenhodan looked back Wencit quickly. "*Walsharno's* a champion of Tomanāk?"

"Why, yes," Wencit said innocently, then chuckled again, louder, at Kenhodan's expression. "It only makes sense, doesn't it?" he went on as Bahzell and Walsharno started back along the trail towards them. "Bahzell's the first hradani champion since the Fall. Who else would be paired with the first courser champion ever?"

◆ ◆ ◆

"Kenhodan, be known to Walsharno, my Wind Brother," Bahzell said with unwonted formality. "It's my life he's saved a time or three, and I suppose if truth be told, I've been after saving his once or twice, as well."

Walsharno had touched noses lightly with the black stallion. Now he turned his head to regard Kenhodan from huge, intelligent golden eyes and nodded slightly.

"Good morning, Milord Champion," Kenhodan said and saw Walsharno's ears flick in what certainly looked like amusement as the stallion shot a mildly accusatory glance at Wencit. "Yes," Kenhodan went on, "*someone* did get around—finally—to filling in a few more blanks." He shot a glance of his own, considerably harder than Walsharno's, at Bahzell. "I can't imagine why it took him this long."

"Well, as to that, I'm thinking it never actually came up," Bahzell responded equably. "Come to that, I'd hoped to be meeting him not so far outside Korun and making the introductions there." He shrugged. "Still and all, as we've just been after pointing out to

each other, plans are a thing as seem to be a mite...
elastic where such as Wencit of Rūm are involved."

"Don't change the subject from your own transgressions, Bahzell," Wencit replied. "And for that matter, you can't fairly blame me for the dog brothers."

"Oh, and can't I just?" Bahzell glowered across at the wizard. "It's in my mind Fradenhelm said as how Chernion was after hunting *you*, not me, Wencit! Aye, and it's not the first solitary word he had to be saying about young *Kenhodan*, either."

"Don't tell me you're actually going to apply *logic* to this," Wencit retorted.

"Well, if pressed I'd have to be admitting logic's not so much a thing as hradani come by naturally," Bahzell conceded. "Not but what I've not been forced to be taking on quite a few things as most hradani don't over the years. The most of them, now I think on it, because of dealings with you."

"There you go again!" Wencit scolded. "That's really very tiresome of you. Especially since, now that Walsharno's joined us, we have someone who can interpret and give us Milord Courser's name."

"Aye, so we do," Bahzell said much more seriously, "and in fact he's been after sharing that with me already. Wencit, Kenhodan—be known to Byrchalka of the Stone Valley herd."

The black stallion—Byrchalka—raised his head in acknowledgment of the introduction and Kenhodan and Wencit both bowed formally from the saddle to him. Kenhodan rolled the name through his thoughts and found it fitting, for it meant "Black Thunderbolt," which certainly suited what he'd seen of the courser so far.

"Byrchalka's fallen brother was Tairsal Lancebearer,"

Bahzell went on more grimly, and Wencit's eyes narrowed. "Aye," Bahzell nodded sadly. "He was after being one of Sir Kelthys' grandnephews, and that's after having made him oath sworn to Balthar. It's glad I am we can tell Baron Chardahn as how Chernion's already paid for young Tairsal's blood. I'd sooner not see him and his in blood feud with the entire Assassins Guild and well you know that's exactly what he'd be doing when he heard."

"No doubt," Wencit said somberly, leaning forward in the saddle to lay one palm on Byrchalka's shoulder. "I know no one will ever be able to replace your Wind Brother, Byrchalka, but I thank you from the bottom of my heart for your willingness to bear *me* on this journey."

The black stallion turned his head, looking back at the wizard, then snorted and nodded in obvious acceptance of Wencit's words.

"And if Walsharno's here," Wencit continued after a moment, turning back to Bahzell and Walsharno, "may I ask where Gayrfressa is?"

"As to that, I've no doubt she's reached Belhadan by now, or soon will have," Bahzell said. "Walsharno says as how himself was after getting both of them on the road back from the Wind Plain about the same time as a drowned rat washed up in the Iron Axe's taproom with as disreputable an old trickster as ever I've known trailing behind. Walsharno was after leaving first, though. Herself had a few things to be looking after at Hill Guard."

Wencit chuckled, but Kenhodan pursed his lips in a silent whistle as he contemplated the incredible distance Walsharno had covered since that night. It certainly put all of the legends about the coursers' speed and endurance into sharp perspective!

"Well, now that he's here, I suppose we should be getting back on the road," Wencit said, as if the accomplishment of such monumental journeys was a mere commonplace. Which, Kenhodan reflected after a moment, they very probably *were* for Wencit of Rūm.

"Let me just be rigging a saddle," Bahzell replied. "Walsharno's firm notions about where a wind rider's arse is best placed, and since Chernion was so very kind as to be gifting us with so many saddles, it's in my mind as how I should be after coming up with something as will work."

◆　◆　◆

<There's something . . . odd about Glamhandro, Brother,> Walsharno said.

Night had found them still several miles inside the Forest of Hev, and firelight danced in gold and black shadows off the trunks of the towering trees. The packhorses and the mounts which had served the assassins were picketed on a line between two of those trees, but Walsharno, Byrchalka, and Glamhandro stood in a companionable knot on the edge of the firelight, eyes gleaming to the flickering jubilance of the flames.

<And is there, now?> Bahzell replied from his place beside the fire. Kenhodan had the current watch, some distance away from the flames' ability to destroy night vision, and the hradani's nimble fingers were repairing a weak spot on the halter of one of the pack horses while he smoked his pipe. *<Now why d'you think as that might not be taking me all by surprise?>*

<Probably because you're actually quite a bit brighter than you'd really prefer for people to think you are.>

Bahzell chuckled, and Byrchalka snorted in matching amusement. The black couldn't speak directly to Bahzell the way Walsharno could, but for the first time since his rider's murder he could at least communicate with someone, and coursers shared many of the "lesser cousins'" attributes. They were creatures of the herd, accustomed to—indeed, they needed—sharing the mind-to-mind flow of thoughts with their fellows.

<Well, as to that,> Bahzell replied, <given as how both Wencit and himself are after telling us young Kenhodan's a mite more than it might be he seems on the surface, I'd not be so very surprised if something was after steering him to a mount as might be just a mite more than he's after seeming, too.>

<Neither would I, but I have to admit I'd feel more comfortable if I knew exactly how Glamhandro came to be available for anyone to steer Kenhodan towards in the first place.>

Bahzell looked up from his leatherwork, glancing over his shoulder in Walsharno's direction, and cocked his ears. As he'd told Kenhodan in Korun, it wasn't entirely unheard of for the coursers' bloodlines to cross with those of lesser horses, but it happened very, very seldom, and it wasn't something coursers often discussed, even with their riders. All coursers were protective where their lesser cousins were concerned, and Sothōii warhorses were the most intelligent horses in the world, but they still weren't coursers. The smartest of them were the equivalent of very, very young foals compared to any courser, and coursers mated for life. So far as Bahzell knew, no courser had ever life-mated with anything but another courser, and the sort of casual dalliance which might have produced a courser-warhorse by-blow was something of which the courser herds strongly disapproved.

<*I'm assuming there's a reason you're finding that a puzzle?*> the hradani asked after a moment, and Walsharno and Byrchalka both nodded.

<*Byrchalka had noticed it long before I ever caught up with you,*> the roan replied. <*It's obvious there's courser blood in him, but neither of us have ever seen—or heard of—a case where it's worked out this way. His link to the magic field is as strong as mine is, Brother, and that's unheard of in any of the lesser cousins, even one with courser blood. And he's far smarter than any lesser cousin I've ever met, as well. Many of them have great hearts and the wisdom that goes with them, but that's a very different thing. It's clear to both me and Byrchalka that he can hear us when we speak to him, too.*>

<*I'm thinking as how you're saying it's more than just his responding to your herd sense?*>

<*That's exactly what I'm saying,*> Walsharno confirmed, and Bahzell drew thoughtfully on his pipe as he chewed that information over.

He himself had acquired the herd sense—the herd stallion's ability to sense the hearts, minds, health, and location of the members of his herd—when he healed the survivors of the Warm Springs herd after Krahana's attack upon it. He still had it, although only Gayrfressa remained of the Warm Springs coursers he'd touched all those years ago, and he knew Walsharno had it, too. Had they not bonded, had Walsharno not become another of Tomanāk's champions, he probably would have become a herd stallion in the fullness of time himself. Unlike Walsharno, however, Bahzell's herd sense was specific to the Warm Springs coursers, so he wasn't surprised by the fact that Walsharno could see more deeply into Glamhandro than he could.

<*You know a herd stallion—or someone who might have been one under other circumstances—*> Walsharno allowed himself a mental chuckle <*can make the lesser cousins understand him when he must. But it's not the same sort of understanding coursers have with one another or you and I have with each other, Brother. It's ... less well formed. Almost more a matter of imposing his will on the lesser cousin, of commanding rather than communicating.*>

Bahzell nodded in understanding of the difference Walsharno was attempting to define.

<*Well, it's not like that in Glamhandro's case. In fact, I'm not sure I could impose my will on him, even if I tried to. He actually hears my thoughts—my words. I'm sure of it, even though he can't reply. And he understands them far more clearly than even the wisest of the lesser cousins understands you two-foots.*>

Bahzell's ears half-flattened at Walsharno's serious tone. And it was a sobering thought, the hradani admitted to himself. He knew how intelligent Sothōii warhorses were, he'd seen how deeply and completely they came to understand and bond with their own long-term riders. Walsharno knew that even better than Bahzell did, so when he said that Glamhandro's understanding surpassed that level of comprehension he knew exactly what he was saying.

<*And there's one more thing,*> Walsharno said now, quietly. <*He's bonded with Kenhodan.*>

Bahzell's ears stood straight up in surprise at that one, and Walsharno shook his head and tossed his mane in agreement.

<*I don't know if Kenhodan's realized that,*> the roan stallion continued, <*but it's obvious to me and Byrchalka. In fact, Byrchalka says he realized they were bonded the instant he first laid eyes on the two of them.*>

Bahzell's upright ears folded slowly close to his head. Something in Walsharno's voice told him the stallion's words meant more than they seemed to.

<*Yes, they do, Brother,*> Walsharno confirmed. <*They were* already *bonded. Whether Kenhodan knows it or not, he and Glamhandro were linked before you three two-foots ever entered Fradenhelm's stable. So I'm very strongly inclined to believe that you rather understated things when you suggested he'd been "steered" towards Glamhandro. And that, as Brandark might have said, gives me furiously to think about how inappropriate words like "coincidence" are when one gets too close to Wencit of Rūm.*>

CHAPTER THIRTEEN

Secrets in Sindor

Three weary riders entered Sindor as afternoon edged into evening.

Eyebrows rose as they passed, for they led eighteen riderless mounts. Obviously something untoward had happened, but only a hardy soul would have stopped the travel-stained trio to discover what. The last weekend had been dry, and they were coated in grit, but dust couldn't hide the identities of the flame-eyed rider on the black courser or the towering hradani on the even bigger roan, and while a handful of those witnesses might have had the temerity to pry into Bahzell Bahnakson's affairs, none of them wanted anything at all to do with those of Wencit of Rūm.

Kenhodan paid the curious little heed as he studied the city's impressive walls and grim battlements. There were two Sindors—one within the walls and one growing beyond them—but the city had kept new structures clear of the main curtainwall, and an extension of the present fortifications had begun. Such a project was hideously expensive; the fact that the city proposed to spend so much emphasized both its own wealth and the chance of trouble.

The walls cut black shadows across the street as they passed the ironbound gates. Guards paced the ramparts, halberds shouldered, but the slight slouch of their shoulders indicated they expected no immediate trouble.

"Well, that's the second stage done," Bahzell said, slapping dust from his chest. "I'd best be turning these horses into the Order's keeping. The bailiff can be explaining to the Guard, which should be after keeping it out of our business."

"A good idea," Wencit agreed wearily, "but somehow I doubt our arrival will go unreported." He gestured at the gawking bystanders.

"And could you be telling me how it might be after being any other way?" the hradani asked dryly. "They'll not see our like here often, Wencit. Still, is it likely to be making much difference either way?"

"It might. We've dealt with one lot of dog brothers, but that's only likely to spur them on. And I'd just as soon give Wulfra as little warning as possible."

"Maybe so, but we've no choice but to be stopping in towns now and again betwixt here and Torfo—South Keep, at the least. After that, it may be we'll have more options, but it's little choice we have for now. It's one threat we've already dealt with—" he nodded over his shoulder at the riderless horses "—and it's in my mind we'll deal with the others as they're arising. For now, what I'm mostly wanting is a bath, a meal, and a bed, and I'm thinking Walsharno, Byrchalka, and Glamhandro wouldn't be so very unhappy as to be finding themselves under a roof with a nosebag full of oats!"

"A masterly prescription," Wencit chuckled. "And you're right. Caution and stealth are one thing; running from shadows is another. You know a place?"

"And would it happen that was a *serious* question?" Bahzell shook his head. "There's times you're after reminding me of a babe just out of diapers, Wencit. Of course I do! The Dancing Unicorn's just down yonder street, and old Telbor was landlord when last I checked, an honest man as welcomes himself's servants. It's after being a mite noisy, but the beds're clean and the food's good. Not up to the standards of Leeana's kitchen, maybe, but then what is?"

Kenhodan sighed. "*I'll* be happy as long as the meat's dead and the bedbugs are no bigger than cats."

"Then the Dancing Unicorn it is, Bahzell. Lead on."

Bahzell grinned and turned down Gate Street, picking his way past taverns, rows of eating places, and the sorts of shops that catered to every sort and grade of traveler. Sindor was larger than Korun, with broad streets and a more sedate population, but Kenhodan was surprised by the number of troops he observed. Everywhere he looked he saw cavalry surcoats or the tunics of royal and imperial infantry. It puzzled him, and his brow furrowed as he considered it, but then his expression cleared as he recognized why they were there. If the southern border was brewing trouble, Sindor was a logical place to mass reserves. Which might also explain the new walls; perhaps the imperial treasury was footing the bill. He looked away from the scenery to raise an eyebrow at Bahzell and twitch his head as they passed a marching squad of infantry.

"Aye, you'll be finding a Purple Lords' caravan guard of soldiers in Sindor most times," the hradani replied with a nod, "but with Angthyr on the boil, the King Emperor's after looking to his defenses."

"So I see. And South Wall Pass is the last pass down this way?"

"Aye. It's naught but twenty-five leagues to the south, but South Keep's after being built clean across it. No army's come that way since King Emperor Forgoth was after finishing the keep three hundred years ago."

"I take it the keep is...formidable?"

"I suppose there's some as might say so. The main wall's after being two hundred feet high and eighty thick."

"Definitely formidable," Kenhodan decided.

"Aye, but that's not to be saying it can't be taken."

"I suppose not," Kenhodan said, although his tone was doubtful.

"Bahzell's right." Unlike Kenhodan's, Wencit's tone was flat and boned with iron certitude. "The walls were strong in Kontovar, but they fell. Not too better generals—I knew Toren Swordarm's generals, and there *were* no finer commanders. Sorcery took Trōfrōlantha and razed the walls of Rollanthia."

Bahzell and Kenhodan exchanged glances.

"Never forget that!" Wencit turned in the saddle to stare at them fiercely. "What happened there can happen here, and that's only as far away as we can hold it! Folk forget how close the peril is. They see the walls of Sindor, of South Keep—of Axe Hallow itself—and they forget that simple force of arms is useless against those willing to twist and pervert the art. They forget it can happen here, but it can. It can!"

His sudden passion shook his companions. Kenhodan looked around uneasily, his mind hazed with images of fire and rapine, and a shiver ran down his spine. Could it really happen again?

He shuddered. Of course it could, and he suddenly realized that Wencit, who'd seen the ruin of Kontovar with his own eyes, was warning them their present mission wasn't simply to deal with a single rogue sorceress. He was telling them it was the first skirmish of the long-awaited final struggle, and what in the names of all the gods had caught Kenhodan up in such a clash?

✦   ✦   ✦

Another mind asked the same question, if from a different perspective. A slim figure leaned against the wall and frowned at the passing travelers.

Well, at least Rosper's fate was confirmed, Chernion thought grimly. It seemed Wulfra's infuriating message had been correct.

The assassin wondered how it had been done, not that it mattered, and growled a mental curse. Rosper should never have been sent after them on his own. Never! And Chernion had known it at the time. Now the dog brothers were committed to kill the targets out of self-preservation, and Wulfra knew it, curse her! Her insolent letter had said as much, if not in so many words, just as it proved she'd witnessed the slaughter with her accursed sorcery. The thought of Wulfra watching what had obviously been a massacre did not endear the baroness to the guildmaster.

Chernion muttered one more curse, then turned and slipped away, considering the next move. The Guild had lost its chance to back away; despite all Chernion's distrust of the wizard breed, the dog brothers were trapped right in the middle of Wulfra's and Wencit's struggle. There was no point weeping over it, but Chernion didn't much care for the Guild's tactical position at the moment.

It was always irksome to work with a craftmaster who wasn't privy to his guildmaster's secret, and while Umaro was a good man, he didn't know Chernion well. Of course, Ashwan was with him, and Ashwan was the only man who'd *always* known Chernion's most guarded secret, but Chernion had no intention of revealing that secret to Umaro if it could be avoided. It could be a deadly weapon, properly used, but it was more likely to slip out with each new mind that shared it, which was one reason Chernion avoided attention and familiarity among the dog brothers as well as in public. The terror of the guildmaster's name rested in no small part on the fact that Chernion was a shadowy, secretive figure even to senior Guild members. Now Chernion might have to admit Umaro to a secret unknown even to the Guild's present Councilors.

The assassin paused in the street, frowning in thought. Perhaps there was another way? The secret had served the Guild before, and it might again—even against Wencit and the Bloody Hand, if the stage were properly set. After several minutes of careful consideration, the guildmaster nodded, stepped silently into the Windhawk Inn, and passed through its taproom, signaling an unobtrusive dog brother to collect his fellows.

It took less than five minutes for them to filter silently into Chernion's small bedchamber, and the guildmaster turned to face them, expression grim.

"They're here . . . with Rosper's horses."

One of the four cursed softly.

"Shall we strike tonight, Chernion?" another asked quietly.

"No." Chernion's answer was soft, and they tensed in disbelief. "No, their guard's up. They've killed eight dog brothers; I see no reason they can't kill five more. Besides, the Dancing Unicorn's a sinkhole of the Order of Tomanāk. We can't take them there."

"You're saying we're going to just let them *go?*"

One of the shocked dog brothers forgot himself enough to blurt out the question, and Chernion's hand flashed. Bladed fingers slashed into the bridge of his nose—not quite hard enough to break it—and he collapsed with a muffled scream, clutching his face. His fellows watched impassively. Fools who angered Chernion could expect sudden punishment and scant sympathy.

"Get up," Chernion said coldly, and he staggered up, leaning against the wall, one hand trying to staunch the flow from his bloodied nose, while the guildmaster continued as if there'd been no interruption at all. "We won't 'let them go,' but it's time to try another way.

"Craftmaster Umaro's been summoned from Morfintan. I'd hoped he would have arrived by now, but obviously he hasn't. Either that, or he already knows the targets have chosen the Dancing Unicorn and he's lying low to avoid attracting their attention rather than risk joining us here. Horum, you'll take charge of this group and find him, wherever he is. Tell him that under no circumstances is he to attack without my direct command."

"Yes, Chernion."

"This is only one of several projects I must attend

to, and I've spent too long on it already. I see, however, that I can't leave the matter unattended, so I'll place a spy among them as a first step."

"A spy? How?" Horum's questions were profoundly respectful.

"There are ways, Brothers. The agent I have in mind is an independent, and while we must always be careful with any such, I've used her before. Yes, *her*," Chernion answered their expressions. "More often than not, men see what they want to see. They don't look for threats in fair places, and the agent I have in mind is fair. *Very* fair."

"But a woman, Chernion?"

"Yes. She's not a dog brother, so we can't trust her fully, but she knows better than to betray *me*. Don't show yourselves to her unmasked. She knows her duties, but I'm the only dog brother she knows, and I wish it to remain so. I'll instruct her, and you'll be guided by her messages. And mark this well: she's valuable to me. In fact, she's more valuable than you are, my brothers. Do you understand me?"

"Yes, Chernion," Horum said carefully, "but may I ask what your plans for her are? Or does Umaro already know them?"

"No, he doesn't, so see that you find him quickly, lest he attack before he learns what I intend. Curse the wizard for choosing the Unicorn! It's too near for comfort, and I can't blame Umaro for staying clear of it, but I don't like how little time we have to rearrange things, and it's always possible he'll act on his own initiative in the absence of direct instructions from me. That's why it's vital that you find him and be certain he knows he isn't to attack in Sindor."

"Understood, Chernion," Horum said. "We'll do our best."

Another assassin might have promised not to fail, but Horum had worked with Chernion before. He knew how little use the guildmaster had for easy promises ... and that Chernion was unlikely to punish anyone who truly did do his best to fulfill his instructions.

"Tell him I want to study the targets," Chernion continued. "If we learn their purpose, we'll be better able to plan their deaths, and beyond that, there are parts of this I don't like. I think our client may be trying to manipulate the Guild, and we have to discover whether or not that's true, as well. Our targets are bound for Angthyr, so we have time to think and plan, and it seems to me it serves the Guild's purposes best to spend some of that time discovering what we can about our client's intentions where we're concerned. At the very least, I think she's trying to ... amass information she might use to control our future actions. That's one reason I want to place my agent in the targets' midst—to learn what she can about their intentions and purpose. That sort of knowledge may give us insight into what our client has in mind and why she wants them dead, and that might be a weapon against whatever plans she has in mind for the Guild."

Chernion paused, and Horum and nodded in understanding.

"Beyond that," the guildmaster continued "I want the targets threatened from as many directions as possible when the time to strike finally comes, so while she joins them and—hopefully—gains their trust, I'll move ahead of them and Umaro will trail behind. If

I need aid, I'll summon it from the other chapters, but I think it's important I reach South Keep ahead of them to find a proper spot between there and Angthyr for a careful attack. In the meantime, the woman will keep us in communication. She knows my codes, and she'll relay messages from me to Umaro, but under no circumstances will he make contact with her. If contact must be made, *she'll* signal *him*."

"Yes, Chernion."

"Very well; go now. Find Umaro, and I'll see you once more when the assignment's completed. Clean killing, Brothers."

"Clean killing, Chernion."

The four dog brothers saluted and hurried away, and Chernion closed the door behind them and shot the bolt, then checked the shutters carefully and paced for several minutes. Umaro wouldn't like the plan, but he had one sterling virtue; his temper was every bit as hot as Rosper's had been, yet he understood control. Besides, he'd have Ashwan to advise him, and Chernion knew Ashwan was adroit enough to control any untoward enthusiasm on Umaro's part without seeming to.

Finally, the guildmaster nodded and sat before the mirror and dark eyes looked unblinkingly into their own reflected depths for a long, silent moment. Then a hand touched the bushy eyebrows, and they came away. A small pot produced a creamy paste for careful application to the dark complexion. A quick rinse, and the darkness fled.

The master assassin of Norfressa looked into the mirror and smiled at what she saw.

◆　　◆　　◆

Bahzell and Kenhodan stretched their legs gratefully under the table, luxuriating in the comfort of their first true safety since leaving Belhadan. A brief explanation had put the Dancing Unicorn's regulars on watch for assassins, and any sorcerous attack seemed unlikely. There were too many witnesses, and Wulfra's attrition rate had been too high. She had to be running low on disciples, Kenhodan thought.

The one thing that worried him was Wencit's prolonged absence. He was uneasy about allowing the wizard to wander unprotected, but Bahzell only laughed at his concern.

"Lad, Wencit's no easily taken bird! Any as care to be hunting him do so at risk, and welcome to it. He's eyes in the back of his head, and you've yet to see him really use a blade, for he's always been after weaving spells when he fought beside you. He's better than you, lad. By the Mace, he's better than *me!* Aye, and he's an interesting technique, too. Much like yours."

Bahzell thumped an empty tankard meaningfully on the tabletop, and a waiter hurried to fill it.

"Like mine?" Kenhodan blinked in surprise.

"Aye. Mind, I'm thinking it's not like to mean much, for whoever it was taught our wizard's after being dust long since, but he fights much as you do. To tell truth, it was that I had in mind when I was after telling you to find the one who'd taught you to be finding your past. It's a few of the oldest elves I've seen fight like the pair of you, but not many even of them, and it's sudden death for aught on two feet you are, both of you."

"That's not very reassuring, Bahzell," Kenhodan said

wryly. "I don't like being so good at killing. It makes me worry over what I was."

"I can be understanding that," Bahzell said quietly "more than many, I'm thinking. But we all of us live as best we can and do the best we may, and Tomanāk and Isvaria ask no more than that. Be yourself, Kenhodan, and wait." He looked across the table into the other man's green eyes. "It's men I've known with hearts of jackals' droppings, and others with a blood hunger none of my poor, cursed folk could ever match. But it's good men I've known, too, and I've seen you with my daughter. Aye, and her with you. Our Gwynna's never been wrong with her trust, lad—never. No, whatever your past, this much I'll say to you as a champion of Tomanāk: you've no cause to fear it. It's no more cause for shame you have than any of us, and there's one advantage at the heart of it. We're after carrying our mistakes with us, but yours are lost."

"I think I might like to feel some honest guilt," Kenhodan said. His smile was wry, but he felt as if Bahzell had lifted a weight from his shoulders.

"Ah, now! If that's the way you're feeling, you'll not be waiting long, for its evil company you've fallen into, what with hradani and wizards and all. And you lacking the strong moral fiber that's made me what I am today, too. No—" Bahzell heaved a huge sigh "—it's always the way of young men to be piling their guilt high. You'll be finding your own share of it soon enough, my lad!"

"Thank you." Kenhodan grinned, once more completely at ease.

"Don't be mentioning it," Bahzell said kindly. "It's a rare gift any champion of Tomanāk has for the giving of advice and counsel, though it might be—and I'm one as says this with full modesty, you understand—as I'm after being a bit better at it than most."

◆　　◆　　◆

Chernion sat at a table and watched Bahzell and Kenhodan talk. Her appearance had changed radically without her leathers, tight breast band, and padded waist, and her sword—longer and straighter than the one the guildmaster carried, but lighter—was clean of the deadly mindanwe poison which coated so many assassins' blades. Chernion seldom needed that sort of edge anyway, and Bahzell had sharp eyes . . . and little respect for one who bore poisoned steel.

She wore the rust and green of the border wardens, for the borderers admitted women to their ranks and were respected everywhere as canny fighters and scouts. She'd used her chosen role often—indeed, she'd firmly established it among the borderers themselves—and it would make her valuable to travelers, if only she could contrive the proper introduction. She knew she needed some compelling means to gain their trust if she hoped to penetrate their ranks and learn their purpose, and neither Wencit nor the Bloody Hand was noted for credulity and childlike trust in chance met strangers.

Finding that means had always been the least certain part of her plan, but she'd find a way. It was dangerous to extemporize against wary and skilled targets, yet she was who she was, and she had no choice. Besides—

She looked up and tensed as four men entered the taproom and found chairs at a corner table near the targets. They wore nondescript clothing, of the sort common in the streets of Sindor, but they gave Chernion pause, for she knew them, and she cursed silently.

Her orders clearly hadn't reached Umaro in time, but it seemed obvious he'd heard about Rosper's fate. And, disciplined or not, there was no doubt at all about how he'd react to that news without a direct order from her to stand down. The quartet was from the Morfintan chapter, and they could only be here to attack.

She ground her teeth, cursing herself for a fool. She'd known the Tomanāk cult preferred the Dancing Unicorn, but she'd expected Wencit to maintain his usual low profile. She'd never dreamed they would come here, and their proximity to the Windhawk had undermined her entire strategy. Nor could she do anything about the present situation. The dog brothers would be strung to the limit as they stalked their prey, and they knew Chernion only as a man. If she approached them now it would touch off a reaction which could end only in their deaths or hers. No, she could only watch and wait, hoping the four might succeed in Wencit's absence. Not that she expected it.

She chewed her thoughts unhappily, uncertain what to do when they attacked. The possibility that she could somehow assist their attack didn't really exist. They'd have no reason to think she was an ally, so they'd have to assume she was trying to help the *targets*, which meant they'd turn on her in an instant. Besides, she wasn't at all certain they'd succeed even with her help, and everyone in the Dancing Unicorn must have heard about Rosper's attack by now. That meant anyone who clashed with the travelers risked being taken for assassins, whatever they actually were, and she could scarcely pose as a friend later if she attacked them now.

No, all she could do at the moment was watch, helpless to affect what was about to happen in any way. That was an unpalatable thought, but a woman hadn't become master of the Guild without overcoming adversity. She would overcome this one, and so she ordered a tankard of ale and carefully eased her sword in its sheath under cover of the table and waited.

The four assassins were in no hurry, and she approved their caution as they ordered ale of their own. She watched them unobtrusively search the room for potential obstacles, then turned her own attention to the targets.

Bahzell and his reputation attracted her gaze first. His sword stood against the table, sheathed, but Chernion took little comfort from that. The strap normally buttoned across the quillons was loose; it wouldn't take the hradani long to clear his blade. Nor was the sword his only weapon. She noted the hook knife and recalled the tales of his skill with it, and his conversation with Kenhodan hadn't fooled her into underestimating him. She knew his eyes had scanned her carefully as he entered, and his attention roamed as acutely as her own, though he was surprisingly good at masking his wariness.

She made a professional judgment: the Bloody Hand was alert, but he could be had with the right plan and enough men. Whether or not the current foursome was sufficient to the task might be another matter, but she was confident of her own ability to take him in the right circumstances. It wouldn't be easy, and it might cost a man or two, but it could be done. So reassured, she turned her carefully incurious gaze to his companion.

Her eyes narrowed in sudden, shocked realization.

By the Scorpion! The redhead was more dangerous than the hradani!

Those trained eyes had measured and respected the Bloody Hand, but she saw deep into Kenhodan with another sense. Something in him touched the darkness at her own core, and she shivered as death called to death.

He was even less obviously watchful than the hradani, but his shoulders never quite relaxed, even in laughter. She'd seen such subtle tension—the tautness of nerves on a hair trigger of constant anticipation—only once or twice, and unlike Bahzell, he'd chosen a backless stool instead of a chair. More than that, he wore his sword across his back, even here, with the hilt against his left shoulder. It was an unusual way to carry a longsword, but Chernion knew how snake-quick such a draw could be, and the scabbard's restraining strap was as unbuttoned as Bahzell's. No, this Kenhodan was a dangerous, dangerous man. He might not even know it himself, but he sat poised for instant slaughter in a way not even Bahzell, champion of Tomanāk though he might be, matched.

She blinked and shivered again in her chair as her subtle antennae vibrated. He reeked of death, yet he seemed unaware of it. Only once before had she sensed so overpowering an aura of lethality: in Regind, the guildmaster who'd taken her oath. But this man wasn't Regind. He had none of the long dead guildmaster's coldness. Deadly, yes, but without the icy stink of blood. He was...contradictory, and in Chernion's trade, contradictions spelled danger.

She was so lost in her thoughts she almost missed the start of the attack.

One of the assassins walked to the bar for fresh drink, his path taking him behind Kenhodan, putting the redhaired man between him and Bahzell. The hradani's gaze flicked over him calmly as he passed, but his purpose was plain, and Bahzell's eyes moved away.

Chernion deliberately looked elsewhere. She hadn't felt so nervous over a kill in years, but there was something in the air. She was a woman of hard logic, yet also one of instinct. She knew false calm when she saw it.

"Ho, Sagrin!" a seated assassin shouted to his partner at the bar. "Don't drink it all yourself, man! We've got thirsts over here, too, you know!"

Chernion recognized the ploy and waited for Sagrin to respond.

"If you need more, then send me another pair of hands. Two of us can *probably* carry enough—even for you sots!"

Chernion watched professionally as a second man stood and walked toward the bar. Innocent banter lent a cloak of normalcy to their maneuver as they boxed their targets: two at the bar, two at the table on the far side of Bahzell and Kenhodan. The attack would come with their prey between them.

The two at the bar each picked up a tankard in either hand and started back. The remaining pair rose and moved casually to meet them, expressing ribald distrust in their ability to deliver the ale undrunk. But the pretext, Chernion wondered. What would be the pretext? If they attacked without some ostensibly legitimate cause, they would never escape alive. Even with one, their chances of escape and survival were less than even, given the Dancing Unicorn's patrons' state of alert, but at least *with* one, they might—

A tankard shifted slightly. It was a tiny thing, so small only Chernion's eyes noticed it, yet it showed her what would happen. She kept her face disinterested but smiled inwardly. She still rated their chances as poor, but she might be wrong.

The man whose grip had shifted passed Kenhodan and suddenly stumbled. The tankard left his hand, as if thrown aside in an effort to regain his balance, and its contents lashed across Bahzell's face.

Fools! Chernion's budding respect for their plan vanished, yet she knew it wasn't truly their fault. They lacked her empathy for death, and they'd misjudged their targets' relative threat. They thought *Bahzell* was more dangerous; she knew better.

"Keep your damned feet under your table, whoreson!" the stumbling assassin shouted, swinging toward Kenhodan in an apparently drunken fury. He dropped the other tankard just too quickly, and again Chernion railed at his blunder. *Into his* eyes, *fool!* But she shouted the mental command uselessly. Bahzell might claw at blinded eyes, but Kenhodan was clear-eyed and deadly.

"Don't talk to me like that!" the assassin roared, his sword springing free, and the most critical witness might have taken it for a drunken reaction to a hot retort. But that was the last bit of perfection. One moment, everything proceeded as planned; the next, chaos and blood ruled the Dancing Unicorn.

Kenhodan's response was instantaneous. His knee smashed against the underside of the heavy table and the top rocketed upward, crashing into the chest and sword of the assassin who'd sprung the trap. That man staggered back, clawing for balance, going to one knee, his sword wavering.

In the same moment, even without rising, Kenhodan's hand unsheathed his sword and swept it back behind him. Chernion knew her own alertness, her own skill and situational awareness, but she doubted even she would have realized what was happening quickly enough to react so unerringly or known exactly where that second foe was to be found. But whether or not *she* could have responded with such flashing speed was beside the point. Steel hissed, exploding into the throat of the second assassin, and the dog brother dropped in a spray of blood with a hoarse, bubbling shriek. He'd drawn his sword just too quickly for a spontaneous brawl, but even so it hadn't fully cleared its scabbard before he died.

Bahzell reacted as well. Ale blinded him, but he knew what was happening. Even as the table bounded up, he grasped his sword blindly and flicked his wrist. The sheath flew, and he whirled with the massive blade to face the attack he knew must be coming from behind him. But he couldn't see. Despite superb reflexes, he was blind, and though his edge hissed dangerously near his attackers, the blow missed.

His assailants gave ground, astounded by the collapse of their trap and the speed of their intended victims' reactions, but they were professionals. The near miss told them the hradani was still blind, and they charged, desperate to finish him before dealing with Kenhodan.

Their brief pause had cost them only fractions of a second...but it was still too long. Kenhodan had recognized his friend's danger, and he launched from his stool. A yard of bloody steel went before him, and he slapped Bahzell's back in warning as he sailed past. His powerful lunge smashed two feet of blade through the lead assassin, but the other—warned by his fellow's scream—backed quickly, using Kenhodan's recovery time to fall into a guard position of his own.

Chernion's mind whirred as if it were made of Dwarvenhame gears and wire. Bahzell's left hand scrubbed at his eyes. They were clearing, but not quickly enough. The obvious ploy was to keep Kenhodan in play until the one who'd been floored by the tabletop took the hradani from the rear. Then both of them would turn on Kenhodan, yet the Bloody Hand must die before his eyes cleared, or they had no hope.

But Chernion had the measure of Kenhodan now. If the man called Sagrin paused to dagger Bahzell, the hradani might die, but Sagrin and his companion were children compared to Kenhodan. They'd never kill him, as well. Her mind weighed the factors fleetingly as she rose and thrust towards the bared steel—to aid her men or be the first to accost them afterward, as circumstances dictated.

Now she took a third option.

"'Ware, hradani! Behind you!" she shouted.

Sagrin turned toward her, warned of the new foe, and his blade hissed. So be it. Kenhodan was more dangerous than the Bloody Hand—she'd staked her life upon it—and unless he died, the attack was useless. Bahzell's death would please the Guild—and Wulfra—but it wouldn't turn Wencit and the redhaired man from whatever mission had brought them to the south. For that matter, the entire taproom was coming to its feet, and none of the men in it were going to accept for a moment that this was no more than a spontaneous drunken brawl. The chance that they would had never been great, and it would have depended entirely upon the affair ending as quickly as it began, a drunken brawl in which none of the combatants had had the time to think things through and step back from the brink. Any hope of that had disappeared forever by now, which meant her dog brothers were already doomed, whatever happened. Yet their deaths might serve her as introduction and guarantee in one.

Steel grated as she engaged her own man. She knew his sword skill was high, as it must be for him and his fellows to have expected this ploy to work, but he wasn't *her* equal.

Sagrin's blade licked at her with dangerous speed, and she parried, cutting in return in a lightning flourish of steel as she matched her greater skill and speed against his greater strength. Her world narrowed to the sharp contact of metal on metal, ringing and pealing. It seemed to have lasted forever, yet the other patrons, many of them trained warriors, were still shocked, frozen as she and Kenhodan engaged the assassins.

Kenhodan heard swords ring yet dared not look away from his foe. He didn't know if it was Bahzell or someone else who fought the other attacker, and fear for his friend stabbed him, but he pushed it down, concentrating on his swordplay. He was the better bladesman, but this man was delaying him. He was a hindrance, and Kenhodan felt his core of fury take command of his left hand, moving it to the hilt of Gwynna's dagger. His right locked blades with a turn of his wrist, and both swords rose high, his chest crashing into his opponent's. For an instant they strained together ... and Gwynna's dagger plunged up under the assassin's ribs and twisted.

The man went down, shrieking, and Kenhodan spun with inhuman speed. Steel belled and crashed as two combatants flashed through a desperate exchange. A woman—a beautiful woman, with black hair flying in a silken cloud—engaged the surviving killer. Kenhodan leapt to her side, but he was too late. Her blade slithered in side-armed, writhing past Sagrin's guard with deceptive ease, and opened a deep gash across his ribs. He fell back in anguish, and the woman's follow-up thrust drove into his belly and ripped upward. He opened his mouth in a silent scream, choked blood, and fell.

He was dead before he landed.

Kenhodan put his back to the woman's and surveyed the room. Scarlet ran from his sword and pearled on his dagger tip, and the hard, bright smell of blood and the reek of opened intestines filled a room which was absolutely motionless. Most of the patrons were fighting men; they knew any move might be misread.

Kenhodan glared at them for a moment, then lowered his sword. The fire in his eyes faded, his daggered foe gave a last moan and was still, and ale still ran from a dropped tankard. It had been that quick.

He drew a deep breath and turned to the woman.

"My thanks," he said formally.

"None needed," Chernion replied with equal formality. Her eyes searched his for a moment and something inside her relaxed ever so slightly as she felt him rechain whatever demon slept at the heart of him.

"My thanks to his," Bahzell rumbled, stepping forward, his eyes cleared at last. "I'm thinking I'd've sprouted a steel backbone, but for you."

"No one likes to see four set on two," she replied, bending to wipe her blade on Sagrin's tunic. She straightened. "And that's what it was from the start. I've seen that trick."

"We're grateful," Kenhodan said, flicking blood from his own blades with the casual wrist snap of a man who'd done it a thousand times before. Then he reached for another fallen assassin's tunic to wipe both of them down.

"But what was it all about?" Chernion wondered innocently.

"I think they were assassins," Kenhodan said grimly.

"*Assassins?*" Chernion put a hiss into her voice. "But why—?"

She broke off as the tavern's owner hurried up, his face dark with anger. He stooped to recover Bahzell's scabbard, then straightened and extended it to him.

"By the Mace, Bahzell, you warned me they wanted you, but I never thought dog brothers would be so bold! To enter the Unicorn...!"

"To tell truth, I'd not've expected it myself, Telbor. I'm thinking I may be after growing soft in the brain, too, for we've killed their fellows and there's more than money in it now. But for my friend and this borderer, I'd never be after making a mistake again!"

His laughter eased the tension.

"And who might it be as I'm after owing my life?" he asked, turning to Chernion.

"My name is Elrytha—Elrytha Sarndaughter," Chernion replied, "border warden from the southern East Walls, of Clan Torm. I'm pleased to have served the Bloody Hand."

"You know me?" Bahzell eyed her intently.

"No." Chernion allowed herself a slight smile. "On the other hand, there aren't so many hradani champions of Tomanāk, are there?" She shook her head as Bahzell's ears flicked in acknowledgment, then frowned slightly. "I hadn't heard you'd come south, though."

"It's Angthyr we're bound for," Bahzell said.

Kenhodan frowned briefly, then shrugged. Their enemies surely already knew their destination. Why not tell a friend?

"Angthyr?" Chernion's tone was surprised. "I have business in Fen Guard in Shespar, and I've been a little nervous about the trip, times being as they are. Perhaps we could travel together for a way?"

She held her breath, afraid she'd pushed too hard but unable to waste the opening.

"That might be a good idea," Kenhodan said slowly, "but I'm afraid we'd have to consult our other companion first. For myself, I'm impressed, and if you don't mind assassins, I'd be pleased if you joined us, Border Warden."

"And I!" Bahzell rumbled, extending his great hand. He and Chernion exchanged the grip of warriors, and his eyes widened in pleased surprise at the strength of her fingers. She smiled inwardly at his expression.

If Wencit was as easily duped as these simpletons, they were all as good as dead already.

◆   ◆   ◆

Wencit returned several hours later to find all three of them at a corner table. He crossed to them and looked down at Bahzell quizzically.

"So, Bahzell." He placed a hand on the hradani's shoulder. "What's this I hear about bloodshed and slaughter? Can't you and Kenhodan stay out of trouble for a moment without me?"

His tone was bantering, but his multihued eyes watched Chernion disconcertingly. She forced herself to remain expressionless, but a tiny flicker of fear flared within her under the weight of that glowing regard. She hadn't bargained on the sheer strength of the wizard's presence.

"Hah!" Bahzell's foot hooked a chair out and he waved at it. "Fine talk! As if these little escapades were owing nothing to our taste in friends! Aye, and as if we weren't after spending half our time keeping your old hide whole!"

"Perhaps, Mountain."

Wencit sat and raised a polite eyebrow at Chernion.

"Wencit of Rūm, be known to Elrytha Sarndaughter of the Border Wardens," Bahzell said. "But for her, the world would be after being the poorer for one hradani."

"I see." Wencit bowed without rising. "My thanks, Border Warden. He may be a noisy lout—in fact, he *is* a noisy lout—but he's also a friend."

"I did little enough. Kenhodan would've finished them without me."

"But not in time," Kenhodan said quickly.

"In time, I think." Chernion shrugged. "Still, I was happy to be of assistance. There are too many dog brothers in the world."

"Aye, that she was and that there are, and she might be after lending still more aid, Wencit," Bahzell said. "She's business in Shespar, and it's our thought we might be traveling together. She's a worthy blade and the skill of a borderer—such might be after serving as well."

"But not unless she knows the risks," Kenhodan interjected firmly.

"Truly spoken, lad. We'd not ask a friend to travel with us blind, but it was our thought we'd best be deferring to your judgment before saying more. You're after being the best judge of how much of our journey should be public knowledge."

"As little as possible," Wencit said dryly. His wild-fire eyes studied Chernion for a moment. Then he smiled slowly.

"A border warden could be of considerable assistance," he murmured. "Very well, Elrytha. Our destination's Torfo. We have a small matter to deal with, one concerning Baroness Wulfra, and she doesn't want us to prosper—thus the assassins. She's attacked three times with sorcery, as well, so any trip with us would be neither safe nor comfortable. Are you sure you want to take the trail with companions so beset?"

"Wulfra?" Chernion found she had no need to feign anger as she said the name. "I owe that one an ill turn or two. Yes, I'll go with you—in fact, I demand to join you!"

"Demand?" Wencit repeated the word softly.

"Yes, demand by my service to your friends! Wulfra cost the lives of some of my close companions, and revenge is my right, I think."

"Perhaps so." Wencit regarded her again, then

shrugged. "Very well . . . Elrytha of the border wardens. Will you take the road with us in the morning?"

"With pleasure," she said, raising her tankard, but behind her smile her brain was busy. Now why, she wondered, had he hesitated over her assumed name? She'd best go carefully with this one. But whatever he suspected, she'd won admittance to his party.

That was worth the lives of four dog brothers.

CHAPTER FOURTEEN

South from Sindor

"Do we *really* have to leave this damned early, Wencit?"

Kenhodan's mournful plaint was low but intense as dawn bled over the city of Sindor and four riders approached the south gate. No one else was abroad except for a few city guardsmen, a single military patrol, and a handful of apprentices sweeping the streets in preparation for business.

"Humor me, Kenhodan," Wencit murmured, glancing around alertly.

"You can't really think the assassins won't find out soon enough anyway," Kenhodan grumbled. "I could've slept another three hours, but for you."

"So you could have. And of course I know the dog brothers have scouts out. Don't worry. They've been taken care of—wherever they are."

"'Taken care of?'" Kenhodan raised an eyebrow. "Didn't you explain to me some time ago that white wizards don't use spells against non-wizards?"

Chernion's nerves went taut at the redhaired man's

question, but her face was expressionless when she glanced at him and the wizard.

"No," Wencit said with a sudden almost boyish grin. "That's not what I said, Kenhodan. The Strictures say a wizard can't *harm* a non-wizard except in direct self-defense. I suppose I could make a case for self-defense against assassins who want to kill me, but that's not really necessary in this case, because I haven't hurt them a bit. In fact," he chuckled gleefully, "they'll find it quite...refreshing."

"Really?" Kenhodan eyed him speculatively. "And are you going to tell us what it is you've done?"

"No," Wencit said smugly. "I'm not."

Nor did he, for all of Bahzell's and Kenhodan's prodding. Chernion, on the other hand, resolved not to try, because something about the wizard's manner whenever he spoke to her made her uneasy. He didn't know she was an assassin—he'd never have let her so close if he'd known that—but instinct told her something she'd done, or said, or possibly left *un*done, had aroused his suspicion. She couldn't imagine what it had been, but she was determined to make no more false steps until she found out. And so she kept silent as they clattered quietly through South Gate and headed for South Wall Pass.

There was no sign of any watcher as they slipped away from Sindor like thieves.

◆   ◆   ◆

Umaro of Morfintan was a hard man whose followers took pains to avoid disappointing him. They were times, unfortunately, when they had no choice about that.

Like this morning.

"It took you *three days* to find me, did it?" Umaro grated. "How did you spend your time? Wenching? You had orders to *find* me, Brothers!"

Umaro's voice was as unpleasant as his appearance, which was to say extremely so. He was a short, slab-sided man, burly as a bear and covered in thick, black body hair. His forehead slanted, his hairline was low, and his eyes were dull as soot, yet surface impressions could be deceiving. He was renowned among fellow professionals as an even better poisoner than Rosper and one of the sharpest witted of the Guild's craftmasters. At the moment, however, his temper—for which he was equally renowned—was on a short leash as he glowered at the dog brother called Horum.

"Yes, Umaro." Horum was sweating slightly. "But we didn't know where you were. Darnosh waited at the Windhawk in case you came there after all while Menik and I searched the city. But you were too well hidden. We just couldn't find you in time!"

"Arrrgh!"

Umaro waved a fist and grunted disgustedly. It was no one's fault, and he knew it, but his fresh losses grated on nerves already raw from news of Rosper's death. Sharnā, but this job was costing dear!

He took a quick turn around the squalid room. Nothing had gone as planned. The fact that Chernion had been right at the start—that the Guild should never have dealt with the sorceress, however good the price—had become steadily more obvious. His own failure only made it worse. Perhaps he should have been warned by Rosper's fate, but the opportunity had looked so good. Yet to have all four of his dog brothers cut down without a single survivor—and without drawing so much as a single drop of blood in return—!

Well, spilt blood couldn't be poured back into his men's veins, and he turned on Horum once more.

"Tell me about this agent of Chernion's again," he growled.

"He says he's used her before." Horum breathed easier at the change of subject. "All I know is that she's supposed to be our relay, and we're to take anything she says as having come from Chernion himself."

"I don't like it," Umaro muttered. "Did Chernion tell her she could kill our men just to gain the targets' confidence? Pah!"

"I think that was her own idea," another assassin said. "In fact, I think it was a case of opportunity, not planning. And I hate to say it, but the fact that she took the opportunity may indicate her judgment's even sounder than Chernion suggested."

Umaro's thunderous expression turned even darker and his jaw clenched visibly as he turned to the speaker, but his tone was almost courteous despite his obvious anger.

"Explain, Ashwan," he said.

"From what I've been able to discover," Ashwan said, "the attack had already failed before she moved at all. No disrespect to our brothers, but they seem to've underestimated the redhead. I don't blame them. Given the Bloody Hand's reputation, I'd've made exactly the same judgment, but that's why they didn't throw the second tankard. They thought blinding *him* would be advantage enough, while throwing both tankards might've looked even more suspicious. On the other hand, it was already going to look 'suspicious' to the

Unicorn's customers, and it would seem—" he drew a fingertip fastidiously across the mean little room's tabletop—"that they should have thrown it anyway."

He raised his finger, gazed down at it for a moment, then blew dust from it and looked back up at Umaro.

"According to the witnesses I spoke with, Sagrin was down at the start—thanks to the redhead. Lerdon died before he cleared leather—thanks to the redhead. And Calth and Freedmark had time for only one cut at Bahzell before the redhead—this 'Kenhodan'—killed Freedmark and turned on Calth." He shrugged elegantly. "I find it difficult to believe he couldn't have killed Calth and Sagrin—after Sagrin picked himself up from the floor again—all by himself." He shook his head. "No. The trap had already fallen apart before Elrytha took a hand, and at least she bought their trust about as convincingly as anyone could have."

"But we might've had the Bloody Hand, at least, but for her!"

More than the frustration of a single failed mission burned in Umaro's angry voice. Like Chernion, he'd consulted the Guild's records when this assignment was accepted. He knew, unlike most of the rest of his men, just how many dog brothers had fallen to Bahzell Bahnakson's sword over the years.

"We might have," Ashwan replied. "But we might not have, either. He barely missed Calth when his eyes were full of ale—I doubt he would have missed Sagrin several blinks later. And be honest, Umaro. I, for one, wouldn't care to face the Bloody Hand when he was only *half* blind."

Ashwan admitted it without apology, and Umaro

only grunted. A killer with Ashwan's record could afford to be honest.

"Maybe you've hit it," the craftmaster growled after a moment, "but whatever happened it leaves us with a hellish mess now. When we took the assignment, the only target was the poxy wizard—now look! We've got the Bloody Hand and this Kenhodan fellow *as well as* a wizard!"

He paused to spit on the floor, and his men stood silently as he worked the venom from his system. Only Ashwan smiled.

"The Council will regret overruling Chernion on this one," Umaro said with bitter satisfaction. "He warned them, and he was right, so I'll abide by his orders. But I'll have all three—wizard or no—before this is over!"

He stopped and yanked out a watch and glared down at it.

"And speaking of orders, where the hell are our gate reports?" he exploded. "It's past ten—surely they must've gone somewhere!"

"True," Ashwan said imperturbably, "but—"

He broke off as another assassin hurried in and saluted, breathing heavily. His face was slick with sweat.

"Well, what bad news brings you here?" Umaro growled.

"Y-Your pardon, Umaro, b-but something strange's happened."

"I suppose you mean something *new?*" Umaro sighed resignedly.

"Yes. Shernak at South Gate. H-He fell asleep, Umaro!"

"He *what?* That's one error too many, by the scorpion! I'll have his heart for this! I'll—!"

"Just a moment, Umaro," Ashwan said softly, holding up one hand, and turned to the messenger. "Why do I feel you have something more to add, Brother?"

"I do," the messenger said gratefully. "The gatekeeper says the targets passed through at dawn."

He flinched at Umaro's volcanic curse, but Ashwan's dark eyes never even flickered.

"And Shernak never saw them?"

His voice was even softer, and the messenger shook his head.

"No. That is, he thinks he did, but he's not certain. If he did, it was just before he . . . fell asleep."

"*Wizardry!*" Umaro snapped viciously. "Gods! If I ever agree to hunt another wizard, I'll deserve to have my own throat slit!"

"Perhaps." Ashwan stroked his black mustache thoughtfully. "But it seems Chernion was even wiser to plant a spy on them than he realized. Without it, they'd probably have escaped. As it is, we have a friend to mark their trail for us."

"*If* she doesn't kill us all!" Umaro growled. "Well, it's nice *something's* working out! Get the horses. We'll have to ride hard to catch up, but I want to be close enough for this Elrytha to contact us tonight. Then we'll see what Chernion has in mind—I hope!"

"Oh, I'm sure Elrytha can tell us that," Ashwan murmured.

◆　◆　◆

"I think we should leave the high road for a while," Wencit said thoughtfully. He touched Byrchalka's neck gently as he spoke, and the black stallion stopped and turned so that they faced the others while the wizard glanced around under the early afternoon sun. "We seem to have the road to ourselves at the moment, so let's try to vanish."

"I thought you'd pulled the assassins' fangs," Kenhodan said.

"Only temporarily. Anyway, I don't want them catching up with us. Not now that we're getting closer to Wulfra."

"Why not?" Kenhodan asked.

"Because," Wencit said patiently, "we're almost close enough for her to try some long-range sorcery, but she can't do it unless she can see us. That's why I want to avoid the assassins' eyes. She can't pierce my glamour from the outside, but if she's set a trap link on one of them, she can use him as a focus to get through."

"A trap link?" Chernion asked the question just a shade too quickly but recovered in time to resist looking away and making it worse.

"Yes, Border Warden," Wencit said, his eyes glowing. "A trap link is a means of turning another person into a sort of beacon for a wizard's scrying spells. You might say it's the same as bearing the wizard's mark."

"I see. And you think these assassins may have been marked that way?"

"I'm almost certain of it," Wencit replied. "It's a favorite trick of dark wizards, usually managed through a gift or a payment. It's easier that way. You place a simple little spell on a valuable object and present it to your victim. The first two or three people to handle it—especially if they covet it—are marked for your spells." He shrugged. "You can do almost anything you want in the way of spying on them after that, even through a glamour. And if they prove unreliable, you can use it to guide a death spell to them."

"That seems like an excellent reason to have no dealings at all with wizards, if you'll pardon my saying so," Chernion murmured.

"Why should I mind, Border Warden? You're quite right, where dark wizards are concerned. But to return to the subject at hand, I want to be safely out of eye range of the road before our friends catch up."

"What about this farm road, then?" Bahzell rumbled.

"It looks promising," Wencit said. "Border Warden, do you know this countryside well enough to guide us?"

"Certainly. How close to the high road do you want to stay?"

"Close enough we can check to watch behind us every so often."

"All right. There's a trail up this lane that leads toward South Keep. It doesn't go much of the way, and it's rough in places, but it tops out every so often and lets you look down on the high road."

"Excellent."

Wencit nodded and Chernion touched heels to her dappled mare, moving up beside Bahzell, grateful she actually did know the lay of the land well. She felt confident she could leave enough signs for Umaro to follow, no matter where they went, but for the moment she let the surface of her mind carry her along while she pondered Wencit's words, and her palms tingled as she recalled the touch of Wulfra's gold. Was it possible?

It was, she thought grimly. And if she could prove Wulfra had forged such a link—or even infer it, for

Chernion was no court of law—the sorceress would die. The safety of the Guild and its master required it.

◆   ◆   ◆

Wulfra felt cautiously satisfied that the spells around her castle were now little short of impenetrable. Wencit could certainly break them, but not without using wild magic, which would both warn her of his arrival and tire him before they met. She'd also augmented her guards, but she didn't rely on them for warnings—only as swords to be sent wherever her trap spells indicated.

Still, it would be far better for Wencit to suffer a mischance on his journey. By her calculations, he must have passed Sindor by now, which put him somewhere on the South Road between there and South Keep. There should be opportunities in plenty for misadventures along that route, but to arrange them, she had to be able to find him. Besides, as the object of his intentions, she had every reason to keep track of his location. The points at which he had to pass through towns ought to have given her an opportunity to do at least that much, but towns were few, far between, and avoidable between Sindor and the border. The only city he *had* to pass through was South Keep and, unfortunately, no wizard's scrying spells could breach the mage barrier maintained around the fortress.

Still, the South Road was chancy enough without arcane enemies, she reminded herself. Winter, when avalanches were more common, would have been better, of course. Such "natural disasters" could eliminate enemies without suggesting the art. That would have been ever so much more convenient than what she might find herself driven to now. The last thing she needed was an investigation by the Council of Semkirk, but if events persisted in forcing her hand...

Yet to attack Wencit at all, she had to find him—and she couldn't. It was maddening to command so much power without having quite enough. With more power, she could have broken his glamour. With more power, she wouldn't fear confronting him. She might not even need her cat-eyed ally at all.

She blanked that thought quickly. It wasn't the wisest thing to be thinking, however hard it was to avoid, given the tight leash on which he kept her. Not that he hadn't made good suggestions. The lightning in Belhadan had been brilliant, but Wencit had guessed at the last minute. The shadows had been a weaker ploy, but worth attempting when the cat-eyed wizard delivered the shadowmage. And she'd entertained strong hopes for the madwind, once more subtly strengthened by her patron, as well.

Unfortunately, none had worked in the end. It was galling to have come so close so often, yet all the tales seemed to be true. Wencit *did* live a charmed life. Whatever she did, he always produced an unexpected ally or counter just when he needed it. How *did* he keep surviving? It was unpleasant of him to be so durable.

Yet none of her attempts had been a complete waste. Each gave a clearer indication of his strength, although the indications to date were uniformly unfavorable. He'd *used* the wild magic more than once, but only as a power source for the most capable *wand* wizardry she'd ever seen. Unfortunately, he hadn't been forced to *rely* on the wild magic to survive any of them, and that had unfortunate implications for the balance of strength between them.

All of which made the cat-eyed wizard's latest refusal to share information with her even more intensely frustrating. He'd made it clear he intended to remain silent on Wencit's doings unless and until she could suggest some plausible means by which she could track the wizard out of her own resources, curse him!

Well, the game might still prove worth the risk, given the power involved. The only difficult bit would be surviving to claim it.

She considered checking Chernion again, but rejected the thought, for she was beginning to wonder just how acute the assassin's senses were. She certainly seemed sensitive enough to have felt it, and it wouldn't do to rattle the killer—or to warn her of the link's existence. Besides, there were other demands on her art. She could no longer put off strengthening the spells on the sword, much as she dreaded it. She'd given the matter considerable thought and expended a great deal of effort on those spells already, enough to give even Wencit pause if he ever got that far, but they could never be *too* strong... not against Wencit of Rūm. Of course, she'd probably be dead already if he did get that far, but it was pleasant to think he might perish shortly after her own demise.

She rose from her desk and turned to the spiral stair into the bowels of Castle Torfo. Its narrow iron treads rang oddly under her slippers as she descended it gracefully, and she held the hem of her gown delicately high.

The walls congealed with damp as she passed the cellars and entered the dungeons. She didn't hesitate as she threaded her way through the cold, dark corridors few of her ancestors had used as heavily as she, and she went still deeper, into a maze of tunnels which were no part of the castle's plans. They were smooth, black, and circular—polished and burned out of the rock by the art. How long ago and by whom she didn't know—not with certainty—but it had to have been one of the Carnadosans. And whoever had done it, the tunnels still tingled with the power which had seared them into the stone's heart, and the years were thick as dust in their dry air.

The castle was five hundred years old, yet until Wulfra's budding sensitivity to sorcery drew her here, the maze had been unknown. Now she knew it as intimately as she knew the power sleeping at its heart.

Muted rustles and scrapes made her smile, for the creatures of her sorcery prowled the darkness. Let Wencit break in! First he must win his way across Angthyr and the Scarthū Hills. Then he had to avoid her spells and patrols, then find a way into the dungeons and from there into the maze. And even if he managed all that, he'd face her pets. His art might protect him, but it wouldn't help his companions very much.

If only she had a few more years to study the sword! Its vast power had eluded her most subtle probing for over ten years, yet she'd learned enough to know its power would have let her stand even against Wencit... if only she could unlock it! But unlocking the sword would be a lengthy and risky business. She needed time for that, and she needed to prevent the cat-eyed wizard from guessing her intent. If he suspected she might actually win control of the sword, his response would be quick and drastic. Normally, a direct attack from Kontovar would have been impossible, but he'd helped her with many of her defensive spells and, for all she knew, he'd installed his own triggers to turn them against her at need. So no thought of mastering the sword must cross her outer mind unless her fortress could be warded against *anyone*—even him.

She turned the last bend and entered the cavern of the sword itself.

A faint silvery-blue light pulsed at its core like cold fire, though the art hadn't created this dark void in the earth. She was certain of that. The maze about it, yes, but not the cavern itself. Yet despite its natural origins, its walls reeked of the power crackling in its cold, damp air. She hadn't suspected the presence of the ancient artifact beneath her castle when first she found the tunnels, but the cat-eyed wizard had led her to it even before she'd acceded to the title, trolling her with a lure of sorcery she'd accepted eagerly. The power pulsing here was neither good nor evil, yet its raw strength had sealed her future, for she'd known the potency trembling about her was only what had leaked through the sword's wards over the centuries, only a pittance beside the furnace of arcane energy trapped *within* those wards. It had whispered to her of a destiny beyond her dreams, that power, yet after long years of study, she was no wiser as to how it came to sleep here.

No matter. The sword was *hers*, and no one would take it while she lived.

She ignored the soft, frightened sounds of her last prisoner as she approached the blade with familiar, avaricious awe. Its power smote her through the corona of its wards, and she stared at it in fascination.

It was longer and narrower than the common words

of Norfressa: needle-tipped and gleaming with the blue wickedness of a razor. The hilt was a deep half-basket set with a spiral of rubies and emeralds that flickered in time with the wards' slowly shimmering radiance, but the pommel was gone, snapped from the hilt in some long-forgotten cataclysm of power.

Her eyes rested on that broken edge, and she shivered. A sliver of red crystal remained, as if the pommel had been a single ruby. Given the strength which still clung to the blade, the exchange of sorcery which had broken it must have been instantly lethal to any wizard within twice a thousand yards.

She let her senses press against the wards, hungry to reach through and take the sword for herself, but she dared not. The power in the cavern might be neutral, but it was only the byproduct of the sword itself, and *that* was far from neutral. She sensed the weight of its purpose, but had no notion what that purpose might have been or whether it would tolerate her touch. Yet she'd learned that the Strictures of Ottovar were artificial in at least one sense. Sorcery might be black or white, but any power—as power— was equally apt to "good" or "evil." If she were strong enough to endure its touch, she might draw the sword and shatter mountains with its strength.

That might explain the struggle the sword threatened to precipitate, but not why it had begun so suddenly. From tiny clues her ally had let slip, she was certain the cat-eyed wizard or one of his allies had concealed it here, though it seemed a strange hiding place. Or perhaps not. If it had been hidden as long ago as she suspected, it had lain here since the Strafing of Kontovar laid the Council of Carnadosa in ruins. Under

those circumstances, hiding it in Norfressa, where none
of his fellows might have thought to seek it, might
very reasonably have struck any surviving Dark Lord
as a very good idea. If that was the case, however,
the cat-eyed wizard obviously knew where it lay now,
so why not simply remove it now that Wencit had
become aware of it? And if, as he claimed, no one
could ever use it, where was the danger in letting
Wencit have it? And if Wencit couldn't use it, why
was he so determined to secure it in the first place?

Her lips tightened as she pondered the same old
questions. They'd troubled her mind often enough to
wear deep channels, flowing beneath her thoughts,
nagging unceasingly, making her wonder to just what
extent and end her patron was manipulating her. That
he *was* manipulating her was a given, and however
glib he might be, there was a core of inconsistency
at the heart of all the "explanations" he'd seen fit to
share with her.

He was mistaken or lying, she thought firmly, and
with Wencit so hell bent on taking the sword, she
suspected it was the latter. But it made no difference.
She would surrender the blade to no one!

She turned from the sword, consciously hearing
the frightened whimpers of her prisoner for the first
time. She smiled coldly at the gypsy girl upon the
altar, then stepped into the pentagram on the cave
floor. She laid the long, silver-bladed knife with its
dried, gory stains before the central candle, and her
captive's weeping grew louder as she lit the wick and
the scent of acrid, sinus-searing incense rose from its
dancing, livid green flame. She ignored the sounds.
The wench would play her part soon enough.

But the sounds reminded her of other tears, and she bent to stroke the lines of the pentagram. They were rusty-red, the color of long-dried blood, which was hardly surprising. She hoped her older sister's ghost appreciated the manner in which her death still contributed to the power of Torfo, but she rather doubted Wilfrida approved any more now than she had then.

No matter.

Wulfra of Torfo lit the other candles and raised her hands, turning pitiless eyes upon the last of the three sisters her guards had brought her. She hated to waste the girl, but she was necessary for the spell to work, and so the baroness pushed the small regret to the back of her brain as she centered on the delicate control her trap spell would require.

◆　　◆　　◆

The cat-eyed wizard watched his crystal and smiled. Such a delightful creature, Wulfra! As cuddly as an asp...and half as trustworthy.

That really was a credible bit of spellcraft, he reflected, given the...unconventional nature of her training, although he often wondered if she truly realized how far above her own level she was competing. He knew all about her designs on the sword, and they didn't concern him. Had it been possible to conquer the sword, he would have done so long since. Unlike Wulfra, however, he knew its history. *All* of its history, from the instant it was forged until the moment its pommel had shattered. There was a hole in that history, immediately following the Fall, for the original Council of Carnadosa had been smashed down to bedrock when Wencit and the White Council strafed the continent.

There was no telling who'd actually placed it under what would become Castle Torfo, although there were hints in the Carnadosans' oldest records that it might well have been Chelthys of Garoth, Herrik Ottarfro's lover and closest ally. It seemed a strange place for her to have hidden it, but she'd certainly have had every conceivable reason to want it far, far away from Kontovar in the immediate aftermath of the Fall! Its jagged, savagely radiating power would have been the last thing any wizard trying to rebuild from the ruins wanted within a thousand leagues of him!

It was remotely possible that it might have been hidden by one of the handful of surviving *white* wizards after the Fall, but that seemed far less likely than the chance that Chlethys had been responsible. The cat-eyed wizard had analyzed the working which had created the tunnels leading to its cavern, and they'd been the work of an immensely powerful and skilled wand wizard, clearly beyond the reach of anyone less skilled than a member of the Council of Ottavar itself, and of all the White Council's wand wizards, only Sharelsa had survived with her power—and mind—sufficiently intact for such a task. Surely if *she'd* hidden it, Wencit would have known where it lay all along, and he hadn't. The Council of Carnadosa knew precisely when he'd discovered its location, for they'd been watching through his glamour when he stumbled across the fact that it still existed. He'd been completely focused on discovering just how Wulfra had killed Queen Fallona's father; his reaction had been priceless when he'd probed the wards the sorceress had set about her castle in search of evidence of Carnadosan involvement in the assassination and turned up the sword instead. It was also the true reason he hadn't involved those infernal pests on the Council of Semkirk in his quest to eradicate Wulfra once and for all. There were some powers so great, some artifacts so ancient and—now—so deadly in their broken, half-mad agony, that even a wild wizard could approach them only with the utmost circumspection and only after years of study and research.

The cat-eyed wizard doubted anyone would ever know precisely how it had come to Torfo, but he knew too many other things about it to worry about Wulfra's pathetic aspirations, for the sword had never been something to be *mastered*. Even before its pommel had been shattered, it had served only those to whom it *chose* to answer and—also unlike Wulfra—he knew the last hand it would ever answer to had died a thousand years and more ago. For that matter, when its pommel had shattered in the long-ago battle that killed its last rightful owner, its power had been forever twisted and snarled, tied into knots of chaotic energy eternally at war with one another and impossible to untwist. Which, he admitted, made Wencit's current mission seem even more quixotic than the risk he'd taken to save Bahzell's half-breed daughter. Why was Wencit so intent on gaining an artifact not even a wild wizard could take against its will when he must know it was useless for the purpose for which it had forged so long ago?

Unless he'd found a way—or thought he had—to use it without touching its power at all? He *had* been studying it for many years now. Had he found a way to at least damp the universe-twisting energies radiating from it? To shut off its power—or, at least, that power's ability to reach beyond the physical limits of its own structure—so that it could at last be once more taken safely from the wards which confined it?

If he'd managed that much, he'd accomplished more than the Council of Carnadosa had achieved, but he *was* the world's last wild wizard. It certainly wasn't impossible he had, and he was clearly worried about what might be brewing in Kontovar. Did he hope to use the sword as a rallying symbol when the final, inevitable conflict began? That possibility had occurred to the cat-eyed wizard, but it didn't worry him. It might, indeed, prove a potent icon, but symbols would be weak reeds in the tempest looming over Norfressa, and without its inherent power, even that sword was little more than edged metal. And in the meantime...

It was unfortunate that the cat-eyed wizard couldn't use it directly any more than Wencit, but he *could* use it to trap Wencit under Castle Torfo. To test him. And if he learned what he expected to learn, the Norfressans were welcome to make what use of the sword they liked, for they wouldn't have long to use it.

He watched appreciatively as Wulfra wove her spells. That was a really splendid demon she was raising, especially for one summoned without the aid of Sharnā or one of his priests. It was true that she couldn't have done it without his own past help and tutelage, but it really was a creditable piece of work. Indeed, it was powerful enough to stand a remote chance against Wencit, though it was unlikely to injure him seriously. And, of course, that tiresome pain in the arse Bahzell had proven himself amply capable of dealing with far more powerful demons or even one of Krashnark's greater devils. On the other hand, it was always possible Bahzell would have suffered a mischief before Wencit ever got that deep into the maze—there were, after all, those other guardians of Wulfra's—and if he were to add a little something himself...

He smiled at the thought. Yes, and without mentioning it to Wulfra. And it might be a good idea to install a trigger of his own, as well, one she didn't know about. It might be amusing to set it off while she and Wencit were engaged and...distracted, as it were. Of course that would kill Wulfra—but, there! One had to make sacrifices.

He propped his chin on the fist as he watched her. Really a very respectable piece of work for a practitioner of her caliber, he thought as he watched her pick up the spell-charged knife and advance upon her twisting captive. His cat-eyes never blinked as the sorceress raised the deadly blade, and all he felt as it descended was impatience for her to finish so that he could improve upon her craft.

Then let Wencit of Rūm beware!

◆   ◆   ◆

Kenhodan squinted up and grunted in disgust as night came with storm clouds. He watched the purple-black banks gathering, then shook his head mournfully. He simply wasn't meant to leave a city dry shod, he decided.

"Rain coming," he said to Bahzell. "Again."

"Aye." Bahzell's glum tone mirrored Kenhodan's disgust. "Chemalka's after working overtime this trip."

"So it would appear. What do you think? An hour?"

"Three hours—at least," Chernion said.

"Those clouds look eager, Elrytha," Kenhodan said doubtfully.

"They are. But see how clear it is to the northeast? Spring storms gather slow in the East Walls, and they don't rain until they're ready. We still have time before it reaches us."

"Aye, so we do." Bahzell sounded noticeably more cheerful. "Time enough to be finding some cover, then, and I've a mind to be sleeping dry, if I can."

"Yes, and with dry firewood, too," Kenhodan threw in.

"I think not," Wencit said. "If Elrytha can find us a secluded spot, we'll pass the night in discreet invisibility."

"No fire?" Bahzell's ears flattened unhappily.

"None. Better cold and damp than dead, Bahzell."

"You've a nasty habit of being right," Bahzell said sourly. "How say you, Elrytha? Would it happen you're after knowing a good spot?"

"I think so. There's a cave up there," Chernion said, pointing up a steep slope, "big enough for the horses—even the coursers—and us. We can even have a fire; there are fissures in the roof to carry the smoke, and it's deep enough to hide the light."

She didn't mention that she'd been making for the cave all day.

"That's after sounding good," Bahzell said hopefully. "Wencit?"

"It sounds suitable." Wencit nodded to Chernion courteously. "You're a woman of many talents, Elrytha."

"Not to match yours, if the tales are true. I can offer only what any border warden might." She shrugged. "No more than that."

"I see. Well, lead us to your cave... Border Warden."

Chernion nodded and nudged her mare to begin the winding ascent of the steep hill, feeling the wizard's strange eyes on her back. What *was* the old bastard's problem? Well, it didn't matter; she was committed, and there was no turning back.

The horses scrambled up the hill as the clouds finished blotting out the sunset, and Kenhodan shivered in a chill breeze and glanced to the east. The tumbled foothills reared high, but the summits of the East Walls proper were far higher, vanishing in cloud, and white snow crowned them with a touch of merciless majesty.

The cave was as Chernion recalled it, even to the pile of wood custom demanded of shelters in mountain country. In a region of sudden snow and howling wind, fire often spelled the difference between life and death. Most travelers left wood ready behind them; those who didn't were always unpopular and sometimes suffered accidents on the trail.

"I'll fetch more wood," she offered. "We'll use a lot of that pile tonight."

She watched the wizard unobtrusively as she spoke.

"An excellent idea," he said calmly.

"I'll be back shortly, then," she said, her voice serene as she throttled her frustration. Damn and blast and Sharnā seize the man! Every instinct told her he knew or suspected something, that he was playing some obscure, devious game. But how? Why? Surely a wizard as wily as he wouldn't let a suspected assassin—or *anyone* he distrusted—slip away to mark their trail! Yet he just had, and she didn't like things she couldn't understand.

She picked her way into a patch of trees and seated herself on a winter-felled oak, pondering from a position which let her watch the cave. Was this some sort of test? Would Wencit send one of the others to follow her? But no one came, and she drummed on her knee in frustration while she sniffed the approaching rain.

It was safer to assume the worst than the best, she thought. So accept that Wencit had deduced she was an assassin. What possible motive could he have for allowing her to join his circle in that case?

Her drumming fingers stilled, and she frowned. There were many forms of manipulation. She herself was using Wencit, in a sense, in an effort to divine just how much Wulfra knew and how blatantly the baroness might have manipulated the Guild. Suppose that . . . suppose Wencit was using *her* at the same time? Suppose he *wanted* to give her information about Wulfra? Wanted to set the Guild at the sorceress' throat? And, of course, by keeping Chernion under his eye, he could control what the assassins learned about him and his mission by controlling their eyes in his camp.

She sighed and rose to begin gathering wood. Whatever his motives, they were too complex to divine with the information she had, but there was still time. She hadn't lived this long without developing a sixth, seventh, and an eighth sense, and those very senses which warned her all was not as it appeared also told her Wencit had no immediate plan to destroy her. If he did suspect her, he was keeping her alive and hiding that suspicion. Which wasn't to say he'd go out of his way to save her from anything else which might threaten, but she was accustomed to facing the world's hazards on her own.

She took her bearings and started back to the cave with a load of wood, grinning wryly. It seemed they were engaged in a game of wits in which he held a temporary advantage, and he *was* Wencit of Rūm. It was possible she'd finally met her match. Entirely possible this was the final game she wouldn't survive—yet the challenge was invigorating.

And she'd scored a few points. By now, Umaro and his thirty men would be on their trail, and they knew about the cave. Assassins often used it, which was why she'd maneuvered her present companions to this spot. She wouldn't be alone and unsupported much longer—and even Wencit would find her hard to dispose of with Umaro at her back. Let the wizard chew on *that!*

She considered ordering Umaro to attack that night, but put the idea away. They were too many unanswered questions. Curiosity was a good way for an assassin to get herself killed, but she knew she'd risk it. She meant to find out just how much Wencit knew, how he'd learned it, who he might have told, and why he'd let her live this long if he knew who or what she was.

She wanted answers to *all* those questions, but most of all she was determined to discover the depth of Wulfra's treachery before she struck.

CHAPTER FIFTEEN

Discoveries Along the South Road

Kenhodan grimaced as he sipped scalding tea, peered out of the cave, and shivered.

Sullen, slanting sheets of rain whipped the hillside shrubs like wet fur. The wind was out of the east, blowing the rain past the cave mouth rather than into it, but when they left they'd be riding straight into its teeth.

"Come look at the morning," he invited glumly as he heard Bahzell stretch and yawn behind him.

"Tomanāk!" Bahzell rested a huge hand on his shoulder as he looked out beside him. "You're after calling *that* a morning?"

"It's as close as we're going to get, I'm afraid. It's been coming down like that ever since I came on watch."

The massive cloud roof was lumpy with rain, and Kenhodan watched his breath plume in the chill air. Spring came late to the East Wall foothills.

"I'm thinking it's going to be a mite unpleasant out there," Bahzell said thoughtfully. "But it's little choice we have, and the dog brothers will be liking it as little as we."

"You're sure they're out there?"

"They're out there."

They turned at Chernion's positive voice. She looked far fresher and more rested than her companions, and she wore the green beret of a border warden. The silver oak tree of its badge winked in the firelight as she shrugged.

"It's not easy to lose assassins. They may fall behind, but they'll be there whenever we stop."

"Aye, you've a point there. At the least, they're after knowing we're out of Sindor, and they've a fair idea as to where we're headed. I'm thinking they'll know we're not on the high road, so they'll be after sweeping the rough lands. Once they start that, it'll not be long before they're after finding this cave."

"I agree," she said calmly.

"Then best we rouse Wencit and get started," Bahzell said reluctantly.

"No need for that," Kenhodan said. "He's already up and out."

"In that?" Bahzell jutted his chin at the rain.

"In that. I asked him where he was off to, and he said he just felt like stretching his legs."

Kenhodan and Bahzell exchanged speaking glances but failed to notice the flicker in Chernion's eyes.

"Which way did he head?" she asked casually. "Perhaps we should go find him if we're in a hurry."

"He was headed into those oaks when I lost sight of him." Kenhodan shrugged. "But I wouldn't be in a hurry to get soaked looking for him. He'll come back when he's ready."

"I suppose so," Chernion said, and returned to the saddlebag she'd been packing.

Interesting, she thought, that the wizard's constitutional took him directly toward the message cairn she'd left for Umaro.

◆　　◆　　◆

"Did you see something?"

"What? Where?"

Two wet assassins huddled under an oak, shivering miserably.

"Over there. Near the edge of the trees."

"I don't see anything," the second said after a moment. "And it's light enough we'd see anything there was to see. Stop imagining things."

"Huh! At least imagining things keeps my brain warm," the first snorted, "which is the only part of me that is!"

Wencit of Rūm paused several yards from the sentries, wrapped in a vision-turning spell, and smiled to himself. He stood just long enough to pat the message cairn's stones companionably, then turned back to the cave.

◆　　◆　　◆

"And where is it you've been?" Bahzell greeted Wencit upon his return.

"Out," Wencit said blandly, accepting a cup of tea with a grateful nod. He looked like a soaked beggar as water dripped from his beard. His boots were muddy to the knee, and the old hat jammed onto his head had gathered enough water to turn down at the brim. With his sword and dagger hidden by his mud-spattered poncho, he hardly looked like a famous wizard.

"And that's all the answer we'll be after getting?" Bahzell asked resignedly.

"Of course it is," Wencit said cheerfully. "If I meant to tell you more, I'd've started out telling you more. Really, Bahzell! All this traveling seems to be softening what brain you had to begin with."

"And aren't you just the world's most amusing fellow so early in the morning?" Bahzell rumbled. "Well, if you're after feeling as clutch-fisted with news as ever, let's be talking of something else. Like the weather."

"What about it?" Wencit asked, bending to lift his saddle as Byrchalka nudged him with a velvety nose.

"I can see as how we've need to be moving on, but I'm thinking we'll be lucky to make three leagues in a day cross-country in this." Bahzell paused, and Wencit nodded for him to continue. "Well, it's in my mind we might be taking ourselves back to the South Road, instead. I've little doubt they've guessed by now we took to the back roads. They'll be hunting us places like this, not on the high road, so like as not, we'd make up time and throw them off again for a while, too."

"That's sensible." Wencit nodded. "Border Warden, can we get to the South Road without too much delay?"

"Probably." Chernion met his eyes coolly and felt a little flicker of amusement in his gaze. In an odd way, she too, felt amused by the elaborate game she was now certain they were playing. "I could get us to the road in twenty minutes, normally. In this, though—"

She shrugged eloquently.

"I see. And your opinion, Kenhodan?"

"I'd like to spend the day rolled in a blanket by the fire, but I gather that's not an option. If we really have to travel, we might as well use the high road. That's what it's there for."

"Not gracious, perhaps, but to the point. All right. We'll take our chances on the high road."

Wencit got the saddle across Byrchalka's back—not without some assistance from the tall courser—and tightened the girth. Then he tossed his saddle bags up to follow and poured the last bit of the kettle's tea into his mess kit cup and stood sipping it while the others completed their preparations.

Chernion puzzled over the strangely unthreatening tension between her and Wencit as she tightened her own saddle girth. She wondered if he saw no *need* to "threaten" her simply because he considered her a negligible danger. The idea hurt her pride, but she made herself admit the possibility. What would be really nice to know, though, was what he'd seen and done out there in the rain.

She fastened her bridle and glanced around. The others were ready, and she toyed with the idea of slipping out to check her message cairn for tampering. But there was no reasonable excuse, so she swung up into the saddle just inside the cave, instead, and waited.

Bahzell pushed up beside her—still on foot, one hand resting on Walsharno's neck. The cave's roof was almost twelve feet above its floor, but that was still too low for someone his size to mount a courser Walsharno's size. Wencit could manage Byrchalka's saddle—barely—as long as he minded his head, but she and Kenhodan had ample room, and so did the packhorses. She felt like a child on a pony beside the towering courser as she glanced over her shoulder and saw the pack animals looking reproachfully at the hradani's back. She watched Kenhodan climb onto Glamhandro's back, arranging an extra cloak carefully over his harp case while the wizard adjusted his dripping hat.

"Very well, Elrytha," Wencit said with a nod. "Let's be going."

She clucked to her horse, and the mare moved unhappily but obediently out into the sodden morning.

Like her companions, Chernion favored a Sothōii-style poncho in this sort of weather, and she was grateful for its warmth as cold water pelted her shoulders. It did little to keep her face dry, however, and she felt the long cock pheasant's feather in her beret whip in the wind as she led the way downhill.

Kenhodan groaned mentally as the wind lashed a volley of raindrops into his face—large, fat, *wet* raindrops, he thought, well chilled by the mountain clouds. They burst over him like a breaker, and Glamhandro snorted his own displeasure as they hit.

The driving rain made the steep hillside treacherous, but they reached bottom without mishap. Thin leaves and early buds tossed about them, wind and water whipping new foliage as their horses shouldered through tangled laurel and rhododendron. Kenhodan shivered, cursing the weather as the slender branches dragged at his riding boots and the raw chill burrowed into his bones.

It took an hour to reach the South Road, for runoff had completed the demolition of an earthen bank already undercut by the spring thaw, and a wet wall of muddy boulders clogged the best trail. The horses were hock deep in the water racing down the only other route to the high road, and everyone was thoroughly muddy and miserable by the time they reached it.

At least the South Road offered secure footing, and rain bounced and bounded on its hard surface and ran down its broad gutters almost cheerfully. That was the only cheerful thing about the morning, however. Sheets of water blew into Kenhodan's eyes, and Glamhandro's mane ran with rain. The big horse snorted water from his nostrils occasionally, sharing his rider's misery. There was no lightning, no thunder—just steady, beating rain, sluicing down with all of nature's blind persistence. Only the wind had a purpose, and that was to get the maximum amount of rain into the travelers' eyes in the minimum amount of time.

Rain and wind paced them as the horses ate wearily at the leagues. Even the coursers lowered their heads and seemed to hunch their shoulders as they pushed into the teeth of the wind, and the riders dripped and shivered, inventing new curses as water picked a way through ponchos and jerkins. Kenhodan watched his drenched companions and the gusting rain and told himself that every weary hour brought journey's end an hour closer, and so was worth its cost in misery.

He told himself that repeatedly; he never believed it at all.

◆　　◆　　◆

Umaro crouched under Ashwan's spread cloak and opened the oiled leather tube carefully. That tube had protected its contents this far, and he had no intention of exposing them to the rain now.

He smoothed the parchment and peered at it. It was Chernion's cipher, all right, and he frowned, shifting mental gears to decode the message. His face was bitter by the time he'd finished, and he balled the long note in a disgusted fist.

"Phrobus!"

"Orders?" Ashwan asked.

"Among other things," Umaro growled. He gestured for Ashwan to reclaim his cloak and glowered moodily as the dripping assassin struggled back into its windblown folds, managing somehow to retain a bedraggled elegance in the process.

"What other things?" Ashwan asked.

"I'm sure you'll be pleased to know Chernion approves his agent's actions in the Unicorn. Can you *believe* that?"

"Yes. I told you what I thought happened."

"Well, Chernion agrees with you," Umaro conceded glumly.

"Is that all he says?" Ashwan asked the question confidently—as well he might, given his status as one of the Council's senior field agents—but his tone was droll enough he managed not to lacerate Umaro's nerves still further.

"Not by a long chalk." The craftmaster snorted. "He and this Elrytha found an opportunity to talk during the night watches, and he's changed plans on us again."

"*Another* change? That's . . . unlike Chernion."

"Aye, but he says this is like no other assignment, too."

"Well, I'd certainly agree with him there!" Ashwan snorted.

"Aye. At any rate, we're supposed to stay close but unseen. Elrytha will continue to mark trail for us, and we're to watch for message drops. Unless we get different orders, though, we're not to attack this side of the pass even if an opportunity seems to present itself."

. "Does he say why not?" Even Ashwan sounded a little surprised by Umaro's last sentence.

"He does." Umaro lowered his voice. "If the brothers ask, we're to say the targets are too alert. When the time comes, we'll have to attack openly, with Chernion's agent to stab them in the back. For that to work, we have to give her time to gain their complete acceptance. That's the official reason."

"Ah!" Ashwan's eyes met Umaro's. "And the *real* one?"

"Chernion's precious spy's turned up more information: something about the client betraying the Guild. As nearly as I can make out, Wulfra may've laid some sort of spy spell on the Guild and maybe even set Rosper up to get killed to keep us after Wencit. Chernion seems to think this Elrytha can worm more information out of Wencit if he gives her time."

"I see. Well, I'm not inclined to argue with Chernion or question his judgment. And between you and me, I'm impressed by Elrytha. She's done better than we have so far, at any rate! We've lost twelve men without a single corpse to show for it. If it weren't for the precedent, I'd say chuck the whole job. It's already cost more than we were paid, and it'll cost more before it's done."

"Agreed." Water trickled into Umaro's beard as he looked up. "But where's the remedy? You and I can no more stop this than Chernion can. We've lost too many, and too many know it. If we give it up as the bad deal it is, what happens to the Guild's reputation? And without that, where are we?"

"Umaro, you know as well as I do that the Guild's tried to kill the Bloody Hand more than once without succeeding. For that matter, I'm pretty sure that if we could look deep enough into the archives, we'd find out we've even been stupid enough to try to kill *Wencit* a time or two in the past! Obviously, they're still here, so it's not as if previous councils haven't decided to cut our losses once the butcher's bill started getting out of hand."

"No," Umaro agreed, although he wouldn't have admitted anything of the sort to anyone besides Ashwan. "But it's been long enough since those other attempts that most people've forgotten them. This memory's going to be fresh in their minds, and I have a feeling the Council's not giving up as easily this time." The craftmaster shook his head. "There's something in the air, Ashwan. Something's changed—or changing—and I don't like the smell of it. But what matters right now, to you and me, is that we both know what the Council's orders would be if we could ask them. Unless Chernion himself orders us off, I don't see where we have any choice but to continue the hunt. And who knows? We may get lucky after all! I'm not sure about the wizard, to be honest, but champion of Tomanāk or no, the Bloody Hand's still mortal. He can be killed just the same as anyone else if we manage to get enough steel—or poison—into him. I'm pretty sure the same thing's true about this Kenhodan, and I can't think of anyone more likely to be able to kill either of them than the Guild!"

He managed to get the last sentence out with what sounded like genuine confidence, and Ashwan nodded.

"I agree," he said. "I didn't say we should let them

go; I only said it would be good if we could. But since we can't, I have a suggestion."

"Which is?"

"Wencit's headed into Angthyr. If there's a chance Wulfra's betrayed us, don't you think it might be wise to let Wencit do whatever he came to do? Wulfra may succeed in killing him, in which case there's no need for us to lose more brothers against him. And if the baroness doesn't kill him, we won't have to worry about anything *she* did to harm the Guild, because Wencit will see to it that she's dead."

"I think I agree." It was Umaro's turn to nod. "At least it's a thought, and we've had precious few of those of late! If I get the chance, I'll pass it to Elrytha for relay to Chernion."

The craftmaster heaved back into his saddle. Like so much else about him, his patently poor horsemanship was misleading. He scrambled up like a mountain climber and sat the saddle like a lumpy sack, yet he could stay there for days on end if he must. Now he reined his horse around to his waiting men. The dripping assassins huddled under what cover there was, soaked to the skin. They'd spent a miserable night in the open while the wizard and his companions used the cave, and there were raw tempers amid the dripping scrub that morning.

"Come on, lads," Umaro growled. "We'll stop long enough to dry our skins a little and make some breakfast, then be on our way again." A few faces tightened, but there was no protest. "I'm sorry, Brothers, but we have no choice. You know as well as I do we have to avenge our losses to clear our reputation."

There was a rumble of agreement. They understood

the importance of that; without the terror of their reputation, their victims might remember assassins, too, were mortal.

Umaro waited with Ashwan as his men's horses scrambled up the hill.

"There goes the best reason of all for letting that bitch Wulfra kill her own game," the craftmaster muttered then, his face bleak as the rain. "How many more brothers can we lose on one assignment?"

◆　◆　◆

The object of Umaro's bitterness was at that moment thinking of the dog brothers. Wulfra hadn't been watching Chernion when the assassin had actually summoned Umaro, but she was certain the guildmaster had called for reinforcements. Unfortunately, Chernion was the only surviving assassin Wulfra was able to locate, so she had no idea who those reinforcements might be or where they might be found.

But now that her defensive spells were complete, Wulfra's mind turned more often to the killer. Little though she cared to admit it, she did feel a slight sense of unease about the trap link. Each time she used it, she increased the chance Chernion might sense it, and sorceress or not, only a fool *wouldn't* feel uneasy at the thought of turning the entire Assassins Guild into mortal enemies. Despite that, the baroness longed to know what the assassin was doing about Wencit. The wild wizard's steady approach to Angthyr was enough to guarantee that!

She chewed delicately on a knuckle as she considered the problem. Prudence pulled one way, curiosity the other—and, as wasn't uncommon with wizards, curiosity won in the end.

She bent over her gramerhain and muttered the incantation. Power rippled through the crystal, flickering for a second...then for several seconds...then over a minute. Wulfra frowned in consternation and tapped the crystal gently. Nothing happened, and her frown deepened as she considered blanking the stone.

She was about to do just that when the gramerhain suddenly cleared, but it took her some moments to recognize the image. Then she gasped in astonishment. She wasn't looking down on Chernion—she was looking out of the assassin's own eyes!

She bent low, almost pressing her nose to the stone, and pouring rain seemed to flick into her own face. The slim, gloved hands on the reins could only be Chernion's, and Wulfra trembled as she realized what had happened. She'd read about this effect, but she'd never actually experienced it. Her simple scrying spell had connected her directly to Chernion, and that happened only in certain special cases—such as when the trap link's object was inside another wizard's glamour. And only one wizard would be simultaneously maintaining a glamour and attracting Chernion's attention.

Wulfra held her breath, torn between exultation and disbelief as she watched for confirmation of her wild hope. If only she could have controlled the assassin's gaze! Unfortunately, she couldn't, but—

Chernion's head turned, and wildfire eyes glowed in the crystal.

Wulfra gasped in triumph, and then Chernion's head turned the other way and Bahzell's face filled the crystal. Not only had Wulfra found Chernion, but the audacious assassin had actually infiltrated Wencit's ranks!

Wulfra blazed with triumph, and blood pounded exuberantly in her temples. Why, she could fix Wencit's exact location whenever she wished!

She gloated over her unexpected achievement like a miser. She could attack at any time she chose! And even if her attacks failed, she could chart his exact progress! Let him maintain his glamour—what did that matter while she commanded that precious set of eyes within his camp?

She threw back her head and laughed, blanking the crystal with a wave. She had to consult her patron. The opportunity was too good to pass up, but first she must clear it with the cat-eyed wizard and ask for aid.

Her urgent request for contact was ignored, briefly. But eventually, the cold cat-eyes blinked lazily in the depths of her stone.

"Greetings, Wulfra," his mental voice purred. "You have news?"

"I do," she replied, fighting to restrain the triumph in her response.

"Then by all means amaze me with it, my dear."

"Very well. As you know, all my attempts to pierce Wencit's glamour have failed," she said flatly, and paused, half-daring him to explain his refusal to aid her efforts.

"Agreed," was all the cat-eyed wizard said.

"Well, I can do it now." She abandoned the effort to hide her soaring sense of triumph. "One of my hirelings has managed to join him, and I have a trap link to her. I can establish his exact position!"

"A sterling achievement. But what do you wish to do about it?"

"I have to attack! Attack at once—before he has an

opportunity to realize what's happened! And for that, I need your help. No spell of mine could succeed at such a long-range, but the opportunity's there. It must be taken!"

She seemed astounded by his lack of enthusiasm, and rightly so, he thought . . . from her perspective.

"Allow me a moment of thought."

His eyes vanished as he withdrew to consider, meshing the new information with knowledge he'd withheld from his minion.

Wulfra's success puzzled him, though he wouldn't admit it, for she must be encouraged to think him virtually omniscient. But he could err. The attack on *Wave Mistress*, for instance, had been a mistake. He'd helped plan it, even given her of his strength for it, yet its only lasting effect had been to show Wencit he was watched.

The result had been predictable . . . or should have been, if he'd taken the time to consider things properly. Wencit was no fool, and he was already suspicious of Wulfra's apparently increased ability, so he'd strengthened his glamour. Indeed, he'd virtually doubled its effectiveness. It cost him something in concentration, but the burden was far from crippling, and the consequences were far worse than any mere inconvenience.

Decades of carefully cherished advantage had been whittled away in an afternoon. Over the years, highly trained teams of Carnadosans had managed to insert delicate probes through Wencit's glamours largely because he'd seen no need to raise first-class protection against second-class opposition like Wulfra. It had been a difficult but relatively straightforward task to spy on the wild wizard under those circumstances.

No more. It was still possible to pierce his shields, but also far riskier. What had been like slipping a needle through a soap bubble without bursting it required far more force, and adding force added risk. It was no longer possible to maintain an hour-to-hour watch on him or even on his comrades when he was near. One simply couldn't manipulate the energy required to breach his new glamour without creating a detectable eddy.

That had resulted from a single miscalculation, and it had gone even further. The morning Wencit left Sindor, his glamour had been so strong not even the cat-eyed wizard had been able to crack it.

The Council had panicked. Wencit's glamour had been so powerful Wulfra couldn't have pierced it even with a trap link inside it; that "proved" he knew about *them*—and he still commanded the spells which had strafed Kontovar.

The panic had eased as Wencit allowed his protection to coast back down to the new level established after the madwind, however, and the cat-eyed wizard had personally relocated him within six hours. His accomplishment had soothed his fellows' near terror and restored their ability to track the old wizard, although not even he dared probe too closely or too often.

Yet even though they'd relocated Wencit, and even though it was once again possible to slip at least occasional probes through his glamour, they dared not pass information to Wulfra. Not as long as that glamour stayed too strong for her to have broken it on her own. That iron rule couldn't be violated, so he'd shut down the flow of information, rendering the wild wizard safe from sorcerous attack until he reached Torfo itself.

But now...

He grimaced in deep thought. All wizards were subtle, and Wencit the most subtle of all. The wild wizard lacked critical information, so his position was ultimately flawed, but another serious error by the Carnadosans might warn him enough to cancel much of the cat-eyed wizard's advantage. Further, it was clear now that Wencit was engaged upon some deep, carefully planned move of his own, one which seemed to be based on information not available to the cat-eyed wizard. That added to the risks, for one side's ignorance might tend to balance the other's. But then, he thought sardonically, if the game was simple, everyone would play.

Yet one thing was certain: Wencit knew about the trap link. He'd have to be senile to miss it. But if he knew, why had he allowed Wulfra to establish it? To misdirect her somehow? Possibly... but if he *wanted* her to be able to spy on him, why cut off the link as he left Sindor?

Ahhhh! The cat-eyed wizard smiled as he suddenly found the answer he sought. The object of this ploy wasn't Wulfra; it was *Chernion*.

Data clicked into place in his orderly brain. Wencit had taken the measure of Wulfra's power and discounted her as a threat at such long-range. He'd judged (correctly, as it happened) that nothing she'd produced to date was a serious danger, and so relegated her threat to a secondary status and turned his attention to his merely mortal enemies.

That made sense of the strong glamour at Sindor's gates. He couldn't be certain how many *other* assassins Wulfra might have snared in trap links like the one on Chernion, so he'd raised a protection strong enough to keep her from directing anyone to him. Then something—some deliberate probe of Chernion, perhaps—had convinced him Wulfra's only link was to the guildmaster, and Chernion was under his own watchful eye, thus neatly beheading the Guild.

The crafty old devil was priming the assassin to turn on Wulfra!

The cat-eyed wizard chuckled in admiration. It was a small thing, but it showed Wencit hadn't lost his touch. It would be easy for him to "let slip" sufficient information to alert Chernion to the trap link. After that, Chernion's plans for the baroness became a foregone conclusion. But the important point was that he'd decided to risk Wulfra's attack as the price of neutralizing her hired killers. It followed, then, that it was feasible to let Wulfra try. Wencit obviously expected her to, and it would never do to disappoint him.

This was a chance to redeem the madwind fiasco, if it was done properly. The attack had to be one Wencit couldn't defeat without using the wild magic, but it must also be one Wulfra was theoretically capable of launching on her own. Something she could do herself if she had the nerve. Hmmm...

There was such an attack. Wulfra would never try it on her own, but she might be induced to with the promise of assistance. And whether it worked or not, it would give him immense pleasure to see it tried.

He threw his eyes back into Wulfra's crystal and studied her taut face, savoring the fear which kept her impatience in seemly check. Dear Wulfra! It would be such a pity when she died.

"Forgive the delay, my dear," he purred. "It was necessary to evolve the proper strategy, you know, but you're quite correct. We *must* attack, and a delightful plan's occurred to me. Here's what I propose we do..."

❖   ❖   ❖

Evening found Bahzell leading them into the lower East Walls. The road wound between steep shoulders, climbing ever upward at a sharp angle. The air was noticeably colder, and Kenhodan shivered under his rain-heavy poncho.

"You wouldn't have another cave handy, Elrytha?" he asked hopefully.

"No." Chernion's teeth chattered, and even her jaunty feather looked miserable. "The nearest shelter I know's a hostel, still some leagues away."

"It's afraid of that I was," Bahzell said sourly, sniffing the air. "We've little option but to be finding some shelter, Wencit. I'm thinking there's snow in this wind."

"Snow?" Kenhodan was startled. "This late in the spring?"

"The Bloody Hand's right," Chernion said. "The year's still young, and even in summer it takes little to turn rain into snow in the East Walls."

"Aye, snow treacherous as a dog brother's heart," Bahzell muttered. He craned his neck to examine the slopes. "We've no very promising campsite here, either."

"No," Chernion agreed, looking about her, then pointed with a dripping arm. "What about those trees? We might shelter under them."

"That's after being a nasty slope," Bahzell said.

"True. But unless you see something better, it looks like our best chance. Or would you rather sleep in the ditch, Bloody Hand?"

"I'm thinking as all I said was that it's no easy climb to yonder trees," Bahzell said mildly. "We'd best be taking it slow and careful."

"All the more reason to get started," Kenhodan said unhappily. "It'll be dark in a few minutes, and then we *will* be in trouble."

"Follow me, then," Bahzell grunted, "but mind the footing! We've no time to be scraping ourselves off the paving."

The climb wasn't quite that bad, but it was bad enough. Even Bahzell and Wencit had to dismount, and they had to lead the horses. In fact, they had to throw their weight onto the horse's leads more than once to get them past particularly treacherous spots, but in the end, everyone scrambled up before darkness fell.

The trees were a mixed collection of gnarled oak and evergreen, and Kenhodan and Bahzell used axes to lop poles for a rough lean-to while Chernion and the wizard cared for the horses. The hradani dumped the cut poles at Wencit's feet, then frowned as Kenhodan dropped wearily to sit on a rough boulder.

"No lollygagging, lad! We've the horses and coursers to shelter, too."

"*More* cutting?"

"Unless you're after wanting Glamhandro to hate you come morning."

"All right. All right! I'm coming!"

Kenhodan groused all the way back into the trees, and Chernion grinned as the axes rang once more. She and the wizard were weaving lopped off boughs through the lean-to's pole frame, and she looked up to see him smiling at her.

She looked away immediately, wondering what had amused him. Then she recalled her own grin and stiffened internally. This was an assignment—nothing more! She had no business regarding her trail companions as anything but targets! She took herself sternly to task and concentrated on the job before her as the lean-to formed under their hands.

Bahzell and Kenhodan returned to build a second, much larger shelter for the horses and coursers. It would provide overhead cover, at least, but it would scarcely offer the sort of protection a proper stable would have given. Wet spits of snow licked out of the rain as they worked, and the hradani shook his head.

"I'm hoping as this is a light fall we're after having, lad."

"How heavy can it be?" Kenhodan asked, holding up one hand and watching flakes melt on his palm.

"Heavy enough. It's no pity at all, at all, the East Walls have, and it's more than one merchant caravan's been wiped out by late snow."

"This far down?"

"As to that, no—but it's higher up for us yet, now isn't it? And the assassins close behind if we're after having to linger."

"You think we'll have to move on in the morning, then?"

"If we can, aye, but it's no sure thing we'll be able to. That slope was after being hard with only rain; we'll likely find it ice tomorrow."

"Well, if we can't get down, assassins can't get *up*."

"Aye. But if they're after guessing where we've gone, what's to keep their bowmen from sitting there and feathering us like geese when we do come down?"

"Nothing, damn you. Why do you always bring up things like this at bedtime?"

Bahzell chuckled and went on laying branches over the lean-to, and Kenhodan joined him, his face icy in the rain. More flakes fell like wet ghosts, and their breath plumed densely as the temperature dropped.

"There, now! Right and tight for our friends!"

They led the horses under the rough roof, and none of them seemed inclined to roam. The well-rugged packhorses and Chernion's mare crowded close to Glamhandro, with Walsharno and Byrchalka shielding all four of the "lesser cousins" with their own bodies. Kenhodan threw handfuls of grain on a flat rock and frowned.

"Three or four nights of this will use up the grain, Bahzell."

"Aye, but once down the hill, we're no more than two days from South Keep. We can be laying in fodder there."

"But first we have to get there," Kenhodan pointed out.

"The price of adventure, lad! Let's go see if those two layabouts have been after kindling a fire for us."

But Wencit allowed no fire, and Bahzell accepted his decision after only a brief discussion. Kenhodan sighed unhappily and crouched against the tree supporting the back of their hut. Blankets closed the open side, and their body heat took off the worst of the chill, but it was still cold and wet as he dragged a stick of jerky from his pack and gnawed disconsolately.

"Lovely weather," Bahzell commented genially after a moment.

"You can have my share," Kenhodan grunted sourly.

"My thanks, but my own share's after being quite enough." Bahzell turned to Chernion. "What weather word have you, Elrytha?"

"I'm not sure." Chernion waved the knife she was using to reduce dried meat to chewable proportions. "The wind's still in the east, so it could push this past us tonight. But if it shifts west, it may snow from here to South Keep with us."

"Ah, me!" Bahzell sighed. "I'm wondering what it is I might've done to upset Chemalka so."

"Even if it passes, it could bury the road," Chernion said thoughtfully, "and spring snows can be heavy."

"Well, snow or no, we'll be needing watches," Bahzell yawned, "so I'll be after taking first turn."

"I'll take second watch," Kenhodan offered.

"Well enough." Bahzell donned his poncho once more and rose, checking his sword. "Best keep your steel close tonight. I'm after smelling something nasty."

"What? Besides the weather, that is?" Wencit asked.

"As to that, I'm thinking you're the wizard." Bahzell shrugged. "When himself's after giving me second sight, you'll be the first to know."

"Many thanks," Wencit grunted, shaking his damp poncho into a bed.

Bahzell grinned and vanished into the thickening snow. Kenhodan heard the rattle of sleet, too, and sighed resignedly as he rolled himself in his own blankets, his sword close to hand.

Chernion wrapped her blanket around her shoulders and placed her own sword in easy reach. She respected the Bloody Hand's instincts, but she also knew—as he couldn't—that there was no threat from the Guild. Which meant it must be something else. Could it be Wulfra?

It was a foolish client who intruded into Guild operations, but it seemed Wulfra had done so, and all this talk of sending death spells down a trap link was enough to make anyone uneasy. Yet Chernion lacked enough information for reasonable deductions or planning, so she suppressed her fears ruthlessly and drifted quickly into sleep.

Kenhodan already slept fitfully, but Wencit was awake, his glowing eyes spangling the darkness. He listened to the night and the sleet, then rolled his blankets tighter. His eyes slitted thoughtfully. Then they closed, and his face relaxed.

◆　◆　◆

Wulfra eyed her notes dubiously. The spell wasn't quite beyond her power, but there was always a risk in pushing the art to one's limits. That was particularly true for this spell, but the chance to simultaneously kill her enemy and touch such rarefied heights with the support of her sponsor was too compelling to refuse.

She studied her apparatus in the circular spell area that covered half the top of the main keep. It centered on a metal brazier, its iron gleaming fitfully with the minor supporting spells already stored in it, and a small beaker of thick blood, the last gift of her three gypsy captives.

She would have preferred to work by daylight, but the dark art's more powerful workings had an affinity for night. By its nature, the dark art relied on shortcuts barred to white wizards (as represented by her vial of blood), but there were other considerations. Night's lower energy level was apt for certain of the darkest manipulations, and she also needed darkness to hide the nature of her summoning. Not only had what she planned already involved an act of murder, but it was designed to accomplish yet more murders—not to mention treason against certain ancient treaties.

She drew a deep breath and relaxed, settling her mind into the twisting lines of the incantation. She must pronounce each word precisely to key the phonetics which unlocked the portion of the art wand wizards dared touch, and this spell verged dangerously near to the well of wild magic no sorceress could control. If she made the slightest slip, that wild magic would seek to enter her, and she lacked the gift to control it. It would destroy her in the blink of a blazing eye.

She ran through the spell mentally once more, and the discipline of years came to her aid. Her nerves steadied, and it was time.

She gestured, splayed fingers throwing something immaterial at the brazier, and red flame billowed, sparks dancing on its crest. She stepped close with a black-winged sculpture in her right hand and the beaker of blood in her left. She moved the sculpture through the edge of the flame, and the wax began to change.

Hard, red light limned her face as her lips moved, forming each word carefully. Power rose about her, wrapped tighter with every phrase, and the statuette grew heavy, tugging at her hand, humming with stored energy as its surface grew hotter and hotter. By the end of the first canto, Wulfra was sealed in the hollow heart of a mystic hurricane.

She hesitated a moment as the brazier's flames billowed up, impaling the night sky. The sheer power she'd summoned was terrifying, but her hesitation was brief, and she lifted the beaker of virgin blood and poured it over the humming, half-molten sculpture. Human blood mingled with wax, smoking, changing it—imbuing it with the dread presence of death. Wulfra's lips firmed, and she hurled the writhing statue into the brazier's heart and spoke three words of power into the hushed night.

The sculpture screamed as flame engulfed it. For just an instant, the entire keep trembled to that scream, and Wulfra held herself rigid in exalted trepidation as a black arrow of sorcery coalesced from empty air. It plunged into the heaving flames after the squirming statute, and a fan of brilliance spewed from the brazier. A flash incinerated everything within twenty feet—except for Wulfra and her notes. A sullen red pillar licked up, and her eyes ached with its fury. Tall as the keep it rose, then twice as tall, and its brilliance dyed the clouds and dripped back like clotted blood.

Watchful eyes widened in fear in cottages beyond the castle as its walls and towers loomed black against the crimson tide. Lips muttered prayers and hands made signs against evil . . . and still the brilliance rose, cresting finally half a thousand feet above the keep until a ball of flame ripped free from its top and streaked off through the heavens to light the sky like an angry dawn.

And then the flames died. The pillar of light vanished in soot and smoke and the smell of burning blood, and Wulfra shuddered in the ecstatic aftermath of power, hugging herself and leaning against the battlements. Her breasts heaved with exultation and she strained her eyes northeast to watch the Scarthū

Hills absorb her fire. The spell was cast, and well cast; she was certain. The summons was set, and she must await her answer and hope her control spells were set equally well.

She allowed herself a tight smile, for she was certain her spells *would* hold her new servant—a servant such as no wizard had known since the Fall! She hugged her triumph tight and never noticed the chill night breeze.

◆　◆　◆

Far to the north, Wencit's glowing eyes opened briefly and rested on the branches which barred his southern view. He didn't move, nor did his expression alter. After a moment, his eyes closed once more.

◆　◆　◆

Kenhodan yawned and awoke unwillingly. His eyes felt dry and sandy, and the cold seemed to have congealed his bones as he elbowed himself up and lifted a corner of the door blankets on a white, silent world.

He shook his head in disgust as fresh white feathers whispered out of the pewter sky. He'd known it would look like this when he turned in, but the confirmation's teeth were colder than he'd hoped. He pulled the blanket about himself like a cloak and stepped out into the morning.

Thick whiteness cocooned every surface, marred here and there by boot prints. His and Bahzell's were mere dimples, but Chernion's were deep and clear. She stood with her back to the lean-to, but the squeak of his boots brought her around to face him. Her breath plumed in the falling snow and flakes of white silvered her green beret. She smiled, and her teeth and eyes flashed in her frost-flushed face.

"Good morning," Kenhodan said, scratching his stubbled jaw.

He considered shaving in cold water, then put the notion aside with a shudder. It was hard, on a morning like this, not to envy the fact that hradani had no facial hair. Bahzell never had to face cold steel and icy water in a grim, snowy dawn. And now that he considered it, a beard like Wencit's had a certain attraction under the circumstances.

"Greetings," Chernion replied. "I don't like the snow, Kenhodan."

"I don't either." He slid a boot through a drift, and ice slithered under his heel. "You think it's going to fall all day?"

"That's what I'm afraid of." She nodded. "The wind died without moving it, and I think the flakes are bigger. It may be twice this deep by tomorrow."

"At least the sleet's stopped."

"Which is precious little comfort when there's already ice underfoot."

"True." He surveyed the white desert and shrugged. "I'd better wake the others, I suppose."

"A moment, Kenhodan."

Her quick words stopped him, and he glanced at her with raised eyebrows. She hesitated as he stood like a tall, broad-shouldered ghost in the snow. Her instinct was to push for information while she had him alone, but should she risk it? Flashing thoughts assessed risk and opportunity and reached decision.

"Forgive me," she said, touching his forearm, "and don't feel you have to answer. But I've noticed that for all your joking with the Bloody Hand, you're sad. Perhaps the saddest man I've ever met. Why is that?"

Kenhodan looked at her for a long, level moment. He hadn't pictured himself as "sad," yet her words forced him to consider the possibility. All too often, he knew, a jester wept inside, hiding his tears in laughter as Wencit often did. Was he the same?

"I'm not sad, Elrytha," he said finally. "Just thoughtful."

"Thoughtful? Why?" She watched him coolly, and he shrugged uneasily.

"I'm just...lost. You see, I have no memory. It was taken from me and sometimes I...miss it."

"Taken? By wizardry?" Her voice was hushed.

"I suppose." He felt restless and exposed. "I don't really know."

Chernion gazed at him, her mind racing, sensing his reluctance to speak further of it. She'd already learned more than she'd hoped, and she mustn't alienate him. Yet of all the frustrating bits and pieces she had to put together somehow, Kenhodan interested her most. Who was he? Where did he come from? He was perhaps the deadliest fighter she'd ever met—more so even than the Bloody Hand, in many ways—but where had he gained his skill? And why was he so important to the wizard?

And now this. Amnesia? How had it happened... and why? Of one thing, at least, she was certain; it was no simple accident. No, his lost identity was the key to all the other questions about him which burned in her brain. Somehow she knew that as she recalled her first impression of bloodshed and innocence.

"I'm sorry, my friend," she said finally. "I didn't mean to pry."

"It's all right. Bahzell and Wencit know—you should, too."

"Thank you," she said quietly.

"Don't mention it."

He smiled crookedly, and his green eyes were somehow gentle, as if softened by sharing his secret. He brushed snow from his shoulders, and she was struck by the odd gracefulness of his strong fingers. Strange that she hadn't noticed how strong he was—and not just physically. He had no past, yet she believed him when he said he wasn't sad. Did he realize how tough and resilient that made him? Yes, he was a strong man, this Kenhodan, and one who might be the key to power....

"I won't mention it again," she said, touching his shoulder lightly.

"Thanks." He looked away. "And now I'd better wake those two sluggards. Not that we're going anywhere very fast."

He vanished into the lean-to, and Chernion watched the blanket drop. She turned to the brow of the hill, looking down on the road, her brain busy—and not entirely, perhaps, with thoughts an assassin should think.

◆   ◆   ◆

Umaro and Ashwan rode at the head of their miserable men. The road was icy under the snow, and the thick flakes were a treacherous curtain. The assassins' horses plodded wretchedly, steaming in the cold while their riders' breath hung in clouds of vapor.

"I tell you, Umaro, they're off the road somewhere," Ashwan said. "They must've seen it coming, just as we did, and they were in steeper terrain. They've gone up a hill, and they're all steep as houses around here. I doubt they can get back down in this *stuff*."

He snorted the last word and scowled at the snow clotting his horse's mane.

"I know," Umaro grunted.

"Then why not stop? We'll only lose a horse if one of them goes down and breaks a leg."

"I know that, too," Umaro said. "And I know we're all cold and miserable, too. But they know we're back here, Ashwan, so I want to get in front of them for a change. Let them follow us. If they see this large a party overtaking them, they'll never believe we're innocent travelers. If *they* overtake *us*, they may."

"All right." Ashwan nodded in agreement. "But I hope the Council never takes another commission like this one!"

"Not damned likely." Umaro grinned lopsidedly. "Leaving aside the minor fact that I'd personally murder anyone who suggested we should, we're after the last of a breed—a white wizard."

There was more than a little bravado in the craft-master's tone, but there was an edge of genuine amusement, as well, and the two of them chuckled as they rode on. Neither of them looked at the top of the northern side of the cut, and so neither saw the slim, poncho-clad figure in the green beret who watched them ride slowly past her.

CHAPTER SIXTEEN

Mage

"Better, Gwynna. Much better! But your concentration slipped. If you can't hold focus all the way through, you'll slip out of rapport before we finish. That's not a problem in a training session, but if it happens when you're under pressure, you could be in trouble."

"I'm sorry, Master Trayn." Gwynna blinked back into focus and nodded slowly. "Should we try again?" she asked humbly.

Trayn caught her pointed chin and raised her head gently, peering into her eyes. They were dark in the shade of the elms, and he frowned. "How does your head feel?"

"It hurts a little," she admitted.

"A little?" He grinned and shook his own head. "If you recall, our last exercise was in truth reading. Would you care to answer that question again?"

"Well . . ." She dimpled, delight briefly breaking through her new, very unchildlike gravity. "All right, it hurts a lot, Master Trayn. But we've *got* to keep going."

"Gwynna, Gwynna! What am I going to do with you?" he sighed. "Some pain's unavoidable when you stretch your talents, but don't overdo it. Too *much* pain is counterproductive—a distraction. It's why you were wavering towards the end. Give yourself time! You're already making faster progress than any student in the Academy's records, you know."

"But you said the proper measure of a mage is against himself."

"And it's true. But any student has to be guided by his or her teachers, as well. Don't push so hard you damage your talent, Gwynna."

"Yes, Master Trayn," she said dutifully.

"Good. And if you think you're not learning fast enough, you're the only person who does."

"I know," Gwynna said sourly, and Trayn looked at her sharply. She refused to meet his eyes, and when he probed gently her shields were locked. He could read her emotions, but not the thoughts behind them.

Gwynna fingered the weave of her dress and nibbled her lower lip, ears half-flattened, as she contemplated one of the more irksome consequences of her talents' strength. She knew some of the other students resented the fact that she was Trayn's only student. He was the Academy's finest teacher, yet she monopolized his time completely.

She sighed. She delighted in discovering her talents, in satisfying the need which drove her like a demon, but she wasn't truly happy.

Those other students disliked her, and she could hardly blame them, though she was enough her father's daughter—and her mother's—to want to pull off a few arms over it. They all knew she was expected to show more mage power than anyone had seen in generations, and that distinction would have been handicap enough without her "preferential" relationship with Master Trayn.

The others saw only that she had what amounted to a private tutor and that in barely more than two months she'd been advanced to second-year status. It hadn't taken long for someone to suggest she was only a half-breed playing on her parents' friendship with the Academy and Wencit of Rūm to receive special treatment. Little did her taunters realize how much they owed to the discipline she'd already mastered, for the rage she'd felt when she heard their remarks had almost launched her at their throats. Yet she also understood that no one with her talents could react as a child, whatever her age might be, so she'd refrained. With difficulty, but she'd refrained.

Trayn touched her shoulder and she looked up. Physical contact was discouraged among student magi as a way to encourage them to reach out mentally, but Gwynna's shields allowed even Trayn to visit only occasionally in the public sectors of her mind.

"They shouldn't taunt you, Gwynna." His face was cold, his normally warm voice chill. "Magi, of all people, should be free of stupid prejudice. I've a good mind to report this to Master Kresco for discipline and a few home truths on the responsibilities attached to their talents!"

"No, Master Trayn." Her hand covered his in a gesture both childlike and heartbreakingly adult. "I know why they say it. They're angry and their feelings are hurt, and they want to hurt me back. I understand that—" she grinned suddenly "—luckily for them! If you tell Master Kresco, they might behave better, but they'd only resent me even more."

Trayn nodded slowly.

"All right, Gwynna. If you really do understand—and if you let me know if it gets out of hand."

"Of course I understand." She grinned again, but a dark ghost of wisdom hovered in her blue eyes. "What's the use of being so 'talented' if I can't sense things like that? None of *them* can shield yet—" she allowed herself a healthy edge of scorn "—so they can't help radiating the truth to me. To themselves, too, but that only makes it worse because they feel guilty but not guilty enough to *stop*, and that makes them even madder."

Trayn nodded again. She was so insightful it was hard to remember her youth. Working with her was almost like working with an adult—until the sprightly spirit which had somehow survived even her mage crisis laughed out at him. He had an idea that spirit would be vital to whatever unimaginable task was to be laid upon her, and he took care to nurse it like a precious flower. Indeed, he often found himself in the peculiar position of actively discouraging a student from acting with all the maturity she could.

"Just between us, Gwynna, you *have* been outshining them—a lot. Not that I want you to get a swelled head, mind you."

"Oh, I do," she assured him gravely, a twinkle lurking once more in her eyes. "It swells up whenever we practice truth reading. In fact it almost *bursts* when we practice so hard."

"You little fraud!" Trayn said indignantly. "It's not my fault you're doing third-year exercises! Semkirk, girl; if you keep going, you'll pack all five years into three or four more months—and then you *will* have some resentful magi on your hands." He smiled as she giggled. "Not that I'll tolerate your being anything less than the best mage this Academy ever produced. I have my reputation to consider, you know."

"Yes, Master Trayn," she said demurely.

"Good! Because right now you need a break from *mental* exercises."

Gwynna's groan was only half-humorous, because physical training was yet another area in which her classmates could resent her. It wasn't her fault she had the strength of her father's people, nor that Leeana had been a war maid, nor even that her own training had begun almost as soon as she could walk. Still, it had outraged the others when she threw Mistress Joslian, the unarmed combat master, out of the training circle that first day.

But at least Mistress Joslian understood. Indeed, she was proud of her prize student, and it hadn't taken her long to set up a private training schedule and to become another of Gwynna's champions.

Gwynna repaid her with possibly even more love than she'd shown Trayn, for she had no need to fear what she might reveal to Joslian. And she was eager to learn, because Joslian was a mishuk, with a style quite different from her mother's. War maids fought with a sort of terrible exuberance, but mishuki were calm, almost cold. For them, combat was an extemporized dance, an almost pure athleticism, and they fought with a sparse, beautiful economy of movement.

Yet the mage-mishuk was even more centered than that, for she fought on two levels, with physical blows and also with the thrust and counter-thrust of mental combat. Combining her psychic talents and her body was unlike her deep rapport sessions with Trayn. In combat, one touched only the fringe of an opponent's mind, for to look too deep was to become confused, but the lower mental tension made her bruise no less easily. If her fellows only knew! Leeana had never seemed lovingly but unwisely easy in her training, yet Mistress Joslian was merciless in comparison.

"Do I really need to go today, Master Trayn?" Gwynna wasn't above using her youth to wheedle, though the Academy's masters were more resistant than non-magi, and her voice was earnest. "Isn't it more important to work on mental discipline? I want to be sure I understand truth reading."

"You, Gwynna Bahzelldaughter, are an unprincipled little baggage," Trayn said, "and you can stop trying to diddle me, young lady! I've known you since you were two years old. I know how far you'll go to get your own way."

"I am not either unprincipled," she said haughtily, lifting her nose with a sniff. "Only practical."

"You *are* unprincipled. Charming, yes, but unprincipled. And if you're late for Mistress Joslian, we'll spend an extra twenty minutes truth reading tonight. *Then* we'll see how your head feels!"

"It might be worth it," she said thoughtfully. "She makes *everything* hurt. And you shouldn't threaten little girls," she added primly.

"Go!" Trayn pointed towards the gymnasium.

"Yes, Master Trayn," she said meekly. "'A student is obedient,'" she quoted from the coda. "'Only by accepting discipline will he learn discipline of self.'"

She managed a tiny sniff, and her head drooped, ears flattening mournfully. "Don't be angry, Master Trayn. I-I'll try to obey."

"Young lady," the empath said in an awful tone, "we both know I can't force your shields, but if you don't take yourself off this second, I'll give them a jolt that leaves you cross-eyed for the next three days. Now *go*, little wretch!" She turned to leave, and he touched her shoulder gently. "And perhaps we'll try distance reading tomorrow night, Little Sister."

"Yes, Master Trayn!"

She curtsied—the gesture of respect slightly marred by the impudent tilt of her ears—and he smiled after her as she sped off and the all-too-rare tinkle of her silvery laugh floated back as she ran.

But his smile faded. It was monstrously unfair that she could share her humor only with the masters. It was hardly surprising the other students resented her astounding breadth of talent, and those same talents made her even less a child than most young magi, yet she *was* a child. She needed to relate to the world of childhood as well as to the world of adults, and she was being robbed of it by her fellow students' fear and resentment.

A light footfall sounded, and Trayn looked up as Lentos stepped into the shadow of an elm. The chancellor stroked the tree bark, examining its texture as if it were the most vital thing in the world, then glanced wryly at Trayn.

"The barriers are up, you know," he said.

Trayn nodded. The barriers were raised a great deal these days.

"I suppose you want a progress report?"

"Only if you have one to make, Trayn. We have no criticism of your work with her, but we're naturally curious as to her abilities."

"You want an honest evaluation?"

"Of course."

"Really?" Trayn smiled in amusement. "All right, here's an 'honest evaluation.' If she left the Academy tomorrow, she could function as well as ninety percent of our regular graduates."

"That well?" Lentos blinked at him in bemusement.

"Better, for all I know. I've never seen anything like it. I know you're tired of hearing that, but—Phrobus seize it, man, it's true!"

"I know it is. Do you think you're the only one who realizes how extraordinary she is? But I need to know what you're seeing—all you can tell me without violating the mentor relationship, anyway."

"All right." Trayn crossed his arms. "It's not on paper—" He raised an eyebrow and Lentos nodded in understanding; paper could be scryed, but minds could not. "—but I can assess her potential. As nearly as I can tell, she's got everything."

"*Everything?*" Trayn was pleased to see that even the chancellor could be shaken on occasion. "Trayn, are you positive of that?"

"Of course not!" Trayn exploded suddenly. "Damn it, how *can* I be? The child can't even lower her inner shields all the way—never! And we're both so strung out from the pace she's setting that it's almost impossible to be objective! But the signs are there.

"She tests incredibly high for basic empathy; her *test* scores are twice as high as mine are *now*. She handles telepathy better than Kresco, and her telekinetic potential's right off the scale. Yesterday she maintained lift for over twenty minutes with fifteen pounds—*pounds*, Lentos—and she's only eleven! Semkirk only knows what she'll lift when she's twenty, and she has better lift and movement coordination now than most fourth-year students.

"Let's see. What else can she do? She tests positive for apportation, teleportation, levitation, and—especially—pyrokinesis. She's a born fire raiser. In fact, she near as nothing melted the testing cubicle the first time she tried it. Then there's empathic healing, perception . . . Phrobus! She's even demonstrating early signs of wind walking and weather control! There are half a dozen talents she *hasn't* shown yet, but be reasonable—she's only been here nine weeks!"

"Calmly, Trayn," Lentos murmured.

"How am I supposed to be calm? Her pace is killing me, but that only seems to make *her* more determined. Listen, Lentos, I'm not even training her—not really. She's improvising her own training as she goes. All I can do is identify her talents for her and try hard to stay in shouting distance.

"For instance, that little girl's driven herself to master the learning trance almost as thoroughly as I have. She retains both conscious and unconscious control at all times, so she can guard herself. Of course, it also means I don't have enough contact to take over quickly if I have to. I don't even know if I could do it at all without killing us both—but I don't know enough about what's happening to insist on handling it any other way.

"Gwynna *knows* what's inside her head, Lentos. I'm sure of that much. But she can't—or won't—share it.

Not even with me, and right now I'm closer to her than her own mother. I don't know if what she's hiding is really that dangerous, but that doesn't matter, because she *thinks* it is.

"She's growing into her talents impossibly fast, far too quickly for us to understand. And she's too inexperienced to be objective herself. That's the crunch point. She's young, scared, and so strong it terrifies me, yet even though she's totally inexperienced, the ground rules are hers to make. As I'm sure you understood when you made me her sole tutor."

"Yes," Lentos agreed heavily. "It has to be that way, if the situation's as dangerous as we think. Someone person has to be there continually, monitoring, watching—ready to do his best if worse comes to worst."

"I understand," Trayn said.

"Do you?" Lentos frowned. "As you just suggested, whatever we think, *she* knows exactly what she's doing, and we don't dare meddle with whatever she's concealing."

"Are you saying I should never push?" Trayn demanded. "Not even in a life or death matter of control? Lentos, I can't promise that. You know some training exercises go sour in the blink of an eye. What if she picks up a resonance she can't damp? What if she panics?"

"I know. But this is such a damnably touchy situation, and we can't even check with Wencit about what's happening!"

"I don't really care about that," Trayn said hotly. "If she goes into a training crisis—and Semkirk knows that's likely, as hard as she's pushing—I can't let her die! I'll have to try to crack her shields, and you and Wencit—damn his eyes!—will simply have to trust my discretion."

"You don't understand," Lentos said softly.

"I understand how important it may be, damn it!"

"No, you don't. You're thinking only of her, and you think I'm thinking only of Wencit's plans for her. Well, I'm not. I'm thinking of you."

"Me?" Trayn blinked in astonishment. "What about me?"

"If she's willing to risk killing herself to hide whatever it is, hasn't it occurred to you she might be willing to endanger others, as well?"

"You mean—?" Trayn looked at him in shock.

"Exactly," Lentos said grimly. "I love her, too, though I haven't been in rapport to deepen the emotion the way you have. But I also have to recognize that she's dangerous. If you have to break her shields, it'll mean she's lost so much control her life's in danger—and that means she'll be reacting on pure instinct. You say she's afraid of her own knowledge? Fine. I accept that. But if fear's her primary emotion when you break her shields—if you *can* break them—she'll *react* out of fear. And if she does—"

"—she'll try to kill me," Trayn finished softly.

"That's precisely what she'll do," Lentos said very quietly.

◆　　◆　　◆

Mistress Joslian Greenoak faced her star pupil and bowed from the waist. She monitored the rise in her adrenaline level, letting years of experience tell her exactly how much boost was useful, and settled into a guard position.

They circled, bare feet silent as they moved gracefully. Gwynna's long braids were pinned atop her
head, the coils flashing red-gold in the sunlight spilling through the skylight, but her eyes were cool and
clear. She and her teacher watched each other and
their hands opened and closed, flexing as patiently as
two cats, total concentration gripping them as they
reached out with hands and minds alike.

Joslian's hands flashed suddenly at the girl and a foot
scythed for her ankles, but Gwynna reacted before the
move was well begun. She slithered through the reaching hands, and one wrist intercepted the swinging ankle
as she threw a rolling block at her instructress' legs.

Joslian leapt over the slender body and landed
in a crouch as Gwynna rolled upright. The trainer
chopped flat-handed at the girl's ribs, but Gwynna took
the blow on a forearm. Joslian followed through the
combination, hard hand slashing for Gwynna's temple,
but Gwynna's head wasn't there. She swayed minutely,
and the hard knuckles skimmed past, close enough to
ripple her hair with the wind of their passage.

She fell backward, somersaulted, and catapulted
feet-first at Joslian. Crossed forearms hammered up
under her ankles, upending her, but she landed rolling.
She vaulted back upright just as Joslian rushed her,
and a crossed-lightning exchange ensued as Gwynna
stepped into her teacher's attack. Their hands flashed
and flickered as they struck, yet the blows flowed with
an almost impossible smoothness.

Joslian stalked her like a cat, but the simile wasn't
really apt, for this was one child it was most unsafe to
stalk. Gwynna was still a head shorter than her teacher,
but her hybrid reactions and strength were incredible,

and they gave her an advantage that forced Joslian to carry the attack to her. Yet speed and strength alone weren't enough, for the older woman was still stronger, with a longer reach, and far, far more experience.

Joslian crowded the girl, using her greater size, her eyes blank with the absent awareness of a mage as she pushed her student mercilessly. Gwynna's serene face mirrored hers as blows landed—hard and punishing, for neither could completely check their attacks in such a blistering exchange. Sweat stained their exercise suits, and Gwynna's breathing grew ragged.

The tempo increased, and for all its flashing smoothness, the blows and counters had a curiously rushed quality, as if each response began before the attack was launched. Joslian filled with warm approval for her student, but her only reaction was to force the pace still harder.

Gwynna tired, and Joslian pressed her advantage, driving the girl back across the mat to pin her against the boundary of the combat area. Her attack redoubled, wrapping around Gwynna's defenses like a net.

And then Gwynna's face went suddenly blank. She stood toe-to-toe with her teacher, and their hands flashed like swords, but the smooth, anticipatory balance vanished, and—abruptly—Gwynna charged.

For the first time, an attack took one of them completely by surprise. Joslian staggered as a sidekick slammed her knee. She had no room to roll—she could only fight for balance, and she didn't get the fractional second she needed. Gwynna's hands locked onto Joslian's smock, and her feet thudded against Joslian's kneecaps as she hurled her body backwards.

Joslian fell forward, arms spread to pin her smaller

opponent, but Gwynna wasn't beneath her. She'd released her hold, throwing her arms high to slither through her teacher's legs. An elbow slammed Joslian's spine, she stiffened as it numbed a critical nerve junction, and Gwynna's hand scythed in what would have been a killing blow in true combat.

But even as Gwynna struck, Mistress Joslian glowed brilliantly. The sworded hand flashed through the corona of her body into the canvas as the teacher suddenly materialized *behind* Gwynna to lock her in an inescapable hold.

The same light flared silver about both of them as Gwynna fought to teleport from her teacher's grip. But Joslian bore down with her mind as well as her arms, and as with their bodies, so with their minds; Gwynna had far more potential, but it wasn't yet developed. The crackling confrontation lasted perhaps five seconds before the girl conceded and went limp.

Joslian released her and they dropped to the mat, panting while the teacher massaged her aching spine and winced.

"Good, Little Sister! Very, very good! I lost you completely when you slammed your shields up. You had me dead to rights, because I was reading too closely to pull back to my physical senses in time. That was excellent—but remember that with your shields up, you can't tell what *I'm* doing, either. You couldn't tell I was gathering energy for the jump."

"I know, but it was all I could think of when you backed me into the corner that way. Besides—" Gwynna managed an impish, panting grin "—you always say to use an enemy's strength against him. And it almost worked."

"It probably would have, if you hadn't been at such a disadvantage when you tried it. I had a tiny bit longer to find a counter—and barely found it in time, as it was. An effective maneuver against a mage, Little Sister, but you won't fight many magi outside the academies."

"No, but the idea's the same, isn't it? To do the unexpected?"

"Yes, Gwynna." Joslian squeezed her shoulder warmly. "Surprise wins—if you don't give up too much advantage for it."

"That's what Poppa says. And he also says there's really no such thing as a surprise in combat unless you make it for yourself."

"He's right about both of those, love. With weapons or hands, there's no substitute for surprise if it has teeth and a plan to follow through. But you understand that; your follow-through would've finished me if I hadn't teleported."

"But you did, and I wasn't ready." Gwynna sighed. "It's so *hard* to read while your own mind keeps ticking away and you have to keep moving. Either I'm so busy reading I miss an opening, or else I'm so busy looking for an opening I forget to read!"

"Shocking!" Joslian said severely. "Nine whole weeks of training, and you still haven't mastered everything. For shame!"

She hugged the girl, and Gwynna smiled as she threw her arms around her teacher's neck.

"It's true, though," she said. "I don't have as much trouble working with Master Trayn, and I never had this much trouble when Momma was teaching me. And she's as good as you are, I think."

"She's better, on the physical level," Joslian said. "But she's war maid-trained. Our styles differ, and so does the mindset required."

"Maybe. But I can keep centered when I work with just my mind or just my body; it's both together I can't manage. Yet." Her eyes were determined.

"You will, Little Sister. But you know why you have trouble combining your talents, really. With Master Trayn, it's a whole new talent, so new there's nothing to distract you, no previous habits to lead you astray. When your mother trained you, you used only your physical senses. She taught you ways to use something you were familiar with, until you were as familiar with the skills she taught you as you were with breathing. Until you could use them well enough to toss me right out of the practice ring."

Joslian smiled and touched the tip of Gwynna's nose.

"But when you combine them, it's hard to ignore the old physical rules—and just as hard to break the new concentration to use your old skills. You're caught between, and it's awkward to keep switching. But it'll come, Gwynna. In fact, it's coming faster for you than for any other student I've known."

"People keep telling me that," Gwynna sighed, "but things are about to happen, and I'm not *ready* for them."

"Little Sister," Joslian said much more sternly, the accent of her native Kosphar stronger than usual in her Axeman, "we all know that what you face is hard. We don't know what it is, but we know your special talents will be tested in special ways. Just don't drive yourself too hard, love. I accept that you need this training, but you have to accept my judgment, too. Trust me to push you as far and as fast as I safely can. Believe that I'm willing to push you almost as hard as you push yourself, because you have potentials no one but you can develop, and I have to teach you what I know quickly so you can move on to things I'll never be able to do. I promise I'll work you till you drop, but only if you'll promise to let me judge when to *stop* driving you, because you won't achieve *anything* if you destroy yourself. Do you understand that?"

"Yes, Mistress Joslian," Gwynna said in a small voice. "I understand. And I'll try. Really I will."

◆   ◆   ◆

"All right, Gwynna, let's try some distance reading."

Trayn touched the candlewick. It sputtered into flame, and he grinned in amusement at his own actions. Had he done that to bolster his ego? He was no fire-raiser, and Gwynna was. Why hadn't he asked her to light it?

He banished the distracting thought with a simple mnemonic and turned back to his student.

"Do you understand what we're going to do, Gwynna?"

"Well . . ."

She squirmed, and he grinned again.

"It's only a different form of clairvoyance, Gwynna, no more difficult than other things we've done. The tests say you can do it. In fact, it should come fairly easily."

"But how does it *work?* I read the notes you gave me, but I can't see how to get started. I mean, the words are all there, and I understand them, but they don't *mean* anything."

"Which is why you have a mentor, Little Sister."

He sat opposite her and looked around her plain little room, pursing his lips.

"You move your viewpoint around—like going to look for something in another room, except that all you send is your mind. Remember the perception exercises?" Gwynna nodded, and he smiled encouragingly. "Well, this is like that. You use the same part of your mind your eyes use, but you use *another* sector to send the part you want to see with to another place. Got it?"

"Sort of." Her tone was doubtful, but it was the sort of doubt that preceded understanding. "That's why you can only distance read someplace you've already seen?"

"Exactly. With clairvoyance, you can see *through* things, but only to the visual horizon. It's a case of the conscious limiting the subconscious. You 'know' you can only see so far, so that's as far as your clairvoyance reaches. But if you're familiar with another place—and have the talent—you can project a viewpoint there. You fool yourself, in a way. You know you can't really see it, but you can build a memory picture and see *that*. When you do, your subconscious is freed and you really do see it."

"That makes more sense than the books." Gwynna nodded. "But if another mage knows the place, and you're in rapport, can you distance read it because *he's* seen it?"

"If it isn't too far away. There's an absolute limit to any distance reading talent, though it's much greater than the clairvoyance limits. The longest distance reading I've ever personally seen was from here to Marfang Island. Old Master Sholt could distance read as far as Bortalik Bay, but that was right at his limit, and all he got were dim images. And he could only read parts of the area he'd actually visited."

"So it's not like Wencit and his gramerhain," Gwynna said slowly.

"No, I can't scry, of course, but as I understand it, wizards send their minds after specific individuals or sets of circumstances. Distance reading is more ... well, more *passive*. Like lying in wait for someone to wander into the place you can 'see.' Understand?"

"I think so." Gwynna nodded. "Can we try now?"

"Certainly. But remember, you probably won't be able to range too far on this first try. Don't strain, and don't be disappointed if you can't."

"I'll remember."

"All right," he said, rising and circling her small desk to stand behind her and rest his hands on her shoulders. "We'll start with something simple, then, and use regular clairvoyance to look into the library, okay?"

"Sure."

"All right," Trayn said again, his voice dropping soothingly. "Watch the candle, just like before. Let your mind rest on the tip of the flame. That's right ... thaaat's riiiiiightttt. . . ."

Gwynna's blue eyes darkened as she dropped into the trance with his hands on her shoulders to strengthen their rapport. His watch lay on the table, its soft ticking like thunder in the quiet of their mingled breathing as she centered. By now, he knew to the second how long it would take her.

"Now, Gwynna," he said after a moment. "Let's distance read. Don't push too hard. Just open like I taught you. Gently ... gently! Not so hard, love. Just watch the candle and listen to the watch. That's good. Pretend the wall is Mistress Joslian, and now ... we'll ... read ... her. . . ."

His voice died away. It hadn't really been necessary, for her mind had melded with his well before he stopped speaking. They were in deep rapport, but her inner core was barricaded still. Yet he hardly noticed the knot of light that forbade his entry, for he'd become accustomed to it. He merely marveled at the power and clarity of the young mind in his keeping. Her mental touch was cool, catlike, clear as a crystal stream and vibrant with life. Each mind had its own unique presence, and hers tasted of cinnamon and autumn leaves, he thought. It blew about him like a breeze whipping in fresh from the sea, and the strength within it almost overwhelmed him.

<Now, love,> his mental voice said, and he looked through her senses at a stone wall, examining it minutely in step with her. <We're going to look through it, just like reading Mistress Joslian, but easier. Walls don't have shields, do they? Just let your mind through....>

The master empath shared her delight as she slid past the wall as if its solid stone were smoke and she a breeze. The empty library was suddenly around them, and he shared her pleasure as her mind's eye roamed the silent shelves. She trembled with elated discovery, and he rejoiced with her.

He moved with her, offering only minimal guidance as she tasted her new ability. She reached out farther, circling the grounds like a windborne hawk. Shimmering privacy shields masked the dormitories, but Gwynna didn't care. All she longed for was the freedom to roam, to stretch out—to test her limits. Her mind quested along the stone walls, touching and tasting grass, trees, even the moss on the stone and the insects in the moss.

She shuddered ecstatically as the world flooded her mind, and Trayn went with her, amazed by her power. Then he scolded himself. If anything could still surprise him, it shouldn't be her strength!

He drew a deep breath and prepared to recall her roving mind for the next step. But before he could, he felt a sudden welling of concentration within her inner shields. He gasped at the sensation, and sudden alarm stabbed him.

What was she *doing*? She wasn't ready for that sort of output!

He fought for her attention, but it was too late. Her astounding breadth of talent had confounded him once again, and even as he prepared to scatter her building strength, he stopped. Too much power had gathered. If he interrupted it, it might ricochet within her. It might kill her to dump it all within her shields, and without breaking those shields he couldn't deflect it from her. All he could do was ride it out . . . and pray.

His flashing thoughts took only tiny fractions of a second. His decision had been made before she unleashed the power she'd gathered.

She pushed. That was the only word for it. It was as if her mind became a spring, wound tightly as possible, only to uncoil. It lashed out, carrying him upon its strength, and he had a sense of rushing wind and darkness as their joined minds whipped out across the face of the night.

They burst from the sheltered Academy, the "mage proof" barriers effective as so much straw against a hurricane. Before the supposed obstruction even registered, they'd vaulted into the night and gone streaming south at a speed that mocked the wind.

Trayn reeled. How could she be *doing* this? What *was* she doing? Blurred, darkness-bound land unreeled below, and mountains thrust brutal peaks at him. He flinched as their image threatened to impale his mind, and he and Gwynna screamed low above the summits, hurtling ever south while bitter snow devils danced on the peaks to envelop them.

Mighty walls loomed, sealing a steep-shouldered pass. A glitter of protective shields flicked Trayn like a lash, but once more Gwynna sliced through them like a meteor. He shuddered in anguish, but then they were past the fortress, circling back, and he gasped as huge, black wings and bone-white fangs flashed above them. The dragon bulked against the moon, vapor pluming from its jaws like steam, and Gwynna panicked. Joy vanished, exultation was quenched by the raw poison of fear—fear for someone *else*, Trayn knew, even then—and a harsh explosion of horror.

Her panic chilled Trayn to the bone, for her fine control vanished as it ripped through her. Precision vanished, balance fled, and in their place there was only the long, terrifying plunge to the mountaintops below them. Gwynna had soared like an eagle; now terror broke her wings and hurled her from the heavens.

She plummeted towards destruction on the waiting peaks, and Trayn reached deep inside himself, grasping the discipline which made him what he was. Exquisite pain ripped at him as he made himself move against the grip of their rapport. It was like opposing his flesh to iron, sweat pearled his cheeks as anguish tore his mind, and every instinct screamed for him to jerk out of their rapport and save himself.

But the mage academies had chosen Trayn Aldarfro for more than just the strength of his talent. They'd chosen him for the strength of his *heart*. They'd chosen a mage who'd fought all the forces of darkness, who'd driven himself to the brink of extinction, who'd *shared* the brutal torture of a sacrifice on the altar of Sharnā, throwing himself between that agony and the gates of hell themselves to preserve the soul of a young woman he'd never met from the demon come to claim it. They'd chosen a *man*, not just a mage—a man who would die where he stood to protect the brilliant, gifted young mind of the child he loved.

It was that man—that mage—whose thoughts flashed as he fought Gwynna's headlong dissolution. Self-preservation beckoned him out of the collapsing ruin of her mind, but he forged a pocket within his half of their rapport and centered his awareness in a tiny island of control. He felt the tremors as her mind toppled, but he slammed panic aside, moving with the assurance of a master mage facing disaster. He gathered himself within his island of sanity as Gwynna's mind thundered to destruction about him in raw terror and did the hardest thing of all . . . he waited.

Trayn's empath soul shuddered in anguish as her ruin crested. He rode a storm front of devastation across her public mind, waiting for the fleeting moment when he might save them both.

It came.

He anchored his identity in the refuge he'd built, and his thought lashed out. He wasn't strong enough to breach her perfectly meshed shields, and he knew it. They stood like a fortress, impenetrable and proud. Yet he also knew panic was destabilizing her control, and he had no choice but to try. He slammed a probe against them like a battering ram...and felt them yield.

He fought down a surge of hope and slammed them again. Again! Bell-like tones of conflict clangored through their rapport. *Again!!*

Her shields shivered, and fresh terror ripsawed through her as she sensed the intrusion. Slivers of her panic lacerated him like flying knives, but he ground his teeth and endured. He hammered once more... and her shields shattered like crystal.

Vast images battered him as he plunged into the maelstrom, ignoring everything else to arrow towards the gleaming life at her center. His mental grasp locked on it ruthlessly, crushing her frantic resistance, and Gwynna writhed.

A flattened hand, its edge like iron, crashed into his ribs, and he gasped in anguish as one of them snapped. The heel of her other hand rammed upward under his chin, but he had just enough warning to ride the blow which should have snapped his neck. She twisted in his grip, her hands rising to his throat, and he fought to block them with his upper arms, for he dared not release her shoulders and break contact. But her strength was unbelievable, and he felt uncontrolled madness guttering through her.

She meant to kill him. In her confusion, she would protect her secrets the only way she could—by destroying the intruder. Her hands tightened about his throat, and he locked his will desperately upon her, slamming her sensory channels shut.

Gwynna went absolutely rigid, her mental voice a scream of terror as all sight, all sound—all perception— was slashed off. Her horror rose past insanity, battering him, but he controlled her at last. He rode the shock-wave of her resistance, weaving his mental grip ever tighter.

She had time for only one last thrust, and a mental needle lashed at him—one fit to burn out any mind. He screamed as it ripped through him, but he refused to yield, and the attack shattered as he hurled her into unconsciousness.

She crumpled like a string-cut puppet, and Trayn went to the floor with her, too spent to stand. He hovered in his little island, hanging on the lip of burning out forever, and gathered the last fragments of his will. He reached out weakly for Lentos, thought he felt a faint response, and then there was only blackness.

◆　　◆　　◆

Trayn's eyelids fluttered unwillingly.

His head was an anvil, ringing with pain. His eyes watered to the fierce throbbing, and he moaned as his hand rose limply to the cold compress which covered them. He gasped as an arm slipped under him, raising him, and another hand caught his on the compress.

"Your eyes are too sensitive yet for that," Lentos said gently.

"Semkirk!" Trayn whispered. "What happened?"

"You tell me," Lentos said dryly. "I felt your message—barely—and got there to find Gwynna in shock and you little better. I thought we'd lost you both, and we almost had."

"*Gwynna!*" Trayn stiffened. "Is she—?"

He reached for her mental presence and moaned as fresh pain roared up.

"Don't try to use your mind yet, idiot!" Lentos sat

beside him. "Gwynna's all right, although I think it will be some time before she regains her confidence. Something trimmed her back—trimmed both of you, I should say—but she'll recover. And probably be the stronger for whatever it was."

"Thank the gods," Trayn muttered weakly. "I thought I'd killed her."

"Well, you didn't. But you'd better tell me what you *did* do."

"Well," Trayn chuckled wanly, "I finally cracked her shields."

"Trayn!" Lentos stiffened. "After everything we've discussed, you actually forced—?!"

"No, no!" Trayn cut off his horrified exclamation. "It wasn't a confrontation, Lentos—or not that sort, anyway. We'd just begun distance reading when something happened in her mind."

He shivered as he relived the moment and felt again the vast strength which had filled her.

"I don't know what it was. No mind should be able to generate that much power, and it wasn't normal distance reading, either. One minute we were right here—the next we were Semkirk knows where, and she was panicking. Something scared her to death, and she lost control. She was on the edge of total burnout, and the only way to stop it was to take control. So..."

"And that *really* scared her," Lentos said as his voice died.

"Oh, it did. It did! But nothing could've scared her much worse than she already was. When I said burnout, I meant it, Lentos. We almost lost her." Trayn pressed the compress with one hand and touched his ribs with the other. "If I'd had time, I'd've been scared to death myself!"

"But you took control? Total control?"

"I had no choice. And you were right about her reactions—she was so busy trying to kill me I couldn't risk just guiding her out. It was either lock her down or watch her self-destruct... and take me with her."

"Did you... see... anything?" Lentos asked hesitantly.

"Not much, and what I did see is hers. Anyway, it was all too fast, and she was still screening even while she was dying. In fact, she was using strength she needed to stay alive to protect whatever she's hiding."

"I understand. But can you at least tell me what panicked her?"

"Yes, but it doesn't make much sense. We were over a fortress—in the East Walls, I think—and we found a dragon. I couldn't see the color against the moon, and I don't know how we got there, but I think she knew exactly where she was, and maybe even what the dragon was doing there. That's what terrified her in the first place."

"A mountain fortress and a dragon..." Lentos murmured.

"Yes, an *imperial* fortress. I caught a flash off its shields. And that's another thing—she went through those shields like they weren't even there."

"*What?*"

"Oh, yes. And here's another tidbit—it wasn't an instant translocation, either."

"Explain," Lentos said, clearly still shocked by the last revelation.

"I'm not sure I can. Distance reading isn't one of my primary talents, and it's just enough of a secondary for me to teach someone else. But whatever she did, she wasn't distance reading. We didn't flash to that fortress—we went *over* everything between here and there."

"Over? Like flying?"

"More like a short-range clairvoyant scan. I think if she'd wanted to, and if she'd known what she was doing, she could have scanned everything we passed over. *I* think she's stumbled onto a totally new talent just enough like distance reading for that to key her into it. And her range! We were a hell of a long way out, but with perfect clarity. If not for that dragon, we might *still* be reaching out! I couldn't stop her. It was like...like wrestling a whirlwind! All I could do was hang on and hope."

"Catch her when she fell, you mean," Lentos corrected warmly. "Thank Semkirk you were able to! And maybe it's as well this happened. At least she may finally see why we warn her against driving too hard. She came close enough to understand, anyway! But back to this vision or whatever it was. Was the fortress in a valley?"

"No, a pass. The walls cut right across it."

"Could it have been South Keep?"

"South Keep?" Trayn frowned, then nodded slowly. "You know, it might just have been. I've never actually seen it from above, and I didn't get much of a look at it as we passed, either, so I can't be certain. But if it was...what a *range* she has!"

"And the dragon was right there, attacking the fortress?"

"No. I think it was on the far side, close to the border but right there in the pass. If it really was South Keep, anyway."

"Trayn, there's no way a dragon could be there on its own."

"Bahzell and Wencit went south," Trayn said slowly, in answer to Lentos' grim tone.

"Of course! She was drawn to their locus by her concern and found a dragon there. Not only that, it must be connected with their mission. By the Scepter, that must be it! And there's only one way a dragon could be there."

"Sorcery," Trayn said grimly. He tried to rise, but his balance was uncertain and Lentos pressed him firmly back.

"No, Trayn. You've done your part. Leave this with me."

"But is there a Council messenger in Belhadan?"

"There's always a messenger in Belhadan. I'll send word at once, but they'll have to touch down outside the shields. And you realize, of course, that even a wind walker may not catch them in time."

"I know, but we've got to try!"

"We will," Lentos said, his voice like iron. "And if we're too late, *someone* is going to pay for it!"

CHAPTER SEVENTEEN

South Keep

Kenhodan eased himself in the saddle and looked gratefully up at a sky which was no longer dropping snow, sleet, or even rain upon his head.

It was a pleasant change he hoped might even last for a day or two.

The snow had cost them four miserable, motionless days, and even after that the weather had been chill, damp, foggy, and thoroughly miserable. The temperature had hovered at or just below freezing during the day (and considerably lower than that at night), and the leaden clouds hadn't broken until late the day before. The cold and mist had oppressed him, but now a stiff breeze had pushed the last fog aside and the sky was a deep, glorious blue, studded with drifting, high-piled white clouds, while the sun was warm on his shoulders. The air was still brisk and melting snow lay all about, but he could almost believe in spring once more.

He settled back, his eyes automatically sweeping

the slopes above them, and felt a fresh surge of the awe he doubted was going to fade any time soon. He'd thought they were into the East Walls before the snow; now he realized they'd only touched their fringes at the time.

Steep mountains shouldered into the sky, with snow still piled on their sides, like ash after a fire. He saw more snow blowing in streamers from the highest crags, and the road swept between majestic slopes clothed in dark pines. He'd watched the mountains grow through yesterday's fog, but he hadn't truly appreciated the sheer weight of earth and stone until the weather cleared. Now he did, and there was something about their bulk that made him grateful for the forests fringing the valleys, almost as if the trees gave him someplace to hide from the peaks' frowning disapproval. As the mountains climbed higher, the trees thinned and ended, replaced by snow-covered grass, then permanent ice and naked stone that had no interest in mere mortals' affairs. Their brooding bleakness was beautiful but oppressive, built to a scale too large for comfort, and he was glad to be this far below those soaring summits, listening to countless rivulets brawl and fume with snowmelt as they raced down the mountains' flanks. The air was clear and clean and the sound of water was a chill, crystal song in the early morning.

"Beautiful, isn't it?" Bahzell's voice startled him.

"Yes. I hadn't realized they were so big—*or* so beautiful."

"Aye, but they're after being more than that, too. The making of the Empire, they were. South to north, it's four hundred leagues they run, though folk

call them the Ordan Mountains up on the edge of
Dwarvenhame. But 'Kormak's Battlements' they were
in the first days, and rightly so. They're after shielding
the Axemen's entire eastern frontier."

"Are they this . . . formidable everywhere?"

"That they are, and passes are few. There's no
more than a handful as might be suited to trade or
invasion. Oh, there's more places than anyone's ever
likely to know as smugglers can be slipping through,
but South Wall, Traitors' Walk, Cragwall, the Pass
of Heroes—those are the only true roads through.
There's North Pass up in the Ordans, but that's after
leading into Dwarvenhame, and it's a foolish, foolish
man takes on dwarves in the mountains. Which leaves
aside the wee problem of slipping past the Sothōii
and my own folk, first."

Kenhodan nodded, but his attention was elsewhere
as the road thrust abruptly out to sweep around the
flank of a mountain. The roadbed's northwest side fell
away in a sheer precipice and he caught his breath
as he gazed down through a thousand crystalline feet
of air into the heart of a hidden river valley. Shadows
cloaked it, but a silver thread ran through snowy forest far below, glittering, and he drew up and stared
down, his heart aching.

"You see?" Bahzell waved at the sight. "It's beautiful
enough the East Walls are to choke your heart, but it's
not beauty as brings us here. The East Walls are after
being worth half a million men when the King Emperor
goes to war. I'm thinking that's why Kormak pushed east
and north from Manhome instead of south."

"It was," Wencit said softly, pausing beside them.
His less-than-new poncho was smudged with slush and

rough travel and his hair and beard were uncombed. He might have been an age-worn peasant staring at a spring he'd never hoped to see, but his eyes burned bright under the red ball of the sun, and his face was ancient beyond belief. The aura of years clung to him, potent with age and power enough to match even the East Walls.

"It was," he repeated, just as softly. "Even then we knew the day would come when the Carnadosans brought their filth and war to Norfressa, and when that day comes, no fortress weaker than these mountains will stand against them."

"When it comes?" Kenhodan's voice was soft as he dared to voice the suspicions which had arisen in Sindor. "Is it coming soon, Wencit?"

He felt Bahzell stiffen beside him as he asked the question, and Wencit looked at both of them for a long, still moment.

"It is," the wizard said, his voice oddly formal, "but not yet. There's still a pause before the storm, but when that storm breaks, it will be like nothing any Norfressan can imagine. Only those who have seen it could understand, and only I remain of those who've seen." He shook his head slowly. "Even the East Walls may not be strong enough to brave that storm," he said softly, and touched Byrchalka with a light, courteous heel. The courser tossed his head, turned away from the valley, and trotted steadily up the high road's steep slope once again.

Kenhodan, Bahzell, and Walsharno stared after him as Byrchalka trotted away from them, the packhorses following. He didn't look like much, especially in the saddle of something as magnificent as a courser. Just a dirty old man with eyes of fire, his face drawn and old in the slanting, early light, whose words had stolen the warmth from the morning.

◆　　◆　　◆

The road grew even steeper as it wound higher, and the air seemed thinner, cold in the shadows and chill even when the sun was brightest. They passed through deep cuttings, their sides covered with tool marks and glistening icicles, some as thick as Kenhodan's body, where wind blew icily through the shadows. The trees ended, and there was no sound but their passing and the wind.

They slowed. Not even royal and imperial engineers could conquer the East Walls, and their way wound through tortuous switchbacks and curves. Spots had been provided where travelers might bivouac beside the high road, and they used them when they must, but an urgency lay upon them, and they pushed hard whenever they had light. Some places they were forced to dismount and lead their mounts up icy grades with the coursers following and watching the lesser cousins alertly, and each downslope led to a climb twice as steep. Twice they heard the rumble of distant avalanches as sun weakened the packed snow.

They were twelve days out of Sindor when they topped out over a steep slope and an east wind swept up it to lash their faces, flap the skirts of their ponchos, and roar softly about their ears like the roll of surf. The day had grown grim and dim once more, the skies like wind-burnished slate, and Kenhodan shivered as the cold dug at him while that same wind seared his lungs.

"I hope that was the last climb of the day," he told Bahzell wearily.

"It was, lad. Look yonder."

Bahzell pointed ahead, and Kenhodan shielded his eyes with one hand, blinking away wind tears and fine, cold drops of rain. The road plunged downward, curving slightly, and the wind came up it into their teeth. A dimness bulked across the narrow pass some miles below them, but he could make out few details through the blowing drizzle sweeping up to meet them.

"South Keep," Bahzell said. "I'm thinking we'll sleep warm tonight."

"Thank the gods!" Kenhodan sighed, and squinted harder, trying to form a picture of the place. The misty rain defeated him, and he shrugged. Any fortress in such a dismal place could only be grim. There ought to at least be fires, though, and hopefully it would have a spare cot somewhere.

"Come on," Wencit said. "It's farther than it looks, and I'd like to be there before gate closing. Believe me, we *don't* want to camp outside the walls tonight if we can help it."

Byrchalka and Walsharno started forward considerably more briskly, followed by Glamhandro, and Chernion's mare. Even the packhorses seemed to catch the mood as they realized the road sloped only down for a change, and Kenhodan watched the keep draw closer, curious about this bastion of the Empire in its bleak and barren surroundings. What sort of men, he wondered, could stand garrison duty in such a place?

He realized only gradually how badly distance and mist had fooled him. What had seemed a low-lying blur slowly resolved itself into a wall; then the wall became a cliff, and his casual curiosity became something very like disbelief. The work of giants lay before him.

Granite walls towered up with a blue-grey arrogance that shamed the natural cliffs to either side. There were three of them, those walls, and they were absolutely vertical, reared out of the East Walls' bones. Kenhodan's muscles tightened as they moved into South Keep's shadow, like ants swallowed in shade, and the walls soared above him, seemingly poised forever on the edge of overbalancing and avalanching down to destroy him.

A deep ravine edged the outer curtainwall, quarried deep and sheer in solid rock. Archers' slits fanged the gate towers—row upon row of them banding the stone to mark the levels within. Gape-jawed gargoyles grinned at regular intervals from battlements so high they seemed tiny, and Kenhodan knew each stony gullet would vomit banefire at need. The effect on any attacker would be dreadful, and the soot streaking their scaled stone snouts spoke of frequent tests. Above all, the scarlet and gold axe banner snapped and cracked, flaunting against the stone-colored sky from at least a dozen staffs.

But it was the gaunt perfection of the wall itself which demanded his attention. It was smooth as ice, without the thinnest line to indicate where stone block met stone block, and his eyes widened as he realized that entire, stupendous wall was a single, seamless stretch of naked rock, as if the mountains' native granite had reared suddenly skyward in a frozen comber of stone. Occasional patches of dark moss softened the hard, powerful stone, but they subtracted nothing from the keep's forbidding power. Rather, they underscored the endurance of the never-taken fortress. It reared like a primeval force, the earth groaning under its weight, between cliffs quarried into knife-sharp vertical precipices. Wing fortresses protected the curtainwall's shoulders, standing on upthrust islands severed from the mountain walls by more sheer chasms. An aura of power brooded over the pass, frowning down on the insignificant mites who'd dared to raise such stony strength.

"Impressed?"

He turned his head to meet Bahzell's amused glance.

"Moderately." He wasn't certain how he'd managed to keep his tone dry.

"Aye, and well you should be. All the passes are after being well defended, but its South Keep lies nearest the Spearmen, and not even Axe Hallow's this strong. The King Emperor was in no mind to take chances when he was after ordering it built, and betwixt the Empire and Dwarvenhame—which wasn't after having joined the Empire in those days—the better part of two hundred sarthnaisks were after working on it for twelve years. That wall yonder—" he flicked his ears at the curtainwall "—that's not after being *built*, lad. It was *forged* in place, and it's after being *tougher* than the cliffs to either side.

"The forts on the shoulders protect the flanks, though Tomanāk knows only a herd of maddened mountain goats could be scaling the cliffs to reach 'em! The garrison comes and goes through tunnels inside the cliffs; there's no other road. They've wells inside, as well, and South Keep's after being stored for a five-year siege, come to that, though I'm thinking as it's an unlikely army as could attack both ends of the pass at once."

Bahzell shook his head as if marveling at the power

he'd described, then Walsharno moved into a canter. Kenhodan followed on Glamhandro, pushing to catch up with Wencit and Chernion, who'd drawn ahead of them.

Two of South Keep's three drawbridges were lowered over the dry moat, and Kenhodan glanced over the edge as Glamhandro's hooves thudded on the thick timbers of the center bridge. One look was enough. The gorge was over fifty feet deep and its bottom was fanged with grim iron spikes. There was another row of archer's slits at its very lip, forty feet above the gorge's floor, and more banefire spouts stretched along the gorge wall just beneath them.

The portcullis was raised—the gods only knew how many tons of weight hung on massive chains, its lower edge glowering with wide flanges designed to lock into iron-reinforced sockets in the roadway when lowered. Halberdiers stood watch before it, and Kenhodan saw colorful splashes of color on the high walls to mark out archers. And this was only the *back* of the fortress—the side least likely to be attacked!

The gate commander stepped into the road as Wencit crossed the drawbridge to him. He shaded his eyes, and a squad of his men trotted towards him, but he waved them back as he recognized the wizard.

"Greetings, Wencit!" To ears which had been buffeted by the East Walls' winds for over a week, his voice sounded unnaturally clear in the calm lee of the keep.

"Greetings, Captain . . . Tolos, isn't it?"

"Aye, so it is." The officer was clearly pleased to be remembered, and Wencit drew up and looked down at him from the saddle.

"I'm pleased South Keep mounts such an excellent watch," he said, "but isn't it a little unusual for travelers to be challenged on sight?"

"I beg your pardon?" Tolos sounded more than a little embarrassed.

"Come now, Tolos! Gate guard's usually a lieutenant's duty, isn't it? And your men are clearly on edge. For that matter, I'm inclined to doubt you studied our faces so closely because you're smitten by my beauty!"

"I think Earl Bostik had best explain, Sir," Tolos said uncomfortably, and something in his tone tightened the wizard's expression.

"I see," he said after a moment. Then he shook himself and grinned almost impishly. "And is the trouble—whatever it is—so bad you feel obliged to detail a guide to keep an eye on us?"

"The Governor would have my ears if I suggested such a thing!"

"In that case, Captain, we'll say thank you and be on our way."

Wencit nodded courteously and Byrchalka strode under the portcullis with his head carried high and proud.

Kenhodan pressed close behind the wizard in the gate tunnel. Hooves rang in the dark, frowning depths of the gut, and he felt crushed by the oppressive weight of stone. The curtainwall was immensely thick; the gate tunnel cut a dark bore through its foundations, and they emerged from it only to see the next wall soaring above them. The killing ground between the walls was dark and shadowed, a deep gulf fifty yards wide, and beyond the second wall rose a third. A new set of bastioned towers flanked the approach road as it passed through each successive wall, and each of those walls had its own massive gates and portcullises. The approach road was designed to be swept by defensive fire in the open, and the thought of the carnage archers could wreak on any attacker was sobering, yet as their way plunged back into each gate tunnel, scattered circles of light gleamed on the dark paving. They fell from openings high above, and when Kenhodan passed under one of them and peered upward he saw a metal-lined hole that reached up to the battlements above. He shivered, recognizing still more outlets for banefire. Anyone who carried the outer gates would find the tunnel a deathtrap.

The passage seemed to stretch forever, and even the dim afternoon light at the eastern end was dazzling when he finally emerged from it.

He blinked, clearing his sight, and stared out over the city those massive fortifications shielded. On the far side, the eastern walls towered even higher than the western walls, and the cloud-hidden sun was a dull pewter patch above the western battlements behind him. The bar of the walls' shadow reached darkly before him, and his eyes widened as they dropped to the city itself. The buildings were of the same granite as the walls, but that was the only similarity. It was if the fortress had two faces: one fanged with steel against its enemies, the other warm and alive to welcome friends.

Multicolored slate roofed the buildings, walls danced with agile frescoes and bas reliefs vibrant with energy, and even the clifflike inner sweep of the third curtainwall was covered with intricate, cunning mosaics. South Keep was a place of war, and Tomanāk's mace and sword dominated many of the carvings and mosaics, but others were peaceful, almost whimsical. Here a maiden peeped shyly up at her lover. There an entire village danced barefoot in the wooden vats of the season's first pressing. And on another wall, children vied in sports and games or raced across alpine meadows with high-flying kites.

The scenes were bewildering in their variety, yet all flowed smoothly together, as if wrought by a single hand, and the colorful roofs completed the composition, turning the inside of the grim fortress into an oasis that celebrated not death, but life. A single structure—citadel and palace in one—dominated its center, its sheer walls and towers alien to the cheerful kaleidoscope about it, yet somehow not marring it, and a tall staff atop its central keep showed the axe of the King Emperor over the crossed swords and axe of an imperial governor.

Kenhodan blinked at that. At first sight, it was ridiculous to equate a fortress commander with the viceroy of an entire province, if that was what the governor's banner implied. Yet it became less ridiculous as he considered it. If South Keep was the most powerful military bastion of the Empire, its commander had better be gifted with extraordinary ability, and it wasn't unreasonable for him to hold rank appropriate to his responsibility.

But as they moved deeper into the fortress Kenhodan's attention shifted from the rank of its commander to the tension about him. Every eye was shadowed, and though several called greetings to Wencit or Bahzell, all seemed subdued. Not with fear—this was more like uncertainty, yet it bit deep, whatever it was, and its cumulative effect was contagious. Even Bahzell seemed affected, and Kenhodan watched his eyes move from side to side, searching for the source of the uneasiness. He remembered Wencit's exchange with Captain Tolos, and a butterfly of nervousness began to beat its wings within him.

A party of horsemen clattered down the street towards them, led by a tall, narrow man in half-plate, his visored helm open to show wary, mud-brown eyes and a drooping mustache. He drew rein when he saw Wencit.

"Greetings, Wencit!" His voice was high and nasal, grating on the ear. "And to you, Bahzell! Of everyone in the Empire, you're the two I'd've asked to see, given a choice."

"Greetings, Milord." Wencit bowed from the saddle. "What's amiss?"

"Damned if I know!" The narrow man hawked and spat into the gutter, then smiled grimly. "I'm a plain soldier. All I ever wanted to be. Whatever this is, it's beyond me. Come to the palace; we'll discuss it over supper."

Kenhodan covered his surprise. *This* was the governor of South Keep? This stoop-shouldered, sharp-toned, staccato-voiced, somehow seedy man?

"Ah," Bahzell rumbled. "I'll not be taking food 'amiss' whatever else might be afoot!"

"You never have." The governor snorted. "Well, come on then! Cooks can find you something, I suppose, Bahzell."

"It's to be hoped so," Bahzell retorted, and the governor gave another snort.

Earl Bostik's escort formed around them and pushed

briskly through the streets, with Wencit and the governor at the party's heart in low-voiced conversation. They looked a bit odd—despite Bostik's height, Wencit had to bend low in Byrchalka's saddle to hear him—but no one seemed disposed to laugh. No one else could catch their words, either, but Kenhodan heard the irritating, drillbit cadence of Bostik's indecipherable voice and shook his head mentally.

Their brisk pace carried them quickly to the governor's palace. Its walls lacked the strength of the main fortress, but it was a formidable castle in its own right. Though an effort had been made to provide a pleasant residence, it could clearly hold its own against attackers for a long period. Unlike the main fortress, it was moated, its walls rising sheer from the water to overhanging battlements. A large stream or small river foamed down from a cliff inside the fortress to fill it, and Kenhodan saw carp darting in the clear water as they clattered over the drawbridge, but for the life of him he couldn't think of a reason to flood it. It was certainly pretty, but no one was likely to be driving any mines through a ditch carved from solid stone, after all!

The courtyard was paved in pastel flags, and stable boys dashed to take the horses. Glamhandro snorted at the strange hand on his bridle, but calmed at a word from Kenhodan. The coursers, though, shook off the ostlers disdainfully and paced majestically in the proper direction. Bostik watched the two of them go and barked a laugh.

"Imagine Walsharno's about to set the stable by its ears!" he said, smiling crookedly up at Bahzell. "And who's the other fellow, if I can ask?"

"His name is Byrchalka, Milord," Wencit replied. "He's agreed to bear me, but his heart's been badly wounded. His wind brother was murdered in Korun."

Bostik's half-smile disappeared, and the muddy brown eyes went bleak.

"Be Krahana's own hells to pay for *that*," he said grimly, and looked back at Bahzell. "Know who did it?"

"Aye," Bahzell replied, equally grimly. "A fellow named Chernion, assuming the little bastard as had Byrchalka locked in a stall was after telling the truth."

"*Chernion!*" the governor hissed. Neither he nor Bahzell noticed the quick flicker of "Elrytha's" eyes. "Now, there's a whoreson whose head I'd like to see over West Gate!"

"That you'll not be doing." Bahzell's ears shifted in unmistakable satisfaction. "The two of us were after having a brief discussion in the Forest of Hev. I'm thinking he'll not have any more of them."

"That way, was it?" Bostik looked up at the hradani in obvious approval. "In that case, looks to me like you've already accomplished one good thing on this trip!"

"I'd like to think we have, at any rate," Wencit said. "And in the meantime, I believe something was mentioned about food?"

"Aye, so it was!" The governor's wide, froglike mouth curved in a slow smile that was the first really attractive thing about him Kenhodan had noticed. "And from Bahzell's expression, we'd best be getting to it quick!"

Bostik chuckled at his own wit, and the travelers followed him into his home. The passages were wide and warm, with coal fires burning on numerous hearths. Colorful tapestries covered the walls, and narrow windows high up under the western eaves admitted the fading afternoon. Their stained-glass turned the gray light into a tangled spill of color despite the dimness of the day.

They entered a large room with an intricately patterned black and white floor. Desks covered half that floor, and maps covered the walls, dotted with little flags mounted on pins. Clerks and officers bustled purposefully, and Kenhodan's respect for Bostik rose. This was clearly a well-oiled team, keeping affairs moving with minimal intrusion from the governor, and Kenhodan recognized the strength of personality needed to head such a staff...and to be willing to delegate to it once it was in place.

A plain wooden chair sat on a low dais, the imperial axe worked in silver and six feet tall on the wall behind it. The floor immediately before it was clear, and as Bostik headed for the chair, additional seats arrived magically for his guests. Small tables followed, and then steaming plates of the best food Kenhodan had tasted since Belhadan. A gray-haired man took Bostik's helmet and battered sword, and the governor wiggled out of his armor and arming doublet with a sigh of relief and sprawled back in a plain linen shirt, left knee bent over one chair arm.

Kenhodan watched him between mouthfuls, and his earlier impression changed steadily. Bostik's voice was hardly that of a leader of men, and his narrow body was long and gawky. His face was homely—to put it kindly—with its long jaw and drooping mustache, but it had an underlying power, and his dark hair, tied back in a warrior's braid, lent him more strength. His fingers were long and powerful, callused from long hours around a sword hilt, and although he lounged sloppily in his chair, his movements were quick and purposeful and his terse, staccato manner hid his swift mind only poorly.

"Now, Wencit," the high-pitched voice cut through the clatter of plates. "Bahzell I know, of course, but make me known to your other friends."

"Certainly, Milord. This is Elrytha of the Border Wardens."

Chernion looked up and nodded respectfully. Earl or no, the governor would receive only an equal's deference from any borderer. Border wardens were the King Emperor's personal agents, charged with keeping order in areas where even the Royal and Imperial Army rarely ventured.

"Border Warden." The dull eyes gleamed as Bostik returned her nod.

"And this is Kenhodan, a comrade of ours from Belhadan."

"Welcome," the governor said, and Kenhodan rose to bow.

"Thank you, Milord. Your cooks have already made me fully welcome, though!"

The governor chuckled appreciatively and waved him back into his chair. He smiled a moment, then turned to other matters with a quick frown.

"What brings you to South Keep, Wencit?"

"Many matters, Earl Bostik," Wencit said formally.

"And none of 'em any of my damned business, hey?" Bostik gave a bark of laughter at Wencit's quick demur. "No, no! Damn me, man, you hold an imperial warrant to go where you will, do as you would. Not prying. But your trip coincides with more worry than I like."

"Worry over what, Milord?"

"Tomanāk! Wish I knew!"

"Come, Bostik. Unless you had *some* idea, you wouldn't worry."

"True enough." Bostik gave another crack of laughter, although there seemed to be little humor in it, and waved one hand. "Look around. How many merchants d'you see?"

"None," Wencit replied. "But surely it's early in the year yet?"

"East Road's clear. Been a caravan a week from Kolvania for a month."

"Then what seems to be the problem?"

"Night before last—" Bostik leaned forward, planting his elbows on his knees, and his voice turned grim "—what was left of a caravan came in."

"It was attacked?" Wencit's face was still, his wildfire eyes on Bostik's face.

"It was," the governor said bleakly. "Thirty merchants. Sixty wagons. Eighty, ninety drovers. Maybe a hundred guards. Four merchants and eighteen guards got here. No one else reached the gate."

Bahzell laid his fork aside carefully and wiped his lips with a napkin. His ears stirred gently, and he watched the governor closely.

"Milord," he said, "there's never a brigand born as would work so close to South Keep, and no caravan as strong as that's such as anyone would be attacking lightly. And you'd not be speaking so to Wencit if you were after knowing what it was had happened, now would you?"

"No. It was dark as the pits of Krahana. Wind and rain right up the pass. Nobody's sure what happened.

Survivors're those who took to their heels at the first screams and had the best horses under 'em when they did. All *they* know is the attack came out of nowhere. One swears it was some sort of creature, but he's a Purple Lord."

"Even a Purple Lord can be accurate, Milord... where his money's involved," Wencit said slowly.

"Maybe." Bostik hawked and spat neatly into a burnished spittoon. "But what eats two hundred men and twice that many horses, mules, and oxen?"

"I can think of one or two creatures which could do the damage," Wencit said softly. "But none of them belong in the East Walls."

"My thought, too," Bostik said grimly. "I sent out a dawn patrol to look for survivors. See if they could figure out what happened."

"And their report explained naught?" Bahzell asked sharply.

"*What* report?" Bostik thumped his chair arm in frustration. "Should've been back this afternoon at latest, but neither man nor horse have I seen!"

"And what strength would the patrol have been, Milord?"

"After those stories?" Bostik snorted. "They went in strength. Three companies of the Axe and two troops of mounted infantry."

"And it's *naught* you've heard?" Champion of Tomanāk or no, Bahzell sounded shaken, and well he might. Bostik's "patrol" had been over five hundred men strong.

"Not a word," Bostik said harshly. "They had experienced officers, too. I'd've taken sword oath at least one messenger would reach me even if they'd run into the whole damned Spearman Army!"

"And I'd not've disagreed," Bahzell said. "But it seems as how we'd both've guessed wrong, Milord."

"True." Bostik frowned gloomily. "That's why I'm pleased to see you. Most things I can deal with—from brigands to a bloody invasion! But I know my limits. Anything can do this is beyond me. D'*you* have any ideas?"

"Most natural possibilities can be rejected at once," Wencit replied. "And that, I'm very much afraid, means you may owe your losses to our journey, Milord. We've been attacked several times, and not always by natural means."

"*Sorcery?*" Bostik half-rose as he spat out the word.

"Perhaps. For that matter, *probably*, truth be told." Wencit shrugged, his expression grim. "There are some—including, let's say, a certain noblewoman of Angthyr—" Bahzell snorted an angry endorsement "—who'd use any means to stop me. They've used the art recklessly from the start."

"Then that's their error," Bostik grated. "The Empire's roads're open to all, and it's flat my job to keep 'em so. I'll tell you this here and now—if someone's killed five hundred of the King Emperor's men, I'll not rest till his head's over East Gate. Whoever he—or *she*—is!"

"With my blessings," Wencit said. "But that still leaves us the question of how to solve your present problem before anyone else is killed."

"And d'you have an answer?"

"Yes. Or, at least, an idea how to begin."

"Well, spit it out! Don't sit chewing your beard at me!"

"Your pardon, Milord. I think my companions and I stand the best chance of learning the truth of this matter."

"*Alone?*" Bostik shot to his feet and planted his fists on his hips. "Fiendark's Furies, man! Think I'm daft? What d'you think the King Emperor'll do if you get killed over *my* problems? Tell you what he'll do—and rightly so! Be up to my arse in snow in some hole in Windfel or Vonderland before I broke wind twice! And I'd *stay* there, too!"

"If my enemies are responsible for it," Wencit said calmly, "then it's clearly my job to deal with it. For that matter, as you pointed out a few minutes ago, I *do* hold the King Emperor's warrant and authority to deal with problems exactly like this one. And I might point out that whatever it is has apparently already attacked two large forces successfully. Do you have another five hundred men you can afford to lose, Milord?"

"I'll lose five *thousand* rather than you," Bostik said flatly.

"I'm flattered, but it would gain nothing, whereas *risking* us may accomplish all you require. And I really hate to point this out, but when you have a white wizard and *two* champions of Tomanāk ready to hand, sending anyone else would probably strike the King Emperor as...questionable tactics."

"Hah!" Bostik snorted and draped himself back over his chair, narrowing his eyes. "Not fooling me, y'know," he said finally.

"Milord?"

"Oh, forget the innocent tone! Don't want me meddling in your affairs, is what it is. I suppose—" his high-pitched voice was edged with irony "—my patrol already did?"

"I'd probably have advised against sending them," Wencit murmured.

"Smooth an evasion as I've heard in months," Bostik grunted. He eyed the wizard smolderingly. "All right! Must've lost what little wit the winter left me, but I'll go along. I'll send no one else down pass till I hear from you—*or* for forty-eight hours. After that, I'll take out a full field force, and neither you nor whatever's out there will stop me. Clear?"

"In that case," Wencit pushed back his chair, rose, and bowed, "we'd best leave at dawn. Which means we'd better get a good night's sleep, first."

• CHAPTER EIGHTEEN •

Death in the Pass

Anxious faces lined the streets as Wencit and his companions rode past them into the dawn, for word of their trip had filtered through the city. South Keep was a fortress, its people accustomed to thoughts of war, but the mystery in the pass was something else, something far more frightening that brought those faces to watch them depart, and the crowd was eerily silent. The only sound was the east wind, cracking the banners like whips.

Kenhodan tried to divert his thoughts from whatever had bested five hundred troopers by studying the fortifications. East Gate's tunnel was twice as long as that to the west, cut into easily defended segments by additional portcullises. The tunnel was wider, too; it had to be, for it was the sole opening in the outermost eastern wall. The sharply angled towers and bastions defending the gate reared high, and the quarried gorge was both wider and deeper than that to the west. Wind howled in its depths, and

Kenhodan shivered as he looked once more on the grimmer face of the fortress.

They crossed the drawbridge, and Wencit gestured them close. Their mounts shouldered together as if to seek the comfort of the herd, coursers on the outside, and wind whipped their ponchos. Cliffs thrust up on either side, fissured and cracked, and the entire pass—much narrower on this side of the fortress—broke sharply downward to the east. It twisted and wove its way away from South Keep, its floor a torment of crevices crossed by the high road, and dove over a sudden, sheer drop—as if an axe had chopped away the side of a mountain across their path—three hundred yards ahead.

"Once we start down," Wencit said, mainly for Kenhodan's sake, the redhaired man realized, "the road is steep—very steep—for about a league. Then it starts to level and the pass becomes very narrow. The merchants were attacked near the foot of the escarpment—they'd stopped to rest their animals overnight before making the climb the next morning. I'm certain the patrol went beyond the point of the first attack even though there have been no reports. At any rate, we need to go at least that far."

"I noticed that you were . . . a bit vague last night," Kenhodan said. "If you have any clearer ideas that you could share with us now that we're alone, I'd really like to know what we're riding into."

"It might be several things," Wencit said slowly, "but it should be impossible for Wulfra to control anything capable of this. Under the circumstances, I'd rather not guess until we know more. Just expect something big and nasty. Anyway, no one in South Keep's seen anything, so I don't expect we will . . . until we're out of sight of the walls, at least. So why worry? You've got time to learn the worst."

"Oh, thank you *ever* so much." Kenhodan shook his head resignedly. "But you're pretty sure Wulfra's behind it?" he added after a moment.

"Who else? The only question's how she managed it, so from this moment I'm holding a glamour *no one* can break, even with a trap link. No point letting her steer anything—or anything *else*, at least—after us, Kenhodan."

"I can agree with that," Kenhodan approved whole-heartedly, and Wencit glanced at Bahzell.

"You and Walsharno are the champions of Tomanāk," he said, "and I suspect this is probably going to end up being at least as much a matter for the War God as it is for sorcery. Is there anything you'd like to add or suggest?"

"Naught until I've been seeing more. I've my own suspicions, but no mind to be speaking before I must. I'm thinking it might be best for me and Elrytha to be taking point, though."

Bahzell's face was grim, and unlike his companions, he wore no poncho. The green surcoat of his order fluttered in the stiff breeze, the golden embroidery of mace and sword glittered in the early light, he'd donned his burnished steel helm, and he'd added a long, heavy lance from South Keep's armories to his usual equipment. Now he glanced down at Walsharno's ears, as if silently seeking the courser's input, and the big roan snorted in what could almost have been amusement.

"And Walsharno's after suggesting that since there's not a one of us knows the least thing at all, at all, he's thinking as it's past time we were after going and taking a look."

"Then I suppose that covers all we can cover at this point," Wencit said philosophically, and Bahzell—and Walsharno—flipped their ears in agreement.

"Aye, it does that. Border Warden?"

Chernion nodded back to him, the wind whipping the feather of her beret and blowing her hair in a black cloud. Her cheeks stung with cold as she urged her mare into a slow trot, and Kenhodan and Wencit let her and Bahzell draw several lengths ahead before they followed.

Kenhodan whistled through his teeth when he reached the knife-edged slash across the pass. Some cataclysm had rent the earth, as if a mountain flank had shattered and sunk into the depths. Raw granite glittered, the road stabbed downward, winding back and forth in corkscrew terraces, and his stomach shifted as he stared down into a gulf almost a mile deep.

The defensive possibilities of the road's twisting descent hadn't been lost on South Keep's designers. As he gazed downward, he saw slots in the cliff faces above the uppermost two of the road's bends. He glanced at Wencit.

"Arrow slits," Wencit confirmed. "Some for banefire, too. The only access to the galleries is by tunnel from the main fortress."

"Is all this—" Kenhodan waved at the defenses "—really necessary?"

"Experience is a hard teacher," Wencit replied. "The Empire once thought a small field force could hold the pass against just about any conceivable threat, given the terrain. That was before Sorfan the First threw the better part of a hundred thousand men up the road in a surprise attack and took the top of the escarpment, though. The Royal and Imperial Army took it back, but the price was steep, and the King Emperor sent in two thousand dwarvish engineers, two hundred sarthnaisks, five hundred magi, and a quarter of a million laborers to make sure it never happened again."

The wizard gazed downward for another handful of seconds, then touched Byrchalka gently on the shoulder, and the courser started down the slope.

Kenhodan followed, his head turning constantly as he surveyed the grim, competent fortifications. Each tier of the winding descent was hacked into the cliff face, its rubble cascading down to form part of the next lower section of road, and the weapon slits above them grinned down as they trotted past, iron shod hooves ringing in the wind. The croaks of ravens carried mournfully in the cold air, and Kenhodan leaned back against the pull of gravity, trying to imagine the labor the road's construction had required.

The roadbed didn't plunge downward; it was the descent's length rather than its sharpness which dragged at minds and muscles. Here and there, the engineers had provided flat spaces where wearied teams or blown pack animals could rest, and each such stop was neatly covered by its own firing slits.

There was little need to stop on the way down, but Bahzell and Chernion drew up to await them at the last rest station. The hradani had dismounted, and Walsharno stood beside him while he propped a boot on the top of the low parapet along the rest area's outer edge and considered the floor of the pass, still some two hundred feet below.

"Whatever it might be we're looking for seems smart enough to be staying away from the keep, Wencit."

"Or else it was ordered to, Bahzell."

"Aye, there's that. But whatever its reason, we've no choice but to go find it. I'll not pretend I'm wild with enthusiasm."

"I don't blame you. Have you had any further thoughts?"

"Not further, so much as more of the same." The hradani turned to look at the wizard, his expression grim and his ears half flattened. "Whatever it is, it's after being big. Like you, I've a thought or three about that, and none of 'em are things as I'd care to be taking home. When we meet, Walsharno and I are thinking it'll likely be fast and sudden. D'you agree?"

"So far."

"Then I've no mind to spread out so far someone— like myself—is after getting too far ahead. The pass twists like a Carnadosan's mind, so I'm thinking it's best we be staying on the same sides of the turns as we go. And, Kenhodan, I'm thinking you'd best keep an arrow on the string."

"An arrow." Kenhodan looked at him with the expression of a man who doubted his own hearing. "It kills two hundred merchants, then polishes off that patrol, and you want me to keep an *arrow* ready?"

"That I do. The biggest creature in all the world's after being mortal. For that matter, I've a mite of experience with things as *aren't* mortal, in a manner of speaking, and this I've found—if it can be after hurting *you*, then you can be after hurting *it*. I've yet to meet anything as can't be killed, assuming as how someone's after hitting it in the right spot with the right weapon. And, truth be told, it's in my mind as how it might not be so very bad an idea to be hitting it from as far away as we can."

"All right." Kenhodan shrugged his shoulders and dismounted to bend his bow, then remounted. "Just remember this is a longbow; I can't use it mounted. If we meet something nasty, you'll have to hold it long enough for me to get down."

"I'll be doing that little thing," Bahzell replied with a grin. "And just you be remembering whose hide it is as'll be keeping it busy!"

"Oh, I will. I will!"

"Then let's get to it," Wencit said dryly.

They clattered down to the floor of the pass, and Kenhodan glanced back almost wistfully as the high road's steep angle of descent eased at last. South Keep looked back down at him from its high, towering perch, and he found himself wishing that whatever stalked the pass had tried its luck on the fortress. He had no doubt what would have happened to *any* attacker foolish enough to do that.

He put the thought aside and followed Wencit, and South Keep quickly disappeared behind them. The gorge was only eighty to a hundred twisting yards wide at this point, making it impossible to see more than a few hundred yards in any direction, and Chernion and Bahzell spread fifty yards apart in front of the wizard. That allowed Bahzell to sweep its right wall while Chernion swept its left, letting one of them to see past each bend as they came to it.

Wencit rode in the center of the pass, eyes slitted in concentration, and Kenhodan followed him, watching their back trail. He felt both empty and tense, and none too confident of stopping whatever could wreak such havoc with a mere longbow. Unless Wencit or Bahzell pointed out some vital spot, he suspected his arrows might just prove a tiny bit less effective than five hundred crack troops.

Chernion's mind was awash with surmise and careful thought of her own, and not all of it was focused solely on her surroundings. She had no idea what awaited them, but she'd deduced a few things. It was fast and powerful, or there would have been more survivors. Worse, it didn't discriminate between targets.

That thought stuck in her brain like a sliver of glass. She was as certain as Wencit that Wulfra was behind it, and the fact that the sorceress had chosen wholesale slaughter as a means of attack told the assassin a great deal. Attacking merchants served no purpose—was, in fact, counterproductive, because it had warned Wencit. Which meant Wulfra either couldn't—or wouldn't—control her agent. And that meant, in turn, that she'd purposely chosen a tool which would attack *anyone* . . . including the dog brothers.

She peered around a fresh bend and saw nothing. She rotated her head to relax her neck, staring upward, and saw an eagle far above. It floated proudly on the wind, disinterested in any business but its own, and she allowed herself a moment to envy it. Then she lowered her eyes and frowned.

She knew Umaro had passed them on the high road, because she'd watched him do it. That meant he and his men must have reached South Keep before her, yet he wasn't in the keep or he would have answered her covert signals. So he'd gone on down the pass and might have met whatever hunted here, and a slow rage burned at her core at the thought. If Umaro and Ashwan—especially Ashwan—had been attacked, there was no question of the price to be demanded of Wulfra.

The narrow, twisting gorge widened slowly but steadily, and she and Bahzell drifted farther apart to stay close to its walls. The dawn had turned into midmorning, but the towering cliffs to either side blanketed much of the narrow, stony gulf's floor in dense, dark shadow. It made the brightness where the sun could reach them almost dazzling, and she didn't care for how hard it was for sunstruck eyes to make out details in the patches of shadow before they actually entered them.

They rounded another bend, and Bahzell's hand rose, halting them. Chernion couldn't see around the bend, but the hradani's attitude made it plain he'd seen something, yet his lance stayed upright, its butt in the holding bracket at his stirrup iron. Clearly, whatever he'd spotted, he didn't consider it an immediate threat, but she loosened her sword anyway and looked about uneasily. She glanced back and up, as well, but even the eagle had vanished.

Kenhodan didn't stop immediately at Bahzell's signal. He pushed farther towards the right and dismounted, nocking an arrow and climbing a boulder to cover the hradani. Unlike Chernion, however, he *could* see around the bend from his new perch, and his face was bleak as Bahzell and Walsharno advanced cautiously on a shattered tangle of trade wagons strewn beside and along the road.

Walsharno moved carefully, ears shifting ceaselessly, and Bahzell sat easily in the saddle. His lance still stood upright in its rest, but his head turned constantly, and Walsharno lifted each hoof with delicate precision, in instant readiness for combat or flight. Yet nothing happened until, at last, they reached the outer ring of the tangled wagons and Bahzell swung down.

Kenhodan strained to watch in all directions at once, yet his gaze returned to Bahzell again and again. The big hradani drew on his gauntlets and picked his way into the wreckage. Even at this distance, Kenhodan sensed the anger in his slow, deliberate movements as he bent and picked something up to study it carefully. He straightened again, and stood in instant longer, looking upward, scanning the narrow slot of sky above the pass. Then he dropped whatever he'd picked up and mounted once more, and Walsharno cantered back towards the others. Kenhodan remained on his feet atop his boulder, bow ready, and the others clustered around his perch.

"Well, Bahzell?" Wencit asked quietly.

"No, it's not after being 'well' at all, at all," Bahzell said bleakly. He held out his right hand, and his thick leather gauntlet smoked in the cold air. Kenhodan sniffed and then coughed on the caustic fumes.

"So," Wencit said softly.

"Aye, it's after being a dragon," Bahzell said, still cold-voiced. "A *black* dragon, from the acid and the fact that it was stupid enough to chew a wooden wagon. And there's never a way in all the world a black dragon's after coming here of its own."

Chernion's head jerked as she stared upward. That eagle had been no eagle . . . and it had been much higher than she'd thought.

"It was Wulfra," Wencit said. "It had to be. But

how? Even assuming she had the courage to violate the treaty between dragonkind and Ottovar, she shouldn't have the *power* to do it. And that's the least of it."

"I'd think that was pretty much the *most* of it," Kenhodan said tartly, his eyes—like Chernion's—sweeping the sky visible above them.

"No," Wencit said impatiently. "For her to send the dragon here means she knew approximately when *we'd* get here. The caravan was attacked two days ago, but Bostik says they've been seeing a caravan a week in South Keep, which means the dragon got here at most seven or eight days ago. Which means Wulfra knew we'd have been here by then, but for the snow. And *that* means she's found a way to pierce my glamour."

"Is she too dangerous to attack, then?" Chernion asked softly.

"No," Wencit replied shortly, "but we're going to have to be more circumspect. To break my glamour without warning me, she must've used a trap link somewhere along the way—" only Chernion saw his eyes rest momentarily on her "—but I'm going to see to it that *nothing* can get through for the rest of this journey. If we avoid her attention, she can't do anything until she and I are face-to-face. Once that happens, Border Warden," he finished grimly, "I don't think she'll be sending any more dragons anywhere."

"I see." Chernion looked away, her mind like ice and no longer uncertain at all. Clearly the baroness must be seen to.

"Well and good," Bahzell rumbled, "but in the meantime, we've a wee bit of a problem here, Wencit. One that'll be running forty feet in length and not so very fond of us."

"True, but we don't have any choice to deal with it, either. Apparently, Wulfra's simply posted it here to attack anything that passes. We can't let that continue, and even if we could tempt it into attacking South Keep—which I doubt her control spells would allow—it might do terrible damage before it died. No, we have to hunt it down."

"I've no quarrel with the notion," Bahzell replied, touching the mace and sword of his surcoat. "Truth to tell, it's in my mind as how that's after being the least of our worries. Like as not, it'll be hunting *us* down."

"Then you should be happy, shouldn't you? Aren't you the fellow who once told me you can't kill something if you can't find it?"

"As to that, aye. That's not to be saying as I've always found it what you might be calling a *pleasant* experience, though."

"Well, if a wild wizard and two champions of Tomanāk can't deal with it, I'm a bit at a loss to think of who else we might send," Wencit pointed out a touch caustically, and a deep chuckle rumbled around in Bahzell's mighty chest.

"And how do we kill it if we do find it?" Kenhodan asked. "Mind you, I'm sure Elrytha and I would be happy to hold your coats while you three deal with it, but it would be nice if we had some small notion about your battle plan. I'm assuming you *have* a battle plan, of course, which I realize might be a little over optimistic on my part."

"A point," Chernion agreed. "Can you kill it with sorcery, Wizard?"

"Not in time. Dragons are virtually personifications of the wild magic, so just controlling them

is hard enough. *Slaying* them with the art requires
preparations I've had no time to make. The good
news—such as it is, and what there is of it—is that
wild magic or not, they're creatures of this world,
not something like a demon or a devil only Bahzell
and Walsharno could hope to stand up to. And they
are mortal. The trick is killing one of them *quickly*
enough. Even mortally wounded dragons have been
known to go on fighting far longer than almost anything else could have."

"Wait a minute. You mean *we* have to kill it?"
Kenhodan waved at the wrecked wagons. "We have
to kill something that can do *that?*"

"Aye, that we must," Bahzell said, "and best be glad
it's black, for black dragons are after being stupid."

"And that helps us exactly how?"

"Bahzell's right," Wencit said. "Black dragons are
little more than appetites with legs and wings, so this
fellow's likely to be a lot less tricky than his smarter
cousins. Of course, even that has its downside, I suppose. The fact that it's stupid—and that it's obviously
being held here by a spell of compulsion—means it's
unlikely to just run away from a fight even if it's losing."

"Wonderful." Kenhodan rolled his eyes. "Does it
at least have a vulnerable point?"

"Well, as to that, not so very many." Bahzell smiled
grimly. "I'm thinking Walsharno and I might be after
getting a lance point into its chest, but that's no
certain thing, given dragon scale. There's no scale as
guards its eyes or its gullet, though. Mind, I've no
ambition to be going for its palate—like enough I'd
only see it as I slid past!—but a black dragon's not
after being smart enough to guard its eyes. If the two

of us are after drawing its attention, I'm thinking it's likely enough to be turning its face toward your bow."

"You want me to put an arrow in its *eye?* Just how big is the bloody thing?"

"As to that, it'll be as much as nine or ten inches across!" Bahzell said bracingly. "It's confident I am you can hit a target that big if you must."

"Are you listening to yourself here, Bahzell?" Kenhodan demanded. "You're going to 'draw its attention' while I shoot…What if I *miss?*"

"Then I'm thinking you'd best have another arrow handy," Bahzell said simply.

◆   ◆   ◆

<I'm impressed by your tactical forethought,> Walsharno said dryly as Bahzell climbed back into the saddle and the two of them circled around the wreckage to head back down the pass once more. *<Thought that up all on your own, did you?>*

"If it's a better notion you have, best be speaking up now," Bahzell replied.

<Oh, no! Far be it from me *to improve on sheer genius when I hear it!>*

"Sure, and you're after being in a fine mood this morning."

<Actually,> Walsharno said more soberly, *<I can't claim that I have any better plan under the circumstances. You* are *putting a lot of pressure on Kenhodan, though. "Might be after getting a lance point into its chest," indeed. Unless this is a really young dragon, you know how much of a chance there is of that!>*

"There's no point at all, at all, in nattering the lad with details as he can't do anything about, anyway. Come to that, though, I'm thinking we've never met anyone less likely to be letting us down in a case like this. Mind, it's better I'd feel with a few score more Vonderland archers at his back, but we've too many other things on our plate to be worrying over might-have-beens."'

<Well, that's certainly true enough! I do find myself wishing we'd brought along my barding, though. I'm much too handsome a fellow to go around with bare patches just because some stupid black dragon spat on me!>

"And you're after being so modest about it, too," Bahzell marveled, and Walsharno snorted a laugh.

<You're right about one thing, Bahzell,> a far deeper voice rumbled like an earthquake through their minds. <You haven't ever met anyone less likely to let you down than Kenhodan. I can't promise things will work out for the best in this case, but I will promise you that if they don't it won't be because he failed you.>

<Can you tell us if there's more than just the dragon waiting for us?> Walsharno asked.

<At the moment, that's all you face, although I imagine it's enough to be going on with,> Tomanāk Orfro said dryly.

"And a great relief to my mind it is, too," Bahzell said politely, and a deep laugh echoed through them both.

<I'm sure it is,> Tomanāk told him. <And now I'll stop distracting the two of you. Call upon me when the time comes.>

The deep voice faded into silence, and the two champions moved steadily into the morning with every sense alert.

✦   ✦   ✦

They moved more slowly now, for Kenhodan went on foot with Glamhandro at his shoulder. He wished the stallion had been willing to stay back with Wencit, but the horse refused to be separated from him and minced along beside him. He clearly sensed danger, and—equally clearly—he would have preferred to have Kenhodan on his back, where he belonged. Kenhodan would have preferred that, too, but he had to be in a position to use his bow. So he concentrated on breathing evenly and wishing his palms were less damp.

Chernion rode grimly down her side of the pass, her expression set as she contemplated the unhappy reality that her only possible role was as bait. If the Bloody Hand couldn't kill the monster, *she* certainly couldn't. And though she was a competent archer, she couldn't hope for a killing shot under the circumstances. No, all she could do was help attract the dragon's attention, and every assassin's bone in her body revolted at the thought. She found herself hoping Wencit, at least, survived... and that whatever he had planned for Wulfra was both slow and lingering.

She stopped suddenly, and Walsharno drew up on the far side of the pass as she dismounted at the side of the road and gazed down at the bits and pieces which had once been men and horses scattered in a deep hollow beside the roadbed. The hollow would have been very difficult to see from the road before the dragon went rampaging through it and shredded the scraggly brush which once had screened it, and it lay in deep shadow, even now. Its sides were heavy with frost the sun's heat had yet to melt and the lighting was poor, yet she could see the details all too clearly.

She drew a deep breath and slithered down into the

hollow, her boots crunching in a red crust of frozen blood. She was no stranger to ugly death, but this sickened her as she stood amidst the carnage, gazing down upon it. Then she turned a body with her toe, and her face tightened—in anger, not surprise—as Umaro's dead eyes glared up at her.

She drew another breath and straightened slowly. That tall, narrow body with the sword in its hand might be Ashwan, she thought through the layer of ice which had encased her brain, but it was so seared by acid she couldn't be sure. She moved closer, looking down, trying to positively identify the body, and her anger was a cold and burning fury when she couldn't.

A sister should recognize her mother's only son.

She looked away and tried to at least count the bodies, but they were in too many pieces. She couldn't match arms and legs with torsos, and their gear had been thrashed and scattered by the dragon. She looked down one more time at the body she thought was Ashwan's, then turned away dry eyed.

She climbed back up to the roadbed and found Bahzell and Walsharno waiting for her.

"No survivors down there, Bloody Hand," she said in a low voice. "Whoever they were, they never had a chance."

"Aye," Bahzell said grimly, "and if we've no better luck than they, there's more than us'll pay for it. Come, Border Warden."

The courser turned, moving off once more, and Chernion remounted. Her dark eyes were colder and more pitiless than any ice as she rode away from that place of death, and she never looked back.

◆   ◆   ◆

Cold wind fingered Kenhodan's hair as Bahzell bent over the acid-burned bodies of a dozen Brothers of the Axe. The hradani straightened grimly, something black in his hand, and sunlight flashed as he extended it.

"Dragon scale," he said flatly.

Kenhodan took it, marveling at its lightness. One side was glossy, shining in the sun, but the other was dull and slick. It was larger than his hand and a quarter-inch thick, yet curiously light.

"They scored a few hits," he said quietly.

"And you see what it was after bringing them. A few bits of scale and—see here where the axe scored it?" Bahzell touched a thin scar across the burnished side. "That was after being a powerful blow, and precious little damage it did. A dragon's three or four thicknesses of these, overlapped like mail, and from the thickness of it, this one's after being older than most. There's never an axeman born as'll get steel through such as that."

"Then I'll have to hit the mark," Kenhodan murmured, dropping the scale. He shivered in the cold and looked around the pass, narrow and gloomy at this point.

"Why didn't they report back before they got this far?" he wondered.

"I'm thinking as they did. From the looks of things, these lads were come on from behind, not the front. If it happens Wulfra's pet's after ranging the pass, I'm thinking as he came up with their messengers first and then trailed them down pass. It's likely enough we'd've been after missing what little a hungry dragon's like to leave."

"I suppose so," Kenhodan agreed. "But there's barely a platoon here. Where's the rest of the patrol?"

"Down below," Bahzell said grimly. "Like as not we'll be finding them stretched out like these lads, unless they were after having Norfram's own luck."

"Then let's go find them," Kenhodan said, gazing at the bodies. His nervousness had vanished, replaced by an anger that pulsed with the battle rage he'd assimilated in the Forest of Hev, and he welcomed it.

"Aye, let's do that little thing," Bahzell murmured, and mounted once more.

◆　　◆　　◆

They made another half-mile and passed a score more bodies before the ebon fury struck. Bahzell and Walsharno had little warning; they turned a bend, and the black thunderbolt whistled into their teeth.

Kenhodan was forty yards back, yet he heard the whine of air over leather wings as the monster hurtled at his friends. Forty feet, Bahzell had estimated, but he'd been wrong. This scaled horror was at least *sixty* feet long, with outstretched forefeet as long as Walsharno and claws thicker than Kenhodan's thigh.

Plated in black iron, the stench of acid venom rippling before it like some pestilence, it hurled itself at the hradani, so close—so quick—there was no time for Bahzell to use his lance. One of those fearsome forefeet smashed at the two champions, brushing the lance aside, shattering it three feet from the hradani's grip, and its head lashed at them.

But the dragon had never met a Sothōii courser. Walsharno neither panicked nor bolted nor froze like every horse it had encountered in its long and hungry life. Instead, the courser swerved, dodging like a dancer, and Bahzell dropped the shattered lance and raised his right hand.

"*Come!*" he bellowed, and his greatsword materialized in his hand, wrapped in a sudden flare of azure brilliance. Walsharno wheeled on his haunches, spinning back towards the dragon, and the pass shuddered as fifty tons of hungry fury slammed down. Dust spurted from the scaly feet, and its claws furrowed the stone.

"*Tomanāk!*" Bahzell's bull voice cut through the hiss of the dragon and the slither of falling stones. Walsharno sprang off his hocks, and the hradani rose in the stirrups to swing two-handed. His muscles corded, razored steel slammed the side of the huge neck like a cleaver, flying bits of shattered scale glinted in the sunlight, and the sound was like a hammer on an anvil.

The dragon scarcely blinked. Its left forefoot flashed with blinding speed, slashing at the midges beside it. Walsharno dodged, barely in time, and Bahzell's sword struck the same spot with the sound of an axe in wood.

Despite his taut readiness, the sudden attack took Kenhodan by surprise. He raised his bow, but the dragon had already turned away, and its venom flashed in a black tide as it sought to destroy Bahzell and the courser.

Walsharno screamed as a droplet seared his quarters, but he never flinched. Instead, he reared, and two steel-shod forehooves, edged with the same blue nimbus as Bahzell's sword, crashed against the dragon's forehead like the mace of the Tomanāk itself.

The dragon shrieked, even its bulk staggered by that titanic blow, and Bahzell thrust for an eye. But the dragon was already pulling back, and the sword point slammed just below the great orb. More bits of scale flashed in the sunlight, shattered as the Axe Brothers' blows had been unable to accomplish, but the eye was undamaged.

Kenhodan bit off a curse. Bahzell and Walsharno had been forced to the left, turning the dragon away from him. He caught a fleeting glimpse of one glaring eye and his arrow flashed away, but it hit the bony eye ridge and skipped, humming as it bounced. Bahzell dared not break back up the pass, yet Kenhodan couldn't move far enough to his own left to get a shot. He could only snatch another arrow from his quiver and pray for an opening.

Chernion gave it to him. Her mare was no courser, but she was war trained and willing. The assassin clapped in her heels, and the mare lunged forward, ears back, while the assassin rose in the stirrups. Unlike Bahzell, she made no attempt to swing. She rode at the thrust, body stretched forward over her horse's neck, and the tip of her blade arrowed straight for the dragon's eye.

For a breathless moment, it seemed she would strike home, but the dragon saw her at the last moment. It jerked away, and her sword slammed into the inner surface of its ear, instead. The scales were thinner there, and black blood flashed, but a huge wing was already swinging. It crashed into the mare, spilling her to her knees, and Chernion flew from the saddle. She hit in a roll, coming to her feet in a supple movement to face the dragon, her blade still in her hand and no hope in her heart.

The dragon turned. Here was a less elusive morsel, and it meant to have it. The head drew back, the long neck curved, and Kenhodan fired again.

The arrow slammed into the monster's left eye, and the orb burst in a hideous shower of fluid. But the barbed head struck the top of the socket and thick bone deflected it. The dragon reared, half-blinded and screaming in anguish. One huge foot snapped the protruding shaft, and pain fanned its fury.

Kenhodan reached for a third shaft. He would have cursed that last shot, but his mind was too cold, too calculating and exhilarated for such emotions. He nocked the arrow and stood waiting, praying for another chance.

Dragon feet thundered on stone, and it bulked over Chernion, hissing. Its jaws opened, forked tongue flickering as it cocked its head to fix the assassin with its remaining eye. But Chernion circled desperately to her right, staying on its blind side. It gave her a precarious chance of escape, but each foot she moved turned the dragon farther from Kenhodan's bow.

Bahzell and Walsharno recognized both her peril and Kenhodan's need and the courser swerved back in front of the beast. Bahzell's sword hammered its shoulder, battering the scales with a blow savage enough for the creature to feel even through its armor, and it turned once more, cat-quick despite its size, slashing at the hradani.

Walsharno reared and struck again, but this time the dragon was turning into the blow. The stallion weighed well over a ton and a half, but weight was meaningless against the muscles of that massive neck. The swinging head slammed up under the plunging hooves and threw the courser end for end like a child's pony, spilling Bahzell from his back. The hradani rolled back upward, almost as quickly as Chernion despite his size and armor, and the hissing head poised above them, mouth opened to strike.

But the turn exposed the ruined left eye once

more, and Kenhodan's bow sang. The arrow flashed
into the oozing socket and the dragon shrieked as
blood splashed. It reared, badly wounded this time,
but once more the arrow had missed the tiny brain
in its massive skull. The mighty wings flailed, blowing
Chernion from her feet, smashing Bahzell back to his
knees, and Kenhodan reached for a fourth arrow as the
remaining eye finally fixed upon the source of its pain.

The monster forgot the others, gathered itself, and
leapt at him.

The redhaired man watched black death flash at
him, and his bow tracked. He needed a perfect shot,
and the angle of approach denied it. He stood perfectly still. If the gods were good, they might give
him a single chance.

The huge beast hurtled towards him, head cocked,
the angle to its brain closed. Kenhodan's hand twitched,
almost loosing, but something inside him—something
cold and deadly—withheld him. He would find the
shot he needed, or he would not loose at all.

Something flared beside him, and he had a vague
impression of Wencit standing in Byrchalka's stirrups,
his right hand cocked at his shoulder. Glaring fury
glittered and burned on the wizard's palm, and then
his arm came forward, and a ball of flame arced to
smash the dragon's cheek.

The monster squalled as the witchfire hit and scales
hissed, blazing like pitch. The shock and pain staggered
it, and its head lurched down. For a moment—one
fleeting instant—the ruined eye was exposed.

In that flicker in the heart of eternity, Kenhodan
fired.

The arrow streaked to its target, slamming through

bone and membrane. Barbed steel crashed deep, the dragon's scream deafened them as the arrow split its brain, and Kenhodan knew his shot had been true. But the dragon didn't know it was dead; it thrashed onward with the deadly vitality of reptile kind, and the gaping stalactites of its ivory fangs were the last thing he saw.

CHAPTER NINETEEN

A Father's Fears

Kenhodan woke to pain. He forced his eyes open, biting back a moan as fire burned his left side, and Wencit looked down at him.

"Rest easy. You're not hurt as badly as it feels, but it's bad enough, and I'm sure it feels even worse!"

"W-What happened?" Even as he heard his own voice ask it, a back corner of Kenhodan's mind decided that was the stupidest question he'd ever heard. Or remembered hearing, anyway.

"Dragons don't die easily," Wencit replied almost absently, ripping at Kenhodan's tunic, and the redhaired man yelped as fresh anguish lashed at him.

"Easy!" he gasped. "That's the only skin I have!"

"And you won't have as much of it unless we do something about the acid," Wencit told him tartly. "Bahzell's just a bit busy at the moment, so do me a favor and behave yourself—" Kenhodan yelped again as more fabric tore in a fresh spasm of pain "—while I at least get it off of you."

"It's not *my* fault your touch isn't exactly gentle," Kenhodan panted through his teeth. He raised his head and looked down the length of his body.

The stony floor of the pass was cold under his spine, and he didn't like the oozing, blistered spots running down his left side from just below the shoulder almost to his hip. None of them were very big—the largest was no wider than a copper kormak coin—but they radiated pain out of all proportion to their size. He'd clearly caught only the very fringe of the dragon's acid spray, but what had hit him was more than bad enough, in his admittedly somewhat biased opinion.

"That's going to upset Gwynna," he said, raising his left hand and not quite touching the burns. They were raw and livid against the pale pattern of his long-ago scars. "She won't like that. Probably think I was careless."

Wencit straightened and looked down at him with a startled expression, and Kenhodan blinked. What an *odd* thing for him to have said, he thought. But it didn't *seem* odd...or did it? He tried to think about that, but it was hard. His mind seemed to be...floating, and the blue sky that framed the wizard's head as Wencit bent over him had a strange, flickering texture. For that matter, it was growing dimmer down here in the depths of the pass. But, no, that wasn't quite right, either. It wasn't growing *dimmer*, it was just that everything was moving away from him, receding into the distance and spinning around him somehow even though he knew it wasn't actually moving. Of course it wasn't. *He* was the one who was moving as the stone under him whirled and curtsied in a strange, steadily accelerating pinwheel dance.

He opened his mouth, tried to ask Wencit what was

happening, but nothing came out. The wizard bent closer, his lips moving as if he were saying something, but the sounds were meaningless. Kenhodan couldn't make them out, and then the whirling world crashed in upon him in a maelstrom of exploding light.

◆   ◆   ◆

Chernion pushed herself shakily to her feet and looked around for her sword. It lay several feet from her, and every muscle ached as she hobbled over to pick it up. The mighty wind from the dragon's wings hadn't simply knocked her over; it had blown her at least ten feet, and she wondered if she'd cracked a rib when she bounced off of the boulder which had intercepted her fall.

She straightened her spine and surveyed the pass.

The dragon lay in a huge, broken sprawl, one wing outstretched across a third of the narrow gorge and the other crumpled under it. Her mare stood a hundred yards up the pass, right forehoof raised and held carefully off the ground. She was surprised the horse hadn't bolted further, even on only three legs, but then she realized Byrchalka had one hoof planted on the horse's reins.

She quirked a smile at the sight, then shook herself. Wencit was on one knee beside Kenhodan, but where was Bahzell?

She turned, searching for the hradani, but it took her several seconds to realize he must be on the far side of the mountain range of dead dragon. That had to be the only reason she couldn't see him, but surely he was tall enough at least his head should have been visible from here, now that she was back on her feet. Only...

She grimaced at the thought and started around the dragon, stepping carefully across its tree trunk-thick tail with her sword still in her hand, then stopped as she realized she'd found Bahzell . . . and why she hadn't seen him before.

Walsharno was down, and one look at the big roan told Chernion he would never rise again. His right foreleg was obviously shattered, blood soaked his side where broken ribs punched through hide and hair, and bubbles of blood frothed from his nostrils with every breath. Not even a courser could survive *that* damage, a corner of her mind told her.

But Bahzell knelt beside the huge stallion with his greatsword in his right hand. His eyes were closed, his forehead was pressed against the sword's quillons, his left hand was on Walsharno's heaving side, and as she watched a faint blue glow enveloped him.

She blinked, not sure she was actually seeing it, but the glow grew stronger, brighter, and she realized what it was. She'd never seen it done, but she knew what Bahzell was doing, knew that at this moment every ounce of concentration, every particle of awareness, was concentrated and focused as he reached out to Tomanāk for the power to repair even those ghastly wounds.

But that would take time, her brain told her. Not even a champion could simply snap his fingers and make injuries like those disappear. And while he was focused, while every scrap of awareness was narrowed into the intensity of his purpose, he was vulnerable. Defenseless. Unaware of any danger and unable to respond even if he'd been aware . . . and she stood behind him with a naked blade in her hand.

She glanced back at the others. The wizard's hands

moved quickly, ripping smoldering cloth from Kenhodan. Clearly the redhaired man was out of action for the moment, and Wencit's shoulders sagged wearily even as he tore the acid-splashed clothing from Kenhodan. Instinct told her that whatever wizardry he'd used against the dragon had weakened him, at least temporarily. He wasn't as distracted as Bahzell, but his focus was entirely on Kenhodan at the moment, and as she realized that, she recognized the opportunity.

She knew her own capabilities, and her mind played out the entire sequence of events. A quick sword thrust to the nape of Bahzell's exposed neck as he bent over Walsharno. A swift turn to her left while the hradani collapsed silently, the viper-quick flash of a throwing knife, and the unwary wizard would sprout steel between his shoulder blades and collapse over Kenhodan. Then three quick strides while Byrchalka was still realizing what had happened and she'd be close enough to hamstring the other courser, bring him down before he could react.

She could kill them all before any of them reacted. Oh, it was possible Byrchalka might react quickly enough to save himself—even kill *her*, instead. But this was what she did, her profession, and she knew in her bones that she could have them all. That Bahzell had saved her life, that Kenhodan had slain the dragon, meant no more to her calculations than her own attack upon it. They'd had no more choice than she had, and chivalry carried no weight in the cool merchandiser of death's scales.

None of those things mattered...but they didn't need to. Wulfra owed a debt not even her own death could ever pay in full, and Chernion's companions were her best chance to collect. So, really, there wasn't even a decision to make.

She sheathed her sword and moved to Bahzell's side, sinking to one knee beside him, and laid her own comforting hand on Walsharno's neck.

◆   ◆   ◆

Kenhodan drifted slowly up from the reefs of sleep and found himself in a soft bed under crisp sheets by an open window. Cool breeze bathed his face, and the sun filled the white-walled room with clear light. He opened his eyes to see Wencit standing beside the bed with Elrytha beside him and Bahzell in an armchair on the other side.

"Welcome back, slug-a-bed," the hradani rumbled.

"From where?"

Kenhodan's voice sounded rusty to his own ear, and he grimaced. It was odd, he thought. He felt as if he'd been hammered flat, wrung out in a ball, and then flattened to dry in the sun. Yet at the same time, he felt curiously tranquil—not so much rested as simply . . . restored.

"You suffered a reaction," Wencit replied, stepping back from the bed and settling into an armchair that matched Bahzell's. "Some people do; some don't, and the only way to find out whether or not someone does, unfortunately, is from experience, so no one's very anxious to find out if they do."

"Reaction?"

"Shock," Wencit said. "Dragon acid's venomous as well as corrosive. Some people have minor reactions to it while others die from it very quickly indeed. You happen to be one of those who react strongly. So am I, if you're interested."

"Actually, while I'm sure that's fascinating, I'm not, thank you." Kenhodan smiled briefly. "Interested, I mean."

"I'm thinking as you should be." Bahzell's deep, unwontedly serious tone pulled Kenhodan's attention back to the other side of the bed, and the hradani shook his head, ears slightly flattened. "If Wencit here hadn't been after recognizing the signs, and doing it quick, we'd not've gotten you back to South Keep alive, lad, and that's the gods' own truth."

Kenhodan's eyebrows rose, and Bahzell nodded firmly.

"It's distracted I was, and that no mistake, when Walsharno went down," he said. "I'd seen you fall as well, lad, but I'd no notion as how you'd been hit hard, and there was Walsharno with two broken legs and half his ribs crushed." Kenhodan's face tightened at the catalog of injuries, but Bahzell raised one hand in a quick, soothing gesture. "It's fine he is now," he said quickly, "and already more recovered than you. But you might be saying as I was a wee bit...focused on healing *his* hurts while Wencit was looking after you. Only then you took it into your head to be sliding down into shock, and if he'd not recognized it double quick and called me over to heal you, you'd not have lasted another five minutes, and that's a fact."

Kenhodan blinked. The thought that he'd come that close to death was strangely intellectual, not quite real, as if it had happened to someone else. Yet even as he thought that, a chaotic memory of a spiraling confusion of light and dizziness flickered through his mind, and with it came the sudden, chill realization that he truly had.

"In that case, I'm deeply grateful—to you both." Kenhodan extended his hand to clasp forearms with the hradani, then looked back at Wencit. "And while we're on the subject, I'm grateful for that fireball, too. If you hadn't—"

"Enough!" Wencit frowned ferociously. "All anyone's done since we got back is thank everyone else in sight for saving everyone else! You're the one who killed the thing in the end, and that's what matters."

"Aye," Bahzell agreed firmly, and Chernion nodded as well.

"Well, then." Kenhodan waved one hand in a half-awkward brushing away gesture and looked for another topic.

"So how did we get back here and why don't I remember any of the trip?"

"Well, for starters, Bahzell was right about the dragon's attacking Bostik's patrol from behind," Wencit told him. "It lost heavily, but Colonel Grantos still had almost three hundred men who'd taken shelter in caves just beyond the point where *we* met the thing. They heard all the racket and Grantos led a troop of his mounted infantry out to offer what assistance he could. He got there about the time I noticed your face was turning blue and that you weren't breathing very well."

Kenhodan grimaced at the last sentence, but the wizard smiled crookedly at his expression and went on.

"Bahzell had Walsharno stabilized by that point and turned to you as soon as he'd recovered enough from the healing trance to pay much attention to the world around them. Truth to tell, I think he had a harder fight getting you back than he did with Walsharno."

"Aye." Bahzell's voice was solemn, but there was the slightest of twinkles and his brown eyes. "Dreadful stubborn you were, and lazy, too. No interest at all, at all, in waking up and being about your responsibilities."

"Actually," Wencit shot the hradani a stern glance, "not even a champion of Tomanāk can make damage like that simply disappear at the snap of his fingers, Kenhodan. He did a remarkable job of pulling the poison back out of your system, but after that you slept like a rock for the better part of a full day. We're just glad you were still around to wake up in the end."

"So am I," Kenhodan said. "But what about our other damages? You said Walsharno had two broken legs. Is he really—?"

"Fine, Kenhodan. He's fine," Wencit interrupted. "Bahzell's had unfortunately extensive experience in healing combat injuries. Of course, until Walsharno'd had a chance to recover his own strength, there wasn't anyone to heal *Bahzell*."

"You're were hurt, too?" Kenhodan looked quickly back at the hradani, who shrugged.

"Naught but four or five ribs and a dislocated shoulder." The hradani waved one hand dismissively.

"A mere nothing for any champion of Tomanāk, of course," Wencit said dryly. "As for me, I had nothing more than a bit of fatigue to deal with, although I believe the Border Warden lost a little skin."

"In a place no lady will discuss," Chernion confirmed demurely.

"I see." Kenhodan's lips twitched and he looked back at Bahzell. "So Walsharno was able to heal you, as well?"

"Well, as to that, no, not precisely." Bahzell shook

his head. "It's no shape he was in for healing at all, at all. Mind you, he and himself would've seen to it quick enough once he was after having his feet under him again, so to speak, but they'd no need. South Keep's an imperial fortress, lad, and Bostik's after having first-class healers on his staff."

"But I—"

A quiet knock cut Kenhodan off in midsentence. A moment later, the door opened and a slender, dark-haired woman stepped through. She wore a blue robe marked with a white patch bearing a golden sheaf of grain and a scepter, and her gray eyes were very calm. They swept the room, resting for a moment on Bahzell, then came to rest on Kenhodan.

"I see your patient is back with us." Her voice was clear and soft.

"Indeed," Wencit said. "Kenhodan, this is a Mistress Sharis—the very talented healer who glued Bahzell back together and then helped us keep an eye on you."

"Oh?" Kenhodan looked at the newcomer and smiled. "Thank you for putting him back together," he said. "He's big, noisy, and thinks he has a sense of humor, but he's also a friend, Madam Healer."

"*Mistress* Sharis," Wencit corrected gently, stressing the title very slightly. "Sharis is a master of the Axe Hallow Academy as well as a priestess of Kontifrio."

"Your pardon, Mistress Sharis." Kenhodan flushed in embarrassment.

"None needed, Kenhodan." Her gray eyes were frankly curious yet strangely unintrusive. "You're an interesting case, but Bahzell did all the heavy work before they brought you back to South Keep. I only had to clean up a little around the edges and damp the last of the venom's effects. I want to monitor you again before I release you from my care—that's why I'm here—but you'd've been fine in another day or so without me."

"Aye, it's a fine healer she is, lad. Why, she'd my ribs and shoulder straightened out quick as quick. It's scarcely a twinge they're after giving me, and that only on cold mornings!"

Bahzell rumbled a chuckle as he pushed himself up out of his chair and he, Chernion, and Wencit started for the door, but Sharis laid a delicate, fine-boned hand on his forearm.

"Sit back down, Bahzell," she said softly.

"I'm hardly thinking as that's needful, Mistress Sharis," he said. "I was only after teasing the lad about my ribs."

"If Mistress Sharis says sit, sit!" Wencit said tartly. "And don't worry about her telling Leeana about your carelessness. Magi are discreet."

"Indeed we are," Sharis said calmly, her eyes flickering briefly to Chernion. "So take your ancient carcass out and let me see to my patients."

"At once! Come, Border Warden. I'd say it's pretty clear we're not needed around here at the moment."

"I agree."

Chernion followed him out, resisting an impulse to eye Sharis searchingly, for she'd never felt easy around magi. Yet even if Sharis recognized what she was, there was nothing Chernion could do about it, and so she closed the door behind her with a silent curse for all wizards and magi alike.

"Now," Sharis murmured as the door latch clicked, and closed her eyes and extended one hand, palm down over Kenhodan's forehead. He looked up at it in puzzlement for a moment, then twitched in astonishment as her hand began to glow ever so faintly with a silvery radiance and she moved it slowly down the length of his body.

Her eyes opened once more and her hand paused. She looked down at him, and he flushed, embarrassed at having revealed his surprise, but she only smiled.

"You haven't seen a mage healer in action before?" she asked gently.

"No," he said, then gritted his teeth. "Or not that I remember, at any rate," he added, looking away.

"Kenhodan, I haven't helped Bahzell and Wencit tend you for the last twenty-four hours without recognizing what was done to your memory. It isn't your doing, and my advice as a healer is to be patient with yourself. Recovery from things like that takes time. Your memory may never come back—or at least, not fully—but that doesn't diminish you or make you any less than who you are. My advice as your healer is to remember that and give yourself time to adjust to it."

"I'll try to," he told her. "Assuming whoever took it does the same, at any rate."

"That I'm afraid I can't help you with." Mistress Sharis smiled briefly. "Now let me finish that monitoring."

She closed her eyes with an expression of concentration, and her hand began to glow once more. It traced the length of his body slowly, never quite touching him, and the glow grew momentarily brighter as it passed over the areas where he'd been splashed by the dragon's venom. He felt . . . something, although he could put no name to what that "something" might be. It was like a cross between a caress and a strange, profound vibration deep inside muscle, sinew, and bone. It wasn't unpleasant, and it certainly didn't *hurt*, yet it was ... unsettling, perhaps. A sensation for which he had no reference and no explanation.

Whatever it was, it took no more than a minute or two for Sharis to complete her examination, and then she opened her eyes once more and gave him a deeper smile.

"Very good, Kenhodan!" she said. "A champion's healing ability's very different from that of a mage, and we don't do things the same way. I hope Bahzell won't take this wrongly, but his healing technique is more of a brute force approach. It puts things back to rights rather more ... forcefully, and sometimes it takes a while for everything to settle back into position neatly. That's what I've been monitoring you for, and it looks like things are coming along nicely. I realize you're still feeling weak and tired, but that's only a lingering reaction to the venom's toxicity. I promise it'll pass quickly now that your system's had time to purge itself. It's my opinion you can be out of bed by tomorrow and probably back on the road to wherever it is you're going by the day after that."

"That's good news," Kenhodan said. "I know you're probably tired of hearing it, but—again—thank you."

"An honest healer will admit she never gets tired of hearing that. It means she's doing her job properly," Sharis told him with a chuckle, but her eyes had slid sideways, to Bahzell. There was something ... thoughtful in their gray depths, and the hradani's ears twitched gently as he noticed the direction of her glance.

"Mistress Sharis?" he asked courteously.

"I asked you to remain because there's a message for you, Bahzell."

Kenhodan's eyes narrowed as the hradani thrust himself abruptly up out of the chair. Bahzell's face paled, his ears flattened, and his cheeks tightened in unmistakable fear. Kenhodan had no idea what could affect him so, but his own nerves tightened in reaction.

"Don't worry, Bahzell!" Sharis said quickly. "Gwynna is *fine*."

"Gwynna!" Bahzell drew a deep breath and closed his eyes. For an instant he stood like a column of hammered iron, and then his eyes opened slowly and he forced himself to relax.

"So it's come," he whispered.

"Yes," Sharis said compassionately. "The word came this morning. You know the fortress is barriered, so they had to send a wind-walker from Belhadan, and I'm afraid he touched down in the middle of nowhere. Wind walking," she added dryly, "isn't always the most precise of talents. In this case, it seems the wind walker was just a *bit* overconfident when he got his orders. He thought he knew where he was going, but he confused two locations in the East Walls when he visualized his destination. Fortunately, the snow wasn't too deep." She rolled her eyes. "It only took him five days to walk out and reach South Keep."

"But how did they know to be sending word here? By our reckoning, we should have been through South Keep long ago."

"I don't know, but at least the news reached you. She survived crisis—not without difficulty, I understand—and Master Lentos says she shows great promise. Very great."

"Thank the gods."

Bahzell fell back into the chair as if suddenly exhausted and buried his face in his hands. His huge shoulders shook, and Kenhodan suddenly realized his friend was weeping—weeping in great, silent, heaving shudders. He looked blankly at Sharis, but she only shook her head to silence any questions and put her hand on the hradani's shoulder.

Bahzell's weeping stopped finally and his hand rose to envelop the small, slim one on his shoulder. He squeezed it gently and shook himself like a man waking from a dream, and his face relaxed.

"My thanks," he said softly. "I'm after owing you much for that word."

"I only wish it had reached you earlier," Sharis said compassionately.

"How . . . how long ago?"

"Almost two and a months now. I understand—" the healer's lips quirked pettishly "—that she's giving the Belhadan Academy fits."

"Aye, she would that." Bahzell grinned with something like his usual humor, but then an edge of anxiety crept back into his voice. "And her mother?"

"Fine, Bahzell. Master Lentos saw her before he sent word, and she asked that he send her love—and Gayrfressa's—as well and tell you not to worry."

"Well, then!" Bahzell said much more briskly, even his ears relaxing. "If Leeana says as all's well, then all's well."

He smiled and leaned back, his eyes going slowly distant as he sank into his thoughts, and Sharis smiled at him again. Then she nodded courteously to Kenhodan and glided noiselessly from the room while the redhaired man lay back on his pillows, brain whirling, and tried to digest what had happened.

✦ ✦ ✦

Evening filled Kenhodan's room with shadow, and still Bahzell sat with him. The hradani seemed unwilling to plunge back into life, and Kenhodan was content to leave him to his silence. Indeed, he felt honored that Bahzell chose to remain with him while he absorbed the news from home. But finally, as the clock in the palace's central tower chimed the hour, Bahzell stirred. Kenhodan could barely see him in the dimness, but he heard the chair creak under the hradani's weight.

"Bahzell?" he asked softly.

"Aye?" Bahzell sounded strange, as if he were both relieved and sad.

"Bahzell . . . is Gwynna a mage?"

"Aye, I suppose she is . . . now." Bahzell sighed, and his chair creaked again. "It's after coming as a shock—not that she's the mage talent, but the *timing*, as you might be saying. Wencit was after warning us long ago as how any child of ours would be mage-born. Truth to tell, it's why we were after settling in Belhadan."

"Why?"

"Belhadan's mage academy's after being the best in the Empire, and we'd reason to want the best. We'd thought as how we might send her to Zarantha's academy in Jashân, but Zarantha herself advised as how Belhadan would be the better choice. Truth to tell, I'd thought much the same even before that, after Master Trayn was after moving to Belhadan. There's never a finer empath's ever been born than Trayn Aldarfro, and we knew as how Gwynna would be after *needing* the best. The more powerful a mage, the worse the crisis when the talent comes upon him. There's few survive it unassisted if they've more than a single talent or two, and it's a hard thing to be judging when it might come. Especially with parents of different races."

His last words caught Kenhodan's attention, more for the tone than the words themselves. There was something in it, something almost like guilt. It was the first concern Bahzell had ever expressed over his union with Leeana, and even now he spoke slowly, shaping his thoughts carefully into words.

"It'll not be easy for our Gwynna," he said. "Oh, we'd not have missed her, but we knew as how we were courting trouble. Folk in the Empire are after being more tolerant than most, and if Leeana and I love one another, there's few would say us nay, yet there's those as eye hradani sidelong, even there. There's some as *would* object, I'm thinking, though there's none brave enough to be saying so in our presence. It's the gods' own jest, but truth be told, there's after being less of that kind of prejudice amongst the Sothōii and my own folk than anywhere else these days. But it's in my mind—aye, and in my heart—as how one of these days, Gwynna will be discovering those bigots, and she'll be after bearing the added burden of the mage power when she does."

"I see," Kenhodan said softly.

"It may be as you do, and it may be as you don't," Bahzell said even more softly. "Gwynna's after being more than just a . . . a *halfbreed*. It's a hybrid she is, like neither sire nor dam. She's after being smart, for starters—Tomanāk, but she's smart!" He chuckled, but it didn't break his tension. "And it's long-lived she'll be. She'll be after outliving Leeana and me both, and we hradani are a long-lived race."

Kenhodan noticed that he didn't say anything about the apparent extension of Leeana's lifespan. He wondered if *he* should mention it, given Bahzell's obvious concerns. But the hradani's next sentence blotted that question from his mind.

"Aye, it's a long life she'll be after living . . . and it's alone she'll be all those years."

"Surely not!" Kenhodan protested sharply. "She's a beautiful child, Bahzell, and not everyone's prejudiced. Surely she'll find someone to love her!"

"Will she?" Bahzell's voice was bleak. "I wonder. Aye, you've the right of it, for it's a beautiful child she is, and I've no doubt at all, at all, she'll be after showing her mother's beauty when she's grown, as well. But who'll be wedding a barren wife?"

"What?" Kenhodan wasn't certain he'd heard correctly.

"Aye," Bahzell said sadly. "Hradani and human—like all the Races of Man, we're after springing from common stock. But not all races bear 'normal' children when they wed. Leeana and I knew that, which is why I know as how Gwynna'll never be after bearing children."

Bahzell paused and looked down at his hands, speaking with quiet determination and difficulty.

"There was a time, Kenhodan, as I realized I'd been fool enough to be letting myself fall in love with someone scarce half my age who'd be after living—maybe, if the gods were good and fortune smiled on us—half as long as a woman of my own folk. There's never a foe I've ever faced as scared me the way *that* did, and it's a hard fight I fought against admitting it even to myself. But Leeana—it's a rare strong, fearless heart she has, and she'd no mind to let any foolishness of mine be tearing away what it was we were meant to be. I told her then, told her plain, as how human and hradani are after having precious few children when they wed, but that was something she already knew, and she told me just as plain as how it was *me* she was after wanting. If the gods were after giving us a child, she told me, she'd love that child with all her heart, but she'd be having me as husband even knowing as how there could *never* be a child."

He looked up from his hands and met Kenhodan's green eyes.

"As it happened, the gods've given us more years than we'd any right to be expecting, and then, greatest gift of all, Gwynna. I've no words—Tomanāk, *Brandark's* no words!—for the joy that gave us both. From the day that baby girl was born, it's my heart she's held in those hands of hers, and the same for her mother. But for all the joy's she's brought us, it's twice as long she'll live, and more, than even my folk. My family, and Leeana's, they're after understanding, and there's no doubt in my mind at all, at all, as how they'll be loving her, come what may. But as *they're* after growing old, as their children—aye, and their grandchildren—see as how she's young and beautiful still, will *they* be feeling the same? And what of folk who *aren't* family? There's some as resent even Wencit, Kenhodan, with all the price he's payed for so long to be keeping them safe in their beds at night. How will folk like that react to someone as never seems to age and who's after being half-hradani into the bargain?"

He smiled sadly.

"Truth to tell, it was that thought led me to buy the Iron Axe, to be showing Gwynna as much of the world as I might as young as I could. Leeana, she's courage enough to face Phrobus himself and spit in his eye. It's not once she ever faltered, ever questioned. But me?" He shook his head. "It's too well I know how other folk look at my own. No doubt there's never a father born as didn't worry about his little girl and how she's like to fare when he's no longer there to watch and ward. But Gwynna . . . it's a long, long time she'll bear the burden of 'halfbreed' in the eyes of some, and there's too many as'll be adding 'bastard' to the tally, as well."

Kenhodan couldn't see his face in the darkness, but he didn't have to. He heard the anguished love of a father in his friend's voice, and he wished suddenly that those who continued to despise the hradani could hear it with him. But they couldn't, and so he reached out and gripped Bahzell's shoulder fiercely.

"Bahzell, you said Leeana told you she wanted *you*, that she would've loved you—married you—even knowing it was *impossible* for you to have children, not just unlikely. Did you feel the same way about her?"

"Of course," Bahzell said simply. "There's not a person in this universe more precious to me than Leeana, unless it might be being Gwynna herself. But children are after being our immortality for most folk, Kenhodan."

"The man who wins Gwynna's hand will be a fortunate man indeed," Kenhodan said firmly. "If he has a grain of sense, he'll know it, too. And your daughter will never be taken in by clever words, never deceived

by promises that aren't meant, just as she'll recognize
the shallowness and stupidity of anyone who hates her
for *what* she is rather than treasuring her for *who*
she is! Trust me when I tell you this. Gwynna *will*
find someone—the *right* someone—to love her and
be worthy of all the love I've already seen in her."

Bahzell smiled in the darkness and gripped Kenhodan's forearm. In all the years since Gwynna's birth,
he'd confided his fears only to Leeana. He hadn't even
discussed them with Wencit—for Wencit had always
known, and Bahzell had never doubted the wizard's
deep, complex love for Gwynna. He'd never feared
Wencit would fail her.

He didn't know why he'd confided in Kenhodan, yet
he was glad he had. Whatever Kenhodan's past, Bahzell
knew he could trust him with his most precious secret.
And his simple assurance reminded Bahzell of Leeana's
so long ago, on the day he'd haltingly confessed he'd
decided to buy the Iron Axe, and why. She'd hugged
him, her eyes wet, and kissed him and told him to
let the future see to itself while they concentrated on
the only time they could control: the present.

And he'd tried. The gods knew he'd tried! He
loved his daughter with all his strength, for if he
and Brandark could cross the chasm of hate between
human and hradani—if his father, and Leeana's, could
bridge that chasm for Horse Stealer hradani and
Sothōii, whose hatred had burned fiercest in all the
world—why should it be impossible for his Gwynna,
the treasure of his heart, to find the man—human or
hradani—meant for her?

It wasn't impossible. *Surely* it wasn't! That was what
he'd told himself then, but now he knew better. She

had no need to cross the chasm; she'd been born on its farther side. Some might hate her for what she was, but not those who knew her—*never* those who knew her! For Kenhodan was right, she *was* a beautiful child, beautiful in every sense of the word, with a heart as open and warm as the sun. Leeana's advice to him had borne that fruit, for he *had* loved his daughter—loved her with all the indomitable strength of his own heart—and that love had built a haven in which she could become what she was meant to be.

The depth of his love for Leeana swept over him like the sea. She'd been so much wiser than he, seen so far past his inner fears from the very beginning. She'd loved him despite his hradaniness, and she'd refused to let him hide from his love for her. She dealt not in stereotypes but in the fierce wisdom of a heart which told her that for every evil there was a good, for every cruelty a kindness. She'd known that Gwynna would create her own life, dealing with pain and sorrow as they arose, and because she was what she was, triumphing. And for Bahzell Bahnakson, Champion of Tomanāk, the weight of the world rested on that one point.

His daughter would triumph.

CHAPTER TWENTY

Farewell to South Keep

The vase was priceless, an heirloom saved out of the wreck of Kontovar. It was a beautiful piece—paper thin, delicate porcelain, decorated with a pattern of galloping horses and the distinctive plum-green glaze of Chanerith, a glaze whose composition was now known only in Saramantha. Had it been offered for sale, collectors in the Empire of the Axe or of the Spear would have bid furiously against one another. The final price would have not only fed but housed and clothed a prosperous family of five for at least ten years...and been far less than it was actually worth.

Wulfra of Torfo held it in her hand, feeling its delicacy, its airy weightlessness. And then, with awful deliberation, she shattered it into fragments, ground the pieces under her heel, and stormed about her bedchamber, cursing viciously.

The last session with her sponsor had not been pleasant. His cold, biting anger had turned his words into flensing knives, and little though she cared to admit it, the distance between Kontovar and Norfressa had seemed far too short in the face of his freezing fury.

Yet what had he expected? Direct control of the dragon would have required moment-to-moment concentration, and if her control had wavered for a second, it would have turned upon and destroyed her. So she'd simply commanded the creature to kill anything that moved in South Wall Pass. How was she supposed to know late snows would delay Wencit? And was it *her* fault he'd slammed up a blocking spell not even the cat-eyed wizard could break?

How *dared* he rant at her? It wasn't he who now faced destruction on every hand! Wencit had undoubtedly discussed who'd been responsible for the dragon with that never to be sufficiently damned Earl Bostik, and the Empire of the Axe had made one point of policy brutally clear throughout its history: *any* arcane attack on the Empire brought retaliation . . . no matter what the cost or risk. And now she was implicated as the arcane killer of hundreds of Royal and Imperial soldiers!

She smashed another vase, twin to the first.

Damn Wencit! And damn Bostik, too! If the wizard didn't deal with her, Bostik would. She'd studied the man too carefully to have any doubt about that. He held his post precisely because he was entirely prepared to act on his own initiative, and he commanded sufficient strength to go through the kingdom of Angthyr like a hot poker through butter. Even if Fallona dared to defend Wulfra (which was now unlikely, to say the least), the army Wulfra had helped factionalize could never resist Bostik if he chose to march straight to Torfo. And that, of course, completely ignored the Council of Semkirk.

She flung herself into a chair. Well, she'd made plans against this day. If she survived—or evaded—Wencit's wrath, she could escape King Emperor, Earl, and Queen alike. There was one bolthole none of them could close against her, one ally who cared naught for their wrath because it was always at war with them anyway.

She smiled thinly, wondering how Harlich would feel when she dropped in on him among the Shith Kiri?

◆　　◆　　◆

The cat-eyed wizard wasn't watching Wulfra, and so he failed to overhear her thoughts. Not that he would have cared about them, given how little chance of survival she had. In fact, her stupidity—and his, he was forced to admit—had lessened her chances appreciably.

He'd blundered massively, rushing into an act which would cost him dear. It had seemed so perfect that he hadn't paused to recognize the true depth of his gamble, or that he could win only if the dragon succeeded. But instead, the dragon had failed—by the narrowest of margins, but still failed—and its failure had cost him a priceless advantage. After all his care to prevent Wencit from guessing he was watched by someone other than Wulfra, he'd forced the wild wizard to another, totally *erroneous* conclusion which—in the short term, at least—was every bit as bad.

He leaned back in his chair, outwardly calm, while a hurricane of wrath spun within him. Damn the old wizard! And damn himself, too! Wencit had known Wulfra could locate him through Chernion, but he hadn't cared...not until the cat-eyed wizard "proved" Wulfra had become powerful enough to control dragons! And since Wencit, for reasons of his own, hadn't chosen to dispose of Chernion yet, he'd taken a perfectly logical step and erected a blocking spell to sever Wulfra's link. Which, of course, just happened to block the Carnadosans, as well.

He drew a deep breath and sought a state of meditative calm. Very well. Accept that he'd committed his first truly serious blunder. What had he lost and how bad was the actual damage?

He could no longer observe Wencit's daily routine or track him, which meant the wild wizard was now immune to attack from a distance. But was that truly so terrible? The whole purpose of the dragon, of the entire gambit with the sword, was to test Wencit. It hadn't worked out that way so far, yet sooner or later Wencit must face Wulfra's guard spells, and when that happened the cat-eyed wizard would be able to see him through Wulfra's crystal, despite his blocking spells. So however frustrating—and infuriating—it might be in the short term, the loss was hardly catastrophic in the long run. Or not yet, at least.

The game was still his, he decided, but he must be careful. Perhaps he ought to regard this setback as a learning experience, one which would make him both more cautious and more effective in the future. He thought about that for several seconds, then sighed heavily as he felt his confidence slowly return.

It would be all right. He'd lost one card, but he still held all the trumps.

◆　　◆　　◆

Mistress Joslian looked up as her office door opened silently. Magi didn't knock on Academy doors; there was no need when thoughts could be sent ahead, and students were encouraged to do just that as they mastered their talents. Yet the physical training master was struck afresh by the utter silence with which Gwynna moved. The child's grace was almost inhuman, she thought, then scolded herself. In one sense, Gwynna was exactly that, but that wasn't the sense in which magi applied the word.

"Good afternoon, Gwynna. What can I do for you today?"

"I need your advice, Mistress Joslian," Gwynna said. The timbre of her voice pricked at Joslian, yet it was the same as ever...wasn't it?

"About what, Little Sister?"

"About...a new talent of mine," Gwynna said diffidently, and Joslian listened to her voice carefully. The girl had made a remarkable recovery from her near-fatal training crisis. To the eye, or even to the casual mental touch, she was just the same as before, yet there was a difference. She was as sunny-natured as ever, and (Joslian smiled inwardly at the thought) almost as flippant with her instructors. But despite all of that, there *was* a change, one that went as deep as the very tone of her voice.

Then Joslian frowned. No, it wasn't her *tone*; it was the voice itself. Still as clear and silver as a bell, yet somehow subtly deeper....

She straightened suddenly, bending talent and eye alike upon Gwynna, and her lips tightened.

"You needn't tell me which talent," she said dryly, and the girl blushed. "Gwynna, Gwynna!" Joslian sighed and waved to the chair. "Why do you *do* these things? Hasn't everything I've said meant *anything* to you?"

"Of course it has, Mistress Joslian."

Gwynna sat in the indicated chair with her feet together, hands folded primly in her lap, mobile ears cocked attentively, her posture of focused respect only slightly marred by the twinkle in her blue eyes. Joslian shook her head reproachfully, yet inwardly she rejoiced to see that glint of deviltry. It would have been a tragedy if her crisis had extinguished Gwynna's core of delight.

She looked absurdly young with her hair pulled back and braided, but Joslian couldn't be fooled. Not now.

"Has it really? Because if it has, if you've really been *listening* to me, just what do you think you're doing, Little Sister?"

"What I have to," Gwynna said. The twinkle faded and she became unwontedly serious. "I have to get ready as quickly as I can."

"But this!" Joslian threw up her hands. "No one's asking you to spend time on the usual journeyman duties. We know you don't have time to work in the message relays or heal a farmer's stock. Those are tasks in which we can all take pride, just as we do in making glass or healing the sick, and it's a terrible pity you can't perform them. But even when that's said and done, you *must* take time to grow into your powers. Don't *rush* yourself so!"

"Mistress Joslian," Gwynna said carefully, "what you say is true, but so is the coda. When a talent *can* be used, the time has come to use it."

"The coda was never written for a student as precocious as you, and well you know it! And don't bother to smile down your sleeve at *me*, girl!" Gwynna hastily assumed a dutifully straight face and Joslian snorted. "That's better. You may be able to bring Trayn around your thumb, but you'll find me a little more difficult than him."

"Yes, Mistress Joslian," Gwynna said meekly. *Very* meekly.

"Gwynna—!"

Joslian glared and then shook her head helplessly. She couldn't restrain an answering smile, but concern banished it as quickly as it had come.

"Listen to me, Gwynna. It's well enough to jest about most things, but not about this. What you're doing is dangerous, child! Age control is a rare and precious gift, but you must *not* use it this way. Control your age, yes, but you can't force yourself to grow like a hothouse flower!"

"The process is controlled," Gwynna said, and Joslian looked at her in momentary surprise. The twinkle had vanished entirely now, and her face was suddenly mature, her voice clinical and impersonal, as if in that moment she'd become fully adult. "The factor's only about two-to-one, and I plan to keep it there until I master the talent completely. But I need your help for that."

"I won't give it to you!" Joslian snapped, love and fear making her suddenly furious. "Damn it, Gwynna— this is *dangerous!* Especially for a woman!"

"A woman, Mistress Joslian?" There was a brittle edge to the strangely adult voice, and Joslian's anger vanished as her heart twisted within her. Gwynna watched her and went on calmly. "I know what I am. I think I've always known, but I learned for certain the day you taught me to scan my own cells. Did you think I'd only scan and not compare? I know I have less need than most to worry about what driving my age this way will do to my hormones and fertility, Mistress Joslian."

"Gwynna—" Joslian's voice was wrung with pain.

"Don't pity me." Gwynna held up an oddly compelling hand, as if she'd suddenly become the teacher. "Not for that, at least. I know I'll have other joys. I *know* it, Mistress Joslian—" somehow, in that moment, Joslian couldn't doubt her calm certitude "—but for that to happen, I have to live. And for that, I *have* to do what I'm doing."

"I see." Joslian bent her head, studying her own clasped hands as they lay atop her desk. "Then what do you want of me, Gwynna? If I can give it to you, I will." She raised eyes that were suddenly bright with unshed tears. "I'll do anything you ask . . . except hurt you."

"I need you to help me so I *won't* hurt myself. I need your help to master this talent and plan my diet and exercises around it."

"I see," Joslian said again, her voice relieved. "At least you know what you'll be asking of your body. But it requires more than that, Gwynna. It requires close monitoring, and not by you. You'll probably lose some fine control of all your talents as your hormones shift."

"I know, Mistress Joslian. That's why Master Trayn sent me to you."

"I'm pleased he had that much sense," Joslian said tartly. "All right, love—just how fast are you planning to go?"

"I need a twelve-to-one factor," Gwynna said quietly.

"Twelve-to-one? That's an awful strain on your system—especially for the age period we're talking about. You're half-hradani, so I suspect your metabolism would be able to handle it better than anyone else's would, but the effects would still be drastic. How long do you plan on maintaining that rate?"

"Seven months," Gwynna said in that same soft voice.

"Semkirk! You haven't even started your cycles yet—are you sure you want to move through puberty so fast? Can't you at least *start* more slowly, child?"

"Not unless I increase the rate later," Gwynna said steadily. "I don't have *time*, Mistress Joslian."

"All right," Joslian said finally. "I'll help you—but only if you promise to do exactly as I bid you!"

"I always do," Gwynna murmured, and the twinkle was back in her eyes.

◆　　◆　　◆

Kenhodan felt very insignificant as he entered the immensity of South Keep's Great Hall.

The stone floor was a shining pattern of white, black, and red squares, stretching away in all directions in the early light pouring through the wide windows. The walls were granite, delicately veined with pink and burnished to a mirror polish. Rich hangings emphasized the purity and strength of the stone rather than hiding the walls, and a carpet runner—its deep, soft pile as crimson as blood—ran from the double doors of ebony to a raised dais at the far end of the hall. The axe of the Empire flashed on the wall above the dais—a massive shape of gold and silver etched with diamonds, rubies, emeralds, and opals. Twenty feet tall it was, from haft to blade, and the precious stones threw spangled pools of green, white, golden, and bloody light across the floor. Below the axe was a massive throne, glowing with beaten metals and rich wood, its cushioned seat stiff with embroidery and gems. The axe motif and the imperial diadem repeated endlessly over the wine-colored silk of its canopy.

Earl Bostik's chair of state sat at the foot of the dais. Only the House of Kormak might sit upon that gloriously uncomfortable throne, and it had been occupied only twelve times in the current generation. Bostik's chair, too, was canopied, but in somber black bearing the crossed swords and axe of his rank in scarlet thread. The earl sat there, waiting, as Kenhodan and his companions walked slowly down the length of carpet past long rows of people.

Kenhodan looked at the faces and swallowed. Bostik's senior officers and Colonel Grantos formed the first line. Behind them stood the families of those who'd died under the teeth and claws of the dragon. And behind them stood every other soul who could crowd into the hall: men, women, children . . . the soldiers of South Keep and their families. The deep bass thunder of male voices rose in welcome, overlaid by the lighter, sweeter voices of women and children. It was the voice of a warrior people, the guardians of their Empire's greatest fortress. It was a stern sound, and it stirred his own pride, for these people knew the value of the deed they cheered.

Bostik rose as they approached through that thunder of voices. He wore the formal garments of his rank. It was the first time Kenhodan had seen him outside the simple armor or garments of a soldier, and with the change of clothing came a change of stature. He was the same man, but another side of him had surfaced. His face was stern, the drooping mustache and deep eyes touched by the hauteur of command and a confidence that stopped short of arrogance but was more than simple pride. This was the face of the man entrusted with the rule of South Keep by his Emperor and King—of a man who knew the responsibilities of his position ... and that he was equal to them. The simple, friendly soldier had been replaced by the hand-picked viceroy of Norfressa's mightiest monarch.

Kenhodan's gaze slipped to the earl's sword of state. The formal, openwork scabbard was banded in malachite and silver set with rubies. Silver chains linked it to a gemmed sword belt, and the hilt was worked in a complex fretwork of gold and silver-chased steel. The pommel was a single emerald, half the size of a robin's egg, that flickered with green glory, but the blade was like Bostik himself: a hard, lethal weapon within the glitter of ceremony and pomp.

Their small party stopped before him, and Kenhodan made to drop to one knee, but Bostik's signal stopped him. The governor surveyed the four of them for a long, still moment, then extended one hand to accept an ornately sealed scroll from an aide. He snapped the seal with a thumbnail, and silence fell as scraps of wax pattered to the carpet. The stiff whisper of parchment was loud as he unrolled the scroll and cleared his throat, and then his nasal voice rang out, projected with clarity, power, and the habit of command.

"From Kormak, of the House of Kormak, of His House and Name the Ninth, Emperor of the Axe, Lord of the East Wall Mountains, Grand Duke of Dwarvenhame, Duke and Protector of Norfressa, Governor of the Colonies of Kontovar, and King of Manhome, to all who hear these words, greetings.

"Know that We are greatly pleased to extend Our

thanks to Wencit, Lord of Rūm; to Prince Bahzell Bahnakson, styled the Bloody Hand, Champion of Tomanāk; to Kenhodan of Belhadan; and to Elrytha, Border Warden of Clan Torm, who have, by their strength and courage, so ably defended Our fortress of South Keep from a creature summoned by darkest sorcery as a bane to Our people. Know that it is Our will that these champions of Our Empire be made free of all borders and fortresses, and that whatsoever they may ask of officers of Our Crown shall be given them as if commanded with Our own Voice. And it is also Our will that when they have achieved their present ends, they shall present themselves before Us in Our capital of Axe Hallow, that We may thank them in person and give to them the gifts they so richly deserve of Us.

"Given under Our hand and seal, this eighteenth day of Yienkonto in the one thousand three hundred and ninety-eighth year of the Fall of Kontovar."

Bostik's voice stopped. He let the parchment roll closed once more with a snap and scanned the assembly like a hawk before he lifted the scroll high.

"Hear the words of our King and Emperor and heed them!"

His voice was drowned in sudden cheers whose roar dwarfed all earlier sounds. The tumult raged for long minutes until Bostik raised both hands.

"My friends," the governor said to the travelers when silence had fallen once more, "the King Emperor has spoken. I stand ready to meet any lawful request in his name, but before that, let us turn to gifts which may, perhaps, express a portion of our gratitude for your deeds."

He struck a small bell beside his chair with a silver mallet, and a crystal note shivered through the silent hall. It was answered by the tread of feet as a small party emerged from behind the dais with a huge and obviously heavy chest. They lowered their burden before him and snapped to attention, and Bostik reached into his formal robes for a silver key. He fitted it into the chest's lock, turned it, threw back the lid, and turned back to his guests.

"You come as travelers," he said, "but clearly you ride to war. No honor is worthy of your deeds, but we beg leave at least to equip you for your peril."

He bent over the chest and rose with an arm full of folded green fabric.

"Prince Bahzell, the Order of Tomanāk has equipped you well as its champion. There is no weapon of war or armor of proof we could give you better than that which you bear already. But your gear did not escape your battle against the dragon unscathed, and so we give you this to replace that which was destroyed in our defense."

He shook out his burden, and a silken surcoat flared wide. It was far finer than the plain, serviceable one Bahzell had worn to South Keep, and the sword and scepter on its breast was worked not in thread of gold alone but edged in sapphires and rubies, as well. They flashed in the sunlight pouring through the windows and the crowd roared its approval.

"May your enemies see these tokens and know fear," Bostik said formally.

"I thank you, Milord—for myself and for my Order," Bahzell said and bowed deeply, his voice like growling thunder after Bostik's.

Bostik returned his bow and reached into the chest once more. This time the weight he lifted from it was far heavier than any surcoat, and he held up a chain hauberk. The sunlight burnished the steely rings from Dwarvenhame's famed smithies with their own chill glitter, and he turned to Chernion.

"To Elrytha of the Border Wardens, this. May it protect one who has served her King Emperor well and remind her always of the thanks of South Keep."

"I thank you, Milord," Chernion said. She bent her neck as attendants lifted the hauberk over her head and settled it on her shoulders, and she wondered what Bostik would have said if he'd known her true trade.

"To Kenhodan, who slew the dragon, we offer these gifts in hope that they will protect and aid him and remind him always that he will ever find a home in South Keep."

Bostik held out a quiver of arrows, and Kenhodan drew a deep breath as he saw the barbed silver and steel heads on their shafts. With the quiver came a hauberk and a light shield covered not with leather, but with scales taken from the dragon. He stood as motionless as Chernion while the mail settled over his shoulders, and he expected to find it burdensome, particularly with no arming doublet beneath it. But though it dragged at his shoulders he felt almost unencumbered, as if it were a weight he knew well, and he bowed very deeply.

"My thanks, Milord," he said. "I accept your gifts with gratitude, and I'll strive to use them as you would have them used."

Bostik smiled at him and then turned to Wencit. He put his hands on his hips and cocked his head to one side.

"For Wencit of Rūm," he said quietly, "no gift is great enough, nor will you accept weapons of war or armor. For generations, the House of Kormak has sought the means to do you proper honor . . . without success. Yet the King Emperor begs that you will accept this gift." One of the aides stepped up beside him with a small, beautifully wrought wooden box in his hands and Bostik looked steadily at the wild wizard. "He ordered this sent from his own vaults in Axe Hallow, delivered by the same wind walker in the Royal and Imperial service who carried us his proclamation, and he charged me to tell you that he will not brook your refusal of it. He bade me say that he knows from whence this gift comes and that yours are the hands in which he would see it bestowed."

Bostik turned and opened the box, and when he turned back to Wencit, silver glory flashed and danced in his hands. He held up the necklet, and the wizard took it slowly. His powerful old fingers trembled as they closed upon it, and Kenhodan stared at the glittering beauty of an exquisitely wrought silver gryphon, rearing with outspread wings. Its clawed forefeet grasped a naked sword, and its head was crowned in gold.

"This pendant," Bostik said, and though his voice was soft it was also clear, for there was no other sound in all that vast hall, "is one of the treasures of the House of Ottovar, preserved by the House of Kormak since the Fall."

"I know it well." Wencit's voice was hushed in reply, wavering ever so slightly around the edges, almost broken. "It was worn by Gwynytha the Wise, wife of Ottovar the Great, and by every Empress of Kontovar after her until Serianna, wife of Toren Swordarm."

"It is the King Emperor's will that it be held once more by hands worthy to hold it," Bostik said, still softly. "Will you accept and guard it as his gift?"

"I will." Wencit raised his head, and now his voice rang proudly as he placed the gryphon inside his tunic, against his heart. "This necklace graced many noble ladies, Milord," he said clearly, "and one day it will grace another equally noble."

Bostik's eyebrows rose and a mutter of astonishment ran through the Great Hall, but the earl said no more. He only closed the box, then set it inside the chest and locked that carefully before he turned back to the gathering.

"And now, my friends, rejoice! We've prevailed upon our guests to stay yet a few more days, and all of you are bidden to table with us this day!"

Another great cheer echoed, and Kenhodan found himself picked up and borne bodily off toward the banquet hall by half a dozen Axe Brothers. Yet even as he was carried away, he saw Wencit in the small empty space his reputation always carved for him. The wizard's eyes were closed, and he moved like a man in a dream with one hand pressed to his tunic as if it cupped something unutterably precious.

◆　　　◆　　　◆

A sharp rap drew Kenhodan's attention to the door, away from the beautiful arrow he was examining.

"Enter!" he called, and the door opened to admit Bahzell, Wencit, Chernion, and Bostik. The earl immediately threw off his mantle, loosened his belt, sank into a chair with a groan, and put his feet on a stool.

"State banquets!" he said sourly. "Give me good,

simple food, and lots of it. No taste for your gourmet cookery!"

"I'm thinking you did well enough by it, Milord," Bahzell chuckled.

"One must," Bostik said, mimicking the fussy tones of a protocolist.

"Ah, and was that the way of it?" Bahzell's ears shifted in amusement. "Well, I'll just be saying it's seldom as I've seen so impressive a devotion to duty."

"I noticed the same thing," Kenhodan said with a smile. "And since I didn't have the opportunity earlier, Milord, I'll take it now to thank you for these—" he lifted the arrow in his hand like a pointer "—and the armor. I'm grateful."

"Damn well should be," Bostik said more seriously. "Should've brought it from home in the first place. And if you didn't have any to start with, Bahzell damned well should've fitted you up with it before you ever left Belhadan! Stealth'll take you just so far. Only wish I could get *this* old fool into armor!"

He glared ferociously at Wencit, but the wild wizard didn't seem particularly fazed by it.

"I haven't worn armor in more than fourteen hundred years, Milord," he observed mildly, "and I don't propose to start now. Besides—" he touched his tunic "—you've given me something far more precious."

"I'm glad," Bostik said simply. "The King Emperor's spent forty years trying to think of something. After the dragon, he decided on this and rushed it out for the presentation."

"I must thank him when next we meet," Wencit murmured.

"As you wish," Bostik nodded, "but I dropped by

for a reason. Take it you're going on? And you'd rather *I* stay home?" It was Wencit's turn to nod, and the earl snorted. "Not surprised. Always were a close-mouthed old rascal."

"Which is precisely why I'm an *old* rascal, Milord."

"Point taken. But I've been thinking. Be best for Wulfra to think you're still here after you leave, wouldn't it?"

"It certainly would be."

"Good. Your spell stops her from spying on you?" Bostik glanced at Wencit, who nodded. "And she can't drive a scrying spell through the mage barrier, so she'll only pick you up if her spies see you. Well, they'll be watching down pass for you, so you shouldn't go that way."

"The secret ways, Milord? Yes, I think that's an excellent idea."

"Thought so myself. Close off your apartments, give out you're resting a few more days, then slip you out tonight. May fool 'em a day or so even if they've got spies in the Keep."

"Thank you, Milord," Wencit said. "Thank you very much."

✦　　✦　　✦

Lanterns glowed on South Keep's mighty ramparts, like bright eyes in the darkness, while shouldered pikes and halberds paced the walls. Guards watched all approaches, alert for any irregularity, but all their watchfulness that spring evening failed to detect the stealthy departure of four travelers with business farther south.

Bostik himself led them down the dark ramp under his palace. It plunged down, down, broad enough for three horses—or two coursers—abreast, stabbing into the bowels of the mountain in a dizzy spiral. Lanterns burned on its walls, glistening on dampness as they passed beneath the moat. Still the tunnel drilled inexorably downward as Kenhodan rode beside Wencit behind the earl while Bahzell and Chernion brought up the rear with the pack animals. His new mail jingled softly, and the air was damp but fresh as it blew gently into their faces.

Kenhodan was impressed but uneasy. He knew from Wencit that the tunnels—"the secret ways"—were, indeed, a carefully kept secret, and escape routes made sense. But they could also be a dagger at South Keep's heart. The tunnel was narrow enough to be easily defended, but still . . .

They rounded a bend, and the tunnel leveled at last, then took an upward angle. Bostik led them across the flat space at the bottom, and his eyes gleamed at Kenhodan, telling him there was something special about this stretch. The redhaired man looked upward and stiffened in Glamhandro's saddle.

"See you spotted 'em." Bostik nodded in unmistakable satisfaction and pointed to the huge bronze valves in the roof, and lantern light glistened from the condensation which dewed them. "From the moat," he said. "We can flood the tunnels in twenty minutes. Hate to do it—takes weeks to pump 'em out again, even with dwarven pumps and windmills, and the moat'd take almost that long to refill—but no one's taking South Keep *this* way, my friend!"

"So I see." Kenhodan tried to sound light, despite a painful awareness of the tons of water waiting patiently overhead.

"Of course, all our defenses are only sound against mortal enemies. Wencit's always reminding me there are other kinds, but we'll do our best. If we meet something too tough for South Keep...well, that's in the laps of the gods."

"True," Wencit put in with a smile, "but the gods never reject mortals' efforts on their own behalf, Milord."

Bostik gave a crack of laughter and led them onward. Steel shod hooves rang as the passage widened, and suddenly three tunnels met. Bostik drew rein, and the others halted around him.

"Three choices here," the earl said. "The left brings you up north of the pass. The center opens into the pass itself, just beyond where Grantos and his men went to cover. This one—" he indicated the rightmost tunnel "—comes out south of the pass. That's the one I recommend."

"Aye, and it's after making sense to me," Bahzell rumbled.

"Then I'll wish you good fortune and good hunting." Bostik clasped arms with each in turn. "Go with our best wishes. Return to us when you can."

"We will," Wencit said, and slapped his back in the first familiarity he'd taken with the earl. Bostik grinned and punched his shoulder in return, then turned to make his lonely way back to his palace as the travelers clattered down the tunnel. They vanished into its dark maw, guided now by a single lantern Bahzell bore at the head of their tiny column.

✦   ✦   ✦

The dark closeness was oppressive, but Kenhodan was soothed by the feel of Glamhandro under him once more. The smooth walls glistened with scattered sparks from Bahzell's lantern, and Kenhodan marveled at the miles of passages. The Empire's engineers were largely dwarves, and they never seemed truly happy without a hammer to hand, but still—!

"Halt! Who rides from South Keep?"

The challenge was crisp, and Kenhodan saw light beyond Bahzell, with a halberdier looming against it.

"Bahzell Bahnakson and companions," the hradani rumbled back. "Sent by Earl Bostik."

"Advance into the light," the crisp voice ordered, and Walsharno minced quietly into a circle of lantern light. He and Bahzell weren't precisely the hardest people in the world to recognize, but the halberdier examined them both carefully before he returned his weapon to parade rest.

"Welcome, Bloody Hand. You may pass."

"My thanks."

Bahzell's reply echoed as if the tunnel had become wider, and he turned in the saddle, waving the others forward.

They joined him, and Kenhodan saw that not only was the tunnel wider, but it bristled with defenses, as well. Most of the light came from lanterns on the walls, but more spilled through long, narrow wall slits in those same walls—slits through which guards peered over heavy arbalests. He counted fifteen slits as he entered the triangular chamber, and five or six arbalesters could fire through each simultaneously. He shuddered to think of the carnage ninety heavy quarrels would wreak in that small space.

They left the chamber under a heavy portcullis of forged steel. Lowered, its spikes would seat two feet into the floor, and he couldn't even guess how far it extended into the roof. Beyond, the passage walls were pierced by more slits, then it narrowed abruptly, forcing them to go in single file for perhaps twenty yards. There was ample headroom for both coursers, yet there was so little width that Bahzell's and Wencit's stirrups barely cleared the walls. Then the passage widened again—this time into a vast chamber wide enough for fifteen horsemen abreast—for the last seventy-five yards as it finally approached the outer world.

Kenhodan smiled in approval. The pinched-in walls narrowed the frontage of any attack into something a few defenders could hold almost indefinitely, while the wider section gave space for two or three hundred horsemen to assemble for a sortie. Whoever had designed this bolthole had exhibited exactly the sort of paranoia a good fortress architect required.

More guards challenged them just inside the tunnel mouth. Then the officer in charge led them to a blank stone wall and barked an order. Every lantern was shuttered as he reached for a chain hanging from the roof, and great weights grumbled in the blackness as the "wall" pivoted effortlessly up on cool breeze and starlight.

Bahzell led the way through the opening, and the breeze strengthened, plucking at Kenhodan's hair as they passed out onto a flat stretch of stone. He turned to look over his shoulder and watched the massive gate vanish once more into the face of the cliff, until only rough rock gleamed dully in the starlight.

He glanced around himself. They were in a natural cleft (at least it appeared natural) with rough walls forty feet high. The cleft bore all the signs of a drainage channel for snowmelt, floored with stone and thin, sparse herringbone eddies of sand, and he chuckled in admiration. Whether the ravine truly served as a streambed or not, its natural stone paving would show little sign of passing feet to betray the entrance.

Bahzell and Walsharno moved cautiously to the end of the cleft under a sky flecked with stars. Looking past him, Kenhodan could make out the terrain, albeit dimly: rolling hills that fell away before them, smoothing gradually into a nearly level plain covered with grass, gray-green and black in the night. The ravine extended into a stone culvert under the high road perhaps a quarter league away, and he smiled again as he noted the unusually gentle slope of the culvert's stone-faced sides.

"Well, Wencit," Bahzell's deeper rumble came through the night, "here we are: the Duchy of Kolvania, and naught but thirty leagues from the capital of Angthyr."

CHAPTER TWENTY-ONE

Brigands and Shadows of the Past

"I've no desire to go to Angthyr City, Mountain," Wencit said. "We'd never evade Wulfra's spies in the capital."

"Desire or no, it's not a matter of choice. I'm thinking it's a bridge you'll need, unless you're minded to be swimming the Bellwater, and if memory's after serving me, there's never a bridge nearer than the Bridge of Angthyr."

"True." Wencit's teeth flashed in a sudden smile. "But perhaps we could use a swim."

"Oh no, you don't!" Bahzell's ears flattened. "Swimming in a little river like the Snowborn's after being one thing, but the Bellwater'll be a league across if it's an inch!"

"So it will. But I will *not* cross at the Bridge of Angthyr." Wencit touched Bahzell's arm lightly. "Don't worry! I'll think of something nearer the river. But for now—" he sniffed the night searchingly "—our way lies due south, so we'll avoid the road from here, if you please."

"And the dog brothers?" Bahzell asked. Chernion stiffened slightly, but no one seemed to notice.

"Are no problem for now," Wencit said. "Even if they know we've left the Keep, they don't know where we are right now. Let's move as quickly as we can in hopes of keeping it that way."

"Good enough," Bahzell rumbled, "but if it's no objection you have, I'll be watching for 'em ahead as well as behind."

"Which," Wencit chuckled, "is how you've lived to a ripe old age."

"And I'm minded to ripen a mite further, despite my taste in friends," Bahzell retorted. He rose in the stirrups to scan the starlit land. "Well, it's not a soul I see out yonder just now, so I'm thinking we'd best be going."

They moved away at an easy trot. The night breeze petted and teased them with quick, laughing fingers and the air was cool, but early summer had come south of the East Walls. It was drier and warmer here, and Kenhodan smelled flowers. The breezy night was quiet, the springy grass absorbed the sound of the horses' and coursers' hooves, and if they weren't as silent as the wind—saddle leather still creaked and harness or mail still jingled softly—they made very little more noise.

The hills faded astonishingly quickly into flat, gentle swells that undulated almost imperceptibly. They rode through a world of grass whose bearded heads swept belly-high on the horses, and the soft hiss of wind pushed gray and black waves across a tasseled sea. Scattered clumps of trees stirred on the wind, and Kenhodan slowly noticed a peculiar odor under the smell of flowers—a not unpleasant acridness that tickled the nose.

The strange smell grew stronger, and he sniffed more loudly. Wencit glanced at him, and he saw the wizard's eyes glow in the dark.

"What's that smell, Wencit?" he asked quietly.

"Smell?" The glowing eyes narrowed for a moment, then widened once more. "Oh. That's just dragon spoor, Kenhodan."

"*Dragon spoor?*" Kenhodan pulled up so suddenly Chernion's mare almost collided with Glamhandro. "You mean there are *more* dragons out here?"

"Not now," Wencit soothed, urging him back into motion. "But there were once—dragons of every conceivable size, shape, and inclination settled this whole area. They were immigrants, too." Kenhodan made a noise of disbelief, and Wencit chuckled. "Surely you didn't think only the Races of Man escaped the Fall? Dragons, you may recall, have wings."

"So what happened to them?" Kenhodan demanded.

"The Dragon Wars," Wencit said, and his voice was lower, almost sad. "The last great war between dragonkind and the Races of Man. Left to themselves, the dragons generally left the refugees alone. Why not? Most of them are much smarter than the black dragons, and very few are actually 'evil' in our sense of the word. But eventually people spilled into the area, and the inevitable happened."

He sighed.

"The wyrms had been here for over a century by then, and they regarded the land as theirs. And, to be fair, the force of law was probably on their side. There was an ancient treaty between the dragons and Ottovar the Great, Kenhodan. Hundreds—perhaps thousands— of dragons had died in the original Wizard Wars of Kontovar because the wizard lords contending before Ottovar and Gwynytha forged the Strictures had used sorcery to enslave them exactly as Wulfra did when she sent the black dragon after us. Ottovar promised he and his allies would never do that. In return, the dragons agreed to aid them against their enemies if the Ottovarans would protect them against the Dark Lords' spells of compulsion. Ottovar agreed, and in recognition of their assistance he guaranteed them possession of the Island of Chersoth and of the Province of Raynkaltha. Chersoth wasn't far from the Isle of Rūm, and for several thousand years the Council of Ottovar and the Council of Dragons regularly exchanged representatives."

He paused, as if to see if Kenhodan was following him, and the redhaired man nodded for him to continue, fascinated by his description of the Races of Man's relationship with the dragons. It was very unlike anything he'd thought he knew about the subject.

"The dragons honored the terms of the treaty, and so did the House of Ottovar. For a time, at least." The wizard's tone darkened and he looked away, gazing out over the grasslands. "Eventually, that changed. When Herrik Ottarfro joined the Carnadosans and turned against his father and his brother, he broke the Council of Ottovar's ability to protect the dragons and the Dark Lords were able to enslave them once more. We shielded Chersoth to the end, but Raynkaltha was beyond our reach, and the gods only know how many dragons died exactly as that black dragon died in South Wall Pass, hurling themselves against their enslavers' enemies."

Wencit's voice fell, softer and lower, hard to hear against the endless sigh of the wind.

"Some of the oldest and strongest of the Dragon Lords fought on Toren Swordarm's side, but few of them survived. The Carnadosans were as good at crafting spells to enslave as we were at crafting spells to protect, and they had the advantage of the initiative. We could only respond to each new spell as it was deployed against us, and in the end, any but the very strongest dragons fell prey to their enemies' control. And too many of the ones who didn't were torn apart by their own enslaved fellows."

He fell entirely silent for a long, brooding moment, then shook himself.

"Some of the wyrms argued that Herrik Ottarfro's actions meant the House of Ottovar itself had broken the treaty. Since the treaty had failed, they held that they were no longer bound by it, either, and they fled to Norfressa on their own, landing wherever they chose. Toren, however, recognized that his house had failed them in the end, whatever his or his father's intentions, and he urged *all* of the survivors to escape to Norfressa. There was room for all, he said, and he promised them his house would recognize their right to the land upon which they settled.

"But the Battle of Lost Hope ended Toren's ability to control what happened in Norfressa. Worse, not all of the refugees from Kontovar landed in the colonies he and his father had established around Manhome. By the end, as the situation in Kontovar crumbled, people fled whenever and however they could and landed wherever their ships touched Norfressa's soil. So while Duke Kormak fully intended to honor Toren's promise to the dragons, scores of enclaves and colonies sprang up far beyond the reach of his own authority. That's how the Spearmen came to found their own empire in the south, and how the Wakūo became lords of the Great Desert, among other things.

"And that meant the dragons who'd fled to Norfressa found themselves facing very much the same situation the hradani did. The refugees and their children forgot—or simply didn't care—how many of the Dragon Lords had died fighting under the Gryphon Banner, but they remembered the dragons who'd been compelled to attack their cities and towns and farms, to devour their stock and murder their children. They saw no reason to allow any dragon to claim territory in Norfressa as his own... and every reason to exterminate the 'servants of Carnadosa.'"

Wencit looked back at Kenhodan, witchfire eyes gleaming.

"On the whole, my sympathies were with the dragons when land-hungry would-be nobles invaded the ranges they'd claimed, but that made no difference. You've proved yourself that a single archer—with great skill, courage, and luck—can fell a dragon. Black dragons are less powerful and more stupid than most, and few archers have your skill, but the armies arrayed against them had hundreds—thousands—of bowmen. Many settlers died, but there were far more of them and humans produce far more offspring, far more rapidly, than any dragon. The plains burned at the height of the war. You could see the smoke for fifty leagues, and the clouds bled fire at night. Dragon venom fell so thick you can still smell it in places, but in the end, the dragons would have been exterminated."

"Would have been?"

"I said dragons are intelligent, and the most belligerent of them—and those least willing to accept terms—died or fled to the extreme east. Those who remained were tired of fighting and willing to negotiate for peace."

"On what sort of terms?" Kenhodan asked, fascinated by the entire concept.

"It was simple enough. The Scarthū Hills lie southeast of here, and the dragons were granted undisputed possession of the northern and central hills in return for a pledge to leave the colonists in peace."

"And that actually worked?"

"As well as most treaties," Wencit said dryly. "Neither the House of Ottovar nor the Council of Ottovar were available to enforce it, of course, and some people always feel their actions are limited only by what they can get away with. But the dragons deal with anyone who violates their territory, and no one misses them much. Then again, the treaty only calls for the dragons to leave the Races of Man in peace, not to stay in the hills forever. They can come and go as they please, as long as they harm no one. In fact, the dragons insisted that wards be set around the hills to guarantee they behave outside them."

"*They* insisted?"

"Certainly. The wiser breeds know their stupider brethren might violate the treaty and that a violation by any dragon might lead to renewed war against all of them. So the wards bar the passage of any dragon bent on evil or a violation of the treaty—not always the same thing, of course—though a wizard can force them through. As Wulfra did," he added grimly.

"These wards," Kenhodan said. "Did you set them?"

"I modestly accept the credit."

"But what stops a dragon from changing his mind after passing them? If your wards work on the basis of what a dragon thinks he's going to do when he passes them, how does that prevent . . . well, *accidents*, I suppose? I mean, even if he genuinely has no intention of doing anything the treaty would forbid, *circumstances* can change, so why can't his intentions change in response?"

"Dragons' brains don't work that way, Kenhodan. They live outside time, peculiar as that sounds. They experience all time—past, present, and future—at once. They know what they'll do before they cross the wards."

"A dragon sees the future? Even the moment of his own death?"

"Certainly. They see the moments of *all* their deaths."

"'All'?" Kenhodan repeated suspiciously.

"Of course. Time's neither fixed nor immutable. It's an infinitely variable series of patterns, of events which might potentially have any number of outcomes, and a dragon sees all his possible futures. But the one which actually comes to pass for him depends on a host of factors, many of which are beyond his control. And as events alter the present, so his possible futures change. The pattern's constantly shifting. I doubt any non-dragon could stand that sort of vision without going hopelessly insane."

"It does sound . . . confusing."

"Oh, it is. But time's even more complex than dragons see, actually."

"Really? How?"

"You might find it interesting to get Bahzell's perspective on that sometime," Wencit said dryly. "The... multiplicity of possible futures is at the very heart of the war between the Light and the Dark. But at least champions of Tomanāk only move one *direction* in time, from the past to whatever future actually occurs. So do dragons, for that matter, but it doesn't *have* to be that way. Not for mortals, anyway; the gods have a... different relationship with time, one which precludes them from meddling with it, although they perceive it much as a dragon would, albeit on a far larger scale. Some magi can see the future, too, but the precognition talent's very different from dragons or deities. Some wizards, on the other hand, can actually travel through time. Fortunately, it's an extremely rare ability. The best estimate I've ever seen is that perhaps one in ten thousand have it, and those who do seldom experiment with it. There are... drawbacks, you see. No one can travel forward beyond the frame of his own experience, so travel into the past is the only really practical 'direction.' But traveling into the past is far less useful than glimpsing the future, and it's very, very risky, because all time is mutable."

Kenhodan looked at him sharply. "You mean—?"

"Precisely," Wencit said softly. "It's hard to even imagine why any theoretically sane wizard would do anything of the sort. A wizard who travels back may alter past events, may actually destroy the future from which he came. It's an interesting theoretical point—if you like, once we get back to Belhadan I can reclaim a few books from my library and let you read the debate between wizards about exactly how it would all have worked out if someone had been stupid enough to try it. There was never any *agreement* on that point, you understand, which is one reason only a lunatic would have attempted it. The question that arose was whether or not his changing the past would create a situation in which he'd never existed, meaning he couldn't come back to change it, thus *not* destroying him. But if he wasn't destroyed, then wouldn't he travel back anyway? Could his actions establish a sort of . . . loop in time which would effectively trap not just him but everyone else in the same dead-end? Or would he have established a preexisting identity before the time change, thus leaving him untouched, thus letting him destroy everything—and every person—he'd left in the future?"

Kenhodan considered that for a long moment and shivered.

"Has anyone ever been crazy enough to actually try it?"

"The longest shift I've ever seen recorded was about five days," Wencit said, "and the wizard who made it did nothing but observe from his own study using his gramerhain. The fact that there's no record of a longer jump may mean it's never been tried, or that the attempt simply wasn't recorded, or that all of the theories about what would happen were wrong . . . or, of course, that the wizard *did* destroy himself and any future in which he might have left notes about his intentions."

"I see." Kenhodan shuddered and forced himself to smile. "That's not the stuff of insanity, Wencit—that's the stuff of *nightmares*! Now I'll lie awake waiting for some time-hopping wizard to wipe us all out."

"Oh, I wouldn't worry too much," Wencit said. "The chances are better that you'll drown in the desert in the middle of a summer heat wave. I said it was a rare talent, and most of the handful of wizards who ever had it couldn't imagine anything compelling enough to take the risk."

"That's a relief." Kenhodan wiped his brow exaggeratedly. "I'll cheerfully leave the processes of time to the dragons."

"Will you?" Wencit chuckled. "I think that would probably be wise of you."

Kenhodan smiled again, more easily. Perhaps it was as well he was willing to leave it to others, since he could never experiment with it anyway. He tried to envision whatever dragons saw, but it was beyond him. The thought was reassuring rather than bothersome, for he rather suspected that if he *could* have understood it, he would no longer have been exactly human himself.

◆   ◆   ◆

Kolvania's grasslands unreeled beneath them, the stars swung towards dawn, and Bahzell led them to a small hollow just at sunrise. Grass grew tall about the depression, hiding them from observation, and a small spring turned its heart into a soft mire around a crystal pool of water for the coursers and the horses. Kenhodan wondered how Bahzell had found the spot, but the hradani only shrugged when he asked. Perhaps thirty or forty years on the Wind Plain would give just anyone such skills, Kenhodan thought. Or perhaps the answer was more prosaic than that, given the keen senses Walsharno and Byrchalka might have brought to bear upon the project.

The hollow was an opportunity to rest, and they stopped gratefully. There was no fuel, but the sun filled the depression with more warmth than Kenhodan had felt since Belhadan, and he relaxed on his blankets in a dreamy doze while morning burned into afternoon.

They started out again shortly after noon. Bahzell and Chernion estimated that they'd made about five leagues during the night, but both hoped to make better speed in daylight. Frequent rest stops were indicated for Chernion's mare and the packhorses, yet Bahzell still hoped to strike the north branch of the South Wall River, which would lead them to the Bellwater twelve leagues west of the city of Angthyr, before evening.

"And I still say as how you'll be needing a bridge, Wencit!"

"Trust me, Bahzell," Wencit soothed. "Have I ever misled you?"

"'Misled,' is it?" Bahzell snorted. "If you're after meaning you've lied to me, why, the answer's no. But if you're after meaning you've never been one as landed me in trouble—?"

He shook his head in exasperation.

"That's an occupational risk of consorting with wizards, Bahzell!" Kenhodan laughed. "For that matter, it probably comes under the heading of normal occupational risks for a champion of Tomanāk, doesn't it? Still, you seem to have survived it so far."

"Aye, though not always by so large a margin as I might've liked!"

"Surviving a wizard's company by any margin's an achievement, Bloody Hand." Chernion looked up from a bridle she was mending. "I've seen little of wizards—nor wish to see more—but that little leaves me no liking for the breed. With exceptions, of course." She nodded to Wencit as she spoke.

"Don't mind me, Elrytha," Wencit said mildly. "Given your experiences, I'm not surprised you don't care for the art's practitioners. I might feel the same in your place."

"My experiences might surprise you, Wizard," she said tartly.

"Possibly," Wencit murmured. "But, then, your experience with *my* wizardry's been fortunately slight so far, hasn't it?"

Chernion conceded the game with a snort and bent back over her bridle. Kenhodan was a little puzzled by the barbed undertones, but Bahzell took it in stride, for he was accustomed to people who eyed all wizards askance. For that matter, the vast majority of hradani would have expressed themselves even more strongly than Chernion, given their people's experience with wizardry. Still, he saw no point in letting the verbal dueling get out of hand.

"If we're to be moving, we'd best be on our way," he rumbled. "Is it finished you are with that bridle, Border Warden?"

"As well as can be." Chernion held up the mended tackle. "It won't win any prizes for workmanship, but it should serve."

"Then I'm thinking as its time we were moving."

They stirred into motion once more, not without reproachful glances from the horses. The grass grew ever taller as they moved deeper into Kolvania. Only Walsharno and Byrchalka towered over the bearded heads now; they were shoulder-high even on Glamhandro, and Kenhodan and Chernion thrust just their torsos and heads above the green sea. Insects hummed in the bright light, and an occasional hawk drifted far above.

Kenhodan drowsed in the peaceful sunlight, for despite the long hours in the saddle, this was the most restful portion of their entire journey since leaving Sindor.

Afternoon wore on and their shadows began falling to their right, rather than the left. The breeze grew brisker, and Kenhodan shrugged back into his poncho. The chillier air brought him back awake, as if the drowsy afternoon had been a dream, and he rose in his stirrups to peer about.

A line of trees broke the grass sea ahead of them. He studied it carefully, eyes watering as the wind blew into his face, and thought he smelled an added freshness. Glamhandro snorted, tasting the same dampness, and he realized those trees marked a river.

So they did. The South Wall River was normally a shallow, flickering stream of rocks and sand. Now the stream was more energetic and the water was high, though dried flotsam showed how much higher it reached during the peak floods. Looking at the necklace of branches and trees the better part of half a mile farther back from the riverbed, Kenhodan was glad to have arrived after that peak had passed.

Those earlier floods had swept the banks clear of underbrush, however, so while tilted rocks were heaped here and there, most of the bank was a firm shingle. Their mounts were relieved to break free of the deep grass, and equally glad for a long drink. Kenhodan didn't blame them, yet he was uneasy as he stood in the shallows and surveyed their surroundings while twilight crept upon them and Glamhandro drank.

The river's rushing, gurgling, rumbling voice drowned other sounds in a bothersome way. It was a small point, but he disliked how it hid other noises. He splashed a boot in the river and rubbed Glamhandro's neck as the stallion whuffled into the water.

Chernion shared his dislike for the masking sound of the river and cared little more for the way the trees along the banks cut off her view of the grasslands, but she said nothing as she rubbed her mare's ears and frowned over her own shifting thoughts and motives. Whether or not Wencit knew it—and she suspected he did—she was his staunch ally until Wulfra was dead. After that, of course, she should execute the original assignment . . . yet she was curiously loath to do so.

She sighed. She could probably avoid it if she really wanted to. No one now living—she stifled a pang over Ashwan—knew about her Elrytha identity. It would be simple enough to slip the Guild Council a message as Chernion arguing that the risks—and the ultimate cost—were too great. If she added that the Guild had been betrayed, the Council would choose to abandon what was clearly a losing endeavor anyway. After all, with Wulfra dead there'd be no one to confirm they'd ever accepted the contract. Any rumors about it, or about the Guild's failure, would fade in time, lost against the far greater terror of all the times the Guild *hadn't* failed. And once the wizard was off the Guild's list, she could abandon the assassins forever, if she so chose, and become Elrytha in truth. Or perhaps more accurately, become Elrytha *again*, for so she'd been born and raised.

The new direction of her thoughts had shocked her when she first recognized it, but it was becoming more acceptable. It stemmed from no sense of comradeship with their targets, but her time with Wencit and his companions had convinced her the Council's suspicions had been correct—that the final struggle between the Council of Carnadosa and the descendants of those who'd fled Kontovar truly was at hand. And the Council might also be right that the Assassins Guild would not prosper in any world in which the Carnadosans failed. But what if the Council had been wrong about the Carnadosans' chance to *succeed*? Chernion's time with Wencit had only underscored all the legends about him, and she was far from prepared to assume he'd be anything but the canny, dangerous survivor he'd been for the last fourteen centuries. In a world where the Council of Carnadosa suffered defeat—again—it might be well for someone with the option to stop *being* an assassin.

Yet that wasn't the only factor, for there was another—one that stemmed from something she couldn't quite lay her finger on. Perhaps it arose from the complex relationships she sensed about her. On the surface, the wizard and the Bloody Hand dominated the group, but underneath it wasn't so simple.

She tapped her teeth thoughtfully, and her brain gnawed at the thought like a dog at a bone.

The puzzle centered on Kenhodan. His lost past was mystery enough, but the way the others reacted to his amnesia was equally instructive. It was as if his past was a puzzle only to him and not to them, which made no sense. At the same time, the blood smell she'd sensed in Sindor was growing stronger, not weaker. He might think what he liked about the dragon, but she'd enjoyed a painfully excellent view of the kill—and of the iron determination which had guided his every move. *He'd* killed it, and no one else, even if the others had done their best to help.

No, it would never do to kill this group off hastily.

There was something at work in Kenhodan, and she intended to discover what it was. If as much power was floating about her as she'd come to suspect, it might be wiser to be its ally than its enemy. After all, she'd chosen her vocation because it offered power; she could always change her trade if a better route to power opened.

◆   ◆   ◆

They moved on after dark, the river singing and chuckling to them as they followed its eastern bank. Stars twinkled, lighting their way dimly. Hooves rattled occasional stones loose to skitter along the flood-packed shingle, and the jingle of harness and mail was louder in the trough of the riverbed.

Bahzell called a halt before midnight and they retreated to the edge of the grass to camp. Driftwood provided fuel, and the river's depression screened them from observation. That allowed a fire and hot food, and Bahzell rose to the occasion by tickling a dozen trout from the river and broiling them.

A restful, uneventful night left them refreshed and ready in the dawn, and cheerful insults passed back and forth as they saddled up for the day.

"I'm thinking as we'll reach Bellwater by evening," Bahzell said around his pipe, trailing blue smoke as they rode. "Would it happen you're ready to be telling me how you're thinking to cross it, Wencit?"

"Something will come to me," the wizard assured him calmly.

"It's happier I'd be if you'd stop saying that." Bahzell pointed his pipe stem into his friend. "You're after knowing exactly what it is you're thinking to do—don't bother denying it! You're only after being so close-mouthed because you know I won't be so very happy about whatever it is."

"Bahzell, you wound me," Wencit said placidly.

"Hah! I'm thinking as one day you'll be after playing something a mite too close to your chest and it's dead I'll end up. And no doubt it's sorry you'll be when I do!"

"You're right," Wencit said, his tone suddenly lower. "I will be."

Bahzell looked up sharply. "Oh, cheer up, man! Its only jesting I was!"

"I know," Wencit said. "But you're right, you know."

"What? That I'll die someday?" Bahzell chuckled. "Tomanāk, Wencit! *Everyone's* after dying doing something!"

"No, Bahzell," Wencit said softly. "Everyone *else* dies."

And to that, the hradani had no reply.

◆   ◆   ◆

Chernion had trotted ahead to scout the trail as they neared the Bellwater; now she cantered rapidly back and her raised hand stopped them.

"Trouble, Border Warden?" Bahzell asked.

"Yes. We're about to run into a nest of bandits, Bloody Hand."

"Bandits?" Kenhodan asked. "Are you certain?"

"Kenhodan, when thirty men in a hidden camp have fifty horses and thirty mules, I start to wonder. When I get close enough to hear them discussing the division of their loot, I *stop* wondering. Trust me; they're bandits."

"I see." He scratched his chin thoughtfully as she turned to Bahzell.

"We'll have to wait for them to move, or else go around them," she said.

"We can't," Wencit said flatly. "I can't be delayed tonight."

"'Can't,' is it?" Bahzell cocked his ears at him. "And would it be you've a mind to be explaining that?"

"You said you wouldn't like the way I'm planning to cross," Wencit said, "but the alternatives are all worse. And if we mean to cross the way I've been planning to do it, we have to be there by moonrise."

"I see." Bahzell tugged at his nose and his ears shifted gently back and forth.

"Well, if they're bandits, we should visit them anyway," Kenhodan heard himself say, and frowned, startled by his own words. What could possess him to take on the odds of seven-to-one? He didn't know, but *something* was ... pushing him. It was almost like a sense of personal affront.

"What do you mean?" Chernion asked sharply.

"What I said," he heard himself say, as if it were the most reasonable thing in the world. "Bandits should be discouraged."

"Has your hair's heat fried your brain?" she demanded.

"Maybe it has." Kenhodan grinned, suddenly reckless, abandoning the attempt to understand his own motives. "But there it is ... and there *they* are."

"The lad's a point," Bahzell rumbled. "It's half a mind I have to be calling on them myself, Border Warden. Me being a champion of himself, and all."

He tilted his ears at her impudently, and she shook her head in exasperation.

"You mean the pair of you have half a mind *between* you!" she snapped, sounding in that moment remarkably like Wencit. But then steel scraped as she drew her sword and fingered its edge. "Still," she sighed, "when you ride with madmen, you have to expect to catch their madness occasionally."

Bahzell's brown eyes twinkled. Despite herself, the hardened assassin chuckled in response, then she shook herself.

"Very well. If you insist on going through them rather than around, let me show you the way of their camp."

She dismounted to draw in the sand with the tip of her sword.

"Here's the river—" she inscribed a sharp line "—and the bank. The mules are downstream in two groups—here and here." She scraped two "X"s beside the line. "They have two men guarding each group, and they're building a fire pit here, below the crest of the bank. There are a half-dozen more of them scattered in an arc away from the river—watching their back trail, would be my guess." She scratched in six more marks. "This center man's farthest out—two hundred yards or so from the river. The rest are pitching tents, except for two men posted right at the ends of their camp—here and here."

"Hmmmmm . . ." Bahzell's ears flattened. "Someone's head's after being better screwed on than I'd like. I'd hoped as how the river'd be clear of guards so we could be after riding down their camp before they knew as we were coming. But this man—" he pointed at the crude diagram "—will be after seeing us as we close."

"How much good would it do them?" Chernion asked pragmatically. "The warning would be short."

"They're after setting sentries and hiding their camp—what if they've seen fit to be taking other precautions? Like a few bowmen with weapons handy?"

"I see. But this guard's the only one that worries you?" Her sword stabbed the diagram.

"Aye. They've no one else placed to see along the river."

"Then leave him to me, Bloody Hand."

"It's confident you are of taking him without an alarm?" he asked, eyeing her measuringly.

"He won't even know I'm there, Bloody Hand." She smiled wolfishly. "He'll die without a sound."

"Well, then!" Bahzell nodded sharply. "That being so, I'm thinking . . ."

✦   ✦   ✦

Glamhandro stirred uneasily under Kenhodan, and he rubbed the stallion's neck one-handed, holding the reins of Chernion's mare in the other. But his attempt to calm the horse was little more than halfhearted as he grappled with his own uneasy thoughts.

He'd been in control of himself since the Forest of Hev, but now he was no longer certain he was, for he was ready—eager—to kill. It worried him, for the thought of killing had become increasingly repugnant to him . . . until now. And this was very different from what he'd experienced aboard *Wave Mistress*. There was no berserk bloodlust in him, only a cold, clinical acceptance that killing the bandits was fitting . . . natural.

He shook his head and glanced covertly after the border warden. She'd changed her riding boots for soft buskins and vanished into the grass like a ghost, flitting away like the shadow of death. That a woman chose the profession of arms as her vocation didn't disturb him, but she'd shown a new face as she checked her weapons with cold, competent expertise. He would have been less disturbed if she'd shown the same grim eagerness as Bahzell; it was the cold, dispassionate glitter in her eyes that had chilled him. He shivered, then took himself to task for his own hypocrisy. Who was he to question her? It was he who'd pushed for the attack—why should her efficiency bother rather than please him?

He shivered again . . . then cursed silently as he smelled his own bitter sweat, for it wasn't fear sweat. By now he knew only too well how his own fear smelled, and this was something else. Something worse. His pulse thundered in his ears, and his thoughts felt swollen and disordered. Hot.

His eyes went suddenly wide. This was more than simple emotional stress. Some buried memory was stirring, and he redoubled his mental profanity, for there could be no worse moment for such a distraction!

Acute nausea stabbed him, and he swallowed desperately as his mouth—dry and scratchy an instant before—filled with a choking rush of saliva. He wanted to whimper and stop the attack, but he couldn't. The border warden already stalked her prey, and the others were too far off to signal without warning the bandits. He rubbed his sword hand on his thigh, scrubbing away sweat. He was clammy and cold under arming doublet and hauberk as he tried to concentrate, tried to force memory to surface . . . or to subside. It refused. Tiny voices nibbled at his sanity, squeaking words he couldn't catch, laughing and shrieking. He was afraid for his reason, for his life if he must fight distracted, for—

The sentry vanished, and Bahzell's hand cut air. Walsharno sprang to instant life, sweeping wide to sweep into the camp out of the sunset with Wencit and Byrchalka behind him, and Kenhodan cursed aloud.

He was barely able to see through red waves of mental anguish, but his sword was in his hand somehow as Glamhandro bolted forward under him like an uncoiling spring. Chernion's mare thundered behind, and his sword was an inert, heavy slab of metal in his hand. Glamhandro's hooves struck sparks of pain in his head, and he felt himself falling into darkness. Wind whipped his face as he charged the camp, and the setting sun glared into his eyes. He fought to cling to awareness as he slithered into the waiting void, but it was useless. A brigand loomed before him, black and stark in his red vision. The man's mouth opened in a shout, but Kenhodan rode in silence, sealed away from the noise about him. He broke free of the world, spinning into a dark cocoon shared with no one, and he felt his sword move as if it were someone else's. Steel glittered and the shouting mouth was silenced forever in a spray of blood. Then he spiraled down, down, into the pit of his own mind and darkness....

Chernion blinked in amazement as Kenhodan thundered by. He released her mare as planned, but he didn't wait for her to mount. Glamhandro swept on past, showering her with dirt as his hooves spurned the grassy slope. His tail floated like a streak of smoke and Kenhodan rode easily, shoulders back, spine straight, sword hand resting on his knee. She watched him hurtle into the astonished bandits like a boulder with no support, no one to cover his flank or back.

Not that the bandits were ready to receive him. Bahzell's plan had brought himself and Wencit into the attack first, fixing the outlaws' attention on them, and when Kenhodan charged, most of them were looking the other way. Some fought to draw steel, others raced for the picketed horses, but their movements had barely begun when Bahzell and Walsharno began to kill.

The hradani's sword moved lightly as a saber, singing through his foes like lightning. Blood hung in its wake, sparkling like rubies in the sunset, and Walsharno fought like another arm. The most superbly trained warhorse in all the world was no match for a courser, for coursers were as intelligent as any of the Races of Man, and the warriors among them—warriors like Walsharno and Byrchalka—trained as hard in their own combat arts as any human or hradani. He and Bahzell weren't simply rider and mount; they were one. Two hearts, two minds, two souls fused by the bond between them into a single, lethal entity. Anything to the right was Bahzell's concern; anything to the left was Walsharno's, and steel shod hooves and jaws that snapped arms like sticks let few escape his wrath.

Wencit curved out of Bahzell's wake to cut the bandits off from their horses, and half a dozen brigands turned at the pound of Byrchalka's hooves. They stared at the thundering courser and the wizard's flaming eyes in horror, but they had no option, and swords shone in their fists as they leapt to engage him, fighting for their lives.

He and Byrchalka weren't the equal of Bahzell and Walsharno, for they lacked the fusion of the adoption bond, and Wencit was no champion of Tomanāk. Walsharno knew what Bahzell knew, saw what Bahzell saw, just as Bahzell shared what *he* saw and knew. He and his rider moved as one, each understanding the other's intent in the moment that intent was born, and they fought with a smooth, polished efficiency not even another wind rider and courser could have rivaled, for it was founded upon eighty years' shared experience in more battles than most men could even have counted.

Byrchalka and Wencit were more than horse and rider, yet less than wind rider and courser. In truth, there was no comparison between their capabilities and those of Bahzell and Walsharno . . . except that no other warrior and no warhorse, however willing and however schooled to battle, could possibly have matched them. If Wencit's sword was of merely mortal dimensions, it moved with equal, flashing speed and the first two bandits to face him found themselves equally if less spectacularly dead. The others tried to work around and hamstring Byrchalka, but too late.

Kenhodan exploded into their backs just as the coursers began to slow. One outlaw heard him and turned to shout a warning, and Chernion watched in disbelief as Kenhodan struck like an adder and the bandit's head flew. She'd never seen a sword move so quickly! And, a corner of her mind noted, she'd never seen a man literally beheaded with a one-handed, *backhand* blow. Then she was clapping her heels to her mare's flanks and pounding along in Kenhodan's wake, her own sword chopping and thrusting.

Kenhodan crashed past Bahzell on an opposite course, his blows splashing the hradani's surcoat with blood. Then he and Chernion broke clear and wheeled—she to join Wencit; he to slash back into the main fight.

The outlaws fought, for they had no choice, but Bahzell and Kenhodan sliced through them like a double-edged sword. The hradani's great war cry rang, and the sounds of his blows were like axes, but foremost—and silent—in the slaughter was Kenhodan.

Even Bahzell's destruction—even *Walsharno's*—paled beside the havoc the redhaired man wrought. His swordplay lacked the fire which had characterized it before, but its deadly efficiency chilled the heart. Overhand, underhand, backhand—straight thrust or lunge—none of that mattered. His blade moved in every direction, and each blow flashed straight to its mark and ended a life. Twice he struck down bandits *behind* him, invisible to him at the moment he killed them, and Glamhandro, infected with the same murderous efficiency, reaped a harvest to rival Walsharno's. They broke through into the open once again and wheeled once more, the gray stallion rearing with a whistling scream before they crashed back in upon their foes.

Shrieks and the wet crunch of steel filled the evening for a very brief time. Then it was over.

Yet *nothing* was over. Kenhodan jerked his steel from the chest of the last bandit and spun Glamhandro on his hocks to confront his companions. A dozen bodies sprawled before Wencit and Chernion, felled as they tried to break through to their horses. Chernion had dismounted to clean her sword, but she looked up as the sudden silence fell and her hands froze in mid-motion. She shivered as she saw Kenhodan's eyes, for they flamed with a green fire to haunt her dreams, and his lips worked silently as he touched Glamhandro with a heel. Hardy soul that she was, she gave back a step as the gray raised his head proudly and paced towards Wencit with the high, measured step of the parade ground.

Wencit sat quietly and watched them come. Kenhodan was blood to the elbow, and more blood dripped from his blade. Glamhandro was scarlet to his knees, and the stench of death rode with them across the field. They halted before the wizard, and Kenhodan shook his sword at him.

"How long, wizard?" His voice stunned them all, for it hissed and gusted with a passion they'd never heard from him. Blood from his sword splashed Wencit and the blade quivered with the power of his grip, but the wizard was silent.

"How long?" Kenhodan's voice became a shout. "How much *longer*? Answer me, damn you!"

"I have answered you," Wencit said softly at last, and Kenhodan's head turned slowly. His gaze pivoted to the west, his eyes flashing at the blood-red horizon while the bones of his face stood out in bold relief, strange and alien and ancient in the ashes of the day's dying light.

"So you have," he whispered in a voice more like his own, but only for a moment. Then his lips locked in a terrible rictus and his sword thrust skyward as if to spear the bleeding sun. Blood spattered from the blade, and he rose in his stirrups under that grizzly shower.

"Damn you, Herrik!" His throat muscles corded, straining with the power of his despairing scream. "*Daamnnnn yooouuuuuuu!*"

And he hurtled from the saddle to the ground.

◆　　◆　　◆

Bahzell and Chernion stared at one another as Kenhodan slammed to the bloody earth, but Wencit sprang down from Byrchalka's saddle and bent over him. He rolled him onto his back and felt the strong, slow pulse in his throat.

"Gods, Bloody Hand! What was *that* about?" Chernion whispered.

"As to that, I've no least idea, Border Warden," Bahzell replied almost absently. "They do say as how strange things follow wizards about."

"Strange!" Chernion was shaken to the core. "Bloody Hand, I don't want to know any more—not now. I'll go make certain no one escaped. Then I'm going to keep watch while *you* sort this thing out!"

"As you wish."

Bahzell watched her canter off, and he didn't blame her for her fears.

<Nor do I,> Walsharno said silently in the caverns of his mind. *<I've never heard of* anything *like that, Brother.>*

"And no more have I," Bahzell replied.

He dismounted slowly and cleaned his blade, one shoulder resting against Walsharno's tall, solid side as he did so, and he needed that contact. He'd recognized Kenhodan's lethality from the very beginning, but this was different. There'd been a smoothness, a deadly efficiency such as he'd never seen from *anyone* to the younger man's swordplay. It wasn't simple perfection of form, either, for there'd *been* no form, no use of learned and practiced parries, cuts, thrusts, ripostes. Kenhodan's sword had simply *been* there, wherever it needed to be at the exact instant it needed to be there. There'd been no waste motion, no hesitation, not even any thought. It hadn't even been *instinct*, for whatever it was, it went deeper even than that, beyond muscle memory into something almost . . . supernatural.

Bahzell Bahnakson knew his own worth with a blade, exactly as he'd advised Kenhodan to learn that first night in the Iron Axe. Yet as he finished cleaning his sword, he realized that even he—champion of Tomanāk and victor in twice a hundred fights though he might be—could never have equaled what he and Walsharno had just seen Kenhodan accomplish.

<*I could wish that this was a moment when He saw fit to give us a little additional information,*> the courser said. <*I know He doesn't lead His champions around by the hand, but I wouldn't object a bit if He could at least drop a hint or two.*>

"Aye?" Bahzell smiled briefly, ears half-flattened, and sheathed his sword. "I'd not take a bit of a hint amiss my own self. Still and all, it's in my mind as how himself's already told us what it is we're truly after needing to know."

<*I don't disagree, Brother. But that doesn't mean I can't wish for more, now does it?*>

Bahzell snorted in agreement and walked forward slowly to kneel beside Kenhodan and stare at the wizard. Walsharno followed him, standing at his back, and Wencit looked up.

"Wencit."

Bahzell's voice was as implacable as the wild wizard had ever heard it, and he recognized the storm of questions wrapped up in his name.

"That . . . wasn't Kenhodan," he said finally, carefully.

"What?" Bahzell sat back on his heels, staring at him, ears flattened.

"It was a shadow of his past, Bahzell." Wencit had placed one of the brigands' packs under Kenhodan's head. Now he smoothed hair from the younger man's forehead, his touch gentle as a lover's, and looked down at him. "He chose his name to mock his ignorance, but what he was remains, fighting to get out. It never will—not entirely—but...parts will still break through. That's what happened this time."

"But what—?" Bahzell began, then stopped as Wencit's witchfire eyes rose like leveled arbalests.

"Shall I tell you that and not him?" the wizard asked sternly, and Bahzell shook his head quickly.

"No," he said. "But is it all right he'll be, Wencit?"

"'All right'?" Wencit shook his head, his mouth bitter. "For as long as I can remember, people have asked me if someone or something was 'all right'! Not everyone can be whatever that's supposed to mean, Bahzell!" The hradani recoiled from the savage despair in Wencit's voice. "Some people aren't given the opportunity to ever be 'all right' again. They don't have that option, that blessing. All they can be is who—and what—they have to be, usually for others, and all too often those others never even guess what they've given—what they've *lost*—for them. I would destroy worlds for Kenhodan, Bahzell. I'd heap the bodies of his enemies from here to *Kontovar* and back to restore what he's lost, and I can't! Only one person in all the world may ever be able to help him rebuild from the ruins, make him whole once more, and even then, the man he becomes will never be the man he was. And I know that, Bahzell. I *know* that, and I can't share it with him, and what does that make me?"

Bahzell gazed into the face of Wencit of Rūm's anguish, then reached out across Kenhodan, resting one hand on each of the wizard's shoulders.

"It's hearing you I am." His deep voice was deeper even than usual, his eyes dark. "But I'll ask you now to be telling me if there's aught as Walsharno and I can be doing. We'll not have him take further hurt from this if there's anything at all, at all, as we might do to prevent it."

"There isn't," Wencit said softly. "He won't even remember it. He wasn't here."

"What?"

"Shadows of the past, Bahzell," the wizard murmured, then shook his head slowly. "Pay me no heed; he'll recover."

He stroked the red hair once more, and then rose. His movement was brisk, focused, deliberately restored to purpose.

"Enough! We won't mend matters standing around till he wakes up. We have decisions to make. Like—" he turned to the mules "—what to do with this."

"Aye." Bahzell accepted the subject change as best he could and began opening packs, though his eyes returned often to his friend.

"It's in my mind we've a problem," he said presently. "There's after being a fortune here, and no mistake."

"Indeed." The wizard was inspecting another pack. "Gold, silver, spices, silk—and something more. A scroll of the Dorfai of Saramantha's verse in his own hand, Bahzell."

"Tomanāk!" Bahzell shook his head. "Brandark would be after killing for such as that! I've no least idea at all, at all, what to be doing about it."

"Pardon me, but aren't you the champion of the God of Justice around here?" Wencit asked quizzically.

"Aye, so I am. And would you be so very kind as to be telling me just how it is Walsharno and I can be dealing with such as this in the middle of Kolvania?"

"You could always claim it by right of conquest," Wencit suggested with a smile. "I seem to recall that Tomanāk doesn't exactly frown on the spoils of combat honestly gained from thieves and murderers."

"That's as may be, but we've no mind as to be coming all over greedy for such as this." Bahzell gestured at the heap of pack frames. "I'm thinking as Tomanāk wouldn't be so very happy if we were after doing anything of the sort." He shook his head. "No, we'd best be returning it somehow."

"No rest for the wizard, I see," Wencit sighed. "I'll see to it."

"How?"

"With a word of returning, if you must know. It's a simple spell, but it'll take them to their proper owners. Still, I'd best give each of them an avoidance spell, too, so no one will notice them until they get home."

"Well..." Bahzell said, then shrugged. "As to that, you're the one's after being the wizard around here."

"You've noticed," Wencit said tartly. "And now, if you don't mind?"

He made shooing motions, and Bahzell backed away with a wry grin, then turned to examine the fallen, though he was certain there were no survivors. While he busied himself, Wencit found his own relief from concern over Kenhodan by considering how best to phrase his spells. Wand magic was always literal, so it was best to think these things through carefully....

CHAPTER TWENTY-TWO

Music by Night

Kenhodan awoke.

The western sky showed just a trace of crimson, and clouds hung in the south in black waves. He lay still, considering the night, making no effort to move.

He was alive, so he knew they'd won. He had vague memories of combat, and his right hand tingled, yet he could form no clear picture of the fight. Some further inner realignment had occurred, but he felt strangely incurious about it. He filled his lungs with the sweet smell of grass and the tang of wood smoke and gazed at the gathering cloud mountains, and all he truly felt was washed out and clean.

Twin pools of light flickered beside him, and he smiled up at them.

"Good evening, Wencit."

"Good evening." The wizard's calm voice was like an echo of the wind as he blended from the darkness and sat on the grass beside him. "How do you feel?"

"Alive. Peaceful." Kenhodan drew another deep

breath and watched the first stars peek out in the
north like scattered gems.

"A beautiful feeling, peace," Wencit said softly.
"Some people are born to it; others aren't. Yet the
one constant I've observed is that those who experience it least value it most."

"You're waxing philosophical." Kenhodan pillowed
his head on his arms. "That's a bad sign. Something
unpleasant always happens when you start philoso-
phizing, Wencit."

"Not always. At least, what happens isn't always
unpleasant."

"No?" Kenhodan's smiled gleamed in the dimness.
"Well, let it go." He drew another breath. "Where
are we, anyway?"

"A few miles south of the last place you remember, near the Bellwater. It's just over there." Wencit
pointed south.

"Was anyone hurt?"

"No—thanks in no small part to Bostik's mail. Our
border warden got a scratch, and Bahzell got a few
cuts that are scratches on him, though they wouldn't
be on me. Other than that, they're fine, and neither
of the coursers—or Glamhandro—got even that."

"Good."

"And you, Kenhodan?"

"Good, Wencit. I feel good." He stared up at the
fragile stars, waiting to feel bitter, but somehow he
didn't. "What does that make me?"

"Yourself," Wencit said softly. "Only yourself."

"Myself? Wencit, will I always be nothing more than
an empty sack around what used to be a memory?"
The words were bitter, but the tone wasn't.

"Not if you live," the wizard said compassionately. "But for now, at least, try to be content. You've lost your past, but you're still you. There's something almost pure about that simplicity, Kenhodan. Treasure it while you can."

"I shed blood like a duck sheds water, Wencit. What's 'pure' about that?"

"Self-pity's the last thing you can afford," Wencit replied a bit more sternly. "You're a superb warrior. Is that reason for shame?"

"To reek of spilled blood?" Kenhodan's voice was still peaceful, yet he sounded unendurably weary. "Yes, it is."

"Really? Would you refuse to kill if that allowed evil to triumph?"

"That's an unfair question, Wencit."

"How? Whose blood can you remember having shed without cause?"

"All right," Kenhodan said finally. "Point taken. But it isn't easy."

"I know—better even than you think. But sometimes, killing is the only way. Sometimes the future can be built only upon death—or by those willing to *dispense* death, at any rate." The wizard's voice softened. "It's never pleasant to learn that lesson, my friend."

"But can anyone really build anything good on death?" Kenhodan asked meditatively. It wasn't arguing. It was more like picking up the thread of a conversation he couldn't remember, yet knew had been interrupted.

"That depends on who you kill . . . and why." Wencit drew a deep breath. "I won't say the end justifies the means, but sometimes someone has no choice but to choose who will die. Possibly which of many will die. And how do you choose them?" He paused, lowered lids turning his wildfire eyes into glowing slits, then went on speaking, slowly. "I have more blood on my hands than any other living man—probably more than any single man who's *ever* lived . . . or will. Does that make *me* evil? Would it have been less evil to let the Dark Lords swallow Norfressa as well as Kontovar? Let them enslave and torture and murder *here* as they already had in Kontovar? I am what I am, and I do what I must, and in the dark of the night . . . in the night I tell myself I've helped preserve a little of freedom and hope. Of love. And that's almost enough, my friend. Almost."

The wizard fell silent for a long, still moment, then shook himself and opened his eyes wider, their glowing circles brightening as he gazed back down at Kenhodan.

"Perhaps my case is a poor example. Someday you may think it's the worst measuring stick of all, and who should blame you? But be as compassionate with yourself as you are with others, Kenhodan. The gods know it's not easy to accept your own faults. Too many times it reeks of sophistry or self-justification, but it's also the only path to sanity."

Kenhodan closed his eyes to savor Wencit's words. Not many could echo the wizard's calm assertion of self—but did he need a memory to try? Perhaps he hadn't been as bad a fellow as he feared. But it hardly mattered, even if he had, for Wencit was right: his life was his. He could kill or not kill, as he chose, and as long as he was guided by honor, he need not feel ashamed.

His teeth flashed in the light, and he thumped Wencit's arm gently.

"You make a good case for the defense," he said softly. "Thank you."

◆　　◆　　◆

Bahzell and Chernion made no comment when Kenhodan and Wencit rejoined them by the fire. Bahzell knew what had happened (or thought he did, which was almost as good). Chernion didn't, but unlike the hradani she meant to find out. She'd recovered from her shock sufficiently to wonder just how important whatever had happened was to the entire puzzle of Kenhodan, and she intended to explore it thoroughly. But carefully! She had no wish to reawaken the killer within him and turn it against herself.

Bahzell handed him a plate of broiled rabbit and he took it with a smile, then settled on a convenient rock and dug in ravenously. The hradani watched him eat, and as he did, he recognized the curious aura of peace which possessed him. The senses of a champion of Tomanāk were too acute to be fooled by surface appearances, and Bahzell felt a vast sense of relief as he recognized the change. The air of tortured memory which had been a part of Kenhodan for too long had all but vanished, as if the process begun in harp music in a forest had been consummated in blood by a river. Bahzell wasn't certain what had replaced it—not yet— but whatever it was lacked the jagged fracture lines and internal, bleeding hurt of the man he'd first met, and he was happy to see it. On the other hand, it left him a little awkward, as if they were meeting for the first time. Kenhodan was the same, spoke the same way, sounded the same . . . yet he was different as well.

Wencit smiled to himself as he noticed the peculiar hesitation—almost a diffidence, if that word hadn't been so utterly foreign to Bahzell Bahnakson—which had afflicted the hradani. If Bahzell had trouble adjusting to *this* change, the experience would stand him in good stead later.

Conversation drifted as the moon climbed slowly, but Wencit said little. He watched the heavens thoughtfully, and the others respected his silence, though Bahzell eyed him occasionally. There seemed little point in sitting here, but Wencit always had his reasons. So what was tonight's?

The wizard finally surprised one of Bahzell's measuring looks and smiled.

"Are you ready to take me to task over the crossing yet, Bahzell?"

"In a manner of speaking. It's a mite puzzled I am, seeing as how we were after risking our necks to reach here by moonrise—aye, and hauling Kenhodan like a sack of meal for the last league or so—if all you've in mind after we've done it is for us to be sitting on our backsides while you watch it."

"You always think in such straight lines," Wencit murmured.

"Aye, so Leeana's said a time or three. It's a little way I have about me. The moon, Wencit?"

"Now, Bahzell! You know wizards are required to study the heavens."

"Hah!" Bahzell sniffed the cool air and cast his eyes over the star-flecked sky. More clouds had massed silently in the south, blotting out half the heavens while moonglow cast silver highlights over them, and the ebon and argent mountain ranges continued to expand. "It's after being a pleasant enough evening, but I'm thinking you've an eye for more than just the moon tonight."

"Why, that's because I do," Wencit agreed calmly, and chuckled as Bahzell glared at him. For all his ancient power, Wencit had never lost a taste for showmanship, and his sense of humor could be...odd. Bahzell sometimes felt like a hard-pressed father who could hold his patience only by reminding himself his wayward son knew no better.

"You're after being the oldest ten-year-old I know," he sighed.

"So I am, old friend." Wencit touched his shoulder and pointed to the moon. "But here's your answer. Hold tight to your courage and trust me."

Bahzell blinked in surprise at the words, then craned his neck to peer at the silver disk. A tiny shape etched itself black against it, growing as he watched. Wings. Two—no, *four* wings, by the Mace! Wencit rose beside him, shading his eyes with a hand as he gazed upward, and his movement caught the others' attention, drawing their eyes, too, to the silent moon.

The shape was smaller than a mustard seed with distance, but it grew, and a glimmer and glow seemed to strike outward from it. Recognition flared suddenly in Bahzell, and the hradani lurched to his feet, reaching automatically for the sword propped upright against a boulder beside him.

Wencit raised both hands. Night breeze whispered as he thrust them at the moon, and a glare of blue light burst upward—a shaft of radiance that pierced the night like a glittering needle. Its backwash illuminated him, etching the hollows of his face with shadow. His witchfire eyes glowed in their craggy sockets like balefires, and his voice rose like thunder.

"Ahm laurick meosho, Torfrio! Ahm laurick!"

His companions stared at him, stunned by his sudden display of power after so many days and weeks of stealth, and the light became a silver streamer. Then it changed yet again, glittering and flowing with all the brilliance of the wild magic itself, shaming the moon as it flared upward to strike the tiny shape. More prominences of wildfire danced before Wencit's eyes, and Chernion looked away uneasily. Even Bahzell stepped back from the power roaring suddenly about the old wizard, and only Kenhodan—to his own surprise—accepted the display without question or qualm.

The flying shape changed course. It arrowed towards them, riding the cable of wild magic like a plumb line, growing until it blotted away first the stars and then the moon, and *still* it grew, dropping upon them like the night come to life.

"Dragon!" Chernion screamed in recognition—and dragon it was, a tremendous beast, dwarfing the one they'd fought. Moonlight flashed from mailed scales in showers of red, gold, and green sparks, as if the creature were wrought of rubies, topaz, and emeralds. The fire from Wencit's hands impacted on its mighty chest in a wash of glitter that purpled the onlookers' sight, and the earth trembled as the leviathan landed.

Not two wings, but four, arched from the razor spine. From scimitar tail to snout was over a hundred yards. Wicked horns jutted, needle-tipped and fifteen feet long. Vapor plumed from the fanged jaws of a multi-ton head, and moonlight and wild magic flashed on ivory teeth taller than Bahzell. It had landed lightly, but the shock of impact shuddered in their bones, and the horses—but for Glamhandro and the coursers—screamed in terror. They tore at their pickets, and their fear woke Bahzell into action. He flung himself among them to calm them, and Walsharno joined him, fastening his own will upon Chernion's mare and the pack beasts.

Kenhodan gaped at the dragon. So vast a creature could never be born of nature! Wencit's description of dragon kind had to be correct. They *must* be the very embodiments of the wild magic itself.

Green dragon eyes flared like bonfires and a chiaroscuro brilliance of shifting color danced in their depths like tongues of flame. It crouched motionless, forty feet away, and its bulk dwarfed the world.

Wencit stepped into the strange smell of the dragon— the smell of burning wood and strange spices, of hot iron and the molten-rock smell of lava. Vapor from its jaws lifted into the cool air, silvered by the moon, and the wizard paused between its towering, taloned forefeet under the shadow of its vast head.

"Ahm laurick, Arcoborus." The voice rumbled like a hurricane, its rolling thunder stunning them deeper into silence. More vapor plumed as the dragon spoke, and it angled its head to peer one-eyed at Wencit, like a bird at a tasty beetle.

"Torfrio." Wencit's voice was tiny in reply. "You come in a good hour."

"The timestorm blows." The dragon's vast voice gusted about them.

"We need your aid, Torfrio."

"I am here. Symmetry demands answer, and so I answer."

"May I introduce my companions?"

"No need. I see them in the timestorm," the dragon rumbled with a huge chuckle. "I know them. Many threads gather here, and my people's fate is in them. Let the young killer meet me."

Kenhodan quivered inwardly, but there was no evading it. He knew who the dragon meant, though not *how* he knew, and he stepped up beside Wencit. The dragon's smell was a hurricane in his nostrils and the green eye hovered over him, slitted like a cat's and deep as the abyss of time itself. The vapor breath stung his eyes and skin.

"I greet you, Young Killer. I am called Torfrio—Son of Fire in the tongue of wizard folk. The timestorm tells me you go to save my people . . . or to slay them."

"I—" Kenhodan groped for words. The dragon's brilliance dazzled him, and he felt like a grub beneath its head. He gripped his emotions and sought the proper words. "I greet you in return, Torfrio."

His voice came out crisp and clear, without a quaver, untouched by uncertainty, and surprise flickered through him as he realized he didn't *feel* uncertain. Frightened, perhaps, but with the clear, unshakable sense that this was the one place in all the world where he *needed* to be at this instant. He looked up into that enormous eye, feeling the century upon century of experience behind it, knowing that in some obscure way he stood before a bar of justice without the knowledge he needed to defend his past or chart his future, and there was no hesitation in him.

"It is well," the dragon thunder muttered. "You have the courage of your past and future, Young Killer. What service shall I render you?"

"Wencit's the one who knows that answer, Torfrio."

"In the timestorm, it is the same," Torfrio said. "Tell me your need."

"I—" Kenhodan hesitated, touched by a different sort of uncertainty. How could he...?

"You see the timestorm, Son of Fire," he heard himself say then. "You know our need."

"I do. But what do you give in return, Young Killer?"

"State your terms, Son of Fire," Kenhodan said levelly. "If I don't agree, I'll tell you."

"A dragon's answer!" Torfrio trumpeted in approval. "Very well! Play for me when the timestorm wills and play for me tonight."

Kenhodan glanced at Wencit in puzzlement, but the wizard only looked back levelly. Clearly, this conversation—this bargain—was his to make and his alone.

"Two tunes, Son of Fire?"

"Two. One tonight, and one when the timestorm wills."

"When will that be?"

"You know the tune; the timestorm knows the time," the dragon voice muttered in thunder. "Play, Young Killer. Play! I must taste the timestorm."

Kenhodan reached for his harp case like a man compelled. His hands opened the fastenings with a nimbleness which belonged to another and drew out the harp as if they knew a secret his mind had yet to grasp. Then he lowered himself to the ground, seated himself on sweet-scented grass within the corona of wild magic radiating from Torfrio, and leaned back against a pillar of dragon claw. He raised the harp, and his fingers kissed the strings.

Power hammered in his blood, pulsing with conflicting emotions as he waited for the music he was somehow destined to play this night. And then his fingers moved, and music spurted into the night—a wild melody...but one he'd heard before. Fierce and proud it was, and it reached deep into its listeners. The dragon's head flung upward, snapping into the heavens, eyes slitted in concentration. Bahzell, Chernion, even Kenhodan himself—one by one they fell into the tiderace of notes, vanished into the music. Only Wencit stood as if unaffected, yet tears slid down his cheeks, burning with wild magic.

The sorcery of his own harping snatched Kenhodan into another place and time. He whirled through unimaginable distances, and then he saw what he'd seen once before, but this time in far more detail. He saw a rich land in the pride of its power...and he saw dark powers, fed on blood and smoke. He saw them raise armies of demons and ogres, of trolls and ghouls, of demons, of Krashnark's devils and Krahana's undead. And he saw twisted parodies of every Race of Man— human and hradani, dwarf and elf—marching to the orders of that darkness, flocking to its banners, yielding to its will. All too many gave themselves willingly to the Dark, but willing or no, the end was the same for all.

Sorcerers led them, raining death on any who opposed them, and flame towered into night skies. Swords drank the blood of man and woman, mother and child, aged and young. Grim ruin enveloped half a continent before its first flooding onrush was checked, and those who died fighting were the fortunate ones, for they were spared the ghastly altars and sacrificial knives.

But the desecration wasn't unchallenged. The Light gathered itself against the stunning onslaught, and armies marched against the tsunami of destruction. Scarlet standards led them, emblazoned with the golden gryphon and crown, and they met the armies of darkness headlong in battles that watered the soil with the blood of hero and murderer alike.

Again and again the crowned gryphon triumphed, but its armies couldn't be everywhere, and with every victory, those armies grew steadily smaller while the power of the Dark swelled with every murder, every atrocity. Desperation beat in Kenhodan's harping as the defenders died and the attackers' strength grew ever greater. The balance tipped further and further against the Light, and if victory had ever been within the gryphon's grasp, it was no longer. Ship after ship fled the embattled land, fleeing ever northward, packed with refugees and the only hope of whatever future might yet be. The gryphon spread its wings, no longer seeking victory or even survival, spending itself, pouring out its life's blood to cover that retreat, protect that seed corn of all it had failed to save in Kontovar. One by one the ports fell and fire and sorcery consumed or enslaved the life remaining in the ruins, yet *still* the gryphon banners—tattered, now, and stained with smoke—fluttered over the ever dwindling armies, and Kenhodan wept as a continent slid unstoppably into darkness in the whirling storm of his harp's notes.

And then the gryphon stood at bay above an army trapped, unable to reach the sea which had been its final destination. Waves of enemies crushed closer, hemming the final warriors in a net of bloody steel.

Desperate sorties struck the encircling ranks, only to fall back or die. Haggard cavalry hewed a path halfway through the attackers, but the horses were hamstrung, the riders dragged down. Less than one in ten of the mounted knights lived to retreat.

Back and back the defenders fell, carpeting the grass and bloody mud with their foes. But the commanders of their foes cared nothing for their own troops' lives. Those lives meant nothing beside their hatred for all the defenders stood for, and every life they spent to crush their enemies only fed the power of the Dark they served. Back and back they drove the gryphon's final warriors, until a tiny knot of warriors stood at bay atop a hill, a desperate ring about a tall man whose sword flashed in the darkness of sorcery. That sword grew to fill Kenhodan's vision, humming and snarling, shining with the fury of the sun, cold as the stars while blood hissed and steamed from its trenchant edge. The blade flamed unquenchable, unsullied by the gore it shed, dragging his heart into his throat and wracking him with sobs.

The music was a dirge as darkness swallowed the hill, overwhelming the gryphon banners, crushing in death what could never be beaten into submission. And as the harp wept, Kenhodan saw the sea-girt island once more as the cold glory of destruction spiraled up from its walls and towers over a sea like a glittering mirror. But this time...this time he saw the fire *strike*.

The brilliance burst, the life stuff of the last white wizards of Kontovar roaring into the heavens in a million flaming pinnacles. They seared the clouds aside and hurled themselves upon the conquered continent, and where they touched was destruction. Soil and stone flared like tinder, ran like wax, and billows of flaming smoke veiled unguessable devastation. Cities burned like pitch, guttering into extinction. Fortresses hissed briefly, like coal newly dropped into a furnace, then exploded into steam and rubble. Armies of slaves screamed in one horrible voice, the hideous death cry of an entire continent as they were consumed, but the destruction was too vast, too terrifying, to be grasped.

Kenhodan cowered before it as the music thundered to its crescendo, crashing over all the world in a hurricane of loss, of destruction, of grief and memory and unendurable loss...and then, mercifully, between one note and the next, it ended.

Silence fell, and Kenhodan shuddered, sucking in air as he escaped the ancient terror. Sweat soaked him, and his muscles were water.

He opened his eyes slowly. The border warden lay on her face, her hands clasped over the back of her head in fragile defense, her shoulders heaving. Bahzell still stood, but only his locked thews kept him on his feet. His eyes were pits of horror, staring at nothing, while his ears pressed close to his skull. Somehow he'd drawn his sword despite the music's spell, but the blade trembled in his hand and firelight shook from the steel in waves. The coursers stood like stone, magnificent equestrian sculptures, carved from eternity's heart by harp song. Even Wencit knelt, beaten to his knees by the harp, and his shoulders shuddered while tears covered his cheeks with flame.

Kenhodan shook his head and tried to rise...and his muscles obeyed him as if nothing had happened. He felt imprisoned in his own body, but that body moved easily, with all its wonted suppleness. He straightened and stood, gazing up the mailed cliff of the dragon's throat, watching the vapor from its jaws streak the moon, and Torfrio's great eyes were half-slitted, jagged green fire spurting from under heavy lids.

Then the head lowered slowly. The sinuous neck curved, bending itself to half encircle him where he stood and press the mighty chin to the ground. The green eyes were no more than a yard above Kenhodan's head, and they opened slowly to show him the incredible depths of those ancient pupils.

"I taste the timestorm," the dragon rumbled slowly. "Truth rides the years, Young Killer."

"You know me," Kenhodan said, and his voice was firm and measured in the shocked hollow of the night. "Do you know the name of that tune, as well?"

"Aye, Young Killer. I know 'The Fall of Hacromanthi.'"

"You know it, Son of Fire—but what does it mean to you?"

"Mean, Young Killer?" The green eyes flared like bonfires. "How strange that you should ask me that! But the timestorm's moment is not now. Not yet!"

Kenhodan swallowed the refusal. He longed to ask more questions, but he dared not. Mystery and danger surrounded him; if he'd ever doubted, he no longer could. Not after his second taste of that devastating music. If he could wreak that with nothing but a harp, what else could he do? What other secrets lay hidden within him, waiting to wake too soon at a single unwise answer? He had only Wencit to guide him, and if the wizard couldn't answer his questions, Kenhodan dared not risk upsetting his plans by asking them of others. For the first time he accepted that fully... and, to his own surprise, without bitterness.

Silence lingered for what seemed a small eternity before Torfrio, finally, broke it once more.

"For what you have done, will do, and may do, Young Killer," the dragon rumbled in strangely formal thunder, "you have my service. I will bear you over Bellwater."

CHAPTER TWENTY-THREE

Wizards' Plans

It was not, Kenhodan discovered—not entirely to his surprise—quite that simple. Torfrio could have carried them in his talons, but not without injuring them severely (assuming the horses didn't simply die of fright), which made *that* approach somewhat short of desirable. And, unfortunately, they had neither the time, the tools, nor the material to build the sort of platforms the black wizards' enslaved dragons had carried in Kontovar. It was left for Torfrio to suggest the means, though he did so with manifest distaste.

"You must ride on my back, Young Killer—you and your friends and beasts. I cannot fly with you to block my wings, so I swim."

"But—"

"My scales are thick; my back is broad. I cannot be hurt by such as you upon me, and you cannot fall. This is the only way."

"I . . . see."

Kenhodan turned helplessly to Wencit, but the

wizard only smiled and nodded in agreement. He seemed to have recovered from the harping, although Bahzell was still shaken and as for the border warden... Kenhodan feared her reason had broken. She showed no more volition than a newborn child, allowing them to push or lead her from place to place but not moving at all of her own will. Wencit saw the guilt shadows in Kenhodan's face and drew him quietly aside.

"Don't worry about the Borderer, Kenhodan. She'll recover."

"But why was she so much more affected? Why isn't she recovering *now*?"

"Perhaps because she had less warning," Wencit suggested. "Unlike Bahzell or me, she'd never heard 'The Fall of Hacromanthi' before, you know. Or perhaps she has less protection from her dead. But she *will* recover, though it may take a few hours yet."

"If you're sure," Kenhodan said doubtfully. "But about this dragon ride..."

"It should work. Torfrio's back is longer and broader than *Wave Mistress*, after all. And he *can* swim, however much he may hate the very thought."

"Why should he hate it?"

"Red dragons are fire wyrms, the mightiest of all the dragons, but they all hate water." Wencit chuckled. "Enough of it will quench even the dragon princes' fire. Of course, that would take a *lot* of water, but the differences between their nature and sphere and that of water go straight to the bone, so Torfrio's making a great sacrifice to aid us."

"But will the horses stand for it?"

"The coursers understand our need as well as you or I do, and Glamhandro's willing enough. After I speak to the others, they won't even know what's happening. And," the wizard went on more briskly, "we ought to do this quickly. It'll be dawn soon, and it would be far better for Torfrio to be far away before anyone sees him and guesses where we crossed."

"That makes sense," Kenhodan said, and turned decisively to Bahzell.

Wencit watched him with a melancholy inner amusement. Kenhodan had somehow assumed command—a not inconsiderable achievement, especially given Bahzell's decades of experience and accomplishments. Yet the change was also inevitable, for the hidden part of him was stirring, driving him beyond the reckoning of any but Wencit himself.

Bahzell Bahnakson's was a strong, tough personality, one fit to stand unbowed in the face of demons, devils, and the Dark Gods themselves, yet he, too, recognized Kenhodan's new strength. There was no change in the hradani's speech or manner, but now it was Kenhodan who stirred their entire party back into motion, oversaw the reloading of their pack animals, and decided how to deal with Chernion . . . and did it all so naturally he wasn't even aware he was giving *directions* to a champion of Tomanāk—*two* champions of Tomanāk, counting Walsharno—and the last white wizard in all the world.

Bahzell looked up as he resaddled one of the pack horses at Kenhodan's instructions and met Wencit's smile with a grin of his own. He was a warrior, a realist, and a champion of Tomanāk. No champion of the war god was a shy and retiring type, and Bahzell was even less shy *or* retiring than the majority of Tomanāk's Swords. But for all his own accomplishments, all the hard-focused, steely purpose of his personality, there was very little arrogance in Bahzell Bahnakson. Where he was equipped to lead, he would lead; where it seemed best to follow, he would follow, with no lessening of his own confidence, his own tenacious fidelity to the goals and obligations which were his. And for the moment, however it had happened, Kenhodan was the person best suited to command.

The wizard prepared the packhorses and Chernion's mare for the crossing with care, laying his hands on their ears and muzzles one by one. His eyes glittered as he whispered to them, and their fear sweat dried and they became as biddable as Chernion.

With the horses quieted and their equipment packed, Bahzell tightened the mare's saddle and lifted the assassin into it. Chernion made no resistance as he picked her up as lightly as a child, and she sat her saddle placidly, but she made no effort to take the reins.

Torfrio lumbered down to the river, and they followed, staying well clear of the sworded tail. The grounded dragon seemed clumsy, but that appearance didn't deceive Kenhodan. He remembered the black dragon's deadly speed too clearly for that.

Torfrio's head swayed as he neared the water. His eyes glittered more brightly than ever, and the breath in his nostrils whistled like a windstorm as he steeled himself and dipped one forefoot into the cold river.

Steam billowed with the hiss of a Dwarvenhame blast furnace, but Torfrio moved steadily onward until water lapped his huge shoulders. White clouds of vapor pearled under the dying moon, shot through with the polychrome glitter of his scales, and he swung his head and peered back with impatient, lambent eyes.

His mighty tail curled into a ramp, and the travelers crossed it to his back.

The tough scales were unyielding even to the coursers' hooves, and the travelers mounted to save space, for the flat area of the massive back was limited, despite the dragon's enormous size, by bulging wing muscles and a sharply serrated spine. Kenhodan and Glamhandro rode at the base of the dragon's neck with the others strung out behind as Torfrio slid forward. His head arched high and his neck cut the water like a ship's prow while waves lapped his sides, their crests erupting into steam at the touch, although none reached the travelers.

Kenhodan smiled quietly as he listened to the whuffling sounds of Torfrio's breath and the deep, grumbling thunder of what were almost certainly muttered—by dragon standards, at least—maledictions upon all water, but it seemed impolitic to comment on them.

The Bellwater was over a mile wide in the driest months, and far wider now. Water gurgled as Torfrio forged towards the farther bank, but it was a lengthy business. Steam cloaked them throughout the crossing, and that puzzled Kenhodan, for Torfrio's scales weren't especially hot. Warm, yes, but not hot. Was the antipathy between his innermost nature and the water even deeper than Wencit had implied?

When they finally reached the farther bank, Torfrio could hardly restrain himself long enough for them to disembark. As soon as the last hoof touched land the dragon bustled out of the water with a massive tail flick that sent a wave over a startled Bahzell in a moon-gilded glitter, and Kenhodan swallowed a laugh as Torfrio shook himself like an angry cat. Not till he'd shed the last, distasteful drop did the dragon turn to Kenhodan again.

"Well, Young Killer. You are across . . . and dry."

Humor might—or might not—have accounted for the emphasis on *to* the final two words, Kenhodan thought.

"We thank you, Son of Fire."

"Thank me not. The bargain is fair, and fairly struck. Until our paths meet in the timestorm, may your sword shine in victory. Farewell!"

The last word vanished in a sudden blast of wind as the dragon launched into the night sky. Mighty wings shivered the river, driving its cool breath into their faces like a hurricane edged with hot spice. Kenhodan staggered, driven backward three paces by the battering backdraft of those stupendous pinions, and Torfrio arrowed upward into the half-disc of the setting moon with preposterous speed. He dwindled with that same startling rapidity, and Kenhodan turned to Wencit.

"What next?" he asked dryly in the suddenly still and quiet night.

"I suggest a secluded campsite," Wencit replied with a smile. "We can all use a little rest after this . . . strenuous evening."

"Hear, hear," Bahzell Bahnakson murmured quietly.

◆　◆　◆

Wulfra of Torfo sat in her rock garden and regarded the morning with sour displeasure. She was surrounded by perfect statues of men and women, each with an expression of horror and shock, and she smiled unpleasantly as she reached out to the delicately carved lady in waiting standing beside her exquisitely carved wooden bench with a hopeless face. A fierce blue flame danced from the sorceress' fingertip to play along a stone arm, and her smile became brighter as a shrill scream filled her mind.

She let the flame burn for long minutes, savoring the exquisite shrieks only she could hear, then closed her hand to quench it. Silent, broken sobs died slowly, slowly, and Wulfra returned her mind to her problems.

Curse the old man! Where *was* he?

She slid her hands slowly over the polished bench's smooth grain while she pondered. She knew no more about Wencit's location now than she had a week ago, and her patron had gone completely silent. He hadn't contacted her in days. For that matter, he'd ignored her own diffident effort to contact *him*, and that silence was even more frightening than his icy rage had been. She could do nothing more without the aid he might have lent, but no aid was forthcoming, and the grim truth had become increasingly clear in the days of his silence. Her death would serve his ends as well as her victory, yet if she meant to survive, she must somehow convince him to give her more power. . . .

Her thoughts were interrupted by a hesitantly cleared throat, and she looked up with suddenly fiery eyes. Her inner anxiety sharpened her anger at the violation of her command that she not be disturbed, and her guard captain flinched as those blazing eyes met his.

"Well, Tenart?" Her voice was soft. "I trust you have a reason?"

"I beg your pardon, Baroness," Tenart said quickly, "but—"

"That had better be an *excellent* 'but,'" Wulfra purred, "or you may spend the next few years here in my garden."

"Please, Milady! I . . . It . . . A matter of urgency, Milady! Very great urgency!"

Sweat greased Tenart's brow. There were compensations for the hearty soul who captained Wulfra's guard, but moments like this weren't among them. He shivered and kept his eyes off the lifelike, suffering statues.

"Such as?" Wulfra's voice was velvet-covered ice.

"The watchers have sent word, Milady!"

"The watchers?"

Wulfra's brows rose, and Tenart allowed himself a tentative breath of relief as her forehead furrowed in thought. The watchers were a legacy from her father, a canny man who'd created a secret network of heliograph-armed observers throughout his own lands . . . and well out into those of his neighbors. The late baron had used them sparingly, in order to keep their existence secret, but their warnings had kept him better informed than most noblemen in Angthyr.

Wulfra had retained the system for several reasons. Its existence, hinted in the right quarters, covered much of her arcane spying, since she could attribute so much of her near omniscience to it. And while she could see farther and more clearly than they, she could look in only one direction at a time. Her watchers sometimes snared tidbits she might have missed.

"Well, Tenart? What was this important message?"

"They reported a dragon, Milady—a red dragon. It left the Scarthū wards last night and returned this morning."

"And you interrupted me to tell me *that?* You'll make a nice birdbath, Tenart."

"No, Milady! Please! There was more!"

"Then tell me before I put a sundial into your navel!"

"Yes, Milady! One of the watchers saw a strange light to the north—how far he couldn't say—but the dragon flew in that direction before the light was seen and came from the same direction this morning."

"Ah?"

Wulfra leaned back in thought, and Tenart resumed breathing.

Strange lights, was it? Wulfra tapped her teeth with an exquisitely manicured fingernail while she thought. Now what could that be? She'd tampered with dragon kind—most definitely, she'd tampered. All the wyrms would be her enemies now, but they couldn't cross the dragon ward to work her harm. Or not directly, at least; it was entirely possible that one of the great wyrms might still find a way of striking at her *in*directly. And the message said the dragon had headed for the light before it was seen, so it was unlikely Wencit had summoned it across the ward. Anyway, her mind was so attuned to the wild wizard that she could hardly miss so potent a spell as that.

"Red, you say?" she asked thoughtfully.

"So the watchers say, Milady."

"Hmmmm..."

Now which red might it have been? Shicolo and Dormandos were too reclusive, and most of the others were either too young or too old for such shenanigans. Torcrach? Possible...he was a bit old, but they didn't call him Fire Fang for nothing. Or possibly Torfrio? He was the most powerful red these days, but he normally paid scant attention to events beyond the Scarthū. Unless her meddling...?

She shook her head irritably. The reds were danger-ous. Unlike their lesser brethren, they understood the wild magic in their blood. They could even use it to a limited extent, so it was possible a red could block her perceptions. But why? Unless it was because of that damned black!

Then again, what had actually happened was unimportant. She needed a pretext to demand more aid, and the dragon might provide it. She wasn't the cat-eyed wizard's equal, but neither was she a fool. If he needed her alive long enough to lure Wencit into whatever trap he'd set, he might at least give her additional protection against the dragons in the meantime. And spells strong enough for that might prove useful against Wencit, too.

She nodded. She would report what her watchers had seen. If he became nervous enough to aid her, well and good, yet if he refused, she lost nothing.

"You may go, Tenart. This time."

She added the threat almost absently, for her mind was busy and her eyes were dreamy as she pondered her next action.

The guard captain backed away quickly, heaving a great—but very silent—sigh of relief for his escape. The decision to disturb her hadn't come easily. In fact, only the fact that death would have been certain if he'd failed to deliver a message which later turned out to have been important had sent him to her. Now he wiped his clammy forehead and breathed deep. Life had been so much calmer when her father was alive! He considered desertion, but once more put the temptation aside. He knew too much. If he ran and was lucky, he'd end on an assassin's blade. If he was unlucky . . .

He shivered and fled the dreadful garden. Phrobus only knew what deviltry the baroness was embarked upon, and Tenart devoutly hoped the Dark One would keep it to Himself. He was a simple soldier, he was, caught in a wizard's web through no wish of his own and sick of it into the bargain. What he really needed was a stoup of wine, and he hurried off to find it.

Behind him, Wulfra walked slowly to her tower and her waiting gramerhain.

◆   ◆   ◆

Chernion woke with sunlight burning her eyelids and lay motionless, searching her memory and setting her identity in place before she showed any sign of awareness. Then her eyes opened slowly and she stared up into a canopy of lacy leaves. Elderberry and willows stirred in the breeze, throwing wispy shadows over the moss on which she lay, and she blinked and turned her head.

Kenhodan looked down at her, his head upside down from her prone position. Her eyes widened in memory, and she threw off her covering blanket and rolled to her feet with one hand on her dagger. She rose cat-quick and angry, her eyes narrowed, and half an inch of steel scraped from her scabbard.

"Good morning, Elrytha," he said calmly.

"Don't waste your good mornings on me!" she snarled, easing more dagger from the sheath. "I've had a belly full of wizard's tricks!"

"Wizards?" Kenhodan shook his head. "I'm no wizard, Border Warden."

"Faugh! You had me fooled—I'll admit it! But if you're not Carnadosa's own, I'll eat this!"

She whipped the dagger free and faced him across its keen-edged menace.

"That would give you indigestion," he said, sitting back on his heels and apparently completely at ease.

"Not as much of a bellyache as it'll give you if you

press me!" she spat, eyeing him suspiciously. Yet even as she snarled, she realized this smiling man wasn't the Kenhodan she'd thought she was coming to know. The old Kenhodan would have been hurt and apologetic; this man wasn't. Had his diffidence been as much a mask as her own borderer's role?

"Then I certainly won't press you," he said. "I only thought you might be shaken by your experiences. It seemed best to try to explain, if you were."

"I want no explanations!" she flared. "You caught me in a spell, but you won't do it again!"

"A spell?" He plucked a grass stem and chewed it thoughtfully. "I suppose I did," he acknowledged after a moment, "and for that I beg your pardon. But it wasn't intentional. If you'll allow me, I'd like to try to explain what happened."

"Hah!" she snorted, but his posture was eloquently unthreatening, and she let herself relax slightly in response. Her dream's terror was less real in this peaceful sunlight, and her predatory instincts told her one fright wasn't enough reason to throw aside the power she sensed Kenhodan offered.

"What I played," Kenhodan said very carefully, "is a very old piece of music called 'The Fall of Hacromanthi.' I don't remember when I learned it, but it's about the end in Kontovar, and apparently it has some very strange powers of its own. Powers which affect anyone who hears it."

"Sorcery," Chernion spat. "You're a wizard."

"I'm not, and I don't know if it's sorcery or not."

"Men who cast spells are wizards," she said flatly.

"Only if they do it intentionally and knowingly," Kenhodan argued.

"Don't fence with me! Either you cast a spell, or you didn't—and I say you did!"

Kenhodan recognized the justice of her accusation and tugged an earlobe as he sought an equally just defense.

"Let me put it this way. You heard a piece of music I'd really rather not play at all, but it was the one I *had* to play when Torfrio demanded a tune as his price for carrying us over the river. In that sense, I suppose a spell was cast on *me* even more than on you. I'm sorry it was unpleasant for you, but it was unpleasant for me, as well—and almost as much of a surprise *to* me, come to that."

"It was a vile trick," she said levelly.

"It wasn't meant to be," he said softly. "I don't play tricks like that on my friends, Elrytha. The visions that song opens are…horrible." He met her eyes levelly. "They're different for different people, I think. For myself, I see visions of the Fall itself. For Bahzell, it's mostly memories of his own battles—and the gods know *they've* been bad enough! Wencit won't say what he sees, which is his right, and no one will ask what you saw, either. I promise."

He seemed so earnest she had to believe him, although she had no intention of telling him her own visions had relived all of her assassinations. She shuddered inwardly. The last part of her dream, when her victims had risen to pursue her with Ashwan at their head, she would tell *no one*, not even herself.

She glared at him for another tense, endless minute. Then she sighed and re-sheathed the dagger slowly.

"All right," she said finally. "I believe you, and I'll accept your apology. You're a good companion and a better fighter, and I can forgive anything short of attempted rape when that's true. But if you ever—" she held up a forefinger "—and I mean *ever*—do that again, I'll skin you out to cover my saddle! Is that clear?"

"Clear and daunting," he assured her. His lips quivered, and her own humor roused in answer. Her eyes danced as morning sun and birdsong drove away the last of her creeping terror, and he smiled. "And I truly am sorry, Elrytha. I'd never willingly cause you unhappiness."

She stared at him, then looked quickly away. Surely Sharnā wouldn't play that sort of trick on her! She had no use for such emotional claptrap as friendship. Yet his words had somehow pierced her armor of expediency.

She glanced at him from the corner of her eye. Ah, no! Surely not. It was impossible—it couldn't be!—for her to become emotionally involved with a target. The very thought shocked her, and she fought for mental balance as she tried to understand what had happened to her.

No, she realized abruptly. Not to *her*. The change was in Kenhodan; the only change in her was the way she reacted to *his* change. He'd always been a powerful personality, whether he'd realized it himself or not. Now that inner strength was even more focused, with a magnetism that reached even into an assassin's heart, and it was frightening to contemplate such power. But her innate hard headedness couldn't evade the conclusion . . . or the worse one that she *liked* the change.

He rose and bowed ironically as that bittersweet pang of realization stabbed her. He extended an arm

to her, and almost against her will she took it in a
whimsical imitation of a court lady, bestowing a half
curtsy upon him in return. Her eyes laughed suddenly, with a warmth foreign to her, and the two of
them picked their way from her thicketed bower to
find the others.

Neither smelled the pipe smoke drifting from the
nearby willows, so neither glanced in that direction to
see Wencit...or the pain in his eyes as he watched
them go.

◆   ◆   ◆

Cat eyes slitted thoughtfully and their owner whistled
tunelessly while he considered Wulfra's latest plaint.
Strange things were afoot, he conceded; things he hadn't
anticipated and for which his plans hadn't allowed.
That was only to be expected, of course, and trying
to allow for all contingencies led to clumsiness, which
was why he normally allowed a certain... elasticity to
his strategies. Too many loopholes, unfortunately, could
be deadly, and he'd seen through Wulfra's half-truths
to the heart of her report. He understood her motives
and dismissed them, yet what she'd reported might still
be worth his attention.

A dragon had crossed the Dragon Ward. That
was rare and nothing to take lightly, but it wasn't
unheard of, either, and his mind ranged the roster of
red dragons as Wulfra's had. Torcrach or Torfrio, he
decided, and he had no wish to engage that father
and son pair just yet. Dragons had long memories,
and it had perhaps been unwise of the Carnadosans
to compel their service in the war. Still, the Dragon
Ward penned them inside their safe little haven in
the Scarthū Hills, powerless to harm anyone outside

it except in direct and personal self-defense. Best to take a few additional precautions, but as long as the ward stood, the threat was slight, even from Torfrio.

Yet even allowing for that, there really might have been a display of wild magic north of Torfo, and that bothered him, for Wencit was the only wild wizard. It was entirely possible Wulfra's watcher might have misunderstood what he'd seen, but it was just as possible he hadn't. So it could indeed have been Wencit, but why should he risk exposing himself that way? He'd covered himself with a glamour he knew Wulfra couldn't possibly pierce, but he also knew about the existence of the baroness' network of watchers. Why give away his position with a burst of wild magic not even a half-blind soldier without a trace of talent for the art could miss seeing after he'd gone to such lengths to deny her any knowledge of his whereabouts? Yet if it hadn't been Wencit, what *had* it been?

He stopped whistling and turned to a bookshelf, running a fingertip down the tooled spines of books which had survived the Fall itself. Many of them had come from the personal library of the first Lord of Carnadosa himself, for the wards protecting that collection had been strong enough to stand even in the face of the White Council's final, despairing counter stroke. True, some of them were a little singed around the edges, but that hadn't affected their contents, and he perched on the edge of his desk as he found the one he sought and opened it with the sort of reverence it deserved.

Dragons were wild magic, and there was no doubt a red with the proper training and strength could shield himself against almost any wizard's scrying. In fact, he had half a memory...

He flipped through the index to the entry he'd thought he recalled, and his lips curled in amusement as he found it and turned to the proper page. His eyebrows quirked as he scanned the text and confirmed his fragmentary memory. It was even more . . . explicit than he'd remembered, and his smile grew broader as he considered the best way to make use of it. Should he contact Wulfra and read her a brief treatise on the mating habits of dragons? It would certainly be amusing, and it might even explain the display in Kolvania. Even if it didn't, it could be made to, and suggesting that one of the reds had sought a partner from beyond the ward would give him a reason to refuse her any further power.

He resumed his whistling as he mentally composed his little lecture, weighing word choices carefully in search of the ones which would extract the maximum entertainment from the situation.

◆   ◆   ◆

"Why are we heading north?" Chernion asked. Afternoon had stretched its weary arms over them as they rode, and her question broke a comfortable silence.

"I have my reasons, Border Warden," Wencit replied cheerfully.

She waited, but he said no more, and when she eyed him askance he looked back with a sardonic smile. Damn him! She no longer had the patience or desire to play games, for she sensed a crisis approaching behind this false calm, and she was ill prepared to meet it. There were too many ambiguities still, too many hints of events sliding towards cataclysmic confrontation, and her own ambivalence over Kenhodan was more unsettling than she cared to admit even to herself.

"And those reasons are?" she asked sweetly, hiding her fuming self-anger at the way she'd risen to the bait he'd trolled so skillfully past her. And her matching anger at him for giving her no choice.

"First," he said after a moment, "Wulfra has more than arcane watchdogs, and her watchers are certainly straining their eyes for us at this moment. We're no more than twenty leagues from her, and I want to skirt the areas they can see."

"And secondly?" she prompted impatiently, thirty seconds later, when he showed no sign of continuing.

"And secondly will become clear in time...Elrytha."

She heard the bite as he used her assumed name, and it took all of her hard-earned skill to simply nod in acceptance. It was almost in the open between them now, but not quite, and she understood his warning. She had far more to hide than he did, and she must accept his secrets or see her own exposed to Bahzell and Kenhodan...at which point she would cease to be a problem for Wencit of Rūm ever again.

Well, let him look to himself. There was clearly a reason he hadn't unmasked her, and that reason— whatever it was—might prove his undoing rather than hers. Some people kept adders as pets, but the pleasure of owning the snakes made them no less deadly. The thought pleased her, and she smiled brightly at the wizard as she reminded herself her fangs were sharp when the moment came to show them. Let Wencit of Rūm remember that!

◆　　◆　　◆

The cat-eyed wizard watched his crystal with silent admiration despite his amusement. Wulfra lay in a canvas chair atop her keep, naked in the sunlight, and he had to admit she was a fine figure of a woman. What a pity.

His viewpoint darted down to probe the cavern of the sword, and he noted that she'd put still more effort into the trap spells between the maze and the cavern proper. That was good—but the presence of her gramerhain in the sword chamber was bad, especially in light of her sunbathing.

He'd spent years studying Wulfra's habits, learning to get inside her mind and thoughts, and because he had, he knew exactly what she was thinking now. It made sense for her to move her command post closer to the sword, yet her decision to soak up all the sun she could argued that she meant to move in soon and remain there for the duration, and that gave one to think.

She hadn't enjoyed his homily on dragon breeding, though she'd tried to hide her fury. But suppose . . . just suppose she planned to move into the cavern to be certain she and Wencit *did* meet face-to-face. Given the balance of strength, the cat-eyed wizard had expected her to stay as far from Wencit as possible, but what if she wanted to communicate with the wild wizard before they engaged? She was scarcely the cat-eyed wizard's equal, but that didn't mean it was impossible for her to have learned—or guessed—far more about his true plans than he thought she had. It was entirely possible she'd learned something valuable enough she might actually hope to betray him in a bargain for her own life. Wencit wasn't known for extending forbearance to anyone who violated his precious Strictures, but there was always a first time for anything. And if Wulfra truly had discovered something significant about the cat-eyed wizard's own identity or intentions, she might well decide it was worth seeing if it would turn her into the exception to Wencit's policy of obliterating any dark wizard who drew herself to his attention. After all, she'd be no deader afterward if she discovered that she couldn't convince him her information was worth her life, and under the circumstances, knowing she'd put a finger into her ally's eye before she died would afford her a certain final pleasure.

The cat eyes danced with silent laughter as they returned to the sunbathing sorceress. Poor Wulfra was *so* predictable! It really was a pity, he thought, eyeing her appreciatively. He could have used a full partner with her beauty and deviousness, if only her power had matched her ambition or her beauty. But it didn't, which relegated her to the role of bait.

It was such a shame. Still, it wouldn't do to let her treachery succeed. He could kill her now, but that lacked subtlety and there was no way it could fail to make Wencit suspicious if he heard of it. Anyway, the poor dear was totally unaware of how he'd improved her spells in the cavern, or that *he* now controlled that particularly nasty piece of nastiness, not she. All he had to do was wait for the proper moment, and then—*poof!*—no more Wulfra...and possibly no more Wencit.

He rocked with mirth and blanked the crystal with a gesture.

◆   ◆   ◆

Kenhodan followed the elusive sound to the edge of a small but steep-sided hollow and blinked in surprise as he realized the humming was coming from Wencit.

Somehow, hummed drinking songs and scandalous ditties about barmaids with an aversion to clothing weren't something he associated with the mighty practitioner of sorcery from all the ancient tales. But apparently he would've been wrong about that, and the eyes which had blinked narrowed as he stepped over the edge of the hollow, slid to its bottom, and came face-to-face with a Wencit who was grinning. Not *smiling*; grinning.

"What, if I may ask, is so amusing?" Kenhodan asked quietly as he slithered to a stop.

"I beg your pardon?" Wencit broke off humming to raise an eyebrow.

"I asked what's amusing you so."

"Oh. I was just considering the nature of black wizards."

"That's *funny*?"

"No, but it *is* amusing, sometimes."

"Amusing, he says!" Kenhodan shook his head and slid enough further down to sit, leaning against the bank opposite Wencit while he eyed the wizard sourly. "All they're trying to do is kill us and—assuming I've got this right from all your hints and forebodings—conquer Norfressa and enslave every single person living on it. If that's amusing, gods preserve us from anything you'd find *hilarious!*"

"Their acts are seldom amusing," Wencit conceded, reaching into his pack for his pipe, "but the way they make their plans really is rather humorous, in a black sort of way."

"Would you like to explain that?"

"Why not?"

The wizard took his time as he filled his pipe,

tamped the tobacco with his thumb, put away his tobacco pouch, and snapped his fingers. A flame kindled at the end of his index finger, and he applied it to the pipe, drew deeply as he coaxed the tobacco alight, and—finally—expelled a sigh of smoke before he banished the flame from his hand.

"Wizards," he said at last, "are extremely predictable when they're black or white. The shades of gray can tax the imagination, but the black and white are easy, because any wizard's decisions reflect—or are shaped by, if you will—his basic orientation. The trick is to figure out what data your opponent has. If you know what he knows, it's fairly simple to deduce roughly what he'll do with that knowledge."

"I can see that . . . I think. But what makes that so amusing just now?"

"Watching black wizards in action, and they don't come a lot blacker than Wulfra. They're all convinced they're vastly more subtle than any white wizard, and she and her allies are no exceptions to that rule." He chuckled and blew a jet of smoke against the dimming sky. "I suppose they think that way because we always keep our promises, which is the main reason white wizards tend to be unwilling to *make* promises very often. On the other hand, it also accounts for the reasons we can trust our allies, but your typical black wizard will never truly understand that, because he equates cunning with treachery. He thinks you can't be *really* cunning unless you're planning to betray—or at least allowing for the virtual certainty of being betrayed *by*—others. It's really rather sad, but every black wizard seems to be convinced deep inside that he personally *invented* treachery . . . or perfected it, at least."

"And you find that amusing?"

"Certainly I do! Think of all the Carnadosans, every one of them scheming to betray the others and simultaneously spending half his energies simply guarding himself against counter treachery. Think of what they might achieve if only they trusted one another enough to really work together! Isn't it amusing for them to cripple themselves trying to be 'cunning'?"

"I suppose so," Kenhodan admitted.

"It's useful, too. They despise us for our honesty, but they don't appreciate that honesty's what lets us find those reliable allies of ours. And they can't seem to grasp that we understand their viewpoint and include it in our own calculations. We're such bluff, unimaginative sorts that they never suspect we might use their own treachery against them."

"How?" Kenhodan asked curiously.

"One way's to make it seem profitable for them to discard an ally for a temporary advantage. Another is to deny them information—or, even better, to feed them carefully *chosen* information. That's risky, but sometimes it actually makes it possible to dictate their strategy without their ever realizing what you've done."

"I suppose that *is* useful," Kenhodan mused. "But treachery—even in an enemy—makes me uneasy. Treachery caused the Fall, after all."

"No," Wencit said softly, his amusement suddenly fled. "No, treachery wasn't the root of the Fall...or not the only one, anyway. The *real* cause was complacency."

Kenhodan's eyebrows arched, and the wizard shrugged. It was a weary gesture, that of a man tired and worn but far from defeated, and he leaned back against the bank beside Kenhodan with a grim expression.

"You see, Kenhodan, the Strictures were never any sort of eternal natural law, and Ottovar and Gwynytha had no moral 'right' to create them in the first place. They did it without really consulting the other wizards of Kontovar at all, purely by virtue of their own power. Ultimately, creating them made their authority stronger, because their subjects knew only the Strictures stood between them and black sorcery, which is one reason the Ottovaran Empire lasted so long. And it's true that the Strictures were built on their determination to protect others. Yet it's also true that the Strictures were always artificial—an eye in a hurricane, but one which could endure only so long as it was *made* to endure, and that was something their descendants could forget only at their own peril, because not everyone *wanted* it to endure.

"In a very real sense, Ottovar and Gwynytha put every wizard into chains. They were right to do it, but denying someone the right to use his own abilities to their fullest, in the way that seems best to him, generates a terrible resentment. That's true for any ability, but it's even more true for wizards, because there's a power, a passion like a fever, for those who can touch the art. It's a *compulsion*, and not every wizard feels compelled to use his abilities for good. Even at the height of their empire, there were wizards who would have liked to be what we call 'black' and saw no reason—other than Ottovar and Gwynytha's brute power—why they shouldn't be exactly that.

"Ottovar and Gwynytha knew it, of course, which is why Ottovar gave Hahnal the Crown of Ottovar. His own ability to create the Strictures in the first place had stemmed from the fact that he was both wizard and warrior—and a wild wizard at that, which meant he was very long-lived. His heirs were much longer-lived than most humans, but they weren't all going to be wizards, and he knew it. So he gave them the Crown, the major function of which was to detect black wizardry. When a black act was committed, the wearer of the Crown sensed it immediately and knew where it had occurred. Then Ottovar deeded the Council of Ottovar the Isle of Rūm as a center for study and teaching of the art, decreed that any wizard must be trained, vetted by a board of his peers, and licensed before he was permitted to practice the art at all. And then he required the Council to punish black sorcery with death under the direction of the Emperor.

"And it worked. In fact, it worked too well."

"Where did they go wrong?" Kenhodan frowned in perplexity. "How could something like that work 'too well'?"

"Easily, I'm afraid. The Crown was too successful, you see. Everyone knew it detected dark wizards before they wreaked major harm—even the Council knew that, and relied upon it for warning rather than developing other means of detection, until the realm's security against black sorcery depended entirely upon the Crown.

"But the Crown had other powers. No device can scry a continent without producing side effects, and one of the Crown's was that it gave the Emperor the ability to sense the very thoughts of those about him. In fact, unless he had an extremely powerful and well-trained personality, he couldn't *not* read them. Worse, everyone knew that whenever the Emperor wore the Crown he was reading their thoughts, whether he wanted to or not."

Wencit shook his head in the dusk.

"No one wants his thoughts known, no matter by whom. The most honest man has some memory he wishes kept secret, and who should blame him? There's a reason the magi are carefully trained and sworn to avoid exactly that sort of intrusion, and the ability of any mage ever born to *intentionally* invade another's thoughts pales into insignificance beside what the Crown did *un*intentionally on the head of anyone not strong enough and sufficiently well trained in that strength to avoid it.

"During the first few centuries, that caused little trouble, because the memory of unchecked wizardry made the intrusion bearable, if not palatable. But time passed, memory and experience receded, and people who'd grown to adulthood under the Gryphon Throne's protection and the rule of the Strictures gradually felt less threatened. It was understandable enough that, under those circumstances, they'd become increasingly uneasy at having their secrets known, and the situation grew worse as Ottovar and Gwynytha's blood thinned and the Ottovarans produced fewer rulers with the inherent talent or strength to control the effect.

"The inevitable happened, and it's not really fair to blame the Ottovarans. I suppose it's true they forgot the dangers their House had sworn itself to stand against, but they were scarcely alone in that. Eventually, as the centuries passed with no resurgence of the Wizard Wars, they decided they owed their subjects mental privacy and wore the Crown less and less often. Finally, they adopted the practice of reserving it solely for state occasions.

"And that was the beginning of disaster. As the

Crown was worn less often, chances to violate the Strictures became more common and a handful of really evil practitioners sprang up. And they'd learned. They formed the Council of Carnadosa to match the Council of Ottovar, to train and discipline their own ranks, but where the Council of Ottovar limited the art to protect non-wizards, the Carnadosans enshrined the unlimited use of the art for the benefit of the minority who could command it.

"And the Council of Ottovar failed to detect them. The Council knew—*knew*—the Crown protected the entire Empire, even when that was no longer true. Yet it was *almost* true, for as long as the Crown was worn even occasionally, no dark act could be too blatant, lest it occur while the Crown happened to be on the Emperor's head."

Wencit paused to relight his pipe and sighed heavily.

"But great evil grows from small evils, Kenhodan, and the Carnadosans grew gradually stronger in secret. The Strictures chained them, but they worked and studied, planning for the day that would no longer be true. And finally they found a way to make that day come."

His voice had become very soft, sad, his earlier amusement vanished.

"Emperor Cleres was a strong ruler, Kenhodan, and he suspected what was happening. He wore the Crown more often than it had been worn in the last two reigns combined, and he started the Council of Ottovar doing what complacency had stopped it from doing long since: perfecting *other* means of detecting black sorcery. But he was too late. The Carnadosans had gathered too much power and forged an alliance that was unholy in every sense of the word—one which combined every faction which hated the imperial authority: dark wizards, those who worshiped the Dark Gods, and—always—the powerful who cherished ambitions for still greater power. Three of the greatest nobles of the Ottovaran Empire defied the Emperor and rejected the Strictures, and civil war began in Kontovar."

Kenhodan watched the wizard's face in the gathering dusk and saw the anguish on his features. His wildfire eyes were wrung with pain, and he looked down into the glowing bowl of his pipe as if it were a gramerhain.

"And somehow—to this day I don't know how—the Carnadosans committed the most heinous crime in Kontovar's history. They stole the Crown of Ottovar and hid it so well that no living eye has seen it since. They couldn't *destroy* it, for Ottovar had bound too much of the wild magic into its making. To destroy it would have released that magic, destroying not only those who released it but every wizard, warlock, and witch within thousands upon thousands of leagues. No one knew how many would have died, and no one dared find out.

"But they didn't have to destroy it, for merely stealing it unleashed the Dark Lords in all their power. Cleres had named me Lord of the Council of Ottovar five years before the Crown was stolen, but that wasn't long enough to repair our neglect, and we were handicapped by the Strictures. They weren't, and they'd spent decades perfecting obscenely powerful offensive spells. We hadn't. It was all we could do to parry their arcane attacks, and we couldn't—*wouldn't*—recruit our armies as they recruited theirs: with spells of enslavement and summonings from the darkest corners of every hell. There seemed no end to the armies they could marshal and hurl against us, yet even then we might have held, but for the final treachery. I saw it coming. I knew it would happen, and I warned Cleres, but he refused to believe me."

Wencit's voice turned even softer, deeper.

"He had two sons, and the younger of them wanted the Gryphon Throne. He wanted it with a hunger that was a madness, and when the Crown was stolen, he joined the Carnadosans. He did more than join them. He was a great noble in his own right—Grand Duke of the Gryphon as his brother's heir—and he took his entire armed might to the side of the traitors. In the end, he sold his very name and soul to Carnadosa herself in return for the power of wild wizardry, and he—an Ottovaran, second in line for the throne—became the Lord of Carnadosa."

Wencit rose slowly, standing like a dark, accusing silhouette against the fading light, and his flaming eyes burned down at Kenhodan.

"And so what had been a rebellion became a dynastic war between Ottovarans, each claiming the throne for his own. It weakened the imperial authority at the very moment when it needed its greatest strength, and the Empire of Ottovar crumbled. Not quickly, not overnight, but inexorably—unstoppably. And I watched it happen."

He turned away in his pain, staring out into the night.

"You know how it ended, and what I did *after* the end. But the worst burden I bear, Kenhodan—the very worst burden of all—is to know that, faced with the same choices and the same knowledge, I would do it all—every single bitter, bloody, step of it—all over again."

He stood very still, and Kenhodan shuddered inside as he finished in an agonized whisper.

"And knowing that, knowing you would kill millions yet again, allow those you loved as dearly as life itself to die yet again...that, my friend, is a weight to crush your very soul."

Wencit walked away into the hum of night insects and the cries of night birds. He left Kenhodan alone, staring after him, humbled by the ancient wizard's sorrow. The redhaired man longed to follow him, to comfort him, but what could ever comfort such pain?

The voices of the night twittered and buzzed about him, and Kenhodan could find no answer to that question.

CHAPTER TWENTY-FOUR

The Hidden Ways

Moonrise found the travelers once more on the move. There wasn't a great deal of conversation. Bahzell and Walsharno had the lead, moving well ahead of the others while their keener senses sought the easiest trail through the darkness in obedience to Wencit's general directions. The two of them were too deeply linked as they focused on that responsibility to spend much time conversing with anyone else. Chernion, on the other hand, rode without speaking for reasons of her own, grimly resolved to avoid giving the wizard an opening for yet another of those disconcerting verbal jabs of his. Kenhodan rode in matching silence, but in his case, it was a silence born of compassion. Wencit seemed outwardly unaffected by their conversation, yet Kenhodan had come to know him too well. Somewhat to his own surprise, he realized he saw even deeper into the old wizard than Bahzell did, and he felt the pain lingering within him.

Eventually, however, they turned south once more

and paused, resting the horses, as a heavy growth of trees loomed before them. The forest had risen slowly as they approached; now it was a dark, solid black mass like some ominous natural fortress entrenched across their path.

"I'm thinking we'd do better turning in and sleeping than traveling on in such as this, Wencit," Bahzell said, gesturing at the trees while they listened to the wind-sigh and branch-rustle of its nighttime breathing. "It's not so very much even Walsharno and I could be seeing under those branches. We'll likely break our necks—or a horse's legs—if we're after keeping on in the dark."

"We won't break anything," Wencit retorted. "Unlike *some* people, I know where I'm going."

"Which is more than I do," Bahzell rumbled. "What about you, Border Warden? Would it happen you're after knowing your way about these woods?"

"I've never traveled through them, but I've heard of them, and none of what I've heard is good," Chernion replied shortly. "This is the Scarth Wood, and people who go into it don't come out."

"Nonsense," Wencit said comfortably. "What you mean is that people who try to go *through* it don't come out. The Dragon Ward lies right down its middle. That's enough to provide all sorts of...accidents for anyone who tries to cross it, and the dragons tend to exterminate anyone who actually gets past it to intrude upon them."

"This is the Scarth Wood?" Bahzell asked, gazing thoughtfully at the ancient trunks before them.

"It is. It's also our path to Torfo. Follow us."

He touched Byrchalka lightly on the neck and the courser pressed forward into the total blackness beneath the towering trees. Walsharno cocked his head, ears pricked, and gave his fellow courser a long, steady look, but Byrchalka never hesitated. He only glanced back with an unmistakable snort of amusement and shook his head hard enough to flap his mane. Then he turned back to the trees and Walsharno gave a snort of his own—this time an encouraging sort of snort to Glamhandro and the horses. Glamhandro moved out willingly enough at the touch of Kenhodan's heel, followed by Chernion and the packhorses while Walsharno brought up the rear of their changed formation.

The tree cover wasn't actually as heavy and complete as it had appeared from outside the woods. Moonlight penetrated patchily, pooling on drifts of long-undisturbed leaves, but Kenhodan felt uneasy, despite the better visibility, as he followed Wencit. If the wizard or Byrchalka felt the least apprehension, they hid it admirably, yet he seemed to feel a humming presence all about him—a sense of barely restrained power looming in the darkness, ready to pounce and entirely too near to hand for his comfort. Or was that simply his imagination, produced only because he knew the ward was near?

Somehow he didn't think so as he watched the others. Neither Bahzell nor the border warden seemed eager to dispute with Wencit and Byrchalka for the honor of leading. Clearly, they, too, sensed that this forest was unnatural, a wood even their formidable skills were ill-suited to deal with, and they picked their way carefully, following their wizard guide without straying from the path he chose.

It was impossible to make much speed, despite the wide spacing of the trees and the absence of any underbrush. The leaf-covered ground was close enough to invisible, even where the moonlight broke through, that the horses—even the coursers—had to move cautiously. Still, they'd penetrated several slow miles before Wencit drew rein once more, and all of the others were relieved at the halt.

"We'll not make much time this way, Wencit," Bahzell said. He wasn't protesting, simply stating a self-evident fact. "I'm thinking as we'd cover the same ground quicker with daylight."

"We might," Wencit agreed. "Except that I couldn't see my guide marks then."

"Guide marks, is it now? In this?" Bahzell sounded frankly doubtful.

"Watch."

Wencit raised a hand and sketched a sign in the air, and his companions' eyes widened as a line of flickering lights glowed suddenly. They burned like tiny beacons in a long line that arrowed under the trees and disappeared in the distance, lost among the trunks. Wencit let the others gaze at them for several seconds, then chuckled and closed his hand, and the lights vanished abruptly.

"You see? I could find them in daylight if I had to, but only by using more of the art than I'd like to so close to Wulfra. Block or no, some of it might leak through, especially if she's laid out a network of kairsalhain charged with guard spells. Of course, it's not likely she'd care to get close enough to the Dragon Ward for that, but there's always the possibility."

"B-But what—?" Chernion bit her lip.

"I beg your pardon, Elrytha?" Wencit asked courteously, and she glowered at him in the darkness before she accepted his challenge.

"Where did those come from?" she asked levelly.

"Why, I put them here, Border Warden," the wizard said lightly. "At the same time I set the Dragon Ward. They lead straight to Castle Torfo."

"So that's how you're after knowing what Wulfra's about," Bahzell mused. "You've a neat little secret highway right into her kitchen garden."

"Perhaps I do, but I've never used it," Wencit replied. "There was never any need to."

Bahzell glanced at him strangely and started to speak, then stopped. Kenhodan wondered what the hradani had been about to say, and then felt his own eyes widen in sudden surmise. If Wencit had never used his "guide marks" before, why had he created them? For that matter, he'd set the Dragon Ward only a century or so after the Fall—over twelve hundred years ago. How could he have known before Angthyr was even settled that he'd someday need a secret path through the Scarth Wood?

The questions burned in Kenhodan's brain, and he longed to ask them. But, like Bahzell, he didn't. The icicle moving up and down his spine suggested that the answers to those questions had entirely too much to do with their current mission and all the unanswered mysteries in his own past, and he discovered he was less eager to hear those answers than he'd thought he was. Not when they led into something like *this*. Besides, Wencit had reasons for everything he did, and if he chose not to volunteer them, it was probably better not to know them.

Wencit's wildfire eyes glowed at his companions, and Kenhodan wondered whether he was amused or simply waiting. Like Bahzell, Kenhodan had come to recognize the wizard's delight in confounding his audience with occasional, offhand displays of knowledge or power. But he'd also come to wonder how much of that was because it genuinely amused the old man and how much was carefully designed to serve an entirely different purpose. A wizard with a reputation for baffling others for the simple pleasure of it might find that a useful cover for the times he had to admit others to mysteries he normally preferred to hide.

Wencit brought Kenhodan's musing to an end with a respectful tongue click to Byrchalka and the courser started off again, lifting his feet high and half-prancing. If the others wondered whether or not Wencit was truly amused, the coal black courser clearly didn't, and he flirted his tail impudently at Walsharno as he forged back into motion.

Kenhodan and Bahzell exchanged baffled headshakes, then Glamhandro followed on Byrchalka's heels while Walsharno fell back into his trailing position. Chernion rode at center of the small party, leading the pack horses, and her own mind was busy assessing suspicions about the wizard which were very similar to Kenhodan's, though considerably less charitable. She knew herself for a subtle web-spinner, but this sort of centuries-long deviousness brought home just how unlike anyone else she'd ever confronted Wencit truly was. If he had surprises like this one up his sleeve for Wulfra's benefit—and if he'd known that long in advance that he'd *need* those surprises—who knew what he might hold in reserve for dealing with *her?*

After another hour, they slithered down a steep bank into a ravine. At first Kenhodan thought it was natural, but then he noticed its absolutely uniform width and the fact that only moss grew along its level bottom. There were neither trees nor undergrowth, and the ravine's floor was as firm and flat as most roads. In fact, the more he studied it, the more it took on the appearance of a highway. A *hidden* highway, for the tops of its banks soon rose well above even the coursers' heads, and the growth crowning them was densely intertwined. It would be almost impossible for anyone to stumble across it, even if they'd dared come this close to the menace of the Dragon Ward.

"This is amazing," he said tentatively, his voice low.

"What? The pathway?" Wencit shrugged. "I had to do quite a bit of local rearranging when I set the ward, Kenhodan. It struck me this might come in handy one day. It wasn't much trouble to include it along with everything else, and the power of the working that set the ward was so great I could be confident no one would notice the energy I used to create it."

"And that was important because it was obvious you'd need to sneak through the area unobserved one day. I can see that," Kenhodan agreed just a touch too courteously.

His manner said plainly that Wencit could be as secretive as he liked, and the wizard glanced across at him, then chuckled and clapped him on the shoulder as they rode side by side. The genuineness of his humor made Kenhodan feel better about him, and Wencit gave him an affectionate shake.

"Kenhodan," he murmured, "I begin to have hopes for you. I truly do."

He gave the younger man another shake, and then Byrchalka stepped forward just a bit more briskly, as if some silent message had passed between him and his rider. The courser flowed away over the smooth ravine's floor, leaving Kenhodan to ride thoughtfully at his heels.

◆   ◆   ◆

They rode all night and all through the next day, pausing only to rest their mounts at regular intervals, and Wencit led them unerringly along the hidden road. It twisted and turned as evening drew on once again, clearly following the line of the most difficult terrain, but it never narrowed, and it never ended.

The moon had set and a second night crept toward a close as they edged endlessly along. They'd made good time once they entered the ravine, but even Glamhandro was beginning to droop by the time pewter-colored dawn seeped back into the woods, and Kenhodan was about to suggest they all needed a longer rest badly when Wencit suddenly stopped unasked.

Kenhodan peered past him and saw that the ravine ended just ahead in a grove of beech and ash. Fresh-budded branches swayed and whispered overhead and the yellow streamers of dead beech leaves swirled about them in a gentle cloud as they eased up out of their sunken roadbed into the softly breathing sunrise. And as Kenhodan drew up beside him, Wencit touched his arm and then pointed to the east.

Dying stars twinkled in a deep blue sky, faint and infinitely distant as the sun stirred restlessly just below the horizon. The eastern sky was salmon and palest rose, and the world was cool and fresh, hushed under the soft sigh of wind and murmur of branches as Kenhodan followed the pointing finger with his eyes and stiffened.

A tall hill stood against the delicately streaked sky, dark and cold with dew. Bare slopes and tumbled rocks climbed up its flanks, barren and dreary in the gray light . . . and atop the hill, there brooded a fortress.

Battlements etched clean lines against the dawn, and a massive central keep thrust high above the inner curtain wall. Shadows hid the foot of the hill, but he saw the vague flicker and white smother of foam of a waterfall far beyond the castle, faint and hard to see with distance in the dimness, and realized the entire hill stood in the midst of a small lake. The fortress sat on its hill, waiting. Yellow torches fumed on the battlements, and lantern light shone through arrow slits, reflecting faintly from rippled lake water as day broke. More lanterns bobbed slowly and methodically along the walls to mark the weary beats of sentries, and light spilled through a barred portcullis in the heavily shadowed western wall to glow on a lowered drawbridge. He could just make out the dark shapes of a strong gate guard in full armor, and the land around the castle had been brushed back to the water's edge, stripping away all cover along its approaches.

"Behold Castle Torfo," Wencit said softly.

◆   ◆   ◆

"Oh, I behold the castle," Kenhodan said wearily. "What I *don't* behold is how you plan to get inside it!"

"Aye," Bahzell agreed. "I'm thinking the lad's a point. It does seem a trifle heavily guarded."

"It is," Wencit agreed. "So we'll simply have to avoid their guard posts, I suppose."

"I see." Kenhodan looked over at Bahzell and grinned. "I'm surprised at you, Bahzell! All we have to do is find the door Wulfra forgot to lock. Every evil sorceress in every story I ever heard forgot to lock the door before the intrepid heroes turned up."

"Actually, you could say she did exactly that," Wencit said calmly. "Not that she *knows* she left any of them unlocked. She's not the most gracious of hostesses, and if she'd known about the door, she certainly *would* have locked it. Since she didn't . . ."

He shrugged, and Chernion snorted harshly.

"I don't especially want to be her guest, or to die trying to break in and failing." She stretched tiredly. "Tell us about this door, Wizard."

"Certainly. But we should rest the horses while I do that; we'll need them again soon enough."

They withdrew deeper into the trees and dismounted, and the horses blew heavily and nosed in the tumbled beech leaves while Bahzell and Kenhodan poured water into Wencit's old hat for them to drink from. The coursers were just as thirsty as their "lesser cousins," but they waited until all the horses had drunk before taking their own turns.

"All right, Wizard," Chernion pressed.

"Very well." Wencit sat on a rock and leaned back against a straight-trunked ash tree as he pointed at the castle's battlements, just barely visible through a gap in the branches. "We'd never make it to the lake, much less across the walls, without being spotted by those guards. Agreed?"

"Aye," Bahzell said, and Kenhodan seconded him with a nod.

"So we won't go that way," Wencit told him. "We'll go there, instead—to that hill north of the lake. See it?"

Kenhodan peered along his pointing finger to find the hill in question. It was perhaps four thousand straight-line yards from their present position and just over a thousand yards back from the lake, with a bare, craggy top, but its flanks were heavily wooded and a dense belt of trees stretched all the way from their present position to it.

"That's the door Wulfra left unlocked," Wencit said. "What we've come for is hidden in a maze under the castle. What Wulfra doesn't know is that there's a backdoor—a secret way into the maze—from under that hill."

"Is there now?" Bahzell murmured. "And it's certain you are as she's not found it?"

"Yes." Wencit's voice was flat with assurance, and the hradani nodded, his ears half-flattened in thought.

"Just what's this 'secret way' like?" Kenhodan asked warily.

"It's a tunnel—too low and narrow for the horses, much less the coursers, I'm afraid. But there's an outer cave big enough to hide them all, with Walsharno and Byrchalka to watch our backs and see to it that none of the 'lesser cousins' stray. The tunnel runs out under the lake and—unfortunately—enters the maze at one side, not in the center, so we'll have to make our way through whatever guards and traps she's set up in the maze itself." Wencit shrugged. "At least we'll avoid her outer defenses."

"So even if we go in through the tunnel, we have to fight our way through her *inner* defenses," Kenhodan mused. "I have to admit, that idea beats fighting our way through her outer defenses, as well. But how do we get out again afterward?"

"If we don't reach our goal, that won't matter," Wencit said bluntly, "because we'll be dead. If, on the other hand, we do reach it, *Wulfra* will almost certainly be dead. And in that case, do you think a black sorceress' guardsmen will really want to face whoever—or whatever—was powerful enough to kill her?"

"I see."

Kenhodan pursed his lips and drummed on his sword hilt, and it didn't seem odd to him that all three of his companions simply watched him think and waited for *him* to pronounce upon the plan's acceptability.

"How likely is she to have arranged something too strong for us to get through?" he asked finally.

"I can't say," the wizard replied calmly. "I would have said she couldn't summon anything we can't handle, but then I'd've said she couldn't control a dragon, either. I don't *think* we'll meet anything cold steel and courage can't match, but—"

He shrugged eloquently.

"It's an unhappy man I am whenever you're after admitting fallibility, Wencit," Bahzell rumbled.

"No one's infallible, Bahzell."

"Aye, but it's a great comfort it's been to my mind over the years to be *thinking* as you are."

Kenhodan paid their byplay little heed while his mind weighed and analyzed. Yet even as he considered his scanty information, he knew there was no point. They'd come too far even to think about stopping now.

"Well," he sighed finally, "I suppose we'll have to try it."

"I'm thinking you've the right of it, lad," Bahzell agreed, rather more seriously.

"And if you three are fool enough to go, I might as well, too."

Wencit glanced at Chernion, but this time she was

too busy wondering about her own motives to notice. Even her Elrytha personality had never agreed to this! Yet she couldn't turn back. Ashwan was dead, and breaking into the castle might get her close enough to Wulfra for the kill. That was her motive, she told herself: vengeance. And the possibility of using Kenhodan for her own ends afterward, of course.

Her thoughts skittered carefully away from her ambiguous emotions where the redhaired man was concerned.

"Very well." Wencit accepted their decision calmly. "In that case, I suggest we move to the hill now, before full daylight. The woods will cover our approach, and we can rest in the cave before we enter the maze."

"Sounds reasonable," Kenhodan agreed, and retightened Glamhandro's girth as the eastern sky turned pale lemon and the rose and pewter light strengthened. He swung into the saddle and the others mounted around him. "How do we get there from here?" he asked the wizard.

"Follow me," Wencit said simply, and they fell back into formation behind Byrchalka once more, with Glamhandro immediately behind the courser and Chernion's mare and the packhorses at his heels. Bahzell and Walsharno followed, covering their rear, and each rider rode with a hand inches from his or her hilt.

Wencit and Byrchalka picked a careful, quiet way through the woods. Their route was well concealed, but its twists and turns made their journey at least twice as long as a bird's might have been, and the horses tossed their heads uneasily as they caught their riders' tension. But the presence of the coursers seemed to offset their anxiety and they made no sound beyond the occasional snuffle . . . usually. Sometimes there was just a bit more noise. When Chernion's mare sent a loose rock clattering down the hillside, the sound threw Kenhodan's heart into his mouth and they all froze, but nothing happened. Of course not, he chided himself. The actual noise must have been far less audible to any sentries than their fear had made it seem.

A gully under the trees offered even better cover . . . fortunately. They'd gone no more than half a mile along it when Kenhodan's suddenly raised hand halted them instantly. Bahzell eyed him questioningly . . . and then sat very still, wondering how Kenhodan's human ears had heard what had been too faint for his own—and Walsharno's—to detect.

The twenty-man patrol rode out of the tree cover between them and the lake and trotted past less than a hundred yards away, and Kenhodan only realized he'd reached for his sword when he felt its weight in his hand. He watched the patrol vanish, then sheathed his blade quietly and heard more steel rasp and click as Chernion and Bahzell sheathed theirs as well. At least their reactions were good, he thought, and wiped a sticky sweat film from his forehead.

Wencit waited until all sound of the patrol had faded before he led them onward once more. Kenhodan followed him, but he couldn't stop glancing to his right, watching the battlements through the treetops as the castle notched the growing dawn more and more boldly. He knew he wasn't as nakedly exposed as he felt, but telling himself that seemed to help very little.

At last the wizard led them up out of the gully, across a slope, and around to the back side of the hill which was their destination, and Kenhodan sighed gratefully as solid earth interposed between him and Castle Torfo. Then Wencit wheeled abruptly to his right and ducked low in the saddle to vanish under an overhanging lip of stone. Kenhodan and Chernion followed quickly, with plenty of overhead clearance, leading the pack animals, but Bahzell had to dismount before he and Walsharno could squeeze under the overhang.

A narrow tunnel pressed tight on them for several yards, then opened into a wider space, and Wencit stopped, murmured a word too soft to hear, and raised one hand in a tossing motion. A globe of light arced from his palm to hang overhead, and Kenhodan looked around at the dry stone walls of a cave the size of the entire Iron Axe Tavern . . . and its stables.

"We can rest here," the wizard said calmly. "We could all use some sleep."

"And you're not worried about Wulfra noticing that?" Kenhodan jutted his chin at the glowing globe, and Wencit chuckled softly. There was an unpleasant, satisfied edge to that chuckle, the redhaired man noticed.

"The cave's shielded, Kenhodan. I—"

"Thought that might be a good idea back when you were setting the Dragon Ward," Kenhodan interrupted, and Wencit grinned.

"Precisely," he murmured with a half bow.

"Well I'm sure it's a great weight off my mind that all's working out to plan so well and all," Bahzell said sourly, "but it's not so very happy Walsharno's after being at all this creeping about like so many worms in a burrow. It's entirely too much of that we've done before—aye, and the most of it with the likes of *you*, Wencit!"

"It's scarcely my fault you and your friend are built on a . . . lavish scale," Wencit pointed out.

"No, but I'm thinking you've quite a penchant for meeting sorceresses in holes in the ground," the hradani rumbled, allowing his eyes to flit briefly—but pointedly—in Kenhodan's direction.

"Perhaps I do," Wencit replied mildly. "On the other hand, most of those previous ventures seem to've worked out fairly well. Which undoubtedly owes a little something to my habit of bringing along the right people when they're needed. Why," he allowed his own glowing eyes to drift even more briefly towards Kenhodan, "sometimes I don't even know they *are* the right people until the proper moment comes along. Still, I'm seldom wrong, am I?"

"Aye, there's that," Bahzell agreed. "Still and all, it's in my mind as that's after being the sort of mistake a man only gets to make once."

"That's probably true enough," Wencit conceded. "This isn't that 'once,' though, Mountain. Not yet. So, as I say, let's get some rest. I want to move in early this afternoon. Wulfra should feel confident we can't penetrate her patrols without the cover of darkness."

"Surprise is always worth having," Kenhodan said, setting his saddle aside, and poured grain into a feedbag for Glamhandro. Then he grinned. "Bahzell might not like caves, but do you realize it hasn't rained on me for over a *week*, Wencit? And with this nice roof—" he waved at the cave walls "—I may even stay dry!"

"Get some sleep, Kenhodan," Wencit advised kindly. "There's no rain in here . . . but there *are* a few damp patches."

Kenhodan looked at him reproachfully as he shook out his bedroll.

◆　　◆　　◆

Kenhodan sat up quickly when Bahzell woke him six hours later, and his heart gave one strong surge before its beat dropped back to normal. The cave seemed dark and threatening, but the smell of horse flesh was comforting and his panic passed. He sat quietly, feeling its echoes vanish into his depths to be replaced by a sort of quivering tension—something more like eagerness than fear.

"Leave the horses saddled behind us," Wencit advised. "I hope we won't be in any hurry when we return, but you can never be sure."

"And if we don't return?" Chernion asked harshly. "This little lady's served me well. I won't leave her tied to starve!"

"Never fear, Border Warden. We won't tie them at all; Walsharno and Byrchalka will see to it they don't stray...or stay here and starve if we don't come back."

Kenhodan listened to them absently as he stroked Glamhandro's nose. The stallion was unhappy at being left behind, but the exit tunnel was far too cramped for him, just as it was too narrow for Walsharno and Byrchalka. Kenhodan soothed the big gray gently until Wencit took up a torch and brought it alight with the touch of a finger. He waited until its flame burned steadily, then waved them all in close about him.

"The cave may be shielded, but I'd prefer not to use the art any further from this point on if I can help it," he said evenly. "Sooner or later, I'll have to, but I want to wait as long as possible. I'm even dispelling my blocking spell—this close to her, even that might sound Wulfra's alarms. Besides—" he smiled wolfishly "—I doubt she's scrying this particular spot.

"I'll go first to probe for trap spells, but we'll rely

as much on your eyes and ears as my spells from here on. Understood?"

They all nodded silently.

"Good. Our way lies there." Wencit's torch waved at a narrow stone cut to their right. "Kenhodan, you'll follow me, please. Then you, Border Warden. Mountain, I'll trust you to watch our backs, but it might be unwise to try raising any of Tomanāk's power this close to Wulfra...until she already knows we're here, at any rate." Bahzell chuckled grimly and nodded, and Wencit continued. "The passage narrows occasionally, but it'll always be wide enough for us to pass. Be ready, but carry no drawn steel! Some of Wulfra's servants will sense a readied weapon long before they can see us."

He paused once more, until each of them had nodded yet again.

"Then let's begin," he said calmly.

◆　　◆　　◆

Wencit's torch cast sharp shadows whose flickering dance confused the eye. Kenhodan wished he were leading rather than the wizard so that he could see ahead, but only Wencit had any idea of their route or of what they might expect to meet.

At first the passage was high and wide enough for even Bahzell to move easily, but then it narrowed, twisting back and forth with serpentine patience. The ceiling lowered as it dove under the lake's water, and the rock grew slimy and damp, covered with algae and odd, knobby projections, almost like rocky mushrooms. The air smelled wet, and a damp breeze pressed coldly into their faces and fluttered Wencit's torch flame. Before long, the passage became so narrow Bahzell was forced to turn sideways, and sword hilts hung irritatingly on rough spots. Kenhodan swore as his bow stave scraped the roof and caught infuriatingly on the walls until he finally slid it from his back and carried it in his left hand. The sounds of their panting breath, the scrape of weapons and mail on stone, the splash of boots in puddles—all seemed magnified by the passage so that Kenhodan felt *someone* must hear them coming.

No one did, and Wencit led them unhesitatingly, lighting fresh torches at need. Their flames fumed, trailing acrid smoke, and side passages opened at ragged intervals, but he never hesitated. Some of those passages gave on mineral-crusted galleries where the torchlight touched flowers of rock into glowing webs, but such flashes of beauty were rare.

Half a mile from its start, the passage opened into a huge cave. Water fretted and foamed through fissures in one wall, plunging fifteen feet into a rippling pool forever beyond reach of the sun. The rush and plunge of water generated the breeze which had blown into their faces on the way in, and the sound of it filled the cavern with a ceaseless, eternal murmur. Stalactites and stalagmites flashed gleaming fangs at the torch, and the floor was coated in fine, liquid mud. Wencit held his torch high and grinned as Bahzell struggled through the narrow slit of an opening into the cave.

"Well, Mountain!" His voice echoed weirdly. "It seems size isn't always an advantage."

"Aye, and it's after making my clothes cost more, too." Bahzell dabbed at a deep scratch on one cheek. "So how much longer is it, this worm warren of yours?"

"The 'worm warren' is over. From here on the passages will be wider and higher. I warn you, though;

don't drink from any water we pass along the way. It's tainted by the power of the thing we've come for."

"You're hunting something *that* evil?" Chernion asked, startled.

"Not evil, Border Warden—only powerful. The art is neither good nor evil in and of itself; it's the use to which it's put which makes it black or white. What we've come for was never a thing of the Dark, yet the power radiating from it could blow out your life like a thought."

"I dislike dealing with wizardry that powerful," she said softly.

"Sometimes we have no choice . . . Border Warden."

She flashed him a daggered look and then fumbled for her water bottle. The act was contagious, and Kenhodan unstoppered his own. It tasted flat, but he preferred its stale taste to the poison of the fresh pool.

Wencit let them rest briefly before he led them across the cave. His companions followed, slipping occasionally on the skim of slickness underfoot, then stopped dead behind him and stared wonderingly at their further path, for this was no natural tunnel.

It was a tube, its round walls glass smooth, and the torchlight reflected from polished black stone like an ebon mirror. The tunnel bored sword-straight into the hill, and runes no one had used in over a thousand years crawled across its lintel. They were deep-cut and black in the torchlight.

"What does *that* say?" Chernion asked edgily, but Wencit didn't answer. Another voice spoke instead, low and soft, almost dreamy against the cavern's water-rustling sounds, and yet crystal clear.

"Wizard wrought by wizard taught,
This gate to death and birth.
The dark road runs through bloody earth
Where future's past is locked."

Chernion and Bahzell stared at Kenhodan in amazement, and only then did he realize who'd spoken. He blinked and shook his head, and the memory of what he'd said fled.

"How did you know that?" Chernion asked softly.

"I-I don't know," he said, his green eyes wondering. "But that's what it says, even if I don't have a clue what it means."

"If it so happened you *did* have a clue, it's worried about your sanity I'd be!" Bahzell said. "It's little enough *I've* understood about this whole Tomanāk-forsaken trip! Wencit?"

"Kenhodan's translation is correct," the wizard said.

"And that's all you'll be saying about it, you vise-lipped old faker?"

"Yes."

"Thought so." Bahzell sounded morosely pleased by the response. "Well, I've no doubt at all, at all, as how all will come clear in time—assuming we're after living so long—but anyone as might expect explanations from you has more faith in miracles than I! I trust you, but I've given over pumping you for information."

"Yes, I've noticed how patient you've been for this entire journey, but I simply put it down to the slowing effect of old age."

"*Old age*, is it?" Bahzell laughed and slapped Wencit's shoulders so hard he knocked the wizard several steps sideways. "I'd not be so quick to be throwing those two words around anywhere as Leeana might be hearing them!"

Wencit grinned at him and made shooing notions with his free hand until the group fell back into formation. Then he stepped under the carven lintel and his torchlight licked ahead into the passage.

Chernion moved up beside Kenhodan as the passage tightened, and the torchlight flowed redly over her face, sparking off the badge on her beret. It fumed and guttered from the mirrored walls, throwing its light down the passage in a spill of blood and ebony that dazzled the eye. Kenhodan had room to sling his bow once more, but he strung it instead, for the reflected light glittered and bounced as much as fifty yards ahead and offered the possibility of shooting if they met something. *When* they met something, he corrected himself grimly.

Yet despite the wider tunnel, they actually moved more slowly. Wencit stopped every few yards to feel for trap spells or other sorcery, and Kenhodan watched him wonderingly. Clearly this passage had been carved by sorcery, and if Wulfra knew nothing about it, then someone besides the baroness must have made it. And, given the hidden highway through the Scarth Wood and the shield protecting the cave in which they'd rested, he had a pretty shrewd idea who that "someone" might have been, but how could even Wencit have guessed such elaborate preparations would someday be necessary?

The tunnel offered no answers. There were no turns or side openings, as if its creator had had no time for frills or decorations. Even the breeze of the outer passages had vanished, and the air was heavy with years, though there was no dust. Kenhodan smiled at that thought. It would take a hardy-souled speck of dust to venture into *this* passage!

He lost track of how far they'd come. The coiled tension, briefly relieved by the byplay between Wencit and Bahzell, flooded back and clamped him in a vise of expectancy that tightened inexorably until he longed for something to break its grip, and his mind wandered back to the inscription. It was baffling enough that he'd been able to read it, but what did it *mean*? It smacked of yet more hidden meanings, and the last thing he needed was mysterious messages he had no idea how to decipher.

His contemplations slithered to a halt as Wencit suddenly stopped before a blank wall. It sealed the passage with the same glossy blackness, reflecting the torch in a long spill of blood until they were surrounded on all sides by the glare. Light bounced off the end wall, the sidewalls, the roof and floor, eating their shadows, and Wencit turned to face them.

"This is where the danger truly begins," he said simply. "The maze is beyond this wall, and I can't open the way without using the art. When I do, Wulfra will know we're here. The maze's nature confuses scrying, but she'll know roughly where we are, and she'll throw everything she has at us. Are you ready?"

"That's a stupid question for someone who's supposed to be such a mighty wizard!" Chernion snapped. "How *could* we be 'ready'? But we're as close *to* it as we're going to be, I suppose!"

"Elrytha's after speaking for all of us," Bahzell rumbled. "But I'm hopeful as there's no need to be going further with weapons sheathed?"

Wencit shook his head, and steel scraped as the hradani drew both sword and hook knife.

"What does this open into, Wencit?" Kenhodan asked as he handed his bow and quiver to Chernion and drew his own sword.

"A cross passage of equal width."

"Which way should we go when we get through?"

"To the right."

"All right. As soon as it's open, Bahzell, you go left and I'll go right. Wencit, you stay behind me from here, and Elrytha will cover you."

Heads nodded, and Wencit hid a smile despite his tension as Kenhodan assumed complete command. Even the wizard must yield in the end, it seemed.

He pushed the thought aside and handed Chernion the torch. She took it gingerly, and her eyes widened as raised his hands to lay them against the stone and his fingers sank into the rock past the knuckles. His brow furrowed with concentration, and brilliant fire washed from his eyes to lick the wall and flare back down the passage. It threw his silver hair into sharp, gleaming relief, and Kenhodan raised his dagger hand to shield his vision against the fierce glare, staring slit-eyed as the light burned savagely.

Wind burst back from the wall in a heated storm that whipped hair and clothing. Wencit leaned into the wall, and the brilliance engulfed him, gusting and glaring and all the more frightening for the utter silence of the violence mirrored in the glossy black walls about them. They were trapped at the heart of a seething cocoon of reflected fire, and their skins prickled as the power crackled.

Silver streaks burned up across the stone, radiating

in a jagged web from the incandescence of Wencit's hands. They veined the stone with white fire, like a web of lightning, and a hissing roar arose at last as steam and the sharp smell of molten rock billowed all about them. The silver lines flared, and Wencit's voice was a shout.

"*Toren ahm laurick! Enlop ef Toren!*"

Kenhodan cringed at the violence of the wizard's cry, but its thunder was swallowed without trace in a sudden tortured scream of stone. The silver lines pulsed once, twice, three times—each beat more brilliant than the last—and the wall shattered, spitting out stone shards in a cloud of steam and dust.

Kenhodan bent his head instinctively, gasping as bits of rock pelted his bowed back and mailed shoulders. More of it flew past him and clattered down the tunnel behind him, but the vast bulk of it blew outward, away from the wizard, and Kenhodan straightened, blinking as the brilliance faded to purple and red afterimages. Then he leapt through the dust, coughing harshly, and landed in a crouch, facing up the passage they must follow. Boots clattered on stone as Bahzell charged through to face the other direction.

"Nothing." The hradani's voice was low and his sword gleamed in the torchlight. Chernion passed the torch back to Wencit, nocked an arrow, and followed Bahzell. She couldn't draw Kenhodan's bow as far as he could, but she could bend it far enough to be deadly.

"They'll be along shortly," Wencit said softly.

"My thanks for the encouragement," Bahzell rumbled.

"Think nothing of it. They may come from either direction, too."

"Lovely. Well, Kenhodan?"

"We may as well meet them coming as going. Let's move." He started down the corridor at a trot, his companions following close behind him. "How far is it, Wencit?"

"Allowing for the need to follow the maze, perhaps two leagues."

"Phrobus!" Bahzell muttered. "Would it happen as there're any good inns along the way?"

"Use your breath for running, Bloody Hand," Chernion advised grimly.

"Sound advice," Wencit agreed. "But be ready to stop if I shout. I smell the stink of spells ahead."

"Better and better!" Bahzell chuckled.

Kenhodan glanced back and smiled despite his tension. The faint blue nimbus he'd seen around the hradani in the battle against the black dragon surrounded him now, yet that wasn't what made him smile. No, Bahzell not only matched their pace but did it trotting backwards without ever once looking over his shoulder at the rest of his companions. His eyes never wavered from the rear, and his sword made little swinging motions, impatient for something to cleave.

All in all, Kenhodan was more than content to leave the rearguard to him.

"There's a three-way split up ahead," Wencit warned. "Bear left."

"Left," Kenhodan muttered in response and went scurrying ahead, alert for attackers and wondering where they were. Well, there was plenty of time for Wulfra's guards to turn up if they had six miles to go, he thought sourly.

CHAPTER TWENTY-FIVE

Swords in the Maze

Wencit's spell exploded in Wulfra's brain. The arcane concussion of the disintegrating wall literally blew her out of her chair, and she crawled to her crystal on hands and knees, gabbling out the activating phrase.

It took her five minutes to find the shattered stone in the maze wall, and she cursed vilely as she spied the unsuspected tunnel through which her defenses had been breached. She was cut off from her guardsmen in the castle; only the summoned creatures on her side of the tunnel could be used, and even her trap spells lay at the maze's known entry! She'd never expected an invasion into the heart of the tunnels, but she shook off the disbelieving shock which threatened to paralyze her and crouched over her glowing stone, sweating palms glued to it, and sent out orders to marshal her scattered servants for battle.

◆   ◆   ◆

Thousands of leagues away, a cat-eyed wizard lurched to his feet in the heart of Kontovar, jarred to the marrow by the same arcane shockwave, for this was no wand spell. Wencit had triggered a massive blast of wild magic...one which had lain hidden for over a millennium, and its echoes shook every wizard of both continents.

A quick gesture woke his stone, and he peered into it, perceiving Wulfra as she hunched over her own crystal. Another sweep showed the broken wall, and like Wulfra, he cursed at sight of the secret entrance, and then cursed more savagely still as the implications seared him.

The tunnels themselves had been carved by wand wizardry; every test the cat-eyed wizard had applied had proved that, yet Wencit had used a spell which could have been left only by the maze's maker...and it had been wild magic. No sorcerer would have used wild magic for such a task even if he could have. It was like cracking an egg with a battleaxe! Yet one huge advantage for a *wild wizard* was that not only could only a wild wizard trigger such a spell, but few wand wizards would ever notice it, however diligently they searched. That made it the perfect application for a working which must lay hidden for decades—or longer—yet be instantly ready to the hand of anyone who knew where it waited. Yet it could be used only *by* a wild wizard...and there'd been only one of them since the Fall of Kontovar. That meant *Wencit* had built the maze—not Chelthys of Garoth—and also that he'd placed the sword there *himself!*

The cat-eyed wizard fought to track his foe through the confusing echoes of wild magic filling the maze. It verged on the impossible, but he didn't head the Council of Carnadosa for nothing. Even from thousands upon thousands of miles away, he found him, and Wencit's presence blazed in his crystal like a torch as the old man readied his art for battle.

"The Trident!" the cat-eyed wizard grated to Wulfra. "It's the Trident!"

The sorceress nodded, her white face intent as she ordered her forces into position, and he backed quickly out of her crystal. He must not distract her . . . and he needed time to calm his own gibbering thoughts.

If Wencit had built the maze, why had he hidden the sword to begin with? Even in its broken state it could have done so much to aid the unity of the Norfressan refugees in the early days of Norfressa's settlement! He could have set wards about its broken magic—wards which would have prevented the century after century of degradation which had snarled that magic so hopelessly not even Wencit would dare touch it directly in its present state—and handed it to Duke Kormak as yet another proof of Kormak's legitimacy as heir to Emperor Toren's authority in Norfressa. Instead, he'd hidden it in a hole in the ground, locked away but growing steadily more deadly, ever more impossible for *anyone* ever to control or contain once more. And if he'd hidden it, why wait fourteen centuries to reclaim it? For that matter, why reclaim it at all, when it was *useless* to him?

Worse yet, it was suddenly and blindingly obvious that he'd *known* he was being watched by the Council all along. Oh, it was still unlikely he'd been actively aware of the Carnadosans' spying, but he'd clearly realized they were watching him far more of the time than they'd ever suspected he'd known about. Why else had he demonstrated such amazement, focused so strongly on "examining" the sword and its surroundings, when he "accidentally discovered" it? He'd known it was there all along; his "discovery" and astonishment could only have been feigned for the spies he knew were watching him from afar!

The cat-eyed wizard's fist slammed his gramerhain. Had he misjudged? With all the advantages on his side, had he blundered on such a colossal scale? It seemed likely, he thought grimly, and something which might have been fear in a lesser man whispered coldly in the marrow of his bones as he remembered all the other times black wizards had underestimated the subtlety of Wencit of Rūm. Many of those who'd thought they were cleverer than Wencit had paid a painful price for their error. Now he'd added himself to the list, and there was no saying how serious *his* mistake might prove.

◆   ◆   ◆

Kenhodan sped through the triple intersection. The hilt of his sword was hard and reassuring in his hand, and his eyes probed for enemies.

"Watch for the second opening on your right!" Wencit called from behind him.

"Second right," Kenhodan panted back. His eyes never stopped their sweeping search. Surely *something* had to be waiting for them?

◆   ◆   ◆

It had seemed so reasonable to set her trap spells on the single maze entrance she knew about, but now she was caught in her own web, for Wencit was between her and the outer world and no spell barrier lay between them. She could depend only on her creatures, and more than half of *them* were behind him now! That knowledge was an icy dagger of panic at her core, but she fought it down and her lips drew back in a snarl equally compounded of fear and defiance. So Wencit knew a few secrets she didn't? Very well! He hadn't reached the sword yet, and by Carnadosa's ebon eyes, he never would!

◆   ◆   ◆

"There! The second right!" Wencit shouted.

"I see it." Kenhodan replied. "But what's that?"

His sword pointed to a shadow lurching towards him.

"A troll," Wencit said. Then his voice flattened. "I beg your pardon—*three* trolls."

"That's what I thought," Kenhodan said, and hurtled down the tunnel towards the hideous creatures.

◆   ◆   ◆

Trolls had only two instincts: to feed and to reproduce. Their great strength, sorcerous vitality, and sharp talons were well suited to both purposes—nine feet tall and armored in scales, they were such as few creatures might choose to encounter, especially underground and at close quarters—yet they were not among the more brilliant servants of the Dark. These three served Wulfra, and they trembled in anticipation, fired by her rage and the sight of food, but they never paused to reflect that no other meal had ever run *towards* them. They only spread their arms to embrace the oncoming bounty as Kenhodan dashed straight at them.

Something within him recognized them as ancient enemies, and he snarled as he plunged into the foremost monster like an avalanche. Words hammered his throat and broke free in a battle cry he could neither remember nor recognize.

"Shekarū, Herrik!" he screamed, and his sword hissed.

Steel struck the troll's right elbow, shearing hide like paper, and the joint burst with an echoing crack. The hideous forearm thudded gruesomely to the floor, and the wounded horror bellowed and clawed with its other arm.

Kenhodan ducked under the six-inch talons and darted inside to slam his sword into the monster's left shoulder. The blow drove the troll to its knees and Kenhodan's blade swept in to sever half the corded neck. Blood spurted in a stinking fan, but the unnatural monster refused to die. Instead, it surged back up, groping for its prey with both mangled arms and Kenhodan stepped back. His sword struck again, shearing through a double-jointed knee, and the troll staggered with another bellow of anguish. It fell, and as it did, Kenhodan hewed through the rest of its neck with a two-handed blow.

The creature went down and stayed down as even its vitality passed its limits, and Kenhodan recovered. He turned into the second monster as a hornet snarled by his ear and Chernion's arrow buried itself to the feathers in the third troll's throat. That creature paused to paw at the galling shaft, but Kenhodan barely noticed. He left the floor in a bound, sword extended before him to slam two feet out of the back of his second opponent's neck. The creature's howl of rage and pain became a bubbling moan as the keen blade severed windpipe and spine alike. The nine-foot killing machine toppled with a dying slash, and Kenhodan dodged easily, turning on his heel to spin behind the last troll even as Chernion put a second arrow into its lungs. The monster screamed, clawing at the fletching, and Kenhodan's sword smashed its spine.

The last troll crumpled, and Kenhodan stood in steaming blood, panting and feeling the ancient fury slink back into the caverns of his mind. His wet blade saluted the border warden, and he bowed to Wencit with a fierce grin.

"This way, I believe you said?" he panted.

"To be sure," Wencit replied, and Kenhodan plunged ahead down the tunnel once more at a run.

The entire fight had taken less than a minute.

✦   ✦   ✦

Wulfra pounded her crystal with both fists. What sort of allies had Wencit *found?* She'd expected *Bahzell* to be a threat, dreaded the thought of confronting a champion of Tomanāk as well as Wencit, yet the hradani hadn't even struck a blow!

She mastered her rage and jerked the crystal back to life. The trolls had been only one line of defense, and there were only a handful of routes through the maze; whichever he chose, Wencit had to pass through the Eye of the Needle. When he did, she would be ready.

✦   ✦   ✦

Kenhodan pressed his back to the stone and wiped sweat from his eyes. The torchlight filled him with a sense of unreality, flashing from every mirrored surface to encase him in a womb of ruby fire while he panted.

He tried to reckon how far they'd come, but haste, fear, and the wavering light made it impossible to be certain. He thought it might be as much as two miles, and so far they'd met only the trolls, yet it was only a matter of time before something worse turned up. He scrubbed his face and shook his head, tossing a fine spatter of sweat against the wall. Then he nodded to Wencit and Chernion and dashed on down the passage.

◆　　◆　　◆

The cat-eyed wizard gnawed his lip and wondered if this was catastrophe or mere disaster. What did Wencit know about the sword that *he* didn't? No one could possibly *use* it, even if it hadn't been broken beyond repair. Yet it was glaringly evident Wencit had hidden it for precisely this moment—and made *damned* sure the Council of Carnadosa would be positive *he* wasn't the one who'd done it. So he thought he *could* use it somehow. But how? *How?*

His fingers drummed nervously on his thigh as he fought the temptation to intervene. It was almost overwhelming, but yielding to it could all too easily prove fatal. Unless he killed Wencit with his first blow, he would almost certainly be killed himself, and killing such as Wencit required preparation. He must be able to deliver the deathblow precisely on target with every ounce of power the Council could generate, and he could neither locate Wencit precisely with his wild magic echoing in the maze nor assemble the Council and browbeat it into risking everything on a single, desperation throw of the dice. Besides, if the old man had misdirected the Council—and the cat-eyed wizard himself—so completely in other things, it was entirely possible he'd hidden some other accursed working in the tunnels. Some working powerful enough to ward against a direct attack from Kontovar which lay concealed as the tunnel-opening spell had lain concealed, waiting only for him to wake it and turn it against anyone foolish enough to attack him from outside the maze itself. The records suggested there *were* such workings, although no one in Kontovar could have created one—and hidden it beyond detection—these days. But as Wencit had just demonstrated, a wild wizard could accomplish things beyond the reach of any wand wizard, be that wizard ever so powerful and well trained.

No. Direct attack was out of the question—impossible. All that remained was the spell in the sword chamber, and as he contemplated the totality of his miscalculation he suspected the trap spell—like everything else Wencit had faced so far—would not be nearly enough.

◆   ◆   ◆

"Stop!" Wencit's shout halted them, and he stepped politely past a panting Chernion and raised his torch to peer ahead down the passage.

"W-What?" Kenhodan puffed.

"There's a dangerous spot up ahead," the wizard said softly.

"What a shame, when the rest of the trip's been after being so pleasant and all!"

"Hush, Mountain!" Wencit continued to study the tunnel. "There are four ways through the maze from here, but all of them use this next bit. See the arch on the left?" Kenhodan nodded. "The passage narrows for perhaps fifty paces beyond that. It's called 'The Eye of the Needle,' and if I were Wulfra, something extra nasty would be waiting just beyond it."

"Any idea what?" Kenhodan asked, panting less heavily as he caught his breath.

"Her sorcery's too thick for a good reading, but I'm certain something's waiting."

"I've got no sorcery at all, Wizard," Chernion gasped,

her breathing still harder and faster than Kenhodan's, "but I don't need any warnings from you to figure *that* much out!"

"True, Border Warden, but then we all have our own talents, don't we?" Wencit tossed her a tight grin. "Just take care, Kenhodan."

"I will." Kenhodan pushed himself off the wall and dried his palms. "Watch my back, Elrytha."

Chernion nodded sharply and exchanged bow for sword as Kenhodan glanced once along the tunnel before he ducked under the arch.

It was indeed far narrower. His body cut off the torchlight, and he moved cautiously, his left hand trailing along the wall while the tip of his blade preceded him. He was just as happy Bahzell was guarding their rear, no matter how comforting it might have been to have the hradani at his side. His friend could never have found fighting room in such cramped quarters, he thought as he counted paces along the narrow stone channel.

Noise echoed ahead of him, and his skin crawled at the sound. It wasn't loud, but the soft, throbbing snarl struck a chill in his heart. Another lost memory warned without identifying, and he drew a deep breath and eased forward.

The snarl came again, louder, and he shuffled on. He must be near the end of the narrow stretch by now, for cool air swirled about him, promising a wider way, and torchlight oozed past him. Strange musk drifted on the breeze blowing into his face, and his stomach knotted in rebellion as he smelled it. Why did—

Black and ivory flashed at his face.

He hurled himself back as a taloned paw wider than

his chest whipped out of the darkness and smashed into the wall. Stone flakes flew, one chip gashing his cheek, and he recoiled from the strength which could shatter fused stone. The paw came at him again on the backswing, and he hammered it with his sword. The blow jarred his shoulder as if he'd driven steel into the tunnel wall, and rage caterwauled from the darkness, yet the flashing paw darted at him yet again, unharmed and undeterred.

He ducked the hissing claws and hurled himself forward. They dared not be pinned down while the gods knew what gathered behind them. Their only path lay ahead, and he couldn't clear the way hacking at an invulnerable limb. He had to face its owner and hope to find a vulnerable spot...somewhere.

He crashed into something as solid as a mountain, and his head rang as he bounced. He clung to his sword, shaking his head as claws raked at him. He squirmed away from the worst of the blow, but those claws caught in his hauberk, ripping, and metal rings jangled as they bounced away.

Chernion leapt through the narrow opening, sword bare in her hand, and more light followed her to show their nightmare enemy. Its enormous bulk clogged the tunnel, cat fangs glistened in an apelike head covered with dinner-plate scales, and white claws flashed, long as short swords. The rest was hidden, stretching down the tunnel, but the broad chest rippled with muscle and venom oozed from its fangs and hissed on the floor.

Chernion threw herself forward in a long, lunging thrust and her blade smashed into the massive throat... without effect. The ape head simply shook itself and darted at her, fangs agape. She eluded the teeth and brought her sword crashing down between the blazing eyes in an overhand blow. The head recoiled, but the forelimbs darted out to seize her.

She was too close for its claws, but the monster locked its forelegs behind her and crushed her mailed body to its chest. The terrible grip threatened to snap her spine, and the head darted at her again. Her sword arm was trapped, but her dagger flashed as she drove it desperately against one pinning limb. The blade snapped, and the creature gripped tighter.

Kenhodan hurled himself at the monster and keen steel whined against the scaled body, only to rebound in baffled rage. He struck again, aiming for the shoulder joint, but his blade only bounced once more. Chernion choked and dropped her sword, stabbing more weakly at the creature's limbs with the stub of her dagger and coughing as the limbs crushed the breath from her. She couldn't live long in that embrace, and Kenhodan cursed in frustration as he gripped his hilt in both hands and swung with the full power of his arms and back. He hammered the monster's neck murderously, scales rang like an anvil . . . and his blade shattered.

He threw the broken sword aside. His left hand snatched Gwynna's dagger from his belt and his right dug into the harsh edged armor as he pulled himself up, climbing his foe as if it were a cliff. The fanged head swept around, striking at him instead of Chernion, but the dagger flashed. One huge eye exploded in hot, stinking fluids and the creature jerked back with a hoarse scream.

Kenhodan hooked a knee over a forelimb and dragged himself onto the ledge of scales. He hammered his slender blade at the gap between two plates, but underlying scale deflected it. He heaved to his feet on the bent limb and his arm darted out to encircle half the huge neck.

Chernion gasped a half-scream as bone crunched and blood frothed suddenly in her nostrils. Her dagger fell from a suddenly slack hand and the monster dropped her limp body to claw at Kenhodan, but the narrow tunnel and his closeness to its body blocked the blows. The head whipped from side to side, battering him against the wall, but he clung grimly and kicked the toes of his boots into crevices between the outer plates. He refused to be thrown off and dragged himself higher, and its efforts redoubled, hammering his body brutally on an anvil of stone. Ribs broke under the pounding and a shattering thunderbolt of anguish burst against his right knee, but he ignored the blows, absorbed the pain, and hauled himself still higher, his total being focused on reaching the only vulnerable point he'd found.

Fetid breath choked him as the creature hissed. A flying talon ripped the heel from his right boot, but he dug his fingers between two scales and leaned back. Fangs hurtled at him, able to strike at last, and his hand snapped forward as he buried the dagger in its remaining eye.

Agony screamed in the tunnel as the steel pierced, and Kenhodan drove the blade inward grimly. Fluids gushed over his hand in a hot tide and he set his teeth in his lip and forced the dagger still deeper into the socket, feeling for the deathblow. Steel grated on bone, turned, and slid into the brainpan. The monster shrieked, and its head bludgeoned the stone in madness. The power of its agony hurled Kenhodan from his stubborn grip at last and a clawed paw lashed in a glancing blow that smashed him into the wall. The blinded, dying creature's braced forelimbs shoved it up from the floor, its head battering the roof madly, and Kenhodan passed out gratefully.

◆   ◆   ◆

Wulfra gasped as death broke her link with the graumau and blanked her crystal. She hadn't believed anything short of wizardry could slay it, but Kenhodan had done it with a *dagger?* She shook her head in shock, yet at least she'd done for the assassin, and possibly Kenhodan, too. She hoped so. She had too few such defenders to wear her enemies down one at a time!

◆   ◆   ◆

Kenhodan opened his eyes and blinked up at a roof of reflected torchlight. Bahzell knelt beside him, one hand on his chest. The hradani's sword was in his other hand, reversed, and as Kenhodan's eyes tried to focus it pulsed with one last flare of blue brilliance.

He felt no desire to sit up, for every inch of his body reported its own pains, yet he seemed remarkably in one piece given what had just happened. He raised his head and saw Wencit standing, sword in hand, gazing alertly back down the tunnel along which they'd come.

"Easy, Kenhodan," Bahzell rumbled. "It's my best I've done, but that's not to be saying as how you're after being right as rain."

"*Easy?*" Kenhodan chuckled weakly. "There was nothing *easy* about it. What in Fiendark's name *was* that thing?"

"A graumau," Wencit said over his shoulder, never looking away from the tunnel. "Many a Kontovaran soldier died of them."

"Died of—? *Elrytha!*"

"Easy, I said!" Bahzell held him motionless. "It's not such very good shape she's in, but I'm thinking she'll live."

"If any of us do," Chernion said for herself in a hoarse voice.

"Can you walk?" Kenhodan asked her, then gasped at an incautious movement of his own.

"Take it easy, and give her a minute, too," Wencit said tartly. "She was hurt far worse than *you* were, Kenhodan. Without Bahzell, we'd be the poorer for one border warden at the moment!"

Kenhodan's jaw tightened as memory replayed that crackling crunch of bone and the blood suddenly bursting from her nostrils. He'd been certain then she was dead, and he reached up to grip Bahzell's forearm as he realized why she wasn't.

"You've been busy," he said.

"Aye?" Bahzell sat back on his heels. "As to that, I'm thinking as the two of you were after being just a mite busier than me."

"Don't sell yourself short, Mountain," Wencit said, and spared a moment to glance over Bahzell's shoulder at Kenhodan. "The border warden's ribs were crushed like a straw basket, Kenhodan, and I'm pretty sure her spine was broken, as well. Believe me, putting her back together again was a challenge, even for a champion of Tomanāk—especially under *these* conditions."

"Maybe so," Bahzell said, "but I'm thinking as she's after feeling none too spry just at the moment, lad, and it's not so very surprised I'd be if you were after feeling a mite less than fit as a fiddle your own self."

"Six broken ribs, a broken collarbone, and a shattered

right kneecap would do that to just about anyone, Bahzell," Wencit said dryly. "At least you got all the bits and pieces glued back together again! I imagine Kenhodan will forgive you for the odd lingering bruise or sprain."

"He's right about that, Bahzell!" Kenhodan gripped the hradani's forearm again, then shoved himself into a sitting position with a suppressed—mostly—groan. Given the wizard's gruesome catalog of his own and Elrytha's injuries, he felt far better—or in one piece, at least—than he had any right to feel. From the weariness which seemed to have sapped—momentarily, at any rate—even Bahzell's elemental vitality, it was clear the repairs hadn't come easy.

"Take it easy, I said!" Wencit's voice was far tarter than it had been. "All three of you need at least a little rest before we move on. What did you and Elrytha think you were doing, Kenhodan? Mountain climbing?"

"Yes—and the mountain fell on us." Kenhodan chuckled again, a bit more strongly. "It was all I could think of." He shook his head cautiously, making certain nothing rattled. "A graumau, eh?"

"Not a pretty beast," Wencit said.

"No argument there."

Kenhodan shoved himself up and nearly fell as he discovered his missing bootheel. He bit off a curse and kicked out of both boots. The stone was cold underfoot, but at least he could stand without falling, and he limped over to kneel beside the woman.

"Greetings, Border Warden."

"Greetings, yourself," she replied.

He reached down to clasp forearms with her, and she winced as she reached up in response. Her face was drawn and haggard, entirely too pale for Kenhodan's comfort, and a dried trail of the blood which had flowed from her nostrils still streaked one cheek.

"Thanks for distracting it," he said.

"You're welcome." She managed a lopsided smile. "Next time, *you* get to do the distracting!"

"It's a bargain," he said with a smile of his own, and Wencit snorted.

"You two make a matched pair of idiots," he grumbled.

"Aye," Bahzell agreed. "And a pretty mess the grau-mau's been and made of our advanced guard and reserve, too. I'm thinking as how the border warden's not likely to be fit for aught more than walking—and that none too quickly—until I've time and opportunity to be seeing to her hurts completely. And I'm not so very sure about *you*, Kenhodan, come to that!"

"I can fight if I have to," Kenhodan assured him. "I'm more or less intact, thanks to you. I'm afraid that's more than I can say for Brandark's sword, though."

"Ah, well! It happens. Here." Bahzell handed him Gwynna's dagger. "It was after throwing it clear in its death struggle."

"Thanks." Kenhodan wiped the sticky hilt and then cleaned the blade and remembered Gwynna's awful contempt for handkerchiefs. "That's three or four times this has saved my life, Bahzell. Remind me to think Gwynna when we get home."

"Never fear, lad."

"Still," Chernion said, her lips tight as she pushed herself into a sitting position, "it's no substitute for a sword."

"Don't worry, Border Warden." Wencit's eyes flared in the torch lit darkness as he smiled. "We'll find another one somewhere."

"Use this until you do," Chernion suggested pointedly, passing Kenhodan her sword left-handed. "It's light for you but longer than that bit of steel. And as the Bloody Hand just suggested, I—" she grimaced wryly "—won't need it for a while."

"Thanks." Kenhodan tried its weight and smiled. "I prefer having a little distance between me and the enemy."

"Speaking of which," Wencit said, "I think it might be best if we were moving on. I don't want to sound alarmist, but something large and unpleasant is headed through the Eye of the Needle behind us."

"Then let's be going," Kenhodan said.

Elrytha's sword was loose in his scabbard, but it freed his hands for climbing. He clambered over the graumau on bare feet and leaned back down to give her a hand, but it wasn't needed. Bahzell boosted the assassin effortlessly up beside him as if she weighed no more than a child.

The dead monster was even larger than Kenhodan had thought. Its armored bulk stretched almost twenty feet, nearly filling the passage. No wonder it had waited here! It could never have squeezed through the Eye of the Needle. In fact, as he scrambled over the catlike hindquarters, he wondered how it had gotten into the maze in the first place. A naked, ratlike tail stretched another thirty feet down the tunnel, thick as his thigh and stinger-tipped. He drew the sword once more and stood straddling that tail's tree-trunk thickness with the sword in one hand and a torch in the other, gazing ahead as far as the spill of light allowed while he waited for the others to join him.

Chernion slid down behind him and leaned back

against the graumau's body for support while Wencit clambered past her to join him.

"What now, Wencit?"

"Now we pick a route," the wizard said. "There are four, separated widely enough to prevent the same guards from watching more than one. Wulfra should have to stretch her creatures thin to cover all of them."

"Could she have another of these?" Kenhodan kicked the inert flesh.

"I doubt it. There aren't many left—thank the gods!—and I was under the impression all of them had been left behind in Kontovar. I haven't encountered one of them since the Fall, at least. Of course, that leads to the interesting question of how she got her hands on *this* one, doesn't it?"

"I'm sure it does, and I'm sure you'll eventually get to the bottom of it. For right now, though, I'll spend my time being grateful she doesn't have any more of them...assuming, of course, that it turns out that way in the end!"

Wencit chuckled without a great deal of humor and took the torch to free both of Kenhodan's hands, and grunting sounds announced Bahzell's arrival as he squeezed between the body and roof.

"Whew!" He wiped his forehead and sat nonchalantly on the graumau's haunch. "I've no idea at all, at all, what's after following us, but whatever it may be, it's a mite too big to be passing this beauty anytime soon."

"Then let's use the delay to move on." Chernion's voice came in jagged spurts and her face was taut with pain, but she was on her feet.

"Agreed." Kenhodan nodded and glanced at Wencit.

"What does it look like immediately in front of us, Wencit?"

"Straight ahead for two hundred paces or so to reach that four-way intersection. Then I think we'd best bear right. It's the longer path, and that may cause Wulfra to pay less attention to it."

"Fine," Kenhodan said grimly. "Elrytha, can you walk alone?" Chernion gave a sharp, ragged nod. "Then you stay with Wencit in the middle. Bahzell, be ready to move up fast if I need you."

"Aye, lad." Bahzell grinned. "So far, so good, seeing as we're still alive and all. If we're after being very good, Tomanāk may be helping us all stay that way, eh?"

"If you don't mind, I'd prefer to give him a little assistance on that point."

"And I'll not disagree with you. Himself's after helping them as help themselves."

They set out once more, urged on their way by wet snufflings and crunchings as whatever followed them stopped to dine, and Kenhodan approved of any delay of something capable of chewing that armored hide. His bare feet were silent on the cool stone as he walked to the edge of the light. Then he stopped.

"Wencit, this light reflects too far ahead. Anything waiting for us will see us long before *we* see *it*, unless we get rid of the torch. Can we?"

"Yes." The wizard nodded approvingly. "There's a simple spell for seeing in the dark—I worked it out some years ago, after Bahzell and I found ourselves in a situation unpleasantly like this one." The hradani's ears flicked in what might have been amusement, but Wencit ignored him. "I'm afraid it will only last for five or six hours, though."

"I hope that's as long as we'll need," Kenhodan replied.

"Why, so it will be," Bahzell chuckled. "One way or the other!"

Kenhodan could have gone indefinitely without that qualifier.

◆   ◆   ◆

Wulfra considered her remaining strength with hard-won calm. She couldn't cover all four approaches adequately, and her survival might well hinge on guessing which one was the true threat.

Her remaining fighting power would be impressive, were it all in one place. But that was impossible, unless she waited to defend the sword chamber itself, and if Wencit got that close, he could attack her directly. Whether he killed her outright or not, half her strength—her golems—would be useless while she defended herself. No, she had to stop them before they got that close.

But how to distribute her strength? Obviously, Wencit was at least as familiar with the maze as she, and that turned the placement of her guards into a guessing game in which he held the edge.

She inventoried her remaining forces carefully.

Most potent where the two demons her patron had loaned her. They could certainly kill any mortal, and wizardry—especially wizardry extemporized in the face of an unexpected threat—would have little effect upon them. Demons were also extraordinarily difficult, but not impossible, for a wizard to bind. That meant it was unlikely—or *should* have been unlikely, at any rate—Wencit would suspect she had them, so he probably hadn't prepared any spells for dealing with them in advance. Unfortunately, he *had* brought along a champion of Tomanāk who'd earned the title "Demon Slayer" the hard way, and neither of her two pets were remotely as powerful as the greater demons Bahzell had slain in the past. Of course, this time he wouldn't have Walsharno's support, and there *were* two of them. On the other hand, the tunnels meant they could only come at him one at a time, and she'd have to deploy them alone. Despite the control spells, they'd be as likely to attack any of her other guardians as to attack Wencit and his allies once combat actually began.

Next most powerful were the chimeras. She had three of them, and Bahzell's link to Tomanāk would avail him no more against them than it had against the black dragon or any other non-demonic threat. That meant they'd have an excellent chance of killing him and Kenhodan, but they'd stand no chance at all against Wencit of Rūm if the others could buy him even a few seconds in which to summon the wild magic.

After that, came her golems. They were potentially the most potent of her remaining guards, yet they had absolutely no minds or volition of their own. They were essentially huge and deadly marionettes; hers would be the mind animating and controlling them in every sense of the word, which was why she couldn't risk using them after Wencit had reached striking range, able to take advantage of her distraction.

Her three stone golems were enormously powerful—considerably more powerful than the chimeras, actually—but they were far too large to fit into most of the tunnels. Worse, she'd required the cat-eyed wizard's assistance to create them in the first place, and if she was right about her suspicions—if he truly had seen her all along as nothing more than bait to draw Wencit into some trap of his own—she might just find he'd buried some nasty little bit of treachery within them. She could think of at least three different spells he might have hidden within the basic working, any of which would have created a blast of destruction which might very well destroy Wencit but would certainly destroy *her* if she was anywhere in the vicinity when it detonated. Better to keep them as far away from her as possible, she decided.

That left only the score of flesh golems. She'd created all of them herself in a working which had effectively depopulated a small village on Darsil of Scarthū's lands. That had been risky, but she'd needed the spare parts from somewhere, and she'd covered her tracks well. In fact, Darsil had blamed Doral of Korwin for the attack, which had helped fan that particular hatred quite nicely.

They were individually weaker than the stone golems, although collectively they were theoretically more powerful than even the demons, for each had the strength and vitality of a dozen men. Unfortunately, like the stone golems they required individual direction, and coordinating all of them would be difficult. She was no warrior, and she doubted she could use their strength fully, for she lacked the trained reflexes for close combat. On the other hand, they were entirely her own creation, with no opportunity for the cat-eyed wizard to have sabotaged the working which had brought them into existence.

North and south were the shortest routes, she thought, and the northern path was the shortest of all. She doubted Wencit would come by so obvious a path, but she couldn't leave it unguarded on no more than a hunch. A quick mental command sent the chimeras off to block it.

South was more likely, she thought. It was short, but less obvious. She rather suspected Wencit would choose south, so she sent the demons to watch that path.

The other routes covered less straight-line distance, but they were longer because of their twists and turns. The more northern of them was the longest of all, and Wulfra suspected Wencit was equally unlikely to choose the shortest *or* longest path, which made the southern approach more likely once more. Besides, it passed through a moderately large cavern which made a natural ambush point . . . and was far enough from the heart of the maze to put her outside the blast radius of any spell the cat-eyed wizard was likely to have embedded in her stone golems. That made the decision for her, and she sent them there while her flesh golems marched stolidly off to protect the last line of approach.

There. She sat back. It was done; now she could only wait and hope she'd guessed right. Given her record to date, she was far from certain she had.

◆　　　◆　　　◆

Her patron shared her doubts. He didn't like her dispositions, yet he could offer no better, and he understood her reasoning, especially—he smiled despite his own inner tension—where the stone golems were concerned. It was really a pity he hadn't considered doing exactly that, he reflected. But however reasonable the deployment of her remaining forces might appear, he was far from confident it was good enough. For all he knew, Wencit had a fifth or even a sixth way to the cavern, hidden exactly as the wall-breaching spell had been and only waiting for his command.

Most frustrating of all was the knowledge that there was absolutely nothing *he* could do. He could no more defend Wulfra—assuming he'd wanted to—than he could attack Wencit directly. That meant only the spell hidden in the cavern itself could prevent the wild eyed wizard from regaining the sword, and given the appalling proof of how badly he'd been fooled by Wencit this far, the cat-eyed wizard no longer regarded even that as more than a hope.

Yet his fear was even stronger than his frustration. It became more plain by the second that Wencit moved with certainty where he could only grope, because the unpalatable truth was that he had no idea at all what Wencit was really doing. The one thing he *did* know was that whatever it was, it *had* to be deeper and far more carefully planned than the simple recovery of a useless sword! That was a thought fit to frighten anyone, given the sword in question, and if the Council—and the cat-eyed wizard himself—could be that ignorant of Wencit's intentions in this, might they not be equally ignorant in other matters?

He snarled a curse and hunched closer to his crystal. The flaming stone limned his face in fire as he sought his enemy once more, but the fleeting scenes in the orb refused to yield the information he needed.

◆   ◆   ◆

Kenhodan leaned against the wall, panting, feeling every single one of the aches and pains which lingered in the wake of Bahzell's healing. The Eye of the Needle lay far behind as he wiped away sweat and looked at Wencit.

"I hope—" he puffed "—it isn't much farther."

"Not much," Wencit replied, and Kenhodan regarded him almost resentfully. The old wizard was breathing hard but showed very little other outward signs of exertion, and Kenhodan wondered how much of his apparent endurance was supplied by wild magic? He hoped he himself would be in as good a shape when he was old. Tomanāk! He wished he was in such good shape *now!*

"Good." His throat felt raw. "Think we've outrun whatever it was?"

"That, or else it stayed to eat graumáu." Wencit shrugged.

"Good," Kenhodan repeated, and slid down the wall.

He sat there, taking a moment to catch his breath. His sight was as clear through the pitch darkness as if the sun shone here in the depths of the maze, and he was grateful. Unfortunately, the fact that he could see clearly didn't make *what* he saw any better, and his jaw tightened as he glanced at Chernion.

She looked terrible. Her pain-wrung face was like wet, curdled ashes, and she was clearly on the point of collapse. But she stood against the wall, supporting her weight on his bow stave, swaying, yet stubbornly on her feet while her closed eyes cut bruised ovals under her brows. Kenhodan didn't understand how she managed it.

Wencit was in much better shape despite his age, yet he, too, settled to the stone floor and sat with weary gratitude. In fact, only Bahzell seemed relatively fresh. Sweat beaded his face and his huge chest swelled rhythmically, but he exuded a sense of fitness and power.

"I'm done in for the moment," Kenhodan admitted with a sigh. "I need to rest—and so does Elrytha."

"I can give a few minutes warning before an attack," Wencit said. "But we can't stay in one place long without being spotted."

"I know, I know," Kenhodan agreed, and massaged his aching legs while his heart slowed and he tried to calculate how far they'd come. He waved his hand and Bahzell squatted beside him, his sword across his thighs. The glittering blue corona which had touched the hradani when they entered the maze had dimmed, almost disappeared, yet Kenhodan knew it would flare back to life the instant Bahzell required it.

"What do you think?" he asked.

"I'm thinking as we've done well so far. You and Elrytha have been after bearing the brunt, but I'll not begrudge it. I'll be having my chance soon enough. We'll have a belly full of it, all of us, if I'm not mistaken."

"You feel it, too, then?"

"Lad, it's a champion of Tomanāk I've been for well-nigh eighty years." Bahzell smiled grimly. "Himself's not in the way of leading his champions about by the hand, but he's not so very fond of leaving us in the dark, either. I've no more notion than you of exactly what it is we're likely to be facing, but I've no doubt at all, at all, as it'll be more than nasty enough to be going on with."

"I thought so. Wencit, how much farther is it now?"

"Perhaps five hundred yards." Wencit's eyes glowed through the darkness. "It's all twists and turns and hairpins up to the last eighty yards or so. Then the passage widens before it narrows again to enter the heart of the maze."

"I see." Kenhodan massaged his sweaty forehead. "Then she'll hit us there—unless she's likely to wait until we're on top of her?"

"No." Wencit smiled unpleasantly. "I don't think she'll do that."

"I thought not," Kenhodan murmured. "All right, Bahzell. Wencit will have to worry about the rear from now on, because I think both of us need to be up front. None of us can guess what it'll be, but I think we can count on it's being the nastiest thing Wulfra still has to throw at us. That means we'd best have both of us ready to meet it."

"Aye." Bahzell tested his sword with a thumb, and his smile was as unpleasant as Wencit's had been. "It's widows we'll make this day, lad!"

"Assuming whatever it is has a wife," Kenhodan said dryly.

"To be sure." Bahzell tilted his ears impudently. "It was only a manner of speaking, after all."

❖   ❖   ❖

Wulfra wanted to pace. Or to curse. Or to kick the wall. Anything but to hunch over the crystal till her eyes burned. But she dared not look away.

They should have arrived by now, especially by either of the shorter ways, and she was sorely tempted to recall her northern and southern guards. But it would be just like Wencit to give her time for second thoughts, time to redeploy her forces, so he could stroll in through the gate she'd left unguarded.

❖   ❖   ❖

"Careful, lad!"

The flat of Bahzell's blade pressed Kenhodan's chest and the faint blue nimbus about the hradani flickered brighter.

"What?" Kenhodan's answering question was equally soft.

"There's something foul ahead through yonder arch, but it's damned I am if I'm after knowing what."

"I don't see anything," Kenhodan said after a careful scrutiny.

"And no more do I, but I've a hradani's nose, and it's more than enough times I've smelled the stink of death."

"That's what you're smelling now?"

"Aye, and something worse. Something I've not smelled before, but it's after having the touch of Krahana about it somehow."

"You think Wulfra's been able to summon some of *Krahana's* servants?" Kenhodan didn't like that thought at all, and it showed, but Bahzell shook his head.

"No, lad. If she'd anything of that sort, himself would have been after telling me plain that she did. There's none of the Dark Gods as have taken a direct hand in this. But that's not to be saying such as Wulfra would be having any scruples about necromancy, now is it?"

Kenhodan pondered. If Wencit was right, that arch ought to lead into the wider space immediately before their destination, so there probably *was* an ambush on the other side of it. And if *Bahzell* was right, the ambush in question was likely to be even more deadly than he'd feared.

"Any idea how we might creep up on whatever it is?"

"No," Bahzell's voice was almost appallingly calm.

"None at all?" Kenhodan asked wistfully.

"Not on how to creep up on 'em, no. But it's an idea or two I have as to what we ought to do."

Large teeth showed in a tight smile, and Kenhodan shook his head in resignation. Then he unsheathed Gwynna's dagger and nodded to Bahzell.

"Tomanāk!"

The hradani's bellow hurled them around the bend like javelins, and Kenhodan's bare feet slapped stone while spell-sharpened eyes probed the dark for foes.

He found them.

Human-shaped but not human, their enemies towered over them. Grossly obese, they stood over a foot taller than Bahzell and spiked maces hung from hands like shovels. Their eyes were empty, untouched by hate or pity, and their stench wafted from them—reeking of death and filth compounded in some queasy corner of hell. Two of them held shuttered lanterns, covers ready to be snatched aside to blind to their prey when they surprised it.

But the prey had surprised *them*. Bahzell's war cry echoed with all the fury of his lungs, the blue nimbus of Tomanāk flared suddenly brilliant against the darkness, and if the golems weren't surprised, Wulfra was. To control them, she must occupy their minds, see through their eyes, hear through their ears. The shout blasted through her from twenty pairs of ears, that terrifying blue glare struck her through twenty sets of eyes, and Bahzell and Kenhodan were upon her before she could recover.

The grotesque front rank hefted their clubs and crouched forward to strike, but they were fatally slow. Twin thunderbolts of steel slashed the blackness, biting deep, and two heads thudded to the stony floor.

"Shekarū, Herrik!"

Kenhodan screamed the half-familiar war cry as he and Bahzell spun into their foes like the arms of a single warrior, but the golems were silent—silent as they struck, and silent as they died. They dwarfed Kenhodan, but his speed and skill surpassed them.

He slid among them like a shadow, entangling them in their fellows as he killed them.

Bahzell was too large to follow into the golems' midst. Instead, he planted his boots in the blood of his first victim and his eyes glittered with the same blue light that wrapped itself about his limbs. His teeth were bared in a wide, savage grin, for this wider stretch gave him fighting room at last and Tomanāk had sent him foes that needed killing. His left hand moved improbably, flipping the hook knife back into its sheath to free both hands for his sword as Wulfra fed her golems into the screaming circle of his steel. Blood flew in salty spray as he took the head from one and twisted his wrists, slashing back in a figure eight to take an arm from another, like a child plucking thistles.

Kenhodan dodged a mace and darted inside it to open the attacker's throat before the golem could straighten. Blood pulsed, but the golem ignored it and reached for him with its free hand. Steel severed its wrist and a bare foot slammed its belly, staggering it back into the hulking shape behind it. Both crashed to the floor, and Kenhodan drove his blade through the unwounded one's throat, severing windpipe and spinal column in the same thrust.

Wulfra fought to control the battle, but her efforts were in vain. She needed light, but while she ordered one golem to smash a lantern into a blazing pool of oil, she couldn't direct others in combat. Even when she turned her full attention to the battle, it was impossible to manage enough awkward sets of limbs. One, possibly even two, she could manipulate as easily as her own body, but twenty were too many. Her enemies moved through them like wraiths of steel and shadow, reaping a red harvest while she flailed at them.

Steam hung in a tunnel floored in blood, and Kenhodan skidded as he engaged another mace. He drove the bludgeon wide, daggered his attacker's heart, and hooked his foot behind its leg, toppling the mortally wounded monster. Air hissed, and he ducked under another fiercely driven mace and slammed steel through its wielder's belly. It folded over the wound, and he recovered, then hacked the creature's neck as dispassionately as a gamekeeper. He and Bahzell moved deeper into the press—dodging, striking, shielding one another. Their salvation was trained speed and motion, and their foes fell away in blood.

Wulfra couldn't credit the carnage. She'd known them for warriors without peer, but she'd never guessed how far they outstripped her golems. The creatures were strong and quick, but they were handicapped by divided control and her own lack of weapon skill. Her fear grew, hampering her further as it manifested in jerkier motion and wilder blows. Her mind began to retreat, but discipline forced her back, and her lips thinned. If she couldn't direct her full numbers, she'd direct one or two of them fully.

Kenhodan sensed a change without identifying it. His mind was focused on survival, not analysis, yet the change was fundamental, forcing itself upon him. The golems were no longer attacking. They stood immobile, ignoring him as he struck. His killing was delayed only by the need to let each body fall, and for a moment he thought it was victory. But then the truth dawned: the mind animating *his* foes had withdrawn to concentrate on Bahzell.

The change surprised the hradani, as well. The golem before him went abruptly inert, but the one to his left took on a sudden cunning and speed none of the others had shown. A mace scythed too savagely to avoid, peeling away his helmet and grazing his skull, and lights flashed before his eyes. Reflex evaded the backswing as he thrust the golem through, but the creature only grunted, ignoring the yard of steel in its belly to slam its mace into his right thigh. Bone snapped, the sound ugly as Bahzell was hurled aside by the blow. His sword flew from his grip, and he bounced twice, skittering across the floor on his back as a third golem raised its mace to crush his skull.

Kenhodan saw it even as he cut down yet another of Wulfra's creatures, but the falling monster blocked him away from his friend as the mace began its downstroke.

Agony pounded Bahzell, but he was a champion of Tomanāk, and he drew his experience about him like armor. He ignored the grating anguish in his thigh and his left hand slapped the hilt of his hook knife. He drew and threw in a single motion, and the knife flashed past the falling mace to drive through the bridge of the golem's nose and into its brain, severing Wulfra's link to it. The whistling bludgeon continued its plunge, but it was an inert mass, without guidance or control.

It nearly sufficed anyway.

Bahzell hurled himself aside, rolling away from the blow while his broken thigh screamed agony. Spikes shattered stone beside him, and one crashed into his shoulder blade, crushing bone through mail and throwing him aside once more. He slammed the wall with a grunt and lay limp as yet another golem loomed above him.

But Wulfra was just too late. Kenhodan vaulted a fallen body and his sword severed the attacker's spine. He straddled Bahzell, levering the monster aside, and spun to face the rest of the pack as it fell mutely into death.

Stone guarded his back, and Wulfra could come at him only from the front. She could no longer confuse him by shifting from mind to mind, and no single golem could withstand the red lightning of his borrowed blade. Oxygen burned his lungs and his muscles ached, but Wulfra wasn't wise enough to wear him down. She strove to crush him, instead, and after only brief moments of singing steel and spattering blood, it was over.

Kenhodan dashed pink sweat from his face, watching the tumbled bodies lest one might be only feigning death. But they were all truly dead, and he dropped to his knee beside his friend.

"Bahzell!"

"Calmly, lad!" Bahzell gasped. "I've taken hurt before. I'll live."

"I know," Kenhodan lied, "but how long are you going to lie idle?"

"A spell, I'm thinking," Bahzell said, his dark face tight with pain, and his ears wiggled feebly. "That as doesn't kill a hradani outright's unlikely to be after killing him at all, and we heal fast, but not that fast."

He tried to sit up and gasped as broken bone ends ground together, and Kenhodan lifted him gently.

"If you'd be so very kind as to be straightening my leg?" Bahzell asked in a pain-tightened voice.

Kenhodan did, his hands gentle as a lover's. Fresh sweat coated Bahzell's jerking face anyway, but he made no sound.

"Better. Much better!" He smiled more naturally once the leg had been straightened and raised his sound arm. "My thanks for my life, Sword Brother."

"I have to bring you home in one piece or Leeana will never forgive me," Kenhodan said, clasping his arm firmly.

"Ah, now, she'd not hold it against you if it was after being my time. But it wasn't, thanks to Tomanāk and you."

"Shut up," Kenhodan told him. "I think they must've hit your head. Something's certainly rattled that pea-sized brain of yours."

Bahzell turned his head as Wencit suddenly appeared.

"Will you be listening at him abuse me, Wencit? Here and I was so careful to be leaving Brandark behind, but not a bit of good did it to me in the end at all, at all! It's a hard life a champion of Tomanāk's after living!"

"Especially for champions with heads made out of solid bone," Wencit said tartly. He knelt and whistled with dismay. "I warned you you might not enjoy this trip."

"Aye, and I've never understood it, such a pleasant time as we've had and all. You're after getting old, Wencit! It's a fine rough and tumble it was."

"Perhaps, but you've been tumbled out of it. We can't move you quickly, and quickness is what we need now."

"Leave me my sword," Bahzell said calmly.

"We can do better than that." Wencit smiled. "The

border warden will stay with you while Kenhodan and I finish what we came to do."

"Just a minute, Wizard!" Chernion broke in. "I've come this far, and I want to see the end of it!"

"You may want what you wish to . . . Elrytha." Wencit's gleaming eyes pinned her. "But whatever you want, you wouldn't survive it."

"But—"

"We haven't got time for buts!" Wencit said sharply. "Someone has to care for Bahzell, and you're in no shape for a fight. That doesn't mean one won't find you anyway if we delay, though. You *must* stay here while Kenhodan and I finish this. We'll return as quickly as we can."

Chernion eyed him rebelliously for a long moment, then bent her head in acceptance. It galled her to realize he not only suspected her but had also guessed enough of her inner thoughts to know she wouldn't finish the hradani while he was helpless. Yet he was right. She *wasn't* in any shape to fight, and they *did* need to finish this quickly. She glared at him a breath or two longer, then drew several shafts from Kenhodan's quiver and knelt painfully to splint the broken thigh.

"Here, Elrytha." Kenhodan laid her sword beside her. "It served me well. Thank you."

"It served you because of your skill," she said stiffly, confused by the sense of gratification she felt at his thanks. "But you'll still need it . . ."

"No," Wencit said quietly. "We'll need no swords from here."

"Ahhh!" she growled in disgust. "Gods rid me of wizardry!"

Wencit made no response. He only touched Kenhodan's shoulder and gestured down the tunnel, and Kenhodan rose and followed him.

◆   ◆   ◆

Wulfra sat quietly by her blank crystal. She'd guessed wrong after all, and it was time to pay for all misjudgments. She made no attempt to recall her other creatures; they were too distant and Wencit was too near. Besides, there was a certain foreordained quality to this moment.

She straightened her gown calmly as she stepped into the rust-red pentagram, and her lips curved ironically. She stood on stone sealed with the blood of her house, and more blood from the same fount might soon anoint it.

Ah, Wilfrida! If only you could see me now, she thought. *Brought to bay by a dotard wizard and a man who wears mystery like a shroud! How you'd laugh—with the last laugh, and the best.*

She bent to touch one powdery line with a gentle finger. She'd never really hated her sister. Strange that she hadn't remembered that in so many years. Wilfrida had simply stood in the way of power and offered an avenue to more, yet it was the quest for that power which had brought Wulfra here, to this moment.

She straightened and tucked her hair under her headdress. She was of the House of Torfo. However she'd acquired her power, whoever had died to secure it, not even Wencit could take her lineage from her.

Her hands rested calmly at her sides as she turned to face the tunnel's mouth.

◆   ◆   ◆

Wencit and Kenhodan rounded the final bend and stopped as a sudden lick of blue fire crawled along the mirrored walls. An arch, small with distance, glowed with an arcane light that flickered down the passage to them.

The wizard looked old and alien in the wash of blue, and Kenhodan shivered as he perceived the power that clung to him. Wencit's strength was near the surface now, and it crawled along the edges of his voice when he spoke.

"We've come far together," he said, the words deep and formal. "You've trusted me with your life and more, even when I withheld your past. Yet I had no choice; what you learn, you must learn for yourself in the fullness of time. But in this moment, you stand in a peril as great as my own, for what must be done now can be done only in part by me...and I can't tell you all that is required of *you*."

"This is a hell of a time to tell me that!" Kenhodan tried to put humor into his voice, but it came out taut and strained.

"It is," Wencit agreed with that strange intensity, "and I wouldn't do it if I had a choice." He took a small, silk wrapped object from his pouch and thrust it into Kenhodan's hand. "Take this."

Kenhodan stared at the folded silk, and his fingers trembled as they opened it. Faint blue light licked at the red, glistening planes and facets in his palm, hard edges pressed his skin, and shadow pooled in carven lines.

Golden eyes winked at him from the face of a carven gryphon, and power bright as blood trembled in its heart. It was two inches long, carved from a single ruby larger than dreams of gems. Thicker than his thumb it reared, wings unfurled, fiercely proud, and its strength burned on the flesh of his face while buried memories whimpered in his heart. He turned the carving and paused; its base was shattered along an irregular line.

"W-what is it?" he whispered, closing his hand upon it and breathing raggedly.

"I can't tell you that," Wencit said inflexibly.

"Then how can I *trust* you?" Kenhodan cried suddenly, tears blurring his sight. "I'm a shadow—a ghost! How much of my heart is my own? How much of it's been built for your own purposes? Even I can feel the power in this thing . . . this *tool* of yours! Am I only another tool?"

"I told you once that if we both live you'll know as much of your past as I know myself."

Wencit's voice was unyielding as steel and his features were set and hard, forged on the anvil of centuries into an implacability which neither asked nor offered quarter, and the unchained might of wizardry burned within him.

Kenhodan closed his eyes against the secret heart of his pain. He longed to believe, to trust—but could he? *Could* he trust the wizard who hid his own past? Who moved all about him like pawns in some vast game whose rules only he knew . . . and wouldn't explain? Yet he'd never forced Kenhodan's will. He'd asked, suggested, argued, and implied, but not once, for all the towering authority of his own legend, had he *commanded* or overborne anyone's will. Yet couldn't that be the ultimate manipulation? There was no way for Kenhodan to *know* . . . but wasn't that the definition of trust? To believe what couldn't be proven.

He opened his eyes slowly and stared into Wencit's wildfire, yearning towards the strength and purpose which had kept the wizard true to a cause down the dusty centuries. That unbending visage gave no hint, no clue to the wizard's thoughts, but Kenhodan's hand rose to the old man's shoulder. His fingers dug deep into aged sinews, hard and strong with their inner core of certitude, and he knew the answer.

"I trust you," he whispered, offering heart and mind like treasure.

"I know." Wencit's face softened and he gathered the younger man into a brief embrace, titanic with restrained wizardry. Then he stood back, a hand on each of Kenhodan's shoulders, and shook him gently.

"Come," he said softly.

CHAPTER TWENTY-SIX

The Gryphon Flies

Wencit passed under the arch with a firm stride, and Kenhodan followed, clutching the ruby gryphon as they entered the very heart of the maze.

He felt a vast power roil and swirl silently about him and the mirrored walls vanished, as though alien to this place's elemental strength. The vast cavern had been clawed out by the fists of nature, ground into the hills by dripping water and the shifting bones of the earth. Wizard lights floated overhead, spangling the air with eldritch beauty, but eternal darkness pressed upon it. Dark patience impregnated the stone and the mineral-bitter pools that rippled and purled to the slow drip of ageless, uncaring water. Kenhodan shivered before the night which had cloaked the cavern for so long, and mortality thrummed in his bones as he measured his life against the endurance of rock and water.

Rough stone collided with water-worn smoothness in twisting aisles of darkness that seamed the raw stone with a web of shadow. Glassy-slick, sunken watercourses tricked the eye away from walls and roof.

And then he saw the rough, tablelike block of stone at the chamber's center, and he shuddered. The terrible beauty of killing had taken form, fleshed in steel and wrapped in plaited light. The sword's wards rippled, curled, reflected dancingly like wind-struck water, yet it was impossible to disguise its lean and lethal perfection, and his soul urged him toward that masterpiece of the swordsmith's art, but Wulfra blocked the way.

She stood on smooth stone within a rusty pentagram. A square, blocky altar stood beside her, its polished stone dark and stained with the memory of lives given to her sorcery, and she rested one hand upon it as she stood motionless. She was proud and tall, stern-faced with power. Rich embroidery and gems proclaimed her wealth, yet the power that burned in her face and posture surpassed the splendor of any garment ever woven. She faced them calm-eyed, without surprise, and threat and sorcery radiated from her, but the flaw of corruption was within her. Kenhodan could almost smell its sickness.

Taut silence filled the seconds as danger crackled between her and Wencit, and Kenhodan had time to compare them. Some extra sense let him see into her heart and feel her power as if it prickled in his own palms. Arcane knowledge filled her with a regal presence beyond diadems, yet her might—great as it was—was less than a shadow of the puissance that infused Wencit's shabby, travel-stained frame. For all her power, she was barely a child in the art of which he was master.

He knew she'd judged the balance as acutely as he, but her eyes never wavered. She gazed upon death, yet a precarious balance of fear and imperious will fused into something like serenity, and her crimson mantle and golden hair gleamed. Wencit outmatched her, but she'd never learned to surrender.

"Wencit."

Her voice was quiet, and she bowed slightly, then straightened and met his wildfire eyes unflinchingly.

"Wulfra."

He matched her tone and returned her bow.

"You have valiant companions, Wencit. Why do they follow you?"

"You might ask one of them," Wencit said gently, and stepped aside. Her eyes slid past him and then, abruptly, widened with wonder as they probed Kenhodan from red-thatched crown to bootless feet.

"So," she whispered. "After so long, you reveal your secret." She smiled. "It's been said you play deep games, but no one ever guessed *how* deep! I salute you."

"Thank you," Wencit said ironically.

"There are those who'd give a great deal to know of this."

"There are . . . but you'll never tell them, Wulfra."

"Oh? Are you so implacable, Wencit of Rūm?"

"I am."

"Noble Wencit!" she sneered. "But your secret will go beyond these walls!"

"Will it? Look to your stone."

His voice was soft, but her eyes dropped to her crystal and widened once more. A formless blur of light glared from it in eye-hurting pulsations.

"That interference will tell others a great deal, Wencit!"

"It will tell your master nothing," Wencit said flatly.

"My 'master'?" Surprise broke Wulfra's calm for the first time, and the wild wizard smiled.

"There's nothing left to hide, Baroness," he said almost gently. "I know far more about him than he knows about me, whatever he may think, and I know he's used you. Now the time's come for him to discard you. He always knew it would. The only real difference is that he won't be able to see it happen...or trigger any of the surprises he's hidden within 'your' trap spells."

"Your tampering with his scrying will tell him you know about him!" she spat. "It proves you're blocking *someone* from seeing or affecting what happens here, and who else could it be?"

"My blocking spells have told him nothing. I've had excellent reasons for raising them that have nothing at all to do with him. You gave them to me."

"But not a reason for *this!*" An index finger stabbed at the stone like a striking serpent.

"I don't need a reason for this. I'm not responsible for it." Wencit's chin jutted at Kenhodan, though his eyes never left Wulfra. "He is."

Her gaze flashed back to Kenhodan. Then it dropped to the gryphon in his fist, and her eyes darkened with final and complete understanding.

"Ahhhh!" Her sigh gusted like pain. "That still exists."

"It does. I've had it all along, hidden in a spell so simple no one ever noticed it. But the proper hand holds it now."

"For the moment."

Her calm tone masked her purpose, and her hands suddenly twisted and a gout of blackness leapt at

Kenhodan like the wings of death. He recognized the danger and flinched, and his fist closed on the gryphon. He raised the carved stone instinctively in a reflex gesture to ward off the death or worse hidden in that pocket of night and knew, even as he raised it, that it would avail him nothing at all.

But the sable arrowhead smashed into his hand and something screamed in the dark. A silent concussion rocked him, jarring him to his heels, and ruby spangles licked between his fingers. They flashed out like darts of fire, stabbing the darkness to its heart. Scarlet serpents savaged Wulfra's attack, swallowed its power into silence, and he stood unhurt.

"Not possible!" She stared at him, breasts heaving, eyes stunned. "That's not *possible!*" she whispered.

"The proper hand holds it," Wencit repeated. "No single wizard can harm him now, Wulfra. The spell's too strong. His death demands skill and numbers."

"Indeed?" she hissed. "Then why hasn't it protected *you?*"

"Because I've chosen to stand outside it. A masking spell, a spell of avoidance . . . such things aren't difficult, Baroness."

"I see." She regained her dignity, her eyes bright and calculating, and suddenly she laughed. "So! You've come for the sword. Suppose I give it to you? Would that even the score between us?"

"Between *us?*" Wencit's brows quirked and his wildfire eyes dropped to the stained altar at her side. "It might. But you owe other debts. You knew the price of your actions; now it falls due, Wulfra of Torfo."

"Why?" she challenged proudly. "Who are you to demand payment, Wencit of Rūm, last Lord of the

White Council? Where's your warrant? You reek of hypocrisy! You want to talk about *my* actions? What of yours? I've done nothing—*nothing*—to rival the blood on your 'noble' hands!"

"I've never denied it," Wencit said softly.

"You can't! You murdered a *continent*, old man! Look at your graveyards and tell me my 'crimes' are worse!"

"The First Stricture convicts you, Baroness. Intent defines the act. What you did, you did for power; what I did, I did to end the *abuse* of power."

"Abuse of *power*?" She laughed harshly and pointed at Kenhodan. "Look at him and tell me you don't abuse power! Power is the heart of your *life*, Wizard!"

"We all make choices," Wencit replied. "I've paid a price beyond your dreams, and I'm not finished paying. Do you wish to judge me? Very well. I'll bear your judgment…but will you bear *mine*?"

Kenhodan listened, grasping for the meaning behind their words, but his mind ached with its proximity to power and his thoughts were sluggish. He knew something vitally important was being said, yet he couldn't understand it.

"I must." Wulfra was cold and dignified. "Yours is the power to act as you will, but don't speak to *me* of 'judgment'! Your Strictures are stone dead, buried in the ash of Kontovar by your own hands. You have no right to levy their ghosts upon others."

"I have every right. And, as you say, I have the power, as well."

"Of course you do," she jeered. "So use it—but spare me your moral mask."

"There's no mask. There never was."

"Bah! Your precious Strictures were always based on power. Nothing else ever supported them, and Ottovar used them only to chain his rivals at the foot of his throne. In the end, they were never any more than that!"

"Power supports them," Wencit conceded, "because there's no other way. Even peace ultimately rests upon the force to defend it—but not the force that feeds upon ambition. See yourself as you are!"

He flung up his hands, his palms flashed silver, and she recoiled as they hurled her own image into her eyes.

"You know only half of power, Baroness of Torfo! You know how to take and to break, but not how to heal or build. No one denies your courage, Lady, but your hunger costs the innocent too much. The Strictures were forged against such as you, to protect those without power from those who know it so imperfectly."

"Fine words!" Wulfra spat, and then composed herself once more in the cold dignity of dispassionate desperation.

"You're empty as the wind. You're no god to judge me. You chose a pattern, and because you hold power, you made others accept it . . . for a time. But yours isn't the only power, and others who hold it won't be denied forever. We reject your right to dictate our lives and work, to tell us what to be and what not to be. Beware, Wencit! Your arrogance has stored up a fate to break a heart of stone! You will know *sorrow*."

She hissed the final sentence, and he nodded slowly.

"Your warning comes too late," he said softly. "I've already known it, and you can neither increase nor decrease it."

"Then let us begin," she said levelly.

"As you wish. Because of what you might have been, I owed you an explanation. But if you tire of it..."

He squared his shoulders and raised one hand in an oddly elegant, formal gesture.

"My name," he said quietly, and the distant rumble of thunderstorm power rolled in the depths of the words, "is Wencit of Rūm. By my paramount authority as the last Lord of the White Council I judge thee guilty of offense against the Strictures of Ottovar. Wilt thou defend thyself, or must I slay thee where thou standest?"

"Indeed?" She gave a laugh like chilled silver. "A formal duel? I *am* honored!"

She dropped a sardonic curtsy, but Wencit's expression never flickered.

"Wilt thou defend thyself?" he repeated stonily, and she straightened, eyes very still, and drew a bone wand from her sleeve. It was ringed with gold, and as she caressed the power it contained, Kenhodan felt the very air throb about him.

She raised her left hand, fingers spread, and a crimson fan grew from it, stitched to her fingertips. A matching arc of multihued fire spread from Wencit's hand, arching from his fingers to meet her crimson and meld with it. Kenhodan stared at the merging streamers, transfixed as he realized the colors bore their life forces, bound together in an intimacy only death could loose.

Wulfra's eyes closed as the colors coalesced into a single sheet of star-shot flame. Her wand lifted, and her lips moved silently as it sought her foe. It pointed at Wencit like a slender sword, and a deep, resonant hum filled Kenhodan's ears, whetted with a snarling edge of hunger, as her grip went white-knuckled.

And then the wand spat black fire.

Banners of midnight flared in the cavern's power-boned air, but Wencit made no gesture of avoidance, and they exploded silently against him. He vanished into the vortex of her attack, and the wizard light of the sword's wards dimmed as negation gouged power from them to fuel the fury hurled against the wild wizard. It crashed over him like a tidal bore, and he stood motionless as it snatched him into its maw, so enshrouded in darkness only his raised left hand and unwavering life force could be seen.

Wulfra laughed—a wild, incredulous bark as if unlooked-for victory lay within her grasp—and Kenhodan groaned. Was this the task Wencit had warned him of? To break Wulfra's spell? But *how?* He gripped the gryphon so tightly its carven wings drew blood, but no answer came.

Yet Wencit didn't fall. Wulfra's red-veined glow of life brightened, and her mouth twisted in a new incantation, its words lost in the subaural beat of sorcery as her power flailed at Wencit with fists of destruction. But Wencit's multihued fire strengthened, burning ever brighter, and Wulfra's jaws ridged as his resistance asserted itself. Kenhodan felt her rage as she urged the blackness to victory, driving it with every ounce of mind, skill, and unquenchable will. Her wand whipped in patterns of subtly diseased geometry which knotted his belly, but though the blackness strengthened, Wencit's fire-streaming hand remained inviolate.

Wulfra's knees sagged and tension blistered Kenhodan's mind. A silent roar battered him as the wild magic blazed suddenly, its brilliance searing out from Wencit to demolish the sorceress' spell with ponderous inevitability.

Stone groaned as power grappled power. Stalactites and stalagmites shuddered, shedding chips like sparks struck from a forge by wizard fire. Rock shards glared like stars and pattered into dark pools, their tiny splashes loud in the titanic silence of the wizards' battle. Stone dust flecked Kenhodan's hair, and he was driven to his knees by eddies of power as Wencit's fire blazed and the dark pools became miniature suns, flaming with inner hearts of deadly light and winged with steam.

Wulfra shouted a word that crackled in Kenhodan's brain, and fist-sized lumps cracked from the roof like hail. The cavern heaved, stone moaning, solid rock popping like ship timbers, and the blackness stiffened.

A moment it stood, dense and dark about a furnace of wild magic. Wencit's light dimmed, but it never faltered, and the blackness hissed and evaporated at its heart even as Wulfra threw more and more power into the attack. And then, suddenly, the wild magic flared like a silent volcano, and the blackness exploded away from Wencit like a forgotten dream.

Wulfra fell to her knees and tormented stone sighed with relief as it settled. Wencit stood motionless. Only the flame of his eyes moved.

"So."

Wulfra's exhausted voice was a whisper of lost hope, but she forced herself painfully back up. She stood with squared shoulders, and her eyes were proud, devoid of hope or appeal.

"So," Wencit echoed, and his soft voice was a sentence of death.

"I think, perhaps, the Council is in for a surprise." Wulfra managed a smile. "I'd hoped to bargain for my life, but it seems you know everything." She shrugged minutely. "Your sanctimony sickens me, but you may yet avenge me. Either he'll destroy you, or you'll destroy him—it hardly matters which. I won't wish you good fortune, but I'll be content with whatever fate befalls you. And—" her smile broadened almost wistfully "—at least the wild magic is swift. Strike your blow, Wizard."

Wencit eyed her silently, then touched his forehead with his free hand and bent his head. Her eyes widened in surprise at the gesture, and he spoke.

"Thine art is an abomination, Wulfra, Baroness of Torfo, but thou dost face death as befits thine house. Defend thyself as thou wilt, Lady."

And he struck.

Fire sheeted from his eyes, crashing out in a flat wall that devoured the very air in its path. Kenhodan staggered back from its power, but Wulfra faced it motionlessly. The flood of flame halted momentarily, inches from her, as if against an invisible wall. But the pause was brief. Isolated flames licked through her wall, breaching it in a score of places.

She pressed her wand across her forehead, and her chant was lost in the crackling sibilance of Wencit's attack as she fought to hold her defenses. For a second, perhaps two, she held . . . but the wild magic surpassed her.

Fire smashed her frail wall. It hurled the wand from her, and it curved outward, striking the stone with a dry rattle and rolling to Wencit's feet. Flame seized the sorceress, engulfing her in jagged splendor, and she convulsed. Her mouth opened in a silent scream, and the brilliance collapsed, pinwheeling in upon itself with a fury that shocked the stone anew. The light snatched her away, whirling her into vast depths and distance. And then the conflagration died with a quiet snap and Wulfra of Torfo was no more.

Her red life force pulsed once, twice, and vanished.

Wencit lowered his raised hand slowly. Calm hovered in the cavern as if frightened of itself, and his shoulders sagged as if in sorrow.

He bent and lifted the bone wand. Its gold glittered as he raised it before his eyes and knitted his brows with power. His eyes flamed once more, consuming the wand to flaky ash that filled his palm, and he blew gently. The ash drifted away, a wispy cloud that settled silently over a pool. It scummed the dim reflection until the next uncaring drop of water broke the surface tension and the pool swallowed its memory.

"Wencit?" Kenhodan said softly, and the wizard turned slowly to face him.

"She was right, you know." His voice was even softer than Kenhodan's had been. "The Strictures *are* based on power, not morality." He smiled bitterly. "It was never morality—only ethics. Ottovar and Gwynytha believed in a world in which those who didn't possess power wouldn't be possessed *by* it. That was morality, if you like, and they built the Strictures to support that way of life with a fist of power. But they were only a code, shaped to a specific end, not an end in their own right. The Carnadosans have never understood that. They can imagine no objective other than the use of power, while the Strictures *renounce* certain uses of power. So they've never understood that when the true end is threatened, a wise man seeks another path to it."

He sighed.

"I told Wulfra, but she couldn't hear me. Intent separates black sorcery from white, and that consideration supports *all* the Strictures, not just the first. Power carries a double responsibility: to renounce it to protect others, and to judge for one's self when the law's letter must be broken to preserve its spirit. *That's* the heart of morality, Kenhodan.

"But I'm rambling!" He shook himself and spoke more briskly. "Come! Let's finish what we came to do."

His hand was warm on Kenhodan's shoulder as he turned back to the blue-hazed stone block. The wards confused the eye, but the sword's sinister beauty transcended sight. Its graceful menace burned into the soul, and Kenhodan's heart thudded. His maimed memory shuddered, fighting against the blankness of his past, yet it couldn't quite break free. He felt history race past him, just beyond his touch—like water trapped under river ice—as he bent above the wards, not daring to thrust his hand into that humming core of power however powerfully the sword called to him, however terribly his fingers ached for it.

The lean blade cried out for release. He tasted the years of its bondage like pain, and his eyes caressed its hard, keen edge. Even through the wards he saw the fine, rippled patterns of the patient hammer, furring the steel with lines of burnished light that danced under the glow of sorcery which imprisoned it.

He couldn't imagine a more beautiful weapon, and he was wrung with need, like a man addicted. Yet he feared and hated it, as well. Its lethality repelled him even as the warrior in him cried out to possess it. It was too deadly dangerous, too killingly beautiful, to be carried by a man. It was a tool of legendry, and any man foolish enough to touch it sealed himself inescapably into its legend forever.

"By...the...gods...." he whispered, and sank to his knees while tears stung his eyes. Hunger choked him, overbearing distrust, and he couldn't help himself. If it were offered, he would seize it avidly, daring even the curse of immortality to possess it. His palm pressed the wards and power pressed back, fluttering against his skin. A spatter of fine sparks danced above his hand, yet he knew he could reach through the wards...if he dared.

"Gently, Kenhodan," Wencit murmured, and pulled him back. The wizard's burning eyes mirrored the blue flicker of the sword, running and flashing through Kenhodan's tears. The dance and wash of their light mesmerized him, and his own thoughts spun away into the silence of forgotten years.

"It's for me, isn't it?" His whisper was half-protest and half-plea.

"It is."

"Who *am* I, Wencit?" Kenhodan's fingers locked on the wizard's arm, shaking him roughly. "*What* am I?"

"You're the bearer of this sword. I can say no more, and that may be too much."

"What sword is it?" Kenhodan whispered.

"I can't tell you that, either—not yet." Compassion blurred the wizard's voice. "But it's served many masters, all well...and it's waited centuries for this moment."

"This moment?" Kenhodan's mind was weary of

implications that muttered just beyond his grasp. "For me?"

"Not for you alone," Wencit sighed. "A certain... conjunction of events was needed."

"Conjunction?" Kenhodan was baffled, and the welter of his emotions—the strain of not *quite* understanding—touched the imperiousness at his core with fear... and anger. He tried to strangle the emotions, but they died hard.

"Yes." Wencit's voice was flatter, as if he sensed the anger in the younger man. "The sword is from Kontovar. It was broken in the Fall, and I've waited fourteen centuries to restore it. But *you* must do the restoring. I can't, because the attempt will trigger a spell which would destroy me."

"*What?*" Kenhodan jerked away from him. "If it can destroy you, how am *I* supposed to survive it?"

"You may not," Wencit said harshly, weariness and something else hardening his expression. "But you have to try. You're the only one with *any* chance of surviving."

"Damn it, Wencit! I—"

"Be silent!" For the first time in all their weeks together, Wencit's voice crackled with anger, and Kenhodan fell back from his whiplash rage. Yet his own anger didn't abate; it grew.

"Do you think you're the only one who's paid a price?" Wencit rasped. "What about the blood on *my* hands? I watched an emperor ride off into a battle he couldn't win—a battle against his own brother. Against a man I *loved*, Kenhodan! He was evil—so evil he'd sold his own name—and *still* I loved him!" Wencit's face was clenched, and his flaming eyes were portholes to hell. "I watched women and children I loved more than life itself die, and I *let* them die when I might have saved them—because I . . . had . . . no . . . choice!"

Kenhodan had seen the pain of Wencit's memories; only now did he see the rage. Yet his own fury answered, burning all the hotter because he knew the old wizard was right, that others had paid as much as he. But it was his life they were discussing, and his smoldering resentment of his helpless ignorance shattered the internal adjustment he'd made. That fury within him blazed back to towering life, and he opened his mouth, but Wencit cut him off ruthlessly.

"You're a key I've waited fourteen *hundred* years to turn." His voice was deadly flat. "You're the one man who can touch that sword with a chance of living, and too much is at stake for you to refuse. Of course it may kill you! But that's a risk I—*we*—have to take!"

"Damn you!" Kenhodan reared to his feet, every muscle quivering in undiluted rage. "What do I know about the prices you've paid? What about the price you demand of *me*? The life I've found these past months is all I have—all you've *allowed* me to have—and you're asking me to throw it away! I'll be damned if I will!"

"You'll die if you don't," Wencit said icily, his coldness all the more cutting on the heels of Kenhodan's bellow. "Are you so blind you can't see that we stand in the heart of a spider's web? Wulfra's dead, but the spells she set can still kill us, still undo all we came here to do—everything I've lived my life to accomplish, that gives any hope of saving Norfressa from the ruin of Kontovar. If you leave that sword lying, you doom us all. Is your life so precious that you'll abandon a *world* to save it?"

The last question was a sneer, and Kenhodan felt physically sickened by the fury that consumed him. So this was a white wizard's friendship! Betrayal. Not treachery born of expedience, but something worse. A deadly entrapment in the name of a soulless cause. Betrayal of the very trust that wizard had demanded of him, and which he'd given. Betrayal all the more bitter because it was inevitable, and because—all the gods help him!—he'd let himself love the wizard who saw him only as a tool, an expendable extension of his own long, corrosive vendetta.

And bitterest, most vitriolic of all, he knew Wencit was *right*. His life *was* less precious than an entire world's and he had no right to save it at such a price. He was trapped, compelled by his own morality as much as the wizard's implacable will, into a risk not of his own choosing, and his soul writhed like white iron in the furnace of his fury as he realized it.

"All right!" he hissed. "I'll do it—and may Phrobus damn your soul to Krahana's darkest hell!"

His green eyes flamed like ice, but Wencit merely shrugged and sank back on his heels. Kenhodan's rage redoubled at his self-assured expression and he turned his back with a snarl and reached for the sword.

The world exploded.

The magic laced about the sword—layer upon layer of arcane weaving: Wulfra's spells, the cat-eyed wizard's spells, the ancient wards, and the deathless wild-magic heart of the sword itself—erupted into Kenhodan with the fury of an avalanche. His brain became a conduit for unbearable power, and his thoughts smoked with shadow and nightmare, gibbering as horror dug fangs of ice into their fragile web. He reeled back—the sword in one hand, the forgotten gryphon in the other, rage in his heart—and coiled power looped about him and clubbed him to his knees. He crashed to the floor, and the sword's tip rang on stone. Sparks sputtered as rock and steel met, and the blade burned inches deep into that unyielding surface. Lightning crackled about his wrist and arm in a tracery of fury, and his head bounced back, hair flying, throat muscles corded like cables. His teeth snapped shut, and bloody froth pearled his lips and trickled down his chin.

To merely mortal eyes, he was gripped by a seizure, but Wencit's eyes saw the truth, and he paled, all pretense of unconcern abandoned, as he watched Kenhodan fight for his life. For Wencit could see the brilliant purple cocoon lapped about him, could see it become an eye-searing violet-green that wrenched at the mind like pincers. The stomach-churning glare brightened as the cat-eyed wizard's spell replaced the last of Wulfra's trap, and the nature of Kenhodan's peril stood revealed, stark and terrible.

A fanged head topped the savage cloud of power, grinning like what it was—the entire essence of a demon, condensed and refined, sealed into a tiny pocket of space and time to claim the soul of whoever released it. The spell had hidden the demon's nature, its presence, even from Bahzell Bahnakson, and the concentrated savagery—focused and directed by that same spell—might have destroyed even a champion of Tomanāk as powerful as him in its sudden onslaught. No lesser strength stood any chance at all against it, and Wencit sat motionless, taloned fingers clutching his knees, as demon laughter roared.

Tension surged like banefire and Kenhodan began

to moan—a high keening that tore through his locked teeth, sharp and growing higher, edging into a shriek of agony as clumsy fingers clawed at his soul. The demon compressed itself around his thought centers, driving spikes of power through him to destroy him, and his torment howled through the cavern.

Yet even as he screamed, the final magic—the deepest magic of all—awoke, and his left hand began to move. Slowly, jerkily, every inch an agony, his left fist crept towards his right. Ruby brilliance showered from the gryphon, and power pulsed in its heart. Red flashes throbbed in time with his flickering life, and Wencit watched the slow, painful progress of that clenched hand with a face as cold as time.

No one could have guessed from the ancient wizard's expression how many thousands of years depended upon that hand's movement, or that he'd deliberately goaded Kenhodan into fury. But he had, and for one purpose—to bury conscious thought in a haze of anger which, however briefly, walled his inner awareness away from the demon that ached to devour him.

Demon tendrils sank deeper into Kenhodan's brain. Anger made him easier to possess, but it hid his innermost thoughts—the thoughts even he didn't know were his. The very ease with which the creature had seized his outer mind fooled it. It underestimated him as it tightened the gibbering stress, drove him into convulsions, so confident it didn't sense the heart of sorcery that moved that slowly creeping left hand.

Ruby fire licked the broken hilt. Time and space hummed in monumental stress, drawn to the breaking point by exquisitely counterpoised forces beyond the ken of nature. And then the gemstone touched the sword.

Kenhodan moaned and his blind fingers rotated the gryphon. Its shattered base moved, pressing against the ancient fracture lines. Ruby grated on clinging bits of ruby, and—at last—the demon sensed danger.

Its rage howled, battering Wencit with the power rebounding from Kenhodan. Fury raved up Kenhodan's arms, driven by demon fear and demon hunger. Energy glared about him, sparks falling like stars, hissing into the stone floor while rock streamed up in stinking steam.

But it was too late. The hidden mind and memory, sealed from the demon by rage, leapt to life at last. Kenhodan of Belhadan's jaws unlocked, blood flowed down his chin, and his voice roared like the thunder of heavy cavalry at sunrise.

"*Shekarū, Herrik!*" he screamed. "*Ottar shen Cleres! Ottar ken Toren!*"

Fire streamed from the sword, and the demon quivered and jerked, straining to destroy him. Ruby brilliance glittered, shivering the cavern with indomitable might, and Kenhodan writhed in torment. His left hand snapped from the pommel . . . but the gryphon remained, and fans of yellow light flashed from the carving's golden eyes, gouging at the demon. The fracture lines had vanished, fused seamlessly, and the gryphon spread its wings and screamed with remembered rage, its golden light like knives against the rags of demon might.

Wencit half rose, crouching towards Kenhodan, and his own muscles mirrored the strain in that sorcery-wracked body. His blazing eyes burned the air about him, and his ancient face contorted in agony . . . or hope.

The sword rose slowly, and the gryphon clawed its

way towards Kenhodan's head. The light of its glowing eyes touched his chin, his mouth . . . and then shafted into his eyes in a flood like destruction.

No human throat could have shaped the noise that rent the air. It sprang from the demon as it confronted its doom, and head-sized chunks of ceiling shattered loose in stony thunder, leaping and cracking as they hit the floor. The sound of battle blazed into the maze, stunning Chernion and Bahzell, for the golden eyes were suns, and the fury of a gryphon's battle cry shrieked through the very bones of the earth.

The violet-green shroud snapped, stressed beyond endurance, and the demon mouth gaped in stricken terror.

Then it vanished.

Kenhodan staggered back under the weight of memory—memory of horror. Of killing blows, savagely given and returned. Of clinging ropes of blackness and an iron mace, battering his armor, snapping his ribs. Pain, his own blade gleaming like lost hope as it sheared and bit. Sorcery raging at his mind, clogging his senses. Blood pumping from his own wounds, more blood gouting over his arm as his sword slashed sorcerous mail, ribs, lungs. His foe's death scream and the thunder of iron on his helm.

Darkness.

He reeled, clutching selfhood as the memories ripped him apart, and breath sobbed in his lungs. Tears of fire traced white lines in the blood from his broken lips, and his muscles trembled and crackled as he fought the merciful darkness which sought to claim him.

He lost that battle. He fell on his face against the

stone, the sword beneath him, and it was no longer a thing of iron or steel, of polished edges and inanimate metal. It glowed, alive and sentient, throbbing with its own fierce life. A distant shriek—a gryphon's scream of triumph—echoed into the darkness with him, but the sword glowed beneath him like a beacon.

The Sword of the South—restored.

Hope Reclaimed

Wencit knelt beside his fallen friend, and hands which had shattered a continent trembled as they brushed the red hair. He took Kenhodan's head into his lap, waiting, and his face was grim.

Kenhodan stirred finally. He moaned softly and his eyes opened, dark and haunted, and Wencit cradled him like a mother with a fevered child.

"Wencit?" The voice was strange: Kenhodan's... and yet not.

"Yes, Sire?"

"How long?" The eyes were wide, unfocused, and the lips moved stiffly.

"Fourteen hundred years, Sire."

"Don't...call me that. Never call me that again."

"Why not? It's what you are."

"No. I'll never be that again. Never!" A callused hand rose to brush Wencit's cheek, gently tracing the angle of the bearded jaw and the deep lines grooved by time and sorrow. "Fourteen hundred years," the strange/familiar voice murmured. "It's too much, Wencit. You use yourself too mercilessly."

"Perhaps. But if I do, I use others just as harshly. Forgive me."

"Forgive?" The voice laughed. "I can't. I made my choices knowingly. There's nothing to forgive."

"There is," the wizard said softly. "Far more than you know. And you must make another decision, one you'll hate. Will you reclaim what is yours?"

"Must I?" The voice was unutterably weary now. "Haven't I paid enough?"

"You have," Wencit said. "But not yet enough for victory."

"Victory," the voice said bitterly. "We cared so much for *victory*, didn't we?"

"Yes, we did."

"And you still do, don't you, my friend? You—sitting there with your burning eyes—you care enough to pay and pay and pay, don't you?"

"Yes, I do," Wencit said simply. "Someone has to."

"Then I suppose I have to care, as well. But I don't want to, Wencit. Oh, *how* I want not to!"

"I know." Wencit touched the red hair gently. "I *know*—better than anyone. But you won't be alone, and with the hurt and pain, there will be love. I swear it, Sire."

Kenhodan's relaxed face writhed at the title Wencit gave him, and the head in the wizard's lap twisted.

"I'll do what I must, Wencit, but I'll have no throne! Spare me that, at least. All I ever wanted was a harp and someone to hear me play."

"I know...my friend," Wencit said very softly. "And

if you wish it so, so it will be. Yet there are things to be done first which only you can do."

"If I must, I must," the not-Kenhodan voice said, "but no thrones! I'll pay what you demand of me, but you have to promise me that. No more thrones, no dynasties. Surely I've earned that much, Wencit?"

"You have," the wizard told him gently, "and I promise what you ask."

"Thank you," the voice murmured. "I could die indeed for that." Then it sharpened, even as it became more distant. "He doesn't know, does he?"

"No, Milord. Not yet."

"Good," the voice said, barely audible now, "but I'll have one more promise from you, Lord of Rūm."

"Milord?"

"Let him live—not me. He's a . . . cleaner man than I can ever be again. Let him conquer me, not be conquered *by* me."

"It will be as you wish," Wencit whispered, and a single tear trickled down his ancient cheek.

"Thank you," the voice was a ghost. "He deserves to live. . . ."

"Farewell, My Lord," Wencit whispered even more softly as the voice vanished and the green eyes slipped shut. But those eyes were closed only for a moment. Then they opened again, and they were Kenhodan's once more, gazing up at the wizard.

"Wencit?"

His voice was unshadowed by the strange timbre.

"Yes, Kenhodan." The wizard rose, lifting him effortlessly. "Forgive me. I goaded you deliberately—I had to for you to survive the demon."

"You knew," Kenhodan said wonderingly. "You *knew* what the spell was."

"I did. Don't ask how, but one day you'll know how I knew."

"Always 'one day,' eh?" Kenhodan laughed weakly and patted the wizard's shoulder. "Somehow that doesn't bother me anymore."

"I know." Wencit hugged him briefly, then stood back. "And in the meantime, I believe I told the border warden we'd find you another blade somewhere, and it would appear I was right. You've acquired a sword of royal lineage, my friend! Look."

Kenhodan stared down for the first time at the blade he still held, seeing the mirror-bright steel and feeling the hum of power. It burned through him, as if the weapon were forged of fire and light, not steel, and the ruby gryphon pommel stared at him with proud, distant eyes of inset gold.

"Tomanāk," he whispered. "It's . . . beautiful."

"It is," Wencit agreed softly, "and only one man may bear that blade: you." Kenhodan swallowed heavily, eyes rising once more to Wencit's face, and the wizard went quietly on. "It was last borne by Toren Swordarm to the Battle of Lost Hope. What you hold is the imperial blade of the House of Ottovar. I still dare not explain everything to you, but I *will* tell you this: you need never feel shame for your past, and in your veins flows the blood of Ottovar the Great and Gwynytha the Wise."

"You're joking!" Kenhodan gasped, his eyes huge. "The House of Ottovar died fourteen hundred years ago!"

"So it was thought. So I *let* it be thought. But that house lives . . . both here and in Kontovar. What began as a battle between Ottovarans can end only in the same way, Kenhodan. The Dark Lords gather power in Hacromanthi. Soon they'll reach out to Norfressa, for I'm an old man, even for a wild wizard, and they know it. My power's peaked and begun its decline. When they're certain of that, when they're confident it's declined far enough, they'll strike. You and that sword—and one other I've awaited until now—are our only hope."

"No," Kenhodan whispered. *"No!"*

"Yes." Wencit was compassionate but unyielding. "You're of a house bred for this battle. You have no more choice than I . . . and you know it."

"Wencit," Kenhodan touched the wizard's arm while the sword hummed in his other hand, "I'm not equal to such as that! You're a wizard—you may be able to endure it. But I'm . . . only me. I can't *do* it!"

"You can, and you must. Wizardry isn't what makes a man endure. It's not even a very good basis for choice."

"Choice?" Kenhodan laughed unsteadily. "You just said I don't *have* one!"

"Every man has choices. You can slay yourself with that sword or bear it into battle. You can run. Perhaps you can even hide . . . but only at the cost of knowing what you've done. Knowing who you've abandoned." The wizard's hand was gentle as he touched Kenhodan's face. "I know about choices, my friend. Believe me. I *know*."

"I do believe you, but—"

Kenhodan broke off as something scraped behind him. He spun like a cat, his sword flaring with power, and two figures lurched into the cavern. Bahzell tottered, glaze-eyed with anguish, balanced on the tip of his massive blade and braced on Chernion's good shoulder. She staggered under that massive weight, little bigger than a child beside him, every line of her slim body eloquent with strain, and both of them were gray-faced with pain, but each carried drawn steel, Chernion in her left hand.

"We heard too much noise," Bahzell gasped. "We came to help."

Kenhodan's face softened, and his sword lowered. He glanced at Wencit, and his face was filled with sorrow . . . and acceptance.

"Choices, Wencit?" He smiled sadly. "I think not— not with friends like these."

"What?" Bahzell's voice was twisted with pain as he stared at the sword and his champion's senses felt its terrible power. "What choice might that happen to be?"

"Never mind, Mountain."

Kenhodan sheathed the blazing glory in an empty scabbard which somehow fitted it perfectly and was once more the man the hradani knew. He and Wencit moved towards their companions and gently eased Chernion aside, taking Bahzell between them. Not even the iron-thewed hradani could withhold a moan of anguish as they lowered him to the floor, and Kenhodan's eyes burned. He gripped Chernion's shoulder tightly for a moment before he bent over Bahzell's crudely splinted leg. They were so battered they could barely move, yet they'd come to help. Worlds were very abstract causes beside the fierce loyalty of friends.

"It really isn't important, Bahzell," he said softly. "Now let's see to that leg properly so we can get you home." He squeezed his friend's forearm and smiled through the haze of his tears.

"Gwynna and Leeana are waiting for you."

Glossary

Ada—the third continent of Orfressa, not inhabited by the Races of Man.

Angthyr, Grand Duchy of—the largest feudal territory of the Kingdom of Angthyr.

Angthyr, Kingdom of—a moderately large independent kingdom south of the Empire of the Axe. The largest of the Border Kingdoms.

Axe Hallow—Capital city of the Empire of the Axe.

Axe, Empire of—the most powerful and populous realm of Norfressa, ruled by the House of Kormak.

Axeman—any citizen of the Empire of the Axe, but especially any civil bureaucrat or soldier of the empire.

Banark Bay—a huge bay on the west coast of Norfressa, subdivided into North Banark Bay and South Banark Bay; the site of the first major Ottovaran colonies in Norfressa, notably Manhome, the main port of refuge.

Banefire—an incendiary compound similar to Greek fire.

Battle of Lost Hope—the final battle of Toren Swordarm, last Emperor of Ottovar, in which his entire army was slain.

Belhadan—the third-largest city of the Empire of the Axe, Belhadan is the largest and most important seaport of northern Norfressa.

Belhadan Bay—the site of the city of Belhadan.

Belhadans—citizens of the city of Belhadan.

Bellwater River—the river border between the Grand Duchy of Kolvania and the Kingdom of Angthyr.

Blue flower, the—periwinkle; the Orfressan flower of the dead and remembrance.

Border Kingdoms, the—small independent states forming a buffer between the Empire of the Axe and the Empire of the Spear. Most of them are allied with the Empire of the Axe.

Bortalik Bay—a large bay at the mouth of the Spear River; a major port, controlled by the Purple Lords.

Bridge of Angthyr—the major bridge across the Bellwater River between the Duchy of Kolvania and the Grand Duchy of Angthyr.

Brothers of the Axe—also "Axe Brothers;" the elite heavy infantry of the Empire of the Axe.

Cape Storm—the major cape marking the southern terminus of the Fradonian Banks off the west coast of Norfressa.

Carchon, Duchy of—a duchy of the Kingdom of Angthyr.

Cardos, Isle of—a large island at the mouth of Belhadan Bay which helps protect the anchorage from winter gales.

Cleres—the next to last emperor of Kontovar; the father of Toren Swordarm.

Coast Guard—the capital of West Barony in the Kingdom of Angthyr.

Corsair Isles—the island homeland of the Shith Kiri Corsairs.

Corsairs—the Shith Kiri.

Council of Assassins—the ruling council of the Assassins Guild.

Council of Captains—the council governing the Shith Kiri Corsairs.

Council of Carnadosa—the ruling council of black wizards in Kontovar, named for Carnadosa Phrofressa. First established to oppose the House of Ottovar in Kontovar and now dedicated to the conquest of Norfressa.

Council of Ottovar—also "White Council"; see below.

Council of Semkirk—a council of magi and mishuki named for Semkirk Orfro, established in Norfressa to train and govern magi in the use of their talents and to combat black wizardry.

Council, White—also "Council of Ottovar"; the council of white wizards originally established in Kontovar by Ottovar the Great and Gwynytha the Wise to enforce the Strictures of Ottovar and govern the actions of wizards in general.

Cragwall Pass—one of the major passes through the East Wall Mountains.

Curse of Kontovar—a hradani term for the inherited compulsion towards violence impressed upon them by sorcery during the final wars in Kontovar.

Direcat—a very large, highly intelligent Norfressan carnivore physically similar to a sabertooth tiger.

Dog Brothers, the—members of the Assassins Guild.

Dorfai of Saramantha—a famous elvish poet, sage, and scholar.

Dragon Ward—a spell barrier created by Wencit of Rūm to confine and protect the dragons who survived the Dragon Wars and their descendants.

Dragon Wars—wars between the Races of Man and dragons in Norfressa, fought over the area now included in the Kingdom of Angthyr and Duchy of Kolvania.

Dwarf—one of the five Races of Man. Renowned for engineering, stonework, and the design and construction of complex machinery.

Dwarvenhame—the most recently added province of the Empire of the Axe, lying between the Dwarvenhame Mountains and the Ordan Mountains.

East Wall Mountains—a virtually impassable mountain range forming the eastern border of the Empire of the Axe, traversable by armies through only a few passes. Generally called simply "the East Walls."

Elf—one of the five Races of Man. The elves were granted effective immortality by Ottovar the

Great and Gwynytha the Wise in return for their renunciation of the powers of unchecked wizardry.

Eloham, Bridge of—bridge of King Emperor Eloham, a long bridge crossing the Snowborn River between Sindor and Losun.

Ephinos—an extremely powerful tranquilizer/anesthetic.

Fall of Kontovar—the destruction of the Empire of Ottovar in Kontovar and the near-genocidal counterattack of the White Council. See also "Strafing of Kontovar."

Fradonian Banks—a very dangerous chain of reefs and shoals along the northwestern coast of Norfressa. Sometimes called "Korthrala's Teeth."

Fradonian Channel—the passage through the Fradonian Banks to the harbor of Belhadan.

Geen Leaf River—the largest river which lies entirely within the Empire of the Axe.

Gramerhain—a crystal used by wizards for scrying purposes. (See also kairsalhain, below.)

Graumau—a large arcane monster combining traits of ape, cat, and rat.

Great Retreat—also "Long Retreat"; see below.

Gryphon Banner—the standard of the Emperors of Ottovar: a red field bearing a crowned gryphon rampant.

Gryphon Guard—the elite personal guard of the ruler of the Empire of Ottovar.

Gryphon Palace—residence of the House of Ottovar in Rollanthia.

Gryphon Throne—state chair of the rulers of the Empire of Ottovar.

Gut, The—a huge fjord north of Belhadan in Vonderland. Completely frozen during the winter months, it is the primary water access to Vonderwatch, the capital of the Province of Vonderland in the Empire of the Axe.

Gwynytha the Wise—wife of Ottovar the Great (see below); cofounder of the Empire of Ottovar and the Strictured of Ottovar.

Hacromanthi—literally "Grave of Evil" in ancient Kontovaran; the name given to Kontovar after the Last White Council's final counterstrike against the Council of Carnadosa.

Half-elf—the half-elves are the result of humans crossbreeding with elves. They are very long-lived, although unlike the true elves they are not immortal. They are not considered a separate Race of Man, a point which they deeply resent.

Halfling—a small, horned humanoid not known in Kontovar and believed to have resulted from mutation caused by wizardry during the final wars. Halflings are widely regarded with suspicion because of their sorcerous origins but are considered one of the five Races of Man. See also Marfang Island.

Healer—anyone who treats wounds, injuries, or sickness, but especially a title granted to magi with the healing mage power.

Hev, Forest of—a very large forest along the Snowborn River in the Empire of the Axe.

Hradani—one of the Races of Man. Hradani are larger, stronger, and longer-lived than humans, but considerably less fertile. Subject to the "Curse of Kontovar" (see above).

Iron Axe Tavern—a tavern owned by Bahzell Bahnakson and Leeana Hanathafressa in Belhadan.

Jewels of Silendros—the stars.

Kaisalhain—a storage crystal, created from grammerhain, which can be charged with pre-cast spells. (See grammerhain, above.)

King Emperor—the title of the ruler of the Empire of the Axe.

King Kormak's Battlements—another name for the East Wall Mountains.

Kolvania, Grand Duchy of—one of the Border Kingdoms (see above). A major feudal state bordering on and allied to the Empire of the Axe.

Kontovar—literally "Birth Land" in ancient Kontovaran; the major southern continent of Orfressa, the original home of the Races of Man, currently ruled by the Council of Carnadosa (see above).

Kormak—coinage of the Empire of the Axe. All coins are called "kormaks," but values vary depending on whether they are made of copper, silver, or gold.

Kormak of Crystal Cave, Duke—the ruler of the Crystal Cave Dwarves in Kontovar, Seneschal of emperor Toren Swordarm, Governor of the Kontovaran colonies in Norfressa, King of Manhome, and founder of the House of Kormak, the ruling house of the Empire of the Axe.

Korthrala—Korthrala Orfro, god of the sea.

Korthrala's Teeth—another name for the Fradonian Banks.

Korwin, Duchy of—a major feudal territory of the kingdom of Angthyr, ruled by Duke Doral. Disloyal to the crown.

Lathe, Princedom of—one of the Border Kingdoms (see above). An independent principality lying southeast of the Empire of the Axe.

Long retreat—also "Great Retreat" (see above); the period of withdrawal from Kontovar as refugees from the Empire of Ottovar fled the wars to Norfressa.

Lord of Carnadosa, The—also "The Dark Lord of Carnadosa." (1) The arch wizard who led the dark wizards against Toren Swordarm in the final wars and was slain at the Battle of Lost Hope. (2) The title of the current head of the Council of Carnadosa (see above).

Madwind—a spell of black wizardry which causes its victims to kill themselves.

Mage—a mental adept of Norfressa; one trained in the use of the mage talents.

Mage Barrier—a psionic barrier maintained by relays of magi around sensitive areas (academies, fortresses, etc.) of the Empire of the Axe. The mage barrier is impervious to all known mage talents and to all wand wizardry (see below).

Mage Talent—also "mage power." Psionic talents mastered by the magi of Norfressa which were unknown before the Fall of Kontovar and are still unknown in Kontovar.

Manhome—the largest of the original Kontovaran colonies in Norfressa. Manhome was given its present name when it became Duke Kormak of Crystal Cave's headquarters in Norfressa and Toren Swordarm named him "King of Manhome."

Man, Races of—the humanoid races of Kontovar and Norfressa, all of whom sprang originally from common stock. They include: humans, dwarves, hradani, elves, and halflings. All Races of Man may interbreed, but some crosses are infertile. The half-elves (see above) bitterly resent the fact that they are not considered the sixth Race of Man.

Marfang Island—a large island off southwestern Norfressa, inhabited by Marfang Island halflings.

Marfang Island Halfling—a particular subset of halflings from Marfang Island. Marfang Island halflings are somewhat larger than most halflings and are noted for splendid seamanship, touchiness, and sometimes rash courage.

Mindanwe—a tree of Norfressa whose sap produces a deadly neurotoxin much favored as a poison by the Assassins Guild.

Mishuk—(plural: mishuki); unarmed combat experts.

Morning Moss Tea—a caffeine-rich tea widely drunk in Norfressa, especially by mountaineers.

Myrea—the mortal maiden taken as a lover by Korthrala.

Norfressa—literally "Daughter of the North" in ancient Kontovaran; the northern continent of Orfressa.

Oath to Tomanāk—a formal oath of surrender which binds followers of Tomanāk to grant quarter but also binds the individual offering "oath to Tomanāk" to abide fully by Tomanāk's code as an honorable prisoner.

Ordan Mountains—a northern subsidiary range of the East Wall Mountains.

Order of Tomanāk—religious order of warriors dedicated to the service of Tomanāk Orfro, god of war and justice. The order is autonomous and enjoys special privileges in the Empire of the Axe and most Norfressan realms.

Ottovar the Great—the first wild wizard of Orfressa, husband of Gwynytha the Wise, with whom he founded the Empire of Ottovar and created of the Strictures of Ottovar, governing the use of wizardry.

Ottovar, Empire of—the enormous and powerful empire which governed the entire continent of Kontovar for almost 10,000 years. Founded by Ottovar the Great and Gwynytha the Wise after they put an end to the Wizard Wars of their time.

Ottovar, House of—the ruling house of the Empire of Ottovar.

Pass of Heroes—one of the major passes through the East Wall Mountains.

Purple Lords—the half-elven oligarchs of the mercantile city states of the Lands of the Purple Lords south of the Empire of the Spear. For centuries they controlled the Spearman economy by controlling all shipping on the Spear River from the great harbor of Bortalik Bay. They are extremely racist, regarding their people as superior to both humans and elves.

Rape of the Rollanthia—the destruction and looting of Rollanthia by hradani slaves of the Council of Carnadosa in Kontovar during the final wars. Begun with the assassination of Toren Swordarm's entire family in the Gryphon Palace.

River of the Spear—the primary north-south river system of Norfressa which flows all the way from Hope's Bane Glacier in extreme northern Norfressa to Bortalik Bay on the continent's southern seaboard.

Rollanthia—capital and fortress city of the House of Ottovar in Kontovar.

Rūm, Isle of—the island home of the White Council in Kontovar.

Saramantha, Princedom of—an independent Norfressa princedom, home of most elves in Norfressa.

Saramanthan—a citizen of the princedom of Saramantha.

Saramanthan Fire Ant—an insect which combines the more objectionable qualities of an army ant and a scorpion.

Scarthū, Barony of—a feudal territory in the kingdom of Angthyr ruled by Davu of Scarthū, a fervent crown loyalist.

Scarthū Hills—a large range of hills in northwestern Angthyr inhabited by dragons.

Sea Scimitar—the flagship of Tolgrim of the Shith Kiri.

Shadow Chill—an icy cold which accompanies shadow-men and can kill on contact by inducing shock and heart failure.

Shadowmen—(also "shadows") creatures created by wresting individuals across the void between alternate universes by black wizardry to serve as slaves of their summoners.

Shadowmage—a shadowman wizard.

Shith Kiri—a corsair confederacy which rules the Shith Kiri Islands, a sizable archipelago south of Norfressa.

Sindor—the capital of South Province in the Empire of the Axe.

Snowborn River—a river in western Norfressa.

Sorceress—a female sorcerer.

Sorcerer—also called "wand wizard." The most common type of wizard: one with limited inherent sensitivity to the art who has acquired his mastery through long years of study and training. Sorcerers use mnemonics, precisely learned harmonics, and carefully crafted rituals/techniques, each set of which taps a small portion of the total "magic field" for precisely circumscribed functions.

Sorcery—also called "wizardry" or "wand wizardry;" the portion of the wild magic which may be indirectly (and very cautiously) manipulated by a sorcerer or sorceress.

Sothōii—literally "Sons of the Fathers" in ancient Kontovaran; humans ruling the kingdom of the Sothōii and claiming pure descent from the noble houses of the Empire of Ottovar. Noted for their superb horses, matchless cavalry, and their relationship with the Sothōii coursers.

Sothōii Courser—a race of fully sentient horses of very large size, human-equivalent intelligence, and incredible stamina and toughness. They are the descendants of arcanely augmented warhorses produced for the army of Toren Swordarm by the White Council in Kontovar. They choose their own riders, with whom they bond permanently, and they and their riders form the elite of the Sothōii army.

Sothōii, Kingdom of the—the third-largest realm of Norfressa, noted for its unmatchable cavalry; an ally of long standing of the Empire of the Axe.

South Keep—the largest and most powerful fortress of the Empire of the Axe, built in South Wall Pass to control the point of access between the Empire of the Axe and the Empire of the Spear.

South March—a province of the Empire of the Axe between the Whitewater River and the East Wall Mountains.

South Province—the southernmost province of the Empire of the Axe.

South Wall Pass—the southernmost of the major passes through the East Wall Mountains. Guarded by South Keep.

South Wall River—a river in Kolvania which drains into the Bellwater River.

Spear, Empire of the—the second largest realm of Norfressa and the primary rival of the Empire of the Axe. The Spearmen are ambitious and expansionist, but not essentially evil.

Spearman—a citizen of the Empire of the Spear.

Strafing of Kontovar—the final counterstrike of the White Council following Toren Swordarm's defeat in the Battle of Lost Hope. The attack did catastrophic damage to Kontovar and prevented the Council of Carnadosa from immediately following the Kontovar refugees to Norfressa and completing their conquest.

Strictures of Ottovar—also known as the "Strictures of Wizardry" or simply "The Strictures;" the code of conduct imposed on white wizards by Ottovar the Great and Gwynytha the Wise in Kontovar. Transgressions of the Strictures was a capital crime in the Empire of Ottovar.

Sword Oath—an oath of truth and loyalty sworn by worshipers of Tomanāk.

Sword of Tomanāk—flagship of the Belhadan Order of Tomanāk.

Toren Swordarm—also known as "Toren the Great" and "Toren the Last;" the final emperor of the House of Ottovar in Kontovar.

Torfo, Barony of—a feudal territory of the kingdom of Angthyr ruled by Wulfra of Torfo.

Torm Fen—a huge swamp south of the kingdom of Angthyr between the Lake of Torm and the Western Sea.

Traitors' Walk—a major pass through East Wall Mountains between South Wall Pass and Cragwall Pass.

Trōfrōlantha—the capital province of the Empire of Ottovar.

Unicorn Inn—an inn in Sindor popular with worshipers of Tomanāk.

Ushian—a powerful stimulant/restorative used primarily by magi.

Vonderland—a northern province of the Empire of the Axe, noted for the quality of its archers, the severity of its climate, and the wealth of its silver and gold mines.

Vonderwatch—capital of the Province of Vonderland in the Empire of the Axe.

Wakūo—fierce desert nomads and city dwellers in southeastern Norfressa.

Wand Wizard—another term for "sorcerer" (see above).

War Maid—a member of a legally recognized female subculture in the kingdom of the Sothōii. Many are deadly fighters, and all are answerable only to their own leaders and the Sothōii Crown.

Warlock—a magic user with an inborn sensitivity for the art so great that he requires no training to use it. Because of his lack of training, however, he never acquires the degree of capability possessed by sorcerers.

Wave Beard—another name for Korthrala Orfressa.

Wave Mistress—ship owned and captained by Brandark Brandarkson.

Walso, Earldom of—a feudal territory in the Kingdom of Angthyr.

West Barony—a coastal barony of the Kingdom of Angthyr ruled by the uncle of Queen Fallona.

Western Sea—ocean waters to the west of Norfressa.

Whitewater River—a river in the Empire of the Axe which flows into South Banark Bay.

Wild Magic—the totality of the "magic field," the energy or force which imbues the entire universe and binds it together.

Wild Wizard—the only type of wizard capable of utilizing the wild magic directly.

Wind Plain of the Sothōii—a huge subarctic plateau/plain which forms the heart of the Kingdom of the Sothōii and is held to be the finest grazing land in Norfressa, despite its severe climate.

Wind Riders—the chosen bonded brothers (and in a very special case, sister) of the Sothōii coursers.

Windfel—a province of the Empire of the Axe which lies east of Vonderland.

Windhawk Inn—an inn in Sindor.

Witch—a female warlock.

Wizard—any trained practitioner of wizardry.

Wizard Wars—the wars between wizards which Ottovar the Great and Gwynytha the Wise brought to an end. This term is sometimes also used to describe the final wars in Kontovar, but the term "the Fall" is more normally employed to denote that war between wizards.

Wizard Wind—a wind conjured by wizardry.

Wizardry—also called "sorcery" or "wand wizardry;" the use of that minute portion of the wild magic which may be channeled and controlled by sorcerers and warlocks. Wizardry manipulates those portions through a series of complex commands, each of which achieves a unique effect. Wizardry is external to the wizard; it requires careful concentration and control but does not place any direct physical strain on the wizard. Any loss of concentration, however, may well result in the spell going wild with generally disastrous effects.

Word of Unbinding—the incantation pronounced by Wencit of Rūm to free the White Council from the Strictures so that it could attack the Council of Carnadosa with wizardry after the Battle of Lost Hope.

A SELECTION OF NORFRESSAN OATHS

"By the Sword!" "By the Mace!" (by Tomanāk's sword or mace)

"By the Trident!" (by Korthrala's trident)

"By the Scorpion!" (by Sharnā's scorpion)

"Sharnā send them scorpions!"

"By Carnadosa's flaming locks!"

"By Carnadosa's ebon eyes!"

"Fiendark's Furies!"

"Krahana fly away with your soul!"

"May the fish lick their bones!" (traditional Shith Kiri malediction)

MONTHS OF THE ORFRESSAN YEAR

The Orfressan year is divided into twelve months of thirty days each, plus Lellandor (the "Festival of Orr"), an adjustment at the beginning of each year. Normally, Lellandor is four days long, but once every eight years the festival lasts six days, with the two extra days given up to meditation and fasting. Lellandor is the high holy season of the Orfressan year.

Month Name	Meaning
Lellandor	Festival of Orr
Blancnachimo	White Ice Fang
Orcimo	Ice Breath
Nienfresso	Rain Maiden
Yienkonto	Flower Birth
Asoyien	Yellow Bud
Haniyean	Green Leaf
Ortomayan	High Feasting
Shomanforg	Harvest Weaving
Siemnach	Wind Fang
Lacrimorfo	Snow Bearer
Barchimo	Black Ice

· APPENDIX B ·

Gods of Light and Dark

THE DARK GODS

Phrobus Orfro

Called "Father of Evil" and "Lord of Deceit," Phrobus is the seventh child of Orr and Kontifrio, which explains why seven is considered *the* unlucky number in Norfressa. No one recalls his original name; "Phrobus" ("Truth Bender") was given to him by Tomanāk when he cast Phrobus down for his treacherous attempt to wrest rulership from Orr. Following that defeat, Phrobus turned openly to the Dark and became, in fact, the opening wedge by which evil first entered Orfressa. He is the most powerful of the gods of Light or Dark after Tomanāk, and the hatred between him and Tomanāk is unthinkably bitter, but Phrobus fears his brother worse than death itself. His symbol is a flame-eyed skull.

Shīgū

Called "The Twisted One," "Queen of Hell," and "Mother of Madness," Shīgū is the wife of Phrobus. No one knows exactly where she came from, but most believe she was, in fact, a powerful demoness raised to godhood by Phrobus when he sought a mate to breed up his own pantheon to oppose that of his father. Her power is deep but subtle, her cruelty and malice are bottomless, and her favored weapon is madness. She is even more hated, loathed, and feared by mortals than Phrobus, and her worship is punishable by death in all Norfressan realms. Her symbol is a flaming spider.

Carnadosa Phrofressa

"The Lady of Wizardry" is the fifth child of Phrobus and Shīgū. She has become the goddess of black wizardry, but she herself might be considered totally amoral rather than evil for evil's sake. She enshrines the concept of power sought by any means and at any cost to others. Her symbol is a wizard's wand.

Fiendark Phrofro

The first-born child of Phrobus and Shīgū, Fiendark is known as "Lord of the Furies." He is cast very much in his father's image (though, fortunately, he is considerably less powerful) and all evil creatures owe him allegiance as Phrobus' deputy. Unlike Phrobus, who seeks always to pervert or conquer, however, Fiendark also delights in destruction for destruction's sake. His symbols are a flaming sword or flame-shot cloud of smoke.

Krahana Phrofressa

"The Lady of the Damned" is the fourth child of Phrobus and Shīgū and, in most ways, the most loathsome of them all. She is noted for her hideous beauty and holds dominion over the undead (which makes her Isvaria's most hated foe) and rules the hells in which the souls of those who have sold themselves to evil spend eternity. Her symbol is a splintered coffin.

Krashnark Phrofro

The second son of Phrobus and Shīgū, Krashnark is the older twin brother of Sharnā and something of a disappointment to his parents. The most powerful of Phrobus' children, Krashnark (known as "Devil Master") is the god of devils and ambitious war. He is ruthless, merciless, and cruel, but personally courageous and possessed of a strong, personal code of honor, which makes him the only Dark God Tomanāk actually respects. He is, unfortunately, loyal to his father, and his power and sense of honor have made him the "enforcer" of the Dark Gods. His symbol is a flaming steward's rod.

Sharnā Phrofro

Called "Demonspawn" and "Lord of the Scorpion," Sharnā is Krashnark's younger, identical twin (a fact which pleases neither of them). Sharnā is the god of demons and the patron of assassins, the personification of cunning and deception. He is substantially less powerful than Krashnark and a total coward, and the demons who owe him allegiance hate and fear

Krashnark's more powerful devils almost as much as Sharnā hates and fears his brother. His symbols are the giant scorpion (which serves as his mount) and a bleeding heart in a mailed fist.

THE GODS OF LIGHT

Orr All-Father

Often called "The Creator" or "The Establisher," Orr is considered the creator of the Universe and the King and Judge of Gods. He is the father or creator of all but one of the Gods of Light and is also known as "Orr Hnarkonto," or "Orr the Unborn" (a more precise translation might be "Orr the Never Born"). He is the most powerful of all the gods, whether of Light or Dark. His symbol is a blue starburst.

Kontifrio

"The Mother of Women" is Orr's wife and the goddess of home, family, and the harvest. According to Norfressan theology, Kontifrio was Orr's second creation (after Orfressa, the rest of the universe), and she is the most nurturing of the gods and the mother of all Orr's children except Orfressa herself. Her hatred for Shīgū is implacable. Her symbol is a sheaf of wheat tied with a grape vine.

Chemalka Orfressa

"The Lady of the Storm" is the sixth child of Orr and Kontifrio. She is the goddess of weather, good and bad, and has little to do with mortals. Her symbol is the sun seen through clouds.

Chesmirsa Orfressa

"The Singer of Light" is the fourth child of Orr and Kontifrio and the younger twin sister of Tomanāk, the war god. Chesmirsa is the goddess of bards, poetry, music and art. She is very fond of mortals and has a mischievous sense of humor. Her symbol is the harp.

Hirahim Lightfoot

Known as "The Laughing God" and "The Great Seducer," Hirahim is something of a rogue element among the Gods of Light. He is the only one of them who is not related to Orr (no one seems certain where he came from, though he acknowledges Orr's authority... as much as he does anyone's) and he is the true prankster of the gods. He is the god of merchants, thieves, and dancers, but he is also known as the god of seductions, as he has a terrible weakness for attractive female mortals (or goddesses). His symbol is a silver flute.

Isvaria Orfressa

"The Lady of Remembrance" (also called "The Slayer") is the first child of Orr and Kontifrio. She is the goddess of needful death and the completion of life and rules the House of the Dead, where she keeps the Scroll of the Dead. Somewhat to her mother's dismay, she is also Hirahim's lover. The third most powerful of the Gods of Light, she is the special enemy of Krahana, and her symbol is a scroll with skull winding knobs.

Khalifrio Orfressa

"The Lady of the Lightning" is Orr and Kontifrio's second child and the goddess of elemental destruction. She is considered a Goddess of Light despite her penchant for destructiveness, but she has very little to do with mortals (and mortals are just as happy about it, thank you). Her symbol is a forked lightning bolt.

Korthrala Orfro

Called "Sea Spume" and "Foam Beard," Korthrala is the fifth child of Orr and Kontifrio. He is the god of the sea but also of love, hate, and passion. He is a very powerful god, if not over-blessed with wisdom, and is very fond of mortals. His symbol is the net and trident.

Lillinara Orfressa

Known as "Friend of Women" and "The Silver Lady," Lillinara is Orr and Kontifrio's eleventh child, the goddess of the moon and women. She is one of the more complex deities, and extremely focused. She is appealed to by young women and maidens in her persona as the Maid and by mature women and mothers in her persona as the Mother. As avenger, she manifests as the Crone, who also comforts the dying. She dislikes Hirahim Lightfoot intensely, but she hates Shīgū (as the essential perversion of all womankind) with every fiber of her being. Her symbol is the moon.

Norfram Orfro

The "Lord of Chance" is Orr and Kontifrio's ninth child and the god of fortune, good and bad. His symbol is the infinity sign.

Orfressa

According to Norfressan theology, Orfressa is not a god but the universe herself, created by Orr even before Kontifrio, and she is not truly "awake." Or, rather, she is seldom aware of anything as ephemeral as mortals. On the very rare occasions when she does take notice of mortal affairs, terrible things tend to happen, and even Orr can restrain her wrath only with difficulty.

Semkirk Orfro

Known as "The Watcher," Semkirk is the tenth child of Orr and Kontifrio. He is the god of wisdom and mental and physical discipline and, before The Fall of Kontovar, was the god of white wizardry. Since The Fall, he has become the special patron of the psionic magi, who conduct a merciless war against evil wizards. He is a particularly deadly enemy of Carnadosa, the goddess of black wizardry. His symbol is a golden scepter.

Silendros Orfressa

The fourteenth and final child of Orr and Kontifrio, Silendros (called "Jewel of the Heavens") is the goddess of stars and the night. She is greatly reverenced by jewel smiths, who see their art as an attempt to capture the beauty of her heavens in the work of their hands, but generally has little to do with mortals. Her symbol is a silver star.

Sorbus Kontifra

Known as "Iron Bender," Sorbus is the smith of the gods. He is also the product of history's greatest seduction (that of Kontifrio by Hirahim—a "prank" Kontifrio has never quite forgiven), yet he is the most stolid and dependable of all the gods, and Orr accepts him as his own son. His symbol is an anvil.

Tolomos Orfro

"The Torch Bearer" is the twelfth child of Orr and Kontifrio. He is the god of light and the sun and the patron of all those who work with heat. His symbol is a golden flame.

Tomanāk Orfro

Tomanāk, the third child of Orr and Kontifrio, is Chesmirsa's older twin brother and second only to Orr himself in power. He is known by many names— "Sword of Light," "Scale Balancer," "Lord of Battle," and "Judge of Princes" to list but four—and has been entrusted by his father with the task of overseeing the balance of the Scales of Orr. He is also captain general of the Gods of Light and the foremost enemy of all the Dark Gods (indeed, it was he who cast Phrobus down when Phrobus first rebelled against his father). His symbols are a sword and/or a spiked mace.

Toragon Orfro

"The Huntsman," also called "Woodhelm," is the thirteenth child of Orr and Kontifrio and the god of nature. Forests are especially sacred to him, and he has a reputation for punishing those who hunt needlessly or cruelly. His symbol is an oak tree.

Torframos Orfro

Known as "Stone Beard" and "Lord of Earthquakes," Torframos is the eighth child of Orr and Kontifrio. He is the lord of the Earth, the keeper of the deep places and special patron of engineers and those who delve, and is especially revered by dwarves. His symbol is the miner's pick.

Flag in Exile pb • 0-7434-3575-3 • $7.99

"Packs enough punch to smash a starship to smithereens."—*Publishers Weekly*

Honor Among Enemies hc • 0-671-87723-2 • $21.00
pb • 0-671-87783-6 • $7.99

"Star Wars as it might have been written by C.S. Forester . . . fast-paced entertainment." —*Booklist*

In Enemy Hands hc • 0-671-87793-3 • $22.00
pb • 0-671-57770-0 • $7.99

After being ambushed, Honor finds herself aboard an enemy cruiser, bound for her scheduled execution. But one lesson Honor has never learned is how to give up!

Echoes of Honor hc • 0-671-87892-1 • $24.00
pb • 0-671-57833-2 • $7.99

"Brilliant! Brilliant! Brilliant!"—Anne McCaffrey

Ashes of Victory hc • 0-671-57854-5 • $25.00
pb • 0-671-31977-9 • $7.99

Honor has escaped from the prison planet called Hell and returned to the Manticoran Alliance, to the heart of a furnace of new weapons, new strategies, new tactics, spies, diplomacy, and assassination.

War of Honor hc • 0-7434-3545-1 • $26.00
pb • 0-7434-7167-9 • $7.99

No one wanted another war. Neither the Republic of Haven, nor Manticore—and certainly not Honor Harrington. Unfortunately, what they wanted didn't matter.

At All Costs hc • 1-4165-0911-9 • $26.00
pb • 1-4165-4414-3 • $7.99

The war with the Republic of Haven has resumed. . . disastrously for the Star Kingdom of Manticore. The alternative to victory is total defeat, yet this time the cost of victory will be agonizingly high.

Mission of Honor hc • 978-1-4391-3361-3 • $27.00
pb • 978-1-4391-3451-1 • $7.99

The unstoppable juggernaut of the mighty Solarian League is on a collision course with Manticore. But if everything Honor Harrington loves is going down to destruction, it won't be going alone.

A Rising Thunder hc • 978-1-4516-3806-6 • $26.00
trade pb • 978-1-4516-3871-4 • $15.00
pb • 978-1-4767-3612-9 • $7.99

Shadow of Freedom hc • 978-1-4516-3869-1 • $25.00
trade pb • 978-1-4767-3628-0 • $15.00
pb • 978-1-4767-8048-1 • $7.99

The survival of Manticore is at stake as Honor must battle not only the powerful Solarian League, but also the secret puppetmasters who plan to pick up all the pieces after galactic civilization is shattered.

HONORVERSE VOLUMES:

Crown of Slaves (with Eric Flint) pb • 0-7434-9899-2 • $7.99
Torch of Freedom (with Eric Flint) hc • 1-4391-3305-0 • $26.00
pb • 978-1-4391-3408-5 • $8.99
Cauldron of Ghosts (with Eric Flint)
hc • 978-1-4767-3633-4 • $25.00
pb • 978-1-4767-8100-6 • $8.99

Sent on a mission to keep Erewhon from breaking with Manticore, the Star Kingdom's most able agent and the Queen's niece may not even be able to escape with their lives. . .

House of Steel (with Bu9) hc • 978-1-4516-3875-2 • $25.00
trade pb • 978-1-4516-3893-6 • $15.00
pb • 978-1-4767-3643-3 • $7.99

The Shadow of Saganami hc • 0-7434-8852-0 • $26.00
pb • 1-4165-0929-1 • $7.99